Affliction

LAURELL K. HAMILTON

Affliction

AN ANITA BLAKE, VAMPIRE HUNTER, NOVEL

headline

First published in the United States of America in 2013 by
the Penguin Group (USA) Inc.
A BERKLEY BOOK

First published in Great Britain in 2013 by
HEADLINE PUBLISHING GROUP

ISBN (HB) 978 0 7553 8902 5
ISBN (TPB) 978 0 7553 8903 2

Typeset in Fournier MT by Palimpsest Book Production Limited,
Falkirk, Stirlingshire

Printed and bound in Great Britain by
Clays Ltd, St Ives plc

HEADLINE PUBLISHING GROUP
An Hachette UK Company
338 Euston Road
London NW1 3BH

www.headline.co.uk
www.hachette.co.uk

GUILTY PLEASURES 1993–2013 AFFLICTION

This one's for Anita and me. Here's to another twenty years of facing our fears, solving mysteries, catching bad guys, and finding love.

Artists and their art, mirror and reflection, yin and yang, the push and the pull, separate but joined, in the end it becomes an act of co-creation, because to truly create art the artists themselves are re-created.

Acknowledgments

We're taught Lord Acton's axiom: all power corrupts, absolute power corrupts absolutely. I believed that when I started these books, but I don't believe it's always true anymore. Power doesn't always corrupt. Power can cleanse. What I believe is always true about power is that power always reveals.

Robert Caro

When power leads man toward arrogance, poetry reminds him of his limitations. When power narrows the area of man's concern, poetry reminds him of the richness and diversity of existence. When power corrupts, poetry cleanses.

John F. Kennedy

I

My gun was digging into my back, so I shifted forward in my office chair. That was better; now it was just the comforting pressure of the inner-skirt holster, tucked away underneath my short royal blue suit jacket. I'd stopped wearing my shoulder holster except when I was on an active warrant as a U.S. Marshal. When I was working at Animators Inc. and seeing clients, the behind-the-back holster was less likely to flash and make them nervous. You'd think if someone was asking me to raise the dead for them that they'd have better nerves, but guns seemed to scare them a lot more than talking about zombies. It was different once the zombie was raised and they were looking at the walking dead; then suddenly the guns didn't bother them nearly as much, but until that Halloweenesque moment I tried to keep the weapons out of sight. There was a knock on my office door and Mary, our daytime receptionist, opened it without my saying *Come in*, which she'd never done in the six years we'd been working together, so I wasn't grumpy about the interruption. I just looked up from double-checking my client meetings to make sure there wouldn't be any overlap issues and knew something was up, and knowing Mary it would be important. She was like that.

She'd finally let her hair go gray, but it was still in the same obviously artificial hairdo that it had always been. She'd let herself get a little plump as she neared sixty and had finally embraced glasses full time. The combination of it all had aged her about ten years, but she seemed happy with it, saying, 'I'm a grandma; I'm okay with looking like one.' The look on her face was sad and set in sympathetic lines. It was the face she used to deal with grieving families who wanted their loved ones raised from the dead. Having that face aimed at me sped my pulse and tightened my stomach.

I made myself take a deep breath and let it out slow as Mary closed the door behind her and started walking toward my desk. 'What's wrong?' I asked.

'I didn't want to tell you over the phone with all the clients listening,' she said.

'Tell me what?' I asked, and fought the urge not to raise my voice. She was about one more uninformative answer away from getting yelled at.

'There's a woman on line two; she says she's your future mother-in-law. I told her you weren't engaged to my knowledge, and she said that she didn't know what to call herself since you were just living with her son.'

I was actually living with several men, but most of them didn't have families to use words like *son*. 'Name, Mary, what's her name?' My voice was rising a little.

'Morgan, Beatrice Morgan.'

I frowned at her. 'I'm not living with anyone named Morgan. I've never even dated anyone with that last name.'

'I didn't recognize it from your boyfriends, but she said that the father is hurt, maybe dying, and she thought he'd want to know about his dad before it was too late. The emotion is real, Anita. I'm sorry, maybe she's crazy, but sometimes people don't think clearly when their husband is hurt. I didn't want to just write her off as crazy; I mean, I don't know the last names of everyone you're dating.'

I started to tell her to ignore the call, but looking into Mary's face I couldn't do it. I'd trusted her to screen callers for years. She had a good feel for distraught versus crazy. 'She give a first name for her son?'

'Mike.'

I shook my head. 'I've never dated a Mike Morgan. I don't know why she called here, but she's got the wrong Anita Blake.'

Mary nodded, but her expression looked unhappy. 'I'll tell her that you don't know a Mike Morgan.'

'Do that. She's either got the wrong Anita Blake, or she's crazy.'

'She doesn't sound crazy, just upset.'

'You know that crazy doesn't mean the emotion isn't real, Mary. Sometimes the delusion is so real they believe it all.'

Mary nodded again and went out to tell Beatrice Morgan she had the wrong number. I went back to checking the last of my client meetings. I wanted to make sure that no matter how long it took to raise each zombie, I wouldn't be too late for the next cemetery. Clients tended to get spooked if you left them hanging out in graveyards too long by themselves. At least most of the meetings were historical societies and lawyers checking wills, with the families of the deceased either long dead or not allowed near the zombie until after the will was settled in case just seeing the loved ones influenced the zombie to change its mind about the last will and testament. I wasn't sure it was possible to sway a zombie that way, but I approved of the new court ruling that families couldn't see the deceased until after all court matters were cleared up, just in case. Have one billionaire inheritance overturned because of undue influence on a zombie and everybody got all weird about it.

Mary came through the door without knocking. 'Micah. Mike was his nickname as a kid. Morgan is her name from her second marriage. It was Callahan. Micah Callahan's mother is on line two, and his dad is in the hospital.'

'Shit!' I said, picking up the phone and hitting the button to put the call through. 'Mrs Callahan, I mean, Mrs Morgan, this is Anita Blake.'

'Oh, thank God, I'm so sorry. I just forgot about the names. I've been Beatrice Morgan for eighteen years, since Micah was twelve, and he was Mike to us. He didn't like *Micah* when he was a little boy. He thought *Mike* was more grown up.' She was crying softly, I could hear it in her voice, but her words were clear, well enunciated. It made me wonder what she did for a living, but I didn't ask. It could wait; it was just one of the thoughts you have when you're trying not to get caught up in the emotions of a situation. Think, don't feel, just think.

'You told our receptionist that Micah's dad was hurt.'

'Yes, Rush, that's my ex, his father, was attacked by something. His deputy said it was a zombie, but the bite isn't human, and it's like he's infected with something from it.'

'Zombies rarely attack people.'

'I know that!' She yelled it. I heard her taking deep breaths, drawing in her calm. I heard the effort over the phone, could almost feel her gathering herself back. 'I'm sorry. When Mike left us he was so horrible, but Rush said he'd found out that Mike did it to protect all of us and that some of the people had their families hurt by these people.'

'What people?' I asked.

'Rush wouldn't tell me details, said it was a police matter. He was always doing that when we were married, drove me nuts, but he said that he'd found out enough to know that other wereanimals in that group had their families killed, and Mike had to convince them he hated us, or they would have hurt us. Do you know if that's true? Does Mike want to see his father? Does he want to see any of us?' She was crying again, and just stopped trying to talk. She hadn't been married to the man for nearly twenty years, and she was still this upset. Crap.

I was remembering that Micah's dad was a sheriff of some flavor, and now his mom was telling me that somehow the dad had found out more about Micah and his animal group than I thought anyone with a badge, besides me, knew. I'd had to kill people to rescue Micah and his group, and I hadn't had a warrant of execution, so it was murder. I was a little leery that Sheriff Callahan apparently knew more about it all than I'd thought. I knew that Micah hadn't talked to his family in years, so how had his dad found out, and how much did he know?

It was my turn to take a deep breath and make myself stop being so damn paranoid and deal with the crying woman on the other end of the phone. 'Mrs Morgan, Mrs Morgan, how did you know to call here? Who gave you this number?' Maybe if I made her think about something more ordinary she'd calm down.

She sniffled and then said, in a voice that was hiccupy, as she tried to swallow past the emotion, 'We saw Mike in the news as the head of the Coalition.'

'The Coalition for Better Understanding between humans and shapeshifters,' I said.

'Yes' – and the word was calmer – 'yes, and you were mentioned in several stories as living with him.'

I wondered if the stories had talked about Nathaniel, the guy who lived with us, or the fact that I was also 'dating' Jean-Claude, the Master Vampire of St Louis? I almost never watched the news, so I didn't always know what was being said in the media about any of us.

'Why didn't you call the Coalition number and ask for Micah directly?'

'He said really awful things to me last time we spoke, Ms Blake. I think I'd fall completely apart if he said that again to me with Rush hurt like this. Can you please tell him, and then if Mike wants to see us, to see Rush, before . . . in time . . . I mean . . . Oh, God, I'm usually better than this, but it's so terrible what's happening to Rush, so hard to watch.'

'Happening? What do you mean?'

'He's rotting . . . he's rotting alive and aware and the doctors can't stop it. They have drugs that can slow it, but nothing slows it down much.'

'I'm sorry, I don't understand. You mean that something preter-natural attacked Mr Callahan and now he's got some disease?'

'Yes,' she said, almost a breath rather than a word.

'But they've seen it before, this disease?'

'Yes, they say it's the first case outside the East Coast, but they've learned enough to slow it down. There's no cure, though. I overheard a nurse call it the zombie disease, but she got in trouble for saying it. The older nurse said, "Don't give it a name that the media will love." I heard doctors whispering that it's just a matter of time before it hits the news.'

'Why do they call it the zombie disease?' I asked, partly to just give myself time to think.

'You rot from the outside in, so you're aware the whole time. Apparently it's incredibly quick, and they've only managed to prolong the life of one other person.' Her breath came out in a shudder.

'Mrs Morgan, there are questions I want to ask, but I'm afraid they'll upset you more.'

'Ask, just ask,' she said.

I took in a deep breath, let it out slow, and finally said, 'You said prolong. For how long?'

'Five days.'

Shit, I thought. Out loud I said, 'Give me an address, phone numbers, and I'll tell Micah.' I started to promise we'd be there, but I couldn't promise for him. He'd been estranged from his family for about ten years. Just because I'd have gotten on a plane for my semi-estranged family didn't mean he'd do the same. I took down all the information as if I were sure of his answer.

'Thank you, thank you so much. I knew it was the right thing to do to call another woman. We manage the men so much more than they think, don't we?'

'Actually Micah manages me more than the other way around.'

'Oh, is it because you're police like Rush? Is it more about the badge than being a man?'

'I think so,' I said.

'You'll bring Micah?'

I didn't want to lie to her, but I wasn't sure the absolute truth was anything she could handle; she needed something to hang on to, to look forward to while she sat and watched her ex-husband rot while still alive. Jesus, Mary, and Joseph, just thinking it was terrible. I couldn't leave her to watch it with no hope, so I lied.

'Of course,' I said.

'See, I'm right, you just say you'll bring him. You manage him more than you think.'

'Maybe so, Mrs Morgan, maybe so.'

She sounded calmer as she said, 'Beatrice, Bea, to my friends. Bring my son home, Anita, please.'

What could I say? 'I will . . . Bea.'

I hung up, hoping I hadn't lied to her.

2

Under other circumstances I would have softened the news, maybe even had Nathaniel with me to help ease Micah into the family disaster, but there wasn't time to be gentle. I had to tell him like jerking off a bandage, because the one thing I didn't want to have happen was his father dying before Micah could say good-bye because I had delayed. So I had to not think too much about what effect it would have on the man I loved and the life we'd built together. Like so often in my life, I just had to do it.

I used my cell phone instead of going through the business lines. He'd see it was me, and he'd pick up without my going through his front office people. My stomach was in a hard knot, and only years of practice kept my breathing even, and because I controlled my breathing I controlled my pulse, which wanted to speed up. I so didn't want to be the one to tell him this news, and yet I couldn't think of anyone I'd rather have done it. Some things you wish you could delegate, and simultaneously know you wouldn't, even if you could.

'How did you know I was just thinking about you?' he asked, not even a hello, just his voice warm and happy that it was me. I could picture him sitting at his desk, his suit tailored down to his slender, athletic body. He was my height, five foot three, but with wide shoulders leading down to a slender waist. He was built like a swimmer, though running was his exercise of choice. His curly, deep brown hair was just past his shoulders now, because we'd carefully negotiated both of us cutting a few inches off our hair, without breaking our deal, which was if one of us cut our hair, the other one got to cut theirs.

I should have said something romantic back to him, but I was too scared, too full of the bad news that I had to tell him. I had to just do it, no hesitation, no games, no words of comfort, because anything but just saying it was only going to make it worse, like I was lying to him, or putting sugar in the poison. I wrapped the sound of his happy, loving voice around me like a warm, safe blanket, and then I said, 'Your mom just called me.'

The silence on the other end of the phone was loud, because I could hear my blood rushing through my ears. My breathing sped up as Micah's stopped, my pulse thundering while his paused, as if his whole body had taken that breath just before you launch yourself over the cliff.

I couldn't stand the silence. I said, 'Micah, did you hear me?'

'I heard you.' There was no happy warmth to his voice now. His voice was as empty as he could make it; if there was any emotion it was a cold anger. I'd never heard him like that. It scared me, and that made me angry, because it was stupid to be scared, but it was that emotional scared – when you acknowledge how important someone is to you and your world and yet know that they are a separate person capable of fucking everything up with a few bad decisions. I trusted Micah not to do that, but I also hated being that dependent on anyone emotionally. I allowed myself to love, but part of me was still afraid of it. That part of me tried to make me angry at him in a sort of knee-jerk reaction, a preemptive strike. If I lashed out first it wouldn't hurt so much, or that had been the idea I'd lived with in my subconscious for years. Now I knew better, but the old habit was still in me. I just had to ignore it and be reasonable. But none of me liked the fact that he was this emotional with just the news that his mother had called me; I hadn't even gotten to the part about his dad. It didn't bode well for how he'd take it.

'What did she want?' he asked, still in that strange, cold voice.

I took in a breath and let it out slow, counting to help calm all the neurotic impulses I had around this much relationship emotion, and spoke, calmly, in a voice that came out ordinary and a little cold. I wouldn't be angry as a first strike, but the old habit of preferring anger to being hurt was still a part of me. I was working on it, but something about the whole conversation had hit an issue of mine. I was better than this, damn it. I wasn't the sad, angry girl he'd first met.

'Your father is hurt, maybe dying. Probably dying,' and my voice wasn't angry now, or cold, but more apologetic. Shit, I so sucked at this.

'Anita, what are you talking about?'

I started over and told him everything I knew, which seemed like damned little under the circumstances.

'How bad is he hurt?'

'I've told you what I know.'

'He's dying? My dad is dying?'

'That's what your mom said; she seemed pretty hysterical about it, actually.'

'She was always pretty emotional. It kind of balanced Dad's stoicism out. Anita, I can't think. I feel stuck.'

'You want to see your father, right?'

'If you mean do I want to make peace with him before he dies, then yes.'

'Okay, then we catch the first plane and get you to his bedside.'

'Okay,' he said. He sounded so unsure, so unlike himself.

'You want company?' I asked.

'What do you mean?'

'Do you want me to come with you?'

'Yes,' he said.

'Do you want Nathaniel to come?'

'Yes.'

'I'll call him and let him know. I'll call Jean-Claude and see if his private plane is available.'

'Yes, good. Why can't I think?' he asked.

'You've just learned your dad is in the hospital and you're running out of time to make up with him. You're having to make up with your whole family during a crisis of epic proportions. Give yourself a few minutes to process, Micah.'

'Good points,' he said, but he still sounded shell-shocked.

'Do you need me to stay on the phone?'

'You can't call about the plane if you're talking to me,' he said. The words were reasonable; the tone was still stunned.

'True, but you sound like you need me to keep talking to you.'

'I do, but I need you to arrange the trip more. I'll give myself a few minutes to process and then I'll arrange for other people to take the business end here while I'm gone.'

'I'll do the same.'

'I love you,' he said.

'I love you more,' I said.

'I love you most.'

'I love you mostest.'

It was usually something that he, Nathaniel and I said to each other, but sometimes just two of us would do it. Sometimes you just needed it.

3

It was late enough in the day that the vampires had begun to rise in the underground beneath the Circus of the Damned, so when I called to see if we could borrow the private jet, Jean-Claude was awake enough to take the call himself. His voice held none of that sleepy edge because he didn't really sleep; he died during the day, so when he woke it was abrupt and instant 'awake.' Vampires sleep more like a switch: on, awake; off, dead. His body would even cool over the hours, not as cold as a real corpse, and there was no color change, because the body wasn't really 'dead,' and it wasn't beginning to rot. If you were really dead, and human, the body began to rot as soon as the heart stopped. It's like cutting a flower in your garden; you can put it into water, delay the process, but from the moment you pick it, it begins to die. The flower looks pretty for a long time, but it's just a waiting game, the end is inevitable. Jean-Claude was a vampire, Master of the City of St Louis, and he'd been dead and beautiful for about six hundred years; his end was not inevitable. Theoretically, he could still be fresh as an unblemished rose five billion years from now when our sun finally gave up the ghost, expanded, and ate the planet. Of course, I'd killed enough vampires in my job as a legal vampire executioner to know that even being master of a territory and head of the newly formed American Vampire Council didn't make him truly immortal, just fucking powerful. That was one of the reasons he was awake with the sun still shining in the sky. If he hadn't been deep underground in what had begun as a natural cave system but had been carved out decades ago into luxurious rooms, even he would have still been dead to the world.

'I can feel your anxiety, *ma petite*. What has happened?'

I told him.

'I can arrange for you and Micah to go, but I will not be able to follow until I have reassured the master of that territory that we are not coming to take over his lands.'

'It hadn't occurred to me that we'd need to clear it with the local vamps to visit Micah's dad in the hospital.'

'If you and he were simply a couple, then no, but you are my human servant, one leg of the triumvirate of power that we share with my wolf to call, our reluctant Richard. If it was Richard, two of us heading into another's territory, they would be certain we were coming to destroy them.'

'We just need to get Micah to his dad's bedside before it's too late, that's all. Surely they can just check and see that the man is in the hospital.'

'It is never that simple to cross from one land to another for master vampires or for the leaders of wereanimal groups. Micah and you are the Nimir-Ra and Nimir-Raj, leopard queen and king, of our local pard. Are there wereleopards in Micah's hometown?'

'I don't know,' I said.

'You need to know,' he said, quietly.

'Shit,' I said, and put real feeling into it. 'This is going to piss me off really soon.'

'The new vampire council is very new, *ma petite*; we cannot afford to be seen as tyrants and bullies. If you enter other territories without at the very least alerting them, then it will be viewed as arrogance. It will seem as if you – we – feel that the entire country is ours to visit and use as we see fit. It will make the lesser leaders nervous and even be used by our enemies to stir up more rebellion against us.'

'I thought we took out the last rebels, or do you know something I don't?'

'I do not know of rebels in our country, but I know with certainty that there is discontent, because there is always discontent. Never in any government of any form is everyone in an entire country happy with being ruled. It is the nature of the political beast to be hated.'

'So you're saying they hate us because we formed a council to keep them safe from all the rogue vampires?'

'I'm saying that they ran to us for safety, but now that they feel safe, they will begin to look at the very power that enabled us to keep them safe, and they will begin to mistrust it, even fear it.'

'Well, isn't that just peachy. So, Micah, Nathaniel and I can't go to see his father.'

'Why Nathaniel?'

'He's our third. Micah wants him to come.'

'Ah, I thought perhaps you were taking Nathaniel as your leopard to call, and Damian as well, as your vampire part of your own triumvirate of power.' A super-powerful vampire could form a three-way power structure between their human servant and a were-animal whose beast form was their normal animal to call, but I was the first human to be able to do my own equivalent of it. Jean-Claude thought that the fact that I was a necromancer and his human servant had enabled me to do the metaphysically impossible, but honestly, we didn't know how I'd done it, just that I had.

'I hadn't planned on taking Damian. He's part of my power base, but he's not our sweetie.'

'He is your lover on occasion.'

'If I took everyone who was my lover on occasion, we'd need a bigger plane.'

He laughed, that wonderful, touchable sound that thrilled down my skin as if he were touching me over the phone. It made me shiver. His voice still held that deep edge of masculine laughter as he said, 'Very true, *ma petite*, very true.'

I had to swallow past the pulse in my throat. He'd made me breathless with just his voice. 'God, Jean-Claude, stop that. I can't think when you do that.'

He laughed again, which didn't help at all. I realized he was doing it very deliberately when I felt the weight deep inside my body like the promise of orgasm. 'Don't you dare!'

The power began to retreat. He'd never been able to make me do the full-blown orgasm over the phone with just his voice until he'd been made head of the new American version of the vampire council. I'd known that it meant that all the master vampires had to make a fealty oath to Jean-Claude as their leader, but I hadn't understood that it came with a power bump, or what that might mean. We'd had no choice. It was us in charge or someone else, and I trusted us.

'I am sorry, *ma petite*, this new power level is a heady thing. I can see why the other masters fear the head of the council, because to be head and take the oaths of their leaders means we have a little bit of all their power. It is a great deal of power.'

'You're saying if you weren't a better person that power corrupts and this much power would corrupt you absolutely?'

'I am not always certain that it is I who am the better person, *ma petite*, but together we are the better person.'

'I don't think I'm always the civilizing influence, Jean-Claude.'

'Nor do I, but through all the metaphysics we have Richard's conscience, Micah's sense of fellowship, Nathaniel's gentleness, Cynric's sense of fair play, and Jade's memories of the terrible use that her master made against her of his ultimate power. The people we have gathered and bound to us have helped make us powerful, but they also help me remember that I am not a monster and do not wish to be.'

'Can you not be a monster just by deciding not to be one?' I asked, and he knew me well enough to know that it wasn't his impending monsterhood I was worried about.

'You are not a monster, *ma petite*, and if we are both conscious of the possibility I believe we can avoid becoming such.'

'So, what do we need to do before Micah, Nathaniel, and I show up at the hospital?'

'Are you intending just the three of you to go?'

'Well, us and the pilot, yes.'

'You must have bodyguards with you, *ma petite*.'

'If we take guards, won't the locals be even more sure we've come to take them over?'

'Some, perhaps, but if our enemies were to realize that my human servant, her leopard to call, and her King of Beasts were all alone and unguarded, I fear the temptation would be too great to see what would happen to the rest of us if the three of you died.'

'Kill enough of our power structure and the rest die with us; yeah, I remember the theory.'

'It is more than theory, *ma petite*. You have seen Nathaniel and Damian almost die when you drained them of energy. You have felt the loss when Richard and I were injured. Let us not test the theory of what would happen if three of us were injured simultaneously.'

'Agreed, but it has to be minimal guards, Jean-Claude. We're going to be seeing Micah's family for the first time. Let's not scare them too much.'

'You feel confident that you can protect yourself and them with minimal guards?'

'With the right ones, yeah, I do.'

'So confident, *ma petite*. It is both admirable and a little frightening to me.'

'Why frightening?' I asked.

'Just because you are dangerous, even deadly, and kill easily and well, does not make you bulletproof, *ma petite*.'

'Or bombproof,' I said. 'I'm not Superman. I know I can be hurt, and I'll have Nathaniel and Micah with me. Regardless of the metaphysical fallout, if they got hurt I don't know what I'd do.'

'And if it were I that were hurt?'

And there it was: This beautiful, amazing man could still feel insecure, still wonder if I loved him, or at least how much. Since we could all feel each others' emotions when we weren't shielding like sons of bitches, it was interesting that we could all still be insecure sometimes. In Jean-Claude, whom I'd once thought the ultimate ladies' man, it was endearing and made me love him more.

'I love you, Jean-Claude; I wouldn't know what to do without you in my life, my bed, my heart.'

'Very poetic for you, *ma petite*.'

'I've been hanging out too much with Requiem, I guess.'

'When this crisis is taken care of, we will need to decide if he should return to Philadelphia permanently.'

'And become Evangeline's second banana for good,' I said.

'Yes,' he said.

'You know, my dad used to breed beagles when I was little. I never wanted to give up any of the puppies, and when I got old enough I always worried the new owners wouldn't take care of them the way we did.'

'I did not know that,' he said.

'We're giving away a hell of a lot more than puppies, Jean-Claude. These are our people, our lovers, our friends, and we're sending them away. I don't mind the ones who are going to rule their own territories as new masters, but the ones we're giving over to other masters as second-in-command, that sort of bugs me.'

'That is why we have a trial visit, or three, to make certain it is a good fit and that our people are being well treated.'

'Requiem doesn't love Evangeline,' I said.

'No, he loves you.'

I sighed. 'I didn't mean for him to fall in love with me.'

'And I did not mean for you to acquire the power of my *ardeur*, my fire of lust, and become a living succubus to my incubus, but the damage is done. We are what we are, and now you know the power that you possess during sex when you feed the *ardeur*.'

'Requiem is a master vampire, Jean-Claude, and he broke the initial unintentional binding.'

'I believe he loves you, *ma petite*, not because of the *ardeur*, but because of you, and him. Love is never about the object of our love, but always says more about us than them.'

'What does that even mean?' I asked.

'It means that Requiem needs to love someone. He has always been a hopeless romantic, and what is more hopeless than being in love with someone who is in love with others?'

'You make it sound like he needs therapy.'

'It would not hurt,' he said.

I sighed. 'You think he'd see a therapist?'

'If we ordered him to do it, he would.'

'We can order him to make appointments and talk to someone, but we can't force him to actually do the work. You've got to be willing to work on your issues. You've got to be willing to face hard truths and fight to get better. That takes courage and force of will.'

'He has courage, but I do not believe he wishes to recover from this sickness of love.'

'I can't help that he cares for me more than I care for him.'

'No, you cannot.'

'Back to the crisis at hand,' I said.

'You've had enough of this topic, I take it.'

'Yeah,' I said. I'd actually had more than enough of it, but . . . . 'One crisis per day, okay?'

'As you like,' he said.

'This isn't what I like, Jean-Claude. I didn't know if I'd ever meet Micah's family, but I didn't want to meet them this way.'

'No, of course not, *ma petite*. The plane is at your disposal. It only remains to choose the guards to accompany you.'

'How many is minimum?' I asked.

'Six.'

'Two apiece,' I said.

'*Oui.*'

'Can you arrange for the plane while I do the guards?' I asked.

'Of course, and I would suggest that most of the guards be your lovers. You will need to feed the *ardeur*, and Micah's grief may make his interest in such things less.'

I nodded, knew he couldn't see it, and said, 'Agreed.'

'I have regretted in the past not being able to take you home to visit my family, because they are long dead, but moments like this remind me that there are worse things than having lost them long ago.'

'Yeah, losing them here and now sucks a lot.'

He gave a small laugh. 'Ah, *ma petite*, you do have a way with words.'

'I am frowning at you right now, just so you know.'

'But you do not mean it,' he said.

I smiled. 'No, I don't.'

'*Je t'aime, ma petite.*'

'I love you, too, master.'

'You always say that with such derision and usually an eye roll. You will never, ever, mean it.'

'Do you really want me to mean it?'

'No,' he said, 'I want true partners, not slaves, or servants. I have learned that is why I chose you and Richard. I knew you would fight to remain free, to remain yourselves.'

'Did you know just how hard we'd fight?' I asked.

He laughed then, and it shivered over my body, making me shut my eyes and shudder at my desk. 'Stop that,' I breathed.

'Do you truly wish me to never do that again?'

My breath came out in a shaking sigh. 'No,' I said, at last. 'I'll call Fredo and see whom he can spare from the guards I want, and if he agrees with the mix of skills.'

'I trust you and our senior wererat to work out such details.'

'Thank you. There would have been a time when you would have insisted on picking them yourself.'

'There was a time when you were attracted to weaker men, but that has ceased to be true.'

'Remember, I was attracted to you in my weaker-men days,' I said.

'You have made me a better man, Anita Blake, as you have all the men, and women, in your life now.'

'I don't know what to say to that. I feel like I should apologize or something.'

'It is in the nature of some leaders to bring out the best in those around them.'

'Hey, I'm not in charge of this little metaphysical bus; you are, remember?'

'I am the political leader, but in an emergency most of our people will take your orders over mine.'

'That's not true,' I said.

'In a fight, they will.'

'Okay, if it's violence, then yeah, it's what I'm good at. You're much better at the politics and dinner party stuff.'

'You have your moments in the political arena.'

'And only a few of the Harlequin are better than you with a rapier.' In fact, I'd been a little amazed at how good he was with his chosen weapon. He'd turned out to have been a famous duelist in his day, as a human and young vampire. He'd explained that his blade work had been what allowed him to survive; the masters of the day had challenged him, and he'd chosen his weapon and he'd killed them. I'd never known until he started practicing in the new gym where the other guards and I could see.

'Are you salving my ego, *ma petite*?'

'I think so.'

He laughed, and this time it was just humor. 'I do not need it. I am king and you are both my queen and my general. One who leads the charge from the front and always will. You know our guards' strengths and weaknesses better than I, because you practice and work out with them. You have quite shamed me and some of the older vampires into exercising more.'

'Most vampires can't gain muscle; the body at death is what it is, unchanging.'

'But I can, and my vampires can.'

'One of the rebel vampires said it's because you take power from them.'

'That helps me be powerful, *oui*, but I believe it is more that my ties to our wereanimals are more intimate. I accept their warm power more as an equal instead of the master/slave relationship that most older masters had.'

'Yeah, none of this treating the wereanimals like pets and property on our watch.'

'It is one of the bones of contention with some of the older vampires.'

'Yeah, they can just suck it up; the wereanimals are flocking to us because of the more equal rights stance.'

'It is impossible to make everyone happy, so in the end we make ourselves happy and do what we can for others. I want no slaves in my kingdom.'

'Agreed,' I said.

'I must hang up to make the plane ready for you,' he said.

'Yes, of course.'

'You are delaying. Why?'

I had to think about it for a minute, and then I gave him the out-loud, honest answer that once I would have died before admitting. 'I don't know if I'll get a chance to talk to you again, and I'll miss you.'

'That makes me happier than I can say, my love. You have quite surprised and pleased me.'

'If I don't say it enough, Jean-Claude, I love you. I love seeing your face across the table while we eat, and watching you root at Cynric's football games, and watching you read bedtime stories to Matthew when he stays with us, and a thousand surprising things, all of it, it's you, and I love you.'

'You will make me cry.'

'A smart friend told me that it's okay to cry; sometimes you're so happy it spills out your eyes.'

'Jason, Nathaniel, or Micah?' he asked.

'One of them,' I said with a smile.

'Smart friends indeed. We must go and do our tasks, *ma petite*. *Je t'aime, au revoir*, until we meet again.'

'I love you, too, and see you soon.' I hung up before I could get any sillier or more romantic. But a little bit of squirming embarrassment was totally worth it for the happiness in his voice. If we'd dropped our metaphysical shields we could have felt every breath and emotion, even some thoughts of each other, but it was still good to say the words and to hear them. No matter how weird and magical we might be, having the people you love tell you they love you and mean it . . . it never goes out of style. Since we're made in God's image, this must be from Him, so even God must need an 'atta boy,' an out-loud, in-your-head 'Thank you, great job on that sunset, and the platypus was a brilliant fun idea.' Maybe that's why we're supposed to pray the way we do, because without it God would be lonely. Sometimes I thought my friends who were Wiccan had something with this whole God and Goddess thing. If people worked better paired up and in love, and we were made in God's image, then logically it seemed like God needed a Goddess. As I got happier in my own love life, I'd started wondering if God was lonely without His Goddess. Maybe I was hanging around with too many pagans?

I said a prayer of gratitude for my own happiness, and a prayer for Micah's dad, and let God go back to taking care of His love life as He saw fit. I called Fredo to arrange the guards and shook my head at my own weirdly romantic religious thoughts; so girly, to wonder if God needed a Wife. That was above my faith pay grade. Picking out dangerous men to guard our backs, that I understood.

4

Micah texted me that he'd called Nathaniel to pack for us so he could meet us at the airport. I let him know I'd gotten his message and called the other third of our couple. Nathaniel answered on the second ring.

'Hey, Anita.'

'Hey, pussycat.' No, most men wouldn't have liked that as a nickname, but he wasn't most men. 'Micah told me you're packing for all of us. Can you bear in mind we're meeting his family for the first time, with the clothes?'

'I am,' he said.

'I need some shirts that aren't low-cut, okay?'

'We love your breasts,' he said, his voice holding that upward lilt that said he was smiling.

I smiled. 'I appreciate that, I even approve, but let's not overwhelm his family with my assets the first time.'

'Would I pack so that all that creamy goodness was on display in every shirt?' he asked in that fake innocent voice.

'Yes,' I said, and laughed.

'I promise to pack some regular T-shirts, but most of your dressy tops are low-cut.'

'That's because the plain silk shell blouses don't lie right when I wear them,' I said.

'They aren't designed for someone with a triple-E cup, Anita. I didn't even know that you could have that big a cup size and be as lean as you are without surgical help.'

'Genetics is a wonderful thing,' I said.

'Yay, genetics!' he said with so much enthusiasm it made me laugh. 'I'll pack so we'll match but won't embarrass Micah. Promise.'

'Thank you. You're the only one I'd trust to pack for all of us.'

'I'll even wear a suit so we all match when we get to the hospital.' Nathaniel had beautiful designer suits, but since his regular job was as an exotic dancer he didn't have to wear them to work like Micah did. The suits were for special occasions like weddings and certain business meetings where all of Jean-Claude's main people had to show up looking businessy.

I realized that Nathaniel was strangely happy. It didn't quite match the reason for the trip. I thought about asking why his mood was so up, but my phone let me know there was another call trying to come through. 'I've got another call; let me make sure it's not Micah.'

'I'll wait,' he said, and again it was cheerful. Was it too cheerful, or was he just better at handling these emergencies than I was?

It was Jean-Claude on the phone. 'Hey, what's up?'

'Are any of the guards you have arranged werewolves?'

'Yes, it's Micah's rule and yours that we try to use as many were-animals for our public bodyguards as possible.'

'You will need to make other arrangements, *ma petite*.'

'Why?' I asked.

'The local wolves have requested that you not bring anyone in who could challenge them. If there is need of a funeral, then they will understand us bringing in our wolves to call, but until that sad necessity they would like none of our wolves, as a sign of good faith.'

'Are you letting them boss us around too much?' I asked.

'If you want this initial visit to be about Micah and his dying father, no. If you want to have to deal with the local werewolves politically, and perhaps even frighten them enough to have it turn to violence, then by all means keep your wolf guard.'

'Okay, I'll switch the guard roster.'

'Good,' he said.

'Is there anything else I need to know?'

'The master vampire of the area has forgone the usual politics and wishes our Micah well. In fact, he offered to put his people at our disposal for transportation and errands so that you could all concentrate on Micah's family.'

'That was very nice of him,' I said, and couldn't keep the suspicion out of my voice.

'It was nice of him, *ma petite*, but we are no longer just visiting masters from out of town. We are council members, or their people, and thus we are owed both allegiance and a certain deferential treatment.'

'So, now that you're on the council we don't have to do all the vampire political shit?'

'In part, yes, but on the other hand, it means we have to be even more conscious of other masters and their egos, unless you wish to feed the whispers of rebellion among them?'

'You know I don't,' I said.

'Then remember that when you are dealing with him and his people, please.'

'Are you afraid I'll be rude and spook them?'

'You, rude, *ma petite*, why would I fear that?' The sarcasm was not that thick, but the very delicate touch of it brought it home.

'I'll be good. It's nice of them to help us out at short notice.'

'They have little choice; the old European council would have seen a refusal of such niceties as a grave insult and would have acted accordingly.'

'What does "act accordingly" mean in this context?'

'You have met envoys from the council, *ma petite*. What do you think they would do to a master who was discourteous to them?'

'Scare the hell out of him, torment, torture, overthrow him maybe if they had someone to put in his place, or in some cases just for the hell of the chaos it would cause.'

'On one hand we are hampered by the old council's actions; it makes the others fear a council here in the United States. They fear we will go mad with power, but on the other hand, they will offer up service and courtesy in hopes of placating us and keeping us from having a reason to be angry with them.'

'So, on one hand the old council's reputation makes things harder for us and scares everyone, and on the other hand they'll probably behave better because they're more afraid of us.'

'*Exactement,*' he said.

'Wait, we had to offer food to visiting council people. Are they going to offer us food for the *ardeur*?'

'I have not arranged it, but if they do not then it is a sign that they are not giving us the same respect that they gave the old council.'

'You're using this as a test to see how Fredrico behaves toward us, toward you.' I fought not to sound accusatory.

'I did not engineer this visit, *ma petite*, but now that we have it, yes, it is a test for the local master. We must discover how well we rule, or how weak our rule is, so that we can decide how tightly we wish to hold the reins of power.'

'I'd rather not use visiting Micah's dying father as a test of loyalty for the local vampires.'

'Not just vampires, *ma petite*, but local wereanimals. Our Micah travels the country talking to various animal groups, helping them deal with their problems. He promotes better relations between normal humans and the lycanthrope community. He has become the public face of the movement and is often called to handle disputes hundreds of miles from our lands.'

'What are you saying, Jean-Claude?'

'We learned that the reason you have no other king of any other animal group as attached to you as Micah is that metaphysically you have your furred king. Through you, he has ties to many more animals besides the leopards.'

'I know, I know, we have ties to all sorts of wereanimals, and Micah is a real leopard king in the metaphysical sense, able to rule by supernatural power and not just force of will and actions. If I hadn't had a wereanimal in my bed that was a true king, then it wouldn't have worked that way, but I thought that was just here in St Louis. You're saying that the other wereanimals across the country are being attracted to Micah's power and don't even realize it?'

'No, I am stating that when he travels and meets them, the power of a true king follows him. People want to be protected, *ma petite*. In America they teach that everyone should be the hero of their own story, but most people are not suited for it. They want, and need, someone to follow. If they are lucky they find someone good to lead them; if they are not so lucky . . .' He let the thought trail off.

'Micah's good,' I said.

'Yes, he is good and strong and thinks of the larger group, the bigger issues.'

'I don't think Micah has called and talked to the animal groups in his hometown.'

'That is why I did it for him.'

'You should probably tell him you did that.'

'I have,' Jean-Claude said.

'What did he say?'

'He was grateful for the help, and he told me that politics was the furthest thing from his mind.'

'Of course it is,' I said.

'But that does not change the fact that this visit is political, *ma petite*.'

'Oh, shit, you're going to say that since Micah can't, I have to oversee more politics.'

He gave a small chuckle. 'Not precisely, but I have spoken with Fredo not about your choice of guards, but about the possible political pitfalls. He said he would inform whatever guards you chose to take with you, though he did say that if it was a political visit he'd have chosen different guards. I told him that your safety is more important than the politics, so go with the original guards, whoever they might be.'

'You know, I totally trust that you didn't ask who we'd picked.'

'In choosing soldiers, *ma petite*, I would trust you implicitly.'

'Thank you. I trust you and Micah politically. Bad timing that it's me with the clearer head on this trip.'

'It is unfortunate,' he said.

I had a thought that I hadn't before, and felt slow. 'I'm feeding off Rafael the Rat King and Reece the Swan King. If either of them had been my lover before I found Micah, would they have been my "king" in the same sense that Micah is?'

'I do not believe so, but I do not know for certain. I do know that the rats and the swans are the only animal groups that have a countrywide ruler. I know you do not feed the *ardeur* on either of them often, but when you do I have felt the energy of everyone bound to their king.'

I shivered, and not from happiness. It was the most amazing feeling to feel people hundreds of miles away give up their energy to their king, and through him to me. I knew the faces of some of the swan-manes and wererats even though I had never seen them outside a metaphysical energy exchange.

'You think Micah is starting to be the overall king?'

'I believe that he has the unique opportunity to become the . . . high king of most of the lycanthrope community in this country. I believe he has taken the wererat model as his working blueprint.'

'You and Micah have talked about this?'

'A bit.'

'Don't you think I should have been included?'

'What did you think was happening, *ma petite*? Micah and his Coalition are called in across the country to settle disputes between diverse animal groups so they can avoid violence and be more "human." When a group of people turn to the same person time and again for leadership, what does that mean, *ma petite*?'

'That he is their leader, or becoming their leader.'

'The fact that you did not see that is because you did not want to see it. You hate the politics. Micah is not wanting to be king, but he is too intelligent a leader not to see the possibilities.'

'Okay, so I've been slow and a little stupid, sorry.'

'Slow, but never stupid, *ma petite*; perhaps oblivious from time to time.'

'Fine, so what do I do with this visit since Micah is going to be too overwrought to do the politics?'

'Concentrate on Micah. Fredrico was very understanding that would be the priority for this visit.'

'Do we know any of Fredrico's background?'

'Yes, he was a Spanish conquistador and nobleman once.'

'Usually ex-nobles aren't very understanding of problems like Micah's,' I said.

'Very true, *ma petite*, but perhaps he is afraid of us. As a nobleman you learn to be very polite to those more powerful.'

'I prefer aggression myself.'

'Ah, but you have never had to survive at a noble court; it teaches you humility, *ma petite*.'

'Humility isn't my best thing.'

He laughed then, and it was a straight-out, laughing-his-ass-off laugh. I wasn't sure I'd ever heard him laugh quite like that. When he didn't stop right away I said, 'Fine, fine, laugh it up. I've got Nathaniel on hold.'

'I am sorry, *ma petite*, but you are one of the least humble people I have ever met when it comes to negotiations.'

'I prefer to negotiate from a point of strength.'

'Even if you do not have one,' he said.

'We are stronger than this Fredrico, right?'

'Much stronger.'

'Then he was gracious because he didn't have a choice,' I said.

'Yes, *ma petite*, but when you see his people, please do not point that out. Let their master and them keep their pride. Fredrico comes from a time when you challenged people to duels to the death to avenge a slight to your honor. Do not make him feel he has been slighted, please.'

'Is wolf his animal to call? Is that why you were so polite with the local pack?'

'*Non, ma petite*, he does not have an animal to call. I was political with the main animal groups because that is how Micah would wish it. We are building our power structure on the equality of all preternatural beings, not just the superiority of the vampires. It is a novel approach, very American, very progressive. The younger among us approve; the older ones distrust it, or even disapprove of welcoming the lycanthropes into a broader position of power.'

'Fredrico is an ex-conquistador, so that makes him older. Does he have a problem with us including the furry in the power structure?'

'Not that he has stated.'

'No animal to call makes him pretty low-power for a Master of the City,' I said.

'It does, which was why his territory was initially in a rural area. No one could have foreseen the spread of human cities until his countryside lands became part of a city rich enough with life to make him a much more important master.'

'If he's that weak, I'm surprised someone didn't challenge him years back.'

'He kept up his sword practice, and as they challenged him he was able to choose the method of the duel.'

'You're saying he won because he's a kickass swordsman.'

'As long as the challenger is not a member of the council, then as the challenged he may choose his weapon, and it would be considered cheating to use animals to call when he has none.'

'So his weakness becomes a strength,' I said.

'In part.'

'But you are a member of the council, so how does that change things?'

'You fought beside me when the Earthmover came and tried to destroy us. As a council member he could have insisted on using every power he possessed. He could have used the very earth against us and reduced our fair city to rubble.'

'The Earthmover wanted to make humans afraid of vampires again. An earthquake wouldn't have done that, because no one would have believed a vampire did it.'

'True, but he would still have been within his rights to do it.'

'So, if you fought Fredrico we could bring all our wereanimals, everything, and just destroy his ass.'

'And put a master of our choosing in his place, *oui*.'

'So, we play nice, and let him save face.'

'*Oui.*'

'Okay, I understand that.'

'Good, now talk to our Nathaniel. Do you wish me to call Fredo and tell him we need a new guard?'

'I'd rather help choose the substitute.'

'Then cut short your talk with our pussycat.'

'I will,' I said. 'Love you.'

'*Je t'aime, ma petite.*'

I switched back to Nathaniel. He said, 'You're on speakerphone; I had to keep packing.'

'I understand.'

'What did Jean-Claude want?'

'I'll tell you on the plane; right now I have to finish arranging the bodyguards.'

'Okay,' he said.

'Love you,' I said.

'Love you more,' he said.

'Love you most.'

'Love you mostest,' he said.

I guess both of my wereleopards were feeling a little insecure. Hell, me, too.

5

I'm usually phobic of flying, and as I tightened the seat belt in my roomy, cushioned seat, it didn't make me like it any better. The seats were bigger, but the plane was narrower. Did I mention that I'm also claustrophobic? It's the combination that makes flying such fun. But the moment Micah sat down beside me and reached for my hand, I stopped worrying about my fears and worried about him. His face was passive behind the dark sunglasses, but tension sang through his hand, his arm, so I knew his body was thrumming with it. In all the rush to get ready to leave, this was the first time I'd seen him since I had to tell him the bad news.

'Are you all right?' As soon as I heard it out loud I knew it was stupid, but it's what you say.

He smiled, but it was sad, and self-deprecating, and held a little anger. It was the smile he'd first had when he came to me. It was a smile, but so full of other emotions that it was never really happy. I was sad to see it back on his face.

I leaned in and wrapped my arms around him, drew him in to me, and let him wrap his arms around me. My seat belt kept me a little pinned so he had to come to me more, but he didn't seem to mind. My chin tucked over his shoulder, because he was the same height as me. He was the only man I'd ever dated who was five foot three just like me. We could wear each other's T-shirts, and some of our jeans. He was the shortest and most physically delicate-looking man in my life, but the strength as he hugged me wasn't delicate. I knew the body under the designer suit moved with lean muscle . . . He ran miles every week, usually outside in all weather. He called it his thinking time.

He spoke with his face buried in my hair. 'I don't know how to do this.'

'See your folks?' I asked.

'Yes.'

I kept hugging him but raised one hand to stroke the thick curls of his ponytail. 'I'm so sorry you're having to go home like this.'

He squeezed me so tight that I almost had to tell him, *too tight*. He loosened his grip before I could do any more than tense. He was a wereleopard, which meant he could crush most metal in his hand, but he was always very aware of his strength.

'I'm sorry,' he said, and drew out of the hug to sit back in his seat, resting his head against it.

I took his hand again and stayed turned toward him. 'It's okay, you're upset.'

'I'll be upset this whole visit probably. How do I see them again, Anita? How do I deal with my dad hurt . . . maybe dying?'

He turned his head, still resting against the seat, and spoke directly on a topic that we'd hardly ever talked about. 'I can't imagine losing a parent as early as you did. This feels awful already.'

I nodded. 'It is awful, but I was only eight when my mother died. You grew up with both your parents until you were ready to go off to college. I had just my dad until I was ten, and then a stepmom that I totally didn't get along with and a stepsister my own age, and then they had Josh together. I can't even imagine what my life might have been like if my mom had lived.'

'I've got a stepfather and half-brothers.'

'You never said.'

He shrugged. 'I wasn't close with my mom's second family. I was on Dad's side after the divorce. I loved my mother, but she left him. He never really found anyone else to love, just her, as if he could only love one person.'

'You were what, twelve, when they divorced?'

'Yes.'

I studied his face, tried to read behind the sunglasses. It wasn't that bright in the plane, but he was used to wearing them in public to hide his leopard eyes. He'd lost his ability to regain full human form because Chimera, the sadistic leader who took over his leopard pard, had punished him by forcing him into animal form so long that his eyes hadn't come back and never would. I loved his green-gold eyes, especially with his summer tan that he got so easily. I had my father's Germanic skin, always pale, never tan.

'You said you had brown eyes originally – whose eyes do you have, colorwise?'

He smiled and this time it was a real smile. 'My father's.'

The smile was full of love, happiness, memories, of a son's pride in having his father's eyes. I knew that Micah had been his father's hunting buddy, as I'd been for mine. We'd both grown up hunting and camping.

'So you look like your dad?'

'He's a little taller, but we're built alike. He knew to put me into gymnastics and martial arts as a kid, not peewee football. He loves watching the games, but he was always too small to play, and he knew I would be, too, so he didn't put me through the frustration of it the way his own dad did.'

'Your grandfather?' I asked.

'Yeah, he's five-eight, built bigger. Dad and I are built like my grandma's side of the family. I don't know why it never occurs to big, burly guys that when they marry the tiny cheerleader some of the kids may look more like her, even the boys. They never think it through.'

'I take it your grandfather isn't your favorite person.'

'My dad and he had issues with my dad not being big enough for regular sports, though Dad went to college on a baseball scholarship. He was good enough for college, but he didn't have the size for the power hitting you need in the majors, and he knew it.'

'Baseball is a manly sport,' I said.

Micah grinned. 'Granddad Callahan played football and wrestled. He also muscled up better than we did. More like Nathaniel.'

As if just saying his name had conjured him, our other sweetie walked up the little steps and into the jet. His shoulders were broader than Micah's, and at five foot seven he carried the extra muscle well. He'd actually had to stop lifting as much in the gym because he was bulking up too much to keep the flexibility he needed as a dancer. Micah fought for every bit of muscle in the gym. Nathaniel's dark auburn hair must have been pulled back into a tight braid because it gave the illusion that his hair was short. He was still wearing his sunglasses, not to hide his eyes, but because it was bright outside. With his eyes hidden and his hair back and a charcoal-gray suit hiding all his body, there was just the line of his face, with nothing to distract the gaze from the near-perfect line that ran from his temple to the cheekbones, the chin that managed to be both masculine and soft. It was the lips that did it, I think, wide, curved lines, just full enough to soften what might have been handsome to make it beautiful. It was his face unadorned, but that was like saying Michelangelo's *David* was unadorned marble.

Micah's hand tightened in mine, and it wasn't sorrow now. Had his pulse sped up, too, just watching our other third walk into the plane? His hand tightened a little more and we turned and looked at each other at the same time. I had a moment of looking at the delicate triangle of his face with his fuller lips that dominated more of his face, and then he burst out laughing, and I joined him. It was as if some horrible tension had just floated away.

Nathaniel smiled and then said, 'Did I do something funny?'

'No,' Micah said, 'just God, you are . . . so . . .'

'Beautiful,' I said.

'Yes,' Micah said.

Nathaniel blushed and gave us one of those big, bright, utterly happy smiles. It made his whole face glow with it, but the blush, that was the rarest of all.

'I've never seen you blush,' I said.

He actually ducked his head as if embarrassed, which I'd never seen either. It was Micah who got up first and went to him. I tried to stand up and the seat belt jerked me back to my seat, reminding me that I'd been a little too safety conscious. It meant I got to sit there and watch them hug each other. It started out as the good-friend guy hug, only upper bodies touching, that distinct hip distance kept, and then Micah moved back enough to look up at the taller man and I had a moment to watch them look at each other. With both of them in sunglasses, suits, hair back, I was treated to their faces in profile in a way I almost never got to see. If Nathaniel was carved marble, then Micah was something more delicate, like carved ivory, if ivory could tan dark and have an edge of curls framing its face even with the ponytail. His hair, like mine, was too curly to behave like Nathaniel's.

They kissed, and I held my breath, watching their lips move, their arms tighten around each other, Nathaniel's hands tensing against the back of Micah's suit jacket so he could feel the muscles underneath the elegant conservative cloth.

They broke from the kiss and looked at me, both of their faces full front, nearly side by side, so that I got the full impact of those clean, sculpted lines, the half-parted lips, their arms still loosely around each other.

I'd like to say I said something profound, or poetic, but what I actually said was, 'Wow.'

Nathaniel grinned. 'I think she liked watching.'

Micah smiled and held one hand out to me, an invitation to join them.

I tried to get up and forgot my seat belt again, and then it was as if I'd forgotten how it worked. I had to fight with it, and the men were laughing as I said, 'You have kissed me stupid and I wasn't even part of the kiss.'

'Do you need help?' Micah asked, his voice full of laughter.

I got free and went to them. They opened up the circle of their arms to bring me in to them. I was suddenly in the circle of their bodies with their deeper masculine laughter, the warmth and weight of them around me, and it was better than almost anything I had ever imagined having. Once I'd thought I could only be in love with one person at a time, but I loved Jean-Claude, and I loved the two men in my arms. I loved them together; as a unit, we were three. Jean-Claude was his own entity, and he and I, even with all the other bed partners, were more a couple. I was in love with him, too.

I stood there in their arms and loving them, and their loving me, didn't take away from Jean-Claude and me; it added to it. All of the relationships added to one another, until we were all happier than we'd ever been. I didn't believe in happily-ever-after, but I did believe in happier-than-we'd-ever-been, because I was living it.

I raised my face and Nathaniel leaned down to kiss me, while Micah held us both, or we held him, and I knew once this kiss was done there would be another one from Micah. Life was great. We could get through this, whatever came when we landed in Micah's old hometown; we could do this, because we loved one another. Love doesn't conquer all, but it can help you conquer everything else.

6

Voices from outside the plane made us look up from the warm circle of us. I tried to look down the steps to see what was making people raise their voices, but I couldn't see past Nathaniel's broad shoulders and chest. He could see, and Micah had a better angle, so I asked, 'What's up?'

'Nicky is blocking the stairs and the other guards aren't happy about it,' Nathaniel said.

'Nilda isn't happy about it,' Micah added.

They moved to either side so I could see for myself. Nicky stood at the bottom of the foldout steps like a wall of blond muscle. He was just under six feet, so Nilda towered over him by five inches; at six foot four she was the second-tallest woman I'd ever met and she hit the gym seriously. It had given her long arms smooth tone and muscle, but she was one of those women who didn't put on muscle easily. She looked strong and imposing, but Nicky's shoulders were almost as wide as I was tall, a huge spread of muscle that nothing would give Nilda no matter how many weights she lifted. I muscled up faster than she did. It was just one of those genetic things. Her summer tan was a light gold that contrasted strongly with her white-blond hair and made her blue eyes stand out in the high cheekbones of her strongly Scandinavian face like an advertisement for Norwegian Vacations-R-Us. Her full name was Brunhilda, after one of the Valkyries, and yelling into Nicky's face, her shoulders and arms straining with tension, her face enraged, she looked it. She was one of the Harlequin who had been the bodyguards, spies, assassins, judges, and executioners of vampirekind for centuries. So deadly that to even speak of them could get a vampire hunted down and killed. They had been the elite guards of the Mother of All Darkness, the legendary first vampire, the darkness made flesh, and she had used them to keep her control absolute. Then she grew bored, or old, and fell into a 'hibernation' for centuries and her control slipped, and the Harlequin began to fracture into those who believed in their original purpose and those who didn't. Nilda was the animal to call of one of the master vampires who had been Harlequin, and she was now with us. There were days when I was pretty sure Nilda would have stayed on the other side with the Harlequin who were still pissed that we'd destroyed their mistress, but Nilda's master was old-school, which meant it had never occurred to him to give her a choice. She was his animal to call, and to the old-school vampires that meant she was just an extension of the vampire, a walking, talking, fighting machine that he occasionally fucked, but sometimes I think he saw it more as masturbating, as if she weren't real to him. No, I didn't like Nilda's master much, but I wasn't particularly fond of her either. She was on this detail in an effort to merge the Harlequin guards into our own, but some of them fit better than others. I wondered what Nicky had done to set her off. Nilda had a temper, but this was off the charts.

I moved toward the open door and could see two of the other guards sort of off to one side. Dev, short for Devil, which in turn was a nickname for Mephistopheles, was standing there grinning like he was enjoying the show. His handsome golden face was shining with happiness, only his blue-hazel eyes were softer, more careful. I didn't have to be closer to know that his body would be tensed and ready to do something if the argument got physical. He was halfway between the other two in height at six foot three; even his shoulders were halfway between Nilda's and Nicky's in width, though both of them had more muscle development than Dev. He was naturally big, naturally athletic, and it made him a lazy cat in the weight room. He worked out like a son of a bitch in weapons and hand-to-hand training, but he didn't like lifting the way the other two did.

Ethan watched it all, face serious, body language unhappy. He was only five-eight, one of our shorter guards, but he seemed to work all the harder for it. He was always the last to leave the practice mat and first to volunteer for learning something new. His short hair was a soft mass of curls, longer on top, so that it almost did a natural pompadour. His curls were a blond that was almost white with what looked like gray highlights in it. There was one streak of dark red from the back of his head to his forehead as if he'd added it for dramatic effect, but it was all-natural color. His eyes were a soft gray that matched the highlights.

'I've never seen Nilda lose it this bad,' Nathaniel said.

'Me either,' Micah and I said together. I moved out from between the two men and went for the stairs and the almost-fight. I'd try to see if I could keep it from turning into a real fight. I would have thought that Nicky had said something to bait her, but I couldn't think of anything that he could have said that would have caused this reaction. The Harlequin guard were supposed to be the ultimate spies, so they had to have iron-willed control, but what I'd noticed was that some of their wereanimal members had serious therapy-worthy issues. Their vampire masters were trying to use it as a way of saying, *See, they need a tight leash, because they're just animals*. I thought it was more that the wereanimals had been abused for centuries, some a thousand years' worth or more, and now they had the freedom to be a person and they didn't know how. Or now that they were allowed their real emotions they were just so angry, and they couldn't take it out on their masters, so they took it out where they could. Apparently, today Nilda was taking it out on Nicky. Fuck.

I came to the top of the steps and called out, 'Nilda, chill out.'

She didn't seem to hear me but poked a finger into Nicky's chest. I watched his shoulders stiffen. She'd touched him, escalated the fight, invited the physical. I yelled this time, 'No fighting! That's enough, Brunhilda!'

She glared up at me with her huge blue eyes gone almost gray. Gray meant that she was close to losing herself to her anger. In the months she'd been with us, we'd all learned that tell from our Viking maiden. The next tell was worse. Energy rolled off her in a wave of heat as if I'd stepped too near to a blasting furnace. In the old system, flaunting this much power would have made most other wereanimals back off and concede the fight or flash their own power. Now it breathed along my skin in a near-scalding heat, power so hot it took my breath away for a second. Even for Nilda this was a lot of power flaunting.

'You say we are one of you, but you always take their side! We served the Dark itself and now we are nothing!' she yelled, and it was as if the scalding heat spilled out her voice so that each word growled power, as if I should have been able to see the words hanging in the air between us like flame.

I kept my voice even but forceful as I said, 'You're the one yelling at me, Nilda. You're the one who's losing control in public like a newbie. Where is the famous discipline of the Harlequin?'

'You do not know what discipline means,' she growled. 'You are a little girl who has not lived a lifetime yet. We are Harlequin!' Her power poured around me, so hot it felt like it should hurt to touch my skin. I fought not to flinch and wondered how Nicky was standing so stoically barely an arm's length from her. Proximity made the effect worse, and touching could be downright painful, yet Nicky stood like a boulder in the rush of that river of power. If he could do it, I could do it.

I stepped down two more steps and it was like wading into a scalding bath, so hot you knew it would leave your skin red and hurting. 'You guys fight good, but so far I haven't been impressed with anything else. And this little girl is in charge of your ass, all your asses.'

'Jean-Claude is in charge; you are less than an animal to call, you are only a human slave. You should not be in charge of anything!'

Ah, here we had it. It was worse than being just the girlfriend, who everyone perceived as being given a management job because she was sleeping with the boss. In the old system of vampireland, preternatural power gave you rank — vampires first, then wereanimals, then human servants. Plain humans were pretty much just food.

'You are not the boss of me, human, and neither is Nicky!' She took a step closer to the big man who stood so silent in front of her.

'He's not in charge of you,' I said, and I let down my shields and very deliberately touched the beasts inside me. I called my own otherworldly heat and let it trickle down into hers. I took two more steps down into the heat of her rage, and my voice growled low and deep as hers. I held tiger, leopard, wolf, and lion in me; all she held was bear. It was one of the brown bears related to Kodiaks and grizzlies, but bigger. Some of the ancient wereanimal lines held the last genetic link to some extinct animal lines. There were several werebears among the Harlequin's animals to call, and they were big fuckers, but a bear was only one beast; I carried a menagerie in me. Jean-Claude's vampire marks kept me in human shape, or had so far, but I held the beasts inside me, including every bloodline of weretiger. 'I am!' I let those two words carry my power.

I was close enough to watch her eyes swim to dark reddish brown, her beast eyes in her human face. The eyes are usually the first to shift when a wereanimal begins to change. In all her displays of temper Nilda had never let her eyes change. Shit. My flashing power back should have calmed things down, because it showed I was ready to back down her threat with my own. Instead her eyes had gone. I so didn't need this today.

'You're behaving like a first-moon rookie. Control yourself or go back to the Circus. We don't need this shit.'

'My orders are that you need six guards. I'm the sixth. I won't disobey my orders.'

'Fredo takes orders from me. If I say you go home, you go home.'

She lowered her head, and I could almost see her power shimmer around her like a heat haze above a summer road. She swallowed it back, and when she looked up again her eyes were just blue and human, though the rage was still there plain to see. That was fine, she could be pissed; what she couldn't be was out of control.

'I will not disgrace my master.'

Things were calming down, but it was too late as far as I was concerned. I didn't have time to babysit Nilda's issues. I felt sorry for her, even understood some of her rage, but Micah needed me and that was my priority. 'I don't have time to babysit your issues, Nilda. I'm sorry that your afterlife has sucked, but it's not my problem today. Go back with the driver and the car. I'll phone Fredo and tell him to expect you.'

She looked up at me, and there was no anger now. She was studying my face, trying to read me. That was another thing I'd noticed particularly about the Harlequin's werebears; they didn't seem to be good with facial expressions, as if they had trouble interpreting human faces. I still had trouble reading the faces of those nearest and dearest to me when they were in animal form, so I hadn't asked about it, but maybe I should. Later I would, but not today.

'I have swallowed my power back. I have done as you asked. Why are you still sending me back?' Her voice was so reasonable, as if I were the one behaving badly.

'Because I can't afford to have you doing what you just did around Micah's family. His father is a law enforcement officer, which means there will be other cops around the hospital, and if you go all otherworldly around them they might just shoot you first and ask forgiveness later. Remember, this is a western state; they can kill you in human form, and if your blood test comes back showing lycanthropy, and it will, it's a legal kill. And if you want to come along and get yourself killed, that's fine, though it'd be a bitch to have your master die with you because you're being a undisciplined baby, but you're likely to get people I care about hurt, and that I won't allow.'

Her wide eyes went even wider, like blue pools in her face, and I realized tears were standing in them. If she blinked the tears would fall, and she was fighting to keep that from happening. Fuck.

'Please,' she said, 'please, if you send me back he will know I have failed. You do not understand what he will do to me if I fail him.'

'He doesn't get to do anything to you without Jean-Claude's permission, so all that will happen is you get restricted guard duty, local only and out of media sight for a while, that's it.'

Her breath came out in a long sigh, and she swallowed convulsively. The tears shone in her eyes but still did not fall. 'You think you control the old Harlequin, but you do not. They hold with the old ways and punish us in private like whipped dogs.'

'I wouldn't let any of our people beat their dogs either. Are you saying that Gunnar beats you in private?'

She covered her face with one hand and stepped away from Nicky and the stairs. I guess that was answer enough.

'Shit,' I said, softly, but real feeling.

Micah stepped up beside me, and I knew Nathaniel was just behind him; without turning to see, I could feel them both at my back. 'I've run into old masters across the country who treat their wereanimal to call like that.'

'We're leading by example, damn it; that means that no one here in St Louis gets to do shit like this.'

'If you send her back, then Jean-Claude has to take care of it,' Micah said.

'We can't take her with us,' Nathaniel said.

We both turned around and looked at him. He was the most submissive of us, so gentle most of the time, and then he'd get a look in his eyes, and you could see the steel inside him. He didn't want to be in charge; that didn't mean he wasn't strong.

'You sound sure,' I said.

'I am.' His face relaxed a little, softening his expression, but he shook his head. 'She feels safer than she's been in years. Sometimes when that happens after a lot of abuse you just fall apart, because you can. You've finally got people to catch you when you fall, but if she's about to uncover centuries of abuse, she can't do it on this trip.'

I looked into his serious, handsome face and realized that he understood her pain better than most, and he was still not going to let her pain manipulate him. It was a type of strength that I was only now learning. I was a dominant personality; my instinct was to take care of people, but Nathaniel was right. Hard, but right.

'I was Chimera's special whipping boy for years; I sympathize with Nilda. When we get back I will help you do anything necessary to keep her from being abused by her master, but right now she is not my priority,' Micah said.

I studied the faces of my two men. 'Am I wanting to help her more than you do because I'm a girl?'

'No,' Nathaniel said, 'because you haven't had as much therapy as I have. It's all about boundaries, Anita, personal boundaries. You've only known Nilda for a few months. You don't love her. You aren't even friends. She tries to cut down all the other shapeshifters, and the humans are just beneath notice, except for you, because she can't ignore you, but she doesn't like you. Don't mistake her cry for mercy for anything but self-serving. It's all about her and her pain. We're all like that, but we have lovers who love us and we love back in that almost-married way; we have our support in place, and she doesn't.'

'I don't think she had a chance,' I said.

'We didn't abuse her, Anita,' Micah said.

'I know that.'

'If we don't take care of ourselves first,' Nathaniel said, 'we can't take care of anyone else.'

It was logical. He was right, so why did it feel so bad?

'Anita,' Micah said, and he put his hands on my arms and made me face him directly. 'Even this delay could be the difference between me seeing my father one more time and him dying before I get there. I don't owe Nilda that.'

I nodded; put that way, he was right. 'I'll call Jean-Claude and Fredo from the plane so we don't delay anymore.'

'Call Jake, too,' Nathaniel said, naming one of the other wereanimals who were Harlequin.

'Why?' I asked.

'Jake will explain to the other Harlequin that you'll be unhappy if Nilda or any of the other animals to call are harmed, until you get a chance to discuss it with everybody.'

'The Harlequin respect Jean-Claude more than me,' I said.

'Some do, but I trust Jake to explain one important difference between you and Jean-Claude.'

'What?' I asked.

'Jean-Claude wants the clout of having the Mother of All Darkness's assassins and bodyguards work for him, so he'll hesitate to kill them; you won't.'

'I'm human, Nathaniel; I can't afford to fight any of the Harlequin. All I can do is kill them.'

'Exactly,' he said.

I frowned. 'I don't want to kill them.'

'But you will,' he said.

'Let's get the other guards on board and get in the air. No more delays,' Micah said, and that was that – though Ethan stayed behind to help the driver keep Nilda in the car. The driver was human and we didn't trust her not to go berserk and tear him up. Strong emotions can bring on the change; grief works almost as well as anger. Which made me worry about Micah as the plane left the ground. I'm usually most afraid on takeoff and landing, but as I held my love's hand, I was too worried about him to worry much about me. Easiest takeoff I'd ever had.

7

It was dark when we landed in Colorado, so all I can say is Denver looks like every other city from the air, all lights like electric stars scattered across the ground. We got off the plane to two black SUVs that came with matching vampires and a white SUV that had a very human woman leaning against it. She was built small and delicate like Micah, with curly red hair trailing around her shoulders. I couldn't see the color of her eyes from where I was standing, but I knew the shape of them, because I'd spent too much time looking into Micah's eyes and face. There was a lot of similar bone structure, though the red hair and freckles were a surprise. I'd pictured his family as darker like him. She smiled, pushing away from the truck, in her blue jeans, blue polo shirt, and cowboy boots, which looked too beat-up and used to be a fashion statement.

Micah went to her with a huge smile on his face. He said, 'Juliet.'

She said, 'Mike.'

They hugged like they meant it, though with that below-the-waist distance that you learn with relatives. Thanks to the nearly four-hour flight, we knew that Juliet was Uncle Steve's daughter, and that Cousin Richie had been Steve's son, but both of them had died in the attack that had turned Micah into a wereleopard. Micah and Richie had both been only eighteen, Richie back from basic and about to ship out to an active-duty post and Micah back from college. They'd come home to have one last deer hunt with their dads, but while they'd been hunting the doe they bagged, something else had been hunting them. Micah's dad had been called away for a suspicious death or he'd have been on the hunt with them.

Nathaniel took my hand. I could feel the tension thrumming down his arm. I turned and looked at him. His face looked neutral but it was a nervous neutral. I fought the urge to lower the mental shields that kept us from getting a direct feed into each other's emotions. We did not need to be drowning in Micah's emotions right now, and once the shields came down, sometimes it was hard to filter strong emotions from anyone I was connected to. It was going to be hard enough to support Micah through the family reunion without actually feeling the emotions with him. So I moved closer to Nathaniel and whispered, 'You don't have to be nervous.'

'Tell me nothing will change between the three of us,' he whispered back.

'Nothing will change between us,' I said, and squeezed his hand. I would have done more comforting, but one of the vampires from the black SUVs walked toward us. Would I have said *glided*, once? Maybe, but he didn't glide, he walked. For graceful movement I had Jean-Claude, Damian, Wicked and Truth, or Requiem, or hell, lots of vampires in St Louis who made the one moving toward us seem rough in comparison. He was dressed in a black suit and white shirt; even the tie was black. It was Jean-Claude's signature black and white, but somehow it didn't work as well for this guy. Maybe it was the cut of the suit being less tailored or the fact that it was a standard suit that anyone could have worn. Jean-Claude always made sure his clothes were his very personal style. This vampire, with his short black hair and run-of-the-mill clothes, looked like someone had looked down a cast list and said, *one generic vampire needed*. It was boring compared to what I was used to, but I put a smile on my face. I knew how to smile at clients even when I didn't want to, and this vampire was from the local Master of the City. I could play nice.

I glanced at Nathaniel and found him smiling brilliantly at the vampire. He had his charming game face on. Whatever he was feeling, he put it off his face and down where it didn't show.

'Ms Blake, I presume,' said the vampire, in a voice as bland and unimpressive as his clothes.

I fought the urge to say, *Well, I'm not Dr Livingston*, but managed to keep the smart-aleck remark to myself. 'Yes, and Mr Graison.'

The vampire looked surprised. 'I'm sorry, our usual protocols don't demand that I acknowledge a *pomme de sang* or an animal to call.'

Pomme de sang was a term for the person a vampire took blood with regularly, but it was more than that, almost a mistress, though often the relationship was only about sharing blood and not about sex. Nathaniel had started out as that for me, but that had been a few years ago. He was my leopard to call, but . . . 'He's our third; that means he's more than just food, or a pet.'

'I'm not familiar with the term *third*, Ms Blake.'

'The third part of our couple,' I said.

'But we are given to understand that there are a great deal more than just three parts to your romantic life, Ms Blake.'

I wasn't sure what to say to that, except, 'Just because I'm not monogamous doesn't mean those closest to me aren't important to me. Think of Nathaniel and Micah as my spouses.'

He gave a little bow from the neck. 'My apologies, I did not realize you took your lovers so seriously, except for your master, of course.'

'It would be a mistake to assume my priorities by normal vampire protocol,' I said.

'I've angered you,' he said.

'It's okay, Anita,' Nathaniel said.

I shook my head. 'No, it's not.'

'So, you're saying this is personal business for you,' the vampire said.

'You know it is,' I said.

'But yet you are wearing your weapons,' he said.

'I rarely go anywhere unarmed.' I let go of Nathaniel's hand so I could stand facing the vampire more head-on. He'd let me know my concealed carry wasn't concealed from his vampire eyes. Or maybe he'd been guessing and I'd confirmed it for him. Shit, I so didn't want to play my-balls-are-bigger-than-yours while trying to support the men in my life. Had I started this game of mine's-bigger-than-yours? Maybe; I hadn't meant to.

'What's your name?' I asked.

'I am Alfredo.'

'Great, okay, Alfie.'

'How did you know my master calls me Alfie?'

I'd actually just used the nickname to irritate him and throw him off his game. The fact that I'd accidentally used his real nickname just made it better. I smiled knowingly. 'Look, I appreciate you coming to the airport to meet us. I appreciate Fredrico behaving like a civilized master vampire, but I'm honestly here to support my boyfriend and meet his family. I don't want, or feel the need, to play who's the biggest and the scariest, okay?'

Alfie looked at me, eyes narrowed. 'I have not . . .'

'Look, just stop, okay? I'll stop, if you will. You had to make a point of letting me know you'd spotted my weapons. I made a point of knowing your nickname, but I'm not going to have time or energy to play games like this, so let's just behave like normal people. Thanks for coming to pick us up. I didn't realize Micah's cousin was going to be coming, too.'

'Normal people?' The vampire laughed, a short, abrupt, very human laugh. I put his age at under fifty years. If I'd wanted to let my necromancy out of the box, I could have told his age within a year or two, five at the outside, but if I trotted any of my metaphysical abilities out like that, he could take it as an insult. 'Normal people do not have bodyguards. Normal people would not be given royal treatment by my master. You cannot be normal, Anita Blake; you are the Executioner, and now you are the American queen to our new king, Jean-Claude. You are a necromancer and I don't know what else; the list of your powers and titles is too long, and thanks to your request that we not be formal I do not have to list them all, but normal you will never be, Ms Blake.'

It was hard to argue with him, though I wanted to, but at that moment Micah came to us. He'd left Juliet at her truck. 'Is there a problem?' he asked, his voice low so it didn't carry back to his cousin.

'No problem,' I said.

Alfie bowed to Micah and said, 'Mr Callahan, I am sorry to meet you under such trying circumstances. My name is Alfie and my master has put me at your disposal in the evenings.'

I thought it was interesting that Micah and I both got a bow, but Nathaniel hadn't rated one, or any acknowledgment until I made a point of it. No matter how hard they tried, there were going to be vampire politics involved.

'Thank you, Alfie,' Micah said. He turned to me and I knew the look. He was asking me if there was something wrong.

I felt, more than heard, some of our people coming up behind us. The look on Alfie's face as he looked up and past the three of us confirmed that the biggest, baddest-looking people with us were now right behind us. The fact that the vampire couldn't keep his worry off his face made me shave another ten years off his undead age: thirty years dead, tops.

I glanced back to see our remaining bodyguards coming up behind us. Bram and Ares looked like dark and light halves to a whole, both six feet, both built tall and lanky; muscle from the mandatory guard workout showed, but neither one of them bulked up fast. They were built for speed and strength. Both still had that military stamp on them, one that lingers if you were in long enough and haven't been out long enough. Ares' desert tan had mostly faded, though he tanned darker than most blonds I'd met. Bram couldn't really tan any darker, though I'd learned that even very dark African American skin could burn; it just took a lot. Bram had been quietly disdainful when he found out that my black curls and dark brown eyes hadn't come with my mother's Mexican skin tone, but my father's blond German so that I just didn't tan worth a damn. Bram's hair was still cut military short. He complained that the tight curl bugged him when it grew out. Ares had let his dark blond hair grow out a little, enough that a woman could run her hands through it, as he'd said, but it was mostly longer on top and still left his neck in no danger of being touched by hair. They partnered each other a lot on guard duty.

Ares grinned at us. 'How are we supposed to guard your bodies if you keep talking to the bad guys without us?'

'One, they aren't bad guys, they're our hosts. Two, not a danger,' I said.

Nicky said, 'I told you.' He walked toward us, the spread of his shoulders making him look shorter than the other two guards, though he wasn't really. His haircut was actually the thing you noticed after the muscles. His hair was short except for half his bangs, which hung in a long yellow triangle down the right-hand side of his face, covering the eye and halfway down the cheek. He used the hair to hide that the eye on that side was missing. He'd lost it when he was a teenager, years before he became a werelion, or he'd have still had the eye. The one eye that was left was a clear blue.

'You told them what?' I asked.

'That you could handle yourself against anything that was on this side of the hangar,' Bram said, in his clear, strong voice. He didn't talk nearly as much as Ares, but when he did it was usually to the point. Ares would joke and tease, Bram almost never.

'Should I be insulted?' Alfie asked.

I said, 'No.'

Ares said, 'Yes.'

Micah said, 'No.'

Alfie looked from one to the other of us, smiling slightly. 'I don't know what I expected from you, Ms Blake, Mr Callahan, but this easy camaraderie is unexpected.'

'Pleasant, I hope,' Micah said.

'Yes,' the vampire said, 'most illuminating.'

'Illuminating, why illuminating?' I asked.

'To shed light upon something; I thought it was a very appropriate word.'

I would have asked more, but Micah's cousin chose that moment to come up and say, 'Who's riding with me?'

'Juliet, this is Anita and Nathaniel.'

I offered a hand to forgo any thought of hugging. I didn't like hugging people I didn't know, and some families just hugged willy-nilly. Her hand was as small as mine, but more callused to match the working cowboy boots. She took Nathaniel's hand, too, and he wasted a smile on her. She smiled back, but it didn't reach her eyes. They were blue, and the frown between them made them look less the shape of Micah's.

'Aunt Bea said you were Mike's fiancée; is that true, or are you just living together? I ask, because if it's just Aunt Bea's way of dealing with her issues about living in sin, I can help head off some of the wedding talk.'

It made me half-smile and half-laugh. It was blunt and I liked it. 'No wedding plans; can't we just introduce me as his girlfriend?'

'Nope, believe me. I lived with my husband before marriage, and *fiancée* is the family's nice, hopeful double-talk for living in sin.'

I looked at Micah, and he knew my expressions, too, because he answered the unvoiced question. 'Some of my relatives are religious in a . . .' He seemed to fumble for words, and finally settled on, 'It's going to be awkward.'

Juliet laughed and shook her head. 'Awkward. Oh, cousin, how I've missed you. You always were the peacekeeper and the master of understatement. You should be able to come home and see your dad and not worry about this other crap, but you know it never works that way. I'm sorry.'

Micah nodded. 'Me, too.'

I was beginning to get a bad feeling that maybe Micah hadn't gotten back in touch with his family after Chimera's death for more than one reason. He and Nathaniel had moved in at the same time; we had always been a threesome, never just a twosome.

'We can call Anita your fiancée and the family will let it pass, but you can't introduce them together like you just did to me, you know you can't.'

'I could,' Micah said, and there was something in those two quiet words that held way more emotion than it should have.

'Micah should be able to just see his dad and not worry about anything else,' Nathaniel said. 'I can just be a friend.'

'No,' Micah said, and he took Nathaniel's hand in his and shook his head. 'No, you can't just be a friend.'

'Oh, Jesus,' Juliet said, 'you're going to force the issue. You haven't changed; you were always so quiet, the perfect son, until you weren't. You'd get something you believed in and you would never back down, no matter what.' She sighed and shook her head. She looked at Nathaniel. 'It's nothing personal. You have to be a wonderful person for Micah to feel this strongly, but I do not want to be in the shitstorm that is going to happen when he introduces you to our family as his . . . what?' She looked at Micah. 'What do you say?'

'Significant other,' Micah said, and his voice was very firm.

Nathaniel said, 'I love that you say that, but honestly, Micah, this has to be about you and your dad. It's just words; I don't want to make this harder on you.'

I saw Micah squeeze his hand and shake his head again. 'It's not just words, Nathaniel, or if it is, words are important, they have meaning and truth to them.' He turned to Juliet still holding Nathaniel's hand. 'I'll let the *fiancée* stand with Anita, because if we could figure out how to marry as a group, we would, but since we can't do that legally, *fiancée* and *significant other* will do.'

Nathaniel looked at him. 'Do you mean that? That if we could marry as a group, you would?'

Micah looked at him. 'Yes.'

Nathaniel threw his arms around Micah, and they hugged. They hugged like they meant it, and I didn't have to see Nathaniel's face to know he was crying. I realized I was, too. Damn. I went to them and wrapped my arms around them both, my two men. And just like that the lines were drawn; Micah wouldn't back down or make Nathaniel mean any less to him, not even to smooth things over with his family. If he could do it, so could we.

8

The three of us rode with Juliet, but the guards insisted on at least one guard riding with us. Since they were here to keep us safe, it was hard to argue with the logic, so we didn't try. What did surprise me was that Dev ended up riding with us and not Nicky. If it was just one of the four I'd expected it to be him. Honestly, I felt odd without Nicky in the car. It wasn't a matter of trust or skill. I trusted Dev to do the job and guard us just fine, but I hadn't traveled out of town with Nicky and Dev since they started being partners so often, and I just plain preferred Nicky's company. I couldn't have put it into words, because God knew Dev was the better conversationalist and tradition-ally charming, but Nicky . . . was Nicky. He fit better. Micah, Nathaniel, and I rode in the back middle seat and we put the last row of seats down so there'd be more room for luggage. The rest of the luggage had actu-ally fit into one of the black SUVs, so Alfie was driving Ares, Bram, and most of the luggage to our hotel so they could unload the regular luggage. Nicky was following us in the other SUV that Alfie had given to us as 'our' car for the time we spent in town. Most of the weapons we'd packed were divided between us and Nicky's follow car. As a U.S. Marshal of the Preternatural Branch, I was duty-bound to keep most of my arsenal at hand, because as a federal officer I could be called up anywhere I traveled. The ruling had come down after a case when another marshal had been unable to perform his duties to the degree necessary to help out a fellow marshal who put out a call for aid. At least they'd changed the ruling that had forced me to either carry most of the 'equipment' with me or have it in a secure lockup at all times. That ruling had come down after an executioner had his bag of dangerous goodies stolen from the trunk of his car and one of the guns was used in a holdup. The ruling had been overturned when a fellow executioner had taken in all his equipment and challenged the judges to carry it. These weren't laws most of the time, but 'rulings,' basically emergency actions taken from some knee-jerk reaction to a tragedy. Since my branch of law enforcement was never called in until people were dead, there was a lot of tragedy to go around. Worse yet, the 'rulings,' even most of the laws that I acted under, were made by people who had never used a gun for real, worn a badge, or had to make a life-and-death decision, let alone that decision in the split second of a vampire hunt or while tracking a rogue shapeshifter.

Juliet asked, 'Do I need to drive slow so your other guard won't lose us?'

'You couldn't lose Nicky if you tried,' Dev said. 'You won't lose him by accident.'

'The roads are tricky after dark.'

'Juliet,' Micah said, 'it's okay; all our people know their jobs.'

Nathaniel and I had put Micah in the middle without talking about it. It was partly just because I knew that Nathaniel would want to keep touching him after the marriage statement and partly because Micah was like most wereanimals in that physical touch made him feel better, and no matter how brave he was being, he needed the comfort. He held on to both of our hands, and I wondered how much hand holding he was going to do in front of his family. In public the two men usually kept the touching to a minimum, depending on where they were; some places were more user-friendly for male-on-male affection than others. Or did Micah intend to shove Nathaniel down his family's throat? I wasn't sure that was the best thing, but I'd support his decision.

A streetlight gleamed onto Dev's hair, bringing out the different shades of blond in his shoulder-length hair. It barely touched his shoulders and was as long as he wanted to grow it.

'Don't take this wrong, Dev, but I'm surprised Nicky didn't argue with you being the guard that rode with us.'

'I stayed with the luggage and made sure the people helping with it did their jobs.'

'I'm surprised you stayed with the luggage,' Nathaniel said.

He turned in his seat to look back at us. 'Nicky pulled rank,' he said.

'He doesn't outrank you,' I said.

Dev gave a wide grin. 'He's a better fighter than I am. He reminded me of that.'

I studied his face for a moment, trying to see if he was offended, but there was nothing but the usual good humor in his face.

'Bram says you could be better than Nicky if you'd work harder in training,' Micah said.

Dev's grin gleamed white in the semidarkness. 'I don't want to work that hard.'

'You're so used to being faster and stronger just naturally that it makes you lazy in practice,' I said, but I smiled when I said it. It was almost impossible to be really upset with Dev.

'I'm faster, stronger, and I practice hard at what I have to do.'

'But only what you have to do,' I said. 'Nicky puts in the extra time to get better, and you don't.'

'No, and I'm not going to.'

'You are a lazy cat,' I said, smiling.

'But I'm *your* lazy cat,' he said.

Juliet said, 'Is there something I should know about Dev, too?'

'He's a bodyguard,' Micah said.

'Are you sure? I'll run what interference I can about you and Nathaniel, but I can't help if I don't know what to protect.'

'Dev isn't my lover,' Micah said.

Dev turned around, his face alight with mischief. The next pool of darkness came and he spoke out of the dimness, 'Oh, but I so would be if only you would say yes.' His tone of voice was teasing.

But Juliet took it seriously, sort of. 'Oh, sweet Jesus, please don't tease in front of the family at the hospital.'

Dev turned to her. 'I know how to behave. Promise.'

'He does,' I said. 'He just doesn't bother most of the time.'

'Well, please, please, bother this time.'

'I may tease in private with Micah, but I would never do anything to make this ordeal worse.' He turned a very serious face to Micah. 'If I haven't said it out loud, I am sorry about your father.'

'Thank you, Dev,' Micah said.

'You are a lazy cat, but a good one,' I said.

'Don't tell. You'll ruin my reputation with the other guards.'

It made us all smile, which may have been part of his purpose. That, and it was Dev. There was more than one reason that his childhood nickname had been Devil and a reason that it was still his name. Of course, when your legal first name is Mephistopheles, almost anything is an improvement.

Micah leaned in against me so that he could bury his face against the side of my neck. Nathaniel moved his free hand up to stroke along the line of neck that Micah had bared by snuggling into me. Juliet talked to us as she drove. We found out that she and her husband did run a working farm. They had two kids. Most of his generation of cousins were either married or in the military, and a lot of them had kids. Being introduced as the fiancée was going to mean a lot of wedding and kid questions. Peachy. Micah asked questions and replied to her, but mostly we petted him, and felt his tension rise, until we pulled into the hospital parking lot, and I could suddenly taste his pulse on my tongue as if the emotion were mine. I redid my shields between me and my leopard king and prepared to go meet the rest of his family. The only concession we made was that Micah took my other hand. It meant I couldn't go for my gun if bad guys jumped us, but Dev was with us, and bad guys were the least of our worries tonight. I'd take a nice straight-up firefight to families and hospitals any night.

9

Juliet pulled into the parking lot with Nicky in the second SUV like a shadow behind hers. 'See,' Dev said, 'you didn't lose Nicky.'

'No one likes an I-told-you-so,' she said, and began to drive up and down the lanes looking for a parking spot. She passed a lot of police cars of every flavor in the parking lot. 'My job just got easier. What's with all the police?' Dev asked.

Juliet pulled into a parking space with a county sheriff car on one side. Nicky had to drive past us. There were no other parking spots as far as the eye could see. 'One of their own is inside,' I said. 'We always come like this.' I unbuckled my seat belt.

Dev turned in his seat, belt free, and said, 'I understand his friends and coworkers, but some of these marked cars are from towns away. There's even one from Wyoming.'

'Dad's been the county sheriff for a long time,' Micah said. 'He knows a lot of people.'

But it was Nathaniel who said the truth. 'There'll be officers here who don't know Sheriff Callahan, but once the word goes out that there's an officer down for any reason, they come to make sure the family has everything they need and that the officer is never alone. They do vigil.'

Juliet turned in her seat so she could see Nathaniel. 'How do you know that? Your dad a cop, too?'

'No, but I've been with Anita for years. I've been at the hospital when she was hurt and visited when other officers were injured.'

'And they accept you as family?' Juliet asked.

'Most of the local police do.'

'They're sort of used to my domestic arrangements,' I said.

Juliet shook her head hard enough to make her curls bounce. 'Well, I don't know about the other cops, but our family is probably going to be embarrassing the hell out of us about your domestic arrangements. I'll just apologize now and get it over with.'

'Appreciated,' I said. Micah squeezed my hand. I gave him a smile. 'If I kiss you, you'll be having to wipe lipstick off.'

'I'll risk it, if we're careful,' he said, and smiled.

We kissed gently, and it left a stripe of scarlet in the middle of his lips. Nathaniel said, 'Share the go-faster stripe, because I may not be able to kiss you for a while.'

Micah turned to him in the narrowness of the backseat. 'I'm sorry.'

'It's okay. We can't kiss in public in a lot of places. I know you love me even when we can't kiss.'

Micah leaned into the other man, and Nathaniel was just taller enough in the upper body to have to bend down a little. It was as gentle a kiss as we'd done, but then Micah slid his arms around Nathaniel's waist, up underneath his jacket so he could run his hands up the muscled warmth of his back with only the thin dress shirt between him and the other man's skin. I loved that pocket of heat just underneath the jacket myself, so I knew what Micah was doing.

Nathaniel responded, sliding his own arms around Micah, and the kiss grew. I knew I had a big, happy smile on my face. I loved watching them together.

Juliet said, 'You really don't mind, do you?'

It took me a moment to realize she was talking to me. I glanced at her, not really wanting to stop looking at my two men. 'Not mind? I love them, and I love seeing them together.'

'I guess I thought you tolerated it, but the look on your face just now . . . You looked so happy.'

I frowned at her. Micah drew back from the kiss, and Nathaniel just sort of wrapped himself around the other man, putting his head on one of Micah's shoulders, so his face was buried against him and he wasn't looking at Juliet.

'I was happy,' I said.

'Why wouldn't Anita be happy to watch us kiss?' Micah said, holding the other man easily, familiarly.

Juliet had the grace to look embarrassed. 'I don't know; I guess I'd be jealous, or . . . I wouldn't want to see two men together.'

'It made you uncomfortable,' Micah said, his voice quiet and almost neutral.

'I'm sorry, but yeah, a little. I didn't know you liked guys.'

'I don't, not really, but I love Nathaniel.'

'Trust me,' Dev said, 'there is a trail of brokenhearted boys back home who wish so much our luscious Micah liked men better than he does. Sadly, where men are concerned he's a one-man boy.' He gave a pouting face as if he were five, and then that slow grin spread across his face. I wanted to frown at him, but that damn Cheshire grin did me in every time. How could someone so big, so grown up, do mischief so well?

Micah looked at Dev. 'There are one or two men back home besides Nathaniel that I notice.' His voice was utterly mild.

Dev's grin faded around the edges, and his eyes were thinking way too hard. You could almost see him reviewing every interaction he'd seen between Micah and the men back home. It was why Micah had said it: to bedevil our devil.

I turned away to hide my own grin.

Juliet said, 'You tease like friends.'

'We are that,' Micah said, his voice still quiet and mild.

'Close friends,' she said, with a little too much emphasis on *close*.

'Dev is bisexual, cheerfully so, but I've already told you we aren't lovers.' He stroked Nathaniel's hair with the other man still entwined around him. 'If we were, I wouldn't hide it.'

She looked at what she could see of Nathaniel. 'I guess not.'

'It bothered you to see us kiss,' Micah said.

She looked down, frowning, then back up, and nodded. 'I'm sorry, but it did. I was all open-minded about it, until . . .'

'It's why we kissed in the car, because you are open-minded compared to some of our family. But it's not just our family; it's the other police, it's everyone. As men we have to be more cautious, or we can end up with other men up in our face.'

'Yeah, I'd rather not have to guard you against a cop. That could be legally . . . awkward,' Dev said, at last.

'You'd be up on assault charges,' I said.

'So what do you want me to do? The police are like a lot of manly men; they react badly to gay.'

'But you're bisexual,' Juliet said, and it was brave of her to make the distinction.

'You're either straight or gay to most people,' Dev said, 'and if a guy touches another guy he's gay, period.'

Nathaniel drew away from Micah enough to say, 'Just like a lot of the gay community thinks a man who touches a woman isn't gay enough. They think bisexual means you haven't made up your mind or won't admit the truth.'

'Really?' Juliet said.

He nodded. 'The gay community can be just as narrow-minded as the straight community.'

Dev said, 'Nicky is almost here.'

I looked out toward the parked cars and the electric glowing darkness but couldn't see him. 'Am I too short to see him from the backseat?'

'Yep,' Dev said.

'I can see him,' Juliet said, 'but I hadn't seen him until your bodyguard said something.'

'Once Nicky gets here,' Dev said, 'if there's still no one in the parking lot, I'll get out first, and when I give you the signal Anita gets out next.'

Juliet looked at the other man. 'You were looking at the parking lot this whole time?'

'Most of it,' he said, and reached for his door handle.

'Why does Anita get out next?'

'Because she's the next best with weapons after me.'

'I'm better with edged weapons,' I said.

He grinned back over his shoulder. 'Yeah, but I make my own edged weapons.' Dev slid out of the car and looked around with the door still open around him.

'What did he mean by making his own edged weapons?' Juliet asked.

'He's a weretiger,' I said.

Nicky was on my side of the car. He glanced down long enough to give me a small smile, then went back to gazing around the parking lot. They were bodyguards first tonight, friends and lovers second. Dev was in charge of the passenger side of the car and Nathaniel. Nicky was taking my side of the car and me. Micah, being in the middle, could get out on either side, and whichever side he used, that guard would have him to keep safe, too. Nicky opened my door, which meant I could finally get out without either guard yelling at us.

'I don't understand; how does being a weretiger mean he makes his own knives?' Juliet said.

'Not knives, claws,' Micah said.

Nicky offered me his hand to get out of the car, which he almost never did. Because it was rare, I took it, though I was perfectly capable of getting out without his hand in mine, but as his hand closed over mine it felt good. He drew me to my feet, and I left Micah to explain our reality to his cousin. I had a moment to look up into Nicky's face; most of the right side was covered by the triangular fall of hair, but the one blue eye that I could see smiled down at me, echoing the smile that curled his lips. I started to go up on my tiptoes to kiss that smile, but his head moved and his expression went very serious. 'Police,' he whispered.

He let go of my hand so I could join Micah and Nathaniel on the other side of the car. Nicky took up his post with Dev at our backs, as Micah reached for my left hand and pulled me forward like a safety net as he and Juliet said hi to three different flavors of uniform. It was reunion time, and thanks to his father being a sheriff, a lot of the members of that reunion would be wearing a badge. The fact that I hadn't realized we'd be wading through police officers at the hospital had been stupid of me. It just showed how much I'd been thrown by his mother's phone call. I'd been thinking I'd have kept Ares and Bram with us. They smelled like military, and being ex-military would have given them clout with the cops. Nicky and Dev were just going to set off their bad-guy sensors, and nothing about the two handsome, physically imposing, armed men was going to endear them to the cops. Crap.

Deputy Al Truman was tall and thin, with disproportionately large hands and feet, as if he'd hit that growth spurt in his teens where the extremities are big and clumsy and his body never caught up with the rest of him. It made me expect him to be awkward, but he wasn't. He wasn't grace personified, but he was normal, and I was betting I wasn't the only person who had been fooled into thinking he'd be clumsy. I wondered how many suspects had expected him to move badly and gotten surprised.

He took off his cowboy hat with its official-looking band. In another part of the country it would have been a more typical Smokey Bear hat. Those big hands rubbed the hat brim over and over like a nervous habit of long duration. His brown hair was crushed by the hat but looked like it had some wave to it, but whoever cut his hair had managed to butcher it so that it was just a mess, hat or no hat.

'I hate that you're coming home to this, Mike.'

Micah nodded. 'Me, too, Al.' He turned to me and Nathaniel. 'Al and I went to high school together.'

'I was best friends with Richie. We went through boot together.'

Al assumed I knew the family tragedy that had turned Micah into a wereleopard, and he was right, but I thought the assumption was interesting. I was betting that Micah's mother, or someone, had told him who I was, and then he said, 'You must be Anita,' and he offered to shake hands. Yep, someone had been talking.

'How did you know . . .' Micah started to ask.

'Your mom said you'd be bringing your fiancée. Congratulations, we were all thinking you were going to be an old maid.'

It took me a second to realize he was still talking to Micah and not me.

'I just had to meet the right people,' Micah said. I don't know if anyone caught the 'people' part, but the next officer stepped up and offered his hand and introduced himself.

Sergeant Michael Horton kept his Smokey Bear hat on; it went with his Colorado state trooper uniform. He was younger than all of us, except Nathaniel and Dev, though I'd noticed that people assumed Dev was older than he was, because he was tall. The taller you were, the more years people added to your age at an earlier age, just like they thought you were younger if you were shorter. Most people would have added years onto Sergeant Horton's age because he was over six feet, but I didn't add them; I knew better. He was twenty-five tops, which would actually make him a couple of years older than Dev and Nathaniel.

The hair that showed around his hat was buzz-cut short and if he hadn't spent a few years in the military I'd lose a bet with someone. I would have bet even money it had been the Marines.

'Sheriff Callahan is a good man,' Horton said as he shook Micah's hand.

'Thank you.'

But Horton looked behind us all at Dev and Nicky, one big, physical guy sizing up the competition. That he discounted the rest of us made me take points off his I-would-depend-on-him-in-a-crisis card.

Sergeant Ray Gonzales stepped into the silence. He was with the Boulder Police Department. He was just under six feet, but built big like Nicky so he seemed taller. His shoulder width didn't come out of a gym, and there was even a slight stomach bulge starting to fight with his equipment belt. Gonzales was just a big-framed man, built like a huge rectangle. He was going a little soft with age, which had to be closing in on sixty, but most of him was more solid than he looked. He reminded me of one of our guards, Dino, who looked out of shape and ran like a lumbering elephant, but all that bulk was solid and he was one of the few guards who I never, ever wanted to hit me for real.

He hugged Micah. 'I'm glad you came, Mike. It'll mean a lot to Rush.'

'I just wish I'd come sooner.'

'You're here now, that's what counts.'

'I know,' Micah said, and something about Gonzales had made him more emotional.

'I've known Mike since he was a baby,' Gonzales said, 'and Al, too, come to think of it. Rush and I are the old guys now.'

'I don't know,' the plainclothes cop said, and offered his hand to Micah. 'Detective Rickman, Ricky; I work with Ray up in Boulder and I wish the younger officers were half as tough as you and Rush.'

'I didn't say we weren't tough,' Ray laughed. 'I said we were old.' He reached a hand out to me and used two hands to shake it. His smile was warm and open. 'I'm glad you're here with Mike.'

'Thanks, me too.'

Detective Rickman said, 'Your reputation precedes you, Marshal Blake. Nice to know one of our hometown boys could make you settle down.'

I didn't like him, and I didn't like the phrasing. I looked at Micah, asking with my eyes how he wanted me to play it.

'I need to get them inside before Aunt Bea hunts me down,' Juliet said. She actually started walking, trying to move us along.

'Who are your friends?' Rickman asked. 'And what's with the dark glasses at night? It's a little Hollywood for here.'

I decided to be a distraction, because I wasn't sure I wanted to give full names to Detective Rickman of our friends and sweeties. Nobody was wanted for anything, but it didn't mean that everyone had unblemished records. I didn't want to mess with it, and I'd just realized that no one here had seen Micah's leopard eyes. He told me he'd had brown eyes once, and that was the color that everyone here would be expecting. 'Detective Rickman, Ricky, no one makes me do anything, and as for settling down I'm not sure what you mean by that.'

'Marriage, Marshal Blake, Anita; that's usually what settling down means.'

Gonzales said, 'Horton, go do the errands that Bea needs.'

Horton opened his mouth as if to tell Gonzales he wasn't the boss of him, but something in the older man's face made him stop. He looked at Rickman. 'You okay with that, Detective?'

'Yeah, we can handle it.'

Horton did what he was told, which was pretty obedient for a sergeant who wasn't in their chain of command and wasn't an old family friend. Either Gonzales had a great reputation or Horton was hoping to get on the Boulder PD and politically he was trying to keep both Ricky and Gonzales happy.

Micah said, 'No one makes Anita do anything, but as for the dark glasses, did you know that if a lycanthrope is forced to stay in animal form too long that sometimes their eyes don't come back to human normal?'

Gonzales and Al said, 'No.'

Rickman said, 'Are you saying your eyes aren't human anymore?'

'Yes. I know that most police are told to watch a lycanthrope's eyes and if they change color then it's the beginning of the shift, but my eyes don't go back to human anymore.'

'What color are your eyes now?' Juliet asked. Her voice was full of some emotion that I couldn't quite read, maybe sadness?

Micah slid the glasses off his face and turned toward the brightest light from the streetlights. Juliet made a sound that was almost a sob and put her hand over her mouth. Gonzales's dark face looked like a world of sorrow had just climbed onto him. Al looked away and seemed sadder than before. Rickman flinched, but he wasn't sad.

'If you could all pass the word to the other local officers, I'd appreciate it,' Micah said. 'I'd really like to be able to concentrate on my dad and family without having to worry about being shot because someone sees my eyes and misunderstands.'

'I'll call up Gutterman and let him pass the word to the cops outside Rush's room,' Al said, and reached for his shoulder mic.

'Good idea,' Gonzales said.

Al spoke low into his shoulder mic and we all waited, while he said, 'It's the sheriff's son, Mike Callahan, and his eyes are stuck on animal.'

A crackly voice said, 'How the hell are his eyes stuck?'

'Just one of those things that can happen with shifters,' Al said. 'Tell the other guys up there. Mike doesn't need someone pointing a gun at him, thinking he's about to shift while he's here.'

'Weird shit,' the voice, I presumed Gutterman, said. 'I'll pass the word around.'

'Thanks, Gutter,' Al said.

Rickman asked, 'You ever have anyone think you're shifting when they see the eyes?'

'A time or two,' Micah said. He slipped his glasses back on, hiding the exotic flash of his eyes.

This was news to me. I turned and looked at Nathaniel, and the look on his face said it was news to him, too. If we hadn't been with so many unknown people I'd have asked Micah to elaborate. Nathaniel gave a small nod, and just like that I knew we'd both be talking to our shared boy later.

'I'm going to walk them in,' Deputy Al said.

'You do that,' Gonzales said.

'Why do you need bodyguards, Marshal Blake?' Rickman asked.

Micah answered, 'There have been threats because of my work with the Coalition for Better Understanding Between Human and Lycanthrope.'

'So they're your bodyguards,' Rickman said.

'Do you really think I'd bring guards to the hospital where my family could see them, if I didn't need them?'

The question seemed to throw Rickman for a minute. He changed tactics and said, 'He's not a bodyguard.'

Micah reached back and took Nathaniel's hand in his and drew him up beside him just like I was on the other side. He gave Rickman solid eye contact as he said, 'Detective Rickman, this is Nathaniel. He's our third, our significant other.'

Gonzales made an inarticulate sound that was loudish. Deputy Al whistled and said, 'Wow, okay.'

'What is it with you and all the gay men, Blake?' Rickman asked.

I laughed, I couldn't help it. It seemed to startle everyone, because most of them looked at me, except for Micah, who was staring at Rickman. 'One, if the men in my life were gay it wouldn't do me a lot of good, would it? Two, why the hell are you this interested in my sex life?'

Micah said, 'Three, why do you have a problem with Anita? You just met her.'

'It's okay, Micah. I make him nervous.'

'Why?' he asked, as if Rickman weren't still standing there.

'My reputation intimidates him.'

'Which reputation, Marshal Blake? The one as a cold-blooded murderer, the one as a voodoo queen, or your reputation as a . . . gentlemen's woman?'

It took me a few moments to realize he'd just switched the sexes on the term *ladies' man* and not called me a slut, though somehow *gentlemen's woman* sounded like a cleaned-up version of *mistress*.

'That's enough.' Gonzales stepped in front of Rickman, and he was big enough that he blocked all our views of the detective. 'You,' he said, pointing at Al, 'take them inside.'

'You don't outrank me,' Rickman said.

'Rush Callahan has been my friend for over thirty years. We served together, bled together, saved each other's lives more times than I can count. We both joined Boulder PD at the same time. He offered to take me with him when he moved to being sheriff. I don't outrank you sergeant to detective, I outrank you because you are forgetting that a fellow officer is down, dying, and this is his son.'

'We do not need Blake here with her hocus-pocus. We do not need the Feds on this case.'

'Make your reputation some other day, Ricky,' Gonzales said. 'Tonight isn't the night for it.'

'I don't know what case you're talking about, but I'm here as Micah's girlfriend, fiancée, whatever. We're here for him and his dad, that's it.'

'You say you're the girlfriend, but you have a federal badge and you're fucking Preternatural Branch, which means you can do any damn thing you want.'

'I am the girlfriend and I don't know what the hell you're talking about.'

'You go' – he motioned toward the hospital – 'go be the girlfriend, be the fiancée, meet the family, but if you try to take this case over I will fight you for it and do everything in my power to make sure you regret stepping on our toes.'

'"Stepping on our toes,"' I said. 'Really, that's the best you can threaten?'

'Anita,' Nathaniel said softly.

He was right, but I'd be damned if I'd apologize to Rickman.

'No, that's not the best I can threaten,' Rickman said, his voice rising.

'Get them inside, Al, now,' Gonzales said.

It was actually Juliet who started us walking, but Al brought up the rear as if he feared an attack from that direction. Gonzales turned to Rickman, and I heard the detective's angry voice rising as we walked away.

'Did you have to bait him like that?' Juliet asked.

I sighed. 'No, and I'm sorry. It was childish.'

Micah said, 'I've seen you have problems with officers who you had a history with, but you've never worked with Rickman, have you?'

'No,' I said.

Juliet's phone rang, and she stepped away from us to take a call from her husband. She apologized and mouthed something about her kids. We all nodded, and suddenly it was just us 'guys.'

'Honestly, after what happened to Rush I'd take any help we could get,' Al said.

'Help on what?' I asked.

'Killer zombies,' he said.

'What?' I asked.

'We've had zombie attacks.'

'You have a rogue zombie?' I asked.

He shook his head. 'Not just one zombie. That's what's weird: It's not the same one. I mean, Sheriff Callahan talks about a flesh-eating zombie they had back in the seventies here, but they trapped it in a house and burned it, end of problem.'

'A flesh eater is incredibly rare; I've only seen one. You don't get herds of them, no matter what the movies and TV shows put out there.' To myself, I amended that I'd seen only one rogue zombie at a time. I had used cemeteries full of zombies that I had raised as defensive weapons against bad guys who were trying to kill me, three times. I carefully did not look behind me at Nicky. He'd been present for one of those moments.

'So it was just the same zombie-eating people when you had to deal with one, right?' Al asked.

'Yeah,' I said.

'This is different ones. We've got at least three different descriptions.'

'Descriptions never match; you could still just have one,' I said.

'One man, one woman, and one child; we think they're a family that disappeared in the mountains about a month ago.'

I shook my head. 'No way, no one would raise a family like that as zombies; no one would do that unless you've got an animator who had a grudge against the family. But it would have to be a hell of a grudge to raise a whole family from the dead, and if they were murdered, then raised from the dead, they'd kill their murderer. It would be their one driving purpose and they would attack people who got in their way, but it wouldn't turn them into flesh eaters necessarily. Were any of the family psychically gifted?'

'Not that we know, why?'

'The only cases I've heard of flesh eaters were animators or voodoo practitioners who had been raised from the dead.'

Al raised eyebrows. 'You mean if you . . .' He stopped abruptly. 'I am so sorry.'

'It's okay; there's a reason my will states I'm to be cremated, Deputy Truman.'

'You're afraid you'd turn into a flesh-eating zombie?' he asked.

'Why take the chance?' I said.

'Can we not talk about the woman I love dying just as we walk into the hospital to see my dying father?' Micah asked.

'Oh, geez,' Al said. 'I'm sorry, it's just someone mentioned calling in the Preternatural Branch, and Marshal Blake was mentioned specifically, before we knew she was with you. I'm sorry, I was being a cop. I'm just . . . sorry, Mike, really.'

'I'm sorry, too,' I said.

Micah squeezed my hand. 'I forgive you, but for the next little bit can you just be my fiancée and not be Marshal Blake?'

'Yes, of course,' I said, and I was ashamed for forgetting that this wasn't a case, this was Micah's dad. But I had a thought. 'Can I ask one more cop question? Just one more while Al is with us?'

Micah sighed. 'One more.'

'Micah's mom said that Sheriff Callahan had been bitten by something preternatural. What was it?'

'One of the flesh-eating zombies,' Al said.

'She said that it was contagious, that he was rotting— Are you saying that the people bitten by the zombies are turning into zombies?'

'No, they just rot and die.'

'But zombies aren't contagious,' I said.

'These are,' Al said.

'How many victims?'

'Five, but we've had witnesses to the last three attacks, so we know what's doing it now.'

'Now?' I asked.

'The first two victims died pretty quick, until Dr Rogers found some cases back east that sounded similar. He used some of the information that they published about it and was able to slow down the spread in the vic before the sheriff.'

'That's more than one question,' Nathaniel said softly.

'No, it's all right, Nathaniel,' Micah said. 'Anita can't be anything other than what she is, who she is, and my dad doesn't have cancer, he has something . . . preternatural, and no one is better at that than she is.'

'Are you saying I can treat this like a crime?'

'You've taught me that zombies don't rise spontaneously from the ground, so someone had to raise these, right?'

'Yes,' I said.

'People have already died, so isn't it at least negligent homicide?'

'Potentially, that's really for a court to decide, but someone raised the zombies and there has to be a reason they're out of control and attacking people, so it's either someone bit off more than they could chew and now doesn't want to fess up, or it's on purpose. Either way, when we locate the person who raised the zombies, it's a death sentence if they're convicted, because it falls under "using magic to kill people." That's an automatic real death sentence, no waiting on death row for years, but executed within weeks to months.'

Micah nodded. He turned to Al. 'You're saying my dad was attacked by a flesh-eating zombie and the bite is rotting?'

'Dr Rogers will explain it.'

'I'm asking you,' Micah said, looking at Al.

'I've said more than I should have shared with civilians.'

'Nicky went with Anita as her deputy on a warrant of execution.' Micah motioned at Nicky, who nodded enough for his bangs to swing out from his face a little.

'I know the preternatural marshals get a lot of leeway with calling in help in the middle of a vampire hunt, but this isn't a hunt.'

'Would you tell Anita more without us standing here?' Micah asked. 'And then she tells you later anyway?'

'She doesn't usually share details about ongoing cases with me, Al.'

'Swear to me she won't share details about your dad with you.'

Micah looked at Al and prepared to lie to him.

'No, Micah.' I squeezed his hand and turned to Al. 'I swear to you that everyone here will keep their mouths shut, and Nicky has been back up on a hunt, and I tell Micah and Nathaniel all sorts of personal shit that they don't blab.'

'What, you going to have them pinky-promise, cross their hearts?'

Al shook his head. 'You know it doesn't work that way. I'm not usually this chatty about an ongoing case. Except it's Mike, and you have a badge.' He looked at Nathaniel, who was still holding Micah's other hand. 'Can I say something that is absolutely none of my fucking business?'

Micah said, 'You can,' but his voice made it clear that Al better be careful what he said.

'Introduce Nate as your significant other, or whatever, but don't meet your family for the first time in almost ten years holding hands. Please, Mike, I know your family, and your Aunt Bertie and Uncle Jamie are here.'

'Uncle Bertie and Aunt Jamie, you mean?' I asked.

'Bertie is short for Bertha. She's my mom's sister,' Micah said. He pulled Nathaniel closer. 'So I'm not supposed to touch him at all, is that it, and his name is Nathaniel, not Nate. I'll let you call me Mike, because that's what I grew up with, but I go by Micah now.'

'Of course you can touch . . . Nathaniel, but can you just put Marshal Blake in the middle for the first meet and greet, that's all I'm saying. And I'll try to call you Micah, but not sure I'll remember.'

Nathaniel leaned over and kissed Micah gently on the cheek. 'Anita sleeps in the middle most of the time at home anyway.'

Micah looked up at him. 'You're okay with hiding?'

'No, but I want to be able to come back to see your family with you, and if you shove me into their faces constantly, then they won't like me. I want them to like me.'

Micah seemed to consider it for a minute. He turned to me. 'You in the middle means one of us has your gun hand.'

'We walk with me in the middle in St Louis when we have guards with us and I'm not on a case,' I said.

'Why am I the only one fighting not to hide?'

Juliet came back with her phone call over, and apparently she'd caught enough of the talk to comment, 'Because you've decided to shove your boyfriend in everyone's face, and once you decide to take a stand you don't back down; you never have.'

'That's more me than Micah,' I said.

He had a stubborn look to his face that I hadn't seen before. It was Nicky who said, 'Sometimes when we go back home to our family and hometown we fall back into old patterns, old actions, old feelings.

They come back up like ghosts, and if you're not careful you sort of become your old self again.'

We all looked at him. Juliet said, 'Well, you're not just handsome muscle, are you?'

He shrugged as much as the muscle development would let him. I knew his comment had come from personal experience. It made me want to ask him how his visit home had gone and how long it had been since he'd visited. His mother was in prison, as far as I knew, and his siblings adopted out. Had Nicky visited his dad? Why was it hard to picture him going home to visit?

'No,' Micah said, 'Nicky is pretty smart,' and he looked embarrassed, which was something else I didn't get to see often. He put his head against Nathaniel's shoulder, more like he was resting against him than holding him, and then he let go of his hand and swung me around so I could walk between them.

I loved walking with both of them holding my hand, and I felt pretty secure that the few seconds it would take me to drop their hands and go for my gun would be filled with Nicky and Dev shooting first.

Micah said, 'Thanks, Nicky, I needed the reminder.'

'You're usually reminding the rest of us to be grown-ups; just returning the favor.' They shared a smile and a nod, which is a particularly male way of thanking and saying, *it's okay.*

Juliet led the way, smiling and more relaxed. Al dropped back behind us and I heard him say, 'Thanks, Nick, or Nicky?'

'Either one is fine,' Nicky said.

'Yeah, I'm Al, or Albert. What's Dev short for?'

'Devil,' Dev said, and I knew he would either keep a straight face or flash a devilish grin. The hospital doors whooshed open, or I might have looked back to see. The cool, antiseptic smell of the hospital wrapped us. I felt both men almost flinch. I glanced at Micah and found him wrinkling his nose, as if something smelled bad. I turned to see an almost identical reaction from Nathaniel. He actually shook his shoulders like a bird settling its feathers, or I guess in his case like a cat shaking something off its fur.

Micah's face was back to neutral as he spoke low. 'I've never gotten used to how hospitals smell.' And I knew he meant since he got super-scenting ability as a wereleopard.

I heard Al from behind us, saying, 'Oh, come on, your name can't really be Devil.'

'My twin sister's name is Angel.'

'I don't believe it.'

'Nicky,' Dev said.

'Dev is short for Devil, and his sister is named Angel.'

Apparently, neither of them was going to tell Al that Devil was a nickname. We were going to need a little humor to get us through tonight, and bedeviling Al about Dev's name was a start.

Juliet and Al took us up in the elevator so we didn't have to ask where to go or what we were doing. Al said, 'You got your badge with you?'

'You know I do; I have to,' I said.

'Maybe put it where the other cops can see it.'

'Won't that make them think Anita has come to butt in on the case, just like Rickman fears?' Micah asked.

'Some of them are going to think that anyway, but cops like other cops, and you being the son of one and the boyfriend of another will make them like you better. It'll make them like you all better.'

The elevator stopped, doors still shut.

'You think we'll need the extra likeability?' I asked.

'You might,' he said.

I looked at him, wondering what I was missing, but Al was on our side, and he had the flavor of the local cops and I didn't, so I paid attention. The doors opened, we stepped out of the elevator, and I dropped the men's hands long enough to move the little walletlike badge cover to the front of my belted skirt, so the badge was visible. I'd have preferred the lanyard that I used at home to display my badge, but I hadn't brought that badge, or the lanyard. Silly me, I hadn't thought I'd need it.

Juliet and Al took us down a short hallway, turned a corner, and half a dozen cops pushed away from the walls, or just turned like magic toward us. One, cops keep their eye on movement, because it can be bad guys. Two, Nicky looked like a bad guy, and Dev looked like a large, physical smart aleck; either one was the kind of person that most cops learn to keep an eye on. With the two of them behind us attracting the cops' attention, it was like being invisible, a magician's trick of misdirection, or maybe they just couldn't see Micah and me behind Al and Juliet? Nathaniel was tall enough that some of him had to be visible.

There were actually only two people in the hallway who I knew for certain weren't cops. They were a man and a woman, a couple if I was betting. The woman was wearing a black polyester pantsuit that had fit twenty pounds ago. The white button-down blouse with its little ruffled collar didn't help. Her glasses were large and black framed so they dominated her face. Her hair was shortish and going from brunette to a tired gray. She'd also brushed her curls out in an attempt to straighten them, and it gave her hair the consistency of wool. When you have hair as curly as mine and Micah's you can never, ever brush your hair. It breaks the curl and makes a mess of it. Jean-Claude, with his only slightly less curly hair, had taught me that. The woman had to be over fifty; you'd think somewhere someone would have taught her how curly hair works. Her only jewelry was a silver cross and a lapel pin in the shape of a crosier, the shepherd's crook that is supposed to mean that a bishop or above is a guardian of his flock, when it's carried in the life-size version. I'd never seen one as a pin.

'Aunt Bertie,' Juliet called out, and went toward the woman, who had flashed an unfriendly look past her to Micah and me. Maybe I was being paranoid about that whole 'me' thing, but fundamentalists of several flavors had hated me on sight; why should Aunt Bertie be different?

It meant that the man with her was probably Uncle Jamie. He was at least five-nine, but he seemed shorter because he was carrying his weight from chest to groin, with only his legs still thin. The legs gave an echo of what he must once have looked like. I knew women who took pride in their legs staying thin, even with the rest of the weight up top. I wondered if men thought the same thing; I'd just be worried about heart attacks.

The man was wearing glasses almost identical to the woman's, but his suit fit better than hers, which probably meant he'd been at his present weight for longer. I just kept thinking I hoped there wasn't any heart disease in the family.

Juliet and Deputy Al tried to intercede for Micah with the pair, but they were having none of it. He was not going to get to see his father without passing through them first. Oh, joy.

Juliet tried, calling out, 'I thought you guys were down in the cafeteria making sure everyone got some dinner.'

Aunt Bertie said, 'I told you we wanted to go with you to meet Mike at the airport, and you snuck off.'

'I didn't sneak off, but I told you they had people with them and there wouldn't be room for you and Uncle Jamie.'

'And how did you know there would be extra people with him?' she asked in a voice that was unpleasant, strident.

Uncle Jamie was in front of us. He had a lapel pin that I thought for a second was a tiny, silver candy cane, then realized it was another crosier. Al stepped back with a shrug and a look of mute apology to Micah.

'So, the prodigal son returns,' Uncle Jamie said.

'I just came to see my father,' Micah said. He let go of my hand and took a step in front as if he wanted to make sure he was taking the brunt of it, or maybe he thought holding hands was a way of cowering? I'd ask him later, maybe.

Nathaniel and I kept on holding hands. It made me feel better and since I couldn't shoot Micah's aunt and uncle for being rude, it gave me something to do with my hands.

'Who are these people with you?' And Uncle Jamie managed to make *people* sound as if what he meant was *fuckers*, but was too polite to say it.

Micah introduced Nicky and Dev first.

Jamie eyed them up and down like he was thinking of buying them and didn't think much of the sale. 'What are they?'

'People,' Micah said, his voice cold.

'Are they unnatural?' he asked.

Unnatural? 'Wow,' I said softly. It hadn't even occurred to me that Micah's being a shapeshifter would be a problem with his family. I'd only worried about the sex part. Stupid me.

'Yes, just like me,' Micah said.

There was a sort of movement, or sigh, in all the police in the hallway. The uniforms, and the two in street clothes, all reacted almost like grass in a meadow when the wind stirs it. I wasn't sure if they were reacting to the growing unpleasantness or if they didn't like that at least three of us were 'unnatural.' We were in one of the handful of states where if someone killed Micah, or Dev, or Nicky, all they had to do was say they had feared for their life, and if the blood test on the dead body came back positive for lycanthropy, it would qualify as self-defense, without a trial or anything. If you had witnesses who said the shooting had been unprovoked you could be up on charges, but if the only other witness besides the shooter was conveniently dead, then it was a clean kill. I hadn't thought what that might mean for my men. My stomach tightened, my shoulders tensing, as I thought about that for everyone I'd brought with me. I was so used to the local police who worked with me seeing my boyfriends as people that I hadn't thought that not all police would be as understanding. That really had been stupid and careless.

I looked at the policemen in the hallway. Two of them were in a uniform like Al's, but the rest were a mix of different uniforms and two were in street clothes. They were all armed, and all had that cop look in their faces as they looked at Micah, Nicky, and Dev for threat evaluation. Was there a time in my career when I would have done the same thing? You hear someone is a wereanimal and you just automatically assume they're dangerous, right? Well, yeah. The cops in the hallway had just been told that Micah and two big, obviously physical, armed men were all faster, stronger, and harder to kill than any of them. I tried to see it from their point of view, but I just couldn't. The men in question meant too much to me for me to be okay with the evaluating looks from the cops. I knew that if anything went wrong they would probably shoot first and ask questions later. There'd been a time in my life when I might have done the same thing.

'Everybody take a deep breath,' I said, my voice calm but clear. 'I'm Marshal Anita Blake and the men who you're sizing up right now are with me.'

'We know who you are,' an older guy in a state trooper uniform said, and he didn't sound thrilled.

'The other beasts are with you in what way?' Jamie asked what the cops probably wanted to ask anyway, so they let him. Except for the beast part, I'd give the police the benefit of the doubt on that.

'First, don't ever call them beasts again,' Micah said.

'That's what they are,' he said, and he raised his hand and pointed at Micah. 'Just like you are.' His silver crosier winked in the light.

'Oh, God, you're wearing the shepherd's crook. Please tell me that the two of you didn't become Shepherds of the Flock?' Micah sounded disgusted.

I thought, *The nut jobs on the news*, but I didn't say it out loud. They were his relatives and I'd do my best not to make things worse, but the Shepherds were a new zealot group that went around to victims of preternatural attacks and tried to 'save' them by telling new lycanthropes they were now animals without souls and new vampires that they were demon-inhabited corpses, so becoming one of those made you an agent of the devil.

'We are here to be guardians for the victims of the beasts and demons,' Jamie said, which was a big yes.

'Sheriff Callahan wasn't bitten by a shapeshifter or a vampire,' Al said, 'so you shouldn't be up here.'

'We're Rush's family. We have every right to be here,' Jamie said.

'Then be here as family, not as Shepherds,' Al said.

'We're here to protect Rush, in case the monster that attacked him comes back,' Aunt Bertie said.

'Leave that to the police,' Al said.

'Not when the police consort with devil worshippers and soulless beasts. You cannot use the devil to protect you from the devil.'

I moved up beside Micah. 'Who are you calling a devil worshipper?' Nathaniel came with me, because he wouldn't let go of my hand. In fact, he had a double grip on my arm now, as if he thought I'd do something unfortunate.

'Don't feel bad, Anita, he just called his own nephew a soulless beast,' Micah said, and now his voice held an edge of anger. The first trickle of power slithered across my skin, raising the hair on the arm closest to him. He had the best control of any shapeshifter I'd ever been around, and sometimes he'd flare power to back down another shapeshifter, like I'd tried to do with Nilda at the airplane, but somehow I didn't think this flare-up was on purpose. His aunt and uncle couldn't feel the burst of power, and if they had it would only have confirmed their fears.

'Easy,' I said softly.

He whispered, 'I need a minute.'

He needed a minute to regain his iron control. I did the only thing I could think to do: draw their 'fire.' 'How dare you call your own nephew a soulless beast, you narrow-minded, poor excuse for a Christian.'

'How dare you question my Christianity, you devil-worshipping, evil—'

'That's enough, Jamie,' Al said, and tried to step between us.

'I'm Christian,' I said, 'and my cross glows just fine. When's the last time you bet your faith against something that could tear your face off?'

Nathaniel's grip on my arm tightened enough to almost hurt. I hadn't meant to step closer to Uncle Jamie, but religious bigots like him pissed me off. The ones who were so sure they were right were usually the most un-Christian of all.

Micah's energy was almost back to normal. The fact that he was having this much trouble getting to normal said just how angry and upset he was, and it wasn't just the crackpot aunt and uncle who were making him raw. His dad was in the room and they were delaying him with their bigotry that masqueraded as religion.

'She's Micah's fiancée,' Juliet said, 'and that alone should make you talk like a civilized human being to her.'

Aunt Bertie pushed up beside her husband and Juliet. 'Are you his fiancée, or is it Beatrice's fancy way of saying you're shacking up together?'

Oh, good, they were going to hate the sex part, too. 'Shacking up together?' I said.

'That's what I said,' Bertie said, and her face looked smug.

'It's just I haven't heard that phrase since I was a little girl; I didn't know anybody still used it.'

She blushed, as if I'd embarrassed her. Interesting, because I had not begun to embarrass Aunt Bertie.

'Are you his fiancée, or living in sin?'

'She could be both,' Juliet said, 'the way I was with Ben.'

'Just because Ben married you when he could get the milk for free doesn't mean it wasn't a sin.'

'Milk for free?' I asked. 'Are you guys for real?'

Jamie gave me a look of utter disdain. 'When a man can get what he wants from a woman, he uses her until he's done with her, and then he abandons her for the next woman who will open her legs for him.'

Nathaniel's hands tightened desperately on my arm, but it was Micah who stepped up beside us and said, 'I am ashamed that you are the kind of man who would fuck a woman and then abandon her, Uncle Jamie.'

'What?' Jamie said, and looked at Micah. 'I would never—'

'You just said that if a man can get sex before marriage, he uses the woman and then abandons her for the next woman.'

'Yes, that's why you marry first and show your commitment before God.'

'I love Anita and I would never abandon her for another woman. I don't need God to tell me that would be wrong, and I'm deeply ashamed that if you hadn't married Aunt Bertie first that you would have fucked her for a while and then abandoned her.'

'I never would . . . I did not say that!'

Aunt Bertie yelled, 'How dare you! Apologize to your uncle! He is the best man I have ever known and he would never do such a thing.'

'And Anita is the best woman I have ever known, and she would never abandon me just because she could get all the sex she wanted without marrying me. She loves me for more than just sex, don't you, sweetheart?' he asked.

I don't think he'd ever called me sweetheart, but I said the only thing I could say: 'Yes, I love you for way more than just the mind-blowing sex.'

He smiled at me, and then he took off the sunglasses that he'd put back on in the lights of the hospital. He let his aunt and uncle see his leopard eyes. They backed up, gasping. Then Aunt Bertie yelled, 'His eyes! He's starting to shift! Oh, my God, help us!'

The police in the hallway knew about his eyes, so they didn't go for their weapons, but Aunt Bertie didn't know they wouldn't. She'd been willing to get Micah killed.

Al said, 'His eyes are stuck in animal form, Bertie. He's not changing.'

She and Jamie kept backing up. She turned to the other officers. 'Protect us.'

'Deputy Gutterman told us about Mike Callahan's eyes being leopard,' the older state trooper said. 'You don't need to be protected from Rush's son, your nephew.' In other circumstances he might have half-agreed with their attitude, but he'd understood, just like I had, that she'd been willing to get her own nephew shot in the hallway outside his dying father's hospital room. None of the police who had witnessed it were going to like either of them now. Some lines you did not cross, and they'd just crossed several.

Micah took my free hand in his, and I said, 'You aren't shepherds, you're sheep. The first hint of threat and you run for protection to the real shepherds, the police.'

The older statie said, 'We're not shepherds, Marshal Blake, we're sheepdogs.' He grinned, and it was more a flash of teeth, like baring fangs, than amusement.

I nodded, because I knew the essay. It was from 'On Sheep, Wolves, and Sheepdogs,' from Lt. Col. David Grossman's book *On Combat*. 'We live to protect the flock, and confront the wolf,' I said.

He nodded and gave that flash of teeth again. It left his eyes cold. 'We do that. I'm Commander Walter Burke, Marshal Blake, and I'm sorry to meet you and Mr Callahan under the circumstances.'

'Me, too,' I said.

He turned to Aunt Bertie and Uncle Jamie. 'Now, some of these nice officers are going to escort you down to the rest of the family.'

'We can't let them see Rush by themselves. He's already been attacked by one monster,' Bertie said.

Commander Burke let out a deep breath and said, 'Deputy Gutterman, Corporal Price, escort these two downstairs to the family lounge. If they resist, charge them with assaulting a police officer.'

'You wouldn't dare,' Jamie said.

Burke turned and let Jamie see his eyes, his face, his attitude, and like a good sheep the other man backed down. 'You're leaving this boy alone to see his father, one way or the other. It's your choice whether you do it in the family lounge or in the back of a police car.'

It was all I could do not to say out loud, *Choose wisely*.

They chose wisely and went with the nice police officers to the family lounge, which meant we'd be seeing them later. That was going to suck.

Burke looked at us. 'I'm sorry that your relatives are going to make this harder than it already is, Mr Callahan, Marshal Blake.' He glanced at Nathaniel's hand in mine.

'Mr Graison,' I said.

'Mr Graison,' he said. He looked at Nicky and Dev behind us. 'I'm sorry you can't come to visit your father in the hospital without body-guards, but if that's your aunt and uncle, I'd hate like hell to see what strangers would do.'

Micah nodded. 'Thank you, Commander Burke. I appreciate that.'

'You're the son of a good cop and engaged to a U.S. Marshal; that makes you family. Now go see your father, and I am sorry that you had to come home to this.'

I wondered if he meant Rush Callahan being hurt or the crazy aunt and uncle? I guess it didn't matter; either way, not everyone in Colorado hated us. Good to know.

12

Micah had told me his dad was five foot six, but he looked smaller in the hospital bed. His hair was auburn, but whereas Nathaniel's hair was a rich brown with red undertones that sometimes you noticed and sometimes you didn't, Rush Callahan's hair was more dark red with brown undertones in it. I wondered if he'd say he had red hair? I hoped he'd wake up enough for me to ask. Right now, his face held that slackness that only heavy drugs can give it; even sleep doesn't smooth out the face in quite the same way as heavy-duty painkillers. His skin was pasty pale, so that the few freckles he had stood out like brown ink spots, but underneath the much lighter skin tone and hair the bone structure was Micah's. Micah was so delicate for a man that I'd just assumed he looked like his mother, but he didn't. He looked like his dad. The biggest difference, other than the faint lines around the eyes and across the forehead, was the mouth. Micah's lips were fuller, more kissable looking. His father had thinner lips, more traditionally Caucasian male. I realized that almost every man in my life had full lips. I guess we all have preferences in partners that we aren't even aware of ourselves. Micah's father's hair was almost as curly as Micah's, though cut a lot shorter. But his dad's reddish auburn curls haloed around his face in a thick circle. His curl was looser than Micah's, or mine, but it was curlier than Cousin Juliet's. She was waiting out in the hallway. She'd wanted to give Micah some privacy, and she'd said out loud that she'd try to head off any relatives so the privacy would last longer. I think she wanted Micah to have a few minutes before he had to deal with any more awfulness from his family. Uncle Jamie and Aunt Bertie had been enough for one visit, though we'd probably be seeing them again, unfortunately.

Micah said, 'That's weird.'

There were so many possibilities for weirdness in that moment that it felt odd to ask, 'What's weird?' But sometimes you have to ask the obvious question.

'Mom used to help him with his hair, but once they divorced he cut it short because he couldn't deal with the curls. I haven't seen his hair like this since the year I was twelve. He must have a new girlfriend, or something, and I've never even met her.' The sorrow in his voice was nearly touchable, but since I couldn't touch his sadness I wrapped my arms around his waist and held him. His arm came around me almost automatically, his eyes staring down at the man in the bed. He'd put his sunglasses in their slim case that rode in the breast pocket of his suit jacket the way other people carried reading glasses. He stared down at his father with eyes that would be a stranger's eyes in his son's face. Like the mystery girlfriend who helped with curls, there would be a lot of catching up to do. I prayed that they'd get the chance to share all of it.

The room was dim, most of the light from the glow of one lamp near the bed. The drapes were drawn against the night, and the small beep of the monitors that let the nurses' station know Mr Callahan was still alive seemed loud in the silence.

Nathaniel came up behind us and put his hand on Micah's shoulder, because there wasn't room for both of us to hug him at once. Micah put up his free hand to cover Nathaniel's hand. There are pains too deep for words, but there's touch to say what words can't.

'Can you both smell it?' Micah asked.

Neither of us had to ask what he meant. Even with my human nose I could smell it: sickly sweet, but with a sourness underneath, so *sweet* seems the wrong word, but rotting flesh does have a sweet undertone to the smell of it. I'd spent most of my adult life smelling it at crime scenes and zombie raisings, though oddly the zombies that I raised didn't smell as bad as some. The amount of smell seemed to get worse the lower the power level of your animator. My early zombies had looked rotted, but they hadn't smelled that way. I'd seen other zombies raised that smelled as bad as a real corpse. The white sheet was raised on a framework so that it didn't touch Rush Callahan's body, like they do with some burn victims. Whatever wound was underneath that white, untouched dome of sheet had a faint scent of rot, like a preview of the corpse to come.

I swallowed hard; my throat was tight, and it wasn't because I was going to be sick. I'd smelled much worse. It was almost as if Micah were keeping such tight control on himself that someone had to cry for him. But damned if it was going to be me; I was here to be strong for him, not to be the first one to cry. I would not be this much of a girl, damn it!

Standing in that room with the smell of death already there, I hugged him tighter, because I didn't know what else to do. He rested his face against my hair and hugged me back. Nathaniel came in at our back, wrapping his free arm around me so that he could cuddle himself against Micah's back and touch us both.

There was a soft but authoritative knock on the door. It opened without our saying *Come in*, and in came a tall, thin man in a long white coat. He flashed a professional smile as he came through, cheerful and empty of meaning, because it makes people feel better when you smile. I knew the smile, because I had a client smile, too, and it meant about as much. You smile, because if you don't people worry more. He was a doctor, and people worried enough around him, so he smiled.

'I'm Dr Rogers; you must be Mike.' He held his hand out toward us, but mainly at Micah. He looked enough like his dad that there was no guesswork between him and Nathaniel.

'Micah. I haven't been Mike in a decade.' He let go of us enough to shake Dr Rogers's hand.

He turned to us, and I said, 'Anita Blake.'

Nathaniel shook his hand, too, and said, 'Nathaniel Graison.'

Rogers nodded and said, 'I'm glad you got here.'

Micah gave him very serious eyes. 'My mother told Anita that it was only a matter of time; is that true?'

'We've slowed the disease, but we have no way of curing it. I'm sorry.'

Micah nodded, looked at the floor, and reached back for our hands. I gave him my left hand, and Nathaniel hugged him on the other side, like I'd been doing when Rogers entered the room. The doctor's gaze flicked to the two men and me, then back up to the men. I thought he was going to say something unfortunate, but he was all professional.

'How long?' Micah asked.

'I can't answer that for certain.'

'Guess.'

'Excuse me?' Rogers asked.

'Guess, give me an estimate how long my father has,' Micah said.

Rogers shook his head. 'I'm not comfortable doing that.'

'All right, then tell me what you're doing to treat my father.'

Rogers was comfortable discussing that. There had been a few cases on the Eastern Seaboard that were similar, but not identical. 'Those patients died within hours, but I used their protocols on our patients here and it slowed the spread of the . . . infection.'

'Is it an infection?' Micah asked.

'Yes.' He sounded very sure.

'What kind of infection is it?'

'It's close to necrotizing fasciitis, and we've treated it the same way, with removal of the necrotic tissue, massive antibiotics, and time in a hyperbaric chamber.'

'How much . . . tissue have you removed?' Micah asked.

'As little as necessary.'

'That's not an answer, that's an evasion.'

'If you insist I can show you the wound, but I wouldn't recommend it.'

'Why not?' Micah asked.

'It won't change anything and it won't help anything. It's just an unnecessary visual for you.'

Micah shook his head. 'I need to know what you've done to my father.'

'I haven't done anything to him, except the best I could under the circumstances.'

Micah let out a slow, even breath.

I said, 'This isn't my father, but you're scaring me. Where was the bite?'

'His left arm.'

'Does he still have his arm?' Micah asked.

Dr Rogers made a face. 'Yes, but if we can't get it stopped we may try amputation, though honestly I think it will just slow it down, not stop it.'

'Did you try amputation with any of the other victims?' I asked.

'Yes, but either we didn't do it soon enough, or once the infection is in the body it hits the bloodstream almost immediately and that takes it throughout the body.'

'I have to see,' Micah said.

Dr Rogers didn't understand immediately, but I did, and Nathaniel did, because he said, 'Micah means he needs to see the wound.'

'Really, I wouldn't . . .'

'Would you really not look if it were your father?' Micah asked, studying the doctor's face. 'I'm betting you would insist on seeing it.'

'I'm a doctor; I would want to see it from a professional standpoint, to understand what was happening.'

'I'm not a doctor, and I'm hoping that what I'm imagining is worse than what you'll show me, but either way I need to see.'

Rogers made a soft, exasperated sound. He got fresh rubber gloves out of a little box that was beside the bed and walked to the far side of the bed with its tented sheet. 'Anything touching the wound site seems to be extremely painful, so we raised the sheet above it.'

'Like for a burn,' I said.

'For some burns, yes,' he said. He unhooked the sheet from the metal framework and looked across the bed at us. 'I honestly don't recommend this.'

'Please, Dr Rogers, I just need to see,' Micah said, his voice low and even. He had a death grip on my hand, and I assumed on Nathaniel's, too.

The doctor didn't argue again, just pulled back the sheet enough for us to see the left arm and part of the chest. I couldn't tell what the original bite had been like, because flesh was missing from the outer part of the lower left arm in a neat oval almost as big as both my fists side by side. The wound placement let me know what had happened. Sheriff Callahan had been attacked and he'd put his left arm up to defend himself and something had bitten him. I had my own share of defensive wounds like that, but none as deep. Even if he lived, I wasn't sure how much use he'd have of the arm. It was an awful lot of muscle and ligament to lose.

Micah's hand tensed around mine, his eyes narrowed, but other than that he showed nothing. His stress sang down his arm into his hand, but it showed almost nowhere else. God, he had such control in that moment. It was impressive and made me proud that he was mine.

He started to say something, swallowed hard, tried again, and just shook his head. I hoped I was about to ask the questions he wanted to ask. 'The edges of the wound look darker than they should, and there's discoloration in the wound itself; is that from the treatment?'

'I'm afraid not.'

'It's starting to rot again,' Micah said, his voice sort of hollow.

'Yes, there are some bacteria in the mix that we've never seen before and they're not responding to the antibiotics.' He started refitting the sheet back over the framework without asking if we were done looking. Micah didn't say anything, so I let it go.

He looked at me and there was such pain buried in the green-gold depths of his eyes. In a voice that was only a little thicker than it should have been, he said, 'Ask.'

'Ask what?' I said.

'Anything you want to know.'

'Not as your girlfriend, but as me?' I asked.

He nodded.

I raised an eyebrow, but I wasn't going to question it. I wanted to know what the hell was going on. 'Okay,' I said, 'what attacked Sheriff Callahan?'

'We're not sure.'

'I heard it was a flesh-eating zombie.'

'Someone's been talking,' Rogers said.

'I am a U.S. Marshal with the Preternatural Division. This is kind of what I do.'

'The local police were worried you'd do just that and take the case away from them.'

'I don't want to take anything away from anyone, but I also don't want people to hoard information between different police agencies. That's a good way to keep the case from being solved and guarantee more victims.'

There was a faint flinching around his eyes when I said that. The other victims had been bad, for Rogers to react like that. If Micah's dad hadn't been the latest it would have been interesting, but now . . . it was scary and interesting.

'You don't want other people hurt like my dad,' Micah said, and I knew he'd seen the flinching, too, and that he'd used 'my dad' deliberately. We both wanted more information and we'd sensed an opening; we'd double-team Rogers. Individually, Micah and I could be relentless, even ruthless; together we were more.

'Of course not,' Rogers said.

'Then help us,' I said.

'You are police, but right now you are the fiancée of a patient's son. That means that you are a civilian, as the police like to say.'

I had a thought. 'Has someone been treating you like a civilian and hoarding information from you, too?'

He looked away from us for a moment. I was betting he was both working to control his expression and debating what to say, or how much to say.

I felt Micah tense beside me, and I touched him, letting him know we needed to wait. This was the first tipping point, and it could lead to spilling all the information we needed, or to nothing; if we rushed it Rogers would clam up, I was almost a hundred percent certain of that. It was like hunting; you needed to be patient and move carefully or you'd step on a stick or a rock and scare the game away.

Nathaniel moved slightly beside us, but I didn't warn him. I trusted him to let us work and not to push.

He looked from one to the other of us, then looked at me and Micah, very hard. It was a good look, not a cop look, but maybe a doctor look. He was looking at us as if we were a mystery illness and he was trying to decide if he could figure out what we really were. 'Are you really his fiancée, or even his girlfriend, or is that just an excuse to butt in on this case, because the local cops would never have asked you in? One of the other doctors suggested you come in for a consult, because no one knows zombies like you do, and you would have thought she asked them to invite the devil in to help. They seem convinced you'll take over.'

'First, I *am* Micah's girlfriend and lover. *Fiancée* is a little harder, because you read the papers, see the news, and you know I'm also dating our Master of the City. I can't marry everybody.'

Dr Rogers looked at Nathaniel standing with us but being so quiet. 'And who are you, Mr Graison? I wouldn't normally pry, but if I help these two then the local police may make my life harder, and before I risk that I want to know who I'm talking to and why.'

'Who do you think I could be that would hurt you with the local police?' Nathaniel asked.

Rogers shook his head. 'No, we're not playing the game where questions get answered by questions. Answer my question, or we are done.'

'Do I look like a cop?' Nathaniel asked.

'No, but neither did Mike here, until he started asking questions and then the energy coming off Marshal Blake and Mr Callahan was very similar. I know he's the son of a cop, so maybe he learned it by osmosis, but your energy feels like hers, too, somehow, and I want to know why.'

Just from his asking the question I knew that Rogers was psychically gifted. He was probably an amazing diagnostician, one of those doctors who came up with leaps of intuition that were right about mystery illness and treatment. It could be luck, but in that moment I was pretty certain it was more than that. He wasn't just seeming to look right through us; in a way he was. It made me feel better that he was treating Micah's dad, but it also meant we couldn't play him. He'd feel the lie, the games, and he'd shut us out. Truth was our only option.

'You must be an amazing diagnostician,' Micah said, making the same logic leap that I had.

Rogers frowned at him, eyes narrowing. 'I am, but flattery is not a good idea on your part.'

'Tell him the truth, Nathaniel,' I said.

Nathaniel moved up and put an arm around both of us. We both put an arm around his waist, so that the three of us faced the doctor entwined. 'The three of us live together and have for nearly three years. I'm an exotic dancer at Guilty Pleasures and a wereleopard just like Micah.'

'That explains why your energy feels like Mr Callahan's, but not Marshal Blake's.'

'I'm their Nimir-Ra,' I said, 'their leopard queen. It's on record that I carry multiple strains of lycanthropy; one of them is leopard.'

'I read the paper that Dr Nelson did on you. You are a medical anomaly. One, multiple strains of lycanthropy, which is impossible since one strain protects you from all other diseases including lycanthropy. Two, you don't change shape. You have all the symptoms and many of the benefits, but you don't shift. I heard the military was very interested in that.'

'So the rumors say; no one's talked to me,' I said.

'Rumors,' he said, softly.

I nodded. 'Yes, rumors.'

'Maybe you're as good as you think you are, Marshal Blake, but I have to live here with the local police after you go home. I'd like someone's okay for talking to you about this.'

'Federal badge means I don't have to have an okay to see the bodies.'

'And talk like that is why the other cops don't like you, Marshal.'

'I'm not here to be liked, I'm here to get things done.'

'I thought you were here to be with Mike and his family.'

'I am, but I'm a cop and no one knows zombies like I do. It would be a bad use of resources for me not to at least consult.'

'I'll ask our local guys about you seeing the bodies in the morgue. Beyond that, talk to the cops.'

I started to try to persuade him to talk now, but the door opened without a knock. I turned automatically, giving myself room to draw my gun if I needed to; I hadn't done it for the doctor, but the last few minutes had made me tense, and I gave in to that tension. Logically I knew that nothing would get through Nicky and Dev at the door, or the cops outside, that I needed to shoot, but sometimes it's not about logic, it's about habit. I was habitually paranoid, like most police.

'I'll let you talk to your brother,' Dr Rogers said, and he left, passing the man who was Micah's brother.

13

The man who came through the door was five-nine, five-ten, with short curly hair the same deep brown of Micah's, but the hair was even curlier so that cut almost military short there was still tight curl close to his scalp. Large gray-blue eyes dominated his face, so that was what you saw first, and I had to look twice to see he had Micah's full lips and a skin tone only a few shades darker, but that was where the resemblance ended. The man's features were clean and handsome, but there was no hint of the delicacy of Micah, his dad, or Cousin Juliet.

'Mike, so you are here,' he said in a voice that was deeper than I thought it would be.

'Hello, Jerry,' Micah said. Unless there was a cousin Jerry we didn't know about it, this had to be his brother, Jerry.

'Beth said you'd come. I said you wouldn't.'

'She was always the hopeful one,' Micah said.

Jerry stood just inside the closed door looking at his brother. 'Little sisters are like that, I guess,' he said.

The two men just looked at each other. Nathaniel and I stood on either side of Micah, but we might as well have been on the moon for all we mattered in that moment.

'I don't know about all little sisters, but Beth was always kind.'

'Softhearted, you mean.'

Micah shrugged. 'Either way.'

I wanted to tell them to hug or something, but I'd never met his brother, and I didn't know enough of their history to push.

'Why'd you come back, Mike?'

'To see Dad.'

'If he wasn't good enough to see while he was . . . before he got hurt, then why the hell do you care now?'

'Jerry . . .'

'What? You expected to come home like the prodigal son and we'd all forgive and forget?'

'No, I didn't expect you to forgive me.'

'Yes, you did. You thought you'd get your Hallmark moment where everyone cries and says nice things, and you get forgiven before he dies. That's why you came home, to be forgiven. Well, if he wakes up and forgives you, remember, I won't.'

'I'll remember,' Micah said, his voice low and even. His face was as blank as he could make it.

'Aren't you going to introduce me to your friends?'

'I didn't think you wanted to be introduced.'

'I don't hate them, big brother, only you.'

Micah did a long blink, and then without any change of expression turned to me and said, 'Anita Blake, this is my brother, Jerry.'

I did the only thing I could think of under the circumstances; I went forward and offered my hand. He could ignore it and be utterly rude, or he could shake it. He looked surprised for a second, and then he took my hand. He didn't seem to know how to shake hands with a girl, or maybe it was me being the girl with Micah. Either way it was a step forward from him just refusing.

'This is Nathaniel Graison,' Micah said.

Nathaniel followed my example and Jerry shook his hand, too. He gave Nathaniel a firmer handshake; maybe he was recovering from the surprise of us being polite?

Micah came up behind us, closer to his brother. 'I'm sorry I didn't come home sooner.'

'Why didn't you?'

'I thought you'd hate me, so there didn't seem to be much point.'

Jerry's eyes were shiny. 'Well, you're right, I do hate you. You said terrible things to Mom and Dad.'

'I know I can't explain it, but I didn't feel I had a choice.' Micah's voice was a little thick now, as if Jerry weren't the only one whose eyes were shiny. I fought not to look at him, not to move too much, as if moving would ruin things.

'Dad's friends with a Fed. He said that he saw files about what would have happened to us if you hadn't convinced some bad-guy shapeshifter that you hated us.'

Again, I wondered how in the hell any Fed knew that and where the information had come from. But now wasn't the time to ask, and Jerry wouldn't know anyway. I wasn't sure if I was looking forward to meeting this friendly Fed or dreading it.

'I saw him do terrible things to other families. I couldn't risk it.'

'You did a good job of making us think you hated us. Mom cried for weeks, and Beth didn't hear it, so she didn't believe you'd said it, any of it. She thought we were lying, because we thought you being a wereleopard made you too dangerous. She thought we'd kicked you out for years.'

'I don't know if I could have said all I needed to say if Beth had been there.'

'I know you couldn't have. No way could you have looked her in the face and been so . . . cruel. You were her favorite brother even though you hunted and killed things with Dad, and she hated that, but she still loved you more.'

'She didn't love me more, Jerry; she loved me different, that's all.'

'You lying bastard.' His voice held the tears a moment before the first of them slid down his cheek. His voice was choking on his tears when he said, 'I hate you, you lying bastard.'

'I know,' Micah said, and something I heard in his voice made me have to look at his face so I could see the tears falling down his face.

It was Jerry who made the first move forward, but Micah didn't wait for more. They were suddenly hugging, clinging to each other and crying. Jerry was still calling him a lying bastard, but somewhere in all the name-calling I heard Micah say, 'I love you, too.'

14

When both men had dried their tears enough so they could pretend they hadn't been crying, Jerry took us to the family waiting room. It had a few couches, chairs, a coffee table full of magazines that almost no one ever read, and a few paintings on the walls, everything in colors that were supposed to be cheerful, or soothing, but never really were. It looked like a hundred other waiting rooms I'd seen, where I'd go to talk to families or police about the person in the other room, in surgery, and what had attacked them. To police it was, *How do we hunt it down and kill it?* To families of victims it was, *What can you tell me that will help me hunt it down and kill it?* It was a room like so many others, except this one had some of Micah's family in it, and that made it unique and strangely more intimidating. We might never walk down an aisle together, but Micah was a permanent part of my life and I was as happy as I'd ever been. Wedding band or not, these strangers were my potential in-laws. Scary, even to us tough-as-nails vampire hunters.

Micah's mom had the same big pale blue-gray eyes as Jerry, and she looked like him, or rather he looked like her. Her shoulder-length hair was the same tight curls, but the color was paler brown, on the borderline between ash brown and sandy blond. She had that clear, soft shade of skin that only nature and some very fun genetics give you. She looked a little more ethnic than her sister, but not by much. Her full lips were lipsticked and her makeup was perfect, but she wasn't wearing that much and if I hadn't known she was Micah's mom I would not have put her over fifty, but she had to be, didn't she? She was heavier than she'd probably been when she was younger, but it was mostly just more curves, so it looked good on her. A nicely tailored suit flattered the fuller figure rather than hid it, which I liked a lot. She was voluptuous, exotic, and beautiful, and Micah's mom. She was also a hugger.

She enveloped Micah in a hug like he was the last solid thing in the world and she was holding on for dear life. We caught snatches of what she was saying through the tears: 'So glad you're home . . . your dad will be so happy . . . love you . . .'

Micah said the only things he could: 'Love you, and I'm sorry.' He said other things, but they were mostly lost to his mother's crying. Nathaniel probably heard more of it, but he stood there holding my hand and waited for the emotional storm to abate enough for us to matter. Dev and Nicky had moved back to the entrance to the waiting area. There was only one way in, so they could guard just fine from there, and give us room for the family reunion at the same time. It was bodyguard multitasking at its best.

Micah extracted himself enough to say, 'Mom, this is Anita, and Nathaniel.'

She hugged me to her, and I had to let go of Nathaniel's hand to return the hug. She started crying again, saying, 'Thank you, thank you for bringing Mike home! Thank you so much.'

I mumbled, 'You're welcome,' and tried to figure out how soon I could break free of the hug and still be polite. My face was buried in her shoulder because in her heels she was at least five foot nine and I hadn't had time to go on tiptoe to keep from being smashed in the hug.

Jerry said, 'Let her breathe, Mom.'

She pulled back, laughing a little, dabbing at her eyes with her well-manicured hands. 'I'm sorry; I'm a hugger, so just a warning.'

In my head I thought, *Too late for the warning*, but on the surface I smiled and nodded, because I had nothing useful to say. People took it wrong if you told them not to touch you in situations like this, so I'd learned to smile and keep my mouth shut.

Micah drew Nathaniel forward. 'Mom, this is Nathaniel Graison.' He didn't add *my significant other* like he had with Cousin Juliet. It was harder sometimes with parents.

His mom looked at Nathaniel, then looked at Micah for a clue as to who he was to him.

Micah took Nathaniel's hand and my hand, took a deep breath, and said, 'Nathaniel is our live-in partner.'

A look that I couldn't interpret crossed her face, and then she hugged Nathaniel as tightly and completely as she had me. He hesitated for a second, then returned the hug, his face a little puzzled, but smiling over her shoulder.

She said, 'So happy to meet you and Anita both; you have no idea how happy I am to meet my son's friends.'

Micah and I exchanged a look. I tried to say with my eyes, *Well, that went well*. I was betting my stepmom wouldn't do nearly as well with it, but then again, Micah had been convinced his mom wouldn't do this well with Nathaniel. Maybe our parents were more grown up than we gave them credit for?

Micah's mom drew back from the hug, and I heard Nathaniel say, 'I'm glad to meet you, too, really.' He was smiling, happy and relieved, because none of us had been betting on it going this well.

A tall man came up behind Micah's mom. He was over six feet by a few inches, completely bald, with what amounted to five o'clock shadow in a thin pale half-circle on his scalp to show that he had started shaving his head after he went bald, rather than as a fashion statement. His eyebrows were thick, nearly black, and arched over dark-rimmed glasses. His eyes were a bright, clear blue. His dark suit, pale blue shirt, and dark tie fit his slender frame well and helped bring out the blue of his eyes and the stark paleness of his skin. The glasses and the baldness distracted me from the rest of his face, so it took a moment to realize he was handsome.

He put his hands on Micah's mom's shoulders in a gesture that, though innocent, was totally a couple gesture. I felt, more than saw, Micah tense. 'So glad you could be here, Mike,' the tall man said, and held out his hand.

Micah took the hand. 'I'm glad I could be here, too.' He turned back to me and said, 'Anita, Nathaniel, this is Tyson Morgan, my mom's . . . husband.'

I had my own stepmom so I knew the awkward moment when you wanted to acknowledge them but not claim them as your parent.

Micah's stepdad's hand was big with long, thin fingers to match the rest of his lanky frame. He smiled. 'Dr Tyson Morgan. I teach at the college with Bea.'

'Anita Blake, U.S. Marshal.'

His mouth quirked, like a small, lopsided smile, and then he shook his head, more at himself, I think. 'I guess I'm prouder than I should be of being Dr Morgan, sorry, but please call me Ty.'

'No need to be sorry, it's a big accomplishment. Doctor of what, since you teach at the college?'

'American literature,' he said.

Micah was searching the other people in the waiting room. 'Where's Beth?'

'She's at home with the other kids,' Ty said.

'Twain has to be what, fourteen now?' Micah said.

They both nodded. 'And Hawthorne is twelve,' Bea said.

I fought to keep my thoughts off my face. Twain and Hawthorne; I realized that the kids were named after Mark Twain and Nathaniel Hawthorne, both American authors, but names like that were usually reserved for cats that lived in the literature building, not for children. *Twain* was tolerable, but *Hawthorne*, for a boy? Elementary school must have been brutal.

Bea added, 'We have two more now; did you know that from our Facebook page?'

Micah shook his head. 'I go online mostly for business. Two more? Boys or girls?'

'One of each,' she said, smiling.

'How old?' he asked.

'Frost is six and Fen is four.'

Micah looked past them to Jerry. He shrugged. 'There's a lot of catching up to do.' He held up his left hand and we saw the wedding band for the first time.

'Who to, and how long?' Micah asked.

'Someone new; she's a nurse here at the hospital, her name's Janet. Less than two years. Before you ask, I did marry Kelsey after high school. It lasted about two years and didn't work from the start. Janet and I are doing good.'

'I don't even know what you do for a living,' Micah said.

'Work at a local engineering firm. I work with Janet's brother. That's how we met. How long have you . . . all been together?'

'Almost three years,' Micah said, and he smiled and took my hand again. He hesitated only a moment and took Nathaniel's hand in his other hand. I had a moment to see a defiant look on his face, as if daring them to criticize. Our patient, diplomatic Micah was more aggressive around his family, more like me. It explained a lot of his patience with me early on.

Jerry's face didn't quite know what expression to have, but his mother beamed at us as if we'd told her she was getting a grandchild or something. Ty's entire body language relaxed, some tension going out of him that I didn't understand. He was smiling. Acceptance was great; this level of happy made me wonder what I'd missed. I was always suspicious if something was too good to be true; it wasn't an old saying for nothing. I'd come into the world with a healthy dose of cynicism, and being with the police for six years hadn't done anything to persuade me otherwise.

Micah squeezed our hands and changed the subject, sort of. 'Is Beth with anyone? I still see her as a kid, but she's twenty-two now, right?'

They all nodded. 'She just graduated with a double major in theology and philosophy,' Jerry said.

'Theology and philosophy?' Micah said. 'I wouldn't have thought that for her.'

'It took her a while to find herself,' Bea said, 'but she's already been accepted into her master's program for next semester.'

I heard Nicky's deep voice murmur something behind us. A woman's voice, much louder. 'Who are you and what gives you the right to question us?'

I turned to find two women trying to get past our bodyguards. Micah said, 'It's okay, Nicky, Dev, they're my aunts.' He went toward them as they walked between our blond guards. One woman had red curls that fell past her shoulders and was wearing work jeans, T-shirt, jacket, and boots that were not a fashion statement. The other woman had hair cut so short there was no curl left, a conservative skirt and jacket over a white blouse with a rounded collar, and sensible pumps. They were dressed so differently that it took a few seconds to realize that other than the superficial differences they were mirror images of each other, or damn close. They both looked a little like Micah, like his dad, and a lot like Juliet, who was hurrying to catch up with them both. There was another woman, or maybe girl, trailing behind Juliet. She was wearing an ankle-length skirt and a button-up blouse untucked over it, hair pulled back in a tight braid that couldn't quite hide the tight curls she'd have if she let her hair go. Where the lack of makeup on Juliet had looked fresh and like she didn't need it, on the girl it made her face look unfinished, or maybe it was the huge black-rimmed glasses that looked like they'd been issued by the military. The kind of glasses that were nicknamed contraceptive glasses, because no one could get laid while wearing them. I thought she belonged to the button-up skirt woman, maybe. Juliet was dressed so much like the woman with longer hair that I made a guess that she was Juliet's mom.

Micah introduced us to Aunt Jody and Aunt Bobbie; Jody was the long-haired rancher-looking woman, and Bobbie was the one who looked like a prim second grade school teacher at a parochial school. Jody did run a farm, and Juliet, her husband, and their two kids lived in a second house on the property and helped run it, but Jody wasn't her mom, Bobbie was. They were Rush's twin sisters. Bobbie was not a schoolteacher or a would-be nun; she was a lawyer.

'I'm sorry Monty couldn't be here tonight, Mike,' she said as she gave him one quick hug and stepped back. The blue eyes that had been warm and showed so much emotion in Juliet's face were cool and unreadable in Aunt Bobbie's. She looked at me like she was studying me for an exam. 'Monty is my second husband; he's a judge now.'

'Congratulations, I remember Monty. He, Dad, and Uncle Steve were friends,' Micah said.

Bobbie smiled with the first true warmth I'd seen. 'He's a good judge.' That one small display said she loved and cared for her husband. It was nice to know Bobbie had found love twice.

'Rex won't be here, I divorced him years ago. He's living in California in a condo where he doesn't have to take care of anything but himself,' Jody said.

Micah gave her another quick hug. 'I'm sorry, Aunt Jody.'

She hugged him and then grinned. 'It's okay, Mike. I've never been happier.'

He grinned back, and I found myself joining in the grin-fest, because there was just something about Jody that had that effect. 'I'm glad,' he said.

'Me, too,' she said, 'and Juliet and her husband are wonderful. Another generation that wants to stay on the farm.'

Bobbie gave a mock shudder. 'No thank you, I am a city girl.' Then she grinned and you could see the same joy in her face as her sister. She took her sister's hand and said, 'I told you when I had Juliet that she was part yours; little did I know you'd make a farmer out of her.'

Jody smiled back at her sister and there was a history and a closeness there that was just good to see. 'Hey, we have a grandchild apiece.'

Bobbie smiled again. 'That we do.'

Juliet smiled at them both and I knew I was missing something, but it was a good something that had formed a bond; maybe it was a twin thing, or maybe not. I'd ask Micah later.

The second girl had drifted back to hug the wall, as if she weren't a part of the happy family moment. Bea called, 'Esther, you remember Mike.'

The girl stepped away from the wall slowly, as if she weren't sure what to do. 'Hi, Mike.' It was almost a whisper.

'How are you doing, Essie?' he asked, his voice soft as if there had always been something fragile, or wrong, with this cousin.

She gave a shy smile. 'You and Beth are the only ones who still call me Essie.'

'I'm going by Micah now; do you prefer Esther?' he asked.

'No, I always liked you calling me Essie,' she said quickly, looking up with big, startled blue-gray eyes that were so like Bea's that I knew which side this cousin was on, which meant she had to be Aunt Bertie and Uncle Jamie's daughter. Poor kid, though she was probably in her early twenties, so not a kid, just . . . she seemed much younger than she looked; maybe it was the awful clothes and glasses?

I heard Dev say, 'Not these guys again.'

It made me look up, but my view was blocked. Ty at six feet plus could see farther and he swore softly under his breath. Bea chastised him, 'Not in front of the kids,' as if we were all five.

'It's your sister and her husband,' he said.

She said, 'Shi . . . Shotgun! I can't take much more of them today.'

I looked at Micah and mouthed, *Shotgun?*

'If you meet my grandparents you'll understand why she doesn't cuss,' he said.

I gave him wide eyes.

Aunt Bertie and Uncle Jamie were being trailed by Al. I heard him say, 'Now, Bertie, it's enough for one night, with Rush hurt like this.'

'Rush knows he's outside God's grace,' Jamie said.

I wasn't sure what that meant, but nothing good. 'What do they want?' I asked.

'To save our souls,' Micah said, and he sounded tired.

'My soul is fine,' I said.

'I know,' he said.

Nicky and Dev looked at us. 'Come on, let us keep them out of the room,' Dev said.

Micah shook his head.

'Sorry, no,' I said.

'Pleeeassse,' Dev said, drawing out the word as if he were three instead of twenty-three.

'Tempting,' I said.

'So tempting,' Micah agreed, 'but let them through.'

Nicky watched the couple pass between him and Dev like he was watching a couple of wounded antelopes and it was just a matter of time.

Al spoke over their heads as they entered the room. 'I'm sorry, I couldn't distract them enough. Apparently, I'm not sinful enough to interest them.'

'You're a good boy,' Bertie said, patting his arm.

Al shrugged. 'Sorry, Mike.'

'Don't apologize to him because you aren't a sinner,' Jamie said.

'I don't think that's what he was apologizing for, Uncle Jamie,' Micah said.

'Leave the boy alone, Jamie,' Aunt Bobbie said. She sounded disgusted with the situation and she'd just gotten here.

'If you hadn't interfered in the first place, Bobbie, there wouldn't be any Coalition, and hundreds of people would have been saved from becoming monsters for them.'

'I checked into your allegations, Bertie, and it's paranoid nonsense,' Bobbie said.

Micah said, 'We do not encourage people to become lycanthropes. We help families deal with members who are already shapeshifters. We counsel people after attacks, but we do not encourage anyone to become wereanimals. We aren't like the Church of Eternal Life; we don't recruit.'

'You and the vampires want everyone to be like you,' Aunt Bertie said.

'That's unsubstantiated rumor,' Aunt Bobbie said.

'I don't know where the rumors started,' Micah said, 'but I can tell you that they are lies. We help people deal with the trauma of attacks the way I wish someone had helped me.'

'I've heard the rumors, but I didn't think anyone was taking them that seriously,' I said.

'A certain branch of religious conservatives have jumped on the bandwagon pretty strongly,' Micah said. He looked at his aunt and uncle.

'The rest of them here will believe your lies, but we know that you've deceived hundreds, maybe thousands of innocent humans.' Bertie turned on Bobbie and pointed an accusing finger at her. 'Innocent lives that could have been saved from evil if you hadn't gone against us.'

'You had no grounds to try to imprison Mike, and a judge agreed with me,' Bobbie said.

'What are they talking about?' Nathaniel asked.

'Jamie and Bertie wanted me to turn myself in to a government safe house when my tests came back positive for lycanthropy. Their church believed that all shapeshifters should be isolated like lepers. When I wouldn't do it voluntarily, they tried to get me declared legally incompetent and be made my guardians, because the rest of the family was too emotionally overwrought to take care of me.'

'The government safe houses are prisons,' Nathaniel said.

I said, 'Once you sign yourself in you can't get out, no matter what they tell you to get you there.'

'I know, and I had Aunt Bobbie to back me up in court.'

'Thank you,' I said to her.

She waved it away. 'They didn't have any right to do it, or legal ground to stand on, but they had a judge who was a church member. Once I got him recused, we were fine.'

'If the monster that attacked you had been in a safe house, Steve and Richie would still be alive and you'd still be human instead of an animal,' Bertie said.

'Aunt Bertie!' Juliet nearly yelled it.

'That's enough!' Bea said; her face was flushed, eyes paling to gray. I was betting that was her angry color of eyes, just a hunch.

'Just tell me these two are the craziest members of your family,' I said.

'Last time I visited, yes.'

'Good,' I said.

Uncle Jamie turned on me like he'd been saving up. 'We know who you are, Anita Blake. You raise the dead from the grave, something only God is allowed to do.'

'I don't do resurrection, just zombies.'

'Of course you can't do what God can do,' Bertie said. 'The devil is only a poor imitation of God.'

I raised an eyebrow at her. 'Excuse me?'

Aunt Jody stepped up. 'You are an evil, narrow-minded person.'

'You are an abomination before the Lord,' Bertie said, in a voice full of such rage it was almost frightening. She'd been yelling at Micah and me, but she was furious with Jody.

'You didn't think that in high school,' Jody said; her voice was bland, empty, but it fell into the conversation like it was anything but.

'We were friends once, before you became perverted,' Bertie said.

'You liked my perversion just fine in high school and then we scared each other. I married the first man who would have me, and you started sleeping with any man who would have you.'

'Mama,' Essie said, and she looked like this was news to her.

'I'm happy now,' Jody said. 'Can you say the same, Bertha?'

'Don't call me that! Don't ever call me that!'

'It's your name,' Jody said.

I felt like I was missing a whole lot. Bertie launched herself at Jody. Al got in the way, keeping the two women apart. Nicky kept Uncle Jamie from joining the fight just by standing in his way and being big. The other man didn't even try to get past him. Dev moved between us and Aunt Bertie, moving us physically back from the almost-fight. None of us told them to stop; I think they were more afraid of what we might do if the fight spread than the other way around.

Jamie yelled around Nicky, 'You are the devil's blood whore!'

'Can I hit him, just once?' Nicky called out.

'No!' I said, and made sure my voice carried.

'Is he calling Micah the devil, or Jean-Claude?' Nathaniel asked.

Dev moved Micah, Nathaniel, and me farther back from the fight. Micah's mom and stepdad, Aunt Jody, Aunt Bobbie, Aunt Bertie, and Uncle Jamie were all screaming at one another. Juliet, Essie, and the rest of us watched like innocent bystanders at a train wreck. It's sort of awful, but you can't look away.

I put my mouth close to Micah's ear and said, 'Can't wait to hear what your family Christmases were like.'

'I've never seen them this bad,' he said.

Juliet and Essie came to stand near us. Essie gave quick covert glances at Dev and Nathaniel, and even Micah. I was suspecting a childhood crush that still had some life in it.

Juliet spoke above the shouting, 'Do you remember Ginger Dawson?'

'I remember the Dawson farm; it was next door to ours.'

'Do you remember the oldest daughter? The one who went away to the army?'

'Vaguely,' Micah said.

'She and Aunt Jody have been living together for about five years.'

'Living together, how?' Micah asked.

'What did you call cutie here? Your live-in partner?'

'His name's Nathaniel,' I said, automatically.

Micah said, 'Yeah.'

'They're living together like that.'

We all looked at one another. Micah said, 'I had no clue.'

'None of us did,' Juliet said.

Aunt Bertie screamed, 'You're bringing up your children with your two catamites!'

'I do not think that word means what she thinks it means,' I said.

'Bertie's gone crazy,' Juliet said.

Essie was hunching in on herself, trying to look like she didn't know any of these people. She muttered, 'I'm so sorry, Mike.'

He patted her arm. 'It's okay, Essie, your parents were never your fault.'

She flashed him adoring blue eyes, and he missed it completely as he watched his mother and aunts fight. Nathaniel looked at me; he hadn't missed it either.

'You contaminated one son,' Bertie yelled. 'Look what he brought home to you! Stop living in sin before you contaminate your other children!'

The three of us, and Dev, all exchanged looks. He said, 'I think they mean Nathaniel, but . . .'

Bertie got a handful of Bea's hair and the fight was on. Hospital security arrived as the two sisters got down to some serious hair-pulling, fingernail-using girl fighting. It was kind of embarrassing, not that it was Micah's mom, but that they fought like girls. I'd have to teach Bea how to throw a punch.

15

Morgues aren't usually my favorite places, but it had been a choice of the morgue or helping Micah talk to the hospital security and police about not having his mom and aunt hauled off to jail. Frankly, I'd have let them take Aunt Bertie if it wouldn't have sent his mom to jail, too. Richard Zeeman's mom, my other almost-mother-in-law, had also had a temper. What was it with the men that I loved having moms who were such . . . live wires? Maybe they both liked women just like dear old Mom? In Micah's case, I was a cop like his dad, so he got a two-for-one deal. It was all too weird and Freudian for me.

I stared down at the first plastic-edged corpse and wasn't happier here with the dead than up trying to figure out the living, but I was less confused. I had felt guilty leaving Nathaniel with Micah and the mess of the living, but he couldn't come with me. Dr Rogers had barely gotten the okay from the local cops for me to see the first three victims. Including my boyfriends would have been asking too much, and besides, I didn't want either of them to see the horrors I saw in my job, especially not if this was what would be happening to Rush Callahan. Previews are a bitch. I pushed away that last thought and looked down at the body.

There would be paperwork somewhere that told me her name, maybe even her background. Had she had a family? But I didn't need, or want, any of that right now. The only way to stay sane was to think *body*, *it*; depersonalize. Background information got in the way of the pronoun *it* and made it more a *her*. Looking down at the body I didn't want it to be a *her*. I needed it to be a thing. Sometimes I worried that I'd become like some legal serial killer with my victims just rogue vamps and shapeshifters, but moments like this made me understand that my empathy was way too good for me ever to be a serial killer. Most of them saw their victims as things like a lamp, or a chair, or a tree, no more real than that. It was what allowed them to do their crimes with so little remorse. You don't feel bad about beating up a chair or breaking a lamp, right?

I stared down at the body and fought to keep in that Zen mind-set where it was all impersonal and I didn't keep seeing Micah's dad in the hospital bed, or think what this woman must have gone through before she died. I fought to keep all that in the back of my head, because in the front it would stop me from being helpful. I couldn't function if my emotions were fucking me over. Yay, I wasn't becoming some emotionless killing machine. Boo, I was staring down at a partially rotted corpse and all I could think was, *What a horrible way to die.*

'Dazzle us, Blake,' Detective Rickman said.

Did I mention I had an audience? Dr Rogers and the coroner, Dr Shelley, I'd sort of expected, but I also had Sergeant Gonzales; Rickman; his partner, Detective Conner; Commander Walter Burke; Deputy Al; and Deputy Gutterman. Al was apparently senior officer while Rush was hurt, but I wondered, if we had two of their officers, how many were left on their force to protect and serve while they stayed down here? It was a small-town sheriff's department, it couldn't be that big, but I didn't question Al's use of manpower. He was in charge and he knew his resources.

The audience had been part of what made Rickman not have a hissy fit about me looking at the bodies. Apparently, he was worried I'd mess up the victims or do suspicious magic. I'd run into officers like him before. Some were ultrareligious, so they thought I was evil, but others just had the same problem with me they had with all female cops, or with a federal cop of any kind butting into their case. I was a woman, a female cop, a godless user of magic, and a Fed – so many reasons for other cops to hate me. The fact that this many different flavors of police were cooperating was rare and good to see. I had a feeling it was Sheriff Rush Callahan's good rep and work that made them all willing to band together. Normally police fought over jurisdiction like dogs over the last meaty bone. It was better than it had been years ago, but it was still a general rule that cops didn't like to share, except when they wanted to pass the buck so that a messy or boring case was someone else's problem. This case was messy, but it wasn't boring, and one of their own was hurt, so it was personal, but more than that, solve a case like this and it could make your reputation. Fail at solving it and it could break you. I wasn't big on failing or breaking.

Though with this many people in the room it was damn near claustrophobic. I felt like I had a wall looming up behind me that kept bending closer. It was actually Dr Shelley who finally turned around and said, 'Gentlemen, you were allowed to observe, not to breathe down our necks. Now, everybody take two big steps back.' She pushed her glasses back up on her nose with the back of her gloved hand and glared at them when they didn't move. 'This is my part of the crime, my domain; you're here because I let you be here. If you don't give us some room to work, then I'll clear the room, is that understood? Now step the hell away from us.'

I liked her. The men exchanged glances as if waiting to see who would back up first. It was Gonzales who stepped back first, followed by Burke, then the deputies, and finally Rickman. Maybe it wasn't just me he didn't like, or maybe it was all women?

'Thank you, gentlemen,' she said in a voice that held no grudge. She turned back to me and Dr Rogers. 'Marshal Blake, now that we can move without bumping into people, do you have any questions?'

Rickman piped up. 'We want to know what she sees that we didn't, not just information that you've already given us.'

Shelley turned around, and I didn't have to see her eyes to know she was giving him her cold look. It was a good look, and we'd all seen it a few times already. It was a look that reminded you of that teacher in elementary school who could make thirty kids go silent with a glance, except this look was more hostile.

Rickman took the full weight and gave his own defiant look back; we'd seen that a few times, too. 'If you feed her information, Sheila, we won't know if she's really an asset to this case or just another Fed to get in our way.'

'This is my morgue, Ricky. I run it the way the way I see fit.' Her voice was very cold, but the fact that he'd used her first name made me wonder if they'd had more than a working relationship once. Of course, maybe he just wanted to point out that her name was Sheila Shelley. He probably didn't get to use names that were almost as bad as his own Ricky Rickman very often.

'She's supposed to be some hotshot zombie expert; let her prove it,' he said, undaunted.

'I can raise zombies from the grave,' I said. 'Can anyone else in this room do that?'

There was silence and a couple of nervous looks.

'Was I not supposed to remind everybody that I raise the dead? Sorry, but it's a psychic gift. I'd exchange it for something else if I could, but it doesn't work that way. I make zombies rise from the dead the way some people are left-handed or have the recessive genes for blue eyes. It's just the way it is; I raised my first one when I was fourteen, so yeah, that makes me a zombie expert, Detective Rickman.'

'Then like I said, dazzle us, Blake.'

'Get out of my morgue,' Dr Shelley said.

'Now, Sheila,' he said.

'Stop using my first name as if that will make us buddies, Detective. You have an issue with women in authority, you always have, and apparently you always will.' She turned to me. 'I'm sorry, Marshal, it's nothing personal, he's always like this.'

'How did he make detective this young if he's always this big a pain in the ass?' I asked.

'Unfortunately, when he gets his head out of his ass he's a really good detective. He solved some big cases early and saved lives by catching the monsters early. I mean murderers, not your kind of monster,' she said.

I nodded, that I appreciated the difference.

She pointed a gloved finger at Rickman. 'But right now you are being childish and unhelpful. Sheriff Callahan has helped everyone in this room do their jobs better. He's saved lives literally and by simply helping all of us do ours. He never grabs credit, but we all know we owe him. Now, we are all going to let the marshal here do her job and respect her expertise with the preternatural, but more than that I hear she's engaged to Callahan's son and that means she deserves respect on that account, too, and you, Ricky, will by God give it to her for one of those three reasons. I don't care which one you pick, but choose one and give her the same credit you'd give a man with the same badge, the same reputation, and the same connection to a wounded officer that we all respect and owe.'

I fought the urge to applaud. Rickman finally looked embarrassed;

good to know he could be. The other officers looked shamefaced, too, as if the lecture were somehow contagious, or as if Rickman had made them all look bad. Either way, Rickman shut up and the rest of them were on their best behavior as if to make up for him.

'Zombies, when they do bite, usually just bite down like a person. The first male victim's shoulder is torn, savaged, more like a wereanimal or a vampire.'

'Vampires don't tear at you like a terrier with a rat,' Burke said. 'They kill neat, almost clean.' He didn't sound happy when he said it, but he sounded sure.

I tried to remember if I'd touched anything in the morgue that I wouldn't want touching my bare skin. I thought and just couldn't be a hundred percent sure. 'I'd have to take my gloves off and reglove, but after we're all done here I can show scars where a vampire did just that to me.'

Burke's serious cop eyes let me know he wasn't sure he believed me.

'I know the literature, and most of the databases treat vampires as sort of organized serial killers, methodical planners, and wereanimals as the disorganized serial killers, making a mess, choosing their victims more by chance like a wounded antelope that falls behind the herd. But I've known vampires that slaughtered and wereanimals that were more organized.' I thought about it for a minute and then shook my head. 'Okay, I've known more vampires that went all slaughterfest than shapeshifters that were methodical in their kills, but trust me, the antelope doesn't always leave the herd by accident. It may look like happenstance, but most predators cause things to happen that will isolate or test the herd, so they get to see who's weak or careless. It's so not accidental most of the time.'

'Predators are all the same, I guess, two legs or four,' Burke said.

'Human, vampire, shapeshifter, a predator is a predator,' I agreed.

'There's nothing in the federal database about vampires eating their victims like a shapeshifter does,' Rickman said. 'I thought they couldn't eat solid food.'

'The commander said worry at a wound like a terrier with a rat, not eat it,' I said.

Rickman looked blank.

'Didn't you ever see a dog savage something just for the hell of it, not to eat it?' I asked.

He shrugged. 'I don't know what you're talking about.'

Gonzales said, 'Did you ever play tug-of-war with a dog that was serious about it?'

Rickman shrugged again. 'Never had a dog.'

We all looked at him. 'Never?' Gonzales asked. 'Ever?' Al asked. 'Are you a cat person?' Shelley asked.

'No, but I hear that Blake is.' The words were innocent, but the tone was not, and neither was the look that went with it.

'Is that some kind of clever reference to Micah Callahan being a wereleopard?' I asked, and made sure that my voice held all the disdain I could manage, which was a lot.

'If the furry slipper fits . . .' he said.

'Detective, I've been called the whore of Babylon to my face more than once; do you really think calling me a "cat person" is going to insult me?' I made little quote marks around *cat person*.

'Yeah, Ricky,' Gonzales said, 'for a ten-year veteran officer that was weak.'

'It *was* weak,' Al said.

'That was a pathetic insult, Detective,' Commander Burke said.

'Come on, Ricky,' I said, 'at least call me a blood whore since I'm sleeping with vampires. Oh, wait, that's not an original insult either; in fact, Micah's crazy aunt and uncle already called me that today.'

'Fine, fine, you've made your point.'

'No,' I said, 'I haven't begun to make my point. The vampire that tore me up the most broke my collarbone gnawing at me. The bend of my left arm has so much scar tissue that they said I'd lose the use of it, but enough weight lifting and stretching has kept me whole.'

'So, you're big and tough, we get it.'

'Shut up, Ricky,' Gonzales said.

Burke said, 'If the vampire wasn't trying to eat your flesh like a wereanimal, then why did he tear at you?'

'Because he meant to hurt me, because he wanted me to suffer before he killed me. You can see what human teeth can do to bodies on these.'

'I saw a ninety-pound cheerleader on PCP tear out a man's throat with her teeth once,' Burke said. He shuddered, and his professional cop look slipped a little and let the haunted look show through. Most cops had a haunted look; they hid it, but we all had it if we'd been on the job long enough. There were always things that happened that left stains on your mind, your heart, your soul. You saw the great, terrible thing and you couldn't forget it, you couldn't unsee it, unknow it, and you were never the same afterward. We had a moment of everyone's eyes remembering something bad, it didn't matter what, different memory, but same effect. We were all haunted; even Rickman's eyes had the look.

I turned and looked at Rogers and Shelley, and the two doctors looked just as haunted. Cops; emergency medical personnel; hell, emergency personnel; firemen; ambulance drivers; all of us . . . you don't need ghosts to be haunted. Memory does that just fine without any supernatural help at all.

The woman's bite had been neater, but it had also been in her face, as if the zombie had tried to tear off her cheek. 'I can't tell how much damage was bite and how much was excised afterward.'

Rogers answered, 'The patient wouldn't sign off on the surgery to excise her wound. It was only after the patient realized that the disease was going to do more damage to her face than the surgery that she agreed to it, but it was too late. The disease had made its way to her brain and there was nothing we could do. I cut away as much of the infected tissue as I could, but when I realized that it wouldn't save her life, I did what I could to make her comfortable. Once this thing gets into a major organ that is needed to sustain life there isn't anything we can do, except pump them full of painkillers and make them comfortable until the end.'

I stopped looking down at the woman's ravaged face and back up at him. 'Is that why Sheriff Callahan is pumped up on pain meds? Has it reached a major organ system?' My pulse sped a little, but outwardly I was calm, my best blank cop face forward.

'No, the disease is also incredibly painful, and since we can only slow it, not stop it, we make the patients as comfortable as possible.'

'You swear,' I said.

He nodded. 'I swear, Rush was lucky it was an arm wound. I was able to take a lot of the flesh. I thought I'd gotten it all, honestly, but it's as if you can't cut fast enough to stay ahead of it. If we hadn't had the earlier patients to treat so we knew to put him on massive full-spectrum antibiotics and use the hyperbaric chamber, it would have spread everywhere by now, but we're learning more with every patient.'

'Why didn't you excise flesh from the man's shoulder wound?' I asked.

'He was the first we found alive. The emergency room doctor tried treating it as less virulent than it turned out to be. In his defense, you see the mess that the wound was. The thing really tore at him, so it was treated as a regular zombie bite, since they carry their own types of infection. By the time the attending doctor called me in it was simply too late. The infection had reached the man's heart, and there was nothing we could do.'

'Are you saying that his heart was rotted away?' I asked.

Dr Shelley answered that question. 'Yes, it was quite decayed. I'd never seen anything like it. You can see that the flesh on most of the chest is clean and looks healthy, but when I did the autopsy the heart looked more like the area around the initial wound.'

'Why did his heart rot? Why her brain? Why didn't it eat the outer healthy flesh first?' I asked.

'We aren't a hundred percent certain,' Rogers said, 'but we think that this infection enters the bloodstream through the bite and rides the blood into a major organ system and rots from both ends, so to speak.'

'So, bad luck about the face bite hitting the brain,' I said.

'Yes,' he said.

'And if you'd known to excise the shoulder wound on the man, then he might have been able to hold on,' I said.

'If he'd been a later victim instead of one of the first, I believe his odds would have been as good as the sheriff's,' Rogers said.

I didn't like the way he said it, not that Rush would make it, but better odds, but we all knew that unless a miracle cure showed up, it was just a matter of time for Micah's dad. He and I had gotten on the plane knowing that, but still . . . I shook it off and concentrated on work, clues, we needed fucking clues. If we couldn't save Micah's dad, then maybe we could find who raised the aberrant zombies and kill them. Revenge wasn't a substitute for saving his dad, not even close, but sometimes it's the best you can do, and it beats the hell out of nothing, or that's what I was going to keep telling myself until I couldn't believe it anymore.

'Where are the earlier victims, the ones who died even faster than shoulder-wound here?'

Rogers and Shelley exchanged a look; it wasn't a look you see often between doctors, especially when one of them is a trauma surgeon and the other is a coroner. They didn't want to see the bodies again. Something about them bothered both doctors. What the hell?

'We'll have to go into the other area,' Shelley said.

'Other area?' I made it a question.

'Where we keep the bodies that are so decayed that we, well, we wouldn't want the smell to contaminate everything. No one would be able to work down here.'

'You mean the room for floaters and bodies like that,' I said.

'Yes,' she said, and she gave me a curious look, as if she hadn't expected me to know that.

'These don't smell that bad; in fact, shouldn't the infection make them smell worse?'

'That is one of the odd things about it; it doesn't seem to have the odor to match the putrefaction process. It's a small blessing for the patients and their families, but it is odd.'

I frowned down at the bodies. 'But you put the other dead bodies in the area with the stinky stuff; why?'

'The early bodies decayed more completely. The infection spread from the initial bite site to encompass fifty to eighty percent of the available flesh in just hours.'

'Wait, hours?' I asked.

They nodded.

'These victims died in hours?' I asked.

'The man did; we were able to prolong the woman's life for three days.'

'Did the early victims in the lockbox die from the infection hitting a major organ group?' I asked.

'No,' Rogers and Shelley said together. She motioned to him.

He continued, 'Actually, the infection seemed to spread faster through the flesh until it hit a major organ. It's almost as if as the patient begins to die, the infection slows. It shouldn't, but it seems to, and I emphasize *seems to*, because we have far too small a sample set to be sure of much with this infection.'

'Understood, you're investigating the disease the way we're investigating the crime,' I said.

He nodded. 'Very much so.'

I shook my head. 'I don't know enough about this kind of disease to hazard a guess, but is there a pattern to the wounds on the other victims?'

'What do you mean, pattern?'

'Well, the neat bite is in the woman's face. The rough bite is a shoulder wound. We know we have multiple zombie whatevers; what I'm asking is, does one zombie bite on the arms and shoulders and the other one bite on the face, or was the bite placement just what they could grab? Do they have a bite preference?'

'Two of the victims had facial wounds,' Burke said behind us.

It was almost startling, as if we'd forgotten the other cops were back there.

'Three of them, including the sheriff, were shoulder, arm, or back wounds,' Al said.

'You said you had witnesses to some of the attacks. Did they report differences in how the zombies attacked?'

Al seemed to think about it and then glanced at the other officers. They all sort of shook their heads and shrugged. 'The witness statements read like a horror movie,' Rickman said. 'I don't mean they're horrible, but more like they're describing a scene from a movie.'

'What do you mean?' I asked.

Rickman looked at the other men, and it was the first sign of insecurity I'd seen in him. I wasn't sure if it made him more human and likable or if it should have worried me.

Burke said, 'My guys were the first on the scene for one attack, and I know what the detective is saying. Zombies are the shambling dead, slow – relentless, but slow. One thing all the witnesses agree on is that these zombies are human-fast, at the very least, and maybe a little faster, which is movie stuff, not reality.'

'The one flesh-eating zombie I dealt with was more than human-fast,' I said.

'Why does eating flesh make them faster?' Rickman asked.

In my head I thought, *I've seen zombies after they've eaten flesh and they haven't been faster, but I can't say it to a roomful of policemen, because I was the one who had raised the zombies and used them as defensive weapons.* I'd done it every time to save my life and the lives of other innocent people, but none of it had been sanctioned by the police, and in fact I wasn't entirely sure the police would have okayed it regardless of circumstances. Technically as a marshal with the preternatural service I could use my psychic abilities to do my job; there were no caveats on what psychic abilities I used to finish my job, and since my job was to execute people . . . technically I was now covered if I did it in the future. In reality I wasn't sure the police would be able to overlook it. At best I'd lose my badge; at worst I might be up on charges of using magic to kill people, which was an automatic death sentence. It was a gray area for the law, but the price was a little too high for me to want to test the limits of it.

'Marshal Blake, Marshal, can you hear me?'

I blinked and realized that Burke had been talking to me for a while, and I hadn't heard. Automatically I said, 'I'm sorry, can you repeat that? I think I was thinking too hard.'

'Too hard about what?' Rickman asked.

'The dead,' I said. I left the statement there for him to make what he would of it: the dead in this room, zombies, vamps, the victims – what dead?

'Why does eating flesh make them faster?' Rickman said, and I realized he was repeating himself.

'I don't know, but I do know that fresh blood allows zombies to speak and helps them be more "alive."'

'What do you mean, fresh blood?' he asked.

'Have any of you ever seen a zombie raised from the grave?'

They all shook their heads. I thought about explaining the whole ritual to them, but it was more information than they needed, and if they didn't have a background in some sort of ritual-based religion it would be way too much. 'We usually kill a chicken at the grave, or some animators cut their own body to get the blood, but either way you need fresh blood to do the ritual.'

'What else do you need?' Al asked.

'A blade, salt, and most use an ointment with herbs in it; the mix is usually unique to each individual animator, because it's homemade. Some animators feel they can't raise the dead without their own mix of herbs and ointment; it's usually partly based on the ointment their mentor used when he or she trained them.'

'Is that all you need to raise the dead?' Rickman asked.

'You need the psychic ability to do it, which is damn rare. You need a buried body that is at least three days dead and you need to know the name of the body you're trying to call from the grave.'

'Why three days dead?' Al asked.

'That's minimum time for the soul to leave the body,' I said.

I got owl blinks from most of them, like I'd startled them or overcomplicated their little heads. It's not a look you get from veteran cops very often. It didn't make me proud; more crap, how did I explain this?

'You believe in the soul?' Rickman asked.

'Yes,' I said.

'Do you believe in God?'

'Of course.'

'Then how can you . . .' Al asked it.

I frowned at him. 'Finish your sentence.'

He shifted a little as if maybe my look and my request didn't match up, but he finished. 'Then how can you use black magic to raise the dead?'

'Oh, for pity's sake, don't you guys read the federal bulletins on religious differences between legal religious practices and illegal ones?'

Al flushed a little, and I didn't want to embarrass him. He was an ally and I would probably need them. Crap. 'Sorry, we're just a little podunk town sheriff department. We don't get all the federal updates.'

'Sorry, Al, I'm just a little tired of being accused of black magic and devil worshipping after Micah's aunt and uncle.'

'Geez, I'm sorry, Anita, really; they were horrible to you. I should have remembered that.'

'You mean Bertie and Jamie?' Gonzales asked.

'Yeah,' Al said.

'Talk to me later and I'll give you some stories that'll make her leave you alone.'

'That'd be great,' I said.

'Okay, I apologize again,' Al said, 'but if raising the dead isn't black magic, what is it?'

'Most people consider it vaudun, or voodoo, but since I'm still a card-carrying Episcopalian, it's not a religious ritual for me, it's just a ritual that helps me focus a natural ability with the dead.'

'Is that what it is to other zombie raisers?' Rickman asked.

I gave him a look. 'If I were a practitioner I'd accept *voodoo priestess*, but since I'm not, the term is *animator*, from the Latin "to bring life."

I know the Boulder PD gets seminars on what's insulting and what's okay to say to various special groups, and animators are about as elite a group as we can get.'

'Elite, in what way?' Rickman asked.

'As in a specialized skill. There probably aren't two hundred people in the world who can raise the dead, at all. Of those, most can only raise the typical kind of zombies, slow, rotting corpses that can barely move like people; most can't even speak. Those of us who can raise the dead so they are able to answer questions with prompting are maybe fifty. If you want a zombie that is coherent enough to answer a lawyer's questions or say the last good-bye to loved ones, well, that narrows it down to maybe twenty-five, thirty. The only flesh-eating zombies I'm aware of have been raised by only the most powerful of us, maybe the top one percent of that. Someone who could raise multiple flesh-eating zombies like this is really rare. There are none in this state that I'm aware of.'

'So it would have to be someone from one of the major animating firms?' Rickman asked.

'I can't imagine anyone from the firms doing this kind of shit,' I said.

'Who else?' Rickman asked.

'There are good vaudun practitioners and not-so-bad ones. A really powerful one who had chosen to do dark magic could do it, but the only one left that I'm aware of is in New Orleans, and Papa Jim is eighty and a good guy from all accounts. There are powerful priests and priestesses, but that doesn't automatically mean they can raise the dead, no matter what the legends say about voodoo.'

'I thought all voodoo priests could make zombies if they were powerful enough,' Al said.

I shook my head. 'No, you can't just pray your way into the ability to raise the dead. It's a gift, like running a mile in under four minutes; practice makes you faster, but some stuff has to be genetic, inherent to you.'

'So you're saying that you couldn't do a spell evil enough to be given the ability to control the dead?' he asked.

I thought about that for a long minute. 'Honestly, I can't answer that. I don't do black magic or mess with the kind of stuff that bargains power for sacrifice or evil deeds.'

'Why does anyone do it?' Burke asked.

'Because they're too weak, or scared, or powerless on their own, and they want to be stronger, scary themselves, and feel powerful.'

'And you don't need any of that?' Rickman asked.

'Nope, do you?' I asked.

He looked surprised. 'No, but I'm just a detective. There's nothing the demonic could offer me.'

I laughed. 'Oh, Detective, there's a certain kind of evil that specializes in finding what a person wants most and pretending to offer it to them at a price.'

'Why do you say pretend?' Al asked.

'Because the demonic can only give you what God has created, or what someone else has; they can't help you create something new and fresh, because that's beyond them. They are a part of the creator's design, not part of the creating of it. They imitate, they bargain, they may know your darkest secret, or worst fear, but they can't create your fear, only exploit the one that's already there, and they can't make you do a damn thing, only know what you've already done and try to use it against you.'

'How do you know all this?' Rickman asked.

'One, I was raised a good little Catholic girl. Two, I've come up against the demonic a time or two.'

'You've fought demons?' Al said.

'Not the way you probably mean, but yeah.'

'And you won?' Rickman said, and he sounded skeptical.

'I'm here, and their victims survived, so yeah, I won.'

'Did you do an exorcism?' Burke asked.

'No, I've assisted a priest on one once; really don't want to do a traditional exorcism again.'

'Why not?'

I just looked at him. 'If you have to ask, you don't want to know.'

'So you help priests fight demons?' Rickman managed to be even more disdainful.

'No, I worked with one priest on one exorcism, but the Catholic Church has excommunicated all of us animators, so I can't help now.'

'Excommunication must make demons harder to fight,' Rickman jibed.

'If your faith is pure, you're safe enough,' I said.

'Pure? Your faith is pure?' Rickman laughed.

'Don't be a dick, Ricky,' Dr Shelley warned him.

'She's sleeping with enough men to field a football team, how is that pure?'

Gonzales and Burke both called him on it, but I raised a hand and said, 'It's okay, I've heard it before, but I have a question for the detective.'

Burke looked skeptical, Gonzales looked worried, Al more curious, Shelley angry, and Rogers like he was ready to be elsewhere, but they all let me ask my question.

'If I were a man sleeping with that many women, would it bother you as much?'

He seemed to think about it and then finally shook his head. 'No, I guess it wouldn't. I wouldn't want the guy dating my sister, but . . . no, it wouldn't bother me as much.'

'Why not?' I asked.

'Why not, what?' he asked.

'Why wouldn't it bother you as much, if I were a man?'

He frowned, thought, and finally said, 'You're a woman, you're not supposed to sleep around. You're a beautiful woman. You don't have to be a slut.'

Dr Shelley said, 'Jesus, Ricky.'

Burke said, 'You aren't in my chain of command, but I will be speaking to your superiors about this.'

Gonzales was shaking his head. 'All I can do is apologize for him, Anita.'

I laughed, not the I-think-this-is-funny laugh, but the abrupt I-can't-believe-what-I'm-hearing laugh. 'I've heard all of it before, unfortunately, but this is the first time I've ever heard anyone's reasoning being that only ugly women sleep around. That's a new one.'

'Beautiful women don't have to; men chase them,' Rickman said, as if he truly didn't understand what he was doing wrong. Maybe he didn't?

'So ugly women sleep around because sex is the only way they can get men?' I asked.

'Please, shut up now, Ricky,' Gonzales said. 'You are embarrassing yourself and the Boulder PD.'

He looked from one to the other of the others, and his expression was plainly confused.

It was Dr Rogers, who had been so quiet through all of it, who said, 'He doesn't understand, does he?'

'Jesus, Ricky,' Dr Shelley said, 'I thought you just hated women in authority and were offensive, but you honestly don't understand that you're wrong.'

'Regardless, I will be reporting this incident to your superiors,' Commander Burke said.

'What?' Rickman said.

'You called Marshal Blake a slut,' Al said.

'I didn't,' he said.

Gonzales sighed and smoothed his hand over his face. 'So that's why when the other women came forward and said you'd called them names, you were so surprised.' He looked at me. 'It's why none of the complaints stuck; he seemed so damned innocent.'

'Because he thought he was,' I said.

Gonzales nodded.

'It's like social dyslexia,' I said. 'He can't see it.'

Gonzales nodded again.

Burke said, 'Regardless, it's unacceptable behavior in an officer.' I was betting he hadn't realized he was sounding more military than cop, but once military enough, it's hard to shake all of it.

'Conduct unbecoming,' I said.

Burke nodded. 'Very much so. I apologize for all the discourtesy you have experienced since you arrived here. I thought the religious zealots upstairs would be the main problem, but apparently not.' He gave Rickman a hard, cold look.

Rickman might not understand why he was in trouble for talking to me, but he understood the look. He tried to give a hard look in return, but his face was uncertain. I think because he knew that not everyone in the room could be wrong, which made him wrong. Maybe, just maybe, he was rethinking all those accusations from other women and wondering if they had been right? One could hope that even men like Rickman could be taught.

Dr Rogers had to go back to his living patients. We were all stripping off the gowns, masks, and protective gear as I asked him, 'Is Micah going to be able to actually talk to his dad?'

'He's basically in a medically induced coma. Normally, I'd bring him out of it pretty quickly, but the last patient to die seemed to go

into shock when the drugs left her system, so I'm going to wean
the sheriff off more slowly and hope his body adjusts better.'

'You mean, one of the victims died just from coming out of the
drugs?' I asked.

He nodded.

'Shit,' I said, softly.

'I am sorry, Marshal. I will do everything I can to give your fiancé
a chance to say good-bye to his dad.'

'I appreciate that, Doctor.'

He nodded, his face a little grim. It's never good when doctors make
faces like that. I turned to the only thing I could do to help: police
work. I got promises to have access to everyone's witness statements.
Al went one better. 'Deputy Gutterman was with Rush when he was
attacked. You can hear his statement firsthand.'

'We can do that next,' I said.

He shook his head. 'Gutter is out on another call. With the sheriff
and me out of rotation, there's not enough people on our force to keep
Gutter at the hospital, too.'

Burke said, 'I could send a couple of cars on extra patrols through
your town if you need it, Al.'

'I really appreciate that, Commander. I may take you up on it, just
depends on how . . . things go.'

I was pretty sure that if I hadn't been Micah's fiancé, he'd have
said something different, because once Rush Callahan died, his small
police force wouldn't feel compelled to keep manpower at the
hospital. I could have told Al that I didn't have to be babied, but if
Micah was with me, then we'd need it; better to get in the habit
now.

There was a moment of uncomfortable silence as all the policemen
knew exactly why Deputy Al had hesitated, and everyone wondered
whether to say something or let the silence spread.

'It's okay, Al, I know that it's a matter of time for Micah's dad,
unless we get a miracle.'

'Do you believe in miracles, Anita?' Al asked.

I nodded. 'Yeah, I do.'

Rickman snorted. 'Miracles are for Sunday school and Christmas
specials. I've been a cop too long to believe shit like that.'

I started to say something, but Dr Shelley beat me to it. 'Be cynical on your own time, Ricky. I want Rush to have his miracle and get to see his son married to Marshal Blake.'

'Not going to happen,' Rickman said.

'Ricky,' Gonzales said in a low, angry voice, 'you are not going to kill Rush before he's dead.'

Rickman looked shocked, and again he didn't know what he'd said wrong. I was wondering if there was maybe something socially wrong with the detective, beyond just being rude. 'I didn't mean anything, Ray, I . . . I want Rush to make it, too, but facts are facts.'

'Fuck facts!' Gonzales said, and he loomed over the detective. Ricky was six feet, the same height as Gonzales, but somehow the sergeant dwarfed the detective. Gonzales did what some people could do, he just seemed bigger. I was told I could do it, too, but I didn't have Gonzales's size, so it couldn't be as impressive.

Burke didn't step between them, but he moved up sort of halfway between where each of them was standing. 'Detective Rickman, go somewhere else away from Sergeant Gonzales for a while.'

'I'm sorry, Ray, I . . .' Rickman shrugged, shook his head, and finally just walked away, but I was betting he was clueless on why the other man was rigid with anger.

Gonzales's voice crawled out of his chest, thick and dark with rage. 'I won't give up on Rush. I do believe in miracles, because I have to.'

I reached out to touch his arm and then stopped myself. Sometimes, when you're angry enough, any physical contact escalates the rage. I didn't want to do that, so I let my hand drop back to my side.

'I believe in miracles,' I said.

He rotated his neck as if the muscles hurt to move, so tight with the tension in his shoulders, and that movement alone let me know how close he'd come to hitting Rickman or how much he'd wanted to do it. 'It's all Rush has got.' It was a growl.

'Let's you and me get some coffee in the cafeteria,' Al said. He gave a small nod to let me know to leave him with his friend. Since I had no clue what to do for Gonzales and I was supposed to be here as moral support for Micah, I let Al take care of it. If I was hand-holding anyone emotionally it had to be my 'fiancé.'

Burke walked me out through the last doors and the hallway beyond. Ares and Bram pushed away from the wall, going from at ease to at attention. Neither of them had been out of the military that long.

They'd come back to the hospital just in time to trail me with the police. Micah had told me to take them because the police would be more comfortable with two ex-military guards than with Dev and Nicky's more civilian-muscle attitude. He'd been right, but the fact that he'd thought of it in the middle of the family chaos made me hug him tight and feel bad that he was having to think about anything but his dad. I looked at the two tall, slender, muscled men, one about as dark as he could get, and the other all honey and golden blond, even his tanned skin. I saw them so often together that I'd started thinking of them as a unit, the way you think of some couples, never alone, but always two. They'd traded military backgrounds with the police, and it had helped put the other men at ease. None of the guards were going to make Micah's family comfortable with their son, brother, cousin, and nephew needing bodyguards because of threats. But seeing Commander Burke nod and smile at them and exchange handshakes was a help here.

Ares and Bram dropped back and took up their posts behind me. It was habit now for all of us, but Burke noticed it. 'I understand that Mike Callahan has threats because he's part of the Coalition, but why do you need bodyguards?'

'I've been tied to Micah and the Coalition in the media, and I'm also tied to the Master of the City in St Louis, Jean-Claude, and the hate groups hate the vampires, a lot. You saw the level of hate from Micah's aunt and her husband; now imagine strangers.'

'Is it that bad?' he asked.

'We had a zealot try to blow up one of Jean-Claude's clubs this year.' I didn't add that he'd tried to blow it up with Nathaniel, Dev, Nicky, Cynric, and me inside it. The zealot had been a human with a few vampire bites on him, the daytime servant of a group of vampires that had decided Jean-Claude was building an evil empire to enslave them all. If they could have killed my leopard to call, two of my tigers to call, and me all at the same time, they hoped it would be enough to kill Jean-Claude. We were all metaphysically connected, which meant we shared a hell of a lot more than just emotional well-being. I'd killed a few vampires myself by simply killing their human servants. You could potentially get the same effect by killing the animal to call their *moitié bête*, literally their beast half? Kill anyone in the psychic power chain and you had a chance to kill them all.

'So you have terrorists,' Burke said.

I thought about it, then nodded. 'Something like that.'

'What happened to your bomber?'

'He died,' I said.

Burke looked back at the other men and said, 'Good to have men of action around when you need them.' He smiled as he said it.

'Oh, it wasn't us,' Ares said.

Burke frowned and hesitated as he walked. 'You mean the other guards upstairs?'

'They were hostages,' Ares said.

'They assisted in their own rescue,' Bram said, and he gave his partner a look that took the smile off Ares' face.

'What'd I say wrong? You're giving me that look again.'

'You mean the look that says you're letting your mouth run away with your head?' Bram said.

'Hey,' Ares said.

Burke laughed. 'You two have been partners for a while.'

'We have, sir,' Bram said.

'Does it show?' Ares asked.

'Yeah, it shows; good partners are like married couples,' Burke said.

'Some people in civilian circles call the partner the work spouse,' I said.

'God knows in police work you see your partner more than you see your wife sometimes,' Burke said.

I just nodded.

'What did I do to earn the look this time?' Ares asked.

Bram glared at him.

'What?'

I said, 'You implied that the other guards with us aren't as good at their jobs as you two are.'

'I did not,' he said, and his face showed that he totally didn't get it.

'Don't you get it, Ares?' Bram said, 'Dev and Nicky don't look like cops, or military, and saying they were hostages just undermines them in Commander Burke's eyes even more.'

Ares looked from one to the other of us, and then his face sort of fell. He took in a deep breath, let it out, and said, 'That is not what I meant.'

'I know,' Bram said with an eye roll, like a long-suffering spouse.

I turned my head to hide my smile.

'I'm just glad Marshal Blake and young Callahan have good men to step in when needed.'

Bram gave him a very direct look. 'None of us saved Marshal Blake that day.'

Burke frowned. 'I'm not sure I'm following.'

Bram sighed. He looked at me, back at Ares, and finally back at me. 'I'm sorry, Anita; having bodyguards with you is going to make all the other cops think less of you as a cop, like a soldier who needs guards.'

I nodded and shrugged. 'Yeah, but what can we do?'

Bram turned back to Burke. 'Let's be clear, Commander. Marshal Blake helped come up with a plan to rescue the hostages and take out the bomber. She went in with SWAT to execute that plan. The other guards upstairs were key players in that plan. In fact, Nathaniel Graison, the other civilian with Micah Callahan, helped save them all, too. If Nathaniel hadn't done his part first, the rescue would have failed. But it was Anita who took out the threat – not the other cops, not the guards, her.'

'You get mad at me for being chatty and now you're just running off at the mouth,' Ares said.

'It's a police case. Everything's on record,' Bram said.

I looked at Bram's stoic dark face. I couldn't read his expression, and hyena wasn't one of my animals to call, so I had no extrasensory hint of what he was thinking. 'Ares is right – this is the longest speech I've ever heard from you.'

'Commander Burke is the highest-ranking officer we've met. I just want him to know that you aren't a victim who needs saving, you're the person who comes through the door and does the saving.'

I smiled and frowned at the same time, puzzling. 'Then why add Nathaniel in?'

'Because he's the kind of man that men like us discount, and Nathaniel deserves better than that. If I had just told Commander Burke how tough you, Dev, and Nicky are, then it marginalizes Nathaniel.'

'You didn't defend Mike Callahan's honor to me,' Burke said.

Bram turned just his head, and there was some change in his energy, not quite his beast peeking out, but almost anger. Ares reacted to it by standing taller and moving slightly closer to his partner. Bram said, 'Micah doesn't need anyone to defend his honor. He is his honor.'

'No offense,' Burke said.

Bram nodded. 'We take Anita's orders because she leads from the front line. We follow Micah's orders because he is our leader.'

'What about your Master of the City, this Jean-Claude?'

'We respect Jean-Claude,' Bram said.

'But he isn't your leader the way Callahan and Blake are?'

It was Ares who stepped forward for Bram this time. 'Excuse my partner here; he's not used to talking this much. I think sharing time is over, right, Anita?'

'Yeah,' I said. It was actually a point of contention between some of the vampires around Jean-Claude that the bodyguards followed my orders better than his and that almost all the shapeshifters followed Micah's orders better. The Harlequin had once been the elite bodyguards of the head of the vampire council, the Mother of All Darkness, but with her defeat they belonged to Jean-Claude now. He was the new head of the vampire council. Not all the Harlequin had agreed with the change, but once the Mother of All Darkness was dead, it was very much 'The king is dead, long live the king.' Though I guess in this case it had been 'The queen is dead, long live the king.'

Burke looked from one to the other of us, but our faces gave him nothing back and he'd been a cop long enough to know when to let it go. What I didn't like was that he'd asked about Jean-Claude in the first place. How much did the other police know about our vampire politics? Looking at Burke's face, I thought maybe more than I'd thought. It made me wonder if Burke had the same mysterious federal friend as Sheriff Callahan had and how much the commander here knew about some of the less public adventures we'd all had, things that hadn't been reported to the police, because we'd handled it old-school. Yeah, I meant illegal.

I needed away from Burke before he asked something even more awkward. Unfortunately, I had the perfect out. 'I need to get back to Micah and Nathaniel. I really wish I'd been able to meet Sheriff Callahan under other circumstances,' I said.

Burke nodded, face somber. 'Callahan is a good sheriff and a good man. I hope like hell that you get a chance to find that out for yourself, Marshal.'

'So do I, Commander, so do I.'

We all shook hands and three of us went for the elevator. It was time to see if Micah's mother and aunt had gone to jail on mutual assault charges. The fun just never stopped on this trip.

By the time we got upstairs, some decisions had been reached. Neither of the women went to jail. Aunt Bertie and Uncle Jamie had been escorted out of the hospital. Aunt Jody and Aunt Bobbie were staying at the hospital with the bevy of policemen who would haunt the place until Rush Callahan either got to go home or didn't. The doctors were starting to wean Rush from the drugs that were keeping him unconscious, but as Dr Rogers had said, they were going to do it slowly because of the other patient going into shock and dying from too rapid a wake-up. We had about two hours, maybe more, so . . . We were invited to go to Micah's mom and stepfather's house. It was close to the hospital and to the university where they both worked.

Micah started to protest, saying, 'I'm not going to leave.'

Nathaniel had moved close to him and spoke low. 'We all need food.'

'I'm not hungry,' Micah said.

'Your beast is, because mine is, and Anita carries more than one hunger inside her.'

We both looked at our third. I don't know about Micah, but I felt stupid for not remembering that we weren't just human. Going without enough food had consequences for wereanimals beyond just low blood sugar. We, and everyone with us, had iron self-control of our 'hungers,' but iron wasn't impenetrable.

'You are under a lot of stress,' Nathaniel said. 'It makes it harder to control everything.'

'I hate to leave him now that I'm back,' Micah said.

I took his hand and said, 'The doctors will call when he starts to come around, and Nathaniel is right. We don't want your family to meet your beast unexpectedly. Do we?'

'My control is better than that,' he said, and sounded defensive, which was rare for him.

Nathaniel hugged him one-armed so I could keep his hand. 'You have the most amazing control of anyone I've ever met, my Nimir-Raj, but no one is perfect, not even you. Don't let guilt make you stupid, not now. You have your family again; let's not scare them by a surprise shapeshift.'

His mother came up then and said, 'Beth is so excited to see you.'

I wasn't sure if it was Nathaniel's common sense or seeing his little sister again, but whichever, we won, and off we all went.

Cousin Juliet drove us, because part of our luggage was still in the back of her SUV. She was going to help us unload and then go home to her own kids and husband. She said, 'I'll give you all some time alone.'

Nicky was in the front seat beside her this time. He turned around and looked back at Micah in the center of the backseat, sandwiched between Nathaniel and me. 'We can stay in the kitchen or living room, if you want to talk privately.'

'Thanks, Nicky,' Micah said. 'I don't know what I want. I can't get past the fact that Mom sold the house five years ago. I've never seen the house we're going to.' He sounded sad when he said it.

I squeezed his hand. 'It would be weird if my dad sold the place I grew up in.'

Nathaniel leaned his head against Micah's hair. 'I don't remember much about the house I lived in until I was seven, and after that I never had a home until now.'

Juliet asked, 'What happened when you were seven?'

Nathaniel raised his head from Micah and said, 'My mother died of cancer, and my stepfather beat my brother to death.' He told the information as if there were no emotional content to it, dry, just facts. I told about my mother's death when I was eight the same way – most of the time.

'I'm so sorry, Nathaniel; I wouldn't have asked if I'd known.' She glanced back at him, her face showing what most well-socialized people look like when a simple question gets a tragic answer.

'It's okay,' he said. 'There was no way for you to know.'

'Car,' Nicky said.

'Turning in front of us,' I said, pulse speeding.

'What?' Juliet said, turning back in time to swerve around the front end of the car that was pulling out. She got the car back under control and said, 'Sorry.'

'No more looking back at us,' I said. 'Just drive, okay?'

'It's just . . .' I watched her hands clutch the steering wheel. 'It's just so sad.'

'There's a lot of sad in the car,' I said.

'What do you mean?' she asked, using the rearview mirror to glance behind at us this time.

I sighed. I had started it, damn it. 'I lost my mother when I was eight.'

I waited for Nicky to give his contribution, but he stayed quiet and looked studiously ahead into the darkened road. His background was as tragic as Nathaniel's, but it was his to share. I wouldn't make him tell.

'I can't imagine losing my mom when I was so little.'

Micah put his arm around my shoulders and pulled Nathaniel's hand onto his thigh, in that casual couple way. It made both of us snuggle into him.

Juliet was turning into a neighborhood of older, modest houses. Most of them were ranch-style with larger-than-normal yards for a suburban neighborhood, but others had smaller yards, because they were tucked up against walls of rock. It reminded me that there were mountains up there somewhere in the dark.

'It seems so weird to be in a neighborhood I've never seen and be on the way to Mom's house,' Micah said.

'I guess that would be weird,' Juliet said as she turned into a cul-de-sac of larger houses.

'My own fault for not staying in touch,' Micah said.

Nathaniel and I hugged and snuggled him from both sides. 'You did what you had to do,' I said.

'You were protecting them from the crazy,' Nicky said.

'Thanks,' Micah said with a smile.

Juliet might have asked what crazy Nicky was referring to as she parked in a driveway, but the door to the house opened, and Micah's mom was framed in the light like an ad for some heartwarming movie. I felt him tense beside me, but not in a bad way. Nathaniel reached for the door on his side.

Nicky said, 'Wait, and let the others get into position.'

'No one is waiting to jump you at Aunt Bea's house,' Juliet said.

'Probably not,' Nicky said, 'but it doesn't hurt to be cautious.'

'Bodyguards are supposed to be paranoid. We sort of pay them for exactly that,' I said.

'I wouldn't have believed you needed them until I saw what Bertie and Jamie did; that was so awful of them.'

Nicky unbuckled his seat belt. 'No one get out until someone has your door.'

'Me, too?' Juliet asked.

'No, you aren't our job,' he said.

'I'm glad,' she said, and reached for her door.

He touched her shoulder. 'Not yet.'

'You said I could get out.'

'I said you didn't have to wait for a guard to have your door, but I don't want you opening your door yet.'

'Why not?'

'You'll illuminate the inside of the car and make a target of everyone in here.'

Juliet's shoulders slumped, and you could almost feel her rethinking the world from a much scarier and more dangerous perspective. She turned in the darkened car and looked at Micah. 'Is this how you have to live all the time?'

'It's a precaution,' he said.

'Is this why you didn't want to come home? You thought you'd endanger everyone?'

'Partly, but now I have enough people to make the bad guys hesitate. They'll see Nicky and the others and know that I'm not unprotected. They'll know that if they harm my family, it won't be without repercussions.' Micah's voice was very calm as he said it, so reasonable. I liked that about him, that he was as ruthlessly practical as I was.

'Do you mean . . .' Juliet said, but Dev was at my door, Ares was at Nathaniel's, and I could almost feel Bram near the back of the truck. I'd noticed that sometimes with Micah physically close to me I could sense the other wereleopards in our group. They opened our doors; we got out and started walking toward the opened door. Micah's mother had already walked down the steps and was partway to us. I wasn't surprised that Bea Morgan was an impatient woman, not after seeing the fight at the hospital. People with tempers are rarely patient. I should know.

We entered the new-to-us house in a circle of bodyguards, with Micah's mother reaching out to lead him inside. We let him go forward to meet her. Ares stayed at his side. Nathaniel and I held hands, with Dev and Nicky on either side of us. Bram brought up the rear, looking back into the darkness. It probably wasn't the welcome home Micah had planned, but if we could pull off some kind of miracle for his dad, it wasn't half bad.

18

We'd had time to see the great room – living room/dining room with the kitchen off to one side, with just half-walls and bar stools around two sides – when a young woman stepped in through the open doorway of a distant hallway. Her curly, dark auburn hair fell around her shoulders. She was maybe five foot four, slender, and dainty except for one part. She had breasts the way Micah had more manly attributes, as if nature had decided to make up for their looking so delicate. But at least Micah could hide his under clothes; Beth, and this had to be Beth, would have more trouble hiding hers.

She walked across the room, face already starting to crumble into tears. Micah went to meet her halfway. She half-fell against him, wrapping her arms around his neck, and started to sob. He held her, patting her back, trying to soothe her.

I heard her saying, 'I knew you'd come. Jerry said you wouldn't, but I knew you would.'

A small voice called, 'Bethy, are you all right?'

Beth pulled away, wiping at her eyes furiously, trying to hide the tears, as she turned around for the little boy in the hallway. He had a halo of golden curls that spilled out around his head and that perfect skin tone that certain mix-and-match genetics can give you. His eyes were huge and shaped like Jerry's and their mother's, but the color was a pale brown, much lighter than the dark brown of Beth's eyes.

'I'm fine, Fen, just happy that my big brother is home.' She half-laughed as she said it, still wiping tears away.

'But you don't cry when you're happy, Bethy.' He said her name like he couldn't quite pronounce *Beth*, and wasn't exactly saying *Betty*, but something in between. He walked farther into the room in his footed pajamas trailing a stuffed toy in one hand, like a modern version of Christopher Robin, except it wasn't Pooh Bear in his hand. I couldn't tell what it was, but it wasn't a bear.

Beth went and picked him up, cocking her hip to one side so he sat better, as she carried him back to us. 'Fen, this is my big brother, Mike. Remember I told you about him?'

The little boy gave solemn eyes to Micah. 'Are you my big brother, too?'

Before Micah could answer, there was a shrill little-girl scream from the hallway. We all looked up and the screamer raced toward us in a Disney Princess nightgown, long, dark gold braid flying straight out behind as she ran shrieking toward us. An older boy with short brown hair was running after her, yelling, 'I am going to kill you!'

Bea said, 'Hawthorne!'

Hawthorne? Oh, right, I remembered. Second husband was a literature professor. Poor kid.

The little girl flung herself into her mother's arms as Ty Morgan said, 'Hawthorne, that is not how we talk to each other in this house.'

'She spilled Kool-Aid all over my backpack! She's not even supposed to be in our room!'

'I did not!' the girl said, with her little arms around her mother's neck and her face buried in Bea's hair.

'Liar, I saw you. If I hadn't had to save my homework, I'd have caught you before you hid behind Mom!' His face was flushed with that peculiar rage you reserve for siblings. He looked like he had a light permanent tan, and his hair was cut very short and old-fashioned, like a 1950s boy cut. He looked about eleven or twelve years old. His bright blue eyes glittered with his anger. He was seriously pissed. I wondered if he had a bad temper normally or if it was special for what was happening at the hospital. Then I realized that Rush wasn't his daddy. His dad, Ty, was standing there, all good as ever.

Micah's mom was stroking the girl's long gold braid. 'It's okay, Frost. Did you spill Kool-Aid on Hawthorne's backpack? Tell the truth; no one will be angry.'

Frost raised her face and looked behind at her brother. All we could see was the back of her head. 'Hawthorne is mad now.'

I thought she had a point.

'You know you're not allowed to drink or eat in the bedrooms,' Bea said.

Frost hung her head. 'I'm sorry, Mommy, I forgot.'

'Apologize to Hawthorne,' Ty said.

She mumbled her apology.

'That's it?' the boy demanded. 'She spills shit all over my school backpack and some of my homework and gets off with an apology?'

'Don't use vulgarisms,' Ty said automatically. 'Frost is going to help you clean off the backpack, and we'll think of something else suitable to remind her she's not allowed to take food back to the bedrooms.'

Hawthorne rolled his eyes. He looked up at us as if we'd just appeared before him. Anger will blind you to a lot, but seven strangers in your living room seemed like something you'd notice. Emotions flowed over his face, and he finally settled on arrogant defiance, but his eyes were wary, almost nervous. He'd looked us over and done a quick assessment of physical potential, which made me put his age up a bit, at least twelve, and he was in some sport that made him aware of physical potential. He'd done the math and knew that there were a lot of other males in the room who could kick his ass.

'What sport do you play?' I asked.

He looked startled at having to drag his attention away from the bodyguards who towered behind us. 'Football and jujitsu.'

I nodded. 'I figured some kind of martial arts.'

'Why?' he asked, blue eyes narrowing.

'The way you sized up the men.'

'What do you mean?'

'You know what I mean,' I said.

He looked at me, and he saw me not as a woman, or a grown-up, but as a person. He was almost my height exactly. 'What martial art do you do?'

'I started out in judo, but now I do mixed martial arts.'

'You do MMA?' he asked, and couldn't keep the suspicion out of his voice.

I nodded. 'I do.'

He looked behind us at the other men again. 'What do they do?'

'Same thing,' I said.

'She trains with us,' Ares said.

Hawthorne looked suspicious again. 'Really?'

'Really,' Nicky, Dev, and I said at the same time.

Hawthorne looked at Micah next. 'You're Mike, aren't you?'

'Yes,' Micah said.

Hawthorne studied his face, then nodded. 'You look like Beth.'

'I know.'

'Do you work out with them?' Hawthorne asked.

'No.'

'Why not?'

'Because in my job my life doesn't depend on my fighting skills.'

Hawthorne looked back at me. 'What's your job?'

I moved my jacket so he could see the badge at my waist.

'U.S. Marshal. Are you here to help catch who hurt Rush?'

'I'm here with Micah, Mike. I'm his fiancée, but yeah, since I'm already here I thought I'd help out.'

He looked at Nathaniel. 'Who are you?'

'Hawthorne,' his mother said, as if he'd been rude.

'What?' he asked.

'I'm Nathaniel,' he said, and offered his hand to the boy.

Hawthorne was obviously surprised, but he took his hand and they shook. 'Do you work out with them?'

'No.'

'Why not?'

'Same reason Micah gave.'

The boy looked him up and down as if trying to figure out what, or who, he was to everyone else. 'They don't all look like marshals,' he said.

'Hawthorne, why don't you take Frost and Fen back to clean up your backpack?' Ty said.

He gave a sullen look to his father. 'Fen is four. How is he going to help with anything?'

Fen rose up from Beth's shoulder and said, 'I can help.'

Hawthorne gave an exaggerated sigh, rolled his eyes again, and said, 'Fine, I'll take the little kids with me, but I know you just want me to stop asking questions and talk grown-up stuff.' He looked worried then, and it was real. 'Did something else happen to Rush?' He suddenly looked younger, the kid peeking through the almost-teenager.

'No, Hawthorne, nothing else has happened,' Ty said.

'Promise,' he said.

'I promise,' his father said.

Hawthorne nodded, flashed us another worried and speculating look, then held his hands out for the kids. 'Come on, brats, I'll supervise while you clean up the Kool-Aid.'

Bea set the little girl on the ground. Frost turned around to face us, hands on hips, elbows out defiantly, and gave us a clear view of her delicate triangular face. Her eyes were small, almost almond shaped, and a deep, solid brown. Except for the hair color she looked like Beth had cloned herself. I was looking at what Micah's daughter might have looked like.

'I am not a brat,' Frost said, stamping her foot.

'Are too,' Hawthorne said.

'Are not!'

'Go with your brother and clean up the mess you made,' Ty said.

I looked at his bright blue eyes, and then at Bea's blue-gray ones. Micah had actually gone pale. How did two blue-eyed parents end up with brown-eyed children? Somehow Fen's golden-brown eyes hadn't seemed so obvious, but these were Micah's and Beth's eyes staring out of a face that didn't look like their mother or her new husband. What the hell was going on?

Beth said, 'I'll go with them and make sure they don't kill each other.' She gave a look to Micah that I think was sympathetic. 'I'm glad you're home,' she said, and carried Fen off after Hawthorne and Frost.

Fen called back over her shoulder, his arms wrapped around her neck, and asked his question a second time. 'Are you my big brother, too?'

Micah turned to look at his mother as he answered the little boy, 'Yes, I think I am.'

Bea Morgan reached for her husband's hand and looked guilty.

19

'Mom, Ty, what is going on?'

Ty stood there straight and tall with an almost defiant look on his face. Bea clung to his hand and looked beseechingly at her son. 'It just sort of happened,' she said.

'Frost isn't Ty's, is she?' he asked.

'She is my daughter,' Ty said, 'but biologically probably not.'

'What do you mean, biologically?' he asked.

'Mike, please, don't be mad. I thought you'd be better than Jerry about it, because you have two people, too.' Her voice sounded apologetic and not sure of itself at all.

The doorbell sounded. Bea went for the door, as if happy to have an excuse to be away from Micah. Bram shadowed her to the door without anyone telling him to; you never left a door totally unguarded, especially if it was about to open. Micah was still trying to deal with the last few minutes. His father hadn't been the heartbroken abandoned spouse but had been at least sleeping with his ex-wife part time. There was an implication of much more.

Nathaniel and I had moved up beside Micah, but I honestly wasn't sure what to say. The look on his face said that part of his family history had just imploded. Nathaniel touched his arm. Micah didn't seem to notice.

It was Jerry at the door. 'You guys never lock the door until bedtime. What's up?'

'I didn't lock it,' Bea said.

'We did,' Bram said.

Jerry looked up at the taller man. 'Why?'

'A locked door gives us a few more seconds to react,' Bram said.

'React to what?' Jerry asked.

'Anything.'

Jerry shook his head and looked past everyone to Micah, who was looking at his brother now. 'The look on your face; you met Frost?'

'Yes,' Micah said in a voice that was almost strangled with tension.

'Surprise!' Jerry said, arms wide in a *ta-da* motion.

'You could have warned me.'

Jerry shook his head. 'Oh, no, wouldn't dream of it. This isn't my explanation to give, I wouldn't even try.'

'Be nice, Jerry,' Bea said.

'Why? I didn't know until Frost was three. I can't believe I was so stupid.'

'Jerry . . .' Bea began.

'No, Mom, just explain to Mike. I'm still working my own issues on this one.' He moved until he was in front of Micah. 'We both felt so sorry for Dad, remember. We were so mad at Mom for leaving him for the professor here, and all the time they were still seeing each other, still a couple.'

'That's not true,' Bea said. 'At first it was everything you thought it was. I loved Rush, but I couldn't live with him anymore. I met Ty while we were separated. Rush could have dated, too, but he chose not to.'

'He was waiting for you to come to your senses and come home, or let him come back home,' Micah said, and that edge of old resentment was suddenly very clear in his voice. Some issues stay fresh every time you open them up. It's like evil magical Tupperware – it stays fresh forever.

'You are thirty years old, Micah David Callahan, too old to believe I can fix something that broke when you were twelve.'

Micah looked a little embarrassed but said, 'So did you cheat on Ty with Dad, or what?'

She looked back at Ty, and he moved up to take her hand again. 'She never stopped loving Rush, and by the time you left for good he was spending more time over here with us and the boys.'

'I remember Twain's fourth birthday party. I was so proud of all of you for being grown-up enough to give the younger kids such a family occasion.'

'Yeah,' Jerry said, 'but what you and I didn't know was that Dad was sleeping over.'

'That long ago?' Micah asked.

Jerry nodded.

'You want to tell this story?' Bea asked Jerry.

'Nope,' he said, and flopped down on the nearest couch.

'Then stop interrupting,' she said.

He spread his hands wide, as if to say, *Sure, go ahead, I'm out of it.*

She turned back to Micah and the rest of us. 'I didn't think I'd have quite this big an audience for the story.'

Bram said, 'We can wait in the kitchen if you like.'

'Thank you,' she said.

He and Ares went for the bar stools around the kitchen. Nicky and Dev looked at me. I nodded, and they went to join them. I didn't have the heart to tell Bea that with their more-than-human senses they'd hear everything she said anyway. Sometimes illusion is all the comfort you get for stories like this.

We all sat down on the nearly perfect square of couches. Ty and Bea were on one couch. The three of us sat on the couch opposite them. Jerry moved to the love seat that sat between them both. When we looked at him, he said, 'I want to see everyone's faces.'

'Jerry, this is not a show for your entertainment,' Ty said.

'I just want to see one of my siblings learn about all of this the way I did, that's all.'

'Beth knew sooner?' Micah asked.

'She was only twelve ten years ago. She lived with Mom. When I asked her after I found out why she hadn't told me, do you know what she said?'

'No,' Micah said.

'She liked having Dad here in the mornings and everyone having coffee together. She said it felt like home. You and I lost everything we thought was safe, but little sister got a second bite at the apple.'

'I don't resent Beth and Dad being happy,' Micah said.

'I do,' Jerry said, 'because I was still on his side about the divorce, and all the time they were shacking up. He let me be all sympathetic and it was all a lie.'

'It wasn't a lie,' Ty said.

'Well, it wasn't the truth either,' Jerry said.

Ty didn't have an answer for that.

Bea tried. 'You have Anita and Nathaniel in your life, and I have Ty and Rush in mine.'

'I only have one wife, not two,' Jerry said.

'You barely have enough social skills for one,' Beth said, as she walked in from the hallway. She looked at Bea. 'I've got Twain reading the kids a story.'

'Good,' Bea said.

Beth sat down on the love seat beside Jerry, and though she wouldn't have said it out loud the way he had, I was betting she wanted a good view, too.

Micah laid a hand on both our thighs and we automatically covered his hands with ours. 'Yes, they are both in my life,' he said, 'but it was that way from the moment I met them. We've always been a threesome, sometimes more.' I wasn't sure if he added that last bit of truth to shock, because two of the extra people were listening, or so that later no one could accuse him of leaving stuff out. It didn't matter; they ignored it. Maybe they felt that explaining themselves was enough for one day. I was all for waiting to try to explain the entirety of our love lives. I wasn't ashamed of what we were doing, but it was a lot to explain. One long story at a time; we still had to get dinner before heading back to the hospital. We'd save our romantic epic for another night.

'I loved Rush, but we couldn't live together. I fell in love with Ty, but I missed Rush.' She wrapped both her smaller hands around his one larger hand and smiled up at him. It was a look of love, but I thought it might have been more a reassurance to the man at her side. Maybe that was just me overthinking.

Bea looked at me and said, 'I know you understand what I'm talking about.'

What I wanted to say was, *Don't drag me into this*, but Micah squeezed my hand, which let me know not to say the first thing that came to mind. Prospective in-laws needed gentler handling than my usual. 'It wasn't exactly like that with Micah and Nathaniel.' In my head, I thought that was more like Jean-Claude and Richard, back when the latter was more in our lives, but since that hadn't worked out well, I kept my mouth shut again.

'I told you that Nathaniel and I came together with Anita at almost the same time. She knew Nathaniel before me, but they weren't a couple.'

Nathaniel leaned into Micah, smiling. 'I think if Micah hadn't come along, Anita and I would never have been a couple.'

'Why not?' Bea asked.

He glanced past Micah at me. I just gave him raised eyebrows, because I had no idea what he was going to say. He smiled wider. 'We work as a threesome. I'm not sure either of us would work with Anita as a regular couple.'

'That's it exactly,' Bea said, and she sounded relieved. 'Rush and I alone weren't enough for each other, but with Ty' – she shrugged and gazed up at him – 'we were.'

'And you were okay with that?' Jerry asked.

Ty looked at him. 'Bea and I were beginning to have problems, and I knew we loved each other, but something was missing.' He turned back to look at Bea, and his face glowed, the picture of a man who was still dead-gone on his wife. 'Rush helped us find that missing piece.'

Micah's hand tensed in mine, and I glanced at him. He looked stricken, or shocked. I wanted to ask what was wrong but couldn't in front of the parents. But Micah saved me the trouble, because he said it out loud. 'I understand that.' He turned and looked at Nathaniel, and whatever look was on his face made Nathaniel glow. I smiled at them both, my two men.

'Oh, for the love of God,' Jerry said.

We all looked at him. 'What's got your panties in a twist?' I asked.

'You guys are all looking at each other in the same damned way. It's the way Dad . . . it's, fuck.'

'Jerry,' Bea said, 'we don't use words like that.'

'The kids aren't here to hear me,' Jerry said, arms crossed across his chest, as he slumped lower into the couch.

'I think it's great,' Beth said. She was smiling at everybody.

'I wanted at least one person in the family who I give a damn about to be pissed like me.'

'You've got plenty of people in the family pissed, as you say,' Bea said, and her face looked suddenly older, strained.

Jerry sat up and reached out, as if to reach past Ty and touch his mother, but he let his hand fall back. 'I didn't mean that, Mom; I would never be as stupid as all of them are being.'

Bea said, 'You've met everybody from Rush's and my family who are coming to the hospital now. His parents will come, but only if Ty isn't there. They'll tolerate me, but not him.'

'What did Grandpa and Grandma get upset about now?' Micah asked.

'Until Rush got hurt, they could do a sort of "don't ask, don't tell" about our . . . domestic arrangement, but we couldn't hide how upset we both were.'

'Have they met Frost?' Micah asked.

She nodded.

'Then they didn't want to know,' he said.

'Probably, but we also had to come back to this house to get Rush's things . . . he lives here. He still owns the cabin, but he hasn't really lived there for almost six years.'

I shifted beside him.

Bea said, 'What is it, Anita? Talk to us, tell us what you think, please.'

I glanced at Micah, and he nodded, then shrugged. We were too far into places he hadn't expected to be able to guide me, I think.

'I think that if they didn't know their son was living here for six years when they live in town – They live in town, right?'

'Yes,' she said.

'Then they've been ignoring the elephant in the room for a long time. I don't think knowing his address would have made them look at the truth.'

Ty, Bea, and Beth exchanged a look.

Jerry sat up straighter. 'What happened?'

Ty answered, 'Your grandfather saw me holding Rush's hand and crying.'

Jerry frowned. 'So?'

'You did more than just hold his hand,' Micah said, and there was no condemnation in his voice, no anger. It was actually the calmest he'd sounded in the last few hours.

Ty nodded and wouldn't meet his eyes.

'It's okay,' Micah said. 'We understand.'

'I don't,' Jerry said.

Beth said, 'Just leave it, Jerry.'

'No,' he said, sitting on the very edge of the love seat and looking from his mom and Ty to Micah.

'Ty,' Micah said.

The other man looked at him.

Micah raised Nathaniel's hand in his and laid a gentle kiss on the back of the other man's hand.

Ty's eyes were shiny with unshed tears as he nodded. 'How did you know?'

'Because it was either that, or you kissed him–kissed him, and Grandpa saw you.'

'Have they disowned their son?' I asked.

Bea shook her head. 'No, they seem to think that Ty is the evil influence. If—' She stopped herself, took a shaky breath, and said, 'When Rush gets better I think they'll either give him a chance to move out of the house or kick Ty out.'

'He won't do that,' Beth said.

'No, he won't,' her mother said.

Micah turned to Nathaniel and me. 'My grandparents aren't as crazy religious as Aunt Bertie, but they are very serious about certain things. They finally accepted me as a shapeshifter because I couldn't do anything about it. It wasn't a choice. If I had chosen to become a monster, they would have disowned me.'

'Rush is their son,' Bea said, 'and he feels like he's outside God's grace now. He loves living here with all of us, but he still believes a lot of what he was raised to believe. It's really hurt him to love us all here.'

'It's made him happier than I've ever seen him, Mom,' Beth said. She got up and went to sit on the other side of her mother so that she and Ty each comforted Bea.

'That's true enough,' Jerry said. 'I've never seen Dad this happy.'

'He wasn't just keeping his home address at the cabin to get around his parents,' Ty said. 'It's also because as sheriff he has to live in the town to serve.'

I nodded. 'Yeah, if he lives in Boulder then he can't be sheriff.'

'No,' Ty said.

'He loves his job,' Jerry said.

'If the worst thing we have to worry about is that he has to change where he's protecting and serving, we'll be doing okay,' I said.

Bea nodded. 'You are so right, Anita, so right.'

'Do the other kids know?' Micah asked.

'We had to sit down with Twain and explain why we all use the same room at night,' Ty said.

'He asked outright?' Micah said.

They nodded.

'You haven't met him yet,' Beth said. 'He's a very serious kid and he'll ask anything if he wants to know. He's like a walking social disaster.'

'He was a serious kid even at four when I saw him last.'

'Hawthorne knows we have one bedroom, but he won't ask outright. He'll just accept it and not ask any questions that he doesn't want to know the answer to,' Ty said.

'Were you all a couple back when Hawthorne and Twain were little?' Micah asked.

'We'd started working on that by the time Twain was four,' Ty said.

'So, while I was still around?'

'Yes,' Ty said.

Micah looked at Jerry. 'We both missed it.'

'Yeah, but at least you've been gone for ten years. This was all happening under my nose.'

'The divorce kept you pretty occupied, big brother,' Beth said.

Micah's hand tensed in mine. I think it was her calling him *big brother*. I wondered if that was a nickname she'd only used for him once? 'I'm sorry that you and Kelsey didn't work out.'

'You never liked her,' Jerry said.

'I wouldn't say never, but by the time you were in college, no. I didn't like her.'

'Why didn't you like her?' he asked.

'It's old news,' Micah said, 'and you divorced her, so it doesn't matter.'

Jerry looked down at his clasped hands, let out a long breath, and asked, 'Did she try to sleep with you?'

Micah's hand tensed in mine again, though nothing else showed his sudden tension. 'It was a long time ago.'

Jerry shook his head. 'Why didn't you tell me, Mike?'

'You were in love with her, and I didn't think she'd approach anyone else. She was a little drunk and it happens.'

'No,' Jerry said, 'even a little drunk, your fiancée does not proposition your brother.'

'I agree with Jerry,' I said.

'You asked me like I wasn't the only one she tried to sleep with; I honestly thought that she wouldn't try for anyone else.'

'Why?' Jerry asked.

Micah hesitated. 'She had a particular . . . interest, um . . .'

'Fetish, you mean,' Jerry said.

Micah nodded. 'Yes.'

Nathaniel and I must have looked puzzled, because Jerry said, 'Everyone else knows that Kelsey was a fur-fucker, beastlover, whatever.'

'She approached you after you became a wereleopard?' I said.

Micah nodded. 'I honestly thought it was just a onetime fantasy and when I said no, she'd let it go.'

'Nope,' Jerry said, 'she's actually living with the local werewolf pack and getting all the furry attention she wants.'

'I'm sorry, little brother,' Micah said.

Jerry nodded, staring at his hands. 'I can't compete with . . . you know how it is better than I do. Kelsey said no human man could compare.'

'I'm surprised she didn't ask you to join the team,' I said.

'She did, but by that time I knew that even if I were a shapeshifter my attentions would never be enough. There's something broken inside her that isn't fixable.'

'I'm sorry,' Nathaniel said.

Jerry looked at him and at him holding hands with both of us. 'It really bothered me when I found out that Dad was a "couple" with Mom and Ty. I didn't like the idea of my dad sharing a bed with another man.'

'Jerry,' Bea said, as if he'd said something rude.

'Are you ashamed of it?' he asked.

'No,' she said.

Jerry looked at Ty.

Ty said, 'No.'

'Then it bothered me when I realized you all shared a bed.' He looked at us again. 'How long have you three been . . . together?'

'Almost three years,' Micah said.

'Mom, Dad, and Ty have been together for double that. I'm the only one who tried for traditional, and by two years in I knew it wasn't going to work. Maybe I need to find a nice couple to settle down with.'

'Janet is a good person,' Beth said.

'I thought Kelsey was a good person, too.'

'Kelsey always noticed other men at parties and stuff.'

'Why didn't you tell me?' Jerry asked.

'Because I was just a kid and I didn't understand what I was seeing. Now, I'd say something.'

'I'm sorry, it's just I feel stupid about Kelsey and about not seeing what was right in front of me with Dad and Mom and Ty.'

'I didn't know you had any doubts about marrying Janet,' Bea said.

'I don't, and then I think how oblivious I've been and I wonder what I'm missing this time.'

'I look forward to meeting Janet,' Micah said.

Jerry nodded. 'Let me know if she tries to sleep with you, okay?'

'It won't happen this time,' he said.

Jerry just looked at him.

'But I promise, I'll tell you if it does.'

Jerry looked at Nathaniel. 'You, too, pretty boy.'

Nathaniel smiled, and then looked uncomfortable and finally just said, 'I'll tell Micah and Anita.'

'We'll tell you,' I said.

'And I don't think I like you calling Nathaniel *pretty boy*,' Micah said. 'It sounds dismissive, and he's too important to me for that.'

Jerry spread his hands wide. 'Sorry, it's just he is pretty, and I'm having a moment of insecurity, okay?'

'My men, they do have that effect on people,' I said. I tried to make a joke of it.

Jerry wasn't really in the mood for jokes, apparently, because he said, 'I'd just make a blanket request that if Janet tries to hit on any of your guys, someone tells me.' He was looking behind me.

I looked back at the guards who were sitting at the counter. I tried to see them from Jerry's point of view. They were all taller, more muscled, and more obviously dangerous. He was as good-looking as Bram or Ares, but Dev and Nicky, not really. Nicky wasn't much ahead of them, but Dev, he was almost as beautiful as Nathaniel and Micah. The real difference was that Dev was a more masculine beauty and my main sweeties were closer to the androgynous and even feminine-beauty side.

'Don't feel bad, Jerry; sometimes it makes me feel insecure to date them.'

He frowned at me. 'Why?'

'I've broken the girl rule,' I said.

'What rule?'

'Never date anyone prettier than you are.'

Jerry looked at me, still frowning. He glanced at Micah. 'Is she teasing me?'

Micah shook his head. 'No.'

'If you think my brother and even Lavender Eyes here are prettier than you are, then you are not looking in the same mirror that I am.'

It was my turn to frown.

'Just say it, Jerry; Anita won't get it any other way.'

'Understand what?'

'You are one of the most beautiful women I've ever seen. The look on your face says you don't know that.'

'Don't believe it,' I said.

'Why not?'

I shrugged. 'My childhood trauma can wait for another day. Didn't someone mention food?'

'You're changing the subject,' Jerry said. 'I've never met a woman who wanted to change the subject after you'd called her beautiful.'

'Anita isn't like any other woman I've ever met,' Micah said, and kissed my cheek. I turned so he could kiss me on the lips and so I could kiss him back.

Bea beamed at us. 'When can I expect grandchildren?'

'I can't have children,' Micah said. He didn't explain that he'd had himself fixed because Chimera had enjoyed getting the female shapeshifters pregnant and then watching them lose the babies when they shapeshifted. Without serious and hard-to-find help, no female wereanimal could carry beyond a couple of months. The change was too violent for the body to hold on to a fetus. Micah hadn't wanted to cause such pain and he'd never expected to be rescued from Chimera, not until he met me.

'I'm so sorry,' Bea said. She smiled gently at her son and then turned the smile on Nathaniel. 'Any children you have with Nathaniel and Anita would be yours just like all of our kids are both Ty's and Rush's. I still want grandchildren no matter who the bio-dad is,' she said.

Nathaniel looked startled, and then looked to Micah, who said, 'I agree with my mom.'

Nathaniel smiled and looked so happy, but . . . 'I am not planning on getting pregnant,' I said.

'Career first,' Bea said. 'I understand.'

'No, my career isn't really the point. I'm just not the maternal type.'

'You don't want to have children?' Bea asked.

'Not really.'

'If I were the girl, we'd already be pregnant,' Nathaniel said. 'I'm more domestic and I love kids.'

I gave him a dirty look.

Micah shook his head and smiled. 'Let's eat dinner before we have to go back to the hospital and before Anita gets too uncomfortable.'

'Okay,' Bea said, 'everyone's brought so much food we could feed a small army.' She got briskly to her feet, as if she had a plan. She was going to either drop the subject as asked, or make sure I was around as many small, cute children as possible, as if there were a pheromone in their tiny bodies that would turn on my biological clock. I'd seen Frost and Fen; they were cute, but they weren't that cute.

20

Three hours later we were back in the hospital and Micah's dad was awake. He raised his one good hand outside the blanket and Micah took it, holding his father's arm against his chest as if clasping him to his heart.

'Mike,' he said in a voice that was still thick with the last of the drugs they'd cleared out of his system so he could talk to his son.

'Dad, I'm so sorry.'

'For what?'

'You know I love you, Mom, Beth, Jerry . . . and all the kids.'

A look passed over his dad's face. He blinked the eyes that were so much Micah's except they were brown, the color Micah had started with. 'You know?'

Micah nodded. 'Once I saw Frost, Mom and Ty had to tell me.'

His dad smiled; it was a good one full of love and happiness, even here and now. 'We didn't plan on her looking so much like my side of the family.'

Micah hugged his father's arm tighter to him, nodding a little too rapidly as if he didn't trust his voice. Nathaniel and I stood in the corner of the room holding hands. We'd have waited outside except that Micah wanted us inside. His mom had been incredibly brave and waited in the hallway.

'You aren't upset about your mom and Ty and . . .' He swallowed hard, closed his eyes, and let out a shaky breath. 'Everything.'

'No, not at all.'

'Jerry's still mad.'

'Jerry's always mad,' Micah said.

His father smiled and gave a little nod, but a spasm passed over his face. The price of this talk was the painkillers being almost out of his system.

'Let me get the nurse; you're hurting.'

He swallowed hard again and let out another shaky breath. 'The painkillers put me out, and I don't want to miss this.'

'Okay,' Micah said. His voice was a little thick, but he wasn't crying. He would be strong for his dad, because that was who Micah was, what he was. Nathaniel squeezed my hand hard. I glanced up and saw his eyes shining with unshed tears. I would not cry, not here, not now, not in front of Rush Callahan. It might be the only time I met Micah's dad; I would not do it in tears. I wouldn't, damn it.

'Who's this?' he asked, and he was looking at us.

'This is Anita and Nathaniel.'

We moved toward the bed, still hand in hand.

'Marshal Anita Blake,' his dad said.

'Yes,' I said.

Those brown eyes so like Micah's moved to look at Nathaniel. He had a small frown between his eyes, as if he was thinking too hard or trying to think of a way to say something.

Micah unwrapped one hand from his father's arm and held it out to us. I took his hand and drew Nathaniel with me. Micah said, 'The three of us have been living together for almost three years.' He smiled, gave a small laugh, and said, 'I thought you and Mom wouldn't approve of me being with Nathaniel.'

His dad laughed, but it ended in another spasm that moved more of his body, as if he were having trouble not writhing with the pain.

He let go of my hand to reach for the call button. 'Let me get the nurse, Dad.'

'No,' and he gripped Micah's hand hard enough to cord muscle along his forearm. He looked up at his son with a fierceness on his face, almost rage. 'No,' he said again.

'Okay, okay,' Micah said. He put his hand back on his father's arm so that he was touching him as much as he could.

'How did you find out I was here?' his father asked.

'Mom called Anita.'

Rush looked at me, and there was a look; it was a cop look. That look that hides most emotions but weighs you, measures you, and sees more than most people understand. 'She appealed woman to woman,' he said.

'Yes,' I said.

He smiled. 'I've read up on you, Marshal. How'd appealing to your feminine side go?'

I smiled. 'I did what she wanted. I got Micah here.'

He smiled a little more. 'You did. Thank you.'

'You are welcome; I just wish it weren't under these circumstances, sir.'

'Me, too, and no need to "sir" me. I'm Rush.'

'Then no need to "Marshal" me,' I said.

He took another breath, and the effort to keep it even was visible. 'Anita, then.'

'Yes,' I said.

'And Nathaniel,' he said.

'Yes, sir,' Nathaniel said.

'Call me Rush.'

'Rush,' Nathaniel said, and held harder to my hand.

'Mom said that you knew why I had been so horrible to all of you ten years ago.'

Rush moved his eyes back to his son. 'I saw some of the photos of what Chimera had done to other families. I understood then why you'd done it.'

I wanted to ask a question so badly, but this wasn't my Hallmark moment. I must have made some small movement, because Rush looked at me. 'Ask,' he said.

'What pictures?'

'He slaughtered and tortured his way across the country before his group got to St Louis. The Feds had a file on the crimes; they just didn't know who, or what, was doing it for a long time.' His body shuddered on the bed, and he gripped Micah's hand hard, not out of affection, but the way a woman in labor will hold on.

In a voice that was breathless with pain, Rush said, 'No nurse, not yet.'

'I don't want to use your time talking police work,' I said.

'You want to know why someone from the federal branch showed me the file.' His voice was recovering its strength, but the strain still showed on his face.

'Yes,' I said.

'Yes,' Micah said.

He looked up at both of us, and again that cop look crossed his face. He looked at me. The force of personality in his eyes was intense, and I prayed that I'd get a chance to see him whole and well. 'Does the name Van Cleef mean anything to you, Anita?'

I blinked and fought to keep my own cop face in place. Van Cleef was the name of one of the people who had helped train Edward, Marshal Ted Forrester, in covert operations after the regular military had trained him in special ops. Two other men that I knew had been associated with him: Bernardo Spotted-Horse and Otto Jeffries. They were both marshals, too, all of the preternatural branch just like me. I knew that Edward had been a professional assassin for years and that Ted Forrester was his Clark Kent disguise. Otto Jeffries's real name was Olaf, and when he wasn't training our military in dangerous things or being a mercenary in other countries, he had a hobby. He was a serial killer, but he only indulged when he wasn't on an assignment, so the government seemed determined to keep him too busy to play.

I honestly didn't know how much the government knew about Edward and Olaf's reality, but Van Cleef had helped train all three of them and some other men who the four of us had met about four years ago. The other men had died. We hadn't.

I'd been quiet too long, because Rush said, 'I see that it does.'

'What does the name mean to you?' I asked.

Micah was looking from one to the other of us, because he didn't know. I hadn't met him when I'd last played with Van Cleef's people. Edward, Olaf, and Bernardo didn't count. Edward was one of my best friends. Bernardo was a work friend. Olaf had a crush on me, because I'd hunted vampires with him, cut people up, killed with him, and he'd thought it was foreplay. The last time we worked together, Olaf had been attacked by a werelion and tested positive for lycanthropy. He'd vanished after that, and so had a female doctor. We'd assumed he took the woman and indulged his hobby. He'd written me a note and basically said he was going to stay away from me until he was sure I wouldn't make him a pet cat like I had Nicky. They had known each other professionally before I tamed Nicky.

'I've worked with Van Cleef's people,' Rush said.

I blinked, fought to keep my face empty, and tried to process that Micah's dad knew people as dangerous as I did.

'Why did they show you the file, and why did they have a file on Chimera and his people?'

'The military has been interested in trying to harness tame shapeshifters for a long time. Chimera interested them.'

'Did the military know what he was doing?' Micah asked.

'Not at first. They were organizing a hunt for him and his people about the time he, and you, got to St Louis. They were going to try to capture him. His DNA on his victims showed he was a panwere. They wanted to study him.'

'Study him,' Micah said; his voice held disbelief and the beginnings of anger.

'I didn't know until this year.' He closed his eyes and took a shuddering breath. Sweat was beginning to bead on his forehead. 'Anita, you interest them.'

'Because I'm a panwere, sort of,' I said.

He opened his eyes. 'The fact that you don't change shape makes them even more interested in you.'

'Are you warning us?' Micah asked.

'They may come to you and try to blackmail you into helping them.'

'Blackmail me with what?' I asked.

'Chimera and his people arrived in St Louis, we know that, but they never left.'

He was looking very steadily at me. I fought to keep as careful a face as I'd shown anyone in a long time. 'What do you want me to say?' I asked.

'Men like Chimera, groups like his, don't just vanish, Anita. But it was your bloodwork hitting the government grapevine that clinched it.'

'I don't know what you're talking about,' I said.

'You killed him. You did it up close and personal enough for him to put his claws, or teeth, into you. Strains of lycanthropy have DNA just like viruses. They know you're carrying some of his DNA inside you, but you have even more control. You have the military's dream of being faster, stronger, harder to kill, better at killing, and you never lose human shape.'

'That's not due to being a panwere,' I said.

'Then what is it?'

I debated for a moment, and then answered. 'We think it's the vampire marks. Vampires can't become shapeshifters with modern strains of lycanthropy, and I was already tied to Jean-Claude when I got contaminated.'

Rush swallowed hard again, closed his eyes, and just breathed for a while. 'So without the vampire marks ahead of time, it won't work.'

'It may only work for me. I'm not sure it's duplicable at all.'

'If I don't wake up again, tell Gonzales what you told me. He'll be able to get it where it needs to go. Don't admit anything; just tell him that your control is based on your ties to the Master of St Louis. Tell them it's not doable.'

'What's not doable?' Micah asked.

'Making more of her.'

'You're joking,' I said.

'I wouldn't waste my time with Mike lying.' He looked up at his son. 'Do you love her?'

'I do.'

'Do you love Nathaniel?'

'I do,' Micah said.

'Good, I'm glad. I love your mom, always have, and I love Ty. It works for us.'

'It works for us, too.'

'Did you know Aunt Jody is living with her girlfriend?'

'Yeah.'

Rush laughed, but it ended in him writhing on the bed, and then making a pain sound. 'Mom and Dad are starting to question what they did wrong, because two of their kids are living in unnatural sin.' He laughed again, but it was a harsh sound. 'Are Bea and Ty here?'

'Just outside,' Micah said.

He looked up at Micah, but his eyes had that fever shine to them, his face glistening with sweat. 'I love you, son.'

'I love you, too, Dad.'

Rush looked at me. 'You take good care of him, Anita.'

'I will.'

'Nathaniel, you love my boy?'

'Very much.'

'Good. Take care of one another.'

'We will, promise.'

Rush nodded too rapidly and too often. His hand convulsed around Micah's and then he said, 'Send them in. If I don't talk to you again, know I love you and I know that you are good and strong and I'm so happy you have two people who love you; that's more than most people ever get.'

Micah used one hand to touch his father's hair. 'I love you, Dad.' He turned to us. 'Get my mom and Ty.'

Nathaniel and I turned and went for the door. We left Micah with his father, saying the things you say at the end if you get a chance and you really do love each other.

21

Back in the family waiting room, Micah sat on the small couch staring off into space, clutching our hands. Nicky, Dev, Ares, and Bram were scattered around the room trying to look harmless and failing. The police talked to Ares and Bram, and Dev had gotten some of them laughing a little. Nicky just found a piece of wall and held it up in classic bodyguard pose near our couch. He didn't usually sweat socializing with the police. He expected them to dislike him. Micah had slipped his sunglasses back on, not to hide his eyes, but so we could all pretend there weren't tears sliding slowly down his face. He made no sound, didn't wipe at the tears, and just let them fall. He sat quiet between us, crying silently. The police and our guards obeyed the guy rule: If a man is crying utterly quietly and pretending he's not crying, you pretend, too.

Deputy Al walked into the room. He started talking low-voiced to some of the other cops. Their stoic, sad faces perked up and went serious. Two of them nodded and left the room like they had a purpose.

I asked, 'What's happened?'

Al looked at us. His gaze lingered on Micah, and his face showed sympathy for a moment, and then he fought it off. He walked over to us with his pleasant cop face in place. He hesitated looking down at Micah, his lips going in a thin, tight line as he debated on being a cop or a friend.

'Mike, is there anything I can do?' he asked finally, deciding on friend.

Micah just shook his head, wordless, not even raising his head enough to make eye contact through the dark glasses.

Al took that as the dismissal it was and said, 'Remember the hiker that Gutterman and the rest were looking for?'

'I remember you saying something about other police business.'

'The hiker was missing two days; this is number three, so we called for volunteers who knew the mountains in that area to help the police with the search.'

I nodded. 'I'd think that's standard in a wilderness area. You don't want more civilians getting lost.'

'Exactly, so everyone we took out with us knows what they're doing. The two men who are missing now, honestly, I'd trust them in a wilderness survival emergency more than most police I know. They are both high-priced hunting guides and can do serious hike-in and hike-out camps with pretty inexperienced hunters.'

'Good teachers, then,' I said.

'Yeah.'

Nathaniel asked, 'What happened to them?'

'They're missing,' Al said.

Micah roused himself enough to look up at Al. 'Who is it?'

'Henry Crawford and Little Henry.'

'They're some of the best in the area, or were ten years ago,' Micah said.

'Henry senior is nearly sixty-five, but he can still hike farther with more in a pack than anyone on our force except your dad, and that includes me. Little Henry is just scarier and quieter than he was, but I'd trust both men in any emergency outside a city.'

'Is Little Henry still an EMT?'

'Yeah.'

Micah finally let go of our hands enough to wipe at the drying tears on his face. 'I can't leave the hospital, Al, I'm sorry. Mom and Ty are still in with Dad, and I'm hoping to be able to talk to him again.'

'I wasn't asking you, any of you, but after the two Henrys going missing I don't want more civilians out there.'

'Is this the same place that the earlier people have gone missing?' I asked.

'Close enough,' he said.

'Something really bad has to be out there for them to be missing,' Micah said. He hunched forward, his elbows resting on his knees. He was staring at the floor thinking nothing good. Was he thinking of the wereleopard that attacked him years ago? It had happened in the mountains around here.

'How long have they been missing?' I asked.

'Three hours. Normally, we wouldn't think anything of it, but one minute Henry and Little Henry were within shouting distance of some of the other searchers and the next thing they were just gone.'

'What do you mean, just gone?' I asked.

'Gutterman says they called out, "We found something." But when the men tried to confirm if they'd found the killer, there was no answer.'

'Did you find anything to let you know where they were last?' I asked.

'It is pitch-black up in the mountains. We can't see shit, and the only tracking dogs are scattered looking for a missing kid and an elderly man who wandered away from his home. Kid is three, man has Alzheimer's, and you know how cold it gets at night here.'

'If they don't find shelter they'll die by morning,' Micah said.

'Our missing hikers are both adults in good health, with some wilderness experience. The Henrys could make shelter and survive a night easily.'

'Did you have dogs here searching for the hiker earlier?'

'One, but it was like its nose went dead. The handler had a word for it: nose-deaf. The dog seemed totally confused, as if it didn't know what the hell it was smelling. He said he'd never seen the dog behave like that.'

'Did it act afraid?' I asked.

He shook his head. 'Why?'

'Some dogs won't track preternatural things, not without special training. They act afraid or just refuse to track.'

'No, it seemed to get the scent at first, but then it hit a clearing and just kept circling. The handler let it take the scent again from a bag of personal effects we had, but it just couldn't pick it out again. Damnedest thing I ever saw with a good dog like that.'

'One of us could follow the scent,' Micah said.

Al shook his head. 'No, no more civilians.'

'Anita isn't a civilian, and if we're in animal form she's our handler.'

'Are you really willing to leave the hospital and risk missing another visit with your dad?' Nathaniel asked.

Micah looked at him, and then back at the floor, shaking his head. 'No, I guess I'm not.'

'I could do it,' Nathaniel said.

'No,' Micah said.

'No,' I said.

'Why not?' he asked.

Micah and I exchanged glances. What did we say – that he was more important to us than any missing strangers? That we felt protective of him, and this seemed like putting him in harm's way?

'What if I went with Anita and Nathaniel?' Nicky asked.

'Civilian, remember,' Al said.

'I'm not a civilian,' he said.

'You're not a cop, and you're not military; that makes you one.'

'I'm not a civvie in the way you mean. I'm not a victim waiting to happen, I won't slow you down, and in a fight I'll vote me.'

'He's good, Al,' Micah said.

Ares and Bram drifted over to us. 'Ex–special forces, remember?' Ares said.

'Micah needs people here with him,' I said.

'Why doesn't Nicky shift and track for you?' Bram asked.

Nicky looked at him, and they both just stared at each other. It was a long, serious look. Neither flinched, but Nicky finally said, 'In animal form I can only kill things; in human form I have more options that Anita likes. Why don't you do it?'

'I'm more versatile in human form,' Bram said.

'I can follow a scent trail in leopard form as well as anyone here, but I can't guard Anita's or Micah's safety, or anyone else's, as well as the rest of you,' Nathaniel said.

'You're one of the guardees,' Dev said, as he joined the conversation a little late. He'd left the other police officers laughing behind him.

'I see you're making friends,' I said.

'They like me now; before they didn't.'

'Dev's right,' Bram said. 'Nathaniel is one of the people we were guarding; that's why originally we were detailed six guards.'

'I'm harder to hurt than any police officer, and even in cat form I can let Anita know more about what I'm sensing than any dog.'

'Can you talk in cat form?' Al asked.

Nathaniel shook his head. 'Not exactly, but Anita will hear me.'

'What does that mean?'

'It means that Anita can read his body language and expressions in cat form the way we can read each other in human form. We know each other.'

'Like a couple or best friends thing?' Al asked, making it a question with the uptilt of his voice.

'Something like that,' Micah said. He'd just lied to his friend. Nathaniel was a black panther. My night vision was good, but not that good. In the dark I would barely be able to see his face let alone the expression on it, but I would be able to hear him in my head. I'd be able to catch his emotions, his thoughts. Hell, if I had the concentration to keep my human body moving through the woods at the same time, I could damn near be inside that huge, sinuous body stalking through the woods on four paws.

Al looked at me, not trying to keep the doubt off his face. 'Really?'

'Really,' I said.

He nodded. 'Okay, Nathaniel in animal form, and you, because you have a badge.'

'Me,' Ares said, 'because my training is perfect for this, even without the beast inside me.'

'How so?' Al asked.

'Scout sniper,' he said.

Al's eyebrows went up, and it was obvious that it impressed him. I'd never been in the military and didn't understand the combination of words. Sniper, yes, but what the heck was a scout sniper? I didn't ask out loud. I'd ask later, after Al had agreed to include everyone we wanted to go.

'I'm as good as Nicky in the woods, maybe better,' Dev said.

'I won't give you better in the woods,' Nicky said, 'but you're better at being charming with the police.'

'You can be charming when you want to be,' I said.

Nicky smiled down at me, and it made his face into something younger, though he wasn't that old, maybe just less cynical. 'I can pretend with the cops, but Dev is more like Micah. He's got better people skills.'

'You're better in the gym,' I said.

'We're all better in the gym,' Bram said.

'Hey,' Dev said, but smiled when he said it.

'Lazy cat,' I said.

He just shrugged, but there was no more debate. The men had just agreed that Nicky and Ares would go with Nathaniel and me. We were winning, so I kept my mouth shut and made a list of questions to ask later.

'We'll need a couple of things before we head out,' I said.

'More weapons,' Nicky, Bram, and Ares said at the same time.

I actually blushed a little. 'I thought that went without saying.' I turned to Al. 'Where can we buy the biggest dog collar you can find, and a good leash?'

'Why do you need it? Is he dangerous off leash in cat form?'

'No, but we're about to go into the woods with a bunch of spooked and tired armed men. Off leash he's a big, black, predatory cat; I don't want anyone shooting Nathaniel by accident. With me holding his leash they'll adjust to the idea that he's helping with the search and rescue like a dog.'

'We don't need to buy a collar or a leash,' Nathaniel said.

'I think Anita is right,' Al said. 'You on a leash will help everyone adjust to you helping out.'

'It's not that,' Nathaniel said.

'You brought yours,' I said.

He nodded, managing to look both happy and shy about it. Asher and I had bought it for him. Asher, who had been Jean-Claude's second-in-command, his *témoin*, which was the word for a second in an old French-style duel. Asher of the golden hair and the angelic face and the devil's own temper. Asher had been Nathaniel's dominant and my top when we played bondage games, but that was before Asher was exiled to another city for behaving like a spoiled, insanely jealous centuries-old master vampire. The collar had been mostly Asher's idea, but Nathaniel loved wearing it. He said it made him feel safe and loved. Me, a collar and leash would just piss me off, but what makes your lovers feel loved doesn't always have to make sense to you, only to them. Some women feel loved if you do the dishes without being reminded; some men feel loved if you'll play a video game with them, others if you buy them a collar and a nice leash and occasionally lead them around by it.

Micah smiled and shook his head. 'I'm not sure I'm going to feel up to helping you use it.'

Nathaniel gave him a solemn face, touching his arm. 'I know that, Micah. It makes me feel better to have it with me, that's all.'

Micah smiled and looked a little puzzled. I think Micah understood Nathaniel's enjoyment of the collar and leash even less than I did; at least I liked to be topped in the bedroom, and he didn't. He let Jean-Claude take blood from him, and to donate blood you had to be willing to submit. I actually found the two of them together incredibly erotic and proved it more than once, but I'd never asked Micah how he felt about the submission. It hadn't occurred me to ask until this moment. Of course, this was probably not the time to ask; uh, no.

'Is it in the bags in the SUV or the ones back at the hotel?' I asked.

'I'm not sure what bags are where. I didn't divide them up,' Nathaniel said.

'Which bag was it in?' Ares asked.

'If I say the small black one, will that help?' He smiled when he said it.

Ares shook his head, smiling, too. 'No.'

'Let's check the back, and if it's not there we'll hit the hotel,' Nicky said.

We all agreed it sounded like a plan, but that meant we had to leave Micah at the hospital. It seemed wrong to leave him behind to deal with his dad and everything. He touched my face. 'It's okay, Anita. I've got this.'

I hugged him, putting our faces close together and our bodies closer, so that we fit against each other like puzzle pieces. I breathed in the closeness of him, let my body sink against his, and felt him do the same. We held each other, and I said, 'I love you.'

'I love you more,' he said back.

Nathaniel came up beside us, wrapping his arms around both of us, so that we all leaned into one another. 'I love you most.' We opened our arms and drew him in to us, so that the three of us fit together and held one another for a moment.

It was Micah who moved away first. 'Go, I'll be all right.'

We each had one of his hands in ours. I nodded and let go of him. Nathaniel held on a moment longer.

'Be careful,' Micah said. He turned to Nicky. 'All of you,' and he gave the guy handshake that turned into a one-armed hug. 'Bring them back to me.'

Nicky smiled and said, 'Always.'

'It's okay,' Ares said. 'We can just shake.'

Micah smiled and shook his hand.

Dev stepped up to me and said, 'I want a hug.'

I smiled and shook my head at him, but I hugged him. I started to pull away, and he put his hand along my face, cupping the edge of my face in his hand. It made me look up at him. The look in his blue-brown eyes was way too serious for our Devil. I might have asked what was up, but he smiled and said, 'Go. I'll be charming to the local cops, since Bram sucks at that.'

Bram said, 'I'm good at my job, that's all the charm I need.'

Dev went back to joking with Bram in that guy way that is affectionate and also hides whatever else they're feeling. What had that serious look been about? If I'd dropped my shields enough I could have known what Dev was feeling and maybe what he was thinking. I could know what the look had meant, but first that was like peeking at someone's diary without permission, and second once I lowered my shields that much, it could open me up to all the men I was metaphysically tied to, and sometimes it was harder to put the shields back in place lately. We had civilians lost out there in the dark; they had to be priorities, or that was what I told myself as I followed Deputy Al through the doorway and into the hall beyond. Nathaniel slipped his hand into my left hand, leaving my gun hand free. Nicky and Ares trailed behind.

22

Nathaniel's suitcase was in the back of the SUV, and so was my extra armament. The guards had kept my extra gear where I could get hold of it on purpose; that Nathaniel's stuff was with us, too, was a happy accident, but it meant we didn't have to go to the hotel for anything. I realized I hadn't even seen the hotel yet. There was a chance I wouldn't see it before dawn, but if we found the two missing Crawford men it would be worth losing sleep.

We followed Al's marked police car, though really it was an SUV, which made more sense for the area. Ares drove our SUV, Nicky rode shotgun, and Nathaniel and I had the backseat to ourselves. I was holding his hand, so warm and real in the dimness of the car as we drove away from the city and farther into the mountains. I wasn't worried about the two men in the front seat. I loved Nicky, but he could take care of himself. Ares was a good guy, but again, he could take care of himself. I'd insisted that Nathaniel go to the range with me until he shot well with almost any gun I could give him. After the bomber in the club, Nicky and I had insisted that Nathaniel learn self-defense. If the bomber had been as well trained as the rest of us we might not have won, but lucky for us he'd been an amateur. If he hadn't been, the man sitting beside me would have died.

I let the hard lump in my gut make me scared. I was taking him into the mountains, the forest, and trusting to his beast, his leopard, to keep him safe. It seemed like a bad plan suddenly. He meant more to me than two strangers. Funny, risking me was one thing, risking him was another. Even though because he was my leopard to call, when I was injured I drained his life to heal mine. For most 'vampires' if you killed their human servant they usually died with them, and vice versa, but animals to call were rarer even among the master vampires. The death of your animal to call could kill you, too, or just weaken you enough to make you easier prey for the hunters. So technically I endangered Nathaniel every time I endangered myself, but that was more abstract than him sitting here in the dark beside me. This felt way more real.

'You don't have to do this,' I said, my voice low not because I didn't think the men in the front seat would hear me but because something about a car at night always made me feel quieter.

He turned to me in the dimness of the car. I couldn't see his face clearly; more the outline of it, and some points, but most of him was lost to shadow. You always forget how dark it is without electric lights, but now he was just inches away and his face was almost blacked out. There was nothing but trees on either side of the road, with almost no lights of any kind but the headlights that plowed ahead into the darkness.

'I want to help,' he said.

'It's not your job,' I said.

'Anita, in leopard form I'm better than in human form.'

'Better at what?'

'Fighting, surviving.'

'Why?'

It was Nicky who answered from the front seat, turning so his yellow hair was a ghost-pale fall covering the shadow of his face. 'The beast lets us react more selfishly. We don't think of the better good or shit like that; we react, we survive. In leopard form Nathaniel will take care of himself more.'

'Really?' I asked, and I was caressing his hand with my fingers as I held it, as if just holding hands weren't enough.

'Yes,' Nicky said. 'It's one of the reasons we're so dangerous in beast form. We don't reason as well. It makes us more dangerous.'

'Half-man form helps you think better,' I said.

'Yeah,' he said.

'But I'll need to be in full leopard form for this,' Nathaniel said.

'Your sense of smell is better,' I said.

'Yes.'

'I understand,' I said.

'You think because Nathaniel can strip on stage and change into his leopard form but not attack the crowd that somehow it's still him in there, but it's his beast with a layer of him in it.'

'So his human form has a layer of beast in it?' I asked.

'Yeah.'

'Because you carry all beasts inside you, but you don't shift, it makes you miss some things about the rest of us,' Nicky said.

'Like what?'

'That we are our beasts, and our beasts are us.'

'I don't think I understand.'

'I'm still me in leopard form,' Nathaniel said, 'but I'm also still my leopard in this form.'

I frowned. 'Micah doesn't talk about his beast like that. Neither does Richard.'

'Don't even compare us to St Louis's local wolf king,' Nicky said. 'He's too conflicted to truly integrate his two halves.'

'What about Micah?' I asked.

'He fights hard to be civilized, human,' Nicky said.

Ares added, 'Micah is still dealing with the trauma of surviving the attack. Those of us who come over involuntarily have more issues.'

'You, too?' I asked.

'Yeah, I hated being a werehyena. I mean, if I had to be attacked by an enemy shapeshifter, why couldn't it be something with a cooler reputation, like a lion or a leopard. Big cats and wolves, now that's sexy.' He laughed, but not like he was actually pleased, more self-deprecating, which I'd never heard from him.

'Are you saying you'd have hated it less if you'd been a different animal?' I asked.

'Yeah, at first, yeah.'

'And now?'

He glanced in the rearview mirror. I got a flash of his eyes as a car passed us on the narrow road. Human eyes didn't reflect like that, which let me know that even in human form his superior night vision was part of his beast.

'I'm a hyena. It's a rougher, more violent world than any other shapeshifter society. We earn our stripes, no pun intended for my stripey brethren. No one, not even the lions, demands the level of toughness that hyena society does. There are many clans of us, but the few that do exist in this country rule whatever city they're in if they go old-school.'

'What do you mean, old-school?' I asked.

'Back before shapeshifters were mainstreamed into human society we handled things less civilized, more naturally.'

'What does that mean?'

'It means the different animal groups would have wars,' Nicky said.

'I thought most animal groups left one another alone outside St Louis and the Coalition.'

'Wereanimals were made legal before vampires were,' he said, 'so you missed the old days when we were able to go into a city and just destroy everything in our path. As long as there weren't any bodies for the cops to find, people just disappeared and my pride and I got paid, and we moved on. Other animal groups hired us to take out their rivals, and we did it without mercy.'

'Wereanimals have been legally humans with a disease for ten years, longer in some states. You can't be that much older than me.'

Nicky leaned into his seat in the dark, his face lost in shadow, only his hair gleaming to show me where to look. 'Lycanthropes age slower than humans, Anita; you know that.'

'How old are you?'

'Thirty-one,' he said.

'So only a year older than me.'

'Yes,' he said, his voice low and strangely intimate in the darkness.

'You don't look older than twenty-five,' I said.

'You look early twenties, too,' he said.

'Good genetics,' I said.

'Are you sure it's just good genetics?'

I looked at his shadowed face as we drove farther into the night-black mountains. 'What's that supposed to mean?'

'I've made you uncomfortable. I can feel you're unhappy and I have to stop. I'm your Bride, which means I'm all about you being happy.'

'I'm not her Bride, or her animal to call; hell, she doesn't even have the ability to call hyenas, so I'll say it,' Ares said.

'Say what?' I asked.

Nathaniel started petting my hand, soothing me.

'You try to ignore Damian, Anita, but he is your vampire to call. He's your vampire servant, and you did fourth-mark with him and Nathaniel.'

'By accident,' I said, and even to me it sounded defensive.

'Doesn't matter how, just matters it happened. I know that Jean-Claude has been waiting to see if Damian starts to age, or if you stop aging, before he brings up sharing the fourth mark with you and Richard.'

'Traditionally, you can't have more than one fourth mark from more than one vampire. You're the human servant of just one vampire,' I said.

'Traditionally, but you're human, not a vampire, and you have a vampire servant, not a human one. There's nothing traditional about you, Anita.'

'What's your point?' I asked.

'You're the first true necromancer in over a thousand years. The rules don't apply to you, Anita.'

'So?' And I sounded sullen. I fought wanting to hunch in the seat. I wanted to take my hand back from Nathaniel and just sulk. I fought the urge off, but just wanting to do it meant this was hitting an old, old issue for me. I wasn't sure which issue it was hitting, but the fact that I wanted to stop touching Nathaniel meant it was something that pre-dated me letting myself love him and all the people in my life.

I forced myself to sit up very straight and keep touching Nathaniel, but his hand had gone very still in mine. I made myself take a nice, even breath and let it out slow. 'Do you have a point, Ares?'

'Jean-Claude's triumvirate with you as human servant and Richard Zeeman as his wolf to call is crippled because Richard won't man up and be the Ulfric we all need him to be.'

'He's doing better,' I said.

'As Ulfric, our wolf king, yes, but as the other third to Jean-Claude's triumvirate he blows. He uses you and Jean-Claude as a booty call and he misses dominating Asher. He can say he doesn't, but it met a need for him to torment Asher. I think Richard misses the bondage games with Asher as much as Nathaniel and you do. He just won't ever admit it.'

'I'm still waiting for your point; so far you're just telling me shit I already know.'

'You have a triumvirate of power with Nathaniel as your leopard to call and Damian as your vampire servant.'

'Again, shit I already know,' I said.

'Do you?' Ares demanded. 'Because the whole time I've worked for you guys I wouldn't know it. You almost never interact with Damian.'

'He's monogamous with Cardinal, and I'm respecting that.'

'I don't mean just sex and feeding the *ardeur* with him, Anita. I mean using him to really make a triumvirate of power, the kind that Jean-Claude wanted to forge.'

'I don't know what you mean.'

He glanced in the rearview mirror again, but this time there was no car to reflect in his eyes, so there was just a shadowed outline of him. 'Nathaniel, is she lying to me or to herself?'

'I would say leave me out of this, but . . .' He sighed, heavily.

I looked at him. 'What's wrong?'

'I feel how drawn you are to all your animals to call and to Jean-Claude. I know how tight we are wound metaphysically, but Damian is always left out. I feel the lack of him, Anita. I can't describe it any other way, but sometimes when you raise power it's like there's a link to him, but it's less. It's . . .' He looked out the window as if searching for inspiration.

'It's what?' I asked.

He turned back to me, and even in the dark I could feel the weight of his stare. 'It's broken. I don't know how, or what, but it's damaged, and that break keeps the three of us from being everything we could be as a power.'

'It's not just me,' I said. I pulled on my hand, but he held on, and I wasn't upset enough to force the issue. 'Damian doesn't want to be bound closer to you and me. He's afraid of being consumed by the *ardeur*, and he's damn near homophobic.'

Nicky gave a harsh laugh. 'Homophobic, really? That's too funny.'

'Why is it funny?' I asked.

'Because if you're not at least comfortable sharing Anita with another man and sleeping in the bed afterward in a big kitty pile, then you are out of fucking luck.'

'London doesn't like other men, or an audience,' Nathaniel said.

'Is that why he's been sent visiting other vampire territories?' Ares asked.

'Part of it,' I said. What neither Nathaniel nor I shared with our two newcomers was that London was addicted to both the *ardeur* and gained power from every feeding. Belle Morte, Beautiful Death, the maker of Jean-Claude's *sourdre de sang*, had addicted London, not me. He had freed himself from her hold and gone cold turkey, running away to England until he'd come to us, and the old addiction had risen again. He was the perfect food for me, but he was already a few centuries older than Jean-Claude and a master vampire. The fact that London had gained power levels from being my food meant that he'd rapidly approached Jean-Claude's own power level, so I'd had to back off. We had sent him to four different territories out of state hoping he'd find a good fit and become someone else's second-in-command. He was powerful enough to be a master of his own territory, but he wasn't good enough at the modern politics needed now. He was still at his last trial run. I couldn't even remember what state he was in this time.

'Damian doesn't want to join with us as deeply as he could, for a lot of the same reasons that Richard fights,' I said.

'I think that if you would take the lead, Damian would be more comfortable sharing a bed with the two of us with you in the middle. He's not as strong as Richard. I don't think he could fight free of us, the way the Ulfric can.'

'You're basically asking me to mind-fuck Damian and forge a stronger triumvirate between him and us, even if it's a kind of metaphysical rape.'

'Put that way, it sounds wrong.'

'It doesn't just sound wrong,' I said.

'You didn't have any trouble doing it to me,' Nicky said.

'You and your pride of lions had kidnapped me and had snipers ready to kill Nathaniel, Micah, and Jason. I was out of options when I made you my Bride.'

'If it's any consolation, I've never been happier,' he said.

It was some comfort, but out loud I said, 'For someone who's supposed to want my happiness and comfort above all else, you say some of the most uncomfortable things.'

He shrugged as much as the muscles would allow and said, 'Sometimes what you need to hear isn't comfortable.'

'Are you saying that you tell me things I need to hear?'

'Sometimes.'

'Which make me uncomfortable, and it makes you anxious if I'm uncomfortable?'

'Sort of.'

I frowned at him and didn't know if his night vision was good enough for him to see it, but I had to frown. 'I'm not sure that I really understand what a Bride of Dracula is supposed to be.'

'We're whatever you need us to be,' he said.

'That you actually mean that,' Ares said, 'makes me glad Anita can't call hyena as one of her animals.'

Nicky turned and spoke directly to Ares. 'Master vampires turn normal humans into Brides of Dracula. Theoretically, it should work on you.'

Ares shivered so hard I could see it in the darkened car. 'Let's not test that theory, okay?'

The red brake lights on Al's car flared and it turned onto a narrow, unpaved road. I'd thought it was dark, but as the trees closed on either side of the car I realized I'd been wrong. This was darker, and I knew it would be even darker under the trees themselves. I'd been raised in the country going camping and hunting with my father. I knew night in the woods. I'd never been afraid of the dark in the woods as a child, only in the house at night. The monsters of my imagination had lived under the bed and in the closet, not in the woods. As a grown-up, I could think of few things I hated more than hunting rogue shapeshifters, or vampires, in the woods. I was just glad we weren't on a hunt tonight. The thickness of the night on the road where there was still some moonlight and starlight overhead let me know that under the trees was going to be thick black night.

I wasn't the only one thinking it, because Ares said, 'It's going to be damn dark under the trees.'

'You have better night vision than I do,' I said.

'Better, but in human form not that much better.'

'You can be the kitty on a leash, then,' Nicky said.

'Hyenas aren't cats.'

'More closely related to cats than dogs,' I said.

He glanced in the rearview mirror again. His face was just a darker shape this time. 'Most people think we're related to dogs.'

'Actually, more closely related to mongoose, meerkats, and civets, isn't it?'

'Yes, it is. How do you know that?'

'Biology degree, and honestly, I read up on hyenas when I realized that it was the second or third largest animal group in St Louis.'

'Better to know your enemy,' Ares said.

'Yes, but you said it yourself, Ares, I don't have metaphysical ties to the hyenas. I don't ken them the way I do lions, or leopards, or wolves, or any of the wereanimals that I can call as mine, or carry a piece of their beast inside me. The werehyenas and wererats are what taught me that a lot of my way with shapeshifters is just another flavor of vampire power. I have to study harder on the beasts I don't carry.'

'Why study? Why not ignore the groups that aren't yours?'

'Micah believes that the Coalition can help all the shapeshifters come together and be a stronger lobbying group, and so do I. It's a good idea, and the only way it's going to work is if we all try to find the things that make us alike, not the things that divide us.'

'That's a politician's answer,' Ares said.

'Maybe, but it's still the truth.'

I got another of those dark glances in the rearview mirror, and then Nicky said, 'I think we're here.'

Ares and I both looked ahead. Al had parked his cruiser. We were here, wherever the hell 'here' was.

23

We were in the Arapaho National Forest. The air smelled like pine, with the ghostly paleness of aspens scattered throughout the darkness of the evergreens. The air hadn't felt that thin down in Boulder, but up here it did. It made me wonder how those of us who had just stepped off a plane from St Louis, which was four hundred fifty feet above sea level, would do above eight thousand feet if we had to run, or fight.

We'd planned on Nathaniel changing shape and just going after the missing men, but I'd forgotten that these were officers who had never worked with shapeshifters before, and they had the western state attitude that allowed varmint laws to still include people like my lovers and friends in the same list as any nuisance animal. Which meant instead of looking for the lost men, we were reassuring the locals that Nathaniel wouldn't eat them the moment he shapeshifted.

'Everyone knows that werewolves have to eat fresh-killed meat as soon as they shapeshift. None of us want to be that fresh kill.' This from Ranger Becker, who was as tall as Nicky and Ares; with her pale brown hair pulled back in a ponytail and the bulky jacket hiding her figure, she'd looked just like the other three forest rangers until I heard her voice.

'It's an old wives' tale that all shapeshifters need fresh meat after they shift,' I said.

'Was that "old wives" comment aimed at me?' she asked, her voice belligerent.

'No,' I said.

'You can make all the girl comments to me you want, but I'm not the one standing on the mountain in the woods in hose and high heels.'

'I've got jeans and boots in the back of the car with my execution gear.'

'And why did you bring your execution gear if you were just here for emotional support for Sheriff Callahan's son?'

'Legally, I have to keep my kit reachable even when I travel for personal business.' I turned to Al, who was standing beside me. 'I thought you cleared this before we came up here.'

'I did,' he said.

'Then these guys didn't get the memo,' I said.

'Look,' Al said, 'do you really think if I didn't trust Mr Graison to shapeshift and help us that I would have brought him up here? He's our best chance at finding the Crawfords tonight, and I don't know about you, but I want to know what could have taken out Henry and Little Henry.'

'Ask Mr Graison,' one of the uniforms called out.

'Who said that?' I called out.

There was a shifting among the men in the dark clearing, and then one of them stepped forward. He was tall, maybe six-five, or even six-six. 'I said it,' and there was that arrogance in his voice that some really big men have, because they've spent their life being the biggest dog everywhere they go.

'What's your name?' I asked.

'Travers,' he said.

'Okay, Travers, do you really think that my men had anything to do with this?'

He mumbled something.

'I'm sorry, when you're making unfounded accusations you're loud enough. If you're going to admit you're wrong, that should be loud, too.' Yeah, I'd about had it with the attitude.

I didn't have to see his face clearly to know he was glaring at me. He stood up very tall and gave me the look that went with the deep, unhappy voice. 'I said, I guess not.'

'Since we have two men lost, maybe hurt, or worse, maybe you should stop wasting time saying shit you don't mean.'

Nathaniel touched my back, lightly, reassuring and probably trying to help me calm down. I didn't always like to be touched when I was starting to get angry, and I had to fight the urge to step away from his hand. When I realized I was thinking about stepping away from

Nathaniel's touch for any reason, I knew I had to calm down. For so many reasons I couldn't afford to lose my temper.

'Little Henry and I go back a long way. I want to find him and his dad,' Travers said.

'Then help us find them,' I said, and my voice was calmer now, less likely to up the ante on the attitude.

Sergeant Michael Horton, one of the state troopers we'd met at the hospital, stepped out of the group and said, 'If you'd brought Mike Callahan, then he'd be Sheriff Callahan's son and the head of the Coalition. We've all seen him on TV and know that he has control of . . . the animal inside him, but Mr Graison here is an unknown. I trust your reputation, so if you trust him for this, I'll just go with it, but some of the other men here need a little more reassurance before he changes into something big and carnivorous. He's not one of us. He's not even ex-military like Mr Ares.' Apparently, Horton had assumed that I'd introduced the guards by last names. 'Mr Nicky's haircut isn't regulation, but he's a guy-guy.'

'Are you objecting to Nathaniel on grounds that he's not masculine enough or because of his sexual orientation?' I asked, and didn't try to keep the incredulity out of my voice.

'No, that is not what I meant,' Horton said, big hands spread wide in front of him as if trying to ward off the sensitivity lecture that someone would make him take if he didn't backpedal pretty damn fast.

'Horton,' Al said, stepping up again, 'just stop trying to explain that comment, okay? If you stop now, maybe we can all pretend you didn't say it.'

Travers said, 'Horton may have said it wrong, but why should we trust Graison? He's a shapeshifter, he's not a cop, he's never been military; how do we trust that he has any control over the animal inside him?'

'Tell them what his day job is,' Nicky suggested.

Ares spoke low. 'You say his job and he'll lose all credibility with these guys.'

'You got a better suggestion?' Nicky asked.

Ares seemed to think for a minute and then shook his head. 'No, sorry.'

'I just need them to let me change and start tracking,' Nathaniel said. 'They don't have to like me or respect me as a person.'

Ares frowned and there was enough light from various flashlights and car lights that I could see it. 'Stripping is what chicks do, not men.'

I grinned. 'Chicks?'

Ares looked embarrassed for just a second, and then he grinned back. 'Hey, you knew I was a misogynistic pain in the ass months ago.'

'Misogynistic,' Nicky said. 'I didn't know you knew any five-syllable words.'

Ares flashed him his middle finger, using his hip to hide it from the other men. Nicky gave that deep, appreciative guy chuckle.

I raised my voice to the assembled men and said, 'Nathaniel's control is as close to perfect as I've seen.' In my head I added, *Except for Micah's.* 'He dances on stage and shapeshifts within a few feet, down to a few inches, of the audience. If he couldn't control his beast just after the change, he'd need a different day job.'

Travers said, 'Dances on stage? What does that mean?'

Someone near the shadowy back of the crowd called out, 'He's a stripper.'

The woman, Becker, said, 'Oh, my God, he works at Guilty Pleasures.'

'How do you know that, Becker?' one of the other rangers asked.

She looked embarrassed even in the dark.

There were more calls of, 'How do you know, Becker? Did you take a road trip? . . . You seen him without his clothes?'

I raised my voice to be heard over it all. 'Yeah, he dances at Guilty Pleasures.'

'Why doesn't he speak for himself?' one of the Boulder officers asked.

Another officer said, 'I heard some wereanimals lose the ability to talk like a person.'

'If that were true, then Anita would have to do all the talking for everybody,' Nicky said.

Ares sighed. 'Great, now they all hate us.'

'It's what we are,' Nicky said. 'I'm not ashamed of it, are you?'

Ares gave him a very serious glare. 'No.'

'Then stop complaining.'

The two tall men looked at each other, and I was reminded that they didn't partner each other much. In fact, I couldn't remember ever having the two of them as a team. Nicky had broken Ares' arm once in a fight. Ares hadn't held a grudge, because Asher had used his ability to control hyenas to force the guard to attack Nicky. It had been one of the things that led Jean-Claude to exiling Asher.

Nathaniel said, 'I hadn't heard the rumor that we lose the ability to talk. It's not true.' He stepped a little ahead of me, with a glance to make sure I was okay with it; I was. 'If I were going to shift to leopard form and eat somebody, it wouldn't be any of you guys. I see beautiful, hot women every night at work. They're worth eating. You guys are so not my type.' They laughed; some of it was a little nervous, but they laughed.

Someone in the back called out, 'Should we be insulted?'

Nathaniel flashed that brilliant smile, the one he used to charm the men who brought their women to the club. 'Yes.' More laughter, and this time it was that deep, rumbling male laughter. 'I could never do your job, but I can trail the Crawfords for you. Anita will put me on a leash just like the dog that was up here.'

'Why put you on a leash if you aren't dangerous?' Travers asked.

'Because I'm going to look like a big-ass black leopard and I don't want to get shot by some hunter. With a beautiful woman leading me around on a leash, they won't shoot me. They may think they're hallucinating, but they're less likely to shoot me by accident.'

They couldn't argue with him, and they stopped trying after a little while. Nathaniel charmed them, kept making them laugh, and we got our way.

'Since when did you get to be this charming?' Ares asked.

'I've always been charming,' Nathaniel said, 'but I've learned how to talk to guy-guys thanks to hanging around with all the guards.'

Ares nodded and sort of shrugged. 'Wow, not just a pretty face after all.'

Nathaniel smiled. 'If I tease you for noticing I'm pretty, it might give the other tough guys the wrong idea, so I'll just strip instead.'

Ares rolled his eyes and turned his back, acting as a barrier to help block everyone else's view. Nicky did the same on the other side. I stopped Nathaniel with his jacket off and the shirt halfway unbuttoned. He looked at me.

'Let me change into my other work clothes, before you strip down.'

'Why?' he asked.

'Because if you're naked at the same time that I'm out of that much of my clothes I may get distracted.'

His smile broadened, and he wrapped his arms around me, drawing me in against his body. We were mostly hidden by the car and Nicky and Ares, but . . . 'Not a good idea to get all romantic on the job, honey.'

'I know, but I love that you can admit how much my body moves you now. You fought so long to not want me.'

I shook my head. 'I wanted you; I just wouldn't let myself admit it out loud even in my own head.'

'Then kiss me now, before we get nude, and maybe you'll be able to resist my charms.'

I laughed, and then he kissed me, and there was no more laughing. I changed clothes and once I was securely in jeans, combat/hiking boots and T-shirt, it was time for me to put on my whole kit.

I started with the vest, specially made to hold the curves that men didn't have. I put on the two wrist sheaths complete with silver edged-blades, but honestly once I put my jacket on they'd be hard to reach. They were for emergency use and had saved my life more than once, but tonight was all about the guns. The Browning BDM moved to a thigh holster, the Sig Sauer P238 .380 went in a MOLLE-rigged holster on the front of the vest for a cross draw if I needed it. In a tactical sling I had my AR-15 M4-styled carbine, which had replaced my MP5, which had replaced the mini-UZI before it. The AR was chambered in 6.8 SPC for literally more bang for my buck. It was also frangible, which meant it shattered once it entered a target, so if I shot bad guy A, the round wouldn't go through him and into good guy B. *Frangible* did mean that if you missed the bad guy and accidentally shot the good guy first, they were going to have a very bad night, but I didn't plan on missing. Normally when I wore the Browning in its shoulder rig, I had a knife sheath attached to the back of it so that the hilt was hidden under my hair. The blade was almost as long as my forearm, but tonight I had something else at my back. It was called a sock, or a sleeve, but it attached to MOLLE straps on the back of my vest and held my Mossberg 500 Bantam. The shotgun was originally designed with the idea that it would fit a tween-age boy's arms and hands better, and it probably did, but it was great for us shorter women, too. I carried the sleeve angled diagonally across my back for a right-hand cross draw over my shoulder. I'd tried it riding straight up my back, but having something tall at the back of my head had just bugged me, so I'd changed it. If I'd been in an urban setting with buildings, I could have had the shotgun and the AR on tactical straps and just pushed one behind me while I carried the other, as needed, but with trees and other vegetation there was too much of a chance of the guns catching on something if they were hanging semi-loose. I needed to be able to run without worrying about getting caught on the trees, and with the butt of the Mossberg just a little above my shoulder it was out of the way until I needed it. My cross was tucked inside my shirt for much the same reason, so the chain couldn't get caught and broken as we moved through the forest. I'd probably feel if my cross got knocked off, but I might not find it if it fell to the leaf-covered floor in the dark. We were hunting preternatural creatures tonight – if they were zombies, the cross wouldn't do a damn bit of good, but if they weren't zombies . . . holy objects were good things to have. Extra shotgun shells were strapped to the stock, and in a pouch on the vest, more shells, extra rifle magazines, and a small flashlight. My off-hand thigh had extra magazine pouches for the pistols. My phone went into a pocket on the pants that I could fasten down. I put a heavier leather jacket over all of it, because it was colder here in the mountains. Someone had said we were over nine-thousand-feet elevation. Yeah, that'd be colder.

Ares and Nicky put on their vests and dangerous toys, too. Once we were dressed and armed to the teeth, it was Nathaniel's turn to take off his clothes, all of them. When he was gorgeously naked, standing in the chill mountain air as if it weren't cold at all, I just stared.

Al called from the front of the SUV, 'Blake, don't get distracted back there, okay?'

I said, 'When I don't get distracted by Nathaniel nude, I'll be dead.'

Nathaniel smiled at me and then said, 'Unless you want your clothes ruined you'll have to step back.'

It took me a moment to realize what he meant, which said just how distracted I was. I nodded and stepped back far enough to be out of the splash zone. With new wereanimals there was blood and clear fluid with the form change. With practice the blood stopped and the clear liquid was less, but there was always some, as if the clear fluid helped grease the works as the man became beast or the beast became man. Though it was almost always less messy to go from animal back to human than the other way around. I'd asked all my wereanimal friends why that was, and they didn't know either. It just was.

Nicky and Ares moved out from the car, too, so they'd be outside the splash zone. Nicky stayed turned outward, watching the dark, but Ares turned around. I might have asked why, but Nathaniel chose that moment to release his beast.

It was a wash of energy so strong it hit me like heat, as if I'd opened the door to an oven I didn't know was there. I'd never felt his beast like this, a wash of heat, energy, power that swept over me, through me, and I felt the beast inside me that matched his rise and snarl white fangs in the coal-black of its fur. My leopard's eyes were a dark gold, like antique coins filled with life and heat. I tried to ground the energy the way I'd been taught, sending it into the pine-covered ground underneath my boots, but my leopard didn't want that rush of energy shoved into the ground to help make the trees grow better. My leopard wanted to come out and play with that heat. I couldn't change shape, but that didn't mean my beasts didn't want me to.

I was breathing hard as if I'd been running, my heart thudding in my throat, pulse pounding in my ears. I was suddenly very aware that I might never have been at this high an altitude. I felt a little light-headed, and then I heard the purr, impossibly loud, as if it thrummed along the air spilling against my skin, sinking into my body until that deep, vibrating purr played along my spine and provoked a higher-pitched echo from between my human lips. I was staring down at a black leopard the size of a large pony, three, maybe four times larger than a natural leopard. He sat there, shaking his fur, kneading the flash of white claws into the ground as if trying to ground himself into the new form. The blackness of him was almost lost to the shadows behind the truck; if he'd been still enough you might have looked right past him. He raised the graceful, rounded head upward and looked up at me with eyes that were blue and gray, an unusual color in leopards, so I'd learned. It was as if his human eyes had bled over into his beast so the eyes had begun to come closer to the lavender of his human eyes rather than have the animal eyes travel to his human face. He moved toward me and I got a gleam of muscled fur in the moonlight. He purred again, and my knees buckled. Ares had to catch me or I'd have fallen. 'What's wrong?' he asked.

Nicky turned around and asked, 'What happened?'

'Not sure.' My voice sounded breathless. My leopard was snarling at me, it just happened to be inside me while it was doing it. It felt as if my body vibrated with the sound that couldn't really be a sound. I purred sometimes, an involuntary happy sound, but I did not snarl, and yet . . .

'She's fever-hot with her beast,' Ares said.

'She shouldn't be,' Nicky said.

'I know that,' Ares said, his voice lowering.

It wasn't until Al peeked around Ares' shoulder that I realized why he'd been whispering. 'What's wrong?' Al said, echoing Ares' question. Al gave wide eyes and was a little pale when he got a good look at Nathaniel in full cat form.

'We're not sure what's wrong,' Nicky said, his voice calm, empty even.

Nathaniel padded forward, giving me worried leopard eyes. He couldn't talk in this form, but we'd counted on me being able to feel, or hear, what was going on inside him, right? The moment his furred cheek rubbed against my hand, my knees gave completely. Ares was holding all my weight. What the fuck was going on? I'd never had a reaction like this to Nathaniel's leopard form or anyone's animal form.

Ares tightened his arms around my waist and stood up. He was strong enough to give the illusion that I was standing, but my feet were taking no weight. Nathaniel sat back on his haunches, looking perplexed at me. I wasn't sure how I could tell he was perplexed; the full leopard form's face didn't move or express the way that even his half-man form did, but somehow I was reading his expressions better than I'd ever been able to do.

Nicky smiled at Al. 'Can you give us a minute, Al, thanks.' As soon as Al was out of sight, the smile vanished as if it had never been. Nicky was a sociopath; it made him the ultimate actor. He whispered, 'Where are you in your cycle?'

I fought to focus on him, my arms wrapped around Ares, trying to hold on as if the werehyena needed my help to hold me effortlessly. 'Cycle, what cycle?' I asked.

'Girl cycle, menstrual cycle?'

'I'm not having that,' I said.

'I know that; what I mean is if you were doing rhythm method, would you be fertile right now?'

I frowned at him. 'What? I'm on the pill, you know that.'

He started to touch my face, then stopped short and rubbed his hand against his pants as if trying to scrape off something he'd touched. 'God, the energy is so thick. How can you stand to touch her like that?'

'She doesn't carry hyena as one of her beasts, remember?'

Nicky nodded.

'What is happening to me?' I asked.

'Have you ever been this close to Nathaniel in full leopard form when you were at your most fertile?'

I was regaining some use of my body, and I used it to tighten my arms around Ares' waist, so that I was finally helping him hold me up. 'I don't know, I don't keep track of my fertility. I'm on the pill, and I use condoms with most of my lovers, so it doesn't matter.'

'In all the time I've been with you, I've never seen Nathaniel or Micah in anything but leopardman form. Have you ever been around them in full cat form before?' Nicky asked.

I tried to think about it. I wanted to say, *Of course I've been near them in full leopard form*, but the longer I thought about it the more I couldn't remember. Nathaniel had gained the ability to be in leopardman form after he'd become my leopard to call. He was proud of having three forms instead of just two. Had I ever seen him like this before? No. Had Micah ever done the full kitty-cat on me? No. Chimera had forced him into his leopard form so long that he'd lost his human eye color. He'd told us both that he hadn't enjoyed being in full leopard form since that time.

'No, I haven't,' I said.

'None of you change to full animal form around her,' Ares said. His arms were secure around my waist, but he wasn't holding as tight, and my legs were working again.

'Because in full animal form she won't have sex with us, can't have sex with most of us.'

'It does cross that bestiality taboo thing,' Ares said.

'That's not it,' Nicky said. 'In full cat form the wereleopards are set up to fuck a leopardess in full cat form.'

'That means more than it sounds, doesn't it?' I said.

'I thought you had the biology degree,' he said.

Nathaniel made a low, disgruntled sound. We glanced back at him, and then back at Nicky. 'Just tell me what you've figured out,' I said.

'If a female is at her most fertile, sometimes changing to full cat form can make her react more than half-form. Theory is that we give off more of the right pheromones in full cat form.'

Ares started to let me go, and I swayed. He went back to holding me, and I went back to holding on. 'I can't do my job like this.'

'Your human mind will think its way out; just give it a few minutes,' Nicky said.

'How do you know all this?' Ares asked.

'Lions are more social than the other big cats. Anita, if you're reacting this strongly to his full leopard form, I'd be careful later back at the hotel; don't be tempted with sex.'

The leopard growled low and deep.

Nicky looked at Nathaniel and said, 'Penis spines.'

I'd never seen a cat look so dismayed, but he did. I had a minute to think it through. 'Crap, in full leopard form he'll have penis spines like most cats.'

Nicky nodded. 'If you're reacting this strongly to him now, I would be careful being alone in the hotel with him. Pheromones can be like being drunk. I know you like it rough, but I'm not sure how rough it would be in this form with you in human form.'

'I wasn't going to,' I said.

'The human part of you wasn't, but the leopard inside you likes the idea a lot, or you wouldn't have reacted.'

I couldn't argue, though I really wanted to. 'Okay, no sex with anyone in full animal form, I got it.'

Nicky looked down, avoiding eye contact.

'What?' I asked.

'Lions don't have full spines like the other cats.' He looked up and he smiled, but his single eye gleamed. His eye had shifted to the rich yellow of his lion form. Something had stirred his own beast. He looked at me with his lion looking out of his eye at me and said, 'Male lions are more ribbed for her pleasure than spiked.'

I looked at that golden-yellow eye set in that handsome face and realized that the idea excited at least part of him, maybe all of him. I didn't know what to say to the eagerness I saw in his face, so I said nothing. We all stood there while the question was raised, and we all ignored it as hard as we could. In a few minutes I could stand on my own.

I fastened the heavy leather collar around the muscled velvet of Nathaniel's neck. It had a flat silver plate attached to the front of the collar. There was a word carved into the metal in swirling letters.

Ares said, 'Pussycat? Does that actually say *Pussycat*?'

'Yes,' I said, as I attached the heavy leather leash to the collar. It was my turn not to make eye contact.

'Pussycat?' he said, again.

'It's her nickname for him,' Nicky said.

'And Asher's for him, too,' I said.

'Asher mind-raped me like I was nothing and made me try to hurt you guys.' He shuddered. 'I've never had anyone roll me like that.'

'There aren't a lot of vampires that can call hyena.'

'Good,' he said. Then he looked down at the shiny silver plate and grinned. 'Pussycat. The cops are going to love it.'

I frowned at him. 'It was supposed to be private; at best he'd wear it at a fetish event. It wasn't supposed to be used around the police – ever.' Nathaniel rubbed his cheek against my thigh, and I petted the thick fur. I pushed my fingers through the thickness and found his skin underneath fever-hot to touch. Most animals run hotter than human-normal 98.6–100 degrees or higher usually. I hadn't touched that many wereanimals in full animal form. Were they all this much hotter?

I sent Nicky to bring Al around so we could finally get started hunting for Henry and Little Henry Crawford.

Ares stayed beside me, grinning ear to ear.

'What is so damned funny?'

'Does everyone have a cute nickname?'

'No,' I said.

'Aw,' he said, 'come on. Micah must have one, or maybe Sin?'

'Drop this topic,' I said.

Nicky came back with the police and it was time to introduce them to the big black pussycat at the end of my leash. I knew we'd won the day when some of them petted him, as if he were a big dog. But there were still more of them who wouldn't approach too close, let alone touch the huge leopard. Al had a jacket and a used rag from the Crawfords' truck so that Nathaniel could know what scent he was trying to follow. I saw Ranger Becker mouth the word *Pussycat* silently to herself as she read his collar. Her eyes flashed up to me, and she smiled, eyes shining so hard with suppressed humor that it showed in the odd light.

It was Travers who said, out loud, 'Pussycat?'

I rolled my eyes at him, and Nathaniel scented the wind and went very purposefully toward the trees. 'He's got the scent.' Nathaniel pulled against the leash hard enough that I started jogging to keep up. He moved faster, and so did I. He gave a small, eager noise, and we started running.

24

We ran in the dark, unfamiliar trees, with me fighting to stay with him. He was faster in this form, as if the extra legs gave him more horsepower, or more all-terrain power. My human body struggled to bend and weave through the pines. Their needles were everywhere on the thin earth, the rocks, so that the world smelled like Christmas trees and the sharp, clean smell of leopard. Just as tattoos stayed on the skin under the fur, so the shampoo and soap he'd used earlier was still there intermingled with the scent of leopard. I could smell the leather of the leash handle as my hand warmed it. The pine needles had killed almost everything on the thin, rocky earth, so that as long as I ducked under the branches I could run full out, trusting that if I turned when he turned, followed his body like a guide through the trees, I'd be fine. I kept my free hand up to guard my face from the branches that he didn't have to worry about but my human form was tall enough to catch.

I felt Nicky to our left, but it wasn't the human part of me that felt him; my lioness knew he was there. It was the first hint I had that he was tied to me as my Bride, and as a lion; as a Bride he sensed me more than I sensed him, but the lion part of me was more aware of him. I glimpsed Nicky like a pale shadow under the trees. I tried to sense Ares, but I had nothing for him, no metaphysical tie and no connection to his hyena. I had to use my human eyes to look to our right and find him racing through the trees to keep up with us. I knew that Nicky could feel me, but Ares was as blind metaphysically to me as I was to him. We had to look for each other; maybe he could smell my scent more than I could his, but even without a stronger connection he was there, at our side, racing on long legs through the trees.

I heard yelling behind us, and I realized it was Al and all the other police. I hadn't thought about them until that moment. The world had narrowed down to the leopard at my side, the uneven ground, the swipe of pine branches against my upraised arm, Nicky like a satellite at our side and the noise and movement that was Ares.

I slowed, and Nathaniel pulled at the end of the leash. I had a sense of just how strong he might be and knew that if he didn't want me to walk him on the leash he would pull me off my feet and 'walk' me.

I said, 'Nathaniel, slow,' a firm command, the way I'd been taught years ago to talk to a big dog when you could tell by body language it was about to do something you'd regret. The very big cat slowed and looked back over its shoulder at me. There was some appeal on its – his – face. I couldn't read it, and I wanted to. I lowered my shields just a bit more and suddenly the night was alive with scent and sound and touch that hadn't been there before.

The smells were everywhere, like a thick, invisible blanket that moved and filled me with so . . . there was something small and furry to our right. It was eatable and smelled like a mouse, but not. The pines were so strong that he'd filtered out the scent the way that a human would react to the constant hum of machinery; eventually you tune it out, but there were so many other things to smell: I would have said I could smell leaves, but there were sharp green smells, old brown smells, and it wasn't the leopard adding the color in my head, that was me, because my human mind had no words for the variety and difference in each scent. I added color, because I couldn't understand without adding some visual cue to all the smells. In human form I didn't have the part of the brain big enough to decipher things purely as smell. I was a primate and we're visual, so I tried to translate all that rich, wonderful information into colors – that smell was sharp, hot, red; that one soft, peaceful, blue; spicy was brown and red; spruce was blue and green; pine was like an ocean of green that we kept having to swim free of to sense anything else. I knew the term *nose-deaf* for hunting dogs, but I'd never realized just how limited my world was to my beasts. How frustrated they must have been to be trapped inside this human body with its limited ability to scent the wind.

I'd always thought my beasts resented this less dangerous body – no claws, no fangs, no way to climb and run the way they wanted to, but I stood there in the forest with Nathaniel's leopard trying to share everything he was sensing and my human brain could not translate it. I got glimpses of it, bits, pieces, and it was amazing, but I knew that it was like trying to explain color to the blind. How do you explain red without resorting to heat? Fire, but that's orange and yellow, even blue, and white-hot heat is a term for a reason. How do you explain red to someone who has never seen it? How did the beast explain scent to my nearly blind human nose?

It wasn't until the leopard rubbed its big head against my hand that I realized I was crying. I was crying because I couldn't understand and for the first time I understood, maybe, just how much I was missing.

Nicky wrapped one arm around me, leaving room for the leopard to rub and lean against my legs. I didn't so much pet him as let him roll the thick velvet of his fur underneath my hand. I wondered how much his leopard understood of why I was crying, but like any domestic cat he knew I was sad and that was enough. Nicky could feel my emotions and was compelled to try to make me feel better. It was part of the compulsion of being a Bride, though as I leaned into the muscled warmth of his chest underneath the leather jacket, I thought maybe we should start calling him my Groom. We'd come up with the term Bride because of Dracula and his Brides. He was the most famous vampire that had held the ability, but it didn't mean that the language couldn't change. I realized I was using the words and their meanings to help me pull away from that world of scent and alien sensations that Nathaniel's leopard had given me. I thought about slang, and how language evolves, because it was something that no animal would have given a shit about. It helped me stuff myself back into me, this body, this mind, these limited senses. I thought things as alien to the leopard and the lion inside me as the world of scent was to me, and it helped me ground and center into myself again.

Ares was standing a little to the side of us, looking out into the dark. 'God, they're loud.'

I raised my head from Nicky's chest and listened. The leopard leaned hard against my leg, and I expected to feel him go still under my head listening, too, but he didn't. He'd 'heard,' or scented the police coming closer minutes ago, while I was wrapped up in my tears, the touch of the two of them, and my human thoughts.

Nicky kissed my forehead. 'You got too much of Nathaniel's leopard in your human mind, didn't you?'

I looked up at him, brushing at the drying tears on my face. 'Yeah, how did you know?'

'I got some of the sensations you were trying to deal with, like bleed-over.' He rested his cheek on the top of my head and pressed me against his chest. The leopard licked my hand and made a small snuffing sound.

'I don't catch sensations from you like that.'

'You can't feel my emotions either, but I feel yours,' he said.

I frowned, thinking about it. 'Being my Bride, my Groom, seems really one-sided, as if I'm not supposed to give a damn about your feelings and needs, just you about mine.'

'Yes,' he said. His body snuggled closer around me and seemed to include the leopard at our feet in the motion, so that Nathaniel rubbed in between our legs, not trying to separate us, but making it a group cuddle. The energy was peaceful, comforting; the only person in the snuggle who thought we shouldn't be so happy about it all was me. It still bothered me that I had possessed Nicky so completely. As if he sensed it, and maybe he did, he said, 'I've never been happier than since you brought me to St Louis, Anita.'

I pulled my face back enough to see his face as I said, 'Doesn't it bother you that it's all vampire powers and mind tricks?'

'No,' he said, and he kissed me, softly, and whispered against my lips, 'I'm happy; why does it matter how it happened?'

I wanted to say, *But it does matter*, but I didn't. I let him kiss me again, let Nathaniel wind his leopard between our legs like a huge housecat. He started to purr and the sound of it vibrated up our bodies like some happy, contented motor wrapped in fur, muscle, and beauty, because he was beautiful in this form, too. I stood there tasting Nicky's mouth and feeling the pull and push of Nathaniel's body, and it just didn't seem that different from the three of us being in bed together when we were all human. Maybe I'd gotten too big a dose of leopard in my head.

'The police are almost here,' Ares said.

We pulled back so that by the time Al and the others arrived we weren't cuddling, just standing waiting for them. Nope, no snuggling going on here, no kissing, and then I realized I'd been wearing red lipstick. I had time to glance at Nicky and see the lipstick tracing the inside of his lips. He was wearing the go-faster stripe. We'd kissed neatly enough that I wouldn't even be smeared, but there was no time to hide the evidence. If he wiped at it now it would just smear worse. Maybe they wouldn't notice in the dark? Of course, they came with the sweep of flashlights, ruining our night vision and theirs. Did some of the lights go back to Nicky's face more than once, or was I just being paranoid?

'I've never seen anything move like you all did,' Al said, as he walked up to us.

'Sorry you had to wait so long for the rest of us mere humans to catch up,' Travers said, 'but I guess it just gave you time to make out a little bit instead of looking for the missing men.'

We couldn't explain, so the only option was a bold front. 'We could just stand here and twiddle our thumbs while you guys catch up, if that would make you happier?'

'Little Henry is a friend of mine, and the thought that you were up here kissing while he could be hurt, or worse, instead of looking for him . . . yeah, that bothers me and it's damned unprofessional.'

Nicky stood up a little taller, and Nathaniel made a harsh sound low in his throat, not exactly a growl, but not a happy noise either. Ares moved a little between us and the police, hands to his side, feet placed to move, but it wasn't that kind of fight.

I took in a lot of air and let it out slow. 'You're right, it was unprofessional. It won't happen again.'

Travers didn't seem to know what to do with the apology. 'I heard you had a temper and never backed down from anything, Blake.'

I shrugged. 'I do have a temper, but when I'm wrong, I'm wrong.'

'While we're on the wrong thing,' Horton said, 'could you all stay with the group a little bit more? It's hard to coordinate our resources if they're scattered all over the woods.'

I nodded. 'Agreed.'

All the flashlights, even pointed at the ground, gave enough light for me to see Horton frown. 'Officer Travers is right; you have a reputation for being harder to get along with than this.'

'When I was younger I was grumpier,' I said.

It made him smile, and then he tried not to. He looked perplexed as he said, 'You can't be more than twenty-five now; how much younger could you have been?'

'I'm thirty,' I said.

'I saw your age on paper, but you still look younger than me.'

'It's because you're tall and I'm short; tall looks older and short looks younger, just does.'

He smiled again. 'True enough.'

'Can we actually start looking for my friend again?' Travers asked.

I looked down at the big leopard sitting at my side. He gazed up at me with the pale leopard eyes. I said, 'Find them; find the scent.'

The leopard gazed up at me. I thought, visualized what I wanted him to find. I pictured the jacket and the rag he'd smelled, just in case words weren't that important to him right now.

He got to his feet, turning in a graceful half-circle to head the way we'd been running. He didn't even put his face to the ground, or scent the wind, nothing, as if he knew where we were going.

25

The body lay in a grove of aspens so that the bare white trunks rose around the dead man like ghostly sentinels. It was a pretty place to leave the body; sadly, what they'd done to the body wasn't pretty at all. It was one of those crime scenes where the eyes don't want to make sense of it at first. If you look away and don't look back, then your brain will protect you. It will keep you from seeing the true horror of it, but it was my job to look, my job not to look away, my job . . . I gazed down at what was left of one of the missing men. I'd never known either of them so I had no idea which it was, only that it was one body, not two. I tried to believe that meant that one of the missing was still alive, but looking down at the remains it was really hard to be hopeful.

From the build and size of the body it was male. The clothes were disarranged as if someone had redressed him after he was dead, or because they'd only moved the clothes enough to get to his flesh. Either way, zombies didn't do that. Ghouls didn't do that. Wereanimals could do it, but why? They could just eat the evidence. Vampires could redress a corpse, but again, why? Also, hunks of flesh had been bitten off of the body. Vampires didn't eat flesh; they couldn't digest it. People could have done it, but even when you had humans who bit flesh off bodies, it would be a few bites. I counted at least ten bite marks. I couldn't be certain, but it looked like at least two distinct bite marks, so two different monsters. Was it the two that had attacked the people in the morgue? The worst was the face; it wasn't there anymore. I'd need to look closer to be sure, but it looked like they'd bitten off everything that made a face a face. Disfiguring didn't begin to cover what they'd done to him. The techs would be here with floodlights soon, so I'd been told. We'd have enough light that we wouldn't be able to unsee anything.

I'd made Nicky take Nathaniel to sit where he couldn't see it, though I wasn't willing for him to be far enough away from me for the smell not to reach him. For all I knew it told him more things than my eyes told me. I'd compare notes later when he could talk again. Right now, I just didn't want my boyfriend to see the really bad stuff I had to see on the job. Nicky had agreed only if Ares stayed beside me. I didn't argue. Ares was a combat veteran; either he'd seen as bad, or worse, or he'd take it and not bitch. Make all the jokes you want about the Marines, but they won't pussy out. I like that in a person.

He stood at my left, because Deputy Al was to my right. Ares and he were the same height, but where Al looked like he'd been stretched too thin for his body, Ares wore it well. He was thin-framed, too, but he'd put on enough muscle so that he just looked tall, lithe, and strong. His brown eyes had gone empty. I would have said he was wearing his cop face, but he'd never been a cop. Was there a Marine face?

A lot of the police and rangers had taken any job that would keep them at the periphery of the crime scene and farther from the body. There'd damn near been a stampede to go back and tell their respective branches and see if there were other duties that needed them. I didn't blame them, but I kept track of who couldn't take it, a little mental list of tough enough, or not.

'Oh, my God,' one of the younger police officers said in a breathy voice.

I glanced at him. Al put his flashlight on his face. 'You okay, Bush?'

I said, 'Go over there,' and pointed.

He looked at me, his eyes bulging a little, throat convulsing. I grabbed him and turned him the other way. 'Don't you fucking throw up on my crime scene! Go!'

He stumbled toward the dark edge of the trees but started throwing up before he made it.

'How did you know?' Al asked.

'I see a lot of bad stuff,' I said.

Someone else started throwing up on the other side of the clearing. Crap. The sharp smell of vomit joined with the smell of drying blood. The body had been fresh enough that it hadn't really smelled that bad. We had two more officers throw up in the woods.

I heard Al swallow convulsively.

'You okay?' I asked.

He nodded, but I watched him struggle. There was something about other people throwing up that can bring it on. Once I'd have been puking my guts up, too, but that had been years ago. I didn't throw up at crime scenes anymore.

Horton came up on the other side of Al. '*Your* crime scene?' he said.

'You've got preternatural shit killing people and I'm from the preternatural crimes branch.'

'We didn't invite the Feds in,' Horton said.

'No,' I said, 'you didn't.' I was suddenly tired.

'I think it's our crime scene until we say otherwise.'

'Fine, knock yourself out.'

He frowned at me. 'You know, you are not the hardass that some of the other staties said.'

'I'd rather get back to Micah and see how his dad is doing than stand here and have a pissing contest over the body.'

'Yeah, sorry again about Sheriff Callahan.'

'Me, too,' I said.

Travers yelled at me across the clearing. 'You're supposed to be some hotshot expert. What killed Crawford, and where the fuck is Little Henry?'

I looked at the big man where he stood in the near dark, hands in fists at his side. He was trying to be enraged, but there was a flinching around his eyes that said the anger might be hiding other emotions. I remembered him saying that he and the son were friends. He had to be looking at the mess on the ground and thinking about that being done to his friend.

I said softly to Al and Horton, 'Could this be your missing hiker?'

'He wasn't this tall,' Al said.

'Okay, how do we know which Crawford this is?'

'Little Henry has shoulder-length hair. His dad is almost bald.'

We all looked down at the corpse. Even through the blood it was obvious that the head was almost bald. 'Okay, this is Henry senior then.'

'Looks that way,' Horton said.

'Why did they eat his face?' Al asked, and it was the kind of question that senior police officers don't ask, because it's a rookie question; there is no *why* to the atrocities that the bad guys do. There may be motive, pathology, but it's not really a *why*, because the only real answer is always the same. Why did the bad guy do the really bad thing to this victim? Because he, they, it, could. That's the real and only true answer; all the rest is just lawyer and profiler talk.

'One of the corpses in the morgue had its face attacked,' I said.

'That was one bite. This is . . . this is not just one bite.' Al had asked a question that most cops stop asking by his age, but the understatement, that was all cop.

'No, it's not,' I said.

'I haven't seen all the bodies in the morgue,' Horton said.

I saw Travers moving this way out of the corner of my eye. Ares moved a little ahead of me, so the taller man would have to come through him. 'No, Ares,' I said.

He glanced at me, eyebrows raised. 'He's five inches taller than me and outweighs me by at least fifty pounds.'

'Yeah, and twenty of that fifty isn't muscle,' I said.

'But thirty of it is,' he said.

'Doesn't matter, you only get to protect me from bad guys, not other cops.'

He looked like he wanted to argue, but he stepped to one side and let me meet Travers on my own. 'Come on, hotshot, dazzle us.' He was half-shouting, but his voice was thick with unshed tears. He hadn't even let his eyes shine with them yet, but I could hear them in his voice. He was fighting so hard not to cry, and anger could help you do that. It had been my coping method of choice for years.

'He wasn't killed here,' I said, voice calm.

'Yeah, there's not enough blood. This is their dump site. Tell me something I don't know.'

'Is Little Henry as big as his dad?'

'Yeah, it's one of the reasons we were friends, because we were both big guys. We were either going to hate each other or be friends. We were friends.'

'Al said that they called out, said they'd found something, and then nothing.'

'Yeah, I was there; why are you telling me shit I already know!' He yelled it at me. I just let the rage wash over me. This was the father of his good friend, who was still missing. I'd cut him slack.

'Did you hear fighting, shouts, cry for help?'

He shook his head. 'No, nothing.'

'Were they trained fighters?'

'Henry was a recon Marine and he worked out at the gym. He was the one who taught Little Henry and me to box. Little Henry was special forces.'

'Two big men – six-five.'

'Little Henry was taller – six-seven.'

'Okay, two very big guys, both trained to fight. There's no person, or zombie, that I know of that could take them both out so quick that neither had time to shout for help or shout a warning.'

Travers seemed to think about it. 'No, they wouldn't go quiet. They'd both fight. Little Henry was different when he got out of the military. He never talked about it, but something bad happened and he didn't like people so much. I think that's why he went into business with his dad. Fewer people and a lot of time out here; they both loved being out in the woods, on the mountain.' I wondered if he realized he'd used past tense for his friend; probably not.

'Then why did they go with the monsters?' I asked.

'I don't know!' He yelled it at me and came close enough to loom over me. At six-five to my five-three he loomed good, but I'd been the smallest kid in class all my life; I was used to being loomed over.

I did have my hands loose to my sides and had put one foot ahead of the other. It wasn't enough of a stance to give Travers a reason to up the violence, but I was ready to move if I had to. He was a cop, but he was also a big guy, and he was processing the loss of the man on the ground and his missing friend. Grief fucks with you; it makes you do things you wouldn't normally do, like take a swing at a coworker.

Horton stepped up. 'Officer Travers, let's take a walk.'

'No, Blake is supposed to be the monster expert. She hasn't told us anything. She's asked questions, fucking questions, and Henry's lying there . . . like that.' He turned away and started walking so we wouldn't see the tears.

Horton started to follow him, but Al said, 'Let him go.' Horton looked like he'd argue and go after him, but in the end he let the older man's advice stand.

Ares asked, 'How did you know he wouldn't take a swing at you?'

'I didn't,' I said.

Ares raised eyebrows at me again and gave me the look the comment deserved. 'You know, it's hard to protect you if you order me off every time large, angry men start getting up in your face.'

'This is the first time I've done that.'

'To me, but I've heard stories from the other guards who do your detail more.'

'Yeah, I'm a pain in the ass.'

'No, well, yes.' He smiled, shook his head, frowned. 'Anyway, you are a bad mark.'

'Yeah, I am.'

'This has to be our killer zombies,' Al said.

'Why?' I asked.

'Because if it's not the zombies that hurt the sheriff we've got a whole new problem, and I just can't believe we have two different kinds of flesh-eating monsters up here. It's an isolated area. Don't you need a population to turn into your monsters?'

'If they started out human, yes.'

'Are you saying that something nonhuman, as in never been human, did this?'

'No.'

'Then what are you saying?'

'I'm saying that I don't know what did this. If it's a zombie it's like nothing I've ever seen. The only flesh eater I ever personally took out ate bodies almost completely, much messier and more complete eating than this, more like shapeshifter kills. This looks almost human.'

'You mean a person did this?' Horton asked.

I shrugged. 'I mean people.'

'People did not do this, only monsters could do this,' Al said.

'You know that human rapists and serial killers bite chunks out of people sometimes.'

'Yes, a bite mark, maybe two, but not like this.'

'Some serial killers take enough to cook later,' I said.

'Yes, but not one bite at a time. When they cook their victims' flesh they butcher the meat off the body.'

'You've done your research, so you know that human beings do horrible shit to each other all the time.'

'I'm not saying people couldn't do this; I'm saying I don't think they did.'

'Why, because you don't want it to be people?'

'No, because human beings couldn't make the Crawfords leave the search for the hikers and go off with them. It has to be something supernatural to have taken them totally quietly and so fast. There were members of the search party who were only yards away from them, Marshal. I don't believe that human beings could have done that.'

I nodded. 'Zombies are just walking corpses, Deputy. They have no special abilities other than being harder to kill, and some flesh eaters are super-fast, and they're all stronger than human-normal.'

'Why is that?' Horton asked.

'Why is what?'

'Why are all the human undead stronger than living humans? I mean, they start out as us; why does being undead make them stronger than we are?'

It was an excellent question. 'Great question, wish I had a great answer, but I honestly don't know. They just all are.'

'I don't mean to complain, but you are supposed to be the expert and so far I'm not hearing a lot of expertise.'

'The attack isn't like anything I've seen. It's not even like the bodies in the morgue, except for the bite marks, but even there it's not the same. Those bodies had one bite apiece. They both died of an infection, a weird infection, but still that's what killed them. Henry Crawford didn't die of a disease, not even a supernatural one. I can tell you it wasn't shapeshifters because the bite marks aren't animal teeth; they look human. A flesh-eating zombie could take chunks, but they eat the body, too. I'm seeing at least two different bite radiuses, and that's without getting down close to the bites. Flesh-eating zombies are solitary. They don't work together.'

'Don't ghouls run in packs?' Horton asked.

I nodded. 'Yeah, but they are tied to the cemetery that contains their graves. It's very rare for them to be able to go outside those boundaries and usually requires some sort of necromancy, or spell, something.'

'But if ghouls could travel out this far, could they do this?' Al asked it.

I looked back at the body and thought about it. 'They could, but again, they usually eat the body. It's food for them just like for the flesh eater. This wasn't done for food.'

'How do you know that?' Al asked.

'Because they didn't eat enough of him.'

'What if they ate the other Henry and just tortured Henry senior?' Horton asked.

I thought about it and finally said, 'Ghouls have no gaze or mind control of any kind. How did they kidnap or lure away the two men without giving them time to call out?'

'Vampires have mind control,' Horton said.

'Yes, but they don't eat flesh. At a glance I don't see fangs, just human teeth marks, or humanlike teeth.'

'What has humanlike teeth and could do this?'

I sighed, and it was too deep a breath. I could smell that the body was already beginning to smell bad, like meat that's gone past its expiration date. I shouldn't have been able to smell it that strongly yet. Had my bonding with Nathaniel's leopard given me better sensitivity to smells? I sort of hoped not, because I wasn't sure it would be an asset in my job.

'There are a lot of things that are more folklore-based that have humanlike teeth and attack people,' Horton suggested.

'Like what?' Al asked.

I shook my head. 'Honestly, this doesn't remind me of anything in myth or folklore. If I think of something that would kill like this I'll share, but nothing springs to mind. I'm sorry, I really am, and I'm not used to coming up this empty.'

'You helped us find Henry, that's something,' Al said.

Horton agreed. He looked past me and said, 'Your other men are coming this way. Maybe it's time for you to go check on Mike and his family?'

Nicky was coming this way with Nathaniel gliding at his side, the leash almost dragging the ground between them. Ares said, 'I motioned Nicky over, Anita.'

'Why?' I asked.

'Because I think I see tracks, but if I'm concentrating on reading the ground I can't guard you.'

'There are tracks all over here,' Horton said.

'It's a popular camping and hiking area,' Al added.

'Barefoot hiking?' Ares asked.

The two men looked at each other.

Nicky and Nathaniel had caught up with us. Ares explained what he was doing and Nicky went on alert, watching out into the darkened woods. Ares knelt down, resting on the balls of his feet, staring intently at the ground near us. He pulled a flashlight from one of the pockets on his vest. He shone it on the ground and began to work his way to the edge of the woods on the far left side of the clearing, if you were facing away from the body. He walked slowly, going to the crowd periodically as he moved back toward us.

'The barefoot print is paired with one that looks like boots. The impression is heavier coming into the clearing and lighter going out.'

'You think they carried his body in,' I said.

'Yes.'

'Can you track them back?' Horton asked.

'The prints are less clear in the trees. There's more dirt here. I can tell you the direction they came and went, but it's going to be almost impossible on this surface in the dark. And if the other Crawford is alive now, he may not be by dawn.'

'If you have a suggestion, now's the time to say it, Ares,' I said.

'Nathaniel might be able to pick up the scent of one of the people who carried the body in. If he can trace them back that way, then I may be able to help track, too.'

'I don't want Nathaniel to get up close with the body.'

'Why, so he won't get spooked?'

I gave a small shrug.

The leopard gave a low, coughing sound.

I looked at him, and those pale eyes met mine, so serious, and though I knew the mind inside there wasn't exactly human, the look in the eyes was not a cat's look. There was too much intelligence, too much . . . personality.

'What do you want to do?' I asked.

His answer was to pad toward the body, delicately, as if he were afraid to smear the evidence. He crouched close to the body and snarled. He rose up and looked . . . puzzled, as if he didn't understand what he was scenting.

'What's wrong, Nathaniel?'

He looked at me mutely. I could have dropped shields and felt more of what he was feeling, but after last time I wasn't sure it was a good idea.

'Are you going to ask him if Timmy is down the well?' Horton asked.

I frowned at him.

'It's just you don't seem to be able to understand him much better than I can.'

'I understood him fine earlier, but the psychic contact was too intense; that's why we ran ahead like we did. I need more control than that.'

'If you can track this monster back to its lair, then we need you to stay close to us,' Al said. 'No racing ahead, okay?'

'I don't know what did this, but I do know that I don't want to take Nathaniel into the middle of it without as much police backup as I can get.'

Al smiled. 'Fair enough. Just don't get carried away with all the psychic stuff again.'

'I'll do my best,' I said. I turned to Nathaniel. 'Do you have the scent?'

His answer was to walk away from Nicky and me to stand in front of Ares. He gazed up at the tall, blond man. I knew they had no psychic connection, but Ares seemed to understand, because he said, 'He wants me to take his leash so we can track together.'

'You with your eyes and him with his nose,' I said.

Ares nodded.

I sighed and went to Nicky. I took the leash from him and then I knelt in front of the big leopard. I held his face between my hands and gave serious eye contact, trying to 'see' Nathaniel in there.

'I love you,' I whispered.

He purred and rubbed along the side of my face so hard it almost tipped me over. I threw my arms around his furred neck and hugged him, then pulled away and said, 'Be careful.'

He rubbed into my shoulder and wound himself around my kneeling body in an almost perfect circle, purring the whole time. I think it was leopard for *I'll be careful, you be careful, too, and I love you*, or maybe he was just scent-marking me. Calling 'mine' so that all the other wereanimals would know, or maybe it was all the above?

I gave the leash to Ares.

'Thank you for trusting me.'

'I trust you both,' I said.

He smiled and then turned around to lead Nathaniel to the edge of the clearing where he had lost the tracks. Nathaniel crouched, sniffing the ground, pulling his lips back so he could 'taste' the smell, too. Nicky put his hand on my shoulder. 'Nathaniel can do this, Anita.'

I nodded, because I didn't trust my voice.

Nathaniel snarled again and then moved purposefully into the trees. 'I think he's got it,' I said. I moved forward with Nicky at my side. Al and Horton followed us, and most of the other police. They'd leave only enough people behind to secure the crime scene; the rest would go with us hoping to have a Crawford to rescue instead of bury.

I prayed that we'd get there in time and that Nathaniel didn't get hurt. Ares, Nicky, and I took our chances with our jobs. Nathaniel stripped for a living. The worst danger he routinely faced was overzealous fans trying to rip his G-string on stage or stalk him off stage. Helping us hunt the things that had eaten Henry Crawford's face off was so not in my sweetie's job description.

26

The leopard tracked, and Ares found actual tracks periodically, or branches broken, or moss disturbed. He was all very Indian scout, which was probably the *scout* part of *scout sniper*, but it was all impressive and surreal in the dark on the mountain with the big leopard padding at his side. We moved slowly, because Ares was trying to gauge how many zombies, or people, or whatever, lay ahead of us. I just wanted it over. The tension between my shoulder blades was tight and tighter. I'd suggested to Al that we call for SWAT, but we were in the middle of nowhere, and technically the small municipality had no SWAT. Unofficially they could call Boulder for help, or even the FBI hostage rescue team (HRT), but in reality we were it.

Was it Nathaniel being here like this that was making me nervous? Maybe, but I didn't like not knowing what had killed Crawford senior. If it was just humans gone crazy, then we'd be fine, but what if it was something else? The only flesh-eating zombie that I'd had to track down before had damn near killed me. But it had been like a disorganized killer, slaughtering wildly and eating more of the bodies. The bites on Crawford's body had been neat compared to that. How had they kidnapped the two men within yards of the rest? We had too many questions and no answers, but if we could save the son . . . if we could get there in time to save Little Henry . . .

I stumbled, and Nicky had to catch my arm or I'd have fallen.

'You okay?' he whispered.

I shook my head. 'We don't have enough information. I don't know what we're tracking.'

He kept his hand on my arm and leaned in to whisper. 'If Nathaniel weren't involved you'd be fine.'

I looked ahead of us to see Ares' blond head almost ghostlike above the dark leather of his coat. The leopard was like a thicker piece of the shadows under the trees as it moved at his side. 'It's not just Nathaniel.'

'Then what is it?' he asked. He was leaned over me, close enough to kiss, and I realized I wanted to, that it would have made me feel better. Touching any of the animals that were part of my list of beasts was like touching a great big living comfort object, but I didn't usually get this distracted in the middle of potential action. What was bothering me? Was it just Nathaniel being here? Was I so worried about him that it made a coward of me? No, the feeling between my shoulder blades was saying, *It's more than that.*

I stopped walking and just stared up at Nicky. 'Why leave the body on display? Why not hide it?'

'They wanted us to find it,' he said.

'Why take two men and kill one of them so quickly?'

'They may both be dead, Anita.'

'I know that, but if they wanted us to find the body, why? What did it gain them?'

'Zombies don't plan things.'

'I never said this was zombies. What did it gain them?'

'We're following them,' he said.

'Or they're leading us.'

'They couldn't plan on us having Nathaniel or Ares with us.'

'I've used shapeshifters to track killers before and it made the news.'

'You're saying it's a trap.'

'Maybe, or I'm overthinking it because of Nathaniel.'

'Don't doubt yourself; what does your gut tell you?'

'The tightness between my shoulder blades tells me they're leading us where they want us to go.'

'If you're right?'

'It's a trap.'

'If you're wrong?'

'Then I could cost Little Henry his life.' I looked up and couldn't see Ares and Nathaniel anymore; that was unacceptable. I started to move, half-jogging through the trees, falling back into the woodcraft I'd learned as a child in the country. You let go of trying to see everything the way you did in daylight, and you sort of felt the trees, felt the ground. There was no undergrowth in these high pine forests; it was so much easier to run through them than it would have been in the eastern woods. I ran, half crouched over to avoid limbs. Nicky stayed at my side, though I wasn't sure how the bigger man was missing the lower limbs, but it didn't matter. We could live with some scrapes and bruises. I wasn't sure I could live if something happened to Nathaniel.

The tightness in my shoulders eased with the run, and that let me know that I was doing the right thing. Horton saw us running and slowed to ask, 'What's wrong?'

I didn't have time to stop and explain. I needed to see Nathaniel and Ares. I needed them in my line of sight; I'd worry about everything else later. The two of them must have started their own run to be this far ahead. Damn it!

The first scream echoed on the thin mountain air. I ran faster. Nicky pulled ahead of me; the nine inches of extra height meant I couldn't keep up. He slowed down, and I said, 'Protect Nathaniel, go!'

He was my Bride; he did what I told him to do, because he had to. I was left alone in the dark running as fast as I could toward the screams of men. The leopard's snarling scream cut through the yells from human throats. Fear tore through me in a burst of adrenaline and I ran faster.

27

I swung the AR around on its tactical strap and kept running. My boots jarred against the ground, branches slapping at me, my chest struggling to breathe past my heartbeat and the thin air; all I could hear was the thundering of my blood in my head. I knew there were other police in the woods running in the same direction, trying to get there to back up the ones who'd gone ahead, but the other officers were just bleeps on my peripheral radar. I spared a second to know that if something wanted to jump me now I'd never hear it coming. I caught flashes of muzzle flare through the thinning trees. I found speed I didn't know I had, willed myself faster, until my breath strangled in my throat and the world ran with spots of white, and I knew if I didn't slow down soon I might pass out in the thin air. I forced myself to slow enough that I could breathe. The starbursts were almost gone from my vision when I saw figures through the tall trunks of the trees. I saw the Boulder PD uniform and a zombie behind him. He was firing at one in front of him. He didn't see the one behind him.

I was farther than I actually wanted to shoot, but he could be dead before I got within easy shooting range. I steadied my shoulder against the bare trunk of a tree, tucked the AR to my shoulder, set my cheek against the stock, tried to force my body to be still enough to make the shot, but the best I could do was hold my breath. My body was one big pulse from the running, but we were out of time. I sighted on the zombie's head and squeezed the trigger. Most of the head vanished in a gout of blood and heavier things. If it had been human it would have been a kill shot, but it wasn't human. The officer startled and turned so he could face both zombies. I pushed away from the tree and was running again, as the headless zombie stopped staggering and started walking toward him again. Headless didn't mean shit to zombies. A finger would keep inching along until you burned it.

I cleared the trees with the AR snugged to my shoulder, a cheek wield between me and the stock, searching the clearing for targets. I'd already fallen into that bent-legged crouching walk that SWAT had taught me back home. It looked awkward, but it moved you along smoother and steadier for shooting than normal walking.

The clearing was bathed in starlight with the spiraling arcs of flashlights everywhere, as officers tried to keep light on their targets. Zombies were everywhere. There was one mound of them crouched on the ground near the only building visible near the middle of the clearing. The zombies were eating someone, I just couldn't see who. I trusted Ares and Nicky, and Nathaniel's leopard, not to end up as food this quickly. I had to believe that and fight my way around to the side of the clearing I couldn't see past the building, because they had to be there. I had incendiary devices on me that would burn up zombies; trouble was, they'd do the same to people. There was no clear way to use anything but the guns.

The zombie I'd beheaded jumped onto the back of the officer. The zombie was twice his size and drove him to his knees. The officer yelled out. He kept firing point-blank at the other zombie looming in front of him. Unfortunately, he was firing into the middle body mass. If it had been a vampire he might have damaged the heart enough to 'kill' it, but the bullets weren't doing more than make the zombie stumble. The zombie on his back was ramming its bloody stump into the back of the officer's head as if it didn't realize it didn't have a mouth anymore, and was still trying to eat him. The officer was screaming as the zombie that still had a mouth leaned down, as his gun clicked empty.

I yelled, 'Guard your eyes!' but I didn't have time to wait and make sure he heard me. I fired the AR almost point-blank into its head. It exploded in a shower of blood, brains, and bone fragments.

The officer was on all fours, blood covering his hair, and he was yelling, 'Get it off of me! Get it off!'

I wasn't sure if he was talking about the brains and blood or the zombie, but I went for the zombie. I put the AR against the zombie's shoulder where the arm attaches to the torso and fired. It blew the arm off and rocked the zombie backward. The officer was able to scramble free of it and almost fell into the second zombie as it crawled around on the ground. It seemed more disoriented about the whole decapitation thing than the first one.

The officer was shoving at the air as if the zombies were spiders and he didn't want them to touch him. I grabbed his arm and helped him get to his feet and move out from between the two zombies. Half his face was covered in zombie blood, but I still recognized him as Officer Bush, who had thrown up first at the crime scene. His eyes were huge, his breathing so rapid he was going to hyperventilate if he didn't stop. I had to find my men, but damn it.

'Bush, Bush, can you hear me?' I shook him until I was sure he was actually focused on me. 'Slow your breathing down, Officer Bush.'

He nodded a little too rapidly.'

'Are you out of ammo?' I asked.

'It didn't do any good. It didn't stop them.'

'Shoot the head,' I said.

'You shot their heads off and they didn't die. They're supposed to die if you take their heads.'

'Only in the movies,' I said.

He clutched at my arm. 'How do we kill them?'

'You can't,' I said.

'What do we do then?'

'Do you have ammo left?'

He nodded, his breathing even, and I watched his eyes fill back up with him and push back the fear. He popped out his empty magazine, reached for his equipment belt and a new magazine. He did the transfer automatically and smoothly. He was going to be okay.

'Shoot their heads, take the mouth out, and then they can't bite.' In my head I added, *so they can't give anyone else the rotting infection.*

'But it still jumped me,' he said.

'Sometimes they do that,' I said. 'Stay with me. Shoot any zombies in the face until they don't have a mouth.'

He nodded, though his face was a bloody mask. He had the gun held upright in both hands; his hands were almost steady, his eyes were good.

'Come on, Bush, let's do this.'

'Right behind you, Marshal Blake.'

'I know you are, Bush. I know you are.' We moved forward and started shooting zombies. He didn't waste any ammo on anything but the faces. Fast learner; good, maybe he'd live to see dawn.

28

We dragged Ranger Becker out from under a mound of zombies. She'd shot off their faces with a shotgun and wasn't bitten as far as I could tell. Her partner was dead, his throat ripped out, eyes glazed even by starlight. The head of the zombie who'd killed him was still eating his throat, even though the bits of him were falling straight out of the neck, because the body was gone, lost somewhere in the clearing. The neck had been shot through, spine severed, but that hadn't saved him.

She said, 'Pete!'

I turned her away from him. 'He's gone, move!' Bush helped me get her moving through the carnage of decapitated zombies and body parts. Any zombie that had made a kill was eating, and other zombies joined them, so in a way even dead they helped the other men. An eating zombie wasn't trying to kill anyone else. I'd never seen this many flesh eaters outside a cemetery. Where the hell had they come from?

I heard the leopard scream over the sound of gunfire and men screaming. It jolted through me as if I'd been shocked. I fought not to reach out to Nathaniel psychically, because it messed with the concentration of both of us for just a second. I blew the head off another zombie. I'd traded for my shotgun, putting the AR back to where it hung in the MOLLE straps on my vest. I didn't have time to be distracted, and maybe he didn't either. I had to trust Ares and Nicky to keep him safe until I could get to them, as they trusted me to keep myself safe.

We had a circle of officers with us now, all of us facing outward, guarding our share of the field. We finally fought our way around the edge of the building, and I could see my men with their backs against the bare rock of the mountain that loomed above them. Nicky and Ares were shooting smoothly. The big leopard was crouched at their feet, snarling. Al, Trooper Horton, and Travers were with them, though one of Travers's arms was hanging useless and bloody. It seemed to be the only injury that they had. Seeing them all standing there loosened the tightness in my chest that I hadn't let myself feel; the relief made me stumble for a second. I shook it off and kept shooting my way toward them.

Nicky blew the head off of a zombie, and the leopard brought down the body and tore it apart. The three humans were way too calm about Nathaniel's leopard tearing up zombies at their feet; it showed that the division of labor had been this way for a few minutes. Long enough for them all to accept that it worked; funny what seems okay in the middle of a fight.

We waded into the zombies around them. We were winning, and then a cold wind blew across my skin. I had time to yell, 'Vampires!'

Bush asked, 'Where?'

The door to the building opened and it wasn't vampires, it was more zombies, and Little Henry Crawford towering above them.

29

Little Henry was nude. I did a quick glance to see if he'd been bitten, but the only mark on him was dried blood all over his groin. His hair fell unbound around his shoulders; his face was traced with the dark edge of beard and mustache. I knew it was called a Vandyke beard, because Requiem, one of our vampires, had told me. Someone shone their flashlight on Little Henry's face and I had the impression that he was handsome and that his brown eyes were empty, as if there was no one home. Was he in shock? If the dried blood at his groin was all his, then he had a reason to be in shock.

The tallest zombie was barely six feet tall, so Henry looked like a movie-handsome island rising above a sea of rotted faces, except for that one part. It looked like they'd started eating there. At least two of the men said, 'Jesus.'

Travers called, 'Henry, Henry, it's me, Hank.'

Henry never even blinked.

Something was wrong, I just wasn't sure what.

The only movement was the crawling zombie parts scattered around the clearing, and then there was another shiver of vampire power, just a breath, not enough to kick the holy objects awake, and then the zombies moved in a blur of speed so that I knew the other police didn't see them. I had enough time to fire into the face of the one coming at me. I heard two other shots echo mine and knew it was Nicky and Ares. We fired and hit three of them, blowing their heads off just like the other zombies. They fell to the ground in three fountains of blood. It was too much blood for a zombie, closer to a person, or a vampire. I remembered that shiver of vampire power.

That left three of them to appear like magic in front of the police.

It wasn't mind tricks; vampires are just that fast. One grabbed Becker and she screamed, but she also shot it through the chest. Her shotgun sounded like an explosion that left my left ear ringing, but the vampire fell to the ground with a hole where its heart should have been. Totally worth it.

Guns exploded behind us, and I had to shove Bush to one side to see Ares on the ground with one of the rotting vampires on top of him. Nicky was there grabbing it barehanded, to pry it off Ares. Travers had the last one on top of him. Horton was trying to get a shot as Travers tried to grapple one-handed with it. Nathaniel's leopard slashed at the zombie's face, and it reared back from the man and screamed in pain. Zombies didn't feel pain.

Nathaniel slashed it across the chest and the vampire, because that's what it was, screamed again, flashing fangs, and stumbled over some of the zombie parts on the ground. It was a rotting vampire, which is damn rare in America, but it was still newly dead, or undead. Old vampires don't stumble like that.

Nicky pulled the vampire off Ares with an arm around its neck and one arm pinned behind its back. He was strong enough to brute-force the vampire back from Ares and hold him. Ares picked up his gun and pressed it to the vampire's chest, growling, 'Stop struggling!' I hoped he remembered that at point-blank range even the handgun would go through the vampire and into Nicky.

The vampire that had been on Travers raised a hand that was rotted enough for bone to gleam in the flashlights. It touched its face, and only then did I realize that it was a woman. She turned and held out her hand toward . . . me? It was a beseeching gesture, but wasted on me.

Bush said, 'Don't hurt her anymore.'

I looked at him and his face was growing slack, like Henry's. 'So beautiful,' he said staring at the rotting corpse.

I hit him in the face with the stock of my shotgun, and Becker put her shotgun to the back of my head. 'Can't you see how beautiful she is? We have to help her.' Her voice sounded dreamy, like she was half asleep. The gun was nice and solid against the back of my skull. If she pulled the trigger I was dead.

My cross flared into white-hot light, and so did all the other holy objects. The glow blazed so bright I was half-blinded by it, but the gun fell back from my head, and I heard Becker say, 'What the hell?'

I aimed at the rotting vampire, but she was gone. I stepped away from the officers and their holy objects, trying to see where the vampire had gone. I got a glimpse of her racing into the trees back the way we'd come. I started toward her, but Little Henry collapsed and I caught him without thinking about it. He was conscious and muttering, 'Beautiful, she's so beautiful.' Then he passed out, and I was suddenly holding the full body weight of someone who outweighed me by about two hundred pounds. Lucky I was stronger than I looked.

There was a cackling, growling sound that raised the hairs at the back of my neck. I glanced in the direction of the sound. Ares' body was a tangle of limbs and flowing fur, golden and spotted in the flashlights that were shining on him. I assumed he was shapeshifting so his wounds would heal. A spotted hyena the size of a pony stood shakily to its feet and then did that all-over body shake like a dog getting out of water. Then he raced across the clearing toward the trees.

I yelled, 'Ares, no!'

He kept running in a mile-eating lope, a blur of golden fur that vanished around the edge of the building. Then a second shadow streaked after him, and the black panther vanished, too.

'Nathaniel, no! Damn it!' I laid Little Henry in the waiting arms of the cops and started running after them. I pulled out my cuffs and handed them to Al. 'These are strong enough to hold the vampire.'

He took them. 'Can't we kill him?'

'We don't have a warrant of execution. If he dies before we have one, it's the same as any suspect dying in custody.'

Becker said, 'That thing doesn't have rights.'

I pulled the AR from the MOLLE straps and shoved the shotgun back into its place. I said, 'Yes, he does.' I ran toward the trees.

Al yelled, 'Don't go out there, Blake!'

Horton yelled, 'It could be a trap!'

I yelled back, 'I know!' Ares I might have left to his stupidity, but I couldn't leave my panther out there.

Nicky yelled after me, 'Anita, wait for me!'

I yelled, 'Catch up,' without looking back. I was well into the trees before Nicky fell in by my side. I ran full out back through the slapping branches of trees, the uneven ground, and that damn thin air. I heard the hyena give its unnerving call, and the panther shriek just after it. Fuck, fuck, fuck!

I promised myself that if Nathaniel went unhurt all night I would never, ever bring him to a crime scene again. The panther screamed again, and we ran until the world was just black blurs and the punishing slap of tree branches. I dropped my shields enough to sense him up ahead, and thought, *What the hell*, and dropped more of my shielding so I could reach out and try to sense the vampire. Sometimes I could, sometimes I couldn't, but tonight it was a could. I sensed her like cold fire up ahead near where Nathaniel's heat pulsed in my head, but there was something else. I sensed another vampire near them. There was a second vampire, and neither of the shapeshifters would know it before it was too late.

I found speed I didn't know I had and came up even with Nicky. He glanced at me and without a word sped up. I stumbled, but I stayed with him. I wasn't sure I was going to be able to breathe, let alone fight, when we got there, but by all that was holy I would get there.

30

My vision was spotted with gray-and-white starbursts, my breath stran-
gling in my throat; my chest was so tight I felt like I was having a
heart attack, but I could feel the vampires close. I saw the dull gold
of the hyena first, and then the blackness beside him moved and I
knew it was Nathaniel. The vampire was in front of them, standing
with her back to a huge, dark tree. They had run her down and bayed
her like a pair of hounds.

I slid to my knees in the pine litter, the AR snugged to my shoulder,
cheek resting against it as I fought to see through the exhaustion
miasma enough to aim. The world swam in streamers. Apparently,
my psychic abilities did not make me immune to altitude sickness.
If I hadn't had to threaten a vampire with a gun, I would have been
happy to throw up.

I felt the energy of the second vampire and tried to see where the
hell it was, but my ruined vision was barely able to keep track of
the one against the tree. 'There's a second vamp, I can feel it.' My voice
was breathless and panting, but Nicky heard and understood, because
he scanned the darkness under the trees for another figure.

'I don't see anything else,' he said.

'Nathaniel, Ares, do you smell another vampire?'

Nathaniel growled at the vampire in front of him but then raised
his head and scented the wind. Ares did the same. I kept most of what
I had left looking at the vampire, but had swimming glimpses of the
panther and hyena sniffing up into the air. The panther drew its lips
back from its teeth in a flehmen, to get as much scent as possible to
the Jacobson's organ in the roof of his mouth. He'd described it to me
as tasting the scent.

Nathaniel lowered his head and made a sneezing sound and shook his head. He was letting me know that he didn't smell a second vampire. So why did I still feel it?

The vampire stood up straight, pushing away from the tree. Her entire demeanor changed; even in the dim light she looked different. Her long, dark hair seemed fuller and moved in the breeze, except there was no breeze.

My cross burst into light like a white beacon. Now my night vision was ruined on top of the exhaustion miasma. Fuck. 'Cut the vampire powers crap, now!' I said.

'But it will be so much more fun if I don't.'

'Nicky, let her know I'm serious; aim just above her head,' I said.

'You usually do your own shooting,' he said.

'I can shoot her, but I don't trust myself to shoot close to her.'

He didn't argue, just did what I asked. The bullet buried into the tree above her head. The shot wasn't as loud as it could have been, a combination of my pulse in my ears and too much gunfire all night. My ears were a little dulled.

The hyena began to pace, and the leopard screamed. Their hearing was way more sensitive than mine. I couldn't imagine how loud everything had been to Nathaniel during the fight.

The vampire's scream was nice and loud. 'Please, please don't kill me!' She had her hands out in front of her as if to ward off a blow, or as if her spread hands would protect her from bullets. They so wouldn't.

My cross began to fade. 'Then stop trying to fuck with us,' I said, my voice still breathless. Stupid altitude.

There were flashlights swinging through the trees. Some of the police were running toward the dying glow of the cross and the sound of gunfire. I like that about cops; they run toward the problem, not away from it.

'One more vampire trick and I'm telling him to shoot you,' I said.

'Shoot to kill, or shoot to wound?' Nicky asked.

I'd rather he not have asked it out loud, but I guess it was an important difference and a misunderstanding would be bad. 'Wound. We can always kill her later, but once you kill someone, wounding seems a little pointless.'

'True,' he said. He kept his AR snugged against his shoulder, his face settled against the stock. He looked very natural, as if he could aim at her all night.

The police were up to us in a whirl of flashlights and noise. Some of them joined Nicky in aiming at the vampire. Others came to check on me.

Bush asked, 'You hurt, Marshal?'

'No,' I said.

'Then why are you sitting on the ground?' It was Becker.

'Too much running like hell in this altitude,' I said.

'You have altitude sickness?' she asked.

'Yeah.'

She gave a small laugh. 'Too funny, that the big, bad Anita Blake has altitude sickness.'

My vision had finally cleared. Yay for that. I got slowly to my feet, still feeling a little shaky. Bush started to reach out to steady my elbow, but then dropped his hand back. He was treating me like he'd treat any of his fellow officers, and I took that as the compliment it was.

I walked over to join everyone gathered around the vampire. They hadn't moved in and tried to cuff her. I realized that they were waiting for me to tell them it was safe. Then I realized that most of the officers in the night-dark woods had been part of the group that I had dragged out from under the killer zombies, or who had joined us when they fought free themselves, and saw that we seemed to have a plan. I had helped them, and now they were willing to chase vampires in the dark with me. Cool.

I stopped at Nathaniel's leopard and Ares' hyena so that I was framed between the two big animals. I trusted Nicky to keep his gun on the vampire. I let the AR hang free on its tactical strap and started to pet Nathaniel's dark fur and laid a hand on the hyena's back. He was taller than the leopard, big enough that I could have leaned my elbow on him like a light pole; he was a big damn beast.

The vampire looked at the two beasts with wide eyes. Someone had put a flashlight on her face like a spotlight so that we could see that one of her eyes was clear and brown and very alive, but the other had that white film that happens after death. Nathaniel's claws had sliced open her face from the edge of the dead eye to the jawline. The wound wasn't bleeding much, as if the flesh had really been dead so long there was no blood to find, but the wounds on her chest had bled a lot. Blood had soaked into the pink A-line dress so she looked like a macabre Valentine. One shoulder had rotted so you could see tendons and bone, but the other one was smooth and perfect. Why hadn't she used her vampire powers to make all of her body whole? Rotting vampires had two forms, human and rotting. Most of them spent the lion's share of their time looking as human and perfect as they could, though most seemed to enjoy the effect their other form had on their victims. This vampire wasn't enjoying it.

'Please, don't hurt me, again,' she said.

'You hurt Henry senior,' I said.

'Who?' she asked.

'The other man that you left up in the aspen grove.'

She looked away from me. 'I didn't want to hurt him. I'd finally gotten strong enough to cloud their minds and make them see me as beautiful. I wasn't done with the first man, but he made us hurt him. He made us hurt him in front of the other man.'

'You killed the father and made the son watch,' I said.

She looked back at me and the fear was naked in her face. 'I didn't want to.'

'No one held a gun to your head,' Becker said.

'Worse,' she whispered, 'so much worse.'

I could feel the other vampire. It was close. 'What's worse?' I asked.

'He is,' she whispered.

'Who is he?' I asked.

She shook her head and a piece of her hair fell down the side of her face. She grabbed at it and started to cry. 'God, maybe I should make you kill me. It's got to be better than being like this.'

'You should be able to make yourself human looking, at least at night,' I said.

She looked at me, the lock of her hair still in her hand. 'What did you say?'

I repeated it.

'If I were able to do that he would have told me. He would have rewarded me. I've done everything he asked.'

'Who would have rewarded you?' I asked again.

She looked up at something I couldn't see and said, 'No, please don't.' She looked at me and said, 'It's not me, don't kill me. He controls me and I can't refuse him.'

'What can't you refuse him?' I asked.

'Anything.' Her voice had gone distant, as if she were listening to something we couldn't hear. I felt the energy flare through her like a cold wind. Her face turned to us, and it was a different person in there looking out of her face. I knew only one vampire that could possess other vampires this completely.

'Traveller,' I whispered.

'No, guess again,' and it was the same voice, her voice, but the tone was so alien that I wanted to say *male*, though I wasn't sure why.

'Who are you?' I asked.

'Guess,' he said, and managed to make that one word hiss, and then my cross flared to life again, and so did every other holy object around us.

'Don't do it, we'll kill her!'

'I'll make more,' the voice said.

'More vampires?' I asked.

'More everything,' and it was an evil whine that didn't match the ruin of the woman he was using.

'Do not look her in the eyes!' I yelled.

'Someone always looks,' said the voice.

I held my cross out in front of me on the end of its chain. 'Leave her.'

'Are you trying to save her?' The voice sounded amused.

'She's got rights, and you possessing her counts as kidnapping and physical invasion.'

'She's mine, mine!'

'No, she's not,' I said, and started forward with the light of my cross held in front of me. Nicky was at my side, gun at the ready, just in case. The beasts growled and chattered at our sides.

'She's mine!' The voice screamed it at us.

'No, she is not!' I yelled back at him.

'Whose then? Who does she belong to, if not I who made her?'

'She belongs to herself,' I said.

The vampire had closed its eyes against the holy light. 'All vampires belong to someone, Anita Blake. If she's not mine, then whose?'

'Mine,' I said, and shoved the cross into her arm.

The vampire screamed, and then I saw it look at me through the white-hot glow, such hatred on its face, and then it was gone. I felt it go, felt it leave her, as she screamed high and hopeless.

I drew the cross back and she collapsed against the tree and slumped to the ground. No one tried to catch her, not even me. She blinked up at us as the holy objects faded like dying stars. She started to cry. 'I'm sorry, I'm so sorry.'

'I know,' I said.

'You chased him away. You chased him away, thank you, thank you, thank you.'

Did she think he was gone forever? That one holy-item burn had chased the monster out of her for good? The relief on her face said that was exactly what she believed. I didn't tell her different, because we needed to interrogate her and if she thought I'd rescued her she'd probably tell me anything I wanted to know. Besides, you shouldn't crush someone's hope if you haven't got anything to put in its place.

One of the other police had a set of the new cuffs, too. She let me put the cuffs on her with no protests. She just kept saying, 'Thank you, and I'm sorry, so sorry.'

Ares collapsed to the ground, still in hyena form, but his legs had gone out from under him. I shoved the vampire at the cop with the cuffs and said, 'Do not look her in the eyes.'

Nicky and Nathaniel, still in leopard form, were crouching by Ares. I went to them. 'What's wrong with him?'

Nicky raised his hand up to the flashlights. His hand was covered in blood that had strands of yellow in it. The smell hit me next. I'd smelled it at the hospital. Shit. I dropped to my knees beside the hyena. 'No,' I said, 'damn it, no!'

The hyena shivered, convulsed, and then the fur melted away, as if his human body were something trapped in ice, revealed by the energy that spilled off him as his body shifted back. He should have been trapped in hyena form for at least four hours, maybe ten. You only changed back early if you were powerful enough to will it, or too hurt to hold form, or dead.

I searched his neck for a pulse, holding my own breath, as I waited to feel it against my fingers. There, there it was, he was alive. I yelled, 'Man down! Medic!'

31

Nicky had put pressure on the wound with his bare hands while we waited for Bush to bring the officer paramedic who was still back at the clearing. I'd shoved plastic gloves at Nicky.

'I can't catch anything from him, Anita.'

'Ares caught it,' I said.

He'd frowned at me, but he hadn't argued after that, just taken the gloves and held his now-gloved hands to the wound.

Nathaniel, still in leopard form, sniffed at the wound and hissed. I started taking off my vest.

Becker asked, 'What are you doing, Marshal?'

'I'm going to give him my shirt to use at the wound, but first I have to get the vest off.'

She was one of only a handful of officers who had stayed here in the woods to guard us in case something else bad showed up. Though I'd heard one cop say, 'We're safer with them.'

I think they meant the three of us.

I got the vest off and spilled it to the ground in a clank of weapons. I peeled off my T-shirt, folded it into quarters, and handed it to Nicky. He reached for it, the gloves dark with blood and streaked with the infection, though I wasn't sure that was what it was, not exactly. Had everyone bitten tonight caught this? The other bites had not looked like vampire bites. They'd been zombie, or human looking. Was this infection something that vampires and shapeshifters could catch? If it was, then it was something new.

I slid the vest back on my shoulders. It was rough with just the bra on, but it was better than not having the vest in case of stray bullets. Besides, it helped me carry my weapons. I used to hate the vests when the government first started making us wear them, but now it was just part of how I carried my stuff.

'Pretty bra,' someone said.

I looked up at the knot of officers around us. I didn't know who had said it, just one of the men, so not Becker. I debated on whether to get angry, but it was a nice bra, all lacy and black. 'Thanks,' I said, and fastened the vest back into place so I could put my jacket back on.

'Do the panties match?'

Crap, the fact that I hadn't been hostile to the first comment had encouraged him. I looked up and said, 'Who said that?'

They shifted uncomfortably, and then the other men stepped back to leave one younger officer standing by himself. He'd been stupid and they weren't going to protect him, not out here, not with people bleeding and dying.

The leopard leaned against me like a big dog. I think Nathaniel was trying to remind me not to kill our friends. I put an arm around him and petted the warmth and comfort of his fur. It did help lower my blood pressure. 'And you are Officer what?'

'Connors, Officer Connors.' He said it clear, no mumbling, and met my gaze steady.

'Okay, Officer Connors, the man bleeding and hurt from fighting beside you against flesh-eating zombies and vampires is my friend. You must have friends back at the clearing who are hurt, or worse, right?'

He nodded.

'Sorry, I didn't hear that, can you use your outside voice?' I said. It was almost a relief to be able to upset about something this small.

'Yes,' he said, and there was the tiniest edge of anger now.

'Then is speculating out loud about a female officer's underwear appropriate under these circumstances?'

'No,' he said, nice and clear this time.

'Good to know we agree on that,' I said.

Bush came jogging back with another officer in tow. He introduced him as Officer Perkins. 'I heard you yell *medic*, but . . . there's a lot of wounded.'

He went down on his knees beside Ares and looked down the nude length of his body. 'This was the hyena?' he'd asked.

'Yes.'

He'd triple-gloved before he signaled Nicky to move back. He shone the light on the side of Ares' neck and just shook his head. 'Travers has a wound like this in his chest. It's the same infection that got Sheriff Callahan.'

'Yes,' I said.

'The wound doesn't seem to be closing. I thought lycanthropes healed better than this.'

'Wounds made by other preternaturals heal slower,' I said.

'So, because it's a vampire bite it's not healing?' he asked.

'Yeah.'

The big leopard rubbed at me. I ran my hands through his fur. 'It's okay, Nathaniel.'

He pushed at me again, and I turned to look into his leopard eyes, but the look in the eyes wasn't animal. He was trying to tell me something. I dropped shields a little more, trying to 'see' what he wanted to share. I was suddenly overwhelmed with grayish images, the scent of the night, and the feel of my body against his, but . . . not the way a person thought of it, more like a . . . I shoved my shields back in place, holding on to his leopard form to keep from swaying. I'd caught glimpses of things, but it was like looking at a jigsaw puzzle that had been swirled around on the floor. You knew there was a picture, but it was just bright bits of color and shapes.

His energy poured over my skin, marching down my nerve endings like electric kisses. His fur flowed under my hands, and for the first time I held him as his human form pulled its way out of the fur and muscles of his leopard. The power of it shivered through my body so that I shuddered as his skin flowed smooth and fever-hot against me.

Becker exclaimed behind us, 'Oh, my God!'

I wondered if she said it from watching him shift form or because he was now crouched naked, hidden only by the fall of his unbound hair. She hadn't said anything when Ares changed form, so it was probably the whole nude-and-beautiful-man-who-wasn't-wounded-and-unconscious thing. It's just bad form to lust after the wounded, but Nathaniel wasn't wounded. He fit into the curve of my arm and body like he always did, as if he'd been meant to be there all along. As nice as it had been to cuddle his leopard, this was better, more comforting to me.

'I've never seen you change back to human this soon,' Nicky said from the other side of Ares and Officer Perkins.

'I've never tried to change back this soon,' Nathaniel said, and his voice was a little shaky.

I hugged him close, marveling at how warm he was, how silken his skin and hair. I buried my face in his hair the way you'd take a stiff drink to calm your nerves. I found the heavy leather of his collar still around his neck, though looser.

'You're supposed to pass out after you shift back,' Nicky said.

'In case I do pass out, Anita, remember the vampire that bit me in Tennessee?' he asked.

I'd known about rotting vampires, but the first time I knew that they could infect people with their bite was when one of them bit Nathaniel. He'd lain on a hotel bed screaming in pain and would have died if Asher and Damian hadn't drained the sickness out of his body, risking their own lives to do it. Asher had been strong enough to be okay, but Damian had nearly rotted to death. I'd saved him by letting him feed on me, and risked dying the same way, but since I'd asked Damian to save Nathaniel, I'd had to try. This was before Nathaniel was my animal to call and before Damian was my vampire servant. It all seemed so long ago and far away now. 'How could I forget?' I said, and hugged him tighter. It seemed unthinkable that once I hadn't loved him, once I had done everything I could to avoid being his lover, and now he was one of the most important people in my life.

'Ares has only one animal form, like I did back then; he's not going to be able to heal this any more than I could.'

I went still as we hugged. I raised my face up from his hair and met his eyes. 'Ares has only one form?'

'You didn't know?'

'He's a big, dominant, athletic guy; I thought that translated into two beast forms.'

'Not always.' This from Nicky.

'I'm not sure what you're talking about,' Perkins said, 'but I've got patients to finish prepping for the helicopter that's coming.'

'What about Ares?' I asked.

'I'll send him when the chopper comes back.'

'No,' Nathaniel said, 'he needs to get to the hospital as soon as possible.'

'Lycanthropes heal anything. There is only so much room in the helicopter that's coming. I cannot triage a lycanthrope ahead of injured humans.'

I looked at Nathaniel. 'You mean it will move just as fast in Ares as it did in you in Tennessee?'

'Probably.'

'See, you healed just fine,' Perkins said.

'I had help, and we don't have any of that kind of help with us,' Nathaniel said, and gave me a long, serious look. He meant we didn't have vampires with us, and even if we did, they'd need to be powerful enough to heal Ares without catching the rotting disease themselves. Asher had been strong enough, but Damian had almost died of it.

I turned back to Perkins. 'Trust me; this will kill him just like it's killing Officer Travers.'

'Lycanthropes can't get infections,' the paramedic said.

'Nathaniel is alive because we had extraordinary . . . healing help, but on his own without that help he would be dead now. It is the only infection I've seen that can be fatal to them. I swear to you that I am not lying to try to get my guy on your chopper. I saw the bodies in the morgue that had this, and a bite near any major artery can travel to organs you need to stay alive. If this gets to his brain or heart, then he'll die from it.'

'You don't know that,' Perkins said, 'and I do know that three of the men waiting for transport will be dead within two hours or less without more medical care than I can give them.'

'Take the brain or the heart of a wereanimal and they won't heal, they'll just die. If this infection rots either of those organs, then it's the same as blowing them out with a shotgun; they're gone either way.'

'They know how to treat it better now; it's not that fast-acting,' Perkins said.

'With treatment it's not, but I'm worried that the higher metabolism he has as a shifter may actually move it through his body faster than if he were human.'

Perkins gave me a narrow look. I fought the urge to yell at him. Nathaniel hugged me closer, trying to soothe me, so I wouldn't lose my temper. He was right. If I screamed at the nice paramedic he would ignore me, and Ares wouldn't get on the first chopper.

'Look, Marshal, we have two men who will die within the hour, and that's not counting Travers.'

'How many will fit on the chopper?' I asked.

'Six. The clearing is only big enough for a Black Hawk.'

'Then there's room for your two critical, plus Travers, and Ares, plus one more,' I said.

He looked grim, never a good sign. 'I don't mean to be harsh, but I have to triage on the basis of severity of injury and likelihood of recovery. If I accept that your friend here has the same thing Travers has, then that doesn't change my mind. My understanding is that they will have to try to cut away the infected flesh. We don't have a lycanthrope blood supply, especially not for AB-negative, which is what Nick said he was. That's the rarest blood type in this country; there's never enough of it.'

I didn't bother to ask how Nicky knew Ares' blood type. I'd ask later after we saved him. 'A shapeshifter can take human blood, it's just the other way around that can give someone lycanthropy,' I said.

'In most of the western states, even Colorado, the blood supply for lycanthropes and normal humans is strictly separate.'

'You're saying that even if we get him there they can't operate in time, because he'll need blood,' I said.

He nodded. 'I'm sorry, but yes.'

'What if you had a lycanthrope with O-negative blood type?'

'One person might be able to donate enough for a conservative operation, but what are the chances of finding a universal donor with lycanthropy?' Perkins said.

'I am.'

'You're O-negative and a lycanthrope?'

'I carry lycanthropy but don't shift form, so technically I'm not a lycanthrope.'

'It's not possible to carry and not shift.'

'So they keep telling me, but I failed my blood test three years ago and so far what you see is what you get.'

He blinked hard, frowning. 'If you are lying to me, Blake . . .'

'I swear to you I'm not. My blood work is on record with the Marshals Service.'

Perkins gave me another suspicious look.

Nicky called out, 'I hear the chopper.'

'I don't hear anything,' Perkins said.

'I don't either, but if Nicky says he hears it, we'll hear it soon.' I'd barely finished saying it when I heard the distant chop-chop-chop sound of the helicopter blades. They were distant but coming. 'I hear it,' I said.

'I still don't,' Perkins said. It was another couple of minutes before he heard it. Sometimes I didn't appreciate that I had super-hearing since I was usually surrounded by shapeshifters and vampires.

I said something I don't say often; I said, 'Please, don't let him die, not like this.'

He frowned at me. 'Damn it, fine, can Nick carry him back to the clearing?'

'Yes,' Nicky said.

'Follow me, and you're going to have to ride along, Blake. We'll have to put you in the helicopter equivalent of a jump seat, and only if the pilot says the weight distribution will tolerate your extra.'

'I'm small,' I said.

'You better pray you're small enough for everyone who needs to be on this chopper, plus one blood donor.'

Nicky picked up Ares easily and followed Perkins. Nathaniel took my left hand in his and spoke low. 'How's your phobia of flying doing?'

I stiffened, stopped walking, and almost stumbled. 'Motherfucker,' I said, softly, but with feeling.

'You didn't think about it, did you?'

'If I can save him, I'm going to,' I said.

He squeezed my hand and said, 'That's my girl.'

'Yes,' I said, 'I am.' We kissed gently as we walked, and the first tree limb caught in his hair. It wouldn't be the last. Becker actually took the ponytail holder out of her own hair and gave it to him so he could braid it. It also inadvertently exposed his body completely. Some good deeds do get rewarded.

32

Other good deeds, not so much. The inside of the Black Hawk wasn't that big. We had a pilot, copilot, room for three stretchers, and two small seats for the medics. One of the medics stayed behind to help Perkins with the wounded still on the ground. We put Travers and Ares stacked to one side and strapped a third wounded officer between the medic seats and the stacked stretchers. By the time everyone was secure it was crowded. Did I mention I'm also claustrophobic?

My view was the stretchers, so no seeing outside, which usually helps with the claustrophobia. I was strapped into the seat, though I had to adjust the AR and the shotgun to sit back in it. The vibration of the chopper beat through my body in a steady, punishing rhythm. The nausea that had hit in the woods after the run came back, and I was left breathing deep, even breaths, trying to control it. I also tried to pretend I wasn't in a whirling machine of death hundreds of feet in the air. There was a gasp that must have been a scream for me to hear it through the earphones and the noise of the blades. I looked up and found Ares trying to sit up. The chopper medic, who had just been introduced to me as Lawrence so I didn't know if it was his first or last name, unbuckled and tried to force Ares back down, but one flailing arm sent him crashing, and only me putting a hand against his back kept him from falling on the wounded man in the middle. Neither he nor Travers moved.

I called out, 'Ares, it's okay!'

Lawrence sat down in his chair, so I could see past him to Ares. His wide, frightened eyes turned and found me. I watched his face get calmer as I unbuckled and moved carefully so I wasn't standing on the third wounded man. I used the other stretchers as part of my handholds, but everyone else was unconscious so they didn't mind.

Lawrence spoke into my headphones. 'Can you calm him down so I can check his vitals?'

'Yes,' I said. The helicopter hit a little turbulence, and I didn't really have my helicopter legs yet. Ares grabbed at me, and I gave him my left hand to hold, our arms bent at the elbow like we were going to arm-wrestle. I felt a spasm that ran through his arm. He writhed on the stretcher, face grimacing in obvious pain. He was mouthing something, saying something, but I couldn't hear it through the headset. I took off one earpiece and bent closer.

'Something's wrong,' he said.

I turned so I could yell into his ear. 'You're hurt.'

'No, it's more, it's . . .' He writhed again, hand convulsing on mine until I almost had to tell him, *too tight*, but he loosened it on his own.

I touched his face, got him to look at me, and said, 'Medic needs to check you. You gotta let him do that, okay?'

His eyes rolled with the pain, but he said, 'Okay.'

I turned and motioned to Lawrence. I started to let go of Ares' hand, but he held on tight, as if he were afraid for me to let go, so I kept hold of him, just moving his arm back with me. It also meant he couldn't accidentally hit Lawrence with it again. If Lawrence needed me to sit down and give him more room, I would, but if it helped calm Ares and I could stay where I was, I'd do it.

Lawrence worked around me, but he'd barely touched him when Ares' body convulsed so violently that if I hadn't had his hand in mine his arm would have swung out again. I held on tighter and yelled next to his face, 'Ares, it's okay. He's helping you.'

'I just need to check you, no needles, nothing bad,' Lawrence said in a voice raised over the noise.

'No,' Ares said in a strangled voice.

'Let him do his job, Ares,' I said, bending over his face. From inches away I watched his eyes turn to hyena gold. The energy of his beast crawled up our joined hands and down my spine. 'No, don't you dare shift in here!'

'Can't help it . . . he wants me to shift.'

'Who wants you to?'

'Vampire, her master, it's . . . he can control my . . . beast.'

'Not through a bite he can't,' I said.

'Land,' he said, 'land, I can't hold on. He's . . . it's . . . calling me.'

'Not possible, not like this.'

'It's like the bite, the rot . . . it carries a piece of him with it. It's not just a disease, it's him . . . it's him.'

'Who?'

He screamed full-throated, wordless, and then he found his voice again. 'Hurts, God, it hurts!'

'Ares! Don't . . .'

He used our joined hands to pull me close and I was left looking at his face from inches away, upside down, as if I'd put his head in my lap. His hand was almost crushing mine. 'I won't be me when I shift. Do you understand? I won't be . . . me. He . . . will control. He will control . . . me.'

'Shit.' I whispered it, but my face must have let him know that I understood, because some tension went out of him. He trusted I'd take care of it. I only hoped I could.

Lawrence said, 'Does he mean what I think he means?'

'We land now,' I said.

Lawrence shook his head. 'We can't.'

'We have to get Ares out of here before he shifts.'

He hit the microphone and said, 'Is there any place to land now?'

The pilot's voice came over the headset. 'That's a negative.'

Ares convulsed again, and the energy of his beast raised the hair on my body. He growled, and the sound vibrated loud enough that Lawrence could hear it over all the other noises. He gave me wide eyes and got back on the headset. 'We've got a problem and we need to be on the ground ASAP.'

The copilot turned in his seat just in front of us and asked, 'What the hell was that?'

'Shapeshifter,' Lawrence said.

'Landing would be good,' I yelled.

'Negative, repeat negative, there is nowhere to bring us down safely,' the pilot said.

I got on the headset. 'Shapeshifter is about to lose his shit, we need him out of here before that.'

'We were assured the shapeshifter had control of himself, or we wouldn't have let him on our bird,' the copilot said.

'Normally he does, but trust me. You want him out of here before it happens.'

'We got no landing site for at least the next ten minutes. Can he hold it together for that long?'

'Ares,' I said.

He looked at me with his hyena eyes. His body convulsed and I almost had to cry uncle. He was going to crush my hand if he didn't stop.

'Ares, can you hear me?'

'Yes,' but his voice had that edge of growl to it.

'Ten minutes, hold on for ten minutes and then they'll land.'

'I don't think . . . not sure.'

'Hold on, we'll get you out of here, but you gotta hold on.'

He writhed again, and I had to pry my hand out of his, or he was going to break me. 'I'm sorry,' he said, and then he screamed again, but the scream ended in a gibbering howl.

Lawrence backed up and had only his little seat to go to. The pilot looked behind at us but spoke through the headset, because of the noise. 'What the hell was that?'

'We need to land,' I said.

'We got nothing for another seven minutes.'

Ares yelled, 'Anita!'

I moved back where he could see me more easily, but didn't offer my hand to hold. 'I'm here.'

'Shoot me.'

'What?'

'Shoot me, before I shift.' He writhed on the stretcher, and screamed in pain again, and then said, 'There's nowhere for you to run in here.'

'Seven minutes, just seven minutes, hold on.'

He screamed, and the gibbering call filled his throat. 'I will attack you. I will not be me . . . I can feel it. Oh, God! God! Shoot me!' He turned wild eyes to Lawrence, pointed at him. 'Shoot me!'

Lawrence shook his head. 'I'm here to save your ass, not kill it.'

'Anita!'

'I'm here, Ares.'

'Don't let him . . . use me . . . like this . . .' And he just started screaming over and over again as fast as he could draw breath. His body began to jerk and convulse. I could see the muscles and ligaments under his skin popping and moving in ways that they were never meant to move. He was fighting the change, which meant it was slower and a lot more painful. He was trying to give us time.

Lawrence asked, 'Does it always hurt this much?'

I shook my head. 'He's fighting it.'

'To give us time,' he said.

I nodded. 'Can you move the other men farther away from him?'

'To where?' he asked.

He was right. There was nowhere to go. Travers was trapped above Ares, and the third wounded man whose name I hadn't even caught was strapped in the middle of it all. Shit, shit, shit!

The screaming gave way to that skin-crawling gibbering, laughing sound. Fur flowed, bones shifted, and it was as if some giant hand crushed the human form and remade it by pulling it apart. I'd never seen anyone change like this, as if they were being dissected and put back together. It wasn't just clear liquid that ran out of Ares. Blood poured from his body and spattered across the inside of the chopper as he fought to hold on. They only bled like that when they fought the change. Blood was hitting the man on the floor of the chopper, and I had a moment to worry about the lycanthrope blood getting in his wounds and then we had other things to worry about.

Ares popped the straps that held his body down and tried to sit up, but there wasn't room with Travers above him. He rolled so his back was to us and the blankets they'd put on him and the shadows hid most of him. We could still see the muscles and bones of his body moving under the blanket like a nest of snakes. I heard the copilot on the radio yelling, 'Mayday Mayday Mayday!'

Lawrence strapped himself into the seat. I stayed standing, got a death grip on the edge of one of the stretchers, and used the other hand to unholster my Browning BDM. Yeah, the AR or the shotgun would be a surer kill, but they would also go through Ares and through the helicopter. The Browning would just shoot a hole in Ares. I didn't want to do that, but I'd had the air marshal training so I could carry on planes, and they'd covered helicopters. They didn't like being shot, even more than airplanes. No matter what the movies showed on screen, damage the rotor blades and it's coming down. You damage the motor and it's coming down. Planes could fly on only one engine, or glide with no engines for a while; once the blades stopped rotating, helicopters just crashed. If I was going to have to shoot Ares anyway, I'd just as soon not kill us all while I did it.

The Black Hawk shuddered and started down. The pilot yelled, 'I found a clearing, but it's gonna be tight. Strap in!'

I debated on sitting down and strapping in, but I wasn't sure I could shoot Ares before he took out the pilot and copilot. The space was that tight. I had assured them that he wouldn't lose it in the air, and I had been wrong, so I stood between them and what was lying on the stretcher in the dark. A low, evil growl trickled through the cabin.

I tightened my grip, braced my legs as best I could, and aimed into the shadowed pile that was Ares. The only comfort I had was that in hyena form Ares was too big to move well in the close space. What made it a nightmare for us made it harder for him, too, or that was what I told myself as I felt something hit the bottom of the copter.

Lawrence yelled, 'Treetops!'

Now that I knew what was happening, I heard and felt the trees hitting the bottom of the copter. I felt the pilot fighting to make a very tight landing. We could skim a few trees as long as the blades weren't compromised. We shuddered, and I could hold on with one hand, but I couldn't keep my feet. I fought to not fall onto the third wounded man and tried to be ready to aim at Ares if I had to. He rolled over and tried to spill out, but he was trapped for a second between Travers's weight on top of him and the frame of the stretcher below him. I had a second to see the werehyena like a pale furred nightmare pressed in the space. I was still half-fallen, only one hand keeping me from the floor, and every angle I had risked Travers just above him.

Lawrence yelled, but I didn't have time to look at him. I had to find a better angle. But the hyena pushed forward with all the power he had, cracking the stretcher underneath him and raising up Travers's stretcher, and the hyena scrambled free and went for Lawrence across from him. He'd gotten his gun out, because it fired before mine did. I got him in the chest, but I knew it wasn't a kill.

I heard Lawrence scream. I was left half-straddling the wounded man on the floor, pushing my gun into the furred body, and fired twice more, but I was just hitting midbody; I didn't have a kill! But apparently I'd irritated him, because he turned and came for me, his weight in the small space pinning me to the wounded man below. I saw the huge bloody jaws, the mad eyes, and I fired into that mouth, as two more guns sounded. I felt like someone had hit me in the side with a baseball bat hard enough to knock the breath out of me, but I knew if I didn't kill the thing on me I'd never get another breath.

An arm showed, and the hyena bit the hand, gun and all. Blood poured over my face, and there was screaming. There was a bump hard enough that it jarred, and we were on the ground. Someone fell into us, and the hyena pushed off me and tore into the man. I thought it was Lawrence, but someone opened the big door on his side, and wasn't that Lawrence, too—

I was trapped underneath the hyena's hindquarters; he was literally sitting on me. I emptied the Browning into what I could reach of him. Even if it wasn't a kill it should have hurt, crippled, but the next thing I knew he was pushing off me and gone.

I pulled myself to sitting and saw Lawrence collapsed in the doorway, his shoulder torn away so badly that it had pulled the jugular vein out with it. He was dead, or dying. I saw lights and a house. We'd landed in a fucking neighborhood and Ares was out there with families, kids – Fuck!

I looked back at the pilot and copilot, but the pilot was putting a tourniquet on the copilot. His hand had been the one torn away, his blood all over my face, mostly.

I made myself move, made myself get to the big door. I dropped the Browning and swung the AR around on its strap and looked for Ares. I didn't expect to see him, thought he'd be long gone, but he was too gone in bloodlust to pass up prey. There was a car in the driveway of the house with children white-faced at the windows, and a woman half-crouched, hair and clothing blown back from the helicopter's blades that were only now slowing, spinning slowly down. I wasn't sure she'd seen the big hyena, but the kids had. It was one of those crystalline moments when everything slows down. You have the illusion that you have all the time in the world. Individual details stand out like they are carved jewel-bright, hard-edged. I saw the children in the car start to scream. I saw the woman shielding her eyes from the dust and debris of the blades, as they slowed and stopped above me. I saw the hyena, his fur shining with blood, start to run toward the woman. I raised the AR to my shoulder, snugged it tight, hit the optics switch, and lit up the hyena's hindquarters. I fired and the 6.8 ammo turned the beast, took his back legs out from under him. He whirled and turned. He looked at me, and it wasn't an animal's look. He turned and started to run away from the woman, away from the children, toward the woods that edged the yard. If he got into the trees we'd lose him.

I used the side of the now-still chopper to steady me; I didn't still my breath, I stopped breathing. I heard Ares' voice in my head from the shooting range. He was a sniper. I did most of my shooting within twenty-five to fifty yards. The hyena was more than a hundred yards away and still moving, shot to hell and still moving well. A hundred, a hundred and fifty yards, it didn't matter, the head was there, I had it in my optics, just like he'd shown me. 'Lead the target, where's the wind.' I always had trouble with wind. I pulled the trigger.

The hyena somersaulted and fell into a pool of darkness on the edge of the woods. I had to know, had to be sure. I stumbled out of the Black Hawk. My side wasn't right, numb, and it seemed like it took a long time to cross the yard with the AR held at the ready at my shoulder. There was a spotlight sweeping over me, following me. I heard another helicopter, but I kept my eyes on the place where he'd fallen.

The pilot was beside me now, his own rifle at his shoulder. He said something, but I couldn't understand it. The spotlight stayed with us so that the harsh white light showed Ares lying in the grass. He was human again, but it looked like he'd been decapitated. Fingerprints, fingerprints would be the way they'd ID him, because it was too late for dental.

I stood over what was left of him and let the AR swing back on its strap. I dropped to my knees beside him. The pilot asked, 'Are you hurt?'

I shook my head and then I realized my side hurt. I put my hand down and came away with fresh blood. 'Fuck,' I said.

'You're hit,' he said.

'Yeah,' I said, 'I am.' I slid slowly to the grass and was on my back staring up at the second helicopter and its spotlight. It was a news chopper. We were going to be live on the local news. Fuck, again.

The pilot was back with the med kit. He was holding pressure on the wound low in my side. I was betting it was the copilot's bullet when he'd been shooting down at the hyena. Damn friendly fire.

I looked at the body just a few feet away. I looked at the man just a few feet away. I looked at Ares just a few feet away. I looked at what was left of Ares. I looked at what my bullet had done to him. He'd have been so impressed that I made the shot. He'd have been so proud that he'd finally taught me to read wind direction. I might have even let him believe I'd calculated the wind that fast, but I hadn't. The truth was I still couldn't read wind direction and make the change in a long shot, but I wouldn't have told him that. It was a guy thing, and for some reason that made me start to cry. I heard the distant *whoop-whoop* of ambulance sirens. The pilot pressed too hard, and I half rose up, saying, 'Ow, damn it,' but it was too much movement. The night swam in streamers of color and shadow, and when the darkness reached up to swallow the world I didn't fight it.

33

The quiet murmur of voices woke me. I tried to move my arm and something pulled. I opened my eyes and found an IV in my left arm. It was taped down to a board, which meant it wasn't the first time I'd tried to move the arm while I was unconscious. The monitor's light seemed brighter than it should have in the darkened room, but it beeped slow and steady by the bed with its metal rails.

'Oh, good, you're awake.' The nurse smiled down at me. Her voice was lower than usual for a nurse, and as if she'd read my thoughts she said, 'Your fiancé finally fell asleep on the couch. Poor boy.'

I looked where she was looking on the far side of the room and found there was a small table with two chairs, and a couch. Micah was asleep on it with a small pillow and a blanket that covered most of him. His face looked pale and his curls like a dark halo where they were escaping from his braid. He looked younger, more fragile lying there.

I whispered, 'How's his dad? Sheriff Callahan?' My voice sounded rough, and my throat was dry. Since I was getting fluids through the IV, it meant I'd been out a while.

'As good as can be expected,' she said, but busied herself with taking my pulse and shoved a thermometer under my tongue before she moved enough that I could see there was someone sitting in a chair by my bed. It was just as well I couldn't talk, because I would have yelled, 'Edward!'

His blond hair was still cut neat and short, as it had been the whole time I'd known him. His eyes were a pale blue, cold as winter skies, his expression almost empty right now, because it was just me looking at him, but he was sitting like his alter ego. He had one ankle on the opposite knee, showing off the rich blue of his jeans and the paler wear marks along the seams, and the cowboy boots with their scrollwork, brown on brown. A white cowboy hat sat on his knee; its brim was creased and folded just right by constant wear. It had aged to a nice ivory, in contrast to the white of his button-down shirt. The sleeves were rolled up over strong forearms; his marshal badge was on a lanyard around his neck, which meant he wasn't Edward right now; he was Ted Forrester, fellow U.S. Marshal attached to the Preternatural Branch. Ted was Clark Kent to Edward's Superman, or maybe supervillain. He was pretty much a full-time marshal now, but when I'd met him his Ted Forrester had been a legal vampire executioner just like me, but as Edward he'd been a very pricey assassin. He specialized in shapeshifters and vampires, because humans had become too easy a prey, and he was bored. I was still a little fuzzy on how much the government knew about Edward, as opposed to Ted, but it was on a case with Edward where I first heard the name Van Cleef and met some of the other people who'd trained, or were trained by, him. Edward would never talk about it much.

'Hey, Ted,' I said, and coughed to try to clear my voice.

He smiled, blue eyes shining and just suddenly a brighter blue. The nurse had turned to look at him, and his face had slipped instantly back into Ted's, but also he was smiling at me, because he'd seen it in my eyes that I would have yelled out the wrong name. 'Hey, back,' he said in a low but cheerful voice, his Ted voice. Edward, now you see him, now you don't. He'd become his Ted persona so strongly that he was engaged to a widow with two children. Donna knew some of what Ted did, but not all. I'd been wicked pissed at him for using her and her kids as part of his disguise until I realized that he really loved her and the kids. I didn't understand what he saw in Donna, but then he wasn't entirely happy with the loves of my life either, so we were even.

The nurse took out the thermometer and smiled down at me. 'No fever. The doctor may want to do one more X-ray before he lets you go, but other than that you seem to be doing exceptionally well. The healing abilities that lycanthropes possess never cease to amaze me.'

I could have argued that I wasn't technically one since I didn't change shape, but I let it go. It was beginning to feel a little like the lady protesting too much.

'Why an X-ray?' I asked.

'You had a crack in your pelvis.'

I gave her wide eyes, then frowned. 'I remember walking after I got shot.'

'You did, but it was a small crack and if the video is any indication, you were pumped up on adrenaline and shock. It helps the body not feel things until later.'

'Video?' I asked.

'You were all over the local news,' she said.

'National news,' Edward said, softly.

'I'll let Dr Cross know that you're awake.'

'Can you take out the IV?' I asked.

'Dr Cross will want to see you first.'

'Can I have water, or at least ice chips?'

'I'll check. My name's Becky; buzz if you need anything.' She pulled a curtain on metal rings closed and went out the door on the other side of it. We waited until the door hushed shut on the other side and then I said, 'How did you get here?'

'Airplane.'

'I mean, why? Who called you?'

'I called your phone until someone answered. They got me to Micah.'

'You saw the news footage,' I said.

He gave a small nod.

'And just like that you flew out?'

'You'd do the same for me,' he said.

I nodded. 'Yeah.'

'What I can't believe is that you didn't call me sooner.'

I frowned. 'Why?'

'You have a zombie apocalypse and you don't invite me.' He put his hand on the hat and shrugged at the same time; it was a Ted gesture and we were alone. I guess if you use cover long enough you begin to blur the lines. It was still a little unnerving to see Edward make Ted gestures instead of the other way around.

'I didn't know it was a zombie apocalypse until we were in it, and for the love of God do not say the phrase *zombie apocalypse* where the media can get hold of it.'

'Too late,' he said.

'Shit,' I said, softly but with feeling.

He nodded. 'But the big news was you killing the dangerous were-animal and saving a mother and her children.'

I looked away then, suddenly interested in my hands on the sheet. I could see the kids with their faces pressed against the car windows, the woman covering her face with her hands as the copter blades blew her hair across her face. I could see the huge hyena . . .

'I'm sorry about Ares. He was a good man in a fight.'

I nodded, taking the high praise for Ares from Edward. 'He was.'

'I'm sorrier that you had to be the one to do it.'

I sighed. 'Yeah, me, too.'

'One thing that the pilot and copilot don't seem clear on is what caused him to go apeshit. Ares had control of his beast, or he wouldn't have been one of your guards. What went wrong?'

'All he could say was that someone was taking him over, making him change.'

'He was bitten by the vampire that was possessed by the other vampire?'

'Yes.'

'The bite shouldn't have been enough to control a shapeshifter like that.'

'I know that.'

'So this is new to you, too?'

'If one of the other regular cops had come back and told me this story I'd have said they misunderstood, that maybe the infected bite drove him crazy with pain.'

'But you wouldn't have believed that one bite from basically a surrogate would be enough to give a master vampire power over someone like Ares.'

'For the level of control "he"' – I made quote marks with one hand – 'had over Ares I'd have said that eye contact would be minimum, or eye contact and a bite.'

'Did you sense this other vampire?'

'In the woods, when he possessed the other female vampire, I fully expected there to be a second physical vampire nearby. That's how strong the energy was.'

'It was strong enough that it infected Ares not just with this corruption, but with the other vampire's power.'

'Yeah.'

'Not possible,' Edward said.

'Nope.'

'But it happened,' he said.

'Yep.'

We looked at each other for a minute.

'Hard to hunt and kill something that jumps bodies that easily.'

'Didn't we just finish doing this?' I asked.

'You mean Mommie Darkest.'

'Yeah, she was spirit and jumped from vampire to vampire.'

'She wanted your body for keeps.'

'If she hadn't wanted to take me over, I'm not sure I could have kept her in one body long enough to kill her,' I said.

'But she didn't do the whole rotting-vampire thing,' he said.

'No, she didn't,' I said, 'though theoretically she was the first vampire, so every flavor of vampire descended from her.'

'I never believed that Marmee Noir was the very first vampire.'

'Me either, but if not the first she was damn old. The only thing I've felt that came close was the Father of the Day.'

'You killed him in Vegas.'

'We did,' I said.

He shook his head. 'I wasn't there for the killing blow, so he's yours.'

'You make it sound like we're keeping score.'

'I am; aren't you?'

I thought about it. 'No, I guess I'm not. I mean numbers, yeah, but then now that we're marshals we have paperwork that makes us keep track.'

'But you don't keep track of which of us is killing the biggest and the baddest?' Edward asked.

I shrugged, shook my head. 'No.'

'Well damn, that makes being ahead of you not nearly as fun.'

'You're not ahead of me,' I said.

He grinned, and it was an odd mixture of Ted and Edward. 'See, you do keep track.'

I grinned and had the grace to be embarrassed. 'I don't keep official score, but I keep track of what you're doing.'

'You keep score; you just don't want to admit it.'

I shrugged again. 'I didn't think of it as keeping score, but I know I have a higher official kill count than you do.'

'Add the unsanctioned kills and I am so ahead.'

'You're older,' I said.

He laughed and it was his real one, one that he'd only started using after he found Donna and the kids. It was like she gave him permission to resurrect some of the pieces he'd had to give up to be Edward.

'Can't a man get some sleep around here?' Micah was sitting up, rubbing at his eyes.

'I'm sorry,' I said. 'Go back to sleep. We'll be quieter.'

'No, you're awake. I want to see you awake.' His upper body was bare, showing the muscles that his clothes hid. Micah would never bulk up, it just wasn't in his genetics, but if you knew what you were looking at you saw the lean muscle as he padded barefoot toward the bed wearing his dress slacks for pajama bottoms. I wanted to trace my hands over his bare skin. The desire to touch him was usually there, but it was strangely more focused than normal.

'How long have I been out?'

Micah was beside the bed now. 'Twenty-four hours.' He put his hand in mine, gently, since it still had the IV in it. I offered him my right hand across my body. 'Compromising your gun hand, you usually don't do that.'

'Edward's here. I think he can handle the door.'

Micah smiled. 'Yes.' He leaned in and kissed me. He meant it to be chaste, gentle, polite for Edward's sake. I slid my hand out of his, trailed it up the warmth of his bare arm, until my hand could cup the back of his neck. His hair tickled along my skin where I held him. I drew him down into the kiss, made it more. He melted into the kiss for a moment, and then he drew back. I didn't want to let him go. He had to move my hand from his neck. He looked down at me, his green-gold eyes studying my face.

'You need food,' he said.

'I don't want hospital Jell-O,' I said.

'I'll just bet you don't.'

'She's looking at you like she's going to eat you,' Edward said.

'Sometimes when she hasn't fed enough she looks like that.'

'I can give you some privacy,' he said.

'Let's see if the doctor will release her. I'd really rather not explain having sex in the hospital room, and besides I need to check on my dad and Nathaniel.'

'What's wrong with Nathaniel?' I asked.

'Elevation sickness, shock, too-rapid change from animal to human form.'

In my head I thought, *and I drained him healing myself*. Edward was one of the few people with a badge who knew the truth about me and my metaphysical connections, but still . . .

'Did Anita drain energy off Nathaniel to heal herself?' Edward asked.

Micah and I looked at him. I'm not sure it was an entirely friendly look. 'I've been around when Anita had to feed the *ardeur* in an emergency. Since she was hurt and couldn't feed like that, she had to get the energy from somewhere.'

'Logical,' I said.

'Most of the time,' Edward said.

Micah looked at me. I nodded. He turned to Edward. 'It's not as simple as just energy drain, but yes. The combination of everything else that had already happened and then Anita being seriously injured made him pass out.'

'How's Damian?' I asked.

'He's fine, though he fed more than normal last night.'

'Is everyone else fine, too?' I asked, trying to ask without asking if Damian had hurt anyone 'feeding' too much. Damian was a vampire; overfeeding could be really bad for the feedee.

'As far as we know.'

'You couldn't just say yes?'

'I have spent the last twenty-four hours going between three hospital rooms that held the loves of my life and my father; I'm entitled to be a little off my polite game.'

'I'm sorry,' I said.

He smiled. 'It's all right, I'm just glad you're awake.'

'Me, too.'

'I'll get dressed and check on Nathaniel.'

'Kiss me good-bye.'

'I don't have shirt or shoes on yet, Anita. I'm not gone.' He went back to the couch area and started rummaging around in a small overnight bag that I couldn't remember packing. He got an armful of clothes and his toiletry case and went for the bathroom, which was, indeed, the door between the bed and the curtained window. He paused in the lighted door. 'If the doctor offers you some of that hospital Jell-O, say yes. You will need to feed the *ardeur*, but real food will help you control it. Not everyone who you pull down into that kind of kiss is going to have my self-control.'

I fought not to squirm. 'I wasn't asking for sex.'

He gave me a look.

'I wasn't.' It sounded defensive even to me, which made me want to sulk about it, which let me know that I was lying to myself. I could feel the craving growing inside me. I'd healed beyond my wildest dreams, but it was going to come with a price, eventually. Of course, Nathaniel was down the hallway hooked up to IVs, too. That was a price that had already been paid.

'I'm getting dressed. If she gets too handsy with anyone else, knock on the door,' Micah said.

'I'm not going to just paw at strangers,' I said, sullenly.

He smiled. 'We have more guards here than when you passed out; most of them are willing food for you, and almost none of them have my self-control.'

I started to cross my arms, but the IV made it too hard. I fought not to pout at him. 'I'll be good.'

'You're always good, Anita; just don't do anything you'd be embarrassed to have Edward see.'

'There are police out in the hallway waiting to help spell me at Anita's bedside. Could we all start calling me Ted, just for practice?'

Micah nodded. 'Anita, don't do anything you wouldn't want Ted to see.'

'You've made your point,' I said.

'How about there are other police in the hallway helping watch over your room just like they are dad's. Don't do anything you wouldn't want them to walk in on, or how about my mom, my sister, my brother. They've been checking on you, too.'

I sank back into the pillow, all the fight and sullen suddenly gone. 'You've made your point.'

'Good. I love you,' he said.

'I love you, too.'

He closed the door behind him and the room suddenly seemed even darker than it had been. There was a knock on the door, but it opened without waiting for me to say *Come in*. I wasn't surprised that it was my doctor. I was a little surprised that he was a vampire and my doctor.

34

Dr Cross, the vampire, was tall and thin, with dark hair that most people would have called black, but I had my hair and Jean-Claude's to compare it to. The vampire laughed enough to show dainty fangs. 'Yes, I know, a vampire called Dr Cross, it is rather ironic, but I was Dr Cross before I became undead.'

'So just a coincidence?' I said.

He nodded happily, unwound his stethoscope from his neck, and began to listen to my heart. The front bangs were thicker on one side, so they fell forward as he bent over, almost falling into his eyes, but not quite. I had a sudden urge to reach up and smooth his hair back from his face. It wasn't like me to want to touch strangers.

I heard the shower start in my bathroom, which meant Micah was in there all naked and soapy. Joining him seemed like such a good idea.

Dr Cross was over six feet and not as comfortable with his height as most of the people in my life, so he stayed bent over me too much, and his hair spilled forward as he opened the neck of my hospital gown enough to reach in and touch the stethoscope to my chest. He kept his hand down the front of my gown as he glanced back at Edward.

'I'm going to have to look at the wound site, Marshal Forrester; I think a little privacy might be in order.'

'I'm fine,' Edward said, watching us.

'A little privacy would be nice,' I said, frowning at him.

He shook his head. 'I don't think so.'

'I won't eat her, promise,' Dr Cross said with a smile, but his hand was still down my gown, the stethoscope held motionless between my breasts. He should have moved his hand out as soon as he was done, but he hadn't. I wondered if he realized he was doing it. My heartbeat was speeding up. What was happening to me? I had better control than this.

'I'm not worried that you'll eat her,' Edward said, smiling back.

I frowned harder at him, and he smiled like all the angels were tap-dancing at his side. I wanted to tell him to leave, at the same time that I knew Dr Cross and I weren't trustworthy on our own. Part of me didn't care.

Cross looked back at me. His eyes were brown with an irregular circle of gray around the pupil. I wondered if he thought his eyes were brown or hazel.

'Dr Cross.' Edward said it sharply.

The vampire startled, as if he hadn't realized he'd been motionlessly bent over me staring into my eyes. 'Sorry, I must be more tired than I knew.' He got very brisk, putting back his stethoscope around his neck, pushing down the sheet, and rolling up my gown. The gown was huge on me, as most of them always were, so it was a lot of cloth to get out of the way until he could see my lower side. 'It might have been quicker to go from the top,' he joked.

'Maybe,' I said.

'One size does not fit all,' Edward said.

The doctor glanced back at him smiling, his hands wound in the cloth of my gown. He was frowning as he gazed at my bare side. He put his back to Edward so he didn't flash my nakedness under the gown to the other man. I appreciated his concern for my modesty. His bangs swung out from his face just above me so that I could actually not see his eyes for the fall of hair. It bugged me. I wanted to see his eyes.

Dr Cross touched my side. 'Remarkable; the scar looks weeks, months old.'

I looked at where his hand was pointing. There was a new white scar tracing the edge of my hip. It looked like it had hit just under my body armor. 'If it hadn't been a silver bullet I'm not sure there'd be a scar,' I said.

He looked up at me, smiling. 'Really? I know theoretically that nonsilver bullets don't hurt you, or me, but I've never tested the theory.' He laughed at the thought of being bulletproof.

'I haven't been shot by a nonsilver bullet in a while. I don't honestly know.' I could see the gray around his pupils again. It made the brown of his eyes seem paler, or maybe they were just that light a brown.

'Dr Cross,' Edward said, his voice a little sharp.

The doctor startled, blinked, and turned to look at Edward. 'Yes, Marshal Forrester?'

'Can Marshal Blake be released?'

He looked at my hip, and the gown spilled back to block his view, so it was just natural for him to move back more of the gown until he bared most of my lower body. His fingers traced the scar, and then his fingertips traced the line where my leg met my groin. He hadn't touched anything he shouldn't yet, and normally I would have been pissed, but his hair had fallen down across his face again. I wanted, needed to see his eyes.

I touched his hair. He raised his head to meet my gaze. I swept his hair back from his face. His eyes widened, lips half opened. He looked startled, almost frightened.

'Anita!' Edward's voice made me startle. I dropped my hands away from the doctor.

Dr Cross stood up abruptly and pulled down my gown over my body. 'I'm sorry,' he said, 'what was I saying?'

'You were saying that Marshal Blake looks good.'

'Well, yes, she does, very good, I mean, she's quite beautiful . . .' The doctor frowned as if trying to gather his thoughts and failing. He knew he was being inappropriate, but he couldn't seem to help it.

'I meant her wound looks good, as in healed,' Edward said.

'It does, of course, that is what I meant.' He tried for brisk again. 'I would like an X-ray just to make a hundred percent certain that the pelvis crack is healed completely. Bones can take longer to heal even with shapeshifters.'

'What would it entail to get her X-rayed?'

'I'm not sure I understand,' Dr Cross said.

'I mean, would she have to be on a stretcher or in a wheelchair?'

'Wheelchair should be sufficient.'

'Who would normally take her to get an X-ray?' Edward asked.

'A technician would come to get her. He would take her down and bring her back when it was done.'

'Why don't you go set that up,' Edward said.

'Ah, yes, good plan,' Dr Cross said. He got tangled in the curtain on his way to the door, fumbling at it. 'So sorry, I seem to be clumsy today.' He finally got free of the curtain and out the door.

'I'll bet twenty dollars that he comes back with the wheelchair and the idea that he'll take you to X-ray personally,' Edward said.

I frowned at him, but I could feel the texture of Dr Cross's hair on my fingertips. The sound of the shower stopped. Micah would be out soon, but if I had a cracked pelvis sex seemed like a bad idea.

'I forgot to ask about getting the IV taken out.'

'You forgot a lot of things,' he said.

I sighed. 'It wasn't on purpose.'

'You captured him at least twice with your gaze, Anita. You vamped the vampire.'

'Not possible,' I said.

'Yeah, neither is you healing a silver bullet in a little over twenty-four hours.'

We looked at each other.

The door opened, letting out a puff of steam and the sweet smell of clean skin and water. I turned to see Micah standing in fresh jeans and T-shirt. His hair was almost black when it was this wet, and straighter, so you could see that it reached midback on him, instead of the inches shorter it would be when the curl contracted it all up. The unbound wet hair I liked; the clothes . . . I was disappointed. I'd really wanted him to come out naked and wet, and the moment I realized that I knew I was in trouble, because that would have been completely inappropriate in front of Edward.

'I need to feed soon,' I said.

'Did the doctor say you could have solid food?'

'No,' I said.

'What did he say?'

Edward answered. 'That he wants an X-ray to make sure the crack in her pelvis healed along with the bullet wound. He's supposed to send a technician to wheel her down.'

'But he wouldn't take the IV out?'

'She forgot to ask,' Edward said, 'and he forgot to offer.'

Micah frowned from one to the other of us. 'What did I miss?'

'She captured the vampire doctor at least twice with her gaze. He damn near groped her.'

'Was he inappropriate?' Micah asked as he moved to the couch and the overnight case.

'Not as inappropriate as the *ardeur* wanted him to be,' Edward said.

Micah looked at me. 'Anita, is he right?'

I sighed and slumped down on the pillow. 'Yes, I think so.'

'We've got a twenty-dollar bet that Dr Cross decides to wheel her to X-ray personally.'

'I didn't take the bet,' I said.

'Because you know he's coming back through that door for you, and you also know that you cannot be alone with him.'

Micah sat down on the couch to put on socks and a pair of ankle-high boots. 'She's not usually drawn to vampires without a connection to Jean-Claude.'

'I can only tell you what I saw,' Edward said.

He pulled the jeans' straight legs down over the boots so that his legs were one nice, long line, or as long a line as our inseams could get. He stood up, smoothing down the jeans, checking his belt with its silver buckle. He'd tucked the forest-green T-shirt into the jeans. The shirt made his eyes much greener, sinking the gold into the background. The green-gold of his eyes was like some humans with gray-blue or green-blue eyes, the color changing with mood, clothes, so that one minute the eyes were one color and the next the other, and sometimes all at once. I wondered if the gray in Dr Cross's eyes would do that in the right shirt?

'Wow,' I said out loud.

'What?' Micah asked, as he walked toward the bed.

'I just wondered if Dr Cross's eyes would change to more gray if he wore a gray shirt the way the green makes your eyes greener, and not as gold. I just met the man; I shouldn't be thinking about dressing him to match his eyes.'

'No,' Micah said, 'you shouldn't.' He was at the bedside now.

I reached for his hand and he gave it to me. The moment our hands touched, heat leapt from me to him, a flare of power that marched down our bodies in a wash of goose bumps.

Micah jerked his hand out of mine. 'Shit!'

'I didn't do it on purpose,' I said, but my voice was breathless with the rush of power. I wanted to pull his shirt out of his pants. I wanted him to climb into the bed with me and let his wet hair spill across my body.

'Stop it, Anita, stop projecting your need!' He backed away from the bed. I could see his pulse in his throat like a trapped thing. I wanted to set it free.

I closed my eyes, took a deep breath, and let it out slow, counting as I did so. I did it a few times, and when I felt steady I opened my eyes. Micah was watching me from the couch.

'You weren't just thinking sex, were you?' he asked in a quiet, serious voice.

I shook my head.

'What else is there to the *ardeur*?' Edward asked.

We both looked at him and then back at each other.

'He's your friend, maybe one of your best friends. I don't know what he knows and what he doesn't.'

It was funny to hear Micah call Edward one of my best friends. By girl standards he wasn't. We'd never shop together, or talk about men, or . . . but we did talk about our relationships, which was somehow different from talking about guys. We trusted each other with our lives, and . . . so many things.

'When Micah pulled away just now I could see the pulse in his neck, and I thought about setting it free.'

'What does "setting it free" mean?' Edward asked.

'I didn't think it all the way through, but I was really thinking about tearing his throat open enough so the pulse could escape, so the blood could escape.'

'Is that the vampire marks talking, or your ties to all the wereanimals?' he asked.

'A little of both, I think,' I said.

Edward looked past me to Micah. 'If you had just given in to the sex, would she have gone to thinking about blood and violence?'

'Not as likely,' Micah said, 'but violence gets sort of mixed up with sex for shapeshifters sometimes. But if she feeds the *ardeur* soon, then she's not going to tear someone's throat out.'

'And if she doesn't feed the *ardeur* soon?'

'If she were a true shapeshifter, then she'd lose control of her beast and shift, unexpectedly, maybe.'

'But she can't change shape,' Edward said.

'No,' Micah said.

Edward looked at me. 'So how long a window do we have before you lose control?'

'Define *lose control*,' I said.

'That soon, huh?' he said.

'I did almost roll the vampire doctor. I could feel that I could mind-fuck him and then fuck him. He feels like food.'

'You're almost entirely immune to vampire gaze, but you've never been able to bespell a vampire yourself,' Micah said.

'Tell that to Damian. I rolled him pretty completely when I made him my vampire servant.'

Micah seemed to think about that for a second or two. 'Interesting; you're right, your ability to control the undead has been growing stronger the whole time.'

'This is a vampire that I have no connection to, Micah; always before it's been one that I've interacted with, or one that was bound to Jean-Claude. This doctor has no connection to any of us.'

'Jean-Claude is the new king of all the vampires in this country, Anita. We've had masters from all over the country come to St Louis and blood oath themselves to Jean-Claude. If Dr Cross's master gave up power to us, then he's our vampire whether you've ever met him or not.'

I digested that bit of information. 'So, every vampire I meet is potentially already sort of predisposed to be connected to me?'

'Potentially, yes,' Micah said.

'Shit,' I said.

'Potentially problematic, yes.'

'Unless she uses them as food,' Edward said.

'You really think it's a good idea for me to fuck Dr Cross?' I asked.

'No, or I would have just stepped out of the room and let nature takes its course.'

'Then what are you saying, Ed . . . Ted?'

'You're in the hospital, and Micah's family lives here, plus other cops are just outside this room. You can't afford to go all predator on the good doctor, but for later why not feed on what's at hand?'

'I don't do casual sex, you know that.'

'I've never understood why it bothers you. It's a need like eating.'

'Said the man who's monogamous and the father of two.'

'Sex with Donna isn't casual, but I don't remember us talking about my state of monogamy, or lack of it.'

I stared at him. 'Are you saying you cheat on Donna?'

'I'm saying that if I'm away from her as Edward, sex isn't out of the question. Ted is a one-woman man; Edward not so much.'

'You do realize that you talked about yourself twice in third person?' Micah said.

'He does that sometimes – creepy, isn't it?' I asked.

'A little bit,' Micah said.

'Why does it bother you that I might have other lovers when you're sleeping with about twenty people?'

'All my lovers know that they aren't the only one. I haven't lied to anyone, not even by omission.'

'We're polyamorous,' Micah said, 'which means everyone knows what everyone is doing. If we were human and could catch sexually transmitted diseases, then the honesty would be part of protecting everyone's health.'

'If that was a reminder that I need to be careful, I have never had unprotected sex since I've been with Donna. I would never endanger her and our family.'

'I don't know why, but it bugs me to think you could cheat on Donna.'

'You don't even like her that much,' he said.

'I don't dislike her, but I don't understand her in your life. I do understand that she makes you happier than I've ever seen you, and that's good enough for me.'

'Same about you and some of your men,' he said.

'I guess that's my point – why would you risk your happiness and your family for extracurricular sex? It seems like a lot to risk.'

'You're that sure Donna wouldn't forgive it?'

'She was jealous of me when we met. She guarded her territory all over you. That is not a woman who would share well.'

'She still doesn't understand you and me,' Edward said.

'Most men and women can't be friends without sex,' Micah said.

'And you can't be friends once you have sex,' I said. 'You can be in love, or be lovers, but not just friends.'

'Jason is one of your best friends and you have sex with him,' Micah said.

I grinned, thinking of the blond werewolf manager and dancer at Guilty Pleasures. 'Jason is different. He's . . . Jason, and he was Nathaniel's best friend before I ever had sex with either of them.'

'That smile is not just a friend smile,' Edward said.

'Jason is the only man I've had sex with where it didn't change the friendship.'

'Why do you think that is?'

I shrugged. 'I'm not sure. I think it's just Jason. His attitude toward it, I guess.'

'Donna told me that it was okay that I was sleeping with you.'

'What?' I asked.

'She assumed that we were having sex when we worked together.'

'We both told her that we didn't,' I said.

'She sees how close we are, and in her mind men and women can't be this close without sex.'

'So she's assumed we were lovers the whole time and just lying to her?'

'Apparently.'

'I thought she liked me.'

'She does.'

I frowned at him. 'She assumed you and I were lovers and lying to her the whole time you've been together. She should hate me.'

'She thinks you've respected our bond, respected her, and she sees that you care about the kids and us being a family.'

'How do you know that much detail about what she thinks?' Micah asked. I wouldn't have thought to ask that, but that's why he was the head of the Coalition and I was mostly muscle.

'She told me that she forgives me for you. That she sees that it doesn't change anything between her and me and that you belong to that other part of my life, the part where the violence stays. She told me that she will be Ted's wife, and she understands that Edward can never marry.'

'She's still seeing that therapist?' I asked.

'Yeah, and yes, it probably is something she and her therapist worked out between them.'

'So both you and Donna think of Ted and Edward as separate?' Micah asked.

He nodded. 'Seems so.'

'How did that make you feel?' I asked.

'Like Donna gets me more than most.'

'So you think Donna will overlook Edward sleeping with other women, because she's okay with you sleeping with Anita?'

'Something like that.'

'But we aren't sleeping together,' I said.

'When I tried to tell her that, she got mad at me and told me that if she could be brave enough to let us have our relationship, the least I could do was admit it.'

'What did you say?'

Edward looked at Micah. 'What do you think I said?'

I looked at Micah. He was looking at the other man as he said, 'You said, *Yes, dear.*'

Edward smiled and nodded. 'Exactly.'

'You told Donna we were having sex?'

'No, I didn't argue with her when she said we were having sex.'

'That's the same thing.'

'No,' both men said together, 'it's not.'

'What?' I asked.

'Oh, and now that she's worked all that out, she accepted my proposal and we're setting a date,' Edward said.

It took me a second to process what he'd said. 'You and Donna are finally getting married for real?'

'Yes,' he said, and he smiled. It was a real smile. He was pleased.

I smiled.

Micah said, 'Congratulations.' He was smiling, too.

'When?' I asked.

'When can you clear your calendar?' he asked.

'Me? Why? I mean, I'll be there with bells on, but we'll all work around your schedule.'

'Good, because I want you to be my best man.'

'I would love to be, but won't the whole Donna-thinking-I'm-your-lover be a problem?'

'She says not.'

I tried to wrap my head around it. 'You know, if you just hadn't told me that Donna thought that, then I wouldn't have felt weird about this, but now . . . wow, awkward.'

Edward laughed, and it was a good, wholehearted laugh, the one that Donna had helped him find. It made me smile. For that laugh I could handle the weirdness, couldn't I? 'I would be honored to stand as your best man,' I said, because in the end, really, what else was I going to say?

'Donna has made one request.'

'What?'

'That one of your men be on her side of the aisle.'

'She's never met any of the men in my life,' I said.

He shrugged. 'I think she believes that if you have a lover in town with you, that will cut down on our time together.'

'So she trusts us, but not really.'

'She never said she trusted us. She said she forgave us, and she understood what we were to each other; she never said she trusted us.'

'That's just weird. Sorry, I know you love her, and everything, but that makes no sense,' I said.

'It's girl logic,' he said.

'I'm a girl,' I said.

'You're too much guy to be this much girl,' he said.

'That doesn't make sense,' I said.

'Yeah,' Micah said, 'actually it does.'

I looked from one to the other of them, trying to decide if I'd been complimented or insulted.

'Do you feel suitably distracted from *ardeurs* and blood lusts?' Edward asked.

'What?' I asked.

'I've noticed that giving you an emergency to handle or a problem to solve helps you ignore all the metaphysical stuff, so have I confused and puzzled you enough for you to get an X-ray without eating the doctor?'

I thought about it, and then I laughed. 'Damn you, but yes, I'm going to be puzzling and puzzling till my puzzler is sore about the convoluted logic of it all.'

The door opened, and Dr Cross came through with the nurse at his side. He was smiling. 'I thought I'd take you to X-ray myself.'

Edward gave me a look. 'Should have taken that bet.'

'It was a sucker bet and we both knew it,' I said.

'And you were never a sucker,' he said.

'Not if I can help it,' I said.

We smiled at each other.

'What bet?' Dr Cross asked, still smiling, but obviously feeling he'd missed something.

'Don't ask,' Micah said. 'They've been best friends for years. Sometimes you just nod and let them have their guy moment.'

Dr Cross frowned harder. 'I don't understand.'

'I'm the wife,' Micah said, 'she's the husband, and he's the husband's best friend. Does that explain it?'

Dr Cross frowned and then said, 'Oddly, yes.'

The fact that it made sense to him made me like him better, which was both good and bad. Good, because liking people is always better than disliking people. Bad, because I was more likely to feed on people I liked.

'You go check on Nathaniel and your dad; I'll play chaperone,' Edward said.

'Thank you,' Micah said.

'Not a problem.'

'Does Donna really not have a preference on which of my guys stands on her side?' I asked.

'Who's Donna?' Dr Cross asked.

'My fiancée,' Edward said.

'Congratulations.'

'Thank you; we're starting to decide who's in the wedding party.'

'That's always fun,' Dr Cross said, and seemed to mean it.

And just like that, this particular vampire was safe from me trying to eat him. I could never eat someone who thought planning a wedding was fun.

35

Dr Cross unhooked the IV and let me use the bathroom but wouldn't let me get dressed. 'Not until after the X-ray comes back clean. I get the feeling if I let you get dressed you'll just make a break for it.' He laughed.

Edward said, 'He does know you.'

I scowled at him, but I took what I could get and went into the bathroom. The door shut and I got the first look at myself in the mirror. My curls had gone every which way. My skin was pasty pale. What makeup I'd been wearing had vanished long ago. My eyes had the beginnings of dark circles under them, which I almost never got. I looked rough. The fact that Micah and Dr Cross had reacted to me the way they had could only be chalked up to vampire mind games, or otherwise I was seeing something totally different in the mirror than they did. I guess we are our own harshest critics.

'Dear God,' I said.

'Did you say something, Marshal Blake?' Dr Cross asked, which meant he might seem ordinary, but he had more-than-human hearing.

'I'm fine, just looking at my hair.'

'You look fine,' he said through the door.

I ignored him. I was able to finger-comb my hair into some semblance of order, but what I really needed was a shower and a fresh start. Food, of all kinds, would help with the rest. I brushed my teeth, among other things, and gave Micah extra credit points for kissing me passionately before I'd tidied up. If things had been reversed I'd have kissed him silly, too. Love means the niceties matter less, especially when you're glad the love of your life is still alive. Yeah, that makes everything better.

I took the lap blanket that the doc offered because I knew the gown got chilly as they pushed you through the hospital. I'd been hurt often enough to know that for a fact. Once settled in the chair, I asked, 'Where's my stuff?'

'You have a bag of clothes by the couch,' Dr Cross said.

'She doesn't mean clothes,' Edward said. He lifted a small backpack from beside the chair he'd been sitting in. 'I got your stuff from the locals when I arrived.'

'My body armor wouldn't fit in there; please tell me they didn't cut it off me in the ambulance.'

He smiled. 'Your armor is safe. I gave some of your things to your guards.'

'What's in the bag?' I asked.

'Enough so you won't feel unarmed.'

'Great,' I said.

'I really don't think you'll need to be armed just to go a few floors to X-ray, Marshal Blake.'

Edward was already unzipping the backpack. 'You can argue with us, but you're going to lose.'

'So I should just give up gracefully, is that it?'

Edward nodded. 'That's it.' Edward handed me the Browning BDM.

I checked it automatically, popping out the clip to make sure it was loaded, though he was the person I trusted most on the planet to give me back my gun. I put it under the thin lap blanket. The weight of it was comforting, my hand on it under the blanket even more so.

'You want any of the blades?' he asked.

I shook my head. 'No, I'll just have to take them off again when we get to X-ray.' I reached out for the whole bag.

'I'm promise not to walk off with your stuff if you let me carry it.'

I thought about it, I really did, but in the end I smiled and nodded.

'Thanks,' he said, and I knew he was thanking me for trusting him with my stuff when it could all sit in the chair. It didn't matter that he'd been in charge of it for hours while I recovered; some things aren't about logic, they're about comfort. I liked having my weapons at hand at any time, but the whole being-shot thing made me really not want to be unarmed right now.

When Edward opened the door and let Dr Cross push me outside,

I was even gladder I had the lap blanket, because there was a damn crowd in the hallway.

There are always police in the hospital when another one is hurt, especially in the line of duty. I don't always have that big a crowd because I'm not usually local and I tend to rub people the wrong way, but I would never complain about the brotherhood in Colorado, because the hallway was packed with Boulder PD, state troopers, and uniforms I didn't recognize. There were plainclothes, too, with their badges at their waists or on lanyards like Edward's.

In among all the handshaking and nods of 'Blake . . . Marshal . . . ma'am,' I caught a glimpse of Dev and Nicky against the far wall. They were just there, strangely unobtrusive for two such big guys. I wasted a smile on them and got some back. They didn't try to push their way through the police to me, just let me know they were there. I was probably as safe as I'd ever be in the ring of police. Bodyguards seemed redundant, but I was still glad to see them. Not so much for the potential protection, but in case the *ardeur* fought its way through the puzzle that Edward had given me. Right now the local PD liked me, thought I was one of them, but one vampire-power-induced orgy involving them and me would so not be on their Christmas lists.

Dr Cross fielded the questions and kept us moving down the hallway. Edward, in full good-ol'-boy Ted Forrester mode, helped the doctor keep us moving. Nicky and Dev trailed behind us. I couldn't see them, but I could feel them like a warm anchor through all the busy, well-meaning human energy like a blowtorch in a field of matches. It all burns, but some people burn brighter. I could feel that brightness.

My stomach cramped so hard that I bent over. Dr Cross bent over me. 'Are you all right, Marshal?'

I let out my breath in a slow, steady flow and said, 'Rapid healing takes energy. I think I need food.'

'Of course, I should have thought of it.' We stopped long enough at the nurses' station for him to order the food.

We had fewer people in our parade as they split off and went to check on Sheriff Callahan and just go do their jobs. Some of the uniforms were probably from small departments like Al's, so they couldn't afford to have all their manpower here.

The door at the end of the hallway opened and Officer Bush walked through. His short brown hair was still hat-flattened, as if he'd been in his patrol car for a while and was still fresh enough from the academy to wear it behind the wheel.

'Marshal Blake, good to see you awake.'

'Good to be awake, Officer Bush,' I said, and smiled.

'I just wanted to come and tell you personally that the vampires that started all this will be dead before dawn.'

'What are you talking about?' I asked.

'The vampires that created the flesh-eating zombies are going to be executed tonight.'

'They aren't the vampire that caused all this.'

He frowned. 'We were there. We saw them do it.'

'You heard what she said, Bush. She was possessed by a much bigger, badder vampire than she is.'

'Everyone lies when they get caught, Blake, you know that.'

'Yeah, but in this case she didn't lie. I felt the other vampire's energy. I felt him on her and knew when he left. His energy was so strong that I kept expecting to see him standing there, but he didn't need to be standing there to control her. He's behind the rotting infection that Sheriff Callahan has, and he's what drove Ares insane and made him attack people. The two vampires we took into custody are our only witnesses to the real vampire behind all this; if they die, then our best leads go with them. Kill them if you want, but the master vampire behind all this will just make more little vampires and keep spreading the infection. Killing the two in custody only helps the bad guys, because then I can't question them.'

'But they're not talking to us, they're not telling us anything,' Bush said.

'I know the questions to ask, Bush. If they're dead before I get there, I can't ask anything. I can't find out who did this to them.'

'Did this to them? What do you mean?'

'Both those vampires are newly dead. They aren't a month old as undead, which means they're some of your missing people. Did you check their fingerprints against the missing people?'

'They're vampires with an order of execution on them; we don't have to do anything but execute them.'

'I know that, but I'm telling you that if they die you've just made it harder to find this bastard.'

'Who's carrying out the warrant?' Edward asked.

'Marshal Hatfield.'

'It's considered courtesy to offer the execution to the marshal who was injured or lost people hunting the vampire,' Edward said.

'We thought Marshal Blake would be in the hospital a few days, at least.'

'I'm a medical miracle. I need those vampires alive to be questioned.'

'I'll call, and I'll get on site to do what I can,' Edward said. He put the backpack with all my dangerous toys in the wheelchair to one side so I could still have a clean draw to the Browning under my lap blanket. Edward never forgot.

'I'll go with you, and I'll radio in,' Bush said.

'Then radio it in,' I said.

He hit his shoulder mic as he and Edward went for the far door. Bush was talking to someone before they hit the door. I trusted Edward to do as much as he could to keep the two vampires alive in custody. I was going to be so pissed if Hatfield executed the only two people who I was sure had actually seen the big bad vampire face to face. Without them, we were back to square one.

A tall officer with short dark hair and brown eyes so dark they were almost black said, 'So the Executioner is saying, *Don't execute the vampires.*'

I looked up at him in his civilian clothes, but there was something about how tall, how terribly in shape he was, muscled, and just a level of energy to him that made me guess he was SWAT or something like it. Special forces military branch tastes the same sometimes.

'I'm flattered that SWAT came down to keep me company,' I said.

The faintest surprise went through those very dark eyes. 'What gave me away?'

I waved sort of vaguely at him. 'This.'

He frowned. 'You just motioned at all of me.'

'Exactly,' I said.

He smiled.

One of the other officers patted his belly where it was pushing over his equipment belt. 'Yeah, Yancey, you don't have all the equipment that the rest of us have.'

He laughed. 'If I had all the equipment you have, Carmichael, I'd get kicked off SWAT.' He patted his own very flat stomach. I was betting he had washboard abs, just a thought, no harm in it. The next thought had harm in it; I wanted to lift his shirt out of his pants and see if I was right.

I called out, 'Nicky, can you take the bag?'

The police had to make room for him to come to my side. Most of them gave him little eye flicks. Officer Yancey of local SWAT looked at him in that way that very fit, very tough men do when they're not used to seeing men who make them wonder, *Could I take him? Would I lose?* Yancey was taller than Nicky, though not taller than Dev, but Nicky's shoulder spread always impressed big men who thought they had nice shoulders until they had to stand next to Nicky.

I smiled, I couldn't help it, and the amusement helped push back the impulse to touch strangers.

'Some of the local PD are really not happy with you surrounding yourself with shapeshifters after what happened,' Yancey said.

'My man was turned against us by vampire mind games just like the officers, including Bush, were mind-fucked earlier by the same vampires.'

Yancey held up his hands as if to show he was unarmed. 'SWAT is delivering more and more warrants as backup for the executioners. We train for what to do if one of us is vamped and turned against the rest of us. You did one of the things that we all pray we never have to do, Marshal Blake. I'm here because SWAT wanted you to know that we respect what you did and we're sorry you had to do it. Hermes of St Louis SWAT speaks highly of you.'

'Thank you,' I said, because what else could I say.

'Boulder won't allow psychics on SWAT yet. The report that vetoed it said they found that most psychics couldn't use their special abilities and do their duty as officers at the same time.'

'Which means most psychics can't shoot straight and use their powers at the same time,' I said.

He smiled. 'Something like that.' Then he looked at me, very seriously, as if he were weighing and measuring me. 'But you can, can't you?'

I nodded. 'Yes, I can.'

'That was a hell of a shot to make under the circumstances, Marshal.'

'It was Ares who taught me how to make that shot,' I said. I took a deep, even breath, because my chest was tight, my eyes suddenly hot. God, I was going to cry.

Nicky put his hand on my shoulder.

'What do you mean?' Yancey asked.

'The man I killed, Ares, was a scout sniper before an enemy attack left him with lycanthropy and they forced a medical discharge on him. Handguns and up-close fighting I'm great at, but long guns, shooting distances, wasn't my thing. He taught me.' I raised my hand and put it over Nicky's where he touched me. His fingers wrapped around mine and it helped me gather myself. I gripped my gun under the blanket, digging the butt of it hard into my hand. The solidness of it helped, too. Funny, that holding a gun made it easier to deal with the sorrow of using a different one.

'I heard he was a scout sniper and that he tracked the vampires for you. I didn't hear that he taught you to shoot.'

'He taught me to shoot far away. I learned to shoot close in a long time ago.'

'I'm sorry, Marshal, I didn't mean to bring up anything . . . hard.'

I nodded and looked down at my lap. I didn't trust myself to look up. I wasn't sure what would upset me more – seeing too much sympathy in Yancey's face, or too little. Better not to know.

'I really need to get Marshal Blake into X-ray,' Dr Cross said.

'Yes, of course,' Yancey said, and backed up.

Dr Cross pushed me toward the elevators. Nicky stayed at my side, hand still in mine. Dev trailed us. The other officers stayed back, and I was grateful. When the elevator doors closed and the only stranger with us was Cross, the first hard, hot tear cut down my cheek. Nicky started rubbing his thumb across my fingers as we held hands. Dev came to the other side of me and touched my hair. 'It's okay, Anita,' he said.

I shook my head, and the tears fell faster. I finally managed to say, 'It's not okay,' and then I gave myself over to the grief and the horror and the unfairness of it all, and I wept.

36

Two protein bars, bottles of water for all three of us, and an X-ray later, we knew the break was completely healed. My phone started ringing as we got off the elevator on our floor. Nicky dug it out of the backpack and handed it to me. It was Edward.

'Vampires alive, or dead?' I asked.

'I've got the execution delayed but can't convince them that the vamps were mind-fucked themselves. You were right that the vampires are two of the missing. They were hikers that came up here about a month ago, so you called that, too.'

'I'm good with the dead,' I said.

'So we hear.'

'What's that supposed to mean?' I asked. It wasn't like him to make snide remarks.

'Some of the locals seem less happy the more right you are.'

'Why?' I asked.

'Since you and I rely on each other to be right, I can't explain why, only that it's happening. My guess is professional jealousy. Marshal Hatfield has a serious hard-on to prove herself, and she seems to feel that your reputation hurts all women everywhere who wear a badge.'

'I take it you don't mean my reputation as a kickass law enforcement officer.'

'No, the other reputation.'

'Oh, that I'm a cold-blooded killer who shoots first and asks questions later?'

He gave a small chuckle. 'Nope, the other one.'

'You mean that I'm one of the monsters and that's what gives me a leg up in the job?' I asked.

He laughed. 'No, the other-other reputation.'

'You mean that I'm dating too many men?' I asked.

'Something like that,' he said, his voice soft again.

'She's right there, isn't she?' I asked.

'Yes,' he said in a normal voice.

'Have you defended my honor to her yet?' I asked.

He lowered his voice again. 'It's hard to defend your honor when everyone believes that I'm one of your conquests.'

I rolled my eyes. 'I'd forgotten that rumor.'

'I hadn't.' There was a tone in his voice.

'Do you get that much grief from the other cops about me?'

'They're just jealous,' he said.

'Of my success rate at the job,' I said.

'Yep,' he said.

'Or that I'm doing you?' I asked.

He did that male chuckle again that he almost never did unless he was playing Ted. 'Some.'

'I'll be there as soon as I can to question the vamps.'

'It's Hatfield's warrant. You have to persuade her.'

'And she already hates me,' I said.

'Oh, yeah,' he said.

'Perfect,' I said.

Nicky held the door while Dr Cross pushed the chair through.

'Make sure you eat before you get here,' Edward said.

'I've had a couple of protein bars,' I said.

'I think you need to eat something beefier than that,' he said.

Dr Cross said, 'I hate to interrupt police business, especially when you're trying to save fellow vampires, but we need this room for sick people. You can go save the day, er, night.'

'Hold on, Ted,' and I turned to the doctor. 'Thanks, doc. About Nathaniel Graison – is he being released, too?'

'Yes, Mr Graison can leave when you do, though I would advise all of you to drink copious amounts of water to keep from having a relapse of elevation sickness. Don't look at me that way, Marshal, it contributed to both of your illnesses.'

'How much water do we need to drink?' Dev asked.

'You know that recommended eight glasses of water a day?'

'Yes,' Dev said.

'Double that, doctor's orders.'

'We'll never have time for that,' I said.

He shrugged. 'Then you or Mr Graison may both suffer ill effects again.'

'I was shot, doc.'

'But he wasn't.'

I opened my mouth and closed it, not sure what to say.

Dr Cross said, 'I know he is one of your animals to call and that you drained energy from him to heal yourself.'

I tried not to look surprised.

'There is a reason they assigned a vampire as doctor on this floor. Sometimes it takes a preternatural citizen to understand another one.'

I nodded. 'So you knew what was wrong the whole time?'

'Not at first, but I'm absolutely serious that the elevation sickness contributed to both of you being hospitalized. It puts extra strain on your bodies.'

'They'll drink the water,' Nicky said.

I scowled up at him.

'I want both of you well,' he said.

And just like that, Nicky won. 'All right,' I said.

'I'll go sign your paperwork. You can shower and get dressed,' Dr Cross said.

'I'm not sure I have time to shower,' I said.

Edward said on the phone, 'You have time and it will probably be your best bet to get your protein needs met.'

'I told you I had two bars.'

'I think you need some beefcake to go with those protein bars.'

'Are you hinting that I need to feed the *ardeur* before I get there?'

'I didn't think I was hinting, but yes.' He lowered his voice again and said, 'I have now made Hatfield walk off in disgust. I believe she thinks the beefcake comment was us flirting.'

'That would be bad flirting,' I said.

'Yep.'

'You're much smoother than that,' I said.

'Thanks, but feed, Anita. You don't want to lose your shit here.'

'Agreed,' I said, but sighed as I said it.

'Are Nicky and Dev still with you?' he asked.

'Yeah.'

'You know there are a lot of women who wouldn't see either of them as a hardship.'

'It's not that; it's the fact that I have to have sex before I can go fight crime.'

'And you healed a broken pelvis and a bullet wound in a little over twenty-four hours, so you have to have sex more often than most for that kind of healing ability. It's not a bad trade.'

I thought about that and then said, 'Good point.'

'You'd be out of this investigation for good if you didn't heal better than anyone I know.'

'I'll feed,' I said.

'But make it a quickie; you do need to question the vampires before dawn.'

'First you damn near order me to have sex, and now you're putting limits on how much time I have to do it. Geez.'

He laughed. 'Just do what you need to do and get over here before dawn.' He hung up, his voice already talking to someone at his end of the world.

'Well, you heard the man; I need to feed and then we go question the vampires.'

'Which one of us?' Nicky asked.

'Me,' Dev said.

We both looked at him.

He smiled and held up his hands as if to say, *Unarmed*. 'The last time you did a major feed on Nicky you almost killed him, remember?'

'I know not to have sex with him twice in a row,' I said.

'He's your Bride, which means he can't shut off his energy when you feed the *ardeur*. We don't want his heart stopping again because of that, right?'

We both agreed.

Then a look came over Dev's face that I couldn't quite read. I just knew it wasn't a happy look. 'Is it such a hardship to have sex with me instead of Nicky?'

I realized what the look was now. He was feeling bad about himself, worried that I preferred Nicky to him. I did, actually, but it wasn't because Dev wasn't wonderful on his own; he'd just gotten to me too late. I was full up for main men by the time our Devil arrived. When he'd first come to us, he'd been so confident he was cocky. It made me sad that I'd made him doubt himself, though I knew that Asher had done a lot to undermine the Devil's confidence in himself, too.

I went to Dev, touched his arm, and studied his face. 'You are handsome and yummy, and I've never said otherwise.'

'You mean that, but it doesn't change the fact that you'd rather fuck Nicky than me.'

'You're prettier than me,' Nicky said.

Dev grinned. 'Thanks, but Anita has a lot of pretty in her life.' His face sobered. 'She needs more than just a pretty face and great sex.'

'I may need more than that, but it's not a bad place to start,' I said. I went up on tiptoe to try and kiss him, but at six foot three, if he didn't bend down to me I wasn't reaching his mouth.

He bent down and let me kiss him, but his blue-brown eyes stayed serious. 'It's not a bad place to start, but I know what it's like to be in love now and to have someone in love with me. I miss it.'

'You miss Asher,' I said.

He nodded.

'If he could stop throwing jealous rages, I'd miss him more, too,' I said.

'I don't like that part of him either, but I love all of him, and he loved me.'

'Have you heard from him?' I asked.

'He told me to go find a girl and settle down with her, that he'd found a boy who liked just boys. He didn't have to be second to the next pussy that came along.'

I dropped back to stand flat-footed. I wondered if he'd given the same talk to Jean-Claude; if so, my main squeeze hadn't shared. 'Yeah, that sounds like Asher when he's being shitty.'

'But the thought that he found another man to replace me really bothered me, Anita. I thought I couldn't live without more people, especially women, but now I don't know.'

'Would you give up women for him?' Nicky asked.

Dev looked at the other man. 'I think I might. It would be hard, but for him I might. I didn't expect to miss him this much.'

'Have you ever missed anyone before?' I asked.

Dev shook his head. It made me remember that he was younger than me and had certainly had a more sheltered life than a lot of the other men in my life. I touched his arm again.

He smiled at me, but it was a sad smile.

'I miss him, too,' I said.

'Do you?'

'I miss the bondage with him topping Nathaniel and me more than anything else, but I'm learning that it can be just as hard to find someone to dominate you in the bedroom as to date outside it.'

'Will you talk to Jean-Claude about bringing him home?'

'I was going to talk to him about it when I got home anyway.'

'Really?'

'Jean-Claude is wasted as the ringmaster at Circus of the Damned. Businesswise we need him back at Guilty Pleasures, which means we need Asher back to manage and be ringmaster at the Circus.'

'Who talked to you about the business side of things?' Nicky asked.

'Jason told me that he can manage Guilty Pleasures, but he doesn't have Jean-Claude's magically seductive voice, and Jean-Claude had some seriously loyal customers who are missing him.'

'Jean-Claude may like women best, but he's missing Asher, too,' Dev said.

'They've been in love with each other for a few hundred years,' I said.

'And Micah doesn't like being introduced as "our Micah" in meetings with other preternatural leaders,' Nicky said.

'He hasn't mentioned it to me,' I said.

'There's a level of intimacy that Jean-Claude is addressing toward Micah just in the last month or so that hints that Micah is more than just your lover.'

'Jean-Claude hasn't mentioned wanting to make Micah more than a blood donor,' I said.

'If Jean-Claude wants another male lover, why hasn't he asked me?' Dev said.

'You'd say yes?' I asked.

He grinned. 'I wouldn't say no.'

'I think Jean-Claude is avoiding Dev because he thinks it would piss Asher off to have his two men fucking each other without him involved,' Nicky said.

I gave him wide eyes.

He shrugged. 'Asher isn't really good at the polyamory. He doesn't like to share unless he's the main focus.'

'And he wasn't the main focus with anyone but me,' Dev said, 'and then I had to try to add a woman who wasn't Anita, and Asher couldn't deal with it.'

'You wish you hadn't done it,' I said.

'Sometimes, but if I hadn't asked for what I thought I wanted, then I wouldn't have realized that I could miss someone like this. I wouldn't have known what Asher meant to me.'

'I don't think any of you would have realized how much he meant if you hadn't had a chance to miss him,' Nicky said.

'I'll talk to Jean-Claude when we get back,' I said.

'Thank you,' Dev said, and then he looked even sadder. 'If he's found someone to replace me and Jean-Claude, then I'm not sure I want him back in town. I don't think I could stand to see him with another man and know that I'd lost him.'

I didn't know what to say to that, so I did the only thing I could think of: I hugged him. He wrapped me in his arms, but there was no heat to it, only comfort. We sort of clung to each other in the debris of Asher's tantrums.

'This is very touching, but it's not going to lead to a quick feeding for the *ardeur*,' Nicky said.

We both turned and looked at him. My look wasn't friendly, and I expected Dev to be in the same frame of mind, but he said, 'Nicky's right. Sad is not an aphrodisiac.'

I pulled back enough to gaze up at Dev. 'What do you want to do?'

'Are you really turning down a chance to feed the *ardeur*?' Nicky asked.

'Just this one time. Would it be totally weird to say I have to call Asher and find out if he's just punishing me with the talk of another guy, or if he's serious that he doesn't want me in his life anymore?' Dev said.

'You want to know the answer before I talk to Jean-Claude about maybe bringing Asher back to town,' I said.

'Yes.'

'Are you giving up Anita along with all the other women?' Nicky asked.

He thought about it and then shook his head. 'I'm her golden tiger to call, and I need to be free to be that in every way she needs. Because of the kind of vampire she is, that includes sex.'

'So, she's the one exception,' Nicky said.

Dev nodded.

'Wasn't one of the reasons you went to other women was that Anita had so many men in her bed that you weren't getting enough pussy?'

I frowned at Nicky.

'Sorry, I forgot you don't like that word, but it's still a good question. It's what started the fight that got Asher exiled in the first place.'

'He's right, Anita, it is a good question.' Dev sighed.

'Okay,' I said, 'do you have a good answer?'

He grinned and then looked sad, like clouds passing over the sun on a summer's day. 'Not until I talk to Asher.'

'You really think talking to him will give you a good answer?' Nicky asked.

Dev smiled, but it was sad around the edges, and in his eyes. 'I'll have an answer; not sure if it will be good or bad.'

Nicky shook his head. 'I'd never have fallen in love with anyone if Anita hadn't mind-fucked me, because I think this is just stupid.'

'Love is stupid?' Dev asked.

'It makes you weak,' Nicky said.

Dev nodded. 'It can.'

I realized that Nicky had said, in a very backward way, that he was 'in love' with me, but since he hadn't made a big deal out of it, neither did I. I'd think about it and decide if we needed to talk about it later. I was voting no.

'Do you think he's learned his lesson?' I asked.

'Asher, you mean?' he asked.

'Yes,' I said.

'No,' he said.

'Me either,' I said. 'He'll be better for a while.'

'And yet we both want him back,' Dev said.

'Apparently we all do.'

'It makes no sense,' he said.

'No, it doesn't, but if it were logical, would it still be love?'

He seemed to think about that for a minute and then shook his head. 'No, I guess it wouldn't.' He smiled down at me. 'But I still think it's too dangerous for Nicky to feed you right now. We don't want another accident where you make his heart stop.'

I looked at Nicky. He looked back. His face was serious, almost unreadable, and I realized it had been even when he was talking about being in love. I went to him and wrapped my arms around his waist. He put his arms around me automatically. We were left staring at each other, me up, and him down.

'I won't risk Nicky like that again.'

A slow smile spread across his face, and he hugged me closer, pressing our bodies against each other. 'Good to know,' he said, voice low and soft.

'But Anita still needs to feed the *ardeur*,' Dev said.

'Who do you want to feed on?' Nicky asked.

'Who's available? Someone told me that we had fresh guards in town, didn't say who.'

'I'll go see who's in Nathaniel's room,' Dev said.

'Where is he?' I asked.

'Farther down the hall,' Dev said.

Nicky hugged me tighter, which made me look at him. 'He's fed you enough; you need fresh meat.'

'I wasn't thinking about feeding on Nathaniel, just seeing him.'

'You have to clean up, so start, and Dev will send someone in.'

I frowned at him. 'I'd like a choice.'

'We won't send in anyone who you haven't already fed on and had sex with, so does it really matter?' Nicky said.

'Yeah,' I said.

He gave me a look, like I was being silly.

'How about it's a surprise,' Dev said, 'you in the shower and your lover strips off and joins you. It's romantic and spontaneous.'

I frowned at him.

Nicky turned me around to face the bathroom door. 'Your soap, shampoo, razors, everything is in there. Go get cleaned up, and before you're finished you'll have food.'

I frowned at him, too.

He gave me a little push toward the door. 'Go, Anita, go so you can question the vampires before dawn.'

'I'd forgotten,' I said.

'When you're really low on *ardeur* feeds, you forget important things. Clean up, we'll bring you takeout, and then we'll go catch bad guys.'

I didn't point out the irony of Nicky calling someone else a bad guy, with his background. I just went into the bathroom and started cleaning up. The fact that I'd gotten this distracted when we were on a time limit for questioning witnesses said just how low my reserves were. I needed a fast shower, fast food, and some fast answers from our vampire prisoners. It was all about quickies tonight.

37

The shower was basically a raised lip in the floor with a curtain that went around the two sides that weren't walls. Nicky was right, someone had put all my stuff on the little built-in shelves ready to go. I'd soaped, scrubbed, done both rounds of hair conditioner, and actually had time to do both legs just above the knees, and I was still showering alone. When I knew I was going to be interrupted I'd started shaving in zones, so at least if I had to stop I'd be even. You can shave or not shave, but one leg completely done and the other not shaved at all just didn't work. So instead of doing one leg from ankle to hip, I did both legs to just above the knee, and then if I had time did the rest of the legs. What was taking the guys this long to decide who was getting in the shower with me?

I actually pulled the curtain back to check the time on my phone, and it had only been fifteen minutes. I'd gotten fast at showers; I guess it was having to get blood off me after most night's work — lots of practice. Fifteen minutes wasn't long to decide who would be feeding me and maybe not be able to do their bodyguard job until they'd slept, or eaten, or both. After this kind of major healing, it would be a drain on whoever I fed upon. We'd be down one guard. I'd give them twenty minutes and then I was calling someone.

I stepped back into the shower and started on my thighs. I might as well accomplish something while I was waiting. Patience was never my best virtue. I didn't so much hear the door open as feel the line of cooler air invading the foggy warmth of the bathroom.

I couldn't see anything through the curtain. I turned to face where the curtain opened, razor still in my hand. My pulse had sped up, my body already tightening, and that was without knowing who was about to come through the curtain. Maybe Dev had something on the whole surprise thing?

The curtain parted and Jean-Claude was standing there, pale and perfectly nude, his dark hair falling past his shoulders, loose and free and covering nothing. Of all the men I'd expected it to be, he hadn't been on my list. I should have chastised him that he was risking himself traveling to another territory. That he was safer at home. That he was basically the vampire president of the country, and he had other responsibilities besides love. I should have said a lot of things, but I didn't. I stepped out of the water and into his arms with a sound that was suspiciously like a sob. I let his arms and body wrap me close and raised my face for a kiss from those lips, that face. I had a moment to gaze into the darkest blue eyes I'd ever seen, as if the midnight sky could be blue, and then he was kissing me and I closed my eyes and gave myself to his lips, his mouth, and his hands gliding over the wet slickness of my body. It was as if that kiss were air and water and everything I'd been needing.

He picked me up, my feet leaving the ground, and I wrapped my legs around him as he shut the curtain behind us with one hand and walked us into the pounding water of the shower.

38

The water poured over our faces as we kissed, so that it was as if the water were part of the kiss: pounding, hot, streaming down our skin, beating against my upturned face as the kiss grew more eager. I could feel him pressed between us, his body growing eager with the kiss. It was wonderful and romantic until I needed to breathe and my vampire lover didn't; then it was like drowning as I tried to hold my breath and kiss him past the point where my body wanted air. I finally had to turn my head to the side and take a breath with the water streaming all around us. My body wanted a gasping, big breath, but I knew it had to be a shallow, careful breath, or I'd swallow water, and there was nothing romantic about choking in the shower, even naked.

Jean-Claude stood there with his face shrouded by the silvering fall of water, like a shining, moving veil. He knew to lower his head enough so the water didn't actually run into his eyes, so he could keep them open and let me see his blue, blue eyes framed by the wet black lace of his eyelashes, and the silvered water, so that it was like looking at dark blue pools through silver mist, while being held by the strength of his body. It was a one-two punch of romance and sex.

He lowered his face, and I raised mine so we could kiss again under the pounding, hot water. When I had to turn away to breathe a second time, he moved us out from under the water to the corner near the faucet, so that only the back of his body was still in the water. He set me on my feet in the corner, my back against the strangely cool tiles, and then he knelt in front of me.

The water had soaked into his hair so that the curl was gone, and all that long, black hair spilled more than halfway down his back, perilously close to his waist. My hair had grown heavy and straight with the water just like his so that it fell to my waist, instead of curling to midback. His hair clung in dark strands to his face; it made his eyes look even bluer than normal, like the sky at sunset when the blue gives one last flash of blue, before the sky drowns in orange and red, and darkness falls. Water beaded on his face, clung to the kissable curves of his mouth, as he leaned in toward my body.

I put a hand on his face and stopped him. My voice was shaky as I half-laughed and said, 'I can't believe I'm saying this, but we don't have time for that much foreplay. I've got to question some vampire suspects before dawn.'

'You will not be able to question them tonight,' he said.

'Why not?'

'Fredrico, their Master of the City, contacted me. He regrets, but when he learned that they had been bespelled, he interceded on their behalf and they have, what is the term, lawyered up. If their testimony is valuable it could save them.'

'Every hour that we waste gives the vampire that's doing this a chance to escape, and spread this sickness to more people.'

He put his hands on either side of my hips. 'That is true, *ma petite*, but dawn will come and trap him as it traps us all. No vampire will be harming anyone once the sun rises.'

'Damn it,' I said.

He smiled. 'You helped make the law that gives the vampires rights to lawyers.'

I gave a small smile. 'I guess I didn't think it would be used against me.'

'We often do not foresee the outcome of our actions, *ma petite*. We strive to do good things, but often there is a bit of bad in with it all.'

I could only nod.

'But there is good with the news; it means we have time for me to lick the water off your body, until we can drown the sorrow from your eyes.'

'There's no sorrow in my eyes. I need to get to work.'

He looked at me, just looked at me. It wasn't vampire powers or his beauty that made me look away. It was the knowledge in his eyes. He knew me too well for me to lie to him, and if I couldn't lie to him, I couldn't lie to myself. Damn it, that's what happens when you let people get too close. You can't hide anymore, not even from yourself.

'I'm trying to concentrate on work,' and even to me it sounded lame and like wishful thinking.

'Work can be a balm for such things,' he said, softly.

I made myself look at him, as he knelt half in the water, his graceful hands resting on either side of my hips. His face was neutral as only the older vampires could be, so that he gave me nothing to judge, or react to, just this patient waiting for me to decide if I was going to lash out in my anger or let him comfort me.

I touched one of the strands of hair that was plastered to his skin. 'When you came through the curtain I was so happy to see you.' I moved the strand away from his face, smoothing it back. 'Even knowing you shouldn't have come, that the local master would see it as a power play.' I touched a strand on either side of his face and smoothed them back into the heavy blackness of the rest of his so-wet skin. 'Even knowing it's dangerous when you travel, because you're outside the fortress that the Circus of the Damned has become.' I pushed back the last stray lock of his hair so that his face was clean and perfect. For once I said everything I was thinking, as if I were too raw to stop myself. 'Looking down at you like this, and I still marvel that you want me, that someone beautiful as you wants me after six years . . .'

His lips parted, as if he would speak, and I put my fingertip against his mouth.

'You'll say I'm beautiful, and I have to believe you. I have to believe the amazingly beautiful people in my life who keep saying it, but I'm saying this, that I never grow used to the beauty of you, your eyes, your face, the hair, the body, everything. I love that you came. You didn't have to. You could have just lowered your shields, reached out to me, and felt everything I was feeling.'

He wrapped his hand around mine and moved it from his lips, laying a gentle kiss on my fingers as he did it. 'When I saw you on the television bleeding and hurt I knew you would not die, because I could feel how hurt you were, and I knew we had power to heal you and bring you safely home to me, to us, but it wasn't enough, *ma petite*.' He pressed my hand to his chest. 'I needed to feel this. I needed to touch your skin, kiss your lips, hold you as close as I could. I would survive your death physically, I believe there is enough power now for that, but my heart . . .' He raised my hand and kissed it. 'My heart, it beats for you, Anita Blake. If there were a way for us to marry without the other men in our lives feeling excluded, I would ask it of you.'

I felt the tears in my eyes and had to concentrate not to blink. I would not cry. My voice didn't show it when I said, 'Micah said almost the same thing to Nathaniel and me.'

Jean-Claude tilted his head to one side. 'Then let us do it.'

'What?' I asked.

'Legally you can marry only one of us, but we could have a ceremony; there is precedence for it.'

'What do you mean?' I asked.

'A group marriage, not legally, but we could handfast, jump the broom as it was once called here in America.'

I was crying, and I hadn't meant to. 'How would we do it? I mean, how many of us? What about rings? I mean, do we all get rings? Do we all get engagement rings? Who would be willing to marry that many people to each other?'

He smiled, and he looked happy, just happy. 'I do not know the answers to most of your very reasonable questions, *ma petite*, but that you are asking them, and did not simply say no, is more than I had hoped for.'

I started to cry harder, so that I had to swallow the lump in my throat to say, 'Did you really think I'd say no?'

'Yes,' he said. 'If I had dreamt otherwise I would have made it the most romantic night of your life and conspired with the other men in our lives to sweep you off your feet. But as it has always been between us, *ma petite*, you put me at a disadvantage and throw all my romantic ideals into the air to land where they may.' He kissed my hand and got to his feet. He kept my hand in his and touched my face with his fingertips, ever so lightly. He studied my face as if he would memorize it. The tears slowed, and I looked up into that most beautiful of faces.

'Anita Blake, will you do me the honor' — he dropped to one knee in the shower — 'the honor and wonder of marrying me?'

I started to cry again, damn it! I nodded and finally found my voice. 'Yes, yes, I will.'

He smiled up at me, his face alight, not with vampire powers or psychic gifts of any kind, but with joy. After nearly six hundred years he was still just a man kneeling in front of a woman, relieved that she'd said yes and happier because of it. And me, for once I let myself be the girl, and I cried, and I let him hold me as I did it. I cried because I was happy and sometimes you get so happy your heart fills up and spills out your eyes, but I cried for Ares, too. I cried for what I'd had to do, and I cried because if I had to do it over again, if I'd known what would happen, the only thing I would have changed is I would have killed him sooner. I wouldn't have risked the officers on the helicopter, and somehow I felt their deaths were on me, even though I knew I couldn't have guessed what would happen. Logically I knew that, but guilt isn't about logic, and neither is love.

Somewhere in all the crying and touching, the kissing grew from gentle to something with force and need. We celebrated my *yes* on the floor of the shower. We started with him on top so I could see all that amazing beauty above me, his body thrusting in and out of mine, but the shower kept spraying around his body and it was a race to see if I'd feed the *ardeur* or drown first. We moved me to my knees, laughing, until he entered me from behind and stole the laughter and the breath from my throat for a moment, with the sheer pleasure of him inside me.

He spread my legs farther apart, his hands controlling my body, keeping me still so he could glide over that spot inside my body over and over again in long, slow, full strokes. The sensation of it was extraordinary.

'Jean-Claude, Jean-Claude, Jean-Claude.' I said his name in time to his body, so that it became part of the rhythm.

My breathing sped, and I could feel the building pleasure, so close. 'Oh, my God, close, so close.'

His rhythm hesitated for just a moment, and then he went back to that long, sinuous stroke of his body inside mine. I could hear him breathe now, and that he was fighting to keep it even, steady, as the rest of his body. Control your breath and you control so much.

Between one stroke and the next, the pleasure spilled over me, through me, so that my body pulsed and beat with it. I screamed my pleasure into the floor, and it echoed back at me, deafening. He held his rhythm, though I could feel his fingers tight against my ass, as he fought to keep me as still as he could, and with every stroke he brought me again, so that it was orgasm after orgasm, or maybe just one long, rolling line of pleasure.

His voice came strained, '*Ma petite*, feed, feed for I will not last, loose the *ardeur* and feed.'

It was there, just below everything, waiting. With less than a thought it was roaring to life, spilling up through me like another pleasure to ride on the orgasm and thrust itself into the man inside me, so that he cried out. I felt his body spasm one more time, and the next thrust was deep and solid, and it brought me again, screaming, my nails scrambling at the wet tile trying to find something to hold on to, to sink into, to anchor myself in the midst of all that pleasure.

I fed on the joy of him inside me, the foolishness of our love, on the memory of his face as he looked up at me, and even the tears I'd shed. It was a good, thorough feeding, because I didn't feed just on our lust, but on our love.

I collapsed onto the tile with him still inside me. I fought to keep my face above the tile, and he fought to keep his upper body from pinning me to the floor and the water underneath us. Our arms trembled in an echo of exertion and pleasure.

'I love you, *ma petite*,' he said, in a shaky voice.

'*Je t'aime*, Jean-Claude,' I said, and my voice trembled as I said it, but that was just great sex, and I was as certain of what I'd just said as anything I'd ever said in my life.

39

Once we cleaned up, I told Jean-Claude about the rotting vampires, the flesh-eating zombies, and the mystery master vampire that was making and possessing the vampires. Somewhere in the telling of it, I realized something.

'The only reason we didn't try to cure Ares the way that Asher and Damian cured Nathaniel in Tennessee was that we didn't have a vampire with us, but you're here now. You could heal Micah's dad!'

We were dressed and Jean-Claude was fussing with my hair, using those long, graceful fingers of his to get the curls to lie just right. I stepped away from him enough to see his face. His expression was not comforting.

'Why can't you?' I asked.

'If it were fresh, I could have tried, but it is days old, *ma petite*. The doctors have cut away the initial wound and the corruption has spread to other places that have no wound to show.'

'How do you know all that?'

'Nicky reported to me on the plane as I traveled to your side. He is a very thorough and dispassionate observer without you awake and aware to feed him your emotions.'

'So you knew everything I just told you about the vampires,' I said.

He moved close enough to pick up another of my curls and begin to wind it around his finger. 'I did, but you gave details that Nicky could not. He has no real psychic ability, or magic, except for being a werelion. It makes his reporting very physical. You add the meta-physical and I need to know that as well. I can ask you questions that he could not answer.'

'Such as?' I asked.

'The Lover of Death is supposed to be dead, killed by other hands, but the Mother of All Darkness was supposed to be dead once before, and she was not. Was this he? Is this the Lover of Death come back from the dead, so to speak?'

I started to just say no, but then I stopped and made myself really think about the question.

Jean-Claude focused on entwining my hair around his fingers, serious as a small child. I let him do it, because my hair would look great, but it was also something that relaxed him. He usually only fussed with my hair as much as he fussed with his own when he was nervous or we were going to be out at some public event.

'I've felt the Lover of Death's energy when he was combined with Mommie Darkest. This didn't feel the same. The vampire didn't do that nifty trick that the council did, kind of appearing in vision above our heads, or in our heads. This one had to use the vampire he'd made as his puppet to talk to us.'

'But you felt his energy, *ma petite*; was it the same?'

'I didn't feel the presence of this one and think, *Oh, it's the Lover of Death*, if that's what you mean.'

'Yes, that is what I mean. So it is not him.'

'No.' I thought about it as I said it. Something was nagging at me, as if I'd forgotten something important.

'What is it, *ma petite*? You look troubled.'

'Was the Lover of Death able to take over the vampires he made like this?'

'No, never.'

'Could he control zombies?'

'No.'

'So how the hell did we end up with a master vampire that can jump bodies like the Traveller, make rotting vamps like the Lover of Death, control zombies like a necromancer, and control shapeshifters through a bite from his puppet vampires?'

'The Traveller can move to almost any body that is his animal to call or a vampire; this master can use only his own creations, which was a gift that the Dark Mother possessed, and when she was in her prime I am told she could control all types of undead, not just vampires.'

'How about the rotting bite and controlling shapeshifters through it?'

'She made the Lover of Death, but like Belle Morte's ability with sex it was something that sprang to life in the Lover of Death's line of vampires. Most powerful master vampires can control their animal to call through a bite.'

'Not a bite through another vampire they've created and possessed, though,' I said.

'I am not sure. I will ask the Traveller if he has that ability.'

'But either way, Jean-Claude, where the hell did this vampire come from? We don't have that many rotting vamps in America.'

'That is true, and one this powerful I should be able to sense, but I cannot.'

I turned and made him stop fussing with my hair. 'Jesus, that's right, you're the king. You can sense vampires that have blood-oathed to you, at least a little.'

'You sense vampires, too, *ma petite*.'

'I can if they're not master level and not trying to hide.'

'I believe that even some master vampires could not hide from your necromancy now. We have all gained power from my rising to the head of this country's vampires.'

'They gave up the power to you so you'd protect them from the bogey vampires.'

'They feared the Mother of us all, and what the Lover of Death forced his descendant to do in Atlanta.'

'He didn't possess the Master of Atlanta, but he drove him crazy and made him and his vampires slaughter people. It's similar enough to what this master is doing,' I said.

'Perhaps this master was hiding not from the human law, but from the Council.'

'What do you mean?' I asked.

'This new master is powerful, but he is not more powerful than the Mother of All Darkness, and if he is a rotting vampire, then he descends from Amor de Morte, which means until they were both destroyed he must have feared them possessing or destroying him.'

'You mean he waited for us to kill everyone he feared and now he's outing himself to us?'

'I am not sure it is that simple, because he sounds quite mad. There is no real logic in madness, *ma petite*, though the mad always believe they are quite logical.'

'Crazy is never logical outside the head of the crazy person,' I said.

'My point,' he said.

'So now that we've destroyed all his competition, this new master is challenging us, or is he too crazy to care about us like that?'

'I think the latter.'

'Shit,' I said, 'does he have a body for us to find and destroy?'

'The Traveller still does, and he is the oldest of us left with the ability to jump from body to body, but if someone destroyed his original form he would die in truth.'

'But Mommie Darkest didn't die when her body was burned up.'

'*Non*, but the body that had been trapped in Paris wasn't her original body, or so I am told.'

I thought about it and shook my head. 'You're right, it wasn't. She'd traded bodies before, which was one of the reasons she thought she could take mine or make me get pregnant so she could take the child over.' I shuddered, as if I could still feel how evil she'd felt inside me. She had been the darkness made real. The night itself giving breath and life so it could slip in your window and do everything you feared would happen in the dark.

He went back to fussing with my hair. I wasn't the only one who had been afraid of the DARK, if you spelled it with all capital letters.

'Killing the spirit-walking vamps is so damned hard,' I said.

'*Oui*, you must first trap them in a body long enough to destroy them.'

'It only worked last time because she wanted to possess my body. It made her stay put long enough for my necromancy and your power to help me kill her.'

'Then you must find what this new master vampire wants badly enough to stay, as you say, put, so you and Edward can slay him.'

'Can you help us find him? I mean, you're king with metaphysical ties to most of the vampires. Can you use those ties to hunt for him?'

'In all honesty, *ma petite*, I do not know. The powers attributed to the old Council head, the Mother herself, were more her magic than any power given to her as the leader of the Vampire Council. I am not the first vampire or the creator of our society. I am a leader, but not that kind of leader.'

'The female vamp was created by him. Maybe if we use her as a link we could trace it back to him like a psychic cell phone. You have her phone turned on, and then you trace where she's getting her messages from.'

'It is a good thought and one worth trying, *ma petite*.'

'But you don't think it will work,' I said.

'I do not know, and that is the truth.'

I took in a deep breath, let it out slow, and changed topics while I tried to think of how to find the new big bad vampire. 'So there's nothing anyone can do for Micah's dad?'

'Nothing that vampires can do for him, I am afraid, but we did save one of your law enforcement officers, Travers.'

I started to turn and look at him, but he kept my face turned so he could keep doing my hair. 'You sucked the . . . corruption out of Travers?' I asked.

'No, Truth did.'

'You brought Wicked and Truth with you?' I said.

'They are my main guards.'

'It was more of a risk for Truth to do it. He's not as powerful as you are,' I said.

'I am the king. That makes me powerful enough to have cured the officer, but it also means that I would have been tempted to drain power from local vampires if it went badly. I would not have allowed myself to rot to death for a stranger if I had the energy available to me to live. If I drain the life from wee vampires the first time I visit another master's territory without asking his permission first, my reputation will be set like the old European council's. I will be a monster and I do not want that.'

'Is it that dangerous to feed on this corruption, even for you?' I asked.

'You witnessed Damian rotting from helping Asher drain corruption from Nathaniel. If you had not been there as his master to offer him clean and powerful blood, Damian would have died beyond all hope of healing, or recovery.'

'But Asher had no problem doing it, and he wasn't as powerful then as he is now, and certainly not as powerful as you are.'

'Honestly, *ma petite*, I would not risk all that I am and all that I have for a stranger.'

I tried to turn again, and this time he moved so I could. 'You wouldn't risk it for Micah's dad?'

'I might have, but he is beyond such cures. No vampire can cleanse his blood now. It is too widespread in his body.' He moved to the other side and started to patiently fuss with my hair.

I wanted to tell him to stop, but then I had another thought. 'Edward mentioned that the media were calling it a zombie apocalypse, and I made international news footage.'

'*Oui,*' he said, winding a curl around his finger and not really looking at me.

'Are we going to have to go through reporters to make the hotel? Is that why you're fussing with my hair?' I asked.

'The police are keeping them well back on behalf of Micah's family.' He placed the curl among all the rest and began to work on that one problem area in the back of my hair that almost every person with long curly hair seemed to have.

'I thought we might have to talk to the press.'

'There is some talk of a conference tomorrow, but not tonight.'

'Then why are you fussing this much with my hair?'

He hesitated and then continued to do each individual curl on the back of my head so it would curl and lie just so. 'It gives me something to do with my hands while I think.'

'So you are nervous?'

'*Oui,*' he said, softly.

I frowned, couldn't help it. 'Are you having second thoughts about the proposal?'

He looked at me then, face showing astonishment. '*Mon Dieu*, no, no!' He hugged me, then moved back with his hands on my shoulders so we could see each other's faces. '*Ma petite*, you have made me a very happy man by saying yes. Never doubt that I am ecstatic with our engagement and look forward to making a more formal presentation of it.'

I frowned harder. 'Formal? Why formal?'

'Because I am the vampire king of America, and kings do not become engaged quietly.'

'What does that even mean?'

'It means that once you, Micah, and whoever else we deem involved have worked out the organization of who is marrying whom, then we will announce what we all wish to announce, whatever that is.'

'Okay, that sounds very reasonable, so why are you nervous?'

'It seems silly,' he said. He drew back from me, running his hands down the lace on either side of the pearl buttons of his shirt. The lace was actually inlaid on either side of the button line trailing up to the collar, which was unbuttoned and lying loose over the black velvet jacket, which hit him just past the waist. The last time I'd seen the shirt, the collar had been high and buttoned all the way up his neck so that the soft, embroidered white-on-white lace framed the edge of his chin. He only wore the collar loose when he was at the end of his day and in private.

'Are you okay?' I asked.

He made a sharp, exasperated sound. 'I am over six hundred years old; you would think I would be past such silliness.'

'What silliness?' I asked.

'We need to gather our young men and retire to the hotel, but I am told that our *chat* has his family with him.'

Chat was French for cat, which meant Micah. Nathaniel was *minet*, kitten, or pussycat in French. 'So we go up and we see how his father is doing. It's hard, but . . .'

He shook his head. 'It is not the sad fate of his father that leaves me so anxious.'

'Then what is it?' I asked.

'The introduction to Micah's family is troublesome.'

'Did he not introduce you?' I asked.

'I came straight to your side, so he has not had time to introduce me.'

'Then I am totally confused,' I said.

He sighed. 'I am being the girl, am I not?'

'If you mean confusing, yes.'

'I want to greet Micah, to comfort him, but I am not certain what he wishes me to do in front of his family. I am a vampire and male. I was told that they are very religious.'

I smiled. 'Some of them are, but his parents will be okay about the guy-guy part.' I explained the domestic arrangements of Micah's parents.

By the time I finished, Jean-Claude was laughing. 'Micah has agonized about being with Nathaniel and what his family would think, and all this time they have had their own ménage-à-trois. It is too perfect.'

I nodded, smiling. 'They were cool about all the wereanimal stuff, so I think they'll be okay with vampires.'

'So they have welcomed both you and Nathaniel into their familial bosoms?'

I nodded. 'It went really well.'

'But a ménage-à-trois is more acceptable than our larger arrangement.'

I had a clue, at last, where he was going with his case of nerves. 'Are you worried about how Micah will introduce you to his family?'

He gave that graceful Gallic shrug that meant everything and nothing.

I went to him and wrapped my arms around his waist, and he put his arms around my shoulders. I gazed up at him and smiled. 'I think the fact that you're worried about Micah and his family is one of the sweetest things I've ever heard you say.'

'It is not sweet, *ma petite*, it is ridiculous. The only man he loves is Nathaniel, and I know this.'

'You don't love him the way you love Asher,' I said.

'That is true, but Asher is no longer with us.'

'Actually, I promised Dev I'd talk to you about Asher.'

'What of Asher and our handsome Devil?'

'Dev misses him.'

'Many of us miss him, *ma petite*,' he said, and there was the slightest tone to his voice that let me know just how much of that 'us' was him.

'Have you spoken to him lately?' I asked.

'I have.'

I studied that handsome, unreadable face. He was hiding whatever he was feeling and thinking from me, which meant it was something he either didn't want to share or thought I'd be upset about. I had a smart thought, or a potentially smart thought.

'Did Asher tell you about the new man in his life?'

Jean-Claude tensed and then went very still, that kind of stillness that people don't have. Snakes can be that still, held frozen and stretched out like a tree branch while waiting for the danger to pass, or the prey to come that inch closer.

'I'll take the silence for a yes,' I said.

'He mentioned his new beau,' Jean-Claude said in a voice as empty and neutral as he could manage. Once upon a time I would have thought he didn't give a damn, but now I knew that sometimes his most neutral tone meant he cared very damn much.

'Dev was supposed to call Asher while I was cleaning up,' I said.

'Was he?' And again the voice was too neutral.

'Yes, he was.' I tightened my arms around his waist. 'Dev wanted to double-check how many of the mean things Asher said were true and how many were said just to hurt our Devil.'

Jean-Claude looked at me then, his face still carefully neutral. 'Asher does have a gift for cruel words.'

I nodded. 'Dev misses him enough that he's willing to give up everyone but Asher.'

Jean-Claude allowed his expression to thaw a little. 'What made Mephistopheles change his mind?'

'He's never missed anyone as much as he misses Asher. I don't think he understood that any one person might be worth giving up all the others for.'

'Has our Devil never been in love before?'

'Apparently not,' I said.

'No, because only love can make of parting such a hell,' Jean-Claude said.

'Yeah,' I said.

His body relaxed around me then, so that he hugged me, rather than simply had his arms around me. That unsettling, almost reptile stillness was just gone, and his body had movement, flow, not just a sense of pulse and life, but as if he could stop his energy, his aura, from moving, too. Maybe that was it? Maybe it was a psychic thing, that vampire stillness, so that they could dampen down not just their physical movement, but all their 'movement.'

I said, 'It's okay if you miss Asher.'

He pulled me in against his body so that my head rested on his chest, cradled against the velvet of his jacket. I snuggled in against him and knew from the softness of the jacket it wasn't real velvet, but some modern synthetic. The modern stuff was always softer.

'Is it, *ma petite*? I miss him and yet I do not believe he has learned the lesson we wished to teach him. He waxed quite eloquent on the phone about his new man and how he is denied nothing from this new werehyena.'

I tried to move back so I could see his face, but he held me in place. I didn't fight it, because sometimes he did that when he wasn't certain he could control his facial expression. The older vampires saw an unguarded expression as something that could be potentially dangerous to them. Centuries of having been punished for the wrong look at the wrong time had taught most of them to hide what they truly felt. Jean-Claude had told me once that it was actually an effort to show emotion. I think that ceased to be true as he got metaphysically closer to all his warm-blooded servants like me. We'd given him some of our warmth, but it had cost him some of his hard-won control.

'I didn't realize it was a werehyena,' I said, with my cheek cradled against his chest.

'Yes, but he is not the leader of the local hyenas, just the prettiest boy to fall under Asher's spell.' He sounded tired.

'Did Asher seducing this werehyena piss off the leader of their pack?'

'Their leader is a woman, and because I sent Asher to her city, he seems to have taken it as a hint that I wanted him to be more heterosexual.'

'Which means he did just the opposite and went for just the guys,' I said.

'Oh, much better than that; he seduced her and then ignored her for this new man.'

I rose up, and this time he let me. 'Holy shit, was he trying to get himself killed?'

Jean-Claude stepped back, shaking his head. 'If he had not been my envoy, the leader, Dulcia, would have made an example of Asher. She called me about a month ago to tell me of his misdeeds.'

'Hyena society is matriarchal, which is why Narcissus won't let women in his clan. He's afraid a woman will automatically take over just like with real wild hyenas.'

'I know all that, *ma petite*.'

'But maybe Asher doesn't,' I said. 'He doesn't do the research that you, me, Micah, Nathaniel, hell, Nicky, everyone does. Narcissus doesn't run his group like most of hyena society, and if they're the only hyenas Asher has spent any time with, maybe he didn't know how dangerous they could be.'

Jean-Claude seemed to think about that for a moment, and then nodded. 'Very wise, *ma petite*; you may be right. Asher was always a weapon to be aimed at someone, or something, by our mistress, Belle Morte. I began as a mere weapon in her arsenal, but I learned to ask more questions and find more answers. Asher was content to follow her plans and then mine.'

'Yeah, he's not a planner,' I said.

'I fear not,' Jean-Claude said.

'He's powerful enough to be master of his own territory, Jean-Claude, but he doesn't have the temperament for it.'

'No, he does not.'

'He's never going to,' I said.

We looked at each other, just a look, but it was enough. 'Either I have to allow Dulcia to kill him for the insult, or I must order him home to us.'

I shook my head. 'We can't let her kill him.'

'No,' he said.

'How long ago did he fuck up this badly?'

'Not quite a month.'

'So he was well behaved for almost five months, and then suddenly he starts trying to commit suicide by werehyena?'

'It would seem so.'

'We originally exiled him for a month, then stretched it to three, because you said he was making a diplomatic success of it.'

'He was, and none of us believed he had learned to value home and his loved ones, so I decided to keep him there for a bit longer.'

'I remember, you were thinking of bringing him home for at least a visit at the six-month mark. You, all of us, hoped that six months away would make him value what he had here with us, and maybe even make him want to try therapy for his jealousy issues and the violent temper that goes with it.'

'All that is very true, *ma petite*.'

'But he didn't know that he only had another month to behave himself and we'd call him home,' I said.

'No,' he said.

'So when five months of good behavior didn't get him what he wanted, he decided to act out like some kind of stupid teenager.'

'There is a part of him that will always be a foolish child. I do not know why, but he has always been so.'

'If he can't get attention for being good, he'll get attention for being bad,' I said.

'Very, very true, *ma petite.*'

'So, Asher hasn't learned a damned thing, and now if we bring him home the bad behavior does get rewarded. Behavior that gets rewarded gets repeated, Jean-Claude.'

'What would you have me do, *ma petite?* You say you will not allow Dulcia to kill him for the insult. After he has harmed all the good diplomatic work that Micah did with Dulcia's group, I do not believe that our leopard king will allow Asher to simply be moved to another city.'

'Moving the problem around doesn't fix it, Jean-Claude.'

'No, no, it does not.' He leaned against the wall and rubbed his fingers on his temples, as if he were getting a headache. I don't think I'd ever seen him make that gesture or known him to have a headache.

'Are you okay?' I asked.

'No,' he said, 'no, I am not. If I did not love Asher, then we could simply let his own actions seal his fate, because in his present mood he will keep pushing until someone pushes back.'

'How do we push back?' I asked.

'I do not know. I wish I did not love him.'

'Ditto,' I said.

He looked at me then. 'You do not love him as you love me, or Micah, or Nathaniel. I'm not even certain you care for him as you care for Nicky, or Cynric. What is he to you, *ma petite?*'

'I do love Asher, but I know that some of my deeper feelings for him are a reflection of you and how much you love him, so I honestly can't always tell where my emotions stop and yours start when it comes to him.'

'I am sorry for that. I would not have you tormented by *mon char-donneret.* One of us so bewitched and bothered is enough.'

'He's not my goldfinch; that's your pet name for him. He tried to get me to call him *master* in the bedroom like Nathaniel does, but you're the only person on this planet that I'll call *master*, and even then only if you need me to do it for vampire politics.'

'Did he truly believe you would call him *master*, simply because he dominated you in the bedroom and dungeon?'

'Maybe, or maybe it was just Asher testing his limits, seeing how far he could push me.'

Jean-Claude nodded. 'That is very him, unfortunately. He must always see how far he can push a relationship. It is a sign of insecurity and of his perverse nature.'

'Like you said, unfortunately.'

We stood there in silence for a minute, and then I said, 'We know all this bad stuff about Asher. He's just confirmed that he's learned nothing in exile, and he'll still be a shit when he comes home.'

'Yes,' Jean-Claude said.

'So why are we even talking about letting him come back to St Louis?'

'Because if we do not get him out of Dulcia's territory she will eventually kill him, because he will keep pushing at her until she breaks or we call him home.'

'Does Asher understand that if she breaks, she'll kill him and worry about the power fallout later?'

'Dulcia fears us, *ma petite*. She fears making an enemy of the first vampire king of America.'

'Does she fear us enough to keep eating Asher's insults?'

'I do not know her well enough to answer that question, but I do know Asher. He is relentless once he decides to be cruel, and he has a true talent for finding that which will alienate, humiliate, or terrify someone.'

'I have a few memories from you, just glimpses of Asher raping people as entertainment for Belle's court.'

'I was forced to help in some of those entertainments, *ma petite*, or risk taking the place of the prisoner. I chose to be the predator to escape being the victim.'

'Asher didn't have to be threatened to do it, though, did he?' I asked.

'He delighted in cruelty once. He is better than that now, but the part of him that enjoys giving pain and fear is still inside him. He has found tame avenues for his interests in the bedroom and the bondage and submission games. He understands now that he must play safe, sane, and consensual here with us.'

'Do you think part of him misses getting to do some of it for real?' I asked.

'How can you ask that about someone that you love?'

'The only part of love that is blind is that first rush of endorphins and craziness; after that wears off, no one knows you as honestly, warts and all, as the people who love you, truly love you.'

'I have found many people over the centuries who stay blind to the faults of their lovers.'

'True love means you love the real person, not an ideal that you have in your head and superimpose over them. That's illusion and lies to me.'

'But if the lovers are happy in their illusion and lies, what then, *ma petite*? Does it cease to be true love because lies are necessary for it to continue?'

'Yes,' I said.

He looked at me, surprised and not trying to hide it. 'Some mystery is needed for love to survive, *ma petite*. If we knew everything about each other, surely the burden of our crimes, or doubts, would destroy us.'

'We know Asher is a perverse, cruel, sadistic bastard, but we still love him.'

'I do not think I would like you to list my faults so clearly. I think it would pain me to know you see me so clearly and so harshly.'

I smiled at him. 'You have faults, and so do I, but your good points outnumber your bad by a lot. We can't say the same for Asher.'

'He is beautiful,' Jean-Claude said.

'Very,' I said, 'and an amazing top in the dungeon. Since he was my first, I didn't really understand how hard it is to find someone who enjoys being as edgy as I like for bondage, and there's no one else sane that comes close to Nathaniel's needs in the area.'

'Our kitten can be quite frightening in his needs.'

'And that's it; it frightens you and me, we don't enjoy topping Nathaniel to a point that satisfies him, but Asher does. In fact, I'm not sure I entirely trust the two of them alone without extra rules from me or you.'

'I believe it is that edge of danger that delights them both with each other,' Jean-Claude said.

I nodded. 'Agreed.'

'So he is beautiful and good in the dungeon, but that is hardly virtue enough to offset his vices.'

'True, but he's also a fabulous lover even without the BDSM,' I said.

Jean-Claude looked away as if he had to control his face for a moment before he turned back to me. 'Yes.' It was one word, but it was enough. There was almost pain in his *yes*.

'You think it's a bad idea to bring him home,' I said.

'Don't you?' he asked.

We stood there looking at each other. I finally said, 'Yeah, I do.'

'Logic would dictate that we leave Asher to his fate,' Jean-Claude said.

'You mean let Dulcia kill him?'

He gave a small nod. His face was very careful as he looked at me. He showed nothing, but the very lack of emotion spoke volumes.

'You're leaving the decision up to me, aren't you?' I asked.

'I have been in thrall to his beauty and his cruelty for centuries, *ma petite*. I cannot rule him as he needs.'

'I can't let someone else kill him.'

His eyes widened fractionally. 'I do not like that phrasing, *ma petite*.'

'Me either, but when he hit Cynric hard enough to knock him out I thought he'd broken his neck, and damage to the spine can act like decapitation for both vampires and wereanimals. If he had killed Cynric even by accident I would have shot him, Jean-Claude. I would have shot him and I wouldn't have shot to wound.'

'That you are strong enough to do it, I have no doubt, but that you could live with it afterward, that I do doubt.'

'I've been thinking about that since Asher left. I know I would have done it. I know that he could still push me far enough that I would do it, but I think it would break something in me that wouldn't heal. Hell, shooting Ares – knowing that I had brought him into harm's way. I practically fed him to the big bad vampire, and then I killed Ares. I loved, but I wasn't in love with Haven, but it killed a part of me to look down the barrel of a gun and shoot him.'

Jean-Claude moved toward me, but I waved him off. 'No, just no,' I said.

'What can I do, *ma petite*?' he asked.

'You've just told me that you believe Asher will need killing and that you can't do it. You've just told me that it's my job, if it has to be done.'

'You do not have to do it either. We can let him behave badly and simply let him be a weakness for both of us. I cannot fault you for being no stronger in the face of his cruel beauty than I myself.'

I shook my head. 'You bastard, you know I can't do that.'

'Being who you are, no,' he said, softly.

'What are we saying then, Jean-Claude?'

'Our wise leopard king says we should bring him home, because too many of us miss him.'

'He didn't just say that,' I said.

Jean-Claude smiled. 'No, he said that we either let Dulcia kill him, or we get him the hell out of her territory so he can try to salvage the goodwill he had built up with her and her hyena clan.'

'Nathaniel misses him terribly.'

'As does our Devil,' Jean-Claude said.

'Even Richard misses having someone to dominate in the bedroom. It gives him somewhere for his darkness to be aimed. He's been more moody without Asher to play with and abuse.'

'*Mon lupe* is surprisingly talented as a dominant.'

'He's trying to embrace all of himself, and part of him really enjoys tormenting Asher with both floggers and whips and sexual denial. Asher loves being the first guy on to deflower a heterosexual man, and Richard enjoys flaunting himself with Asher and never letting Asher touch him.'

'They do seem to fill a need in each other, as does Asher for Nathaniel, and you, *ma petite*.'

'And you,' I said.

'And Narcissus, our own hyena leader, pines for Asher.'

'So he fills needs that no one else fills for a lot of us,' I said.

'It would seem so,' Jean-Claude said.

'I wish we didn't love him.'

'I have wished that off and on for centuries.'

'I bet. Asher is just so . . . damaged, and he won't go to therapy and work on his issues.'

'Therapy will be part of the price for his return,' Jean-Claude said.

'We can make him go sit in the therapist's office, Jean-Claude, but we can't actually force him to do the therapy.'

'That is true,' he said.

'The fact that I want him home, too, means that you aren't the only one who has a weakness for him.'

'Love is both a great strength, *ma petite*, and a great weakness, which depends on the day, the hour, the moment.'

I went to him, and he met me in the middle of the room. We hugged, but I kept watching his face. 'We bring him home because we're not strong enough to tell him to bugger off, is that it?'

He smiled. 'Something like that.'

'Ain't love grand?' I said.

'Yes,' he said, as he bent to kiss me. 'Yes, whatever it may hold of pleasure, or pain, or even grief, I would not trade it for its absence.'

We kissed, because we needed to feel the touch of each other, to reassure ourselves that we weren't being damned fools about Asher, or at least if we were being fools, we were in it together. Sometimes love isn't about being smart. Sometimes it's about being stupid together. I hated those moments, but I'd grown to understand that love, real love, is full of choices that make no sense, that should go horribly wrong, but you make the choice anyway. Why? Because love is about hope; you hope that this time it will be different. Sometimes it is – Jean-Claude and I were proof of that – but sometimes it isn't, and Richard and the three of us were proof of that.

Faint heart never won fair lady; I guess the same goes for winning the fair lad. Here's hoping.

40

Some of the local police were like Yancey from SWAT and accepted me as one of them because I'd held my shit together under fire, but others . . . were very busy trying to blame me for what Ares had done. They needed to blame someone, and I'd killed the only other person they wanted to hate, so they hated me.

Dev and Nicky had driven with me to the station. We'd meet up with Edward/Ted and get introduced to Marshal Hatfield and the rest. There were witness statements to read, crime scene photos to look at, and the pictures of the missing, some of whom had turned up as the walking dead of one flavor or another. I hated to waste darkness on doing stuff I could do in daylight, but the vampires in custody were safe behind their lawyer for tonight. Maybe by the time I got to question them tomorrow night I'd have a better handle from reading up on the case. That was what I told myself to keep the frustration down. We had two perfectly good suspects who had seen the big bad vampire that was the real danger, and we couldn't ask them a damn thing.

The plan was for the men with me to wait out in the public area until I was done, or until they were relieved of duty by the next pair of bodyguards. They knew the drill. They also had carry permits for their guns with them, and they were willing to give their guns up to a lockbox if the local PD demanded it. What we weren't prepared for was Detective Ricky Rickman to be passing through the check-in desk. One of the things people fear most about shapeshifters is that they look just like everybody else, because they *are* everybody else. It's just a disease, and short of a blood test or a change of form, you can pass for straight human. I wasn't trying to sneak them past anybody; I just didn't think about it.

'Get your animals out of here, Blake!' Rickman yelled it; he wasn't that angry, he just wanted everyone within earshot to hear. He was full of an I-told-you-so self-satisfaction. It masqueraded as righteous fury, but he was too pleased with himself for that.

'They aren't animals, Rickman,' I said, my voice calm.

One of the uniform officers said, 'Are they wereanimals?'

'Yeah, all of them are,' Rickman said.

'How can you tell?' the officer asked. His eyes were a little wide, which made him look even younger than he was. Perfect.

'I can just tell,' Rickman said.

I whispered to Dev and Nicky, 'Whatever happens, stay out of it. Don't do anything that feeds this.'

Nicky gave a small nod. Dev said, 'Okay, boss.'

'If you want to whisper sweet nothings to your fur-bangers, do it somewhere else,' Rickman shouted; he was moving up on us, on me, trying to use his height to intimidate.

I was calm but made sure my voice carried. 'First, bullshit, Rickman, you know they're lycanthropes because I told you. Second, they aren't animals, they're people.'

'Your last pet killed Baker and tore Billings's fucking hand off!' Rickman towered over me, shouting into my face.

We had a crowd gathering around us. There were mutterings of, 'They don't get to come in here.' 'Get them out of here.' 'Animals.' 'They're monsters.'

'First, he wasn't my pet, he was a Marine. Second, he was bespelled by a vampire just like some of the other officers,' I said.

'He wasn't an officer' – Rickman spat it in my face – 'he was a fucking animal!'

I wiped the spittle off my face as I smiled up at Rickman. I didn't want to smile. It was an involuntary expression, one that usually preceded me doing something unpleasant and usually violent. I was angry. I controlled it, but the smile most unpleasantly showed it.

'What the hell are you smiling at, Blake?' he yelled.

I have no excuse for what I did next; I deliberately stepped into Rickman. I didn't hurt him; I even kept my hands at my sides, so that the body armor under our shirts was all that barely brushed against each other, but I understood violence and men. That one small move-ment was an escalation. I'd touched a man who was leaning over me, spitting his rage in my face; the lightest touch can tip that into something physical. A lot of women don't understand the rules, that most fights among men start like dogfights with trash talk and body language and that one delicate brush against him went through his adrenaline-pumped body like a jolt of electricity, sharp, nearly painful. To his anger, his body, I might as well have hit him.

We were too close for him to swing at me, so he pushed me hard enough that I stumbled back from him. I thought about falling on purpose, but I debated too long and lost the chance to make him look like a bully, but when someone is that angry you get other chances.

I said, 'You fight like a girl.'

He swung at me, and no matter how stupid he seemed, he was a cop and had been one long enough to make detective, which meant he knew how to fight. I was still fast enough and good enough to block the blow, but I was also fast enough and good enough to take the hit. I needed to show Rickman for what he was.

His fist connected solid on my cheek, and I went down. Rickman was just human, but he was six feet of in-shape human, and he was a cop; they know how to hit, because sometimes their lives depend on putting someone down and making sure they stay there. I ended up on my ass on the floor, my head ringing with the blow. I staggered to my feet before my head had cleared, because one rule in a fight is that you get to your feet as soon as you can. The only thing I could have done from the floor was dislocate his knee with a kick. I wanted more options than crippling him, so I got to my feet and faced him hands up, already in a stance, weight springy and even, slightly on the balls of my feet so I could move.

Rickman was faster than he looked, because he had another fist headed my way. This time I blocked it with my forearm and hit him with my other fist in the side of the body. I pivoted on my feet, throwing my weight into the blow and twisting my fist at the end just like you do when you work the heavy bag. I did what I'd trained to do, but it had been years since I'd fought a normal human. Rickman had hit me full out, and I returned the favor, but I forgot that I was stronger than any human being of my size and sex. I forgot that I carried multiple strains of lycanthropy and had metaphysical ties to vampires. I just hit him and forgot everything but making the blow count.

I felt his ribs give, heard a low-pitched crack as something broke, and knew it wasn't anything on me. Then there was a wall of men in uniform separating us, pushing us back from each other.

I expected to hear Rickman cursing me, but there were no yells over the crowd. I spotted a familiar face among the men pushing me back; Officer Bush had a hand on my shoulder and was trying to divide his attention between me and the men behind him. The right side of his face had bloomed into amazing bruises. Him I'd been able to knock out when the vampire mind-fucked him. I had a moment of regret so sharp that it took my breath away, because I had one of those ridiculous thoughts that guilt will give you. Why hadn't I tried to knock Ares out? Answer: Once the change begins, that kind of shit doesn't work. In fact, it can make things worse, because you can knock out the human but leave the beast more in control. Logically I knew that, but regret isn't about logic, it's about emotion, and that's got no logic to it.

I stood in a little bubble of isolation even with Bush and others touching me, holding me back as if I were fighting to get free. I wasn't struggling to get to Rickman. The fight was over as far as I was concerned. The only reason there'd been a fight at all had been my emotions about losing Ares. Motherfucking son of a bitch, I knew better than this.

Bush grinned down at me. 'You pack quite a punch, Marshal Blake.'

'Hey, you were going all vampire-controlled on us, I had to do something.'

'Not me,' he said, 'the detective. They're saying you broke one of his ribs.'

'It's only a floating rib,' I said, 'they bust up easier than the ones higher up.'

A plainclothes officer with a head full of unruly black hair said, 'How's your hand, Marshal?'

I flexed my right hand and nothing hurt. 'I'm fine.'

He smiled, flashing a dimple to one side of a nice mouth. His eyes were a nice, solid brown, not too dark, not too pale. 'You're going to need ice on your face, though.'

It had hurt when Rickman hit me, but it wasn't until the new detective said something that it started to ache. The fact that it hurt this much with my healing abilities meant Rickman had intended to hurt me badly. I felt less bad about the rib thing.

'I'm MacAllister, Detective Robert MacAllister; friends call me Bobby.'

I wanted to ask if we were friends, but comments like that were taken as either hostile or flirting, so I took it for what it was. 'Glad to meet you, Detective, Bobby. I'm Anita.' I said it on automatic, my attention on the cluster of men I could see through Bush's and MacAllister's chests. I felt separate from it all, distant and almost floating. Fuck, I was in shock. How could I be in shock from a puny fight like this?

Dev was at my side. He touched my face, gently, turning so he could see the mark. 'If you keep ordering us to stay out of the fights, all the other bodyguards are going to make fun of us.'

That made me smile, which was probably his goal. 'I'll bear that in mind.'

Nicky moved up beside us. 'You did just get out of the hospital.'

I turned to look at him. What I could see of his face through the fall of his hair was set in bored, stoic lines, but I realized that I'd ordered him to stay out of the fight no matter what. Would he have been forced to watch someone hurt me badly, try to kill me, and been helpless to help me, because I'd given him a direct order? I wasn't sure, and I should have thought of that before I spoke. I felt off my game.

I reached my left hand out to him and he wrapped his bigger hand around mine. I didn't normally hold hands with my lovers when they were being bodyguards, but it was the best I could do to apologize for making it impossible for him to do his job, maybe, by not thinking my words through. I should have been able to know if what I said had crippled his ability to guard me that much, but I couldn't seem to think my way through the maze in my head. His hand was warm and real in mine. It helped.

He smiled, and that was enough to make me happy that I held his hand even in front of the cops.

Bush said, 'Hey, Nicky, does the marshal ever let you guys actually protect her?'

Nicky grinned at him. 'Every once in a while.'

'Naw,' Dev said, 'she's usually protecting us.'

Bush looked up at the taller man, as if waiting for the joke, but something in Dev's face stopped him and made him frown instead. He might have asked if we were kidding, but someone came up behind us who made Bush stand at the cop's version of attention. MacAllister was suddenly all serious. The other officers cleared out around us as if we were all suddenly contagious. Whoever was behind me was someone in charge. They weren't in charge of me, but I was in their house, and that meant . . .

'Marshal Blake, Detective Rickman, I need to see you both in my office, now.'

With a serious face, MacAllister leaned over and whispered, 'Called into the captain's office first time you step inside; fast work.'

'About par for me,' I said, and then turned with a professional face, but a hand going up to the blossoming bruise on my cheek. I'd let Rickman hit me so that everyone wouldn't get all hysterical about Dev and Nicky being wereanimals, because nothing undercuts someone's accusations like being made to look unprofessional and a bully. It had worked, but a sympathy bruise is a sympathy bruise, and I was going to see if this one could be multipurpose. I was going to milk it, just in case the captain was upset about me breaking one of his detectives.

41

Captain Jonas was a large African American man who looked like he'd probably played high school ball, maybe college, but the desk job had started to round out his middle to the point where I wondered if he had to pass the same health standards as his patrol officers. He sat behind his desk glaring at us. The 'us' didn't include Rickman. He was on the way to the hospital. The 'us' was U.S. Marshal Susan Hatfield, Edward, and me. Apparently my doing something bad enough to get called on the carpet by Jonas had renewed Hatfield's fighting spirit and she was trying to get me kicked off the case again.

Hatfield was about five foot six, which made her almost as tall as Edward. He gained about two inches from his cowboy boots and she was in the same flat treaded boots as I was, so she seemed shorter, or he seemed taller. Her chestnut-brown hair was back in a small, neat ponytail. She moved her head as she gesticulated angrily, and the overhead lights picked out deep red highlights in her hair. She was about two tones off from going from chestnut to a nice deep auburn. She was thin, but it was a thinness that came from genetics and working out, not starving herself. Her forearms had lean muscle on them as she gestured, and what I could see of her upper arms wasn't bulk. She was all long, lean muscle, almost mannish hips, and small breasts. She was one of those women who managed to look delicate and feminine without having the curves to go with the triangular face. Her chin was a little sharp for my tastes, but then I wasn't shopping to date her, I was just noticing things while she ranted. She was basically accusing me of being too close to the monsters to make good choices. I wasn't really listening, because I'd heard it all before, and I was a little tired of hearing it from anyone. I just stood there and let her words wash over me like white noise.

It was Edward saying, 'Anita, Anita, the captain is talking to you,' that made me blink and pay attention again.

I looked at Edward standing a little behind and to the other side of Hatfield, and then I looked at Jonas behind his desk. 'I'm sorry, sir, but I didn't hear what you said.'

'Are we boring you, Blake?' he asked.

'I've heard the song and dance before, sir.'

Edward stepped forward in his best good-ol'-boy Ted persona. 'There's a beaut of a bruise blossoming out on Anita's face. I think she got her chimes rung pretty good when Rickman hit her.'

'Are you making excuses for her?' Jonas asked.

'No, sir, just pointing out that she just got released from the hospital and she may heal like a son of a bitch, but the healing isn't perfect or instantaneous. I'm just wondering if she's more hurt than she's letting on.'

Jonas narrowed his eyes at Edward and then looked back at me. 'You hurt, Blake?'

'My face hurts,' I said, but my voice was as empty of emotion as Hatfield's had been full of it.

'I can't see the bruise from here. Turn so I can.'

I turned to give him the right side of my face where the throbbing was beginning to spread into the beginnings of a really nice headache. It put me looking at Hatfield, who glared back at me.

I heard Jonas's chair slide back. 'It's swelling a lot for just a bruise.' He'd come around the desk so he could see it better. He pursed his lips, scowling. 'Ricky hit you just on the bone there. You think he cracked the bone?'

'I didn't hear it break,' I said.

'How bad does it hurt?'

'Not bad enough to be broken, I don't think.'

'You had broken bones?' he asked.

'Yes, sir.'

'So you know what it feels like,' he said.

'Yes, sir, I do.'

He let out a big huff of air. 'You need some ice on it at least before it swells into your eye. Can't send you out looking beat to hell.' He went to his door, opened it, and yelled out at someone. 'Need an ice bag and some towels wrapped around it.' He seemed to expect it would get done, because he closed the door and went back to sit at his desk. He steepled his fingers, elbows resting on his stomach, because he'd gained too much weight to use the chair arms for it. It looked like a habitual gesture from before the stomach came on. He looked at us over his fingers.

'Marshal Hatfield holds the warrant of execution on these vampires, and she wants you and Marshal Forrester to mind your own damn business.'

'That much I heard,' I said.

'Technically, I'm not in charge of the three of you – you're federal – but we're the local PD who will be backing your move. Hatfield here is the local executioner. I know her. Why should I give either of you any consideration?'

'If we just needed to kill the vampires, fine,' I said. 'Wait until dawn and then chain them to a metal gurney with some holy objects and stake their asses, but we want information from them, and for that we need them alive.'

'They aren't alive!' Hatfield said, and there was way too much emotion in that sentence. She was one of those, a vampire hater. It was sort of like giving a Ku Klux Klan member a badge and a license to kill the racial group of his choice, and could get just as nasty.

'Legally, they are,' Edward said in a friendly, almost joking voice.

Hatfield turned on him with an accusing finger and said, 'Of course you'd defend Blake; you're sleeping with her.'

'Hatfield,' Jonas said, and the word was sharp.

She turned to the captain, and underneath the anger was uncertainty plain enough for all of us to see.

'Actually,' Edward said, 'I'm defending the law, not Marshal Blake. Legally the vampires in custody have rights as citizens.'

'The only reason I couldn't kill them tonight was because of the law that she' – and she pointed a finger at me without really looking at me – 'helped create.'

I resisted the urge to grab her finger and break it as it pointed in my face, but her face stayed toward Edward. 'If you kill the two vampires we have, then what, Hatfield?'

She finally deigned to look at me. 'Then we'd have two less vampires walking around.'

'So you're more about killing the vampires than solving cases,' I said.

'Once they're dead, it is solved,' she said.

I looked at Jonas. 'The two vampires in custody only went missing as humans about a month ago, or that's what the locals have told me. I'd come down here tonight to read over the files, but are they about a month missing?'

'About,' Jonas said.

'So who made them vampires? Who made the rotting vampires that we killed in the woods?'

'The bastard that runs the bloodsuckers in this city made them!' Hatfield said, her voice strident and just this side of yelling.

'They were rotting vampires. That means that your Master of the City couldn't have made them, because he's not a rotter.'

'They're all walking corpses, Blake; they all rot in the end.'

'Everyone rots in the end, Hatfield,' I said.

'Fredrico has disavowed all knowledge of the vampires in the woods,' Jonas said.

'Of course he has,' Hatfield said. 'What else could he say? That he lost control of some of his bloodsuckers and they slaughtered people?'

'Entire families are missing,' I said. 'Vampires don't take out families. It's illegal to make children into vampires.'

'I've killed kid vampires,' she said.

'How many?' I asked.

She looked sullen and finally muttered, 'Two.'

'They were older than they looked, though, weren't they?'

'What's that supposed to mean?' she asked.

'I mean they looked like kids, but they weren't,' I said.

'They were kids,' she said, and sounded so certain.

'Did you talk to them at all?' I asked.

'Talk to them? Talk to them? Who talks to the vampires? Oh, wait, you do, and a hell of a lot more than just talk.'

Edward said, 'Have you spoken to any of the vampires before you killed them?'

She wouldn't meet his eyes full on before she said, 'No, they don't do much talking during the day.'

'Have you ever even served an active warrant?' Edward asked.

'Once you serve it, it qualifies as an active warrant,' she said.

'Have you ever been on a vampire hunt?' I asked.

She just stood there glaring at us.

'Have all your vampires been morgue kills?' I asked.

'No, I've tracked the bloodsuckers to their lairs and killed their asses in coffins and fucking sleeping bags. I've been lucky and found them in daylight most of the time, so there wasn't a lot of talking happening; besides, they're not afraid of me. I'm not the Executioner.'

I exchanged a look with Edward. Hatfield wasn't exactly a newbie, but she wasn't us. Maybe it showed on our faces, because she said, 'I am a legal vampire executioner; I do my job, I'm just not the Executioner,' she said. 'The vampires haven't given me some cute pet name yet.'

'They don't hand those out to every marshal,' Edward said.

'Yeah, I know you're Death,' she said.

For a second I thought Hatfield knew about Ted's big secret identity as Edward, because he'd been Death as long as I'd been the Executioner, but the nickname had been his before a badge and falling in love with Donna had tamed him down some. But the vampires had dubbed Edward Death once as an assassin/bounty hunter and once as a bounty hunter/marshal. It was convenient of them to use the same name twice.

I fought to keep my face blank as Edward drawled in his best Ted voice, 'If you know I'm one of the Four Horsemen, then you know that Anita has two earned names among the vampires.'

She looked sullen. 'Yeah, I know she has two pet names.'

'I don't,' Jonas said. 'Enlighten me.'

We both looked at Hatfield. She glared at both of us, then finally back at Jonas. 'Forrester is Death and Blake is War.'

'Who are the other two Horsemen?'

'Otto Jeffries is Pestilence, and Bernardo Spotted-Horse is Hunger.'

'I've met Spotted-Horse and I know Jeffries by reputation; they're both ex-military, and so are you, right, Forrester?'

'Yes, sir.'

'Then why is Blake "War"? She's never been military.'

'She has a higher kill count than I do,' Edward said, 'and the vampires see Death as a one-on-one killer, whereas War kills a lot all at one time.'

'You asked the vampires,' Jonas said.

'I did.'

'But why not Jeffries, or Spotted-Horse?'

'You've met Bernardo, right?' I asked.

'I've met him, too,' Hatfield said. 'He didn't seem that scary.'

'He's Hunger,' Edward said.

'I don't get it,' Hatfield said.

'The vampires said Bernardo looks good enough to eat, but no one's ever tasted him, so he leaves them hungry.'

She frowned.

Jonas seemed to think about it, and then he grinned wide and happy. He laughed. 'He's tasty like food, I get it.'

'Dangerous food,' Edward said. 'He has the fifth highest kill count of any marshal.'

'I've met Jeffries once. He had a way of looking at women when he thought no one else was looking, like we were meat, and that was before he caught lycanthropy on the job. Now I guess we really are meat to him.' She shivered, shoulders hunching a little, and then seemed to realize what she'd done and stood up straight, shoulders back.

The fact that she'd noticed made me think better of Hatfield. I knew Otto Jeffries as Olaf. Olaf's hobby was being a serial killer, never in this country, and never on government work, so if you could keep him working he was 'safe.' The military kept him busy, and since he got a badge he was even busier, and being a part of the Preternatural Branch of the Marshals Service meant he could torture and kill vampires and rogue shapeshifters to his heart's content, and as long as he killed them in the end, there were no rules to how he carried out the execution or how long he took to do it. Olaf was one of the scariest people I'd ever met, alive or undead, and that was an impressive list to be near the top of. Hatfield was right; he'd been that scary before he got cut up by a werelion and tested positive for lycanthropy. He'd gone AWOL after he got his test results, but he'd resurfaced a few months later. If he'd done anything unfortunate while he was learning to control his beast, the human authorities hadn't heard about it.

Micah had asked around in the preternatural community, and Olaf seemed to be playing the part of a nomad lion. He had stayed away from any group. Where he'd gone to learn to control himself, no one seemed to know. I actually wondered if he hadn't gone anywhere, if the serial killer part of him was actually so close to an inner beast that he'd understood how to control both?

Since Olaf had considered me his little serial killer girlfriend because we went out and killed people together, I'd avoided him before he learned to turn furry; now he was avoiding me as hard as I avoided him. He'd known Nicky before he became my Bride, and Olaf was afraid of my taming him the same way. Anything that kept Olaf away from me was fine in my book.

'I haven't seen Otto since he caught lycanthropy either.'

'You're a fur-banger; why would him being a wereanimal bother you?' Hatfield asked.

I turned and looked at her. 'What did you call me?'

'So you don't deny that you slept with Jeffries, too.'

'I didn't sleep with him, but I've learned two things. One, it's impossible to prove a negative, to prove I didn't do something. Two, when a woman sleeps with more than one man, she gets accused of sleeping with damn near everybody. But let's get back to you calling me a fur-banger.'

'I'm not familiar with the term,' Jonas said, 'so before I yell at someone for saying it, tell me what it means.'

'It means someone who fucks shapeshifters,' Hatfield said.

'No, it doesn't,' I said. 'It means people who will fuck any shapeshifter just because they are one. It's like badge bunnies are about cops.'

'Hatfield, that sounds pretty insulting to a fellow marshal.'

'I heard you were living with Sheriff Callahan's son, Mike, and another wereleopard from his group; that true?'

'Yeah, it's true.'

'The two blonds you brought in with you tonight. They're shapeshifters just like Rickman said, right?'

'Yeah,' I said.

'You sleeping with them, too?'

I took a deep breath in and let it out slow. I counted slow, before saying, 'Yes.'

'So four shapeshifters,' she said.

'I never said I didn't date shapeshifters.'

'And Forrester here, too, right?'

I looked at Edward. 'Will it do any good to deny it?' I asked.

'If she wants to believe it, she's going to,' he said, but his voice was losing the Tedness and getting colder and more empty. The real Edward was beginning to seep through.

'And I hear your Master of the City flew to your side, so you're also screwing him.'

'You know, Hatfield, I was going to try to like you, but I don't think I want to work that hard; let's just hate each other and get it over with.'

'You're fur-banging coffin bait and helping Forrester cheat on his fiancée who has two kids; I was never going to like you, Blake.'

'Hatfield,' Jonas said, one word, sharp and unhappy with her.

'If I'm really doing Ted here, then why is Donna, that's his fiancée, okay with me being in the wedding? She's wanting one of my fur-bangees to be in the wedding, too. I know some of the other law enforcement people will be at the wedding; maybe when they see me standing at the altar with Donna and Ted, this stupid rumor will go away.'

Hatfield's mouth opened and then closed; unfortunately it opened again. 'If that's true, I'll apologize after the wedding.'

'Fine, what's the longest-term relationship you've ever had?'

'I don't see how that's any of your business,' she said.

'You call me names and get up in my face about my personal life. You spread rumors about me and Marshal Forrester, and you get insulted because I ask a simple question?'

She went back to looking sullen. There were lines around her mouth that showed she frowned a lot more than she smiled. Smile lines are happy exclamations; frown lines just makes you look old before your time. If Hatfield wasn't careful she was going to do the latter.

'Blake is being polite after everything you've said to her, Susan,' Jonas said.

She frowned harder but said, 'Three years. I was married for three years.'

'Okay. Micah Callahan, Nathaniel, and I have been living together for three years. I've been dating Jean-Claude, my Master of the City, for almost seven. The blonds, as you call them, have both been with me over a year.'

'It's not the same thing as being married,' she said.

'It's not my fault that it's illegal to marry multiple men at the same time; that's like saying that a gay couple isn't as serious as a straight couple because the straight couple is married, at the same time you make it impossible for the gay couple to marry.'

'Are you saying that you would marry all of them?' She made sure I didn't miss the disdain in her voice.

'Not all of them, but a lot of them, yeah.'

'A lot of them?' Again, she made sure the disdain dripped all over her words.

'We're still working out who's going to marry whom,' I said.

'Are you telling me that the engagement to Callahan's son is real?'

'Something like that, yeah.'

'It's not just so the sheriff can die knowing his son is okay, and not gay?'

I laughed; I couldn't help it. She obviously knew nothing about the sheriff's domestic arrangements.

'What's so funny?' she asked.

'Hatfield,' Jonas said, 'you may be our local vampire executioner, but you haven't been here long. You don't know all the local PD all that well yet.'

She looked from him, to me, to Edward, and back to Jonas. She knew she'd stepped in something, but not exactly what. I had no intention of enlightening her. I wasn't sure that Edward even knew about Micah's dad's love life, but no one living did better poker face than Edward, so it seemed like the only one in the room who didn't know that Sheriff Callahan was living with another man, and a woman, was Hatfield.

She decided to go back to something she was certain of and said, 'This is my warrant and I don't need Forrester or Blake looking over my shoulder. It's just two vampires to execute.'

'There were more than two vampires in the woods,' I said.

'You saw them die, Blake. From what I hear you helped blow some of them away with that arsenal you carry.'

I turned to Edward and said, 'Please tell me that someone burned the remains of the rotting vampires that we blew to hell with the guns?'

'Ask Hatfield; she was the marshal in charge by the time I got here.' Ted's cheerful voice was wearing around the edges so that Edward's coldness was leaking out. He didn't like Hatfield either.

'They all either were decapitated or had their chests blown open, and all of them had their spines damaged. That's dead enough,' she said.

'Didn't you follow what happened in Atlanta when the Master of the City went crazy?' I asked.

'Yeah, the police used flamethrowers on the vampire lair and ruined most of the evidence. They still haven't identified all the victims' remains. Local police say you were the one who told them they had to use fire to cleanse it, which is bullshit and overkill.'

'Fire is the only surety with rotting vampires,' I said.

'There are still people waiting for news of their loved ones, thanks to your suggestions in Atlanta,' she said.

'Anita's right,' Edward said, and his voice was cold now. 'Fire is the only way to make sure the rotters don't heal and rise again. Tell us you burned their bodies, Hatfield.'

She was looking from one to the other of us. 'Nothing keeps moving after a decapitation except zombies.'

'Exactly,' I said, 'and rotting vampires are a lot more like zombies than most vampires.'

'The Master of Atlanta may have needed fire, but that's a master vampire. They're all harder to kill. These were all newly risen, right?'

'New makes them easier to kill,' I said, 'but I burn all rotting vampires regardless of age just to be safe, and then sometimes I do the whole scattering of the ashes in different bodies of running water.'

'You are just trying to spook me now,' she said.

'I travel with a flamethrower when I drive,' Edward said, 'and sometimes I can even get it on the plane if I promise there's no fuel in it.'

'I heard you liked fire, Forrester. Were you a bed-wetter and terror to the neighborhood pets?'

Edward ignored the insult. 'Captain, where did the bodies from the woods get transferred?'

'The hospital morgue has a special room for vamp and lycanthrope undead.'

'Is it more heavily armored so they can't get out?' I asked.

'No, it's just separate so that the human dead don't get . . . contaminated.' He sounded a little apologetic when he said the last word.

'To my knowledge normal dead just stay dead even if you mix them with a whole bunch of vampire and lycanthrope bodies, but are you telling us that all the dead from the woods are now in the morgue in the basement of the hospital where Micah and Nathaniel are? Where Sheriff Callahan is?' Jean-Claude and the rest of the vampires had gone for the hotel because dawn was only two hours away, and traffic accidents happened, and there was no saving throw between a vampire and sunlight, so he was safe, but he also had some of the most dangerous guards with him, so it was a mixed blessing, damn it!

'Yeah,' Jonas said, 'tell me for real, can these things heal enough to attack people again?'

'Rotting vampires are really rare, but I wouldn't trust anything short of burning them up like zombies,' I said.

'Agreed,' Edward said.

'You did burn up all the zombie parts from the woods, right, Hatfield?' I asked.

'We couldn't burn them in the woods; the fire danger's too high.'

'What did you do with the parts?' I asked.

'Once dawn came, they stopped moving,' she said.

I wanted to grab her and shake her, but I forced myself to be calm and dig my fingernails into my palms as I made fists so I wouldn't do it. 'What-did-you-do-with-the-zombie-parts?'

'They're in the morgue with the vampire bodies.'

'Shit,' I said.

'It's been dark for hours, Blake; if anything was wrong we'd have heard by now,' Hatfield said.

'Call the morgue,' I said to Jonas. 'If they say everything is hunky-dory, then Ted and I are wrong. I'm good with that. I'd love to be wrong.'

The captain called, because calling didn't cost him anything. I'd never actually seen a rotting vampire this young in undead terms, so maybe they got their uber-healing powers after a few years. Maybe a few weeks wasn't enough time to be that scary?

The phone rang a long time; I was getting nervous, and Jonas was looking worried.

'See,' Hatfield said, 'you've both been on the job too long; it's made you paranoid.'

'Crap,' Jonas said, and Hatfield and I looked back at the captain. 'No one answered at the morgue,' he said to whoever was on the phone. 'No, I do not want you to send someone down to check. This is Captain Jonas of Boulder PD, and I want all the hospital staff to stay away from the morgue until I have some officers check it out.'

Whoever was on the other end of the line was talking, and he was trying to tell them, no, he didn't want any of the staff to go down to the morgue. They wanted to know why and Jonas didn't want to tell them, because in case it wasn't vampires and killer zombies, but just a bad phone line, he didn't want to scare everyone at the hospital.

We didn't have time for this. I got my cell phone out and dialed Micah. It went to voice mail. I dialed Nathaniel's phone without letting myself think about why Micah hadn't answered. He was in with his dad, had turned off the ringer, that was it, that had to be it. Nathaniel would answer. When he picked up I thought my heart was going to choke me, so I sort of croaked out, 'Nathaniel, everything all right there?'

'Micah's dad is struggling in his sleep like he's having a nightmare. The nurse says he shouldn't be able to move with all the drugs in him.'

'Is he saying anything?'

'No, he's just struggling like a nightmare we can't wake him up from. Micah and his parents are in with him now. Why would you ask if he said anything?'

'Ares was possessed just by being bitten with the rotting disease. I wondered if it would work the same way on regular people.'

'Wouldn't Micah's dad have manifested some sort of weirdness by now if it worked that way on humans?' Nathaniel asked.

'Probably me being paranoid. Do you recognize any of the cops in the hallway? Anyone who I've met since we landed and who didn't hate me on sight?'

'Having more trouble with the local police?' Nathaniel asked.

'A little, but I really need to talk to someone there right now if possible.'

'Anita, what's wrong?'

I had to swallow past a lump in my throat as I said, 'They stored the vampire bodies in the morgue there, along with the zombie parts.'

'They didn't burn them?' he asked. That was my boyfriend; he knew more than Hatfield did.

'No,' I said.

'Why not?'

'Fire hazard in the woods, and later I don't know. Do you recognize anyone in the hallway?'

'Deputy Al is here.'

'Good, can you put him on?'

'I love you, and you'll explain everything later,' he said.

'I love you, too, and yes, I will.'

He didn't argue, he just did what I needed. I loved him, but in that moment I loved him even more. The next thing I heard was his voice, distant, saying, 'It's Anita, she needs to talk to you.'

'Hey, Anita, what's up? Your boyfriend here has a serious face on him.'

I explained about the vampire bodies and zombie bits being in the morgue. Deputy Al said, 'The fire hazard makes burning anything in the forests too dangerous.'

'I accept that, but . . . Al, Captain Jonas can't get anyone to answer the morgue extension. He's trying to get someone in the hospital admin to let him send someone to check on it without panicking anyone. I don't care about that, I just want someone I trust to see if the dead vampires stayed dead. I'm not sure if the zombie bits will be moving around, but it's the rotting vampires that I'm most concerned about.'

'We blew them to hell, Anita. Brain, spine, heart, all splattered. That's dead for a vamp, according to most of you marshals.'

'It is for most vampires, but rotting vamps are different, much harder to kill. Fire is the only sure thing, and even then I'd deposit the ashes in different bodies of running water.'

'Really?' he said, and sounded skeptical.

'Look, if I'm wrong, I'm wrong, but if there is even the faintest chance I'm right, then the vampires have been walking around down there for a while. I have no idea how long it took for them to heal the damage we did to them, but by now, if they can heal it and walk again, they will be.'

'Now you're scaring me.'

'Good, you should be scared,' I said.

'Shit, okay, I'll grab a couple of other men from up here and we'll go check in with hospital security and see if the morgue is full of dead people or not-so-dead people.'

'Thanks, Al, and watch your back.'

'Always,' he said. 'I'll give you back to Nathaniel.'

Then Nathaniel was on the phone again. 'I heard enough. So you think they killed everyone in the morgue.'

'It's a possibility, and I'd rather be paranoid and wrong than reasonable and really wrong. You and Micah be careful. Who's with you for bodyguards?'

There was a knock on the door and a uniform finally came through with an ice bag wrapped in paper towels. I took it, because they'd gone to the trouble, but I'd actually forgotten my face hurt. I had to use my right hand to hold the ice in place since I was using my left for the phone.

'Bram and Socrates. Micah sent everyone else home to get some sleep.'

'Shit,' I said.

'What?' Nathaniel said.

'I'd just like you and Micah to have more than two guards with you, that's all.'

Edward held up his car keys and just raised his eyebrows. I nodded, and we headed for the door.

'I'm not done with you, Blake,' Jonas called.

'You can yell at me later, and yell at me more if I'm wrong about the morgue. If I'm right, we don't have time to wait.'

'They're sending hospital security down to check,' Jonas said.

I paused with my hand on the doorknob. 'What's their security armed with?'

He asked the person on the phone. 'They don't know. They say the guns are black. Does that help?'

'Shit, did you have someone who doesn't know guns at all send security down to the morgue? Do they have any idea what they're walking into?'

'They aren't walking into anything,' Hatfield said. 'I did my job.'

'I hope you're right, Hatfield. God knows I hope you're right.'

Edward said, 'Captain, with respect, talk to someone on security personally and warn them, or they'll just be more bodies.'

Jonas hung up and redialed. 'I know an ex-cop on their security; I'll call him.'

I opened the door and said, 'Good.' I wasn't sure Jonas had heard me, and I know I didn't care.

Hatfield yelled after us from the open door. 'There's nothing wrong at the hospital. I did my damn job!'

Edward and I both ignored her. We'd pick up Dev and Nicky from the front of the station and head to the hospital. If I was wrong, we'd get down there and look silly, but if I was right, people would already be dying, or dead. If I was right, Micah and Nathaniel were just a few floors up from half a dozen rogue vampires and a whole bunch of zombie parts that would do their best to tear people to pieces. God, I hoped I was wrong.

42

We were standing outside the morgue with the windowed door barricaded shut, because there were zombies inside eating the remains of two morgue attendants and the security guard who some genius had sent down here by himself after Jonas called them. By the time Al got down there it was all over except the eating part. I'd been worried about vampires, not so much the zombies. I'd never heard of zombies putting themselves back together once you blew them into pieces with guns. We didn't have to worry about the vampires, because according to Al and the police with him the zombies were eating them, too.

We had two more hospital security officers with us now. One man looked to be in his early forties, built sort of square, with a high-and-tight haircut that said ex-military as if he had a sign around his neck. He'd introduced himself as 'Macintosh, yeah just like the apple, but call me Mac.' The other guard, Miller, looked to be early twenties, a slender, dark-haired kid with glasses. He'd already been sick down the hallway where we made him run when we realized he was going to do it. Throw up outside in the woods, or at a graveyard, and the out-of-doors sort of took away the smell and made things better. In a hallway in an area with no windows the smell of vomit lingered; at least it lingered a little farther away from us. I hadn't yelled at him; I mean, how many times do you have a coworker, maybe a friend, eaten by zombies? Besides, once he got sick he calmed down. I'd been the rookie once, too. Everyone throws up at least once.

Have you ever wondered why there are windows in the doors of most morgues? It's so attendants can look in first and make sure nothing has risen from the dead and is waiting to eat them. Whoever had put the windows in these doors must have a been a tall motherfucker, because Edward had to stretch to see in the windows and he had me by five inches, plus the two inches of his cowboy boots.

'Tell me what you see,' I said.

'It's like Nicky described from the zombies in the mountains; they're just huddled down over the bodies like vultures.'

'They'll be safe-ish until there's nothing left to eat; then they'll try to get out and find something fresh. What kind of zombie can take out a vampire?'

'This kind,' Edward said.

'Are they eating the other dead bodies, or just the vampires?' I asked.

'There are no bodies on any of the slabs.'

'Shit, I need to see them,' I said.

Edward looked down at me and smiled; even with the sounds coming through the doors, he smiled that Ted smile. 'Need a boost so you can see for yourself?'

I scowled at him.

'How can you smile looking at that?' Al asked; he looked a little green.

'I can smile looking at a lot of things,' he said, and this time it was more Edward looking out at the deputy. He let his inner sociopath show through more than he ever did on a case, which was a sign of just how much he was bothered by what he was seeing.

To distract Edward from terrifying Deputy Al, I distracted them by saying, 'Yeah, I need a boost.'

Edward moved toward me, but it was Nicky who went down on one knee and made a stirrup of his hands before my fellow marshal could get started.

'You could have picked her up and been all romantic,' Dev said.

'It's only romantic if Anita thinks it's romantic,' Dev said, 'and right now she wouldn't think so.'

'That's more insight than I'd have credited you with, son,' an older uniformed officer said. He was about Edward's height, but the way he carried his weight made him look shorter. He was mostly bald with a fringe of white hair that looked like it would be soft to touch like baby duck fluff. His eyes were a clear, brilliant blue, like an echo back to when the rest of him was as vibrant.

'I'm not your son,' Nicky said.

'No offense meant . . . just giving you a compliment.'

'A backhanded one.' Gonzales looked at Nicky. 'Don't let Jenkins here get your goat. He calls everyone *son*, and he doesn't know how to give anything but backhanded compliments,' Gonzales said. The big sergeant had been upstairs when Al had called for volunteers. I had a feeling he was spending most of his time near Rush Callahan's rooms.

Nicky didn't respond, just stayed waiting to give me a boost. I didn't know what to say, because Nicky's dislike of being called *son*, or *boy*, probably had something to do with his abusive family background, and that was no one's business. I ignored it all and put one foot in Nicky's hand. He trusted me to be able to hold myself steady enough for him to lift me up, and I trusted him enough to lift me smoothly so I could see. The only concession I made was to put my fingertips against the cool wood of the door as he lifted, and that was for balance. He lifted me until I said, 'That's great.'

It was great, sort of, in that I could now see into the room for myself, but what I had to see was awful enough that I wished I hadn't. I get that a lot in both of my jobs. Like most truly awful sights it took my mind a moment to process it; at first it was just images, shapes, that didn't want to make sense. I knew what I was supposed to be seeing; the fact that my eyes refused to 'see' it meant it was going to be bad. It was the brain's way of giving you a chance to look away, to not see the awful thing, but it was my job to look when everyone looked away. So I kept looking, and suddenly all the jumbled shapes snapped into focus.

It looked like every zombie movie you'd ever seen, except that I knew they got it wrong, so why did this match it? We'd sent a handful of vampires to the morgue, and maybe a dozen zombies in bits, but the room was so full of the walking dead that I couldn't count them as they huddled over the bodies. Edward had compared them to vultures, but vultures squabble over the dead, fighting for the best pieces, or any piece. The zombies ate in near silence, except for the wet, tearing sounds that I'd been hearing through the door long before my mind wanted to acknowledge them. I hadn't realized that my hearing might try to protect me just like my vision did; interesting. The zombies huddled around four distinct piles of 'food.' There were only supposed to be three dead, so why four piles? I couldn't see the bodies because the crouched undead hid most of the corpses from view. I got bits of red flesh glinting in the overhead lights, white bone gleaming like polished nightmare pearls, and the shining colors of organs as they were torn from deep within the bodies and consumed by . . . people.

Some of the zombies were decayed, but the one munching on someone's heart looked fresh as a newly minted undead penny. None of the zombies we'd sent here had looked that good, and just like that my poor, horrified brain put the impossible together.

'Oh, shit,' I said, and I sounded afraid, even to me.

'What?' Nicky asked.

'What's wrong?' Edward said. 'What are you seeing that I don't?'

'We sent less than a dozen zombies in pieces here.'

'There's got to be more than twenty,' he said.

'Yeah, and none of them looked this human, Ed . . . Ted. They were all decayed, a lot, not fresh like this.'

'It's some of the bodies that were in the morgue when we unloaded,' Al said.

I turned and looked at him, with my fingers holding on to the edge of the window. 'What did you say?'

'Far as I can tell it's every body that was in the morgue when we dropped off the vamp bodies and zombie parts.'

'Let me down, Nicky,' I said.

'You look spooked,' Gonzales said. 'That can't be good.'

'It's not,' I said.

'Why do you both look like you just saw a ghost?' Jenkins asked.

'A ghost wouldn't spook me,' I said.

'It's a saying, Anita,' Edward said, as if it mattered.

'Talk to us,' Gonzales said.

'Zombies rise from graves, not morgues. They need to be buried before they can be called from the grave as zombies. Even I couldn't raise a body that's just been sitting around the morgue.'

'What do you mean? Dead is dead, right?' Jenkins said.

'No,' I said, 'you don't get it. Zombies don't rise without a vaudun priestess, or necromancer, to call them from the grave.' I pointed back behind me to the doors of the morgue. 'They don't rise spontaneously just because you put older zombies in the same area, and let me just say that zombies don't put themselves back together once you've blown their legs and heads off. They keep moving and will kill and eat you if they can, but they don't heal. Dead flesh doesn't heal, and zombies are the most dead of the undead.'

'So if all that's impossible, then what the fuck is going on?' Jenkins asked.

I shook my head. 'I don't know.'

'Oh, I don't like that at all,' Gonzales said. 'You're supposed to be *the* expert on zombies in the Marshals Service. If you don't know, then . . .'

'We're fucked,' Jenkins finished for him.

No one argued with him.

Something heavy hit the door, and I screamed like a fucking girl.

43

'We have to burn them,' Edward said, 'we have to burn them all to fucking ash and then scatter it into different bodies of running water.'

'Burn them how?' Gonzales asked.

'I got a flamethrower in my car.'

'This is the basement of a hospital,' Gonzales said.

'Evacuate the hospital,' Edward said.

'We can't order that,' Jenkins said.

'We have killer zombies in the morgue, and unless we can use fire we might not be able to stop them. I think that's an excellent reason to evacuate the hospital,' I said.

'Fuck,' Gonzales said, softly but with feeling.

The zombies were beginning to throw themselves clumsily against the doors, but flesh-eating zombies aren't like the regular shambling dead. They wouldn't stay clumsy; they would learn, evolve into better killers, better predators. I'd never heard of a flesh-eating zombie being kept 'alive' longer than a few days. They didn't hide themselves well enough; we found them and killed them, or vampires did, because they drew attention to all the dead. It had been the Harlequin that had told me that they destroyed rogue zombies the same way they had killed rogue vampires, and for many of the same reasons. It was bad for business in that this-will-get-us-chased-through-the-countryside-by-torch-wielding-mobs sort of way.

The doors shuddered under the next shove. We all looked at the axe handle shoved in the door handles. 'Whatever we're going to do, we need to do it before the doors give,' I said.

Macintosh Call-Me-Mac's phone sounded. Everyone jumped but Edward, Nicky, and Gonzales. Yeah, that included me.

'Mac here. We may need to evacuate the hospital.' He was quiet, and then he went pale. 'Say again, you have reports of zombies on three different floors.'

We were all quiet, listening hard.

He hit speaker so we could all hear and said, 'I've got cops with me, and you're on speaker. Can you please repeat that, Ida?'

Ida said, 'We have reports on three, five, six, and some kind of disturbance in ICU. They called on the hospital line. The line went dead, but I could hear people yelling in the background before the call cut off.'

'What floor is ICU on?' I asked.

Mac held up his hand and opened and closed it twice. ICU was on the tenth floor. That was the floor that Micah's dad was on. I hit Nathaniel's number, because Micah was probably still in with his dad.

Nathaniel answered with 'Anita,' and there was something in his voice that I didn't like at all.

'You have a zombie reported on your floor,' I said.

'I'm looking at it,' he said, his voice odd, as if he were trying to stay quiet and calm so as not to spook it. That didn't really work with zombies.

My mouth was suddenly dry. 'Tell me there are cops with you.'

'Yeah.'

'Bram, Socrates?'

'Yeah, but, Anita,' and now he was whispering, 'it's not a zombie, it's a vampire.'

'A rotting vampire,' I said, 'so people are reporting it as a zombie.'

'Yes,' he whispered.

Al said, 'Mother of God.'

'We are on our way; barricade yourself into Micah's dad's room.'

I heard a man's voice yell out with authority, 'Stop, or we'll shoot!'

'Shoot, tell them to shoot!' I yelled, and I was starting to run down the hallway.

Mac yelled, 'What do we do with the zombies?'

I realized that Al, Gonzales, Jenkins, and Edward were with us, leaving the two guards by themselves with that fragile door. I slowed, because if the zombies got out . . . shit!

Nathaniel said, 'We're in the room. Bram and Socrates are on the door.'

Edward yelled to Mac, 'Evacuate the hospital. We're going to have to burn it.'

'You cannot use a flamethrower inside the hospital, it'll set off the sprinkler system,' Mac yelled.

'Fuck!' Edward said.

'What did he say about flamethrowers?' Nathaniel asked.

'That we can't use them; the sprinklers will put out the zombies before they can burn.'

We stopped in the hallway. 'I'm going for Micah and Nathaniel,' I said.

'Anita, do what you have to do,' Nathaniel said.

There were more shots, muffled because now they were on the other side of the room's door. 'I'm coming to you,' I said.

Micah was on the phone. 'Anita, we're safe for now; do your job.'

'I am coming to you.'

'We have a hallway full of police officers. We will be okay.'

'I love you, and I love Nathaniel, but this isn't a debate. I'm coming,' I said, and I hung up on him.

'I've got some phosphorus grenades with me, but I've got more in the car,' Edward said, and held out his car keys to me.

I didn't take the keys. 'I'm getting to my guys first.'

'I know,' he said.

I reached down and took two grenades out of one of the pockets low down on my tactical pants. I put the grenades into his hand and took the keys. 'I couldn't use them in the forest without setting it on fire.'

Edward smiled, a tight, fierce, and strangely happy smile. There was a part of him that wanted to meet a danger that was more dangerous than he was – so far he really hadn't, but he kept looking.

Gonzales said, 'I'm going for Rush.'

'I'll stay with Forrester, Jenkins, and the guards,' Al said. 'Tell Rush . . . tell him I'm doing my job.'

Dev said, 'But the sprinklers will put out the grenades, too.'

'Phosphorus burns hotter when you get it wet,' I said. Edward and I had a moment of remembering ghouls running through a stream screaming as they burned. It was old-fashioned phosphorus, and about the only people who still wanted it were vampire executioners. 'Don't die on me,' I said.

'I won't,' he said, and he leaned forward, lowering his voice so the other cops wouldn't hear. 'I've got European grenades in the car.'

I gave him wide eyes, because in parts of Europe where vamps and shapeshifters can be killed on sight just for being, they had grenades designed to burn longer than even the old-fashioned phosphorus over here. They were designed to explode, get nasty burny stuff on the targets, and the burn kept burning until it burned through the target. They were illegal as hell here.

I smiled and shook my head. 'I'll be back with more stuff when I can.'

'I know you will,' he said.

I looked at Al, and didn't know what to say to him. Jenkins and the guards I'd just met, but Al had grown up with Micah.

I heard the doors bang as the zombies started working better as a unit. I'd never seen this many of them without a necromancer in control of them. I should have stayed with Edward and kept them contained. That would have been the best use of resources, but I was going for the loves of my life. Once they were safe I'd save the rest of the world; until that moment the world could take care of itself. Or that was what I told myself as I started running for the elevators with Nicky and Dev at my side and Gonzales bringing up the rear.

44

The elevator doors opened just as a huge crash came from behind us. I had to look back. Edward and the rest had thrown themselves against the door. He yelled, 'Anita!'

'Shit,' I said.

Edward yelled, 'They're using a gurney as a battering ram. I need my gear now! I'm sorry.'

In all the years we'd worked together he'd never apologized for the job and the choices we had to make. Dev was in the elevator. He held out his hand. 'Give me the keys, and you go on to Micah and Nathaniel.'

There was another huge crash, and the men at the end of the hallway all put their shoulders into it, holding on. 'Anita, you know how I pack. You can find them faster. We need them faster!' The doors bucked as if some giant hand had slapped them. They weren't going to hold.

'Anita, now!'

I got in the elevator. 'Stay and help hold the door. I will be as fast as I can.'

Nicky stepped out. 'Don't make me stay.'

'I'll keep her safe,' Dev said.

Gonzales stayed beside Nicky. 'Hurry,' Gonzales said. There was another thunderous crash at that far door.

The elevator doors began to slide shut and I had one of those moments of revelation. I knew Nicky was stronger, more ruthless, and better at fighting than Dev; he was the one to leave. The only reason not to leave him was that I loved him. I love-loved him, and I hadn't known it for certain until this second. I moved as the door closed and said, 'I love you, Nicky.'

He smiled then, and the doors closed.

I wished there'd been time to kiss him good-bye.

45

I dug the earpiece for my phone out of one of the pockets and called Micah from the elevator. He answered on the second ring. 'Anita, vampire on this floor is dead. We're okay.'

'The morgue is not okay; I've got to help Ted contain it. I had to leave Nicky there to back him up.' As soon as I said it, I realized I was looking for absolution, someone as strong as I was to tell me that it had been okay to leave someone I loved who wasn't a cop down there with the other cops and the monsters.

'What made you willing to leave him down there with Ted?'

'Grenades and shit in Ted's car, Dev and I are fetching.' I transferred my badge from my hip to tuck it in a MOLLE strap on the front of my vest. We didn't have any uniforms or locals with us this time. I wanted witnesses to know we were the good guys.

'Because you know where the stuff is in Ted's car,' Micah said.

'Yeah,' I said, and the elevator doors opened.

Dev paused before he went through, checking to make sure it was clear; he gave a small nod and held the door for me, leaning against it with his gun already out. Most handguns wouldn't do much against zombies or rotting vamps, but Dev had never seen real combat like Nicky had, or I had, which meant he was more comfortable with handguns than long ones. I had my AR to my shoulder checking the hallway – left, right, and up. Vampires fly, or float, sometimes. The hospital ceiling was too low to really be a place to hide, but checking up was a habit that was good to have when you hunted vampires that could fly and shapeshifters that could climb.

'U.S. Marshals,' I said, for the startled nurses and doctors. 'Police.' I added that just in case. I yelled 'Police' again and kept Dev and me moving toward the outer doors. I ignored the questions, because they would slow us down too much and I didn't know what to say. Captain Jonas had said out loud that he didn't want to start a panic; if I told them what was in the basement and wandering the hallways, they might panic. They should panic and evacuate everyone they could, but I wasn't in charge, not like that.

Dev flashed them all his melt-in-your-socks smile. 'We'll be back, I promise.'

One of the scared nurses actually blushed at him. That was some good flirting.

'We're going outside,' I said to Micah, low voiced, over the headset.

'Be careful,' he said.

'I think it's safer outside, but I'll be careful,' I said, as I moved toward the outer doors with the AR snugged to my shoulder.

'I love you,' he said.

'I love you and Nathaniel. I didn't get to kiss Nicky good-bye.'

'You'll get another chance to kiss him,' Micah said, and that was it, he'd given me my absolution, my that's-okay-you-didn't-leave-your-lover-to-die pat on the ethical back.

'Thanks, gotta run. I love you.'

'I love you more,' he said.

'Love you mostest.'

He laughed, softly, and hung up.

Dev and I were outside now. I looked up at the night sky, electric-kissed with the pools of light from the hospital behind us and the light poles rearing over the cars. Nothing moved in the darkness above us. The parking lot stretched empty and so still you should have been able to hear city crickets if it hadn't been too cold for them.

'Can we run now?' Dev asked.

'Yes,' I said.

He took off like something elemental, so fast that his speed left me immobile for a heartbeat, and then I ran, too. I ran fast, going from a dead stop to making the parking lot a blur to my vision like some movie special effect. I moved and it wasn't just to be fast to save everyone and get the weapons, it was a release of tension to be able to move as fast as we could even for a few moments, to be able to RUN! I arrived at Edward's SUV to find Dev there catching his breath. My heart was in my throat, trying to creep over my tongue and into my mouth. I felt alive, full of blood and thunder; it was the kind of energy that made you want to leave the guns in the holsters and wade into a fight with your bare hands. I wouldn't do it, but I understood the urge.

Dev grinned at me, a fierce baring of teeth that still managed to be sexy and charming. I grinned back and unlocked the back of the SUV with my pulse thudding behind my own fierce smile.

Dev and I moved our gear out so I could get to where Edward kept his incendiaries. There was a reason he drove his SUV if the crime scene was close enough, or sometimes if it wasn't. He had several compartments in his truck where the really bad things were hidden. If someone broke in and stole stuff, they wouldn't get anything more dangerous than guns. Even if they stole the whole truck they'd likely never find the hidden shit unless they dismantled the truck piece by piece like at a chop shop, but even Edward couldn't plan for all eventualities. Besides, some of the hidden stuff was illegal. I hadn't known he had the European grenades. I'd read about them, seen videos of the effect, even photos of the victims. Some people in parts of Europe were using the grenades in my hands as a reason to give vampires and shapeshifters human rights, because the effects were too terrible to do to anyone, almost. No one cared about zombies, strangely. Not all dead are created equal.

Under other circumstances I might have hesitated to use something illegal while I was wearing my badge, but today . . . the European grenades gave us a real chance. I grabbed all that were in the compartment, shoving them into pockets on my tactical pants and handing some to Dev to carry, too. The grenades would burn long enough to actually destroy the zombies, if we could cut them up first so that they didn't catch us, or the hospital, on fire. It was looking at Edward's extending magazines that gave me the idea. I grabbed his, and mine, and an extra cross-draw bag because Dev and I couldn't carry all of them in the pockets, or even the MOLLE straps on the vests. Usually it was overkill to travel with this many magazines for the ARs, but tonight it might just get the job done.

We shoved everything back in the truck. Dev shut the back. I hit the key lock and without asking each other we ran back to the hospital. The world blurred past as I tried to keep up with Dev. He was a foot taller and a lot of that was leg, oh, and the whole weretiger thing, too, but I wasn't far behind as we whooshed through the doors.

The nurse who had smiled at Dev looked even paler, eyes huge in her face. 'You're not human, are you?' she asked.

'No,' I said.

'Human's overrated,' Dev said with another sex-on-wheels smile as we went for the elevators.

My phone rang in my earpiece, 'Bad to the Bone,' which had been Edward's ring tone since Nathaniel put it on as a joke back when I didn't know how to change it. I hit the button and said, 'Yeah.'

'Bring all the extra mags you can,' he said, and I could hear shooting in the background magnified oddly over the headset.

'Already have them,' I said, as we stepped into the elevator.

'You had the same idea,' he said.

'We have enough ammo to cut them into pieces and then . . .'

'Use the Euros to burn them in place,' he finished for me.

'Yeah,' I said.

'Yeah,' he said, and then he laughed that deep, masculine sound that most men reserve for sex or moments more private with the lovers in their lives.

'I love the way you think, too,' I said.

He gave that date/sex laugh. I guess there was more than one reason that Donna thought I was his lover. Someone yelled, and a man screamed. Edward said, 'Gotta go,' in a voice so serious it was as if the laugh never existed.

I whispered, 'Edward,' to empty air.

'He all right?' Dev asked.

'I don't know. It sounds like the zombies are on top of them.'

Dev holstered his handgun and unhooked his AR from the back of his vest where the MOLLE straps kept it.

'A head or heart shot won't do anything but irritate a zombie. We're going to use the ammo to cut off the arms, legs, anything that makes them mobile, and then decapitate, or explode the entire head. When that's done we burn 'em.'

'You and Ted didn't discuss details; how do you know that's why he wanted the extra magazines?'

The elevator was slowing. I snugged my AR to my shoulder and said, 'I just know.' The doors opened, and a zombie fell into the elevator.

46

Dev yelled like a guy. I tried to tell him *don't do it*, it was already armless, but he was already pulling the trigger. He shot the zombie in the head while it was trying to bite his foot. The reverberation of the shot was actually painful in the metal box of the elevator, as if someone had stuck something sharp and hard through my ears.

His hearing was better than mine, and he wasn't expecting it. He hunched over, free hand to one ear, face grimacing with pain. I didn't bother trying to say anything; I let him have his moment of disorientation while I stepped over the armless zombie as it tried to push itself to its knees, leaving most of its brains on the floor of the elevator.

I put my shoulder against the open doors to hold them, AR snugged to shoulder, and tried to use my eyes to see what was happening in the hallway while my hearing recovered. I'd learned to push through the disorientation of that kind of noise in small spaces; it let me stand there and see the hallway while Dev was still struggling for his brain to process anything but the pain and shock.

I gave myself a second of eye-sweep to see Nicky's blond hair and Edward's white cowboy hat, upright and firing in the direction of zombies, and then I was able to take in the scene. They'd taken their stand in front of the elevator doors, but the line had crumbled to the right of the doors, because the young guard, Miller, was sitting against the wall bleeding, with the other guard holding pressure on a neck wound that gushed crimson over his hands. Jenkins had moved up to take their place in the half-circle of guns, but he had a handgun and the zombies didn't give a shit. Two of them launched themselves at him and the weak part of the circle. Damn smart for zombies.

Gonzales was there firing point-blank into their faces. He had a .45

and at that range it blew one head to pieces, so that it was just left with hands reaching blindly, but he was dry-firing into the face of the second, and it turned to him with a hungry, evil expression. I fired into its head from less than two feet away with the frangible round, and the head exploded in a fountain of blood and brains. There was bone in there, but it was always the soft, wet parts that made for the spectacular visuals.

Gonzales glanced at me with wide eyes, his naturally dark skin paled almost gray. The look was enough; he'd known he was almost out of ammo when he stepped up to shield Jenkins and the two guards. Dev was beside me; he still seemed shaken and didn't have the AR to his shoulder yet. I didn't have time to babysit him, but in that moment I realized he'd never seen combat. He'd seen action – shootings, violence, hand-to-hand, and hand-to-claw – but he'd never been in this kind of chaos. I counted him out for the fight and started shooting the zombies that were trying to pour through the gap in the defenses. I tried to take their lower faces out first, because once they couldn't bite, they were half-disarmed. I blew off most of a zombie's shoulder and arm as it reached for me with its remaining arm. The ruin of its face meant it couldn't bite me, but it could still strangle me or tear out my throat if I let it get a good grip.

Al was on the other side of me firing his own .45 into the reaching hands and gaping mouths of the zombies. The slide on his gun slid back and stayed there, showing he was out of ammo.

Gonzales moved back up beside me with the bull pup shotgun in his hands. Dev had recovered enough to start handing out the extra weapons and ammo; good.

Al fell back; I hoped to get more ammo, or another gun, and I kept shooting anything that moved outside our small circle. Nicky was beside me now; he shot the face off one zombie, then let his AR swing on its tactical strap so his hands were free, grabbed the zombie at the shoulder and upper arm, and pulled. I had a moment to watch his muscles strain, the veins on his arms raising with the force of what he was trying to do, and then he pulled the zombie's arm out of its shoulder socket. It was fresh zombie, so basically he'd just pulled a man's arm off with his bare hands. It wasn't just a matter of being fucking strong, but he'd known where to grab to disarticulate the shoulder joint. Maybe later I'd ask him how the hell he knew that.

No matter how impressive it had been, it meant Nicky was out of ammo.

Al was on my other side between me and Gonzales. Al's .45 had the slide back in place, and I didn't ask if he was locked and loaded; I knew he was. Let's hear it for grabbing all the extra ammo we could carry.

I stepped back, letting them know they needed to cover me if they could, and both of them stepped up. I opened the flap of the bag I was carrying and Nicky was close enough to reach in and get his own fresh magazine. He swung his AR on its strap, slapped the magazine home, and we started to move up again.

Edward's voice was in my earpiece. 'I'm out!'

I dropped back, and Nicky and the others moved up to cover the gap. I had the AR magazines, just like Dev had most of the handgun rounds. I reached in the bag one-handed and had an extended magazine in my hand as Edward's hand came into view. He took it like we were running a relay race and we'd made a smooth pass of the baton. He slammed it home, and I moved back out to the circle with him on one side and the freshly armed Nicky on the other.

Dev was finally up and shooting on the other side of Nicky. When we all survived I'd talk to him about how long it took him to orient himself, and we'd have to figure out some kind of training to prepare him and any other newer guards for the serious shit, but that was later. Tonight, right now, it was just shooting zombie heads, blowing shoulders away from bodies, or shooting their legs out from under them, anything to make them immobile and disarmed.

Most of the time in a firefight you are full of adrenaline, on hyper alert, but sometimes battle becomes a grind of horrific sameness. You begin to shoot without really thinking, your body is almost on automatic, because it's just too much – too much noise, too many visuals, too much to see, hear, feel, from the sweat that begins to trickle inside your vest, to your hands actually aching from shooting so much. I'd have changed guns just to rest my hands, but the AR was the right tool for the job, and there was a lot of job to do. But when you go to that battle haze, it's all distant, echoing in your gun-deafened ears, your body vibrating with the force of shooting, fighting, hitting when an enemy gets too close for anything else. It's beyond survival mode; it's mechanical, exhausting, with moments of breath-stealing terror sprinkled like chocolate chips in a cookie, reminding you how much you want to live and how much you have to make the other guy die to do that.

It's in moments like this that mistakes can happen; you see a face and you just fire without processing that this new stranger wasn't a soldier, but you've killed so many, and had so many people try to kill you in this one breathless, horrible fight, that it's only later you think, *Wait, did I miss something? Did I shoot a face that wasn't trying to kill me?* Until you have been that exhausted, that traumatized by sheer fighting, you can't understand how such a thing can happen. It is inexplicable to most people, because you haven't been there, and until you wade through bodies, hands grabbing at you, teeth snapping at you, trying to kill you with whatever weapons they have left, you don't understand that there comes a point when everybody who isn't 'us' is a 'them,' and you just shoot them.

If you've never reached that moment of battle haze, then you don't understand what's happening, which is why when the elevator doors opened behind us, and I knew Dev was back there, I turned away from the fight to check on him, because he was my responsibility, and that's what you do when you bring a greenhorn to a slaughter fight.

It was SWAT in full gear, and I watched Dev bring his AR to bear on them. There wasn't time to yell, and he likely wouldn't have heard me anyway; our hearing was blasted at this point. I aimed in front of him, between them and him. It wasn't even a conscious thought, it was see, act; even saying *I reacted* was too slow for what happened in my body, because it acted before my brain caught up to the rest of me.

It made the SWAT guys aim at me, so I held a hand up to show I was okay, but it made Dev startle and look back at me. I had a moment to see his eyes refocus, and then he watched SWAT spill out of the elevator and I knew he'd be all right. I turned back to shoot more zombies, but there was nothing standing in front of me. The hallway was full of wriggling bits and pieces, but nothing left that could run at us or do much except try to grab on to our feet with dismembered hands. It was the stuff of nightmares, but it wasn't actively going to kill us, not anymore.

It was Yancey from the police station who pulled up his face protection enough to say, 'Looks like we missed it.' If I hadn't been able to watch his lips move, I'd have never known what he was saying.

'You haven't missed it; we still have to burn the motherfuckers,' I said.

'You'll set off the sprinklers, or burn the hospital down,' he said.

'Sprinklers, yes,' I said. 'Burn down, no.'

'How?' he asked, and he was nicely skeptical.

I grinned at him, with my face still covered in zombie bits and blood. Yancey didn't flinch. 'We'll show you,' I said.

He grinned back, eyes taking in the knee-deep pile of moving corpses around us. 'I look forward to it.'

I liked Yancey; he was okay.

47

Normal phosphorus, or even thermite, grenades are designed to burn for a short time and then go out. They cause damage that would discourage vampires, ghouls, or even lycanthropes and humans, but not zombies. They don't get scared, they don't panic, they don't give up because you hurt them, because it doesn't hurt them. Scientists have tried to figure out how the nerve impulses keep zombies able to walk but not able to feel pain. If they could figure it out, then maybe they could use it as a way to get paralyzed humans walking, but so far it is a mystery, because once you've cut an arm off a body it should just lie there. They shouldn't even flop around like cut-in-half snakes, because the human nervous system works differently, and zombies start out human.

The pile of body parts that SWAT had helped us gather into the middle of the hallway burned. They burned because we'd piled the European grenades all around them. They weren't designed for a quick explosion and a quick burn like the American ones; they were meant to explode and cover whatever was near with fire. Fire that clung and continued to burn until there was no more flesh for it to eat.

Don't picture orange flames like a fireplace; it's white-hot flame, so bright that it will sear your retinas and steal your sight if you look too long. We'd warned everyone who had stayed not to stare. The heat was so intense it felt like it was shearing the skin off us, but we had the bodies in the pyre to compare to, and we weren't close enough to the fire to have our skin sheared. We all stepped back anyway.

Yancey asked, 'Do zombies always burn so bright?'

'No, it's the phosphorus,' I said.

The smell of burning flesh isn't always that bad; sometimes it just smells like cooking meat, but hair burning, and some of the internal organs that you normally remove before cooking a big piece of meat, that makes it smell . . . odd. It didn't always smell bad, and zombies usually smelled better burning than not, so . . . I tried to remember, but either I was finally nose-deaf to the smell of rotting zombies or these hadn't smelled bad. My zombies didn't smell bad, even if they looked rotten. I'd had an older animator explain to me that the magic that called it from the grave made it not rot for a little bit, and it was the rotting that caused the odor.

I touched Edward's arm. 'Did the zombies smell rotten to you?'

Edward seemed to think about it, then said, 'No.'

I looked past Edward to Dev, who was standing against the wall. His eyes looked too wide by the light of burning bodies. 'Did they smell like rotting corpses to you?'

He just shook his head, taking too long to blink. He looked shocky, but I'd worry about it later.

I turned to Nicky, on the other side of me. 'Were you able to smell them rotting?'

'No, but zombies don't smell like rotting corpses.'

'Mine don't,' I said, 'and those are the ones you've been around.'

'True, but you're scared; why?'

'Most zombies smell like what they are – corpses; the amount of smell comes from the amount of rot. My zombies don't smell bad because I'm powerful enough that they don't rot right away. But rotting vampires don't smell bad until they want to; they look bad, but they don't smell. The vampires and zombies in the mountains, they didn't smell bad, did they?'

'No,' Nicky said.

'I'm missing something,' Yancey said. 'Why are you saying that like it's a bad thing?

The fire alarm started to scream around us, but with our hearing still recovering from the shooting, it was like hearing it down a tunnel, as if it were echoing a long way off instead of just above us. The sprinklers kicked in, and suddenly it was raining.

Water pounded down on us and helped ease some of the battle fatigue, like a quick, sharp slap of ice-cold water. For the first time I wished I had the helmet I usually hated to wear when I enacted a warrant with SWAT backup. I had to look at the floor to keep the water from running in my eyes and had to wipe my face to keep the blowback of blood and other things from running into my eyes or mouth. Yeah, I knew to keep my mouth shut, but still . . . there was just something about certain things touching your lips that was an ick, and zombie bits were an ick.

Dev made a sound that I heard above the water, the alarm, and the fire blazing up like a white-flame version of hell, which meant it was a louder sound that my ear could make out right now.

He was wiping at his face frantically, and I realized he didn't know the rule that plumbers and monster hunters know – keep your mouth closed.

He stumbled away from the wall, fell to his knees, and threw up next to the burning pyre, while the water rained down on him. I went and knelt beside him. I tried to smooth his hair back from his face, but it was so plastered from the water that I had to pick up the wet locks of it and put it behind his ear. His hair was short enough and fine enough that the water kept it back where I'd put it. He looked sideways at me, his eyes flashing too much white, like a horse that's about to bolt. Then his eyes tracked something behind me that made them go even wider, and fear was plain on his face. I whirled still on my knees, bringing the AR up to bear, and found nothing but the white flames and the writhing of the body parts like octopus tentacles trying to get out of boiling water.

I glanced back at Dev, tracked back where his sightline was, and found a zombie arm with a hand still intact enough to finger-crawl coming toward us. I let my AR swing back on its strap, unholstered my Browning, and shot the hand so it wouldn't move so well, picked the arm up, and tossed it back into the fire.

When I turned back to Dev, he was looking at me with something like horror in his face, as if I'd done something terrible. I started to touch his shoulder, then realized he might not want me to touch him with the same hand I'd just touched the zombie with, so I let my hand drop.

'Go, up top, check on the guard, Miller.'

Dev nodded, a little too fast, a little too often, and he mouthed, *I'm sorry*.

I didn't ask, *Sorry about what?* I knew the what. He was my body-guard, but being at my side tonight had broken something in him. It remained to be seen whether the break could be mended or whether it was permanent. There'd been a time when I'd thrown up at crime scenes, but Edward had taken me into the thick of things at about the same time and I had managed not to break, but that had been me.

Dev got to his feet, steadying himself against the wall. He stumbled when he took his first step, and I caught his arm to help him. He tensed but didn't pull away. He smiled at me, weak and uncertain, but he tried. I took it for a positive sign that he could smile at all and hadn't pulled away from me. I'd had other friends and lovers over the years who had pulled away and never been able to close the distance again.

He went to the elevator, still a little shaky on his feet. I could have gone with him, helped him, but honestly I didn't want to. He was supposed to be taking care of me, and instead I was having to take care of him. It wasn't what bodyguards were for, and I wasn't getting enough out of my relationship with Dev to make up for this kind of loss. A loss of what, you might ask? Trust. I would never trust him to stay by my side and hold his own against the horrors in my life again. I would remember this moment and it would color things, just as he would remember.

Edward leaned over me and said, 'Why is it bad that the zombies and vampires don't smell?'

I smiled up at him; trust Edward to go right back to business. I followed his lead and said, 'It means that something, or someone, is controlling these things, or at least keeping enough power over them to keep them from rotting.'

Nicky leaned over us, talking into the roar of water and flame. 'But the vamps and zombies in the mountains were rotting. Bits fell off them.'

'I've seen rotting zombies lose bits off, but when they changed to their human form the parts they'd lost were still there, and whole.'

'How does that work?' Yancey asked.

I told the truth. 'I don't know. I just know it works that way, or can.'

'Are you saying sometimes it doesn't work that way?' he asked.

I wiped water and something thicker off my face before I answered. 'Rotting vampires are special; a lot of vamp rules don't apply to them.'

'So is the vampire that possessed the vamps in the mountains the one raising the zombies?' Nicky asked.

I started to say yes, then stopped myself. 'I don't know.' If Yancey hadn't been with us I'd have just brainstormed out loud, but I wasn't sure where the thoughts would go, so . . .

Dev called out, 'The elevator won't work.'

'Once the alarms are triggered, it goes to the lobby and waits for the firemen to use a key to override it,' Yancey said.

'You could have said something before he went and pushed the button,' I said.

Yancey shrugged.

'I knew, too,' Edward said.

'And you didn't say something, why?' I asked.

Edward just looked at me. It was an eloquent look.

I looked at Nicky. The water had plastered his hair to the right side of his face like it had been glued in place. 'And your excuse?' I asked.

'I'm a sociopath; I don't have to be nice,' Nicky said.

I gave him a look.

'You're mad at him. I can feel it, which means I really don't have to be nice to him.'

'I thought you were friends.'

'What part of *sociopath* didn't you understand?' he asked.

The water stopped pouring down and the sudden absence of it seemed loud, as if my body had gotten used to the pounding cold of it. I actually heard myself gasp; that meant my hearing wasn't permanently damaged, which was nice to know.

Dev leaned against the wall and slowly slid down it until he was sitting with his knees drawn up, and tears shone in the overhead lights. I looked at the men standing around me and realized that though they'd all help me kill monsters and burn the bodies later, they were so not helping me do the emotional stuff.

'Well, fuck,' I said, softly, and went to give what comfort I could. I spent a lot of that short distance trying to make my face more neutral, instead of irritated. I also upped my psychic shields, because Dev could feel my emotions sometimes, not all the time, but this was one moment I didn't want him to feel with me, just like I didn't want to feel his emotions with him.

I stood over him, debating what to do with him. He spoke without looking at me. 'You knew I was going to shoot at them. How did you know?'

It took me a minute to realize he meant SWAT. 'I've been in these kinds of battles before. It was Edward who saved me.'

'I'm good with a gun, and hand-to-hand, but I don't think I can do this, Anita. This isn't being a bodyguard, this is war.'

'Yeah, sometimes that's what I do.'

He looked up at me, fresh tears shining in his eyes. 'I didn't understand.'

I knelt beside him and debated on whether he wanted a hug, or if it would undo him completely, but he decided for me. He reached for me and I wrapped my arms around him. He buried his face against me and wept huge, racking sobs that shook every inch of that six-foot, three-inch body. He was strong and fast and brave, but I would never take him out again as my bodyguard. This had been killing zombies; what would he have been feeling if it had been humans, or shapeshifters, or vampires? Our Devil wasn't hard enough for my job.

Movement made me look up from murmuring sweet, comforting nothings into Dev's silky blond hair. Nicky was standing, talking to Edward and Yancey. He met my eyes and that one look was enough. He wasn't shaken. He'd been through battles like this before on his own job back when he was a mercenary, before the *ardeur* helped me tame him. We had the long look, and then he went back to talking to the other men, and I went back to holding Dev. Nicky and I both knew that we would never bring Dev out on a job again. He wasn't a soldier; there was no shame to that; we all have our strengths and weaknesses, but I needed someone . . . harsher. Nicky and Edward turned and looked at me, as if they'd felt me thinking. Nicky could have felt it because he was my Bride, and Edward, well, best friends know what you're thinking sometimes. I looked at the two of them, and I knew that Edward would be fine with Nicky coming out to play with us again. It was a pure Edward look in his face; Ted was gone like a dream, and what looked out at me was the same man who had threatened to torture and kill me when we first met, and he'd have done it if the job called for it. Now I was his friend, he cared for me, would miss me, depended on me, but that killing coldness was still in there. Nicky's face held the same look: distant, cold, able to do what needed doing to survive and finish the job, whatever that job was, whatever it called for, no matter how terrible. Nicky was probably capable of things that even I wouldn't do, maybe even things that

Edward wouldn't do, but sometimes a little bit of a sociopath was about right for my world. I'd told Nicky I loved him and realized for the first time just how much. Seeing him standing there, all stone-cold-killer calm, didn't make me love him less, it made me love him more. I hadn't been in love with Dev, but as I held him in his tears, I knew I never would be.

48

The elevator opened and spilled firemen in full gear out into the hallway, while I was still comforting him. I was pretty sure they'd be pissed about the fire that water didn't put out, so I concentrated the hell out of holding Dev and being all girly and comforting, and after we assured them that neither of us was physically hurt, they left us alone.

I smoothed his wet hair, and he buried his face against my chest, which was less sexy than it sounded because of the body armor, but it was the desperate strength of his hands, his arms, as he held me so tight that eased my anger and even my disappointment with him. If I hadn't used him as a beard to keep the firefighters from bitching at me about the fire, I'd have hugged him and been up and on to something else, but I couldn't hold him in that moment and not be moved. I would still never take him to work with me again, or let him bodyguard me outside normal St Louis events, but something hard and unpleasant that had been trying to take root against him eased.

Maybe what I saw as a weakness wasn't, and maybe the rest of us, in our strength, had lost something that this man would never lose. If I had ever been the kind of person who would have fallen apart in front of the other men like this, it was long gone. Pride would have kept me more together than this, or maybe stubbornness; whatever it was, or wasn't, I held our Devil, our Mephistopheles, and murmured, 'It's okay, it's okay. I've got you.'

He raised up his face and looked at me with his blue-on-blue tiger eyes so sad. 'I'm supposed to help you, supposed to protect you. I'm sorry.'

'You stood at our side and fought all the way through. You didn't run, didn't flinch, you did the job. A lot of people couldn't have done that, Dev.'

'But I'm a mess now.'

'Once the fighting is over, the danger past, it's okay. You stayed in there until it was over.'

'But you think less of me for falling apart, I know you do.'

I smiled at him, and with me on my knees and him sitting flat, I was barely taller than him. 'I won't take you vampire hunting again, but you're brave enough to admit you're in love with another man, and I know a lot of people who wouldn't do that. They'd hide from themselves. I still haven't gone out in public with Jade on my arm even though she's been in my bed for over a year. There are all different kinds of bravery, Mephistopheles; this just isn't your kind.'

The moment I said it, I promised myself I'd talk to Jade when I got home and see about going out with her and maybe Nathaniel for a dinner out. Why not just the two of us? Because Jade puzzled me; she was more than a thousand years old, originally from ancient China, and there were cultural differences that went beyond her being the first girlfriend/lover I'd ever had. I needed a wingman to date Jade in so many ways.

The firefighters were yelling at Edward about the phosphorus. I caught one loud male voice saying, 'What the hell is this stuff?'

Firefighters do not like saying that about burning things; they're used to knowing what and why things burn. I caught the comforting tone of Edward's Ted voice, though not what he was saying. We were too far away for that, and my hearing wasn't a hundred percent yet.

'I think if I could shower and get the blowback off me, I'd feel less freaked,' Dev said.

I remembered the first time I'd gone home and realized I had a piece of a vampire's brain in my hair. I'd stared at myself in the mirror and started to shake and ended up on the floor of the bathroom a lot like Dev was sitting now, but there'd been no one to comfort me. I'd been so alone for so many years that maybe I'd have reached out for someone, too, if there'd been anyone to reach out to.

Would I be less hard now if I'd had someone to turn to, or would I still be me? Maybe I'd just have been a lot happier, a lot earlier? There was no going back, but looking down into Dev's earnest face, I wondered. I wasn't sure I'd ever wondered before, not about that.

'I need to make sure the rotting vampires that were reported on other floors are all executed, and check on Micah and Nathaniel, and then we can go clean up.'

'Showers?' he asked.

I nodded.

'Can you help me make sure I get all of it off me?' he asked, and his eyes looked uncertain again.

'Are you asking me to join you in the shower?' I smiled when I said it, made it teasing.

He smiled back, and the change in his eyes from uncertain to happy anticipatory lust was worth it. Would I normally have maybe moved Dev off the list of lovers after this? Maybe, but for the gloom to lift from his face and eyes, sex in the shower with him was not a hardship.

'Yes, I am,' he said, and this time when his arms went around me it wasn't a desperate grip, but a caress with a promise of more to come. Sex may not be the answer to everything, but it's also not the worst answer to a lot of things. It beat the hell out of anger and killing things.

49

We stepped off the elevator into a mass of police, medical professionals, and first responders of every flavor. It was as if the hospital population had tripled between the time we went down to the basement and now.

A uniform who I remembered from the hallway earlier that day, though it seemed like a hundred years ago, said, 'What the hell happened to you guys?'

We all looked at each other. The men's hair was plastered to their heads, and even my curls were dripping wet, as were our clothes. I looked down to find that we were making a puddle on the floor. We had to have done the same thing in the elevator, but we just hadn't noticed.

The uniform laughed. 'How did you get that wet and still look like you walked out of a slaughterhouse?'

I blinked at us all and realized that the sprinklers hadn't exactly gotten all of the mess. It was like I was seeing the world in pieces, which meant that though I was handling it better than Dev, I might be a little shocky. Interesting.

'Zombies,' I said.

'What?'

'They were killing zombies,' Hatfield said as she walked up to us.

'We were killing vampires, but none of us look this bad,' he said.

'Zombies are messier,' she said, and then she said, 'Just give it a rest, Lewis. I need to talk to the marshals.'

He started to say something else, but she said, 'Now, Lewis.'

He frowned, but he walked away.

Hatfield was in full gear like we were, though we had more weapons on us, but then Edward and I tended to overpack. A gurney with a covered body on it wheeled between us. There was blood soaking through the covering, which meant it was a very fresh body.

Hatfield watched it being wheeled into the elevator. She kept watching it as the doors closed behind the dead body and the orderly pushing it. Her eyes reminded me of Dev's earlier. He'd rallied, and to strangers he probably didn't look any worse for wear than the rest of us, except for Yancey, who had gone to find the rest of his squad. He still looked fresh compared to the rest of us, but then he'd only helped with cleanup. The real mess had been the dismembering by shooting; he'd missed that part.

'We've got five dead,' she said, and her voice sounded harsh, angry even, but I knew she wasn't angry with us. She was just angry; I knew all about that.

'Did the guard, Miller, make it?' Dev asked.

She shook her head. 'I've never seen anything like these rotting bastards. They don't die like regular vampires.'

I opened my mouth, and Edward must have been afraid that I'd say *I told you so*, because he touched my arm. 'They're the hardest type of vamp to destroy,' he said.

'The vampires' bodies have already been put in the incinerator in the sub-basement here. The incinerator is designed to destroy medical waste, and I watched each vampire go into the fire. Is that dead enough?'

'It'll do,' I said.

There was a flinching around her eyes, and she said, 'Could they climb back out of an incinerator? Medical waste has to be destroyed completely, so I thought it was enough; if it's not . . .' Her voice broke, and she stared down at the floor, one hand resting on the butt of her sidearm. There was a time when I touched my gun like that, like a dangerous teddy bear.

'Fire destroys even the rotting vampires,' I said.

She looked up at me, and the only word I had for her eyes was haunted. She looked haunted. 'I've hunted vampires in the field. I'm not just one of those newbies who's only staked them in the morgue. I know what it's like to hunt them and have them hunt you back, but I've never seen anything like this.'

'Rotting vamps are real rare in this country,' Edward said in his best Ted voice.

She nodded. 'How did they heal the damage to their brains, hearts, and spinal cords? That's supposed to kill anything, even vampires.'

'The rotting vampires are more like zombies,' I said, 'and that means fire is the only certainty.'

'Except daylight, right?' she said.

'I've seen two rotters that could walk in daylight and not burn. Daylight shows them as rotting corpses and they can't pass for human, but they could still walk around and do everything else.'

'Day walkers, that's just legend,' she said.

I shook my head. 'I've known a few other vamps that were powerful enough to walk in daylight. Some are just so damned old that daylight doesn't hurt them anymore; for others it's a power curve, almost like being able to call an animal, or levitate.'

'Every time I think I've seen the worst of these bastards, I'm wrong,' she said, and she wasn't looking at us anymore. She was staring off into space, seeing some horror from the fighting and the dying playing over in her head. How did I know that was what Hatfield was thinking? Because I'd been there, done that, and was tired of collecting that particular T-shirt.

'The rotting vamps are the worst of it,' I said.

She looked at me then. 'Really?'

I met those haunted eyes and said, 'Yeah.'

She gave a laugh, but it was a bitter sound. 'I want to ask you to promise me, like I'm fucking five or something.'

I smiled to take the sting out what I was about to say. 'I wouldn't promise, sorry.'

'You said this was the worst.'

'I did, but there are things that have scared me more. Vampires that scared the fuck out of me.'

'Like the one you killed in Vegas.'

'Yeah, he was pretty scary,' I said.

'Is it true that he could call jinn, like make-a-wish genies?'

'Yeah,' I said.

'I didn't even think jinn existed outside of old stories,' she said.

'Me either,' I said.

'Well, fuck,' she said.

I nodded, shrugged, and said, '*Fuck* about covers it.'

'But these vampires are dead, right? It's over, except for the two in custody that I can kill later today.'

'We need the master vampire behind this, Hatfield. Until he's dead he'll make more rotting vampires, and we'll have more flesh-eating zombies. We need the two vampires alive so I can question them tomorrow night. They're our best chance at finding out his daytime location and destroying him once and for all.'

She nodded, and like Dev downstairs it was a little too rapid and a little too often. 'Forrester persuaded me not to kill them earlier, but if you tell me they're more valuable alive than dead, I'll believe you, Blake. I didn't believe you once and people died. It'll be dawn soon; what can we do until the vamps wake up to be questioned?'

'They've lawyered up,' Edward said. 'Questioning them won't be as easy as normal.'

'That fucking new law,' Hatfield said, and then she looked at me. She studied me as if she were trying to see inside my head. 'Knowing all that you know about them, how could you help draft a law that gave these bastards rights?'

'I've worked serial killer cases where the perp was human, but I still support human rights.'

'That's not the same,' she said.

'How many serial cases have you worked?' I asked.

'Every vampire case I've ever worked had multiple deaths.'

I shook my head. 'Most vamps kill to eat or because they're trying to make more vampires. They don't have the same kind of pathology as a serial killer, even though that's technically what they're classed as a lot.'

'What does that even mean?' Hatfield said, and she sounded irritated, a hint of her earlier attitude.

'It means I've seen human serial killers who did things so awful that as horrible as the vampires and shapeshifters can be, it's not as terrible to me.'

'Why not?' she asked, and the irritation was melting with something that was almost tears.

'Because we're human beings, damn it, and we're supposed to remember that and act accordingly. Serial killers don't remember that.'

'It can be worse than we saw tonight.'

I didn't know whether to pat her on the head or laugh in her face.

Edward saved me from either. 'Marshal Hatfield, the worst monsters I've ever seen have all been human.'

Her eyes were shiny. 'I don't want to believe that.'

'No one wants to believe that,' he said, 'but that doesn't make it any less true.' He sounded sympathetic, kind even, and I knew he wasn't, not about this kind of thing. He was the consummate actor when he needed to be, and he had his Ted act down to an Oscar-worthy performance. I still didn't understand how he did it, but watching Hatfield look at him with her eyes held wide so the tears wouldn't fall, I watched her buy his sympathy, hook, line, and sinker.

She said, 'I need to go . . . do something. I'll . . .' She went for the doors and the outside air. Maybe she needed air, but I was betting she just didn't want anyone to see her cry. No cop wanted the other cops to see them cry, but as a woman, once you cried at a crime scene you never really lived it down. Throwing up at a crime scene was better than crying at one.

'What next?' Dev asked.

'Kiss Nathaniel and Micah, and then I'd like to finally see the hotel, clean up, and get a few hours of sleep.'

'I usually have to make you sleep on a job,' Edward said.

'Maybe I'm getting old,' I said.

'You're younger than I am,' he said.

I smiled. 'Maybe I just got out of the hospital after being shot and spent the last few hours in a brutal fucking battle against killer zombies, and so I'm a little tired.'

He grinned and settled his hat a little lower on his head. 'A little tired,' he said.

'A little tired,' I said, and smiled.

'Well, I'm fucking exhausted,' Nicky said.

'I thought lions were supposed to have stamina,' Dev said, and his eyes were wide and innocent, too innocent.

Nicky raised an eyebrow at him. 'We've got more stamina than tigers, but that's not saying a lot.'

Dev grinned. 'I can think of one way to prove what cat has the most stamina.'

Nicky grinned back.

'I don't know whether to put my fingers in my ears and go *la-la-la* or find more of your guards so we can take bets,' Edward said.

I frowned at him.

He grinned, and with all of them grinning at me, what else could I do but grin back. 'Fine, but I'm not sure I'm up to anything bet-worthy tonight.'

Dev pretended to pout. Nicky just looked smug. I narrowed my eyes at them. 'Pouting I get, but why smug?'

Nicky grinned again. 'You're dead tired, and you just got out of the hospital, and you've already fed the *ardeur*, but you still didn't say no.'

I rolled my eyes.

He leaned in close and whispered, 'I love you, too.'

It took me a moment to realize what he was referring to, which let me know just how tired I was, but when my brain caught up to the comment I blushed. Red, hot, to-my-roots blushed, which I'd almost stopped doing.

Nicky laughed, high and delighted. It was such a happy sound that it made people look at us.

'I haven't seen you blush like that in years,' Edward said.

'Fuck you both,' I said, and went for the elevator. I was going to see Micah and Nathaniel and then go to the hotel. I might not be as freaked about it as Dev had been, but I could feel thicker things than blood drying on my skin as I moved. I didn't even want to know how much, or exactly what, was in my hair.

It occurred to me after I'd pressed the button that we were covered in rotting flesh and fresh blood, and Micah's dad had an open wound that they were leaving open to the air. We couldn't go near him.

I hit the earpiece and hoped that he and Nathaniel could come down, or out to us. I needed to see them, touch them, and know they were all right with more than just a voice over the telephone. I felt exhausted and yet, weirdly, wasn't sure I'd be able to sleep. It was like that after a fight sometimes, exhausted but jazzed.

Nathaniel answered the phone. They could come down and say good night. Yay, so very yay! There, the edge of tears now. I didn't usually get this emotional this soon after the violence, but sometimes it was as if my mind didn't know how to cope so it kept trying out different strategies—humor, sarcasm, exhaustion, embarrassment, sadness. Once I'd just been numb, that was how I'd survived, but the problem was that in trying to cope with my job I'd become numb to everything. It had been damn depression, and then Jean-Claude had found me and broken down the walls that I'd so carefully built around myself. The good news was that I'd never been happier. The bad news was that in feeling love, I felt other things, too, and some of them were not so good.

The elevator doors opened and Micah and Nathaniel were there and it was everything I could do to not fall into their arms and start to sob. Two things stopped me. One, I'd have gotten zombie bits all over them and then Micah couldn't have gone back into his father's room without a shower. Two, if I threw myself into my boyfriend's arms and sobbed like a freaking girl I'd never live it down. The other cops would see me as a girl, and I needed them to see me as one of the guys, but as I reached out a hand to each of them, rather than flinging myself on them like I wanted to, I wasn't sure being one of the 'guys' was worth it.

50

The front desk clerk of the very nice hotel took one look at the four of us as we walked through the doors at an hour till dawn and assumed that something was wrong at the hotel. I wanted to see Jean-Claude before dawn, so I didn't have any patience left for it.

'We're just going to our room,' I said.

He looked us up and down, and his face said clearly he didn't believe we had a room in his fine establishment. I think the room rate was probably above most cops' salaries.

It was Edward who touched my shoulder and made me realize I'd taken a step toward the desk clerk. He spoke under his breath. 'Ease down.'

I tried to swallow past the pulse that was suddenly trying to jump out of my throat. What was wrong with me? I nodded to let him know I'd understood.

It was Dev who smiled and charmed the man, flashing the room card that he had. He'd actually seen the rooms while I was off in the mountains hunting vamps with Nicky and Ares. Thinking his name caused that tightening of the chest, the reaction in the gut that would happen for a while. At least he hadn't been a lover, and the moment I thought it I felt bad for being relieved that I hadn't been closer to him, but I was relieved all the same.

We had a suite of rooms, and basically Jean-Claude had taken over a floor of the hotel, which was why we'd invited Edward to come stay the night. There'd be a bed somewhere, or so Dev had said. I might not want him as my backup on a warrant of execution, but I trusted him to report the rooms and the sleeping space available. There are a lot of people I trust to coordinate my life who I wouldn't trust to guard my life, just as there were people I trusted at my back in a fight who would have sucked at the organization part of things. We all had our skills.

I watched Dev, his hair still slimed on one side with drying blood, charm the frightened hotel clerk. He wasted that smile on him that was usually reserved for sexual prospects, and either the clerk was into guys or Dev was just that charming. I didn't know which, and if it would get us up to our rooms sooner I didn't much care which.

The three of us went to the elevators, and Edward had me hold the door while he and Nicky loaded in the bags of weapons; normally I would have insisted on helping load, but it would be bad to have the doors close with our bags in there and none of us with them. So I held the door while the men loaded until there was barely going to be room for us to stand. Edward leaned on the open door, holding it, and Nicky and I got in, and when he put his arm around me I didn't protest. I cuddled under his arm, as close as the body armor would let me get. I let him hold me and tried not to feel much, except that it felt good. Dev trotted up to us, and Edward stepped in and let the doors close.

'He offered us help with our bags,' Dev said.

'Is the clerk into guys, or is your ability to charm devoid of sexual promise?' I asked.

He grinned at me. 'Devoid of sexual promise; you must not be as tired as I thought.'

I scowled at him.

Nicky hugged me a little tighter, and I scowled at him, too.

Dev's grin did not fade; in fact it widened. 'Yeah, the clerk is into guys.'

'You imply that you might see him later?' Edward asked.

'Nothing as strong as that,' Dev said.

'What does that even mean?' I asked, and it sounded grumpy even to me.

'It means he didn't pimp himself out, but he let the clerk think that he liked guys, too,' Nicky said.

I glanced up at him from under his arm, so it felt like being a child and too small and . . . I moved out from him.

'What did I do wrong?' he asked.

'How did you know that?'

'Flirting for distraction is the same no matter if it's women or men, Anita.'

'You're saying you've done the same thing.'

'I've been the young, cute distraction on a few jobs back when I was with my first lion pride, so yeah.' His face was neutral as he said it, empty of emotion. It was the way he hid when he was feeling something, because Nicky wasn't a born sociopath; his feelings had gotten tortured and abused out of him. It meant he still had feelings, but they were . . . hidden and a little twisted.

'You do more than just flirt on the job?' I asked.

'Don't do this,' Edward said.

I glared at him. 'Do what?'

'Pick at the people you love, because you've finally got a minute that isn't an emergency and all the feelings you've been shoving down inside are trying to find a way out, and if you won't give them a nice clean exit wound, they'll tear their way out of your life and everyone near you.'

We looked at each other. I wanted to ask who he had torn up that had been close to him, because I knew it wasn't Donna and the kids; whoever he was referring to had been before that, before I knew him. If we'd been alone I would have asked, but he wouldn't answer in front of anyone but me, and maybe not even me.

The doors opened and Dev moved first like a good bodyguard. It moved Edward to check the hall and Nicky to move so that his broad body blocked me from view, though knowing that I loved him meant that him taking a bullet for me had taken on a whole new suck.

There was a murmur of male voices, and then I heard more clearly, 'Sorry, man, but it's orders.'

'What's wrong?' I asked, fighting the urge to peer around Nicky's body.

Edward answered from the door that he was holding open. 'Claudia is in charge of the detail and apparently she's upset.'

'Why? What'd we do?' I asked.

'You aren't in trouble,' Dev said. 'We are.'

'Why?' Nicky asked.

'Apparently, for letting Anita get hurt.'

'When I'm on the job you guys can't protect me.'

A second male voice said, 'Claudia got put in charge of Jean-Claude and Anita's safety, so she's going to yell at both of you.'

'Lisandro, is that you?' I stepped around Nicky then, and he let me, only sliding his hand into mine so we walked out hand in hand.

'It's me,' he said, and there he was, six feet of tall, Hispanic handsome, his long black hair tied back in a ponytail. He was wearing a black T-shirt under a black suit jacket, over black jeans and boots. The suit jacket didn't hide the gun at his waist as well as it would have if his waist had been less slender and his shoulders a little less broad, but Lisandro did the same workout as the other guards, and unlike Dev he worked hard at it. He was built more slender than Nicky and would never muscle up like that, but what muscle he had looked good on him. He was better in a fight than he looked, but . . .

'You aren't supposed to travel out of town on guard work,' I said.

'When Jean-Claude decided to come out here, Rafael wanted the best guarding him, so Claudia is in charge and I'm her second-in-command, because we are the best.' He said it with no trace of attitude, just a statement of fact.

I opened my mouth and closed it, because what was I supposed to say, that ever since he'd nearly died on an out-of-town guard detail with me, I hadn't wanted him with me again, because I didn't want to tell his wife and kids why their father had died keeping me alive? Or that we'd had one emergency feeding of the *ardeur* when the Mother of All Darkness and the Lover of Death had messed with us, and his wife had told us no harm, no foul, but if he ever had sex with me again then she was divorcing his ass and taking his kids, and I didn't want to risk it?

'Hey, that makes me the best, too,' and it was Emmanuel, who was five foot eight with short, pale brown hair and the only blue-gray eyes I'd ever seen on someone who was Hispanic. He tanned in the summer, but never as dark as Lisandro was normally. Emmanuel was also one of our younger guards, under twenty-five, though I wasn't honestly sure just how much under.

'You must have been training behind our backs, because last I checked you couldn't beat me in anything.' Dev said it with a smile that let the other man know he was teasing.

'Well, you didn't do so hot at keeping her safe, did you?'

And that was a little too close to home, because Dev stopped smiling. In fact, for a moment a much more serious person looked out of that handsome face, and the first trickle of otherworldly energy whispered through the hallway, which meant he was really pissed, because the golden tigers prided themselves on ultimate control over their inner beast.

'Hey, I'm sorry,' Emmanuel said. 'That was out of line.' He looked genuinely embarrassed, and he should have.

'We're supposed to turn Anita over to the guards in the main room and then escort the two of you to Claudia. I don't have orders for . . . Marshal Ted,' Lisandro said.

'I figured we had room for him, and if it's a fight, him with us is better,' Dev said.

'I can't argue about the fighting part, and you're right, we have the whole floor to ourselves, so there's a bed for him.'

'Thanks,' Edward said in his Ted voice, even smiling.

Lisandro gave him narrow eyes, because he knew exactly who Edward was; the Ted was so he wouldn't forget around the other cops.

'I didn't think Claudia traveled out of town for guard duty either,' I said.

'We didn't have time to get Bobby-Lee back in town to be point on this, and Fredo had a family event, so that left Claudia and me.'

'I'm sorry for that,' I said, and I wondered if he understood what I was apologizing for.

He smiled bright in the dark handsome of his face. 'You almost died, and you're apologizing because we had to travel out of town at the last minute.' He shook his head.

'I want my weapons in the room near me; if we all carry stuff it'll be quicker,' I said.

They didn't argue. We all picked up bags and Lisandro led the way to a door. He gave a knock that sounded like a signal: two short, one loud. The door opened, though I couldn't see who opened it around everyone's taller and broader bodies. I was used to being the smallest person in the room and certainly the smallest person when the guards were with me. They deposited the dangerous bags just inside the door, because though the room was large there was barely space for this many new bags.

I finally got to see the hotel suite. I'm sure it had looked roomy once, but with all the coffins in it there was barely room to thread a path from the window to the bathroom. Jean-Claude could have slept in the bed just fine, but two things. One, a lot of the older vampires preferred to travel with a coffin. Two, a maid opening the drapes, by accident or on purpose, would be very, very bad. A lot of the maids were devoutly religious and from sections of the world where vampires weren't legal and could still be killed on sight, if you could manage it before they killed you. It just wasn't worth the risk. Some of the newer vamps traveled with mummy sleeping bags. They folded up better in your carry-on bag. Coffins were for vampires who had servants and flunkies to tote and fetch. Jean-Claude had those. In fact, some of the coffins were for the flunkies.

I kissed Nicky good luck as Lisandro led him off to get yelled at by Claudia, about something that wasn't his fault, but I understood chain of command enough to know that my interceding for him would just piss her off more. Claudia was six foot six, the tallest woman I'd ever personally met, and had the shoulders and muscle to go with her size, though she still managed to look feminine, dangerous but beautiful. With no makeup to grace the high cheekbones, and her long hair usually pulled back into a tight ponytail just like Lisandro's, she was still one of the most striking women I'd ever met.

Lisandro led them and Edward off to find her and a bed for Edward and his own bags of dangerous toys. Dev poked his head back in at the last minute. 'You still going to help me clean up?'

I smiled at him, I couldn't help it. 'Yeah.'

He grinned at me, and Emmanuel gave him a halfhearted push through the door. 'You are such a horndog.'

'Yes, I am,' Dev said, and the door closed behind them. I turned to see past the bags, mine and the mountain of Jean-Claude's, and the coffins, to find what guards I'd been handed off to, and smiled.

The Wicked Truth had come as Jean-Claude's bodyguards. Wicked and Truth were tall, broad-shouldered, handsome, with shoulder-length hair. Wicked's hair was straight and thick and very blond. Truth's hair was brown with a slight wave to it. They both had gray-blue eyes, which meant that sometimes they looked blue and sometimes not so much. Once Truth had an almost-beard, nicely scruffy, but he'd shaved it and like most vampires he wasn't able to grow it out once he'd shaved it, so now you could see that they both had a deep dimple in the square, manly chins. Without the facial hair the brothers looked even more like twins, though I knew they'd been born a year apart. I also knew that Wicked had dressed them both in designer suits; his was a pale gray with a blue dress shirt that made his eyes look very blue. Truth was in charcoal gray with a shirt almost the same shade of blue so his eyes were as blue as I'd ever seen them, so that when they turned and looked at me it gave a startling mirror image, and then Wicked's arrogant, teasing smile spoiled the illusion. Truth was far too serious for that smile.

Wicked was still smiling as he said, 'It doesn't do any good to send bodyguards with you if you keep insisting on hunting monsters without us.'

'You are a fool, brother,' Truth said, and moved toward me through the coffins. It looked like an undertaker's showroom.

'I had a bodyguard with me,' I said, quietly.

'I am a fool,' Wicked said, 'and I am so sorry about Ares.'

Truth hugged me, and I let him. I let the strength and solidness of him hold me close. I could trace his shoulder rig under the suit jacket, and my hands found his weapons without thinking about it. The suit jackets were tailored to hide the guns and blades. His torso was long enough that he had a short sword down his back in a back sheath modeled after one I used to hold my biggest blade, though I was short enough that mine was just a big knife. His short sword was longer than my body from neck to waist. I knew that somewhere in his luggage was the great sword, his real sword. He'd fixed up a back harness for it, too, but there was no way to actually wear it concealed, just more modern-looking. His battle-axe didn't really fit under modern clothing either, but then axes are like machine guns; concealment isn't really the point, intimidation and blood is the point. He had several smaller axes, too, but only the smaller throwing axes actually fit under modern jackets, and then barely.

I liked that hugging Truth was always an obstacle course in weapons placement. Some of the men in my life probably felt the same way about me, though I wasn't sure about the 'liking' part.

He stroked my hair and just held me close. Truth was a man of few words, which meant he didn't expect much from others. There were moments when that was a very good thing.

Truth and I pulled back from the hug at about the same time. I looked up into his face and those surprisingly blue eyes and found them grayer than when we'd started the hug. I realized his eyes had changed shade because he was sad, or knew I was; blue-gray eyes did that.

Wicked was at our side now. His handsome face was very serious as he said, 'We understand what it is like to be forced to kill a friend and comrade in arms, Anita.'

I realized that they meant it. Centuries ago the head of their bloodline, their *sourdre de sang*, had gone insane and been possessed by a blood frenzy that had spread through all the vampires he'd created, except for the two brothers standing with me. They had executed the others of their line, a bloodline known for its warriors, before the Vampire Council's executioners could arrive to carry out the death sentences.

I wrapped an arm around Wicked's waist, while still having a loose arm around Truth. They hugged me together, but it was Wicked who bent over for a kiss. He was the bold one in certain areas.

'We were never allowed such liberties with our Dark Mistress,' a man's voice said.

We turned, and it was one of the executioners sent to carry out that death sentence oh so long ago. Mischa was one of the Harlequin; he had been Graziano, one of the early names of the *Dottor* or Doctor in the *Italian Comedy*. He'd spent centuries wearing a mask that matched that name. The only people who saw his real face had been those he spied upon or those he killed. His real face had been the last sight on earth for thousands, maybe millions. Some of the Harlequin were more than two thousand years old. You could rack up a pretty impressive kill count in that space of time.

Many of the Harlequin were what real spies looked like: nondescript for their day, or their country. Real spies weren't James Bond; you didn't want to stand out or attract too much attention. If you were well known enough that bartenders all over the world knew you preferred your martini shaken and not stirred like old-school Bond, then you were a stalking horse, not a spy. You were sent in to attract attention so the real spies could be sneaky and find out things, or assassinate from the shadows and then vanish back into those shadows.

Mischa was tall for one of them, almost six feet. He had thick blond hair that was as straight as Wicked's, but his hair was a paler, almost white blond, which meant it must always have been that pale, because sunlight hadn't touched his hair in more than a thousand years. Wicked's hair was an almost golden blond from lack of light to pale it.

Mischa looked at us with blue eyes that should have looked like warm summer skies, but they were cold, no matter how pure the blue of them might be. Wherever he'd been recruited for the Harlequin, it had been somewhere that all that pale hair and those bright blue eyes would have fit in without anyone blinking – somewhere Scandinavian.

'Anita is a kinder mistress than the Mother of All Darkness,' Truth said.

'Jealous?' Wicked said.

'The Mistress of us all isn't supposed to be kind, she's supposed to lead.'

'Anita leads us where we need to go,' Truth said.

'You believe she leads well enough,' Wicked said. 'You are just jealous that we have her favor and you do not.'

'That is not true, and you know it. You say such things only to try to anger me.'

'I was jealous of the other guards who shared her bed until I was added to the list,' Wicked said.

'That is you. I am made of sterner stuff than that,' he said, and walked farther away from what looked to be a large bathroom behind him.

'You have yet to best me at sword practice or outdo my score at the firing range with a handgun,' Wicked said.

Mischa flushed, hands curling into fists at his side; for a really ancient vampire he was surprisingly easy to bait. Most of the really old ones could control their emotions to a degree that was frightening, almost . . . inhuman.

'I have bested you both with knife and long gun,' he said, hands in tight fists.

'But neither of us with sword or handgun,' Truth said, 'and you won't even try to practice with me and an axe.' Truth would have stayed out of it, but the other vampire had said *both*. Truth would seldom start a fight, but he would finish one. Wicked would pick a fight but leave it laughing without caring who won most of the time. Truth cared more once you got him going.

'Even I've bested your score with a handgun,' I said.

'That is at the range, not real combat,' Mischa said.

'I shoot just fine in real combat,' I said.

Mischa looked almost pained as he said, 'I was impressed with the shot you made on the news. I would not have thought you capable of it.'

'I had to make it, so I did.'

He nodded. 'Needing to make it does not automatically give you the ability to do it, Anita Blake. That you had the skill within you under trying conditions was . . . impressive.'

'Bet you hate saying that,' Wicked said.

Mischa glared at him. 'Our Dark Mistress was a weapon; she had no need of guns and blades and training with us. She was more dangerous than any of us could ever be.'

'So does that mean that Anita is more dangerous than all the remaining Harlequin?' Wicked asked.

'No.' Mischa almost spat that one word.

'You said that the Mother of All Darkness was more powerful than any of you; then wouldn't whoever killed her be more powerful than any of you, too?' Truth asked.

Mischa shook his head but said nothing.

'They debate between themselves on how a mere human woman could have slain their dark mistress.' A man stepped out from the adjoining bedroom. He was taller than Mischa by several inches, broader through the shoulders, just bigger all over. He had short brown hair that curled carelessly and eyes that were deep reddish brown. If you didn't know what you were looking at you'd think they were human eyes, but they weren't; they were bear eyes, big fucking ancient cave bear eyes. His name was Goran and he had been a werebear before most of the great cities of the world had been more than a wide place to sell your cattle, and Mischa was even older. If I let down my shields and let my necromancy feel them, they were old enough to make the bones along my jaws ache.

'There isn't a human being in this room,' I said. 'Where's Jean-Claude?'

'He's on the phone in the other room,' Wicked said, and there was the faintest tone to his voice. Whoever Jean-Claude was talking to, he didn't like it.

Mischa had no problem saying out loud what he didn't like. 'Our lord and master is on the phone to the sodomite who has him pussy-whipped.'

'Sodomite?' I asked.

'He's talking to Asher,' Wicked said, 'but I wouldn't let Jean-Claude hear you talk about his beloved that way, Mischa.'

'Wait, you can't be both a sodomite and pussy, or did the slang change?' I asked.

'It didn't change, he's just trying to be objectionable,' Truth said, and gave the other vampire an unfriendly look.

I walked toward the vampire and his big bear of a sidekick. 'I can't argue the sodomy part, but wouldn't it be pecker-whipped, or maybe cock-whipped?'

Mischa glared at me; he knew I was making fun of him, but he wasn't quite sure how. I'd noticed that almost all the older vampires had trouble with modern slang; even the ones who'd mastered some of it hadn't mastered all of it. Slang didn't travel well from one language to another either.

Truth was at my back, and Wicked was moving up through the coffins on the other side of the huge conference table that dominated the main part of the room. There was also a couch and coffee table pushed to one side of the room to make room for more coffins. The kitchenette wasn't movable, so it just took up the room it took up.

'The fact that our Dark Master is begging that sodomite to come back to St Louis is embarrassing to all of us.'

'I let you call him that once,' I said, 'and I let you know I didn't like it, but maybe I'm too tired for subtle.'

'You yourself said that you cannot argue the charge of sodomy against them,' Mischa said.

'What we all do in the privacy of our bedrooms doesn't matter to you unless you're our lover, and since you're not, why does it matter to you what we do or who we do?'

'It is an insult to all of us who call him our prince that he lets another man use him so.'

I frowned at him. 'So you're objecting because you think Jean-Claude is bottoming to Asher?'

Mischa seemed to think about it, and then he nodded. 'I've never heard it called that, but *bottoming* is quite accurate under the circumstances.'

I smiled, almost laughed, and was just too tired to not say what I was thinking. 'Well, if that's all that's bothering you, don't worry about it, Mischa. Jean-Claude isn't bottoming to Asher; he definitely tops him, not the other way around.' The fact that I was using BDSM terms that really had little to do with actual sex, homosexual or otherwise, went over the vampire's head, way over.

'You mean Jean-Claude uses him and is not used by him?'

'If you want to put it that way, yeah.' I had recovered myself enough to think, but not say, *As far as I know, when I'm with them.* If they switched the other way around when I wasn't with them, that was their business and I wasn't sure it bothered me anyway, but I hadn't seen it swing that way, but that didn't mean . . . oh, hell. I was too tired to worry about something that didn't bother me anymore.

'You know, Mischa,' I said, 'I like men. I like watching the men I love together, knowing that all that strength and beauty will be aimed at me later, so stop being all homophobic. I'm too fucking tired to mess with it tonight.'

I don't know what he would have said next, because the door opened behind them and Jean-Claude stepped out. Mischa gave a look to us, and the look was enough. He would never have said what he'd just said to me to Jean-Claude. The ex-Harlequin might have been saying mean things about Jean-Claude and Asher, but he said them only to me, which showed a lack of respect for me. He feared what Jean-Claude would do, but not what I would do. I filed the thought away for later when I wasn't achingly tired and covered in the drying blood and bits of the dead I'd helped make deader.

Jean-Claude's eyes widened just a bit. '*Ma petite*, you have had a busy night, I see.' His French accent was as thick as I'd heard it in a while, which meant he was feeling strong emotions that he couldn't quite hide, but he was trying. I appreciated the effort, because the accent alone meant that what he wanted to say was his version of, *You are covered in blood and worse, which means you were in horrible danger and probably nearly died . . . again! How can you keep risking yourself like that when I love you so much?* Instead of picking a fight he just glided toward me and held his hands out to me, as graceful as if he meant to dance when he got to me.

It was one of those moments when I felt very ordinary, or maybe clunky. I had good hand-eye coordination, and speed, and skill at using my body, but I would never rival his grace and beauty of movement. He had too many centuries of practice on me, and nearly all of it showed as he walked toward me. It was that, that finally clued me in on the fact that maybe fear of my being in danger wasn't the only strong emotion he was fighting not to show.

He'd been talking to Asher. The conversation had gone either really well or really badly. Even as he took me into his arms, I couldn't tell which. I went up on tiptoe to meet him bending down over me, and the moment his lips touched mine I felt the excitement in him. The kiss grew from our normal tender, but fairly chaste kiss in front of the newer guards to one so passionate that I had to work to make sure we didn't cut my lips on the dainty fangs just inside his mouth.

I drew back from the kiss breathless and smiling almost stupidly up at him. I was energized, befuddled, and entirely too happy. It wasn't vampire powers; it was just the effect Jean-Claude had on me.

He smiled down at me so broadly that he flashed fangs, which he almost never did with just a smile. He was so obviously pleased with himself that I knew the talk with Asher had gone well, better than well.

'It is almost dawn, my lord; there is no time for sex,' Mischa said in a voice that dripped with disdain.

Jean-Claude looked at him, and the look was enough. Mischa bowed, sweeping his arm down and close so that you could almost see the hat with its feathered plume that should have been in the hand to go with that gesture. All the Harlequin had great bows and gestures of obedience, but a lot of them also had Mischa's gift for making the gesture only after they'd insulted us or turning the gesture into a snide remark of its own. The only thing that made them worth putting up with was that they were almost as good as they thought they were, and good enough that when Claudia wanted to bring the best with her she'd picked some of them.

Jean-Claude's voice came smooth and nearly devoid of accent, centuries of control sliding back into place within seconds. 'Tell me, Mischa, how did you stay alive being so snide with the Mother of All Darkness?'

There was the faintest stiffening of his shoulders, but Mischa's voice was rich and almost empty of emotion as he said, 'She valued my skills as an assassin and spy above petty concerns of flesh and hurt feelings.'

It was another insult, and perhaps even a threat. I wasn't the only one who thought both, because Wicked and Truth moved up on either side of us, a little ahead, not blocking our view of the other men, so not technically between us, but they were in place if needed.

'Do you delude yourselves that you could win in a real fight outside the practice arena?' Mischa asked.

'Yes,' Wicked and Truth said together. Their hands were already near weapons. I stepped away from Jean-Claude's embrace so I could have my hands free for weapons, too. Logically, Mischa was just being shitty, which was very him, but logic is seldom what starts a fight.

'I value your skills, Mischa, Goran' – Jean-Claude nodded at the second man – 'or I would have left you both back in St Louis, but I do not value your skills enough to be insulted, and if I will ask plainly, did you mean to threaten me?'

'No, my lord, I did not,' but his voice was tight when he said it, as if the words and the emotion behind them didn't match.

'Then you are admitting that your language is that imprecise,' Jean-Claude said in a voice that was mild, even pleasant.

'No,' Mischa said, as we'd all known he would.

'Then you did threaten me.'

Mischa looked confused. 'No, my lord, not . . .' He seemed to think about what he'd said and finally added very lamely, 'not on purpose.'

'Goran, is your master this much a disaster as a spy?'

'No, my lord Jean-Claude,' Goran said, but there was the quirk of a smile on his lips as he bowed. He was so much bigger than Mischa that you expected the movement to be less elegant, but it wasn't. The werebear's bow was as graceful as the vampire's had been. I guess he'd had nearly as many centuries to practice.

Mischa's hands were in fists at his side. He was obviously fighting to control his temper, and that was just weird in a vampire this old. They were the ultimate in control. He'd been like that from the moment I met him, whereas most of the other Harlequin were smooth and controlled, even empty, as if they waited for the next emotion to be given to them, rather than already owning it themselves. I found that a little disturbing, but that was just vampire creepy; Mischa had a temper.

'It must gall you and many of the other Harlequin that I am your new lord and master. I know that the Dark Mother sent out her guard to spy on the vampires she felt were powerful enough to be on her council, or powerful enough to be a threat. I am betting I wasn't on the watch list, that I never entered her mind as a threat or rival to anyone, let alone her, am I right?'

'Yes, my lord,' Mischa said.

'It was a game of patience and subterfuge worthy of one of us,' Goran said, and he smiled as he said it.

'A lovely compliment,' Jean-Claude said.

Mischa scowled at them both.

'What bothers you more, Mischa: that Belle Morte's concubine is your ruler, or that none of the all-knowing Harlequin saw me as a power to be reckoned with until it was too late?'

'You make them wonder what else they might have missed,' Goran said. 'It undermines their sense of superiority.' He smiled when he said it.

Mischa whirled in a movement faster than the eye could follow, or faster than mine could. I actually didn't see him hit Goran in the face, just the blur and the big man staggering backward, blood scarlet on his mouth.

Wicked and Truth were just there, one second beside us, the next on either side of Mischa. Truth was there to block Mischa's arm as he tried to strike Goran backhanded as his fist returned its arc from the first blow. Mischa's other hand came at Truth, and he blocked that, too, which led to a knee coming up, and the fight was on.

I had trouble following the moves, but it looked like neither of them was landing a blow on the other, so it was like a full-speed, full-contact practice bout, except they meant to harm each other, if they could get through the other's guard. Then Goran moved at Truth's back, but Wicked was there to back the bigger man up, and suddenly we had two impressive fights in a space barely big enough for one.

Why didn't the guards from the hallway come rushing into the room? Because they were all nearly silent; only the impact of flesh against flesh and sharp exhales of breath, cloth, shoes on the carpet, noises I never heard when I was fighting were suddenly loud in the silence of the room. Jean-Claude watched, and I debated on what to do. They were all four our bodyguards, his bodyguards, and here they were fighting one another. They could end up wounded themselves, until we'd be down some more guards. If it had just been me I might have tried to stop it, but Jean-Claude was right there, and he was the king, the prez, the head of all the vampires. If he didn't stop it, was it my place to step in, or did I wait? Question was, what was I waiting for, and if I did decide to try to stop the fight, how would I do it?

Mischa tried for the beginnings of a roundhouse kick, but there wasn't room, and his leg hit a coffin, which stopped the movement and tumbled the coffin over. It also made him stumble, hesitate, and that was all Truth needed.

He hit Mischa in the solar plexus enough to double him over and followed it with a blow to the face that spun him half around and collapsed him over another coffin.

I heard the outer door open and glanced away from the fight long enough to see Lisandro and Emmanuel spill into the room, guns drawn. I held up my hand, not sure if it was needed; I didn't want anyone to get shot, but the silence was suddenly nothing but the labored breathing of fewer men. I turned back to find Goran collapsed on the ground and Mischa still draped motionless over the coffin.

Wicked and Truth stood, chests rising and falling with their breaths, which you didn't always see in vampires, because they didn't always breathe. It meant they'd worked hard to win the fight, but they had won; more than that, they'd knocked them both cold, which wasn't easy against either a vampire or a wereanimal. The brothers grinned at each other, a fierce baring of happy teeth. Wicked grinned wide enough to flash fang, which I'd never seen him do; I could only see the back of Truth's head, so I missed seeing his fangs do their happy, tired flash. Blood started to trickle down the side of Wicked's face, proving that Goran had landed at least one blow.

'Wow,' said Emmanuel.

'I can smell that Goran's alive, but is Mischa?' Lisandro asked. His gun was pointed at the carpet, but not holstered.

It hadn't even occurred to me that when vampires fight among themselves, they might be able to kill each other by snapping the spine. I said out loud, 'Mischa's too ancient and powerful to die from a snapped spine, isn't he?'

Lisandro shrugged.

I glanced at Jean-Claude.

He sighed and started forward.

Truth started to bend over Mischa, as if to check for a pulse.

'No,' I said, loud and firm.

Truth looked at me but kept back from the fallen vampire. 'What's wrong?'

'Other than the fact that you may have killed one of our bodyguards?' I said.

Truth had the grace to look embarrassed then, but he said, 'Yes, besides that.'

I took out the Browning Hi Power and placed it against Mischa's temple, gun to flesh. 'Now check for signs of life,' I said.

Truth looked a little puzzled, but he bent over the fallen vampire.

I didn't keep looking at where my gun was pointed; I'd feel if his head moved. I looked farther down the body like you do in a fight; you look at the center of the body where the arms and legs attach to see if they move, because if the center does not move, nothing moves. I saw his hand tense not on his holstered gun, but near it.

'Don't move, Mischa, not an inch.' My voice was low, careful, honed down with practice and control, because when you have the barrel of your gun pressed to someone's temple, your finger on the trigger, you have to have control, because without it you might flinch and blow their brains out.

'How did you know he was bluffing?' Truth asked.

'I hunt vampires, remember?'

'Lisandro is going to disarm you, Mischa, just until you cool down.'

'I can disarm him,' Truth said.

'No, you can't,' I said. 'If you touch him he might try to kill you, and then I'd have to shoot him.'

Wicked said, 'Goran is coming around.'

It was Jean-Claude who said, 'Goran, can you hear me?'

The werebear's voice was a little shaky and too deep from the dregs of the extra testosterone from the fight. 'I hear you, my lord.'

'This fight is over, do you understand me?'

'I understand.'

'Lisandro is going to disarm your master so he will not do anything unfortunate.'

Mischa spoke carefully, and I could feel the small movements against my gun as he enunciated his words. 'That won't be necessary. I am quite calm.'

'You were going to shoot Truth as he bent over you,' I said.

'I thought about it,' he said, 'but your gun against my head dissuaded me.'

'And when my gun isn't against your head, what's to dissuade you then?' I asked.

'My temper is hot, but your cold steel has dampened the flame of it.'

'Fancy talk, but how do I know you won't get all hot and bothered later?'

'Mischa,' Jean-Claude said.

'Yes, my lord.'

'Give us your word of honor that you will not in any way, through any means, seek retaliation against Truth, or Wicked, for this incident.'

Mischa went so profoundly still that I could feel the change in his body through the barrel of my gun against his head. I knew that if I'd dared to raise my gaze from his center body mass to his face, it would have that unreadable emptiness to it that the old vampires got when they went very still, as if they were well-crafted statues rather than people.

'Mischa,' Jean-Claude said, 'give your word.'

'And if I do not?'

'Then *ma petite* will finish this argument for you.'

'My death may take Goran's life, as well.'

'It would be a shame to lose him for such an inexplicable reason, but he understood the risks when he joined the battle at your side.'

'Truth stopped Mischa from hitting you a second time,' Wicked said. 'Why did you join the fight on his side?'

'He is my master,' Goran said, as if that explained everything.

'Wives attack the police when they try to take their abusive husbands to jail. It's one of the reasons that police hate to go on domestic disturbance calls,' I said.

'Why would you help your abuser?' Truth asked.

'I don't know, but they do,' I said.

'Better the devil you know than the unknown,' Jean-Claude said.

'What?' I asked.

'Never mind, *ma petite*; Mischa, give us your word and we can all go to bed for the day.'

Now that he'd said it, I could feel the press of dawn above us like the hand of some giant hesitating over a butterfly, except we were the butterflies and knew what was about to happen.

Mischa gave his word.

'You may put up your gun, *ma petite*. Old-school vampires are many things, but we are not oath breakers.'

I hesitated for a fraction of a second, but he was right. It was one of the few things that made dealing with the really old vampires better than dealing with the weaker modern ones. Modern vampires lied just as easily as people did, and their word wasn't worth shit.

I took my finger off the trigger and eased my gun back. The mark of my barrel was imprinted on his skin where I'd pressed it tight. If he'd been human it might even have bruised. I stepped back before I raised my gaze enough to meet his blue eyes. I expected to see anger in his eyes, but instead I saw respect, even admiration. I had not expected that.

'May I get up?' he asked.

Jean-Claude said, 'You may.'

Mischa kept looking at me and didn't move.

'You heard your lord and master,' I said.

'But he will not kill me and you will.'

'He won't shoot you,' I said. 'That's not the same thing as not being willing to kill you.'

'Fair enough, my dark queen, but you have the gun and he does not.'

'Get up, Mischa, but don't do anything stupid.'

He sat up carefully, never taking his gaze from me. 'You would have killed me.'

'It's my job description,' I said.

'Killing someone you have a warrant of execution for, who has already taken human life, is one thing, but you would simply shoot me for thinking about harming Truth. Either you value him as your lover more than we thought, or you would have done it to protect any of your guard.'

'I don't point a gun at someone unless I'm willing to pull the trigger. I don't pull the trigger unless I'm willing to kill. And I never bluff, Mischa; do we understand each other?'

'No, but if you are asking, do I believe that you will kill me, then yes, yes, I do. I'm looking in your eyes and there is no remorse, no relief that you didn't have to shoot me. You simply don't care one way or the other, no real emotion at all about what has just happened. I didn't know that about you.'

'Know what?' I asked.

'That you killed coldly. I thought you would kill in hot blood like you fuck.'

'I don't enjoy killing,' I said. 'I enjoy sex.'

'I enjoy killing,' Mischa said, and smiled just a little bit when he said it, which was disturbing. He watched my face and I knew he'd caught that flicker of distaste from me. 'That bothered you, that I enjoy killing. Why did that bother you? I am no worse than your werelion, Nicky, but he is your lover. If you were squeamish about such things, why would you fuck him?'

'Enough,' Jean-Claude said, and his voice was harsh enough that everyone looked at him.

Mischa and Goran bowed low again. Truth and Wicked did more bows from the neck and put their right fists over their hearts. I couldn't see what Lisandro and Emmanuel did, but I doubted either of the wererats showed that formal a reaction. I just stood there not quite sure why everything had turned so stylized.

'Dawn is almost upon us.' He held his hand out to me and I went to him, holstering my gun as I moved. He took me in his arms and kissed me less thoroughly than he had earlier, but I could feel the sun on that edge of hovering nearness. There had been nights when I fought just to have the sun rise and help save me from the vampires, and now I was in the arms and heart of the biggest vampire in the country. The irony wasn't lost on me, but I'd stopped worrying about it.

Jean-Claude spoke low, but quickly. 'Asher will be here tomorrow night. The territory he is visiting is close enough that he will be driven here and then fly back with us when we leave.'

'And he wanted to see you sooner,' I said.

'He wanted to see all of us,' Jean-Claude said.

I sort of doubted that, but I kept it to myself. I knew who Asher loved best, and it sure as hell wasn't me, or Nathaniel. I was pretty sure it was Jean-Claude but wasn't positive where Dev fell in the list of Asher's affections.

'So the talk went well?' I asked.

'Very well,' Jean-Claude said, and smiled, giving that flash of happiness

I'd noticed when he first walked out of the back room. It made me smile and I went on tiptoe to press my smile against his, because when someone you love is happy, you're happy for them, even if what they're happy about is another love of their life. Or that's how it works for us. The only person in our little group who suffered from jealousy was Asher. Here was hoping that when he came back to us, he left the green-eyed monster behind. I'd have crossed my fingers if they hadn't been too busy touching Jean-Claude.

51

It was an hour past dawn; all the vampires were tucked in their coffins. Lisandro and Emmanuel took Goran with them; I wasn't sure if he was going to be in the duty rotation, or if Claudia was going to give him the third degree, because I'd taken Lisandro to the side and told him about Mischa hitting Goran and about Nilda's anger and panic at the plane in St Louis that had gotten her kicked off the detail. I wanted to know if others of the Harlequin vampires were abusing their animals to call, and how bad the abuse was, because it wasn't okay in my book.

Nicky and Dev were with me, and the three of us were still covered in drying bits of zombie. I'd learned years ago that no matter how tired you are you never go to sleep without showering first, so . . . 'We've all got to shower,' I said.

Dev grinned at me. 'You said you'd help me clean up.'

'I didn't agree to giving up shower sex,' Nicky said.

Dev looked at him. 'Hey, I've been traumatized.'

'Just because you got your combat cherry popped doesn't mean you get to have shower sex with Anita and I don't.'

'You keep this up and I'm showering alone,' I said.

They both looked at me as if I'd spoken in tongues.

'You love shower sex,' Dev said.

'You love sex,' Nicky said.

'I'm tired, I'm cranky, and you're arguing over who gets to have sex with me in the shower without asking me if I have a preference. I'm standing right here, guys.'

They looked at each other, and then Dev looked embarrassed, and Nicky gave me a very direct look, as if he were trying to read more than just my expression. He probably was. 'Who do you want to shower with?' he asked.

'Right now, neither of you,' I said, and it sounded cranky even to me. I wasn't even sure why I was saying it. They were both wonderful lovers. It was easier to get the dried crud off with someone to spot and help.

'So, what, Nicky helps me get the stuff out of my hair?' Dev asked, and the look on his face was almost funny.

'Not my job to be your shower boy,' Nicky said, but he was looking at me.

My phone rang; I would have ignored it, but it was Edward's ring tone. I hit the button and said, 'Yeah, Ed . . . Ted, what's up?'

'Don't fuck this up,' he said.

'What? Fuck what up?'

'Dev and Nicky, to start with,' he said.

'You warned me in the elevator, I remember.'

'You remember, but you still sound pissed. I know that tone. It means you're being hostile and bitchy and are going to say, or do, something that you'll regret.'

'Did you even take time to shower before you called to give me advice on my personal life?' I asked, and I sounded angry. I was angry, but I was also confused. 'Since when did you start giving me advice about men?'

'I just got out of the shower, but I figured if I waited to dress you'd have started a fight with one or both of them. And we've been criticizing or giving each other advice on our personal lives almost from the moment we met, which was sort of weird if you think about it,' he said.

That stopped me, because he was right. 'Your advice used to be that I complicated my life and I should just find someone to fuck.'

'I didn't understand you, or me, back then; now I'm telling you to not take your mood out on Nicky and Dev. Nicky's a good guy, and Dev stayed in the fight and cleanup afterward until it was pretty much over, when he was probably scared shitless and overwhelmed. Don't sell either of them short and don't aim your bad mood at them.'

'Well, aren't you just a wellspring of dating advice?'

'If you think it's bad advice, then don't take it,' he said.

'I didn't say it was bad.'

'Then don't pick a fight with them. Remember, you love one of them and like the other one a hell of a lot.'

'Yes, sir,' I said, but it sounded petulant, even pouty.

'You can do what you want to do, Anita, but in the mood you're in, sleeping alone may not be the best idea.'

'I used to sleep alone all the time.'

'Yeah, and you were miserable. I may not understand how your life works with everyone in it, but this is the happiest I've ever seen you. I'm not sure how much of that happiness is due to Nicky, or Dev, but some of it is, so keep that in mind in the next few minutes. I'm getting sleep before someone with a badge calls with another emergency.' He hung up.

I was left standing there with the silent phone and the two men. Dev was looking a question at me. Nicky was trying to be all neutral, and he was, except the very emptiness of his face and body screamed just how not neutral he was feeling.

I sighed and looked at them. Finally I said, 'I'm sorry.'

They looked at each other, then back to me. Nicky said, 'For what?'

'For being pissy and taking my bad mood out on both of you.'

'It's okay; I'm your Bride, you can treat me the way you want.'

'Do you know how much I hate that you mean that?'

'Yeah, but it's still true, and, Anita, if you hadn't made me into your Bride I would have killed you and helped my pride kill Jason, Micah, and Nathaniel. I was, and am, a very bad person. I am a bad guy, or would be if your sense of moral outrage didn't control me.'

'I know, I know, I'm your Jiminy Cricket.'

'No, you're more than that,' he said, and took a step closer to me. 'You said you loved me tonight. I felt that you meant it.'

'I did mean it,' I said.

He held out his hand, and I took his hand in mine.

'That's okay,' Dev said. 'You guys have fun. I'll find another room.'

Nicky and I looked at each other. I raised my eyebrows at him.

'He doesn't have to go on my account,' Nicky said.

'Stay,' I said.

Dev looked at us both. 'You just said you loved each other for the first time. You should have a night to yourselves.'

'Why?' Nicky asked.

'Because you love each other,' Dev said, as if that made perfect sense.

'Anita saying she loves me doesn't change everything,' Nicky said.

'But shouldn't it?' Dev asked.

'Why should it?'

Dev looked to me then. 'You explain it to him.'

'Explain what? I agree with Nicky.'

'Shouldn't you want a night alone to sort of celebrate the love thing?'

I squeezed Nicky's hand and smiled at him. 'One of the reasons I love Nicky is that he's okay with sharing me with Nathaniel and Micah, and Cynric, and Jean-Claude, and Asher, and' – I shrugged – 'all the people in my life.'

'It doesn't bother you to share her?' Dev asked, and I knew he was asking Nicky.

'Nathaniel says you share better than I do, so why are we having this discussion again?'

Dev smiled, shook his head, and said, 'Because I keep getting hung up on the clan tiger idea that eventually you fall in love and become monogamous, and when Asher comes back I'm going to try to be monogamous, so . . . I guess it's how I'm thinking. Honestly, I don't know, but somehow love should change everything, shouldn't it?'

'If you're doing it right, love makes you more of who you are, not less,' I said.

'What does that mean?' Dev asked.

'It means if we were a happy little polyamorous group before I said I loved Nicky, why should saying it and meaning it change that?'

Dev seemed to think about it, nodded, rolled his lower lip under, and then nodded again. 'Okay, your logic beats out my sentimental whatever. Now what?'

'Shower isn't going to be big enough for all three of us,' Nicky said.

'Regular hotel shower would fit me, Nathaniel, and Micah, but not the two of you. Your shoulders alone won't fit.'

Dev grinned suddenly, the serious mood gone so that his blue tiger eyes sparkled with it. 'The shower is one of the biggest I've ever seen in a hotel, almost as big as the one that Jean-Claude had put in at the Circus.'

'Cool,' I said.

'So we clean up and then we see about shower sex for all of us,' Nicky said.

'Sounds good,' I said.

Dev laughed. 'Sounds better than good, sounds amazing. I never thought I'd get you out of your clothes.'

'I don't think he's referring to me,' I said.

Nicky sort of hung his head and sighed, and then he laughed. 'If you hadn't said anything, you could have groped me and said you misunderstood.'

'I've seen you hit a heavy bag; I don't want any misunderstandings between us,' Dev said, smiling.

Nicky laughed again. 'Fair enough; we're sharing Anita, not each other.'

'You okay with accidental touching?'

'Sure,' Nicky said.

Dev's smile blossomed back into that grin of his, the one that was part mischief, part sex, and all charm. 'Cool.'

And it was.

52

There are moments when undressing isn't sexy; being covered in dried blood, guts, and brains is one of those moments. Weapons first and there were a few bits of dried zombie on them, too. We'd clean them later. Our body armor had left a clean spot on our shirts underneath. The vests were all going to need cleaning, and since mine was a custom-fit job I didn't have a backup vest. Men's vests didn't fit right on women, though I could borrow a man's vest and because it was really too big for me it didn't crush my breasts the way it did on women who were bigger through the shoulders and rib cage. But holding up the vest and looking at some of the stains on it, I thought a second vest might not be a bad idea.

The three of us paid attention to our weapons and body armor, and it was sexless. Shirts first, and Nicky looked at my bra, all right, he looked at my breasts, they just happened to be in a black satin bra.

'I like that about you,' Nicky said.

'What, my breasts?'

He grinned. 'Those, too, but you don't bitch if I stare at your breasts.'

'I'm wearing a push-up bra; if I didn't want people to look at my breasts I should probably wear something else.'

'Yeah, but I know that Nathaniel packed for you, which means it's all going to be push-up, satin, or lace.'

I smiled and shook my head. 'I'm not sure I own anything else.'

'I like that about you, too,' he said. He took off his shirt in one movement. I heard the cloth stick on one shoulder as it came off, but at least the vest meant the whole shirt hadn't been covered in gunk; bad for the vests, but good for our peace of mind and a lower ick factor. I concentrated on the muscled expanse of his chest and shoulders; they almost distracted me from the flat plains of his stomach.

'Hmm . . . an eight-pack.'

He grinned. 'Some of the other guards are pissed, because they can only do a six-pack, if they work their asses off.'

'Eight is genetic; not everyone can do more than a six-pack no matter how hard they work out,' I said.

'Yeah,' he said, and he looked pleased with himself.

There was a small sound in the room, the kind that makes you look up and try to locate the source, and depending on who was making the sound, you'd either pretend you hadn't heard or comfort the person making the noise. Dev had his belt unbuckled, but his shirt was only partially untucked. He held his hands sort of awkwardly away from his body, as if he didn't want to touch something or already had touched something and didn't want to transfer it from his hands to his clothes.

Nicky and I looked at each other and, without a word, went to Dev. 'Let me help you out of those clothes,' I said, trying to put teasing and sexiness in the words.

Dev looked at me, eyes too big, face sort of slack with the edge of panic he was fighting. He held his hands out to me like he was five and had hurt himself. There was no mark on his hands; they looked clean to me, but sometimes you have a sort of Lady Macbeth moment, and even after washing away the blood, it's like you can still see it, feel it, ingrained on your skin.

I reached out to touch his hands, but he jerked back. 'I've got . . . stuff on me.'

'Me, too,' I said, my voice soft.

His eyes fluttered and flashed white like a horse about to bolt.

'It's okay, Dev, it's okay.'

He shook his head.

'You said you thought you'd never get me out of my clothes, and you haven't even said how cute I look,' Nicky said.

That got a smile from Dev; it was weak, and a little uncertain, but it was better than I'd gotten out of him. He looked at Nicky then, really looked at the other man. He looked at his bare, muscled chest, the way Nicky had looked at my breasts. There were some men in my life who, even as comfortable as they were sharing a bed with me and other men all at the same time, they wouldn't have taken that look from Dev without it being a fight, or at least severely uncomfortable, but Nicky took it in stride.

'That's better,' Nicky said.

Dev put his head to one side and said, 'You don't like men, so why do you care if I admire the view?'

Nicky shrugged as much as his shoulder muscles would let him. 'I like knowing that you're not just kidding about it.'

'You like knowing that I'd do you if you'd let me, and you're still going to get in the shower with me. Most straight men would be totally creeped by it.'

'I'm secure in my masculinity.'

'Well, that's the truth,' I said.

Nicky smiled at me, and I smiled back.

'But you wouldn't be doing me; I don't bottom to anyone,' Nicky said.

'That works for me,' Dev said.

I was no longer certain we were joking.

Nicky grinned. 'If I come across for you then I'll have to fight off Jean-Claude and Asher. I think I'll stay on this side of the heteroflexible divide; it'll make things less complicated.'

Dev pouted at him, and if you've never seen a handsome, athletic, six-foot-three man pout and be able to make it totally work for him, then I'm sorry, because it was way fun to watch.

Nicky laughed. 'Let's get naked and wet.'

The look on Dev's face at such a bold comment from the other man ruined the pout and stripped his face to something uncertain and hopeful. I hadn't known that Dev thought Nicky was cute, but Nicky's maneuvering of the other man let me know that my werelion had known. Was I that blind, or was Nicky just that observant?

Dev stripped off his shirt in one fast motion and threw it on the floor as if he didn't want to touch it any longer than he had to, but he unzipped his pants and stripped them off to join his socks and boots, which were already on the floor beside him. He was suddenly totally nude and beautiful, but he wasn't looking defiantly at me, he was looking at the other man. It was almost as if he thought Nicky would chicken out and have a moment of heterosexual panic, but I knew better. If it was a test of nerves, my money was on Nicky.

He didn't disappoint me. He just unfastened his pants and stripped them off – okay, he had to peel them off due to some fluid that had dried on one leg, but he got them off and let them fall on top of his own boots and socks. He stood there naked and yummy and stared at Dev like he was daring him to say something.

Dev opened his mouth, closed it, and then laughed, head back, eyes closed, totally delighted. Nicky looked at me and smiled. I decided then and there that I would never try to bluff Nicky, because he was out of my league. I could lie, but I couldn't manipulate like that, not even for a good cause.

Nicky held his hand out to me, and I went to him. 'You have too many clothes on,' he said.

'We can fix that,' I said.

'Yes,' Dev said, his voice still holding an edge of laughter, 'we can.'

We did.

53

We helped one another get clean. It took three times through the shampoo for Dev's hair to get clean. He'd gotten hit the worst from something, or maybe it was the baby-fine texture of his hair; whatever. Nicky helped me pick bits out of the back of Dev's hair. He started shivering even though the water was steaming hot, but there is cold that no amount of hot water will warm. I think we could have turned his skin pink with heat and he would still have shivered.

He put his hands on the tile of the wall and leaned, as if he were trying to take strength from the wall to keep standing. Nicky and I exchanged a look; he motioned with his head for me to get closer to Dev while he kept picking bits of zombie out of the other man's hair. I touched his arm, and he jumped.

'It's me, Dev, it's just me,' I said.

'I'm sorry,' he said. 'I don't know what's wrong with me.'

I let that go; we both knew what was wrong, but knowing doesn't always fix it. I touched his arm again, and this time he stood still for it. I slid in under his arm, and even with him leaning against the wall he was tall enough for me to look up at him and not have to bend over at all. He was a foot taller than I was, and standing there with his arms on either side and above my shoulders, his face above mine, I was suddenly aware that he was really big, not just tall, but wide through the shoulders, broad through the chest. If he had spent half the time that Nicky did in the weight room, Dev would have been massive. I wasn't sad that he didn't; I might have felt physically overwhelmed, but then again, maybe I wouldn't. I could see Nicky's shoulder on one side of Dev's, and I didn't have a problem with Nicky. I didn't think a few inches of extra height would have tipped the difference for me.

Wet, Dev's hair fell a little below his shoulders, framing that square and very masculine jaw. His blue-on-blue eyes blinked a little too quickly as he stared down at me. I slid my hands over the slick wetness of his chest as Nicky kept working on his hair.

'I don't think I'm in the mood, Anita. I never thought I'd say that, but I can't stop thinking about what Nicky is cleaning out of my hair. Now I know why you insist on a shower before you greet everybody some nights.'

I touched his face, made sure I had serious eye contact. 'The thing in the basement tonight was bad, Dev; even by my standards it was a slaughter. I don't do that every night. Hell, I don't do it most of the time.'

'You mean I'm not being a serious pussy?'

I smiled at him. 'Well, you are a pussycat, but no, it was bad, worse than normal even by my standards for mess and brutal fighting. Flesh-eating zombies just don't stop coming. I've never, ever seen that many of them.'

'Really?' he asked, and his voice was fragile, like the look in his eyes.

'Really,' I said, my hand on the side of his face.

His head pulled back as if Nicky were moving his hair too much. Then I saw Nicky's hands come up and he ran his fingers through Dev's hair. 'There, all clean.'

Dev let out a shaking breath, but he straightened, pushed away from the wall, and ran his own hands through his hair. He did it a second time, a look of relief on his face as he smoothed his hair back from his face.

'Thanks, Nicky,' he said.

'You can return the favor sometime,' Nicky said.

Dev looked over his shoulder at the other man. 'Are you inviting me to shower with you again?'

Nicky smiled. 'So far you've been a perfect gentleman; I think my virtue is safe.'

'You have virtue to keep safe?' I asked, peering around Dev's body.

Nicky raised an eyebrow at me. I realized he'd swept his wet hair back from his face, completely exposing the scars that covered the socket of his right eye. He usually hid the scars with that triangle of bangs, so I valued when he didn't. It meant he was comfortable. I liked that.

'No, no, I don't,' he said, and there was something about the way he said it, more sad than teasing back, that made me remember that he'd been abused as a child both sexually and physically by his mother. She'd been the one who took his eye. I suddenly felt stupid and slow and . . .

I went to Nicky, stroking my hands down his bare, wet arms. 'I wasn't thinking. I'm sorry.'

'It's okay,' he said.

I wrapped myself around him, nakedness to nakedness, and it wasn't erotic, because he didn't hold me back, he stayed upright and didn't meld into the hug.

'I missed something,' Dev said behind us.

Nicky said, 'Yeah, you did.'

I looked up at the man in my arms, searched that closed-down face. He'd turned away from me just enough to hide the scars, not to be pretty the way Asher would do to hide his, but it was either that or reach back up and smooth his wet hair down over them, and that would have been admitting it mattered to him and Nicky wouldn't do that.

'Look at me, please,' I said.

He did, but the look on his face was arrogant, distant as his body still felt because he wouldn't hug me back.

'I'm sorry, I forgot.'

He glared at me, and I felt the first rush of heat as his anger hit his lion and it stirred. 'How can you forget when you have to look at this every time you see me?' He touched his finger to the edge of the scars.

It was the first time he'd said out loud that the scars bothered him, reminded him every time he looked in the mirror. The way he wore his hair let me know that it bothered him, but he'd never actually said so before.

'It's just a part of you,' I said. 'That's what I think when I look at you; that's all I think.'

He stared down at my face, studying it. 'I can feel that you mean that.'

'I like the scar,' Dev said, 'and the fact that you are as good as you are with weapons and hand-to-hand having to compensate for the lack of depth perception is impressive.'

Nicky shifted in my arms, and that flare of anger was like heat marching down my body, as if the heat of the shower were starting to emanate from his body and not the taps behind us. 'He really does like scars,' I said. 'Dev's a texture junkie.'

He relaxed a little in my arms and finally put his arms around me. He wasn't holding me tight, but it was progress.

'I'll prove it to you, if it won't freak you out,' Dev said.

Nicky gave him a look, as if nothing he could do would be that freaky, but I knew Dev better than Nicky did. I was betting there was plenty that the weretiger could do to freak out the werelion. The reverse was also true, but Dev's would be sensual and Nicky's would be more violence. I didn't really want them to try to freak each other out, though; I feared it would go badly.

Dev moved in behind me until his body was pressed up against mine, which pinned Nicky's hands between my body and the other man's. Nicky was only touching against Dev's stomach; he didn't complain or move his hands. Neither man's body was excited to be there yet, so though it was nice, it wasn't as erotic as it might have been. He reached out to touch Nicky's cheek.

Nicky jerked back.

Dev let his hand fall and smoothed his hands down my arms. 'See, it freaks you out.' He leaned down to lay a kiss on the top of my head, nuzzling against my wet hair.

I wriggled into Dev's touch, raising my face so he could kiss my lips. We kissed, and the kiss grew until it tightened my hands around Nicky and made me grind myself against Dev. His body was already beginning to react, which encouraged me to grind harder against him. Nicky's arms around my back kept me from grinding as much as I could have, which forced me away from Nicky's body in an effort to touch more of Dev's.

Nicky's body pressed in tighter from in front. It brought me back from kissing Dev and to move my face toward Nicky. This time he leaned over so I could reach his lips. We kissed and it was a soft brush of lips, then a more urgent press of his mouth on mine. He moved his arms from between Dev and me, and at the same time I was suddenly pressed tight between both of them. With one of them thick and growing thicker against the front and the other against the back of me, the sensation of being pinned between their bodies tore my mouth from Nicky's and made me cry out.

It was only when Dev leaned over me for another kiss that I realized why they were both pressed so close. Nicky had moved his arms so he was holding on to the other man's waist and Dev had done the same, so that they were using their strength to press themselves in tighter against my body. Nathaniel and Micah called it making a sandwich, and I loved being the middle of it.

They took turns kissing me, until I writhed and ground against both their bodies and they were both hard, and thick, and achingly ready. With their skills at foreplay it seemed a shame to skip most of it, but sometimes the urgency of the need is its own foreplay.

Dev rose up from kissing me and touched Nicky's scar. When he didn't protest Dev leaned over me, which pressed him even tighter against my ass, and he laid a soft kiss on the scar. Nicky didn't really react to it, so it encouraged Dev to move one hand up to the side of Nicky's face. He leaned in and kissed the scars where Nicky's eye should have been more thoroughly. I looked up to watch the kissing, my body still pinned between theirs. Nicky had gone still, and his body wasn't quite as happy to be pressed against me, though Dev had no way of knowing that.

He kissed down Nicky's face, one soft kiss at a time, and I got to watch each kiss get closer and closer to Nicky's mouth, until finally Dev kissed him.

Nicky drew back from it, shaking his head. 'No,' he said, not angry, but firm.

Dev dropped his hand from the side of the other man's face and kissed me as if he were trying to kiss me as deeply and completely as he could. He drew back from the kiss, lips half parted, his face so eager, so excited, that it made me laugh, a little breathless and shaky.

Nicky kissed me then, and it was gentle, tender, as if he were making love to my mouth. He drew back and left me with my eyes still closed, lips half parted. I was even a little weak in the knees, just from the kiss.

'Wow,' Dev said, 'I feel like I need to try again.'

I opened my eyes enough to see Nicky smiling down at me. He looked utterly pleased with himself. It made me smile up at him, but the smile spread until it was more an evil, happy grin.

'Now I know I need to try another kiss,' Dev said, 'because that is a really good smile.'

'Yes,' Nicky said. 'Yes, it is,' and his voice was already deeper with the first rush of testosterone, and a smile that held all the heat you wanted to see in a man's face. It was full of love, yes, but it was also full of lust, and the thought of everything he was going to do to you and with you.

'Why do I feel like I need to catch up when I've been standing here the whole time?' Dev asked.

'She loves me,' Nicky said, as if that explained everything, and apparently it did, because Dev said, 'You are a lucky man.' That's usually something a man says when what he means is, *Your woman is hot and I would totally fuck her, but either it's morally wrong or you would kill me for it.* It seemed weird that Dev felt the need to be so polite with his nakedness pressed against my ass and knowing that he was getting sex, too, but sex isn't everything. It's nice, it's great even, if you're lucky, but everyone, eventually, wants love.

I went up on tiptoe to kiss Nicky again, and Dev moved back a little so that we could use hands and arms on just each other, while the kiss grew from tender to urgent. When we drew back just to look at each other, Dev said, 'I'll offer just once more to give you guys privacy, and I should get major brownie points for offering, at this point.'

I looked over my shoulder at him, with Nicky and me still holding each other. I wasn't sure what I would have said, because Nicky said, 'Breast, or ass?'

'What?' Dev said, frowning, obviously puzzled.

'Do you want to fuck her first, or have her suck your dick first?'

I turned back to look at Nicky; the look was enough, because he said, 'You love me and I love you and it's amazing, but at heart I'm a thug, Anita. I'm crude and rude and violent, and you've taught me the only gentleness I've ever known, but I'm still me.'

I nodded. 'Okay, it's not that I don't agree with the division of labor; it was just a little crudely put, that's all. You surprised me.'

He smiled. 'Okay, Mephistopheles, are you a breast or a thigh man?' Nicky looked at me, head cocked to one side. 'Better?'

I grinned. 'Yes, thank you.'

Dev watched us like he'd never seen us.

'What's wrong?' I asked.

'I'm just wondering when you guys became a couple and why didn't I notice?'

I looked back at Nicky and he slid his arms more securely around, bringing me in against his body in a way that was less sexual and more romantic. It seemed weird in the shower all naked with another man, but there you are; if it works, don't poke at it. I was trying to be smarter.

'You were busy worrying about Asher,' Nicky said.

Dev nodded. 'True, and I'll take thighs.'

Nicky grinned quick and fierce, more a baring of teeth, like a happy snarl. 'We fuck both ends.'

'I'd like to go down on her, while she goes down on you.'

'That's hard in the shower,' I said.

'Bed?' Dev asked.

'Normally, I'd say not only yes, but hell yes! But if the police call before I get some sleep I'm going to cry, so just this once let's just have intercourse,' I said.

Dev's face showed a conflict of emotions, but finally he smiled and said, 'Who am I to argue with the Queen of Tigers?'

'Still not sure I like that title,' I said.

'You hated Mother of Tigers more,' Nicky reminded me.

'True.'

'But I don't think we'll be fucking right away,' he said.

'Why not?'

'Too much talking, not enough sex,' he said, and motioned that he wasn't hard anymore.

I glanced at Dev and found similar deflation. 'I can fix that,' I said, and knelt between them on the shower tiles, the water rushing around my knees.

'So we get oral and intercourse; seems unfair,' Dev said.

'I like and can orgasm from both,' I said, looking up at him from my knees.

'I've had women orgasm from intercourse, but you're a first for oral,' he said.

'Anita, will you please shut him up?' Nicky asked.

I went down on Dev while he was still talking, stopping him in midsyllable. The feel of him in my mouth was, as always, amazing. I liked the sensation of men when they were small and soft and it was easy to take them all in my mouth, roll them around with my tongue, and bury my mouth against their bodies as close and tight as I wanted without choking or fighting my gag reflex, and as long as I kept him deep in my mouth he'd stay smaller. It was only as I began to draw back off him and suck him back into my mouth that he began to grow longer and thicker.

Nicky ran his hand through my wet hair and turned me to him. He wasn't as small as he had been; just watching me go down on Dev and anticipating his turn had made him grow bigger, so that he filled my mouth more, and I had to fight a little around the beginnings of my gag reflex to bury my mouth against his body as far and tight as I could.

Nicky put his hand on the back of my head, holding me on him, but moved my hand from his thigh to wrap it around Dev so I could feel that the other man was thick and hard in my hand. The double sensation of my hand and mouth filled up with that eager hardness . . . They were both so warm, skin soft like muscled velvet to suck and stroke, so that it made me suck harder and faster on Nicky and stroke my hand up and down Dev's shaft to curve over the round, thick silk of him.

Nicky wrapped his hand in my hair and pulled me away from his body. 'I want inside you first,' he said, his voice breathless. He used his handhold on my hair to push me toward Dev. I slid my mouth onto Dev but kept my hand on him, too, so that I was stroking the shaft and sucking and licking the head and first few inches.

He whispered, 'Oh, my God.'

I felt Nicky's hands on my waist and hips as he pulled me into place. I started to turn and say something, or look, but he pushed his hand into the back of my head, holding me down on Dev for a second. Without words he was clear what he wanted, me to go on Dev while he . . . I felt the head of him brush against my opening, but being in the water, even just a shower, had made me tighter even than normal, so that I felt the brush of his hand as he guided himself in place and then began to push the head of him against the tightness of my opening. Just feeling him do that made me begin to suck faster and deeper on Dev, my hand wrapped around the base of him against his body.

'I won't last long,' Dev said.

Nicky pushed his way inside me, fighting for every inch against the tightness from the water. It made him feel even bigger, thicker than I knew he was, and the sensation of him pushing his way inside made me cry out around Dev.

He made an inarticulate sound. I could taste salt from the precome now; he was close, but I didn't care as Nicky finally found enough room to shove himself into me, and my body finally opened for him so that he pulled himself almost out, put his hands on my hips to hold me in place or move me with him, like leading on a dance floor, except this was the water-slick tiles of a shower. Then Nicky pushed his way in again and found a fast, deep rhythm that made me scream as I buried my mouth down the length of Dev's body.

'Close,' Dev said, his voice strained as he fought to last.

Nicky picked up his rhythm, fast and deep so that his body smacked against mine in a sharp, repetitive sound of flesh on flesh, and between one quick deep thrust and the next he spilled me over and I screamed my orgasm around Dev's body. It was too much for Dev, and he thrust into my mouth rather than waiting for me to suck, but with Nicky's orgasm riding my body I wanted as much of both inside me in that moment. Dev responded to my eagerness by grabbing the back of my head and forcing me down as he thrust up, and it was almost too much down my throat even with orgasm. I had to fight not to try to breathe, because I couldn't have. It isn't always a gag reflex; sometimes it's a suffocation reflex. I relaxed my throat as much as I could while I was still trying to scream my own orgasm, but Dev had shoved himself so far down my throat that there was no sound possible. I felt him pulse inside my throat all the way along his shaft where it lay in my mouth and knew that he was going, before I felt that moment of hot as he spilled himself inside me and I fought to swallow. If I'd let the *ardeur* loose there would have been no problem, because when that rode me I had no gag reflex, it was like magic and took away all the issues; but I'd fed already and I was trying to do certain things without the *ardeur*'s help, because if I could do it just as me, then I could do things more frequently without risking draining my lovers to death. Such a mood killer.

It was while I was struggling to take all of Dev in that Nicky intensified his rhythm and let me know he'd been aiming for that sweet spot nearer the opening, because now he searched for the deeper spot that he could hit from behind. Most women will go from the G-spot being caressed long enough, but not all women go from the two deeper spots; for the longest time I thought I enjoyed having my cervix bumped until I learned that wasn't what the men were hitting, not at all. From behind, Nicky slid the head of himself into the spot deep and high within me, and the orgasm that had been fading spilled into a second one from deeper within me, so that when Dev drew himself out of my mouth I screamed loud and deep-throated. Nicky drove himself one last time deep inside me, his hands pulling me backward against his body at the same time, so that he thrust as deep into me as he could in that last moment as his body convulsed inside mine. That last thrust was almost too deep, almost hurt, but in the middle of the orgasm, topped by the sensation of him going inside me, the almost-pain translated into a bigger pleasure.

'I'll go,' Dev said, and stepped out of the shower on slightly unsteady legs. The water that he'd been blocking suddenly cascaded down on me. I hung my head down so it wouldn't get in my eyes and mouth. I wanted to ask where Dev was going, but I couldn't figure out how to say words yet. I was still quivering happily from the orgasm; coherent speech was a few minutes away.

Nicky was still buried as deep as he could be, hands still holding my hips in place, so that even if I'd wanted to, I couldn't have moved. He leaned over me and laid a kiss on my back and said in a voice growling deep, 'You'd think they'd get used to the fact that you're a screamer.'

Apparently, Nicky and Dev had heard the other guards pounding on the door. I tried to be embarrassed that they'd all heard me screaming, but Nicky chose that moment to lean over me and growl. The sound of it seemed to vibrate through my body as if as long as he was buried inside me I would resonate with the growling depth of him.

I shivered for him.

He leaned his face close to mine, so that the water splashed over us both. 'If Dev hadn't been here I would have set my teeth into your shoulders and marked you as mine, but mustn't scare the tigers.' And he growled again with his chest curved over me, his face touching mine. I made a small, helpless noise of happiness, and he laughed so deep a sound that it should have had teeth and claws around it.

54

I woke blinking into a bar of golden sunlight, made more gold by the blond hair that was spilling across my face. The sunlight was a slit in the curtains. The bed was moving, and I blinked through the hair and sunlight to see Nicky sliding out of the bed. That meant the very warm and softly muscled someone wrapped around the back of me was Dev. I tried to sweep the hair out of my face and realized my arms were pinned by his arm. He snuggled closer, arm flexing as I tried to move. Apparently Dev was a serious snuggler.

I heard deep voices soft and low at the door. I was able to turn my head and see around Dev's head enough to see Nicky naked at the partially open door, but couldn't see who he was talking to. Then he opened the door, and Edward walked in, which made me suddenly look down to see how much of me was covered with sheet. It hadn't seemed that important a minute ago.

Dev had not only my arms pinned, but the sheet trapped at about my waist level between us. At the moment his arm covered some of my breasts, but some is not enough when the person who just walked into the room isn't a lover. Yes, Edward was one of my best friends, but it wasn't the same as having a best girlfriend.

I could reach my sheets with my hands pinned, but I couldn't actually get any more sheet to cover me because it was caught between Dev's body and mine. Crap! I did the only thing I could: I hid behind Dev and said, 'Just a minute, Edward.' I planned on my voice being calm and matter of fact. I failed.

Edward laughed, that rare real laughter for him, and the fact that he did it in front of Nicky meant he approved of him in some way. 'I'll turn my back until you cover up.' His voice was made up mostly of laughter. I wasn't sure I'd ever heard him sound quite that pleased. It wasn't just this moment of embarrassment for me, as I poked Dev and made him blink awake so I could grab covers; I thought it was Donna and her working her issues, so that there would be a wedding. Maybe I was being all girly and projecting, but Edward was happy. When we met years ago we were both pretty miserable; I just didn't know it.

'I'm moving, I'm moving,' Dev said, as I pushed at him a little furiously.

Edward was standing with his back to the bed like he'd said, but his shoulders were shaking with laughter. Nicky stood beside him totally nude and totally comfortable, as he watched me struggle to hide my nakedness and drag all the covers off Dev. He didn't care any more than Nicky did – stupid wereanimals and their lack of modesty, and stupid me still caring this much.

Edward was bent almost double, laughing so hard it sounded like he was having trouble breathing. 'Glad I could lighten your morning,' I said, grumpily.

It made Dev grin, and then Nicky chuckled.

I pointed a finger at Dev. 'Don't you dare.'

Dev's mouth quirked as he fought not to laugh. Nicky's face was alight with suppressed laughter. I fled to the bathroom with the king-size sheet wrapped around me like the most oversized robe in the world, grabbing my overnight bag as I moved, so that I actually tripped over the sheet and fell in the doorway to the bathroom.

'Motherfucking son of a bitch!'

That was it; both of them laughed out loud. I gathered my sheet and what was left of my dignity and closed the door to the bathroom to the sounds of masculine laughter. I rolled my eyes at myself in the mirror and realized that I had no idea why Edward was in our room. I was betting it was business, which meant crime to solve, bad guys to catch, and a mysterious master vampire to find. That took the smile off my face, but I realized not entirely. Yeah, things were bad, and last night had been brutal, but I could still hear the men laughing to themselves. It was a good sound, and not a bad way to start the day.

55

Marshal Hatfield sat in Deputy Marshal Chapman's office on the edge of her chair with the warrant of execution spread on the edge of his desk. She wanted to sign it over to me. There was precedent for it, but for some reason Chapman didn't want her to do it.

Hatfield gazed up at him with hollow eyes. I wondered if she'd slept at all. Her hair was coming loose in strands as her ponytail sagged at the nape of her neck. She'd looked so crisp and together yesterday; now she looked like she needed a hug. I wondered if she had anyone in her life who could give her one.

'I don't understand, sir. It would have been Marshal Blake's warrant in the first place, if she hadn't been shot.'

'The warrant was assigned to you, Hatfield, and we expect you to fulfill it.'

A look of near pain came over her face; lines that hadn't been there before showed sharp and harsh. I'd have put her under thirty, but in that moment I put her over, but it wasn't age it was just stress. It'll mark you up. Sometimes the marks fade and sometimes they don't. Just as smile lines are the mark of every happiness you've ever had, so some lines are the mark of every disappointment carved into your flesh as surely as any scar.

'Technically, sir, Hatfield is a part of the Preternatural Branch of the service just like we are,' Edward said.

'I'm aware of that, Marshal Forrester.'

'Well then, sir, you are aware that we are not in your direct line of command because you're regular service and we're preternatural service.'

Hatfield blinked at Edward, as if she weren't tracking everything, but she'd heard something that seemed important.

'Hatfield was in my direct command for several years, Forrester; she knows her duty.'

'I thought our duty was to execute each warrant in the most efficient way with the least loss of life,' I said.

Chapman frowned at me. 'Of course,' he said.

'Then Blake should take this warrant,' Hatfield said. 'I'll still work with her and Forrester to complete it, but I'd feel more comfortable with her in charge of the overall investigation.'

'You have been a law enforcement officer longer than Blake. You have five years more experience than she does,' Chapman said.

'I do, and there are men on the force who are ex-military and she's never been that either, but none of us have her background in dealing with the undead, sir. I believe that my lack of experience in that area led directly to the five deaths yesterday.'

'You can't blame yourself because Blake and Forrester here didn't share information.'

I pushed away from the wall. 'I was unconscious in the hospital, Chapman. How was I supposed to share information?'

He looked at me, then gave a little nod. 'Perhaps that was unfair; if so, my apologies.'

'I didn't arrive in the state until after Marshal Blake was shot,' said Edward. 'I didn't know the facts of the case until dark the next night; in what way did I conceal information that would have prevented the deaths yesterday?' His voice was quiet, calm, but held enough suppressed anger to set fire to something. I'd never heard Edward sound this angry as Ted.

Chapman shifted on the balls of his feet, hands clasped behind his back like an echo of being at ease in the military. His gray hair was cut high and tight. I'd have said Marines, but it felt more like Army. Marines fucked about a little less and were less likely to rise as high in rank as Army, due to a certain cussedness that seemed to go with being a nonpracticing Marine. You had Marines who rose to high rank, and you had ex-Army who were as stubborn as a Marine, but it was usually the other way around.

'Sir,' Hatfield said, 'I knew about the rotting vampires in Atlanta. I read the same information that Blake and Forrester did, but I failed to make the logic leap that these vampires might need fire just like the ones in Atlanta did. I'd never seen anything like them, and I thought . . . heads blown up, spines damaged, hearts . . . I could see through their chests, sir. I thought that was dead enough; I was wrong.'

Hatfield's willingness to fall on the grenade for what had happened made me like her better, and it was even true. She should have erred on the side of caution, and she hadn't, and people were dead because of it, but . . . she was letting the guilt tear her up.

'They were missing civilians, Marshal Hatfield. We owed it to their families to identify them before the bodies were burned,' Chapman said.

'Are you saying it's become acceptable practice to not burn vampires once we've taken their heads and hearts?' I asked.

'Outside of special circumstances, it has worked very well. We've closed missing-person cases that were decades old.'

Huh. 'I honestly hadn't thought about that, sir, that some of the vampires that go bad would be filed missing persons from decades and probably cities away.'

'It's given closure to families who had given up on ever hearing news.'

'But you need an intact head for dental records, so only decapitations, not blowing the face away with an AR or shotgun, right?' Edward asked. His voice was a little less hostile, but not much.

Chapman nodded. 'Exactly; many people don't have their fingerprints on file.'

'If you're looking at people missing for decades, then dental records don't always help either,' Edward said. 'It's routine that when a dentist retires, old patient records aren't kept track of if the patient isn't being referred to another dentist.'

'That is true.'

'How are you identifying the dead vampires then?' I asked.

'DNA of surviving family members, female in particular.'

'Because the maternal line carries the most direct DNA,' I said.

He nodded. 'Yes, most people don't know that.'

'In my misspent youth I got a BS in biology,' I said.

'I read that in your file. There's been some discussion that your science background is part of what makes you so effective at this job; do you believe that's true?'

I thought about it, then nodded. 'I actually took preternatural biology classes and classes on myth and folklore beasts and beings that exist in the real world, so yeah, it gave me a jump on knowing what I was supposed to be up against.'

'You had no police background, no military, nothing but the biology, and yet new marshals who have come straight from the classroom to the Preternatural Branch aren't doing as well as you did at the beginning of your career.'

'I was trained in raising the dead and hunting vampires by a fellow animator, and by Marshal Forrester here when he was a bounty hunter specializing in monsters.'

'The animator you're referring to is Manuel Rodriguez.'

I nodded.

'He has no background in police or military either.'

'No, sir, he was an old-fashioned vampire hunter. What we call a stake-and-hammer man.'

'That's still standard for morgue executions,' Chapman said.

'Yeah,' I said, and couldn't quite keep my disdain for it out of that one word.

'You disapprove, Marshal?'

'You try putting a stake in someone's heart while they're chained to a gurney and begging you not to kill them, then come tell me how much you liked it.'

'It's supposed to be done during daylight when the vampires are comatose.'

'Yeah, it is, but when I was new to this business I let people bully me into executing as soon as possible; sometimes that meant the vampire was awake. A few executions like that, sir, and I lost my taste for it.'

He nodded again, rocking on the balls of his feet, hands behind his back. I think it was a nervous gesture. Hmm . . . why was he nervous? 'I can certainly understand that, Marshal Blake.'

'Good to know,' I said, and studied his careful eyes and face. Either there was more and worse to come, or something else.

Hatfield looked at me from the chair, and her eyes were even wider. 'God, you mean you put a stake through someone who was begging and struggling?'

'Yeah.'

'I've shot ones that were begging, but that's . . .' She turned back to the paper, pen poised.

'No,' Chapman said.

She looked up at him. 'Why not, sir? Why shouldn't I sign this over to the best person for the job?'

'We've started fielding new preternatural marshals with older, more experienced ones, much as Forrester and Blake did on their own, but, Hatfield, you have the field experience. You're a good marshal, a good cop.'

'I am, sir, but I am not a psychic anything. When they did the mandatory testing in the Marshals Service, I came up as a total blank. Blake has a psychic ability with the dead and with shapeshifters. She has skills with the very creatures we are hunting that I will never have no matter how many more years I have with a badge. I cannot learn Blake's skills with the monsters.'

'Preternatural citizens,' Chapman corrected automatically.

'Whatever you want to call them, but no amount of time behind the badge will give me the skills Blake has naturally. A lot of the SWAT are starting to put psychics on their teams, and police forces across the country are pairing up cops with psychic ability with partners who have none. I believe that the preternatural service should do the same thing. I've spent all night trying to think how I could have done things differently, and the only thing I can come up with is that I needed someone who was psychic to tell me the bodies weren't dead, or warn me that it was a bad decision. With the information and the standard practices as they are, sir, I did my best, but I believe that I did not have all the information I needed to make an informed decision. I will happily work with Blake, and I am eager to see how her psychic abilities change how we do this job.'

'Forrester barely tested on the psychic profiling,' Chapman said. 'How do you explain his success?'

'I don't know, sir, but I know that the psychic testing isn't perfect.'

'You believe that Forrester is more psychic than the testing showed?'

'Or maybe he's spent years fighting monsters, and the rest of us just don't have his wealth of experience, but I know that he listens to Blake even though he started out as her mentor. They work as a team, sir, and I believe that's part of the key. They don't seem to care who gets the credit or rises in rank; they just do their job to the best of their ability, which I believe saves lives.'

She bent over the piece of paper again. He protested, but this time she signed it and handed the pen to me.

'I'm not sure this is the best course of action,' Chapman said.

I had to walk past him to take the pen from Hatfield.

'You aren't the boss of us,' Edward said, 'not even of Hatfield, because she's one of us now.'

I signed my name, then turned and held the pen out to Edward. 'Want to witness it?'

'Sure,' he said, and he had to walk past Chapman, too.

'And the fact that I am not the boss of any of you is precisely the problem. The Preternatural Branch of our service is like a speeding car with no one at the wheel; eventually it's going to crash and then we'll be expected to clean up the mess.'

'If by *we*, you mean the Marshals Service, don't sweat it; I heard we're about to be spun off into our own bureaucratic entity.'

'If they do that, Blake, you will be what amounts to legal death squads hunting legal citizens in the United States.'

'I didn't say it was a good idea, or even that I agreed with it, but it still looks like it's going to go through,' I said.

'I don't believe it will.'

'We'll see,' I said.

'Yes, we will.'

Edward looked at the other man. 'The problem is that you keep trying to treat this problem like it's a police and civil liberties issue, and it's not.'

'What is it then, Marshal Forrester? You tell me.'

'Have you ever had a nightmare so real that when you wake up in a cold sweat, you look around the room and you feel that rush of relief to know that it wasn't real?'

Chapman shrugged. 'We all have.'

Edward nodded. 'Have you ever felt that rush of relief and then heard a noise that shouldn't have been there, because you're supposed to be alone?'

Chapman just looked at him, controlling his face and giving blank face back. 'I can't say I have.'

'I have. Anita has. We know that the nightmare can be real, and we have the skills, the will, and the tools to fight the nightmares and win.'

'You and Blake are tough motherfuckers, I get that, Forrester.'

Edward shook his head. 'That's not it.'

'Then explain it to me,' he said, and his irritation sounded in his voice.

'The newer marshals think like cops, which means they're trained to preserve life. Blake and I think more like soldiers; our job is to take lives, not save them. In killing the monsters we save lives, but our actual job is to take life. We aren't Officer Friendly coming into the classroom to reassure the kids. We aren't the person with a badge who the nice elderly lady can call for help when her cat's up a tree. We aren't the patrol officer who will give you directions when you're lost. We aren't the state trooper who will stop you when you're drunk so you don't kill anyone else or yourself with your car. We aren't any of those things and neither of us ever has been; we weren't trained for it. All the best executioners come from backgrounds that do not include police work but often include military, or a civilian background where they hunted and killed large game.'

'Blake is not a great white hunter,' Chapman said.

'No, but her dad took her hunting for deer, which was the biggest game they could hunt in her home state.'

He glanced at me. 'That's not in your file.'

I shrugged.

'We hunt and kill things. When it comes to a stand-up fight like it did yesterday, we are soldiers first, cops second, because even if we negotiate with the bad guys, they know, and we know, that we are going to kill them. We are assassins with badges. We are death squads, and the fact that Hatfield and all the good police officers in our field don't understand that is why they aren't as good at the job as we are, and Bernardo Spotted-Horse, and Otto Jeffries, or . . . All the best of us started out as bounty hunters, or vampire hunters who were supplementing the police.'

'You're admitting that you're just killers with badges,' he said.

Edward nodded. 'Yes.'

'I can't endorse the Marshals Service being a party to that.'

'I know,' Edward said, 'because being a police officer is about preserving life, liberty, and safety.'

'We put the bad guys away, so the innocent aren't hurt,' Chapman said.

'The police are really good at that if the politicians let them do their job, but the monsters are real, Chief Deputy Marshal Chapman. When the government decided that the monsters were too dangerous to put in jail and that executing them was the only way to keep the innocent safe, then it stopped being a job for the police.'

'You have badges; you are the police,' Chapman said.

'We have badges and we are police officers, but you don't really believe that. If you did, you wouldn't have cared that Hatfield was giving the warrant to Anita.'

'It's the lack of control, the lack of checks and balances for you and her,' he said.

'We make you nervous.'

'No, you don't make me nervous.'

I wanted to say *Liar*, but wisely kept my mouth shut.

Then Chapman looked at us, and finally at Hatfield. 'You're a good marshal, Hatfield; if you want to leave the Preternatural Branch and come back to our side of things I will fully support you. I'll personally see that you don't suffer any ill effects careerwise.'

'Thank you, Chapman, and I may do that, but I feel I have to stay with this case until it's done. I wouldn't be able to live with myself if I didn't.'

'When it's over, you can come back to regular service,' he said.

'Thank you, sir; I think I'd prefer that.'

He turned to Edward and said, 'You and Blake, Spotted-Horse, Jeffries, the rest of you, don't make me nervous, Forrester; you scare me, because you aren't cops, and I don't like people thinking that just because the monster has a badge it ceases to be a monster.'

'Are you calling us monsters, Chapman?' I asked.

'They've let two marshals who tested positive for lycanthropy keep their badges. They're in the field again, but I saw the damage that Blake's shifter friend did to the officers in the chopper. Are you really comfortable letting something like that have a badge?'

'I will hunt down the vampire that made Ares attack us. I will hunt him down and I will kill him.'

'In revenge?'

'No, sir, because it's my job.'

Chapman shook his head. 'You're right, Forrester; you're death squad soldiers with badges. I suspected that, and it was one of the reasons I was pushing so hard to have people like Hatfield join your branch. I was hoping it would help balance the rest of you, but now I'm afraid that instead of her balancing you, you will corrupt her.'

'I'm a little too old to be corrupted, sir,' Hatfield said.

He looked at her and his eyes were sad. In that moment I knew that

Chapman had seen real combat; there's a look that only real violence, real survival, and real survival guilt can give you.

'Until the devil takes your soul, Hatfield, you're never too old to be corrupted.' With that he turned and walked out, leaving the door open behind him.

We gathered up our stuff and went to talk to witnesses, read over the police reports, and hope we found a clue.

56

The local PD gave us a small room in the depths of the building to spread the papers around. There'd been some reluctance, but I had the warrant now and that made this my case. I tried not to be too rude, but I also was all out of taking shit. We had until nightfall to learn what we could from the reports, pictures, and witness statements. I was hoping to talk to some of the human witnesses, the few who had lived through being a witness, but first the reports. Yeah, they can be tedious and even boring, but there's a reason we write reports and take pictures and measurements from every angle, and not all of it's for court; sometimes you learn new things that help you catch the bad guys.

The three of us divided the reports into three piles: the missing-person reports, most of which were now solved; the crime scenes where people had been killed; and the reports from the doctors about the survivors' injuries and the rotting disease. I skipped the last pile, because I'd talked directly to the doctors, and Edward had spoken to Micah about his dad while I was unconscious, so Hatfield got that pile. She hadn't taken time to read any of it through; most of the time if you're given a warrant against vampires in custody, there isn't time to study up on it. The marshal can insist on reading about the crime, but most don't. They ride into town, perform the execution, and ride out again. We're sort of the Lone Rangers of Death, and yes I do know that the Lone Ranger was a Texas Ranger, not a U.S. Marshal, but it's still what most people think of when we show up. One modern inner-city slang term for us was Lone Rangers, or just Rangers. We don't usually solve the crime, but we sure as hell end the investigation. Death is about as final as you can get – mystery solved, time to ride off into the sunset on our pale horse with our blood-spattered scythe. I'd started reading before I did custody executions, because if I was ending someone's life, I wanted to know what they'd done to earn it. I wasn't called out on morgue kills anymore, partially because they knew I'd be a pain in the ass about it and actually insist on seeing case files, and because there were plenty of marshals like Hatfield and one of my fellow marshals back home who would be happy to ride into town, take care of your vampire problem, and ride out without asking a damn thing.

Edward read the crime scenes to begin with and I read the missing persons. It was interesting that some of the missing would turn out to be victims and others would be moved over to 'vampire.' Vampires were never considered victims in these cases. Once you moved from human to vamp you were the enemy; it was like you started out as the princess waiting to be rescued and ended up being the dragon to be slain. I'd theoretically known that this was the way things worked, but seeing the missing people divided up so neatly made me have to look at it differently. I even agreed with the change, because when a person was first made a vampire and the rogue master that made them was still controlling them, the new vampire was like a loaded gun in the hands of a killer. It would take weeks for them to be self-aware enough to be anything more than blood-seeking killers. New vamps were the most likely to tear out people's throats by accident, because they could sense the blood in the body, and they wanted it, but there is a practice curve to learning to use fangs. Hell, once a person had been captured by vampire gaze, they could turn into an enemy. I'd had more than one fellow cop try to shoot his own men after a vamp mind-fucked them. So I agreed it was just standard because the evil master vampire would control them until he or she was killed, and if the master was new enough, killing him or her would turn the newbie vamps into damn near revenants that attacked and killed anything. Some vampires' minds could survive the deaths of their masters, and some couldn't, and those had to be put down like a rabid animal, because that was probably all they'd ever be. But as I read through the reports about families with children, engagements announced just before they disappeared, parents asking after their grown children on a weekly basis, I began to wonder if given enough time even the most insane new vamp could become more like who they had been?

There was no way to test the theory, because they were animals with superhuman strength and super-speed that lived off the blood of the living. They weren't much more alive than a flesh-eating zombie. You couldn't cage something like that and hope it improved over time, but looking at pictures of the vampires before they became vampires made me wonder how many people we'd killed who might have recovered to be law-abiding citizen vamps. It was like wondering if a serial killer could be reformed. The answer was no, but it was still something you wondered about when you heard of one who could go twenty years without a kill while he raised his kids to be teenagers. Apparently being the parent of teens was enough to send him back to killing. I've heard having teenagers was stressful, but geez.

'You've thought of something,' Edward said.

I looked up from the files, blinking because I had to drag myself back from the files, and the smiling faces, and the bloody faces, and my own thinking.

'Not really, or not in the way you mean.'

'Share,' he said.

I glanced at Hatfield, who was looking at me now, too. If had just been Edward then I would have shared, but . . . 'Just a weird thought I had about how new these vampires are. I've never been called in where this many people were listed as missing and then changed to killer vamps; one or two, yeah, but not dozens.'

'It's not dozens,' Hatfield said.

'I requested they send me all the missing-person reports for this area in the last three months, even ones they didn't think were linked. A lot of people vanished in the same area, but over about a three-month time period. They found three bodies so decomposed that they thought they'd all fallen to their deaths and then animals got to them. That may be what happened; animals do that in wilderness areas and it's routine to just accept it as accidental death.'

'But you don't think it was,' Hatfield said.

'If a vampire is powerful enough, it can go inactive for years and sustain itself, but when it wakes, or gets out of where it was trapped, whatever, it usually is a little crazy. It feeds in a more animalistic fashion, like a newbie vampire again, until it's had enough blood to sort of get its head back to a point where it's not crazy anymore. Some vampires never come back after being trapped without food for too long.'

'Trapped how?' Hatfield asked.

'Cross-wrapped coffins, usually,' I said.

'Who traps them in cross-wrapped coffins? We'd just kill them,' she asked.

I debated on what to say, and finally Edward said, 'Vampires have what amounts to jail when one of their kind goes crazy and they don't want to kill them.'

'I thought they just killed each other like any other predator.'

'Even animal predators don't like killing one of their own friends, but vampires are just like regular people. They find it hard to kill someone they've known a long time, so they try to imprison them and hope they can cure them.'

'You mean rehabilitate them?' she asked.

'Something like that,' I said. In truth, being trapped in a coffin was usually more punishment than trying to save you. I'd known vampires that had been driven crazy from long coffin imprisonment, but that wasn't something I was sharing with Hatfield. She was being friendly, but she wasn't my friend, not yet.

'So, say you had a vampire wake up, or escape being imprisoned, whatever; they'd go after the nearest food, which would probably be animals, right?' Hatfield asked.

'Animals are harder to catch than you'd think,' I said, 'but maybe you can't actually sustain yourself on animal blood, not even freshly killed animals.'

'Why not?' she asked.

'Because you need that spark, that extra energy, whatever it is from humans to go with the blood.'

'You mean like drinking someone's soul?'

'That presupposes that animals don't have souls and I wouldn't be willing to say that,' I said.

'Okay, then what? What makes us so special for vampires?'

I smiled. 'If you can answer that question in a definitive way, Hatfield, you'll be doing better than hundreds of years of religion and philosophy.'

'Oh,' she said, 'I get that. But why do you think it's an old vamp that just woke up?'

'Because it's a really rare talent, and I've only seen it in ancient vampires. If there were a vampire that old and this powerful, we'd know about it. You just can't hide this much power from both the vampire and human community, not to mention the shapeshifters. He was able to mess with my friend through the bite of one of the vampires he possessed, not even his own bite, and he was able to control Ares, or drive him crazy, from a distance.'

'I've never even heard of a vampire being able to possess its vamp followers in any of the literature. You should write a paper about it, publish it for the rest of us to read.'

I looked at Edward and he looked back. 'Not all the really old vamps like their secrets being that out in the open, Hatfield.'

'Oh, you mean they're still alive. I guess I thought you killed them.'

'I don't kill every vampire I meet, Hatfield.'

She looked a little embarrassed. 'I guess not; I mean, you are with your Master of the City. No offense meant.'

'None taken; I am dating him.'

Hatfield had a moment where thoughts chased across her face so quickly I wasn't sure what she was thinking; maybe she didn't even know what she was thinking exactly.

'Just say it, Hatfield,' Edward said.

'I don't think I could ever get past the fact that he was dead, but if you had to be dating a vampire, your Master of the City is pretty gorgeous – again, no offense.'

I smiled. 'Why should I be offended? Jean-Claude *is* gorgeous.'

'I'm sorry I said pretty horrible things to you earlier about him, and Micah Callahan, and . . . oh, hell, I was awful and it was just that you cast a long shadow over the Preternatural Branch of the Marshals Service for the rest of us female officers.'

'I'm sorry if my dating preternaturals makes it harder for the rest of you, but I'm not going to stop dating the men I love because people are bothered by it.'

'Now that I've seen you in person, I realize a lot of it's jealousy. You're as tough as you are beautiful, which means a lot of women must hate you on sight, and the men can't decide whether to try to compete with you or sleep with you.'

I frowned at her. 'Sorry, I spend most of my time around men who make me look like the ugly stepsister, so I don't get the beauty-being-intimidating part, but on the tough part, most of them can't compete.'

'If you're the ugly stepsister, then your guys must be even prettier than their pictures.'

'They're pretty spectacular,' I said.

'And you let the men know they can't compete,' she said.

I shrugged. 'In our job we can't afford to baby anyone's ego. They're either up to the job or they're not.'

She gave a small laugh. 'Oh, yeah, a lot of your haters are just insecure around you. I didn't think anyone could live up to your reputation, but you made a believer out of me, Blake.' Her face sobered. She looked down at the papers in front of her. 'This disease is pretty terrible. I'm sorry about Sheriff Callahan for a lot of reasons, but if he really is your future father-in-law, I'm sorry that Micah Callahan had to come home to this.'

'The best thing I can do for Micah and his dad is find the vampire that started all this. Until night falls and we can question the vampires, we look at what the victims can tell us. I want to see how close the missing-person reports are to each other geographically. I need a map to see if I'm right, but if I am, then it may be where our master vampire is hiding his body. If the missing persons are clustered originally in one area like I'm thinking, then I'd send police up to check on anyone living up in the area. There are always people in the mountains who don't come to town much if you go far enough up. Some because they're just good old-fashioned mountain people and antisocial. Or, the new mountain people have money and some of them have helipads at the summit of their mountains, so either way potentially no one would know they're missing for a while.'

'You really think we have a lot more people missing?'

'I'm half-hoping we do, because that will give us someplace to start looking for the master vampire's body.'

'You say *body* like he's not in it,' Hatfield said.

'A vampire that can take over his created offspring this easily usually does leave their body somewhere safe and just uses other bodies as a sort of stalking horse. That body gets damaged, they abandon it like a sinking ship and find another boat to take over.'

'They jump bodies that easily?' she asked.

'I've known a couple that could, and I'm thinking worst-case scenario here.'

'If the bad vamp can jump bodies that easily, how do you kill it?'

Edward and I spoke in unison. 'Destroy the original body.'

She looked from one to the other of us and almost laughed. 'You've done this before.'

Edward and I looked at each other. Then I said, 'Yeah,' and he said, 'Yes.'

'Okay,' she said, giving us wide eyes, 'let's go find that map.'

57

They found a map, and the cluster of pins – red for known victims, green for missing people, yellow for missing people found dead of presumed natural causes – did form a pattern, but not the one I was hoping for. There was a cluster at the beginning in a remote spot in the mountains, but then the next cluster was miles away and less isolated, and the next one closer to one of the small towns in the mountains, and then bypassing it and heading toward Boulder.

The big surprise was that Travers joined us for the planning/briefing session. I'd known that Truth had sucked out the rot, but I'd assumed he'd been more hurt than just the vampire bite. He was bandaged up enough for the dressing to show at the collar of his shirt, and he moved carefully as he leaned against one of the pillars in the room, wincing as he settled his six-feet-plus frame. Everyone had said how glad they were to see him and hadn't expected him. I'd said hi and good to see him. He'd given me a tiny nod, his face guarded. Last I'd seen, me and my people had saved his ass twice. Something told me he was going to be weird about it. Sigh.

'How did we not see this?' Detective Foster asked. He was an older detective who was down to that fringe of hair, and in his glasses he looked more like a high school math teacher than a cop, until you noticed the width of his shoulders and the small muscles that played in his forearms.

'We didn't see it, because there's nothing to see,' Travers said, in his big, deep voice, all gruff like when he'd been trash-talking me in the mountains. 'That is every hiker and tourist gone missing for three months. It is not vampire victims.'

'You guys usually lose that many hikers in a three-month period?' I asked.

There was a moment of silence, and then Foster said, 'No, and that's what I mean about how did we miss it? Even if it wasn't vampires or some other preternatural, it's still too many people to lose. Someone should have red-flagged it.'

Captain Jonas stepped up beside the map. 'This is the first time that all the cases have been put together. Individually it was a bigger number of missing and accidents than normal, but not that much bigger.'

'It's the same problem we run into all the time as marshals. Different law enforcement agencies covering different areas mean that you don't share information unless there's a reason for it. Different jurisdictions, hell, different ranger stations cover at least two of these areas. Some of them could still just be runaways; an elderly man who wandered off and was found dead by a presumed fall and exposure may be just that. People die by accident all the damn time, especially in wilderness areas if they don't have experience and they don't understand how fast the temperature can drop or the weather can change.'

'How do you know so much about mountains? You're from St Louis – that's what, a few hundred feet above sea level?' Travers called out.

'I've executed warrants all over the country. I had one in the mountains where a snowstorm came up so fast we were lucky to find shelter, so I did more research on weather patterns and survival for this kind of terrain, because you're right, I'm a flatlander, and it damn near got me killed once. I've worked to make sure it doesn't happen a second time.'

'Aren't you just the little Boy Scout,' he said.

'What is your problem with Blake?' Hatfield asked.

He looked surprised. 'Since when did you become her biggest fan? I heard you called her a fur-banger and coffin bait.'

Hatfield looked embarrassed. 'I didn't know Marshal Blake then, and when I did I jumped on her bandwagon, Officer Travers. Since five people died last night, because I didn't have her expertise with the undead.'

'The vampires looked dead; they were dead. No one could have known the vampires weren't dead enough,' Travers said.

'Blake knew. Forrester knew.'

'Bullshit,' he said.

'Travers, what the hell is your problem? Everyone else who came off that mountain with her has nothing but good to say about her. I hear one of her vampires saved your life,' Captain Jonas said.

'Yeah, one of her vampire lovers fixed me all up.' He sounded bitter.

'Travers, shut the fuck up. If Blake has to keep defending her honor against all our people, I'm going to run out of people to send into the field,' Jonas said.

'I heard about Rickman. He's good in a fight; she got a lucky shot,' Travers said.

Edward laughed.

Travers glared at him. 'You got a problem, Forrester?'

'Anita didn't get in a lucky shot.'

'I say she did,' Travers said, and pushed away from the pillar and winced, but he straightened so all six foot five of him towered over the room, and by implication Edward.

'Anita didn't need luck to win the fight,' Edward said.

'You were there, right?'

'No.'

'Then how the hell do you know what happened? You ever even meet Rickman?'

'I don't have to meet him,' Edward said.

'What does that mean?'

'Anita doesn't win because she's lucky. She wins because she's just that good.'

'Well, I guess you'd know how good she is,' Travers said.

Edward pushed off the desk where he'd been half-sitting.

Travers started moving toward him slowly, stiffly, but moving. He was smiling. I knew that kind of smile. It meant he wanted a fight, but he wasn't picking on me; he wanted a piece of my 'boyfriend.'

Jonas said, 'That's it, Travers; go home.'

'You need every man you can get,' he said.

'I need every man and woman who wants to work as a team and do their damn jobs. I know Rickman is like one of your best buds, but now that Blake beat his sorry ass, you don't need to take his place as her bully.'

'I got no beef with Blake.'

'Then stop trying to pick a fight with her and Forrester. Make one more out-of-line remark and I will send you home and write your ass up officially.'

'Write me up for what?'

'Sexual harassment, for starters,' Jonas said.

'I didn't sexually harass anybody.'

'Maybe my memory is better than yours, Travers, so I'll quote you back to yourself: "Well, I guess you'd know how good she is." That was a sexual remark aimed at both our visiting marshals.'

'I wasn't talking to Blake, so how is that harassing her?'

'Did you sleep through the last sexual harassment seminar? Comments made in the presence of a female officer can also constitute harassment.'

Weirdly it sort of hurt my feelings that Travers seemed angrier with me now than before I'd saved his ass in the mountains, and then I wondered if he hadn't liked being saved by a woman and a bunch of preternaturals? If that was it, it pissed me off even more.

Hatfield stood up for me. 'If one of her vampires hadn't sucked out that rotting disease, you'd be dying like the sheriff.'

'I didn't ask for the help,' he said.

'Ungrateful bastard,' I said.

He turned those angry eyes to me. 'You want a piece of me, Blake?'

'If you mean sexually, no thanks.'

He flushed, his face coloring.

'If you mean a fight, I'll wait until you're healed. It wouldn't be fair while you're wounded.'

His face darkened even more, and he started walking toward me, which meant toward Edward, too, since we were beside each other.

'Don't finish walking over here, Travers,' Edward said, 'because I don't care if you're wounded.'

'You think you can take me?'

'I know I can,' and he smiled as he said it, which was the guy equivalent of saying he didn't want the fight at the same time he was encouraging it.

Travers kept coming. Captain Jonas intercepted him. He looked small beside the other man, but there was nothing small about his attitude. 'Go home, Travers. I'll be recommending you get some counseling, because you're obviously traumatized by recent events.'

'I'm not hurt that bad; I can help find this bastard.'

'I didn't say you were hurt, I said you were traumatized. Now go home while I can still give you the benefit of the doubt. If you touch either Forrester or Blake, I will suspend you without pay, now – go home right now!'

He turned to go but had to throw a comment over his shoulder. 'I don't owe your vampire anything, Blake.'

'Truth didn't save you so you'd owe him something. He saved you because it was the right thing to do and he respects fellow warriors.'

'He is not a fellow warrior. He's just a damn bloodsucker!'

'Would you rather be rotting away in the hospital like Sheriff Callahan?' I didn't yell it, but my voice was getting louder.

'Why didn't your vampire save *him*?'

'Because the disease has spread through his body, and there's no one place to suck the poison out.' I felt the bite of tears behind my eyes. I would not cry in front of this bastard. 'It's too late to save Micah's dad, but we were able to save you, you fucking ungrateful, misogynistic, prejudiced, racist, undeserving bastard.'

Travers's face sort of froze, and then it was like he looked lost – that was the only word I had for it. That one expression was enough; something about the fight in the mountains, being wounded, being saved by Truth, had affected him deeply, and not in a good way. He just turned without another word and walked out.

'What the hell was that about?' Jonas asked, to no one in particular.

Since the question hadn't been directed at anyone in particular, no one answered it. In fact, the silence was a little thick.

It was Deputy Al from the back of the room. 'Sorry I'm late, but damn, Anita, you cuss real pretty.'

It made people laugh, at least a little. I smiled as Al walked farther into the room. He smiled at me, and the look on his face let me know he'd heard enough of what had just happened to want to make it better. Travers might be an ungrateful bastard, but for every one of those there was an Al, and a Hatfield, and a Jonas. I had more friends than enemies in most cities. It was just that I didn't understand why some people kept resenting me; I just didn't get it, and I never would. I wasn't much for hating people for things they couldn't change, like the way they looked, or psychic gifts, or whatever. I was grumpy and killed people almost everywhere I went, but I didn't hate them. That probably wasn't much of a comfort to the people I executed, but hey, sometimes you take what you can get.

58

Once upon a time, hunting vampires was all about daylight. You hoarded the hours while the vamps couldn't be up and hunting you back so you could find them in their daytime lair and put a stake through their hearts, or decapitate them while they were dead to the world and couldn't fight back, but we had two vampires in custody that might be able to answer all our questions. They probably knew his daytime retreat, but while the sun was up they couldn't talk to us. Yes, there was that pesky lawyer thing, but now that the warrant was mine I could use all the power it granted me. That power included being able to force the lawyer to let me question them with him present, if I believed more lives would be lost without their information. We'd lost five people last night, and only two of them had a job that put them in harm's way; the other three had been innocent bystanders. I had all the proof I needed to be able to question the vampires once the sun went down. I was looking forward to nightfall and being able to talk to them, at the same time that I was worried what this rogue master had up his undead sleeve. The zombies at the hospital and the rotting vampires that wouldn't die had been pretty terrible, even by my standards. So, on one hand I was eager for the day to pass, and on the other hand, not so much.

Deputy Al went out with all the officers who could be spared to hunt up some of the more isolated people who weren't answering their phones and hadn't been seen in a while. Now that the warrant was officially mine I could include our guards in the investigation. It was a clause in the Preternatural Branch that had come into place after several marshals died because they were alone and hunting very bad things but couldn't involve civilians. When they did, some of the civilians had been charged with assault and in one case murder, because it had happened in states where self-defense wasn't as broadly defined in that individual state's laws. Most people don't realize how different some laws are from state to state. We are still the United States of America, and the founders of our country worded it that way for a reason. We're supposed to be a bunch of individual entities under the umbrella of America, not just one entity known as America, or that's how it was originally set up. The states may not be the nearly separate countries that the Founding Fathers thought they'd be, but legally there can be some surprising differences. In the days before I had a badge but was still expected to carry out legal executions, I read up on the laws of individual states, a lot. The Supreme Court had ruled in favor of some of the civilians who had saved the marshals' lives, but they'd been in jail until that time, so a new 'law' had been piggybacked onto the Marshals Service. It was really an old tradition given new language and new legality. As the warrant holder I could recruit civilians if I thought they had skills that would help me stay alive and help me keep civilian casualties lower.

It was basically a legal version of the sheriff standing out in front of the saloon in the Old West and saying, 'Let's form a posse and go get these guys.' It meant that I could have Nicky with me officially.

I found a little privacy in a corner of the room as everyone cleared out and called him to join me; he'd asked, 'Do you want Dev?'

'I think Dev has had enough of my day job for a while,' I said.

'Do you have a preference of who I bring with me?'

'I don't know who all is here now. Lisandro said that they'd only brought the best; with Claudia in charge I believe it.'

'So let Claudia pick?' he asked.

'As long as her choice isn't someone that you or I don't like to work with, and it has to be someone who works well with the police.'

'I'll see who Claudia wants to send. Do you have a preference where Dev goes in the rotation?'

'Do you? He and you partner a lot for guard duty,' I asked.

Either he made a small pleased sound, or I could hear him smile over the phone. 'I love that you asked my opinion, when you could just make your Bride suck it up.'

I smiled. 'I guess I'm just not that kind of Groom. Honestly, until you made that remark in the hospital I thought you and Dev were good friends.'

'I don't know if I can explain it to you, but he's a friend up to a point. When he lost it after the basement fight, his status in my friend list went down.'

'Because he was weak?' I made it a question.

'And because if that fight bothered him, then he doesn't want to know most of what I've spent my life doing. You can't really be friends with someone who only likes parts of you. I can be work friends with Dev, and share you with him like in the shower, that was fun, but he couldn't stomach who I really am, Anita. I know that now.'

Edward came up to me. 'Can I put a vote in?'

I nodded. 'Ted wants to put his two cents' worth in,' I said.

'I'm cool with that,' Nicky said.

I looked at Edward, raising my eyebrows. 'Who do you want to play with?'

'I don't know everyone they brought with them, but if I can't have Bobby Lee or Fredo, I'll take Lisandro. If they brought him, Socrates would be okay, too. I'd say Claudia, but she's not sure she likes me.'

'Claudia's never said she doesn't like you, at least not to me,' I said.

'She suspects I get you into more danger than I help you get out of.'

Nicky chimed in. 'I don't want Claudia. She's great in a fight, but she's not comfortable around me.'

'Why?' I asked.

'I'm a big, dominant male werelion; after what happened with your last lover who fit that description, she doesn't trust me.'

He very delicately hadn't said Haven's name, because he knew having to kill him had hurt me in ways that I was still discovering. Claudia had never liked Haven, and when the shit hit the fan she'd helped me kill him, after he shot Nathaniel and her and killed one of the other werelions. It had been a mess.

'Okay, I guess I can understand that,' I said, 'but I'd rather not use Lisandro.'

'He's good at the job,' Nicky said.

'Yeah, but he almost died last time he came out on a case. He's the only one on the list who's married and has kids. I'd rather not have to explain to his wife and kids why they're down one husband and father.'

'Lisandro knows the risks,' Nicky said.

Edward said, 'If you leave Lisandro home when it gets dangerous, then you've effectively ruined him as a guard.'

I sighed. 'Maybe, but humor me, okay?'

'If you're talking to me, just tell me what you want and I have to humor you, remember,' Nicky said.

'I remember, Nicky. I was talking to Ted.'

Edward said, 'Is Socrates in town?'

'Socrates is good,' I said.

'Yeah, but he doesn't trust me, makes it hard to work together.'

'Why doesn't he trust you?'

'I'm a bad guy and he's an ex-cop,' Nicky said.

'You're not a bad guy,' I said.

'Yes, I am, Anita.'

'We'll agree to disagree,' I said.

He gave that deep chuckling laugh. 'No, Socrates's cop sense goes crazy around me, and it should. I'm exactly what he thinks I am. I just don't hide it as good as Ted.'

I started to say, *But Ted isn't a bad guy either*, and then stopped myself. *Bad* and *good* were relative terms when it came to my best bud and to some of my lovers. I took a deep breath and let it go. It was a philosophical problem for another day.

'No, of the people they brought I'd prefer Lisandro or Domino. Pride would be okay, but he was raised and trained with Dev. He might have the same issue in a rough fight. Ethan is good, but I don't know if he can handle your job either,' Nicky said.

'Pride is here, really? Our other golden tiger guard hasn't ever come out on an away job,' I said.

'Apparently Claudia volunteered him and he didn't say no,' Nicky said.

'Who else?' I asked.

Edward came close and said, 'Anita, let Lisandro do his job.'

'I just remember how I felt when I thought we'd gotten him killed last time out. All I could think was I didn't want to tell his kids and his wife.'

'I have kids, and I'm Donna's husband except for a legal piece of paper, but you aren't leaving me home.'

I looked up into those blue eyes. He was saying something warm, but the eyes had bled to winter sky pale. I realized we were the last in the room, except for Hatfield. She wanted to ride with us, to learn the job the only way that seemed to work well, in the company of someone else who already knew how to do it. She was standing across the room, giving us privacy. Everyone else had taken their share of the addresses to check and left. Edward didn't have to pretend to be Ted when it was just me.

'Compromise,' I said. 'We bring Lisandro and Socrates. I'll talk to him about toning down his spider-sense about your thugginess.'

'You really think having Socrates along will keep Lisandro safe?' Edward asked.

I shrugged.

'You have to let him do his job, Anita.'

'No, no, I don't.' I looked at him.

He frowned at me. 'You can't be like this just because people are married and have kids. Your guards are going to have a life outside of their job, and that's going to include more kids eventually.'

'I know that,' I said, but I sounded defensive even to myself.

'Then stop letting your issues with your own childhood mess with Lisandro's ability to do his job,' Edward said.

'I don't know what you're talking about.'

'Anita,' he said, and just looked at me.

I wanted to pout, or get unreasonably angry, all things I'd done for years as a coping mechanism. 'Fine, but I still want a third guard to come with them.'

'Will you trust Nicky to pick the third guard?' Edward asked.

I sighed and then said, 'Yeah, sure.'

'Me, too,' he said.

I looked at him. 'Really?' I said, and didn't try to keep the surprise out of my face.

'Lisandro and who?' Nicky asked.

'Edward and I agree that you can pick whoever else comes with the two of you.'

'You used his real name,' Nicky said.

'Sorry, he just surprised me.'

'What'd he do to surprise you that badly?'

'I'll explain later,' I said. 'Just be ready. We'll pick you up on the way out of town.'

'Will do. Love you,' he said.

'I love you, too,' I said, and it was automatic, because I was still studying Edward's face. When Nicky had hung up, I said to Edward, 'You trust Nicky's judgment that much?'

He gave one nod.

'High damn praise,' I said.

'You know me, Anita; I like working with sociopaths who are willing to do anything to get the job done.'

'What's that say about me?'

He grinned, and it was all back to good-ol'-boy Ted. 'You'll never be as good a sociopath as I am, Anita, and neither of us will be as good at it as Nicky. It means he won't let emotion color his choice. It isn't that his feelings are hurt about Socrates not trusting him, it's that the lack of trust makes Socrates hesitate to follow Nicky's lead in a fight, and that makes for a bad team, and more than any sport, combat means you need a good working team.'

I stopped arguing, because Edward trusted Nicky. It was unprecedented that he had that much faith in one of my lovers. He liked Micah and Nathaniel. He didn't dislike Jean-Claude, but that wasn't the same thing as trusting any of them. I shoved it all away, put in a box to look at later, because we were running behind. I admitted to myself that the reason I'd argued about Lisandro had been about me losing my mother when I was eight. I knew how much damage that had done to me, and I didn't want to do the same thing to Lisandro's kids; there, that was the truth. I hated when my own issues interfered with me doing my job. They'd gotten in the way of my personal life for years, but my job was usually safe from my neuroses – well, most of the time.

We got Hatfield and went for Edward's SUV. I told her we were picking up some deputies on the way out of town. She didn't argue, just asked, 'Are we picking up the two blond men?'

'One of them,' I said.

'And new friends?' she asked.

'New to you,' Edward said.

'I look forward to meeting them,' she said.

I glanced in the rearview to see if she was being sarcastic, but her face looked open and honest.

'What?' she asked.

'Just trying to decide if you meant that.'

'If there's anyone, or anything, that can help me do my job better, I'm all for it. I got those people killed last night. I can't bring them back, but I can get better and not do it again.'

'You didn't kill them, Hatfield,' I said.

'Neither of you would have stored the body parts in the morgue of a hospital. If either of you had been in charge last night, all five victims from last night would be alive now. Tell me how my ignorance didn't cost them their lives.'

I didn't know how to answer her.

'We all make mistakes until we know better,' Edward said.

'Exactly, and I'm going to follow you both around like your fucking shadows and learn all I can before you leave.'

I wasn't sure I wanted Hatfield following me that closely, but I couldn't tell her no. Edward and I exchanged a look. He didn't tell her no either. I guess we had a third wheel. I wondered how she'd like Lisandro and whoever else Nicky picked. For that matter, I wondered what they'd think of Hatfield.

59

We were at the third house on our list. If someone had come down the two-wheel track by accident and driven past, the house would have looked ordinary from the front. You had to get out and walk around to the back of the house to see the broken windows, the shattered door, its pieces scattered around a small deck that had a view off the side of the mountain that people would pay millions for in other towns farther north. They'd tear down the little house and put up something more elegant and a lot more expensive, but the view wouldn't be one bit better off a bigger, fancier deck than it was from the little one.

The mountains marched off and off until the front range rose in white, snow-capped peaks, stark and so beautiful that it looked like a calendar shot instead of someone's back porch view. I took in deep, even breaths of the crisp, clean air, but took too deep a breath because I caught the whiff of what lay inside. The elderly couple had been eaten by zombies. Had they been bled by vampires first? There was no way to tell from the scattered bones and what little flesh was left on them. It was amazing how bad just a little bit of meat smelled after a few days. If the bodies had been dragged outside, the scavengers would have cleared up the mess by now, but the wrecked furniture had partially blocked the door and even the windows. The windows I thought the couple had tried to board up with the tall dresser, but the door . . . why and how had the kitchen table gotten in the wrecked doorway? If the couple put it there, then why were they ripped apart and eaten? We'd had to move the table to get inside ourselves.

Nicky came to stand beside me. 'You saw worse than this last night,' he said.

'I know.'

'Why is this bothering you so much, then?'

It was a fair question. I thought about it. 'Did you see their pictures?'

'Yeah.'

'They have all their pictures up. You can watch their family grow from babies to grandkids. They loved each other. You can see it in every damn picture, and after forty years of marriage they died in terror and . . . it just seems like I've spent too many years seeing the bad end of a lot of happy.'

'Pictures don't tell the truth, Anita. Anyone can lie long enough to have a picture taken.'

I looked at him and realized he was looking out at the view. I knew he'd grown up on a big cattle ranch somewhere, but I'd never asked where. Had there been mountains like this where he grew up?

'You think they lied in all those pictures and they actually hated each other?' I asked.

He smiled, still looking out at the view. 'No, you're probably right that they were great people. They raised their family and were the kind of parents that Hallmark commercials tell you everyone has, and yet the abusive bitch who cut my eye out is still alive, she's in jail, but she's alive. The kids in those pictures . . . I thought childhoods like that were fiction. I thought everybody was abused like me, that it was this big secret that nobody said out loud, but it happened to everybody, and then one day I realized that it wasn't everybody. It was just my shitty family.'

I wrapped my arms around him as much as our both being in body armor and packing more weapons than most people would have thought necessary would allow. It was a lot cozier out of work stuff, but in that moment touching was better than not touching.

'When I see pictures like that, it pisses me off. It makes me feel cheated. Stupid, huh?'

'No,' I said, 'not stupid at all.'

He looked down at me. 'I can feel that you mean that. I think if I couldn't feel what you're really feeling, I wouldn't believe in it.'

'In what?' I asked.

'In us, in love. If I didn't have to feel your emotions, I could have kept convincing myself that none of it was real, and everybody was lying, at least a little. That nothing could be as good as those pictures in there, but you won't let me believe that. I feel how sad you are, how much you want to make me feel better, and because it's my job to make you feel better, I have to feel happier, because you want me to feel happier so much.'

'When you love someone, their happiness is important to you,' I said.

He nodded. 'I'm beginning to understand that.'

Edward came out to join us. Hatfield trailed after him. Lisandro and Seamus came last. Seamus was tall, dark, and handsome, and very African, which made his name jarring. Someone who looked like he should have been hunting lions with a spear shouldn't have been named the Irish equivalent of James. He blinked rich, brown eyes at me. If hyenas hadn't had slit pupils, more like you think a reptile would have, you could have mistaken the eyes for human, but the pupils were wrong and the color was odd. It wasn't coppery red like the werebear Goran, but it wasn't human brown either. I wasn't sure I could explain the difference, but I was beginning to know it when I saw it.

I'd been informed that the vampire, Jane, that he called master had made him his animal to call hundreds of years ago and had forced him into animal form at one point until his eyes had never changed back. They, like Micah's, were stuck. It just seemed worse that Seamus's master had done it. I'd helped Micah escape from Chimera by killing him. There was no escape for Seamus, because if his master died, very likely he'd die, too. He wouldn't have been my choice for rounding out our little party of crime busters. It wasn't his fighting skills I questioned, because I'd seen him in the practice ring. He was eerily graceful for such a tall, long-limbed man. Fredo had described him as 'dark water,' because of how liquidly he moved. The nickname had stuck and some of the guards called him Water. He didn't seem to mind. He didn't seem to mind anything. He was a big, dark, graceful killing machine who seemed to have fewer emotions than all the other sociopaths.

Hatfield watched him out of the corner of her eye, her hand moving toward her duty weapon without her really thinking about it. He was just so big, so self-contained, and so neutral that it was actually unnerving. It was nice to see that I wasn't the only one who thought it was unsettling.

If there had been more strangers with us, Nicky and I wouldn't have kept hugging each other, but Hatfield was going to have to either get used to it or tag along with someone else. I needed the cuddles.

'What the hell happened here?' she asked.

'The nice older couple got eaten alive by zombies,' I said.

She gave a small shudder. 'I know that, but why is the table in front of the door and the broken window covered? I mean . . . shouldn't that have kept the zombies out?'

The fact that she had figured out the puzzling part made me like her even more. 'Yes, it should have.'

'Even if there was a reason for them to put the table and dresser back in place, that would have trapped them in the house, and they weren't trapped in the house. They ate the victims and then they left,' Edward said.

'So how did they get out?' I asked.

'Did you see the corkboard with all the keys in a row?' Lisandro asked.

We all nodded or said, 'Yes.'

'Want to see if the house key is there?'

'They'll have a spare,' I said. 'They're just that kind of people.'

'Okay, then let's check and see if their keys are here. Personal keys have stuff on them, they aren't just bare keys,' he said.

'Did anyone see the lady's purse?' I asked.

No one had.

'Let's find her purse,' Edward said.

I didn't want to go back in the house with the smell and the happy parade of pictures. Nicky didn't want to go back in either. For once even Edward looked a little worn around the edges. The only one who seemed unmoved by it all was Seamus. I would have asked Nicky if he found the other man's lack of emotional affect bothersome, but he'd have said no.

The other two houses that we'd seen had held the remains of dead bodies; they'd been broken into, but they hadn't been barricaded. As attacks by killer zombies went, the other two houses had been normal. The only puzzle was this one, so we went back inside to figure it out, because that was what we did when we weren't shooting things or setting them on fire.

60

We couldn't find her current purse. Hatfield suggested that not every woman carried a purse, but we couldn't find her wallet, a change purse, any form of identification. We found her husband's wallet with his ID, money, and credit cards all intact on the bedside table, where it looked like he put it every night.

'There are three purses in the closet, but they're dressier, or older. She should have a purse,' Hatfield said.

I knew what she meant. The female victim – I had to do my best to think of her as just that. Where was the woman's purse?

'Zombies don't take purses,' I said.

'What if they're made of leather?' Seamus asked; his voice was as deep as you expected it to be.

'Flesh-eating zombies only eat fresh kill or fresh-ish carrion. Treated leather, even the most expensive, would still be too dead for them to eat it.'

'A ghoul would eat it,' Edward said.

I agreed. 'But if ghouls did this, they'd have eaten the man's belt and a lot of other stuff in the house. They live on carrion and garbage.'

'I thought ghouls wouldn't leave the cemetery where they spawn?' Hatfield said.

'They don't normally,' I said.

'There's no cemetery for miles and miles,' she said.

Edward and I looked at each other. We both remembered a case where ghouls followed a necromancer who had accidentally raised them. 'I don't think it's ghouls,' I said, to that look in his eyes.

'No,' he said.

'If the zombies didn't take the purse, who did?' Nicky asked.

'Maybe somebody broke in after they were dead and took the purse,' Lisandro said.

'Then why not take the man's wallet? There's over a hundred dollars in it, and a full set of credit cards,' I said.

'If it wasn't robbery, then why take the purse?' Hatfield asked.

'If it was robbery, why not take more stuff?' Lisandro asked.

'So it wasn't robbery,' I said.

'There were vampires with the zombies in the mountains; was this a mixed group, too?' asked Nicky.

'Maybe,' I said.

'Why would a vampire take some nice old lady's purse?' I asked.

'What was in the purse that wasn't in the wallet?' Edward asked.

Lisandro, Nicky, and I all said, 'Keys.'

'They didn't get in the window or the door. The couple barricaded themselves in, but then for some reason they opened the front door.'

'Vampire mind powers?' Hatfield asked.

'Not if they were already fighting off zombies in the back. The fear and panic would keep almost any vampire from being able to get a hold on their minds unless they'd had previous contact. If they'd been mind-fucked earlier, then maybe,' I said.

'Unlikely, though,' Edward said.

'Agreed.'

'You have killer zombies at the back. You've barricaded yourself in. What would make you open the front door?' I asked.

'Who would you open it for?' Nicky asked.

'Someone you know,' Hatfield said.

'Help,' Edward said.

I turned to him. 'What?'

'You'd open the door in an emergency to help. If the house is on fire you'll let the firefighters in; if you're being robbed you'll open for the police.'

I looked at him. 'You're saying a cop.'

'I'm saying either a cop or someone they trusted and thought would protect them. Maybe an officer they knew,' he said.

'We can't accuse another officer of conspiring with vampires and killer zombies on this much guesswork,' Hatfield said.

'We're not going to accuse anyone in particular, Hatfield, but think about it. Every house we've seen has been torn apart in the area of the house that wouldn't be seen by someone just driving by. Zombies, even killer zombies, don't think that well. If they were being controlled by a vampire, then maybe, but if what I saw and felt in the mountains is any indication, then this vampire isn't that cool a customer.'

'Maybe he's getting more disorganized as he keeps killing?' Edward suggested.

'You mean like a serial killer disintegrating as he feeds his compulsion?'

'Yes.'

'Maybe,' I said.

'But someone let the zombies and vampires out, then took the victim's purse and calmly locked the door behind them,' Edward said.

'We're all agreed on that,' I said.

'I'm not sure we're all agreed on that,' Hatfield said.

'Would you agree it's most likely?'

'No,' she said. 'Everything I learned in class and in the field is that this does not happen. Flesh-eating zombies are incredibly rare. They do not run in packs, contrary to every zombie movie out there, right?'

'Right,' I said.

'Vampires do not hang out with zombies, right?' she asked.

'Right,' I said.

'And now you want me to believe that a human, maybe a cop, is helping scout the houses, lead them in from the most unobtrusive way, and helping cover their tracks.'

'Maybe,' I said.

'If he's covering their tracks, then why leave the table in front of the door?' Lisandro asked.

'Why take the purse? He could have thrown it back through the opening at the edge of the door. There was room to shove a purse back inside,' Nicky said.

That time we did all agree it made no sense.

'What if he doesn't want to cover for them anymore?' Seamus asked.

'What do you mean?' I asked.

'What if something about these victims made him rethink his allegiance?'

'It goes back to him knowing them,' Edward said.

'Yes, or perhaps he looked at the pictures on the walls as I've seen all of you do and it affected him, too.'

'So he's beginning to want to get caught?' I asked.

'Not in the front of his head,' Edward said, 'but maybe in the back of it.'

'You think he'll just keep making more mistakes until he gives himself away?' Hatfield asked.

'Maybe, but that would mean we'd have to see more crime scenes to catch his mistake. I want to catch him before they kill again,' I said.

'Of course,' Hatfield said, 'but how?'

I shook my head. 'I don't know yet.'

'Yet,' Edward said.

'Yeah, yet, it's always yet, Ted, you taught me that.'

He nodded and gave that small, cold smile that I knew so well. It was one of the ones he wore when he killed.

'We don't know yet,' he said.

'But we will,' I said.

'And when you figure it out, then what?' Hatfield asked.

'We kill all of them,' I said.

'Even the human, if it is a human helping them?' she asked.

'Yes,' I said.

'He'll get a trial. His lawyer will go for an insanity plea and get a reduced sentence.'

'No lawyer can help anyone connected to this,' I said.

'What do you mean?' she asked.

'She means that the warrant of execution doesn't differentiate between perpetrators.'

Hatfield frowned. 'I don't understand.'

'The language of a warrant of execution allows me to kill anyone who participates in the crime, Hatfield.'

'You mean you can just kill a human just like that, no arrest, no trial, just bang?'

I nodded.

She gave me wide eyes. 'If they're trying to kill me, or someone else, I could pull the trigger, no problem, but you're saying that if they were handcuffed, chained down like a vampire in the morgue, you'd just kill them.'

'No, I'm saying I could legally.'

'Humans don't go dead at dawn. They'd be staring up at you, begging for their lives.'

'Yeah, just like vampires do if they're awake.'

'You really don't see a difference between taking human life and the undead, do you?'

'No,' I said.

'Did you see a difference once?'

'I believed sincerely that vampires were evil and I was saving the world by killing them, but that was a few years ago. I haven't believed that for a while.'

'If I start seeing vampires as people, I don't think I could keep killing them.'

'Then stay away from Anita's friends,' Edward said. 'You can't keep seeing them as monsters once you see them as people.'

Hatfield shook her head. 'I don't know.'

'Let's have the rest of this discussion outside, where it smells better,' Lisandro said.

'Wererats have one of the most sensitive noses in the animal kingdom,' I explained to Hatfield.

She looked at Lisandro. 'Wererat?' she asked.

'I know I'm too handsome to be a wererat – you were thinking werewolf, or wereleopard – but no, I'm just a great, big, giant rat.'

Hatfield fought her face, and finally lost and showed her disgust. She even shuddered.

'You afraid of rats?' he asked.

She gave a little nod.

He smiled, but it was more a snarl, a curl of lips that didn't match the handsomeness. 'Then you do not want to see me in animal form.'

'No,' she said in a small voice.

I hadn't thought that she might literally be phobic of rats. Snakes, spiders, I might have thought of, but not rats. Funny, how you get used to things and it just stops occurring to you that it might bother someone else.

We all trooped out onto the porch again. The view was refreshing, but there was still that smell of corpses. 'Is the fridge working?' I asked.

'I know what you mean,' Lisandro said. 'The smell shouldn't be this strong, but I checked, and the food is fine.'

'Then why does that little bit of flesh smell this bad?' I asked.

'It's almost as if there are more bodies we haven't found,' he said.

I looked at Edward. He said, 'There's a basement.' He pointed to the side of the deck. I went to look where he pointed, and there were stairs leading down to a door tucked up under the deck.

'I didn't see a door into the basement from the inside of the house,' I said.

'I didn't either,' Hatfield said.

I looked around at everyone. 'Anyone see a way down besides this outside door?'

They all shook their heads.

Edward walked back into the house, and we trailed him. He was standing in the back bedroom looking at the huge dresser. It towered up over the window, but the room was so small that it effectively blocked the entire corner of the room from view. He got one side and Nicky got the other. There was a shorter-than-average door in the wall.

'They weren't blocking the window. Someone else was blocking the door,' I said.

'Were they blocking something in, or out?' Hatfield said.

'Or were they just hiding the door from this end?' Nicky asked.

'Don't know,' I said.

'The smell is worse near the edge of the door,' Edward said.

'You can't usually find zombies just by the smell of the rot,' I said.

'Not usually.'

He and I looked at each other. 'It's either a hell of a lot of zombies, or more bodies,' I said.

He nodded. 'I have my flamethrower in the truck,' he said.

I smiled. 'Not yet; let's see what's down there first. If it's zombies you can barbecue it all.'

'We need crime scene techs up here to at least take more pictures than just a few with our phones. They need to collect evidence,' Hatfield said.

'Technically I can call it without doing anything else,' I said, 'but we can call in the techs after we find out what's down there.'

'Let's let someone know that we have more zombies, or more dead bodies here, before we confirm,' Edward said.

'You want to call for backup before we know if we need it?' I asked.

'If this turns into another hospital basement, backup might be good.'

I didn't know what to say; in all the years I'd known him I wasn't sure he'd ever said that before, which meant that maybe I owed Dev an apology. If it had bothered Edward, then it had been bad. That it hadn't bothered me more made me wonder about myself. Maybe it would hit me later, or maybe Edward needed more emotional backup than I could supply. I had my sweeties with me to cuddle, and say what you will, that helps.

'Okay, we call it in,' I said, and we did.

Edward made the call. He told them that we suspected there was something preternatural or just bad in the basement, and if anyone wanted more pictures of the crime scene than we'd taken with our phones, then they needed to send techs out now. When they suggested sending more cops to back us up, Edward didn't say no. He was mellowing.

'Do we wait?' I asked.

He shook his head. 'No.'

'If we're going in before backup arrives, then why call it in at all?' Hatfield asked.

'So they'll know where we are, just in case,' Edward said.

'Just in case what?' she asked.

'Just in case whatever is in the basement tries to eat us, or trap us, or in case the basement is all one great big trap,' I said.

'If we think it's a trap, then we should wait,' she said.

'Probably,' I said.

Edward turned on the flashlight mounted to his AR.

'But we're not going to wait, are we?' she asked.

'No,' he said.

'No,' I said.

'Why aren't we waiting again?' Hatfield asked.

'Because they're Death and the Executioner,' Seamus said.

'I thought they were Death and War,' Hatfield said.

'That, too,' Nicky said.

He seemed to think about it for a minute and then nodded. 'Maybe if we follow you around enough on cases, we'll get nifty nicknames,' he said.

'Like what?' Nicky asked.

'Minions,' Seamus said.

'What?' Lisandro asked.

'We're her minions, all of us are,' Seamus said, as if that made sense.

'War doesn't have minions,' I said.

'Yes, actually he does: strife, panic, anger, discord, to name a few.'

'Are we delaying until backup arrives?' Hatfield asked.

'I am,' Lisandro said. 'The basement smells bad enough from here.'

'Pussy,' Nicky said.

'Ratty, actually,' Lisandro said.

'Who's Mole then?' Nicky asked.

'Anita's shortest,' Lisandro said.

I was about to remark that they'd just made a *Wind in the Willows* joke, but Edward had had enough of games.

'Shut up,' Edward said. 'Anita, get the door while I cover it.'

'No,' Nicky and Lisandro said together.

I glared at them.

'Anita doesn't go first if we're here to be her bodyguards,' Lisandro said.

'I'm on the job,' I said.

'So are we,' Lisandro said, and eased past me toward the door.

I moved into his way.

'Anita, you can let me help Ted through that door, or we can argue about it until the other cops arrive, your choice.'

I looked at Seamus. 'You'd let me go first.'

'Yes.'

'Why?' Nicky asked him.

'Because there can be nothing down there that is scarier than she is.'

'Thanks for the vote of confidence, I think,' I said.

'You have destroyed the greatest vampires to walk the face of the earth, Anita Blake; what could possibly be in this small basement that would compare to the prey you have already eaten?'

Again, I didn't know what to say to that, so I let it go, but I also let Lisandro open the door for Edward. I wasn't as scary as Seamus thought, Lisandro was harder to hurt, and he wasn't letting me go first through the door, so unless we wanted to twiddle our thumbs for an hour . . . I let Lisandro put his shoulder up with Edward. I went next with Nicky, then Hatfield, and Seamus bringing up the rear. We had our marching order. We had our guns out and ready and were carefully not pointing them at anyone in our party. Lisandro opened the door, and the smell of rotting meat swept up and over us. Hatfield choked a little behind me. I started breathing shallow through my mouth, though that really didn't help as much as you wished it would. Lisandro tried the light switch, but the mouth of the basement stayed black and untouched.

'Why do the lights never work at times like this,' I said, softly.

The flashlight attached to Edward's rifle flared to life and trailed into the darkness like a shiny coin tossed into endless night. Okay, it wasn't that black, or that bad, was it? I realized that I hadn't liked the dark as well since I killed the Mother of All Darkness. She'd been the night itself made real, alive, and hungry. I'd destroyed her, but for the first time in my life I was afraid of the dark. It seemed like I should have been more afraid when she was still alive, didn't it?

'Stairs,' Edward said, quietly, to the unasked question. He saw stairs, and he went down them; Lisandro followed, making a face at the smell. I followed Lisandro, my own flashlight sweeping ahead of the barrel of my AR. There was nothing to see but bare walls and stairs going down, but the smell made me dread what was to come.

61

Trying to feel my way down the narrow, unfamiliar steps in boots made me wish for my jogging shoes. I didn't dare lower the rifle to shine my light on the steps, because that would have taken the barrel across Lisandro and Edward's bodies. You did not cross a loaded weapon over your team, especially not on narrow steps where tripping was a real possibility. Normally, with killer zombies on the loose, I'd have had my finger on the trigger ready to fire, but I'd weighed that extra second before I could fire against possibly shooting my friends and decided the danger of tripping on the stairs was higher than being eaten by a zombie, at least on the stairs.

The swing of my light showed glimpses of railing just ahead. Once I was surrounded by open railing I'd reassess the dangers; until then I'd keep my finger off the trigger.

The smell of decomposing flesh got stronger with every step down. I just hoped that there'd come a point where my nose would get used to it and it would just cancel itself out. I'd smelled rotting bodies before, but never this many, or maybe just nothing this big. It was a lot of meat going bad. It didn't have to be bodies. Maybe they had a meat locker that had lost power and we were smelling rotting cow and pig and . . . Part of me really hoped it was something like that; the other part of me hoped it was something horrible that would give us a clue to find the rogue master. If he was down here in the basement, even Lisandro with his superior rat nose would never smell such innocent things as a bloodsucker over the overpowering stench of rotting meat. I didn't think the rogue vamp was down here – most vampires are picky about odors – but it certainly would keep casual visitors away.

Hatfield cleared her throat sharply behind me. I prayed silently that she wouldn't throw up on me. Not just for the obvious reason, but because if she did I would so throw up, too. It could be a chain reaction sometimes, not often, but once one person lost it, sometimes it was harder for the rest of us to hold on, or hold in. My stomach rolled at the smell and the thought and Hatfield's nervous cough. I realized we hadn't eaten breakfast, and I was glad.

I heard Lisandro make a sharp hissing sound between his teeth, as if he had held in a louder noise. I wanted to ask what had startled him, but I was inches away from the banisters and seeing for myself. If it had been something dangerous, Edward would have said something. I trusted him to warn me, but I'd seen Lisandro tortured and he hadn't made a sound that sharp.

Edward and his rifle pointed to the left of the stairs, Lisandro took right, and as I stepped out of the sheltered area and into the open space of the next section of stairs I took left and knew that Nicky would know to take right. I had to trust that Hatfield and Seamus knew how to quarter a room. They both had the training, but until I see someone use that training I reserve judgment.

My flashlight slid over the darkness and I saw the first pile of bodies. They were stacked on top of each other and, except that these bodies were plump and rotting instead of thin and starving, it reminded me of the photos from the Nazi concentration camps. There they just stacked the bodies up because there were too many of them to stay ahead of even mass graves. There weren't as many bodies here as those thousands, but there were dozens. In the dark, coming upon them suddenly, it seemed like more.

Nicky made no sound of surprise as he hunched down the stairs behind me. Hatfield asked, 'Are they zombies?'

'No,' I said.

'How can you be sure?' she asked.

'They're bloating with gases. Zombies rot, but they don't make gas. Theory is, either moving around dissipates the gas, or something about being a zombie means they rot differently from regular dead bodies. No one's really sure, but zombies go thin and wear down; they don't swell and expand like real corpses.' I sounded so ordinary, like I was lecturing. Sometimes in the midst of horror you hold on to the ordinary, so I explained our job to Hatfield and it helped me stay calm.

'If they're not zombies, why are we still pointing guns at everything?' she asked.

'Because something put the bodies down here,' Edward said.

'Oh,' she said, and a glance back showed me her gun pointing out past Nicky's body. It was enough for me to know that she was taking the opposite side of the stairs behind Nicky. We split the room the same way, with me following Edward, and Nicky peeling off with Lisandro. I hadn't known for sure that he would follow protocol if it meant being farther away from me, but I guess he trusted Edward, or he trusted that he and Lisandro would be fast enough to protect me from one side of the small basement to another.

The six of us split the room like we'd been trained to, and we had our guns on as much of the space as possible without risking shooting one another. 'Zombies don't hoard food,' I said, softly.

'Ghouls will,' Edward said.

'I thought we decided this couldn't be ghouls,' Hatfield said from her part of the room.

'We did, but that was before we saw the bodies.'

'Is it food storage, or are they hiding the bodies?' Seamus asked.

'I don't know,' I said.

'I thought zombies would just eat everything, and ghouls would eat even the bones,' Hatfield said.

'Yep,' I said.

'The bodies are almost untouched,' she said.

'Yep,' I said.

'Then if this wasn't zombies, or ghouls, what, or who, put the bodies down here?'

'Don't know,' I said.

'Forrester?' she asked.

'I don't know either,' he said.

'Aren't the two of you supposed to know?' she said.

'I thought so,' I said.

'If this is food storage, then we could use it as bait,' Edward said.

'You mean like staking out a kill for a maneater?' I asked.

'Yes,' he said.

'And what if it's just a body dump?' Nicky asked.

'Then they may want to put more bodies down here,' I said.

'So either way we stake out the place and see who, or what, comes back,' Edward said.

'Not if they see the police here,' Lisandro said.

'He has a point,' I said.

I heard the distant wail of sirens.

'Too late,' Nicky said.

'Maybe,' I said, 'or maybe whatever is doing this won't know, because it's daylight. We clear everything out before nightfall and it still might work.'

Then power ran through my head and over my skin. I had a second to feel it wake, and then yelled, 'Vampire!'

'Where?' Hatfield called.

'Here,' said a voice that wasn't any of us.

62

There was a scream, and then Hatfield and Seamus fired at something I couldn't see. Even in the lightning flashes of their guns I couldn't see the vampire, but God, I could feel it like a pressured magic against my skin. Edward and I were moving, guns up, lights searching for what they'd seen to shoot. Where was it? Where the fuck was it? I could feel it all around in me in the dark, as if the air were turning into it. My chest tightened down, as if I didn't want to breathe it inside me.

I felt movement in the dark and knew before Lisandro yelled, 'Zombies!' They'd been scattered among the dead like spies. The vampire's power was animating them. He was a motherfucking necromancer, just like the Mother of All Darkness had been. Motherfucking son of a bitch!

I yelled, 'Retreat! Daylight, get to daylight!' Once we were out we could burn it all.

I retreated backward toward the stairs and hoped everyone would come with me, but they didn't. It was too late for a clean retreat. Hatfield screamed and fired again. I could see Seamus like dark on dark, wrestling with a zombie that had knocked her to the floor. Edward and I moved toward them, because they were closer to us. Nicky's and Lisandro's guns sounded like thunder as they fired into what looked like a moving mass of zombies.

I peeled off to the right for Nicky and Lisandro. I didn't have to tap Edward; we were aware of each other in combat the way you knew your partner on the dance floor. I did the shuffling, bent-legged walk that I'd learned with SWAT. My light showed a wall of zombies snarling and reaching. The snarling was the clue that these were flesh eaters;

regular zombies were a lot deader. Three of them were headless already. Lisandro was a quick study: take out the mouth and they can't bite, take the arms and they can't grapple, take the legs and they can't move. We weren't going to stay here long enough to do it all like we had in the hospital, but Nicky was showing him the combat math of a zombie apocalypse, and Lisandro was learning it.

The three of us worked back toward the stairs, shooting zombies as we moved. Their heads exploded nicely, but they still kept coming, relentless as only the dead can be. We backed up until we touched shoulders with Edward. He and Hatfield were still firing with their rifles. Seamus was down to a handgun; something was wrong with his right arm, but I didn't have time to see what. We formed a half-circle around the stairs and sent Seamus and Hatfield up first. Sending the wounded and the rookie up first made sense, but I didn't want to go next, and Lisandro and Nicky wouldn't go either.

Edward yelled, 'Anita, go!'

I cursed, but I went, and there was no way to help them shoot zombies once I was in the covered area of the stairs; I had to go up and trust that they'd come after me.

I heard Hatfield scream, 'Blake!'

Shit, what now? I thought, and ran up the last steps into the small bedroom. They weren't there, so I ran out into the living room beyond, AR to my shoulder scanning for what had made her scream. Hatfield knelt on the far side of Seamus with a bare pillow in one hand and its pillow slip in the other. Seamus lay in the middle of the floor beside the bentwood rocking chair. There was already a pool of blood expanding out from the nice hooked rug, spreading dark and thick across the scrubbed wooden floor. His arm was a bloody mess where the zombie had torn at it with that more-than-human strength and the all-too-human teeth.

'Tourniquet him,' I told Hatfield, and turned to go back to Edward and the others.

'He won't let me touch him.'

'A cut on her hand and my blood could bring her over,' Seamus said.

I'd totally forgotten that, my bad. 'He's right. Hatfield, cover their retreat.'

She handed me the pillow slip. I let the AR hang by its strap and took it as she went for the bedroom. I turned to the big man on the floor. His skin was dark enough that the blood didn't show as clearly, but the torn muscle and bone glistened surrounded by the darkness of his skin like some macabre art piece. So much of violence is both beautiful and horrible.

'Shapeshift; it will heal at least part of the damage,' I said.

'I dare not,' he said.

I didn't ask why he dared not; I'd stop the bleeding and then play twenty questions, so I knelt above his head, out of the pool of blood. I wrapped the pillow slip around his arm and started looking around for a tool to help fasten the tourniquet.

'You're faster than this. How did you let it hurt you this badly?' I asked.

'I don't know,' he said.

I got up and went to the rocking chair. It was the only thing I saw in the room that might do what we needed. I tore one of the smaller curls of wood out of place. It came away with a sharp crack. Edward and the others were still shooting in the other room. Until we burned the zombies, they'd keep coming. Zombies didn't like daylight, but it wouldn't stop them with food – us – this close.

I wrapped the piece of wood in the pillow slip and tightened it until the blood stopped spurting out. 'Hold it tight. I'll call for an ambulance.' I wiped my bloodstained hands on my pants and fished my phone out of the pocket it rode in.

Seamus held the tourniquet tight but said, 'Don't call.'

'You're not dying,' I said.

'I can feel him inside me. He's telling me to change form. He wants me to kill you. That's why I don't dare shift to heal the damage.'

I stared at him with the phone half-dialed in my hand. 'Who wants it?' I asked, but I knew.

'He does – the vampire. It was a zombie that bit me, but somehow it was him, Anita. Somehow the vampire was using the zombie's body just like the Traveller and the Dark Mother used vampires. He bit me, do you understand, Anita?'

'I understand,' I said, and put my phone back in its pocket.

'I am Harlequin, and I am bound to my master. It helps me fight the compulsion, but I do not know if I will win this battle.'

I drew in a deep breath and let it out slow. I didn't feel anything. I was numb, as if I'd been numb for a while and just hadn't known it.

'The compulsion is that strong?' I asked.

'It should not be. I am fully bonded to my master. I should be proof against all vampires except for my master. The only one who could tamper with such bonds was the Dark Mother, and she is gone.'

'Yeah,' I said.

'This master should not be this strong; no wonder Ares fell to him.'

'What do you want me to do?' I asked.

'If you kill me, then my master may die and never wake, but you cannot allow me to shift forms. If I do that, then you must kill me, because there is something in this power that wants me to kill things, not just you, but everything. He likes death, Anita, in all its forms.'

'Does the vampire have a name?' I asked.

'He does not tell me. I am an animal and he does not owe me his name,' Seamus said, and shuddered, his eyes fluttering closed.

'Is that your thought, or his?' I asked.

'Both.'

'You are not an animal,' I said, 'and he does owe you his name.'

Seamus smiled at me. 'I like your modern ideals, but it is too late for me to enjoy them.'

'No,' I said. I touched his arm, bare skin to bare skin, and a flash of warmth passed between us. I could feel his beast, could see it behind my eyes where dreams show themselves. The werehyena looked up at me, and I felt something stir inside me that was new. I had a new beast.

Seamus's brown hyena eyes stared up at me. 'You cannot be one of us.'

'A bullet went through Ares' body and into mine. I didn't think it would be enough.'

'His call is softer now,' Seamus said.

'Just from my touching your arm?' I asked.

'Yes.'

I wanted to call out to Edward, because I wanted someone to be able to shoot Seamus if it needed doing, but I wanted to keep touching him, and if he went apeshit I didn't want to be this close to him while I was trying to shoot him. Out of reach would be really good. But I didn't want to distract Edward in case he needed all his concentration to stay away from the zombies that were probably trying to climb up the stairs and into the bedroom. I did the only thing could; I kept my left hand on his arm and drew the Browning with my right.

Seamus looked at the gun and then back at my face. 'Shoot me if you have to.'

I just nodded. I had every intention of it. I'd failed Ares by not shooting him sooner. I wouldn't fail again, not like that.

Someone called out, 'Police, hello in the house!'

I called back, 'Living room!'

Deputy Al walked in from the kitchen. The smile on his face changed when he saw us. 'What happened?'

'Zombies in the basement,' I said. More shots sounded, as if to make the point.

He drew his sidearm. He looked in the direction of the shots and then back to us. 'He's another shifter, isn't he?'

'Yeah,' I said.

He started to point the gun in Seamus's direction. Sirens sounded in the distance. The rest of the backup was finally here. Al lowered his gun and looked uncomfortable, bordering on embarrassed. Until he'd made that movement toward Seamus, I might have asked him to help me guard the shapeshifter, but now . . . I wasn't sure Al wouldn't be a little trigger happy. I couldn't really blame him, because I knew he'd seen the damage that Ares had done, but that wasn't Seamus's fault, and yet . . . if I had to this time I would shoot him. I would not let another of my guards hurt anyone else. I couldn't. The cynical part of me thought, *Well, at least I'm not as attached to this one*. I hated that I thought it, but Ares had been my friend; I barely knew Seamus.

Seamus suddenly grabbed my left arm, too tight, his eyes flared wide. 'He doesn't want to burn.'

Edward and the others came running toward us, and only then did I smell the burning flesh. Nicky and Lisandro caught one arm and the opposite leg of Seamus as they moved through, lifted him, got him balanced, and kept going for the door. I followed them, because when the people blowing shit up start running, you try to keep up, just a rule.

Edward unlocked the door from this side and they carried Seamus through. Hatfield went after them. Edward said, 'Outside, now.' He followed his own instructions and I ran to comply. Al didn't ask questions, he just ran with me. The two of us were on the grass of the front yard when the first explosion rocked the world and staggered us. I kept moving away from the house, and when he got his footing Al followed.

The second explosion was even bigger and made us all cower from the blast wave and the rush of heat.

'What the hell did you do?' Al asked.

'They had extra propane tanks in the basement. One of the grenades must have hit them.' He made it sound like an accident.

I looked at him, but his face was mild and unreadable. He held out a hand to wave at our backup with their lights and sirens. I wondered if they'd stop a safe distance back or drive up to the house. Another explosion made the ground shiver and the air smack into us like a giant hand. Al fell to the ground on all fours.

'You okay?' I asked.

He nodded.

A third explosion rained down burning bits and pieces.

'How many tanks were down there?' I asked.

'Enough,' he said.

Then Nicky yelled, 'Anita!'

Seamus was beginning to writhe on the ground. I still had the Browning naked in my hand. Damn it, the vampire should have been blown up, dead, and when he died Seamus should have been free. Which meant the vampire wasn't dead. Fuck!

'The vampire isn't dead,' I said, and went to put my hand on Seamus. Either I'd help him control his beast until the vampire burned up, or I'd shoot him before he could change. Either way, my place was beside Seamus. Edward had his rifle up and was watching the house. If anything crawled out, he'd shoot it. Enough of the house had blown up that we could see if anything went out the back now, but the vampire could have run out that back basement door before the biggest explosion. Shit, if we'd waited for backup they could have had men back there to shoot him as he ran.

Seamus cried out. Nicky and Lisandro were holding him down, pinning him to the ground. I jogged the last few yards and fell to my knees beside them. I laid my hand on his arm again. His skin was hot to the touch, and his beast snarled up at me. It wanted to come out and play. My new beast growled up at me, or maybe at him.

'If he shifts we have to kill him,' I said.

Nicky said, 'Understood.'

Lisandro said, 'There's got to be another way.'

Seamus spoke through gritted teeth. 'She's right.'

'You smell like hyena,' Lisandro said, 'but you don't carry that beast.'

'I do now.'

'Let him smell your skin,' Nicky said.

I had to stop touching his arm to put my arm in front of his face. His eyes rolled back into his head, and his energy calmed. When he opened his eyes they were peaceful, he was in there again.

'He's not trying to control me anymore.'

'Why not?' I asked.

'I don't know. It's like he's gone. I would have said dead, but I don't think that's it.'

'Gone is good enough,' I said.

Al said, 'You've set a fire over in the trees there. It's been a dry year; we need to put that out.' He looked tired, as if something about the last few minutes had taken a lot out of him.

'You okay?' Hatfield asked.

'I knew the couple who lived here. I don't want to tell their kids in town that their folks got eaten alive.'

'Tell them they were murdered,' I said.

'The families always ask how, always, as if that will make them feel better.' Al shook his head. 'Some truths don't make you feel better. Some truths just hurt more.'

No one argued with him; we'd all been around violence and death too long to argue with something that true.

63

If Seamus hadn't been injured we'd have had to stay at the scene longer, but they let us take him to get patched up. I wasn't risking him in the ambulance; it was too close to the scenario with Ares in the chopper. No one argued with us. I think they thought the same thing. The EMTs put a dressing on his wound to keep him from bleeding all over the car and then let us go. We implied, though didn't state, that we were taking him to the hospital; we didn't. I called Claudia from the car and had some of the guards waiting to help take him upstairs. They'd help him shift form and if he went apeshit they'd kill him. If he was calm, they'd let him heal in animal form for a few hours.

We dropped Hatfield at the station for her to pick up her own car and drive home to clean up. The rest of us went to our rooms to shower with the industrial-strength cleaner that Edward and I had both started carrying in our go bags. It smelled like bad fake orange, but it was better than smelling like corpses. It was weird that zombies didn't smell as bad as plain dead people, but they almost never did. Metaphysics was weird that way.

Edward went to his room across the hall from Nicky and me. Lisandro had a room farther down the hall. The guards on hall duty informed me that Nathaniel was asleep in the room. I asked, 'And Micah?' but was told no, just Nathaniel. I had a moment to wonder how Micah and his family were doing and why Nathaniel wasn't plastered to his side, but then I wasn't plastered to Micah's side either and I was his 'fiancée.' I opened the door with his key card and tried to be as quiet as possible. The room was dark, the blackout curtains pulled except for that rim of sunlight. If they hadn't told me Nathaniel was in the bed, at first glance it would have looked like just a pile of covers. When he slept alone he cuddled down like he was making a nest. It was always impressive how invisible he could be in a bed by himself.

Nicky and I threaded our way through all the coffins and past the bed. I might have kissed him if I hadn't smelled like rotting corpse. I did not want the smell on the sheets. Nathaniel was a heavy sleeper, but to sleep through both the noise and the smell meant he was exhausted. I tried to remember if he and Micah had slept at all in the last twenty-four hours and couldn't remember, which probably meant, no.

Someone had tidied the bathroom since the last shower that Nicky and I had taken. We had fresh towels, but no soap or shampoo that the hotel had would take care of this smell. I got the bottle of the same all-around body cleanser that they used in morgues, which was actually where I'd first used it on my hands. We'd use Febreze on the body armor vests and bag the clothes and talk to the hotel about laundry. They wouldn't be happy with us if we let them put the clothes in with any other guest laundry. It was definitely a separate load for all five of our clothes. Of course, Seamus had bled all over his, so they might be a loss anyway.

Nicky and I made two separate piles of our weapons, then stripped. Much like last time, there was no teasing or foreplay, it was just strip as quickly as possible. He got the water as hot as we could stand it and then we did a quick cleanup with the heavy-duty orange-smelling stuff top to bottom. It was hell on my hair, but it was about the only thing that worked for certain occasions. When we both smelled like overdone orange something, I got the conditioners for my hair, because otherwise it would do its best imitation of a white-girl Afro, which was so not a good look for me. Nicky got his own shampoo and conditioner. His straight hair would be more forgiving except for the extreme triangle-cut one-sided bangs; it meant that he had to baby his hair more than he would have otherwise. If he didn't, the bangs didn't lie right over his eye.

We stood in the shower waiting for the conditioner to sit for a minute or two, and Nicky grinned at me.

'What?' I asked.

'Do we have to go back and play detective after we get cleaned up?'

'Yeah, I need to make sure they don't vacate my warrant because they think the big bad vampire got burned up.'

'The body he was using probably did get fried,' Nicky said.

'Maybe, but we couldn't see the back door from the basement until after the house blew up. He was in a zombie body; he could move in daylight without frying in the light.'

'Shouldn't he have not been able to do that, take over a zombie body, I mean?'

'No, he shouldn't have,' I said.

He touched my face, turned me to look up at him. 'I didn't mean to make you look all serious.'

'It's a first for me, Nicky. This vampire is breaking all the rules.'

'When you and Edward don't know what's going on, it's bad, isn't it?'

I nodded. 'Yeah, it's bad.'

'So no time for more sex,' he said.

I smiled, then laughed. 'You aren't tired yet?'

'I'm a werelion, Anita. Natural lions can fuck every fifteen to thirty minutes for days.'

'Yeah, for about ten seconds at a shot. Your stamina is much greater, and the lions do nothing but sleep and fuck for days. We've been busier than that.'

He laughed. 'I love that you research the animal side of us.'

'Hey, biology degree; once I thought I'd be a field biologist specializing in preternatural creatures. Some of the stuff I knew going in, but yeah, I research my guys, um, people.'

'It still weirds you out that Jade is a girl.'

I shrugged. 'Yeah, but when I'm around her I like her; I just never saw myself with a girlfriend.'

'The *ardeur* overwhelms you as much as your people sometimes,' he said.

'Yeah, let's get the conditioner out and get changed.'

He suddenly wrapped me in his arms. 'I'm sorry I keep bringing up things that take your smile away.'

I hugged him back, and even naked in the shower it was more comfort than anything else. It felt incredibly good to simply hold him and be held as close in return. He laid his cheek on top of my head, and I snuggled in against him. That was enough to make his body begin to respond.

I laughed. 'We need to get the conditioner out, remember.'

'Anything you say,' and he backed us into the water still holding each other. It made me laugh, and that may have been his main goal all along. We finished our hair and then used Febreze on all the clothes, even the ones that were going to be laundered. It helped. Febreze was actually invented for stuff like body armor that got really smelly but couldn't be traditionally cleaned.

The big hotel towel was so long it covered me from armpits to mid-calves. Nicky just dried off and didn't bother with wrapping himself in the towel. Micah was the most body-modest wereanimal I'd ever met, and he wasn't that modest. Nicky was like most of them, totally comfortable nude. I was more comfortable than I'd ever been, but I still covered up more than I didn't.

I looked down at the weapons. Without the MOLLE straps to hold all the weapons, there was really no way to carry them all except piled in my arms like firewood, which made them useless as actual weapons, so I left most of them in the bathroom and just kept my Browning. Yes, I was in a room with Nicky, surrounded by our bodyguards, but there was still a window and this vampire had broken every rule so far. Sometimes I felt paranoid, sometimes I just felt careful.

Nicky slung his AR over one shoulder on its tactical strap. I felt less paranoid, and it was an interesting look with him buck naked. It made me smile.

'What?' he asked.

'I was feeling paranoid until I saw you were toting your AR.'

'You said it yourself: This vampire is breaking all the rules. I like to be prepared.'

I started to ask if he'd ever been a Boy Scout, but then realized I'd never been one and I liked to be prepared, too.

Nicky made me let him open the bathroom door and check the room. 'There are guards in the hallway,' I said.

'There's still a window,' he said.

Since I'd already thought the same thing it was hard to bitch about it, so I didn't.

He opened the door quietly, and when he'd looked around the room enough he moved to one side and held the door for me as if we were in public and he was on guard. I walked out into the hush of the room, and the pile of covers moved on the bed.

Nathaniel's voice came thick with sleep. 'Hey, was it as bad as it smelled?'

'Almost,' Nicky said.

'Hey, Nicky,' Nathaniel said.

'Hey,' he said with a smile.

I smiled; I couldn't help it and went to the bed, where I still couldn't see any of Nathaniel, just his voice from the nest of covers. I started to sit down on the edge of the bed, and he wiggled enough to make room. One arm came out of the covers first, and then his face peered up at me. He blinked at me, his face haloed by the sheets; it made him look younger than he was, like a glimpse into some little boy who must still be in there somewhere. He leaned upward, the covers spilling down to reveal the muscled shoulders and upper chest, the illusion of childhood vanished as the very adult body sat up to kiss me.

He was unbelievably warm straight from his nest of blankets as he stretched to kiss me, his hand on the side of my face, tracing the edge of my wet hair. He murmured as he pulled back from the kiss, 'Come take a nap with me.'

'Is this the first sleep you've had in what, twenty-four hours?' I asked.

'Yes,' he said, and wrapped his arms around me, trying to drag me under the covers.

I moved so he couldn't do it, and he lay back against the bed, pouting at me. His hair in its thick braid curled around him like an auburn-haired Rapunzel. He kept my hand. 'Come to bed.'

'I have to get dressed and go be a cop,' I said. 'We only came back to shower and change.'

Nicky was already rummaging in his own luggage, getting clothes.

'You can both come take a nap,' he said.

'No, we have to catch bad guys,' I said.

'I have to follow her around and pretend I'm not the bad guy,' Nicky said.

'Then you have to eat solid food, before you go back to work,' Nathaniel said.

'There's no time for food,' I said.

He sat up enough so that the covers pooled into his lap. 'Make time, Anita; the reason I had to leave Micah at the hospital is that you're draining energy from me. Dev started getting tired, too. You can't ignore your physical body without affecting all of your animals to call, and Damian your vampire servant.'

'I'm sorry, you're right. How is Micah holding up?'

'He won't let himself cry. He's just holding it inside. He holds my hand, lets me hold him, but he's trying to be strong for his family and me. Sometimes it's hard to take care of the two of you.'

'I'm sorry we're difficult,' I said, 'and doubly sorry I'm a pain in the ass.'

'Want me to order room service?' Nicky asked.

'Go tell Edward we're getting food and see if he wants anything.'

'Have one of the other guards order the food and have it delivered to the conference room on this floor,' Nathaniel said.

'Conference room?' I said.

'Yeah, it's got this huge oval table almost big enough for all of us to eat at once.'

'How did you have time to see the conference room?' I asked.

'I knew you hadn't eaten, so I asked where we could have food set out.'

'Why didn't Micah come back with you?' I asked.

'He won't leave the hospital.'

I held Nathaniel's hand. 'I'm so sorry I had to leave you and Micah to deal with it all.'

'You saved Henry; that's what Micah wanted you to do.'

I nodded.

Nicky pulled on jeans. 'What do you want for food?'

'Get protein,' Nathaniel said.

'I always get protein,' I said.

He smiled. 'That's true. I'm the salad eater.'

'You take your clothes off for a living, you have to watch your girlish figure,' I said, and kissed him again.

'Food order,' Nicky said.

I ordered a burger, fries, and a Coke. Nathaniel surprised the hell out of me by ordering the same thing, except for the Coke. 'I don't have to watch my figure for a day or two, and I need the protein,' he said.

'I drain that much energy from you?' I asked, and now I was worried. He almost never ate a burger; lean steaks, but not hamburger.

'Not yet, but you should feed the *ardeur* before you go back to work.'

'If I'm already draining energy from you, I think feeding the *ardeur* would be bad.'

'Feed on Nicky, have sex with both of us.'

'I like the way he thinks,' Nicky said from the door.

'I thought you would,' Nathaniel said with a grin.

'It's a fancy hotel and we have the whole floor; they'll be fast on the food service. Thirty minutes tops,' Nicky said.

'Then you should write down what we all want for food, hand it to someone, and get into bed,' Nathaniel said.

Nicky grinned at him, then got the bedside pad of paper and wrote down our orders and his. Then he strode to the door with the AR still on his shoulder. He left the door slightly ajar. I heard him knock on Edward's door. There was a murmur of voices, and then Nicky was back in our room, closing the door firmly behind him.

'Who's ordering the food?' I asked.

'Edward is,' he said, and walked around to the far side of the bed, the one closest to the window. He laid the AR on the floor.

'That was really quick. What did you tell him?' I asked.

'That we were going to have sex and to text you when the food arrives.' He unfastened his jeans and started peeling them down his hips, a little more carefully around the front, because his body was already partially erect, anticipating the sex.

I wanted to say, *You did not just tell Edward that*, but I knew Nicky had. It was Nicky; he didn't see anything wrong with being honest. Nothing much embarrassed him so he didn't always understand it might embarrass someone else, or maybe he didn't care.

Nathaniel put my hand with the gun still in it on the bedside table. 'We're not that dangerous. I don't think you need to be armed.'

I laid the gun on the table.

'I am that dangerous, just not to you,' Nicky said, as he pulled the covers out from the tangle Nathaniel had made of them.

Nathaniel raised up the covers, like an invitation. 'You don't need the towel either.'

I dropped the towel to the floor and crawled into the warm nest of the covers and Nathaniel's body. 'You sure you don't need to sleep more than you need sex?'

'Sex energizes me; you should know that by now.'

Nicky loomed over both of us, propped up on one shoulder. 'I vote you as an honorary lion.'

'High praise,' Nathaniel said.

Nicky nodded hard enough that his bangs swung back and forth with the movement. 'It *is* high praise; now let's fuck.'

Nathaniel and I both laughed, high and delighted. 'You sweet-talking bastard, you,' Nathaniel said.

'Thirty minutes, or less, tick-tock,' Nicky said.

'Don't get spoiled by quickies,' I said.

'Never,' Nathaniel said, and rolled me over his body so I was in the middle. I liked being in the middle.

64

Nathaniel kissed me loving and long under the warm nest of the covers, and then he moved gently back from me and Nicky kissed me. He kissed me like he had in the shower, a slow caress of lips, and his hand playing on the front of my throat like he was petting me with a hand that was almost big enough to encircle my entire throat. Nathaniel laid a gentle kiss on my upper chest, as Nicky continued to kiss me. Nathaniel kissed me again, a little lower, so that he touched the upper mound of my breast. Nicky's mouth pressed more eagerly on mine, and I opened my mouth to him, arching my neck against his hand. Nicky squeezed his hand around my neck, just a little. It made me arch into his hand and kiss him harder.

He wrapped that big hand around the front of my neck and squeezed hard enough for me to make little protesting noises as we kissed, my body arching against the bed. He kissed me as if he would crawl in through my mouth, all tongue and teeth and eager fierceness.

Nathaniel licked my nipple, and then suddenly he was sucking me hard and fast with an edge of teeth. It made my spine arch, my body writhe, and me scream my pleasure into Nicky's kiss.

Nicky's hand clamped down on my throat so hard and sudden that there were no more eager noises, because I had no air to make them with. Nathaniel bit harder at my breast, sinking his teeth into the mound of it, so hard and sudden that I would have screamed for him, but I couldn't make a sound. Nicky kissed me deeper, forcing my mouth open so wide it almost hurt, as if he were trying to reach things with his tongue that you were never supposed to touch. I writhed for them both, and then my body hit that moment where it began to panic for lack of air.

I fought the panic as long as I could, because I liked the feel of his hand so strong, so dangerous around my neck. The force of his kiss and Nathaniel's teeth biting down on my breast were all amazing, but in the end I had to tap out, literally.

Nicky eased his hand and drew back from the kiss, so that I could draw my breath in a long wheezing gasp. Nathaniel raised his mouth from my breast. Nicky stared down into my eyes and said, 'Are you having fun?'

I managed to gasp, 'Yes.'

He grinned, showing a fierce flash of teeth. 'Good, because so am I.' He let me have two good deep breaths and then he squeezed my throat shut again. Nathaniel reached across my body and cupped my other breast in his hand. Nicky moved so that his body acted like a prop to give Nathaniel more room. He bent over my breast. Nicky eased his grip enough for me to catch a few shallow breaths, and then when Nathaniel had sucked my breast down, as if he meant to deep-throat it, Nicky squeezed his hand tight and cut off my air again. Nathaniel bit down and the feel of his teeth in my flesh, as Nicky held my throat tight and kissed me deep and hard, made me writhe on the bed, my hands grabbing at the sheets, knotting them under me. Nathaniel bit down hard and harder, a steady, growing pressure until it was just this side of too much, and my body began to scream for oxygen. My feet began to struggle and push against the bed, I couldn't seem to help it. I tapped out, hand against Nicky's arm, and he eased his hold, so that my breath came in a near-sobbing gasp for air.

Nathaniel rose up from my breast. I tried to focus on him but couldn't make my eyes work quite right. They kept fluttering back into my head. Nicky gave a low chuckle. 'I think she liked that.'

I felt Nathaniel move up higher on the other side of me so he could look down into my face, too. I could almost focus on him as he grinned down at me. 'I think you're right,' he said, and he laughed, too.

I heard my text tone go off. I tried to say, *Don't answer it*, but couldn't remember how to form out loud words. It was like the afterglow to an orgasm.

Nathaniel reached for my phone from the bedside table. 'Food will take at least forty-five minutes; apparently there's a banquet.'

'More time, awesome,' Nicky said; his voice was a deeper bass with an edge of growl to it. Not werelion growl, but just that deep, dominant rumble that some men get when the sex is rough, or just like they want it.

Nathaniel bent over my breast and licked, very delicately, along the bite marks he'd left. It was an exquisite pain, almost pleasure and almost not, as if my body couldn't decide which it would be.

I whispered, 'Oh, my God.'

'If we had a gag, I'd use it.'

'Anita doesn't like gags,' Nathaniel said, and sounded a little sad.

I managed to say, 'Would try it.'

Nathaniel came back up where I could see his face. I was able to focus on him now, though the look on his face was one I hadn't seen before. 'If you offered because you didn't think we had any, you should know that I packed more than just the collar and leash.'

It took me a minute to realize what he meant. 'You packed one.'

'I packed two,' he said.

'Even though you knew we probably wouldn't get to use them,' I said.

'High stress makes me want more bondage; even having some toys with me makes me feel better, and I figured this would be a high-stress trip.'

They were both propped up on one elbow looking down at me. 'Will you wear a gag for us?'

Looking up at them, I had a moment of doubt. I didn't believe they'd hurt me for real – if I did, I wouldn't have sex with them – but it was the pretend, the almost threat, that made some kinds of bondage work. Either you were titillated by the idea, or it couldn't be explained to you. I was titillated, and a little nervous. Nathaniel was right, I didn't like gags; they were uncomfortable and I didn't find it an attractive look. I had tried one on once, but I'd just put it in without any bondage happening, and without some other fun and games, I did not like them, but Nathaniel loved having one during certain kinds of bondage. I thought it was a ruin of a good and useful mouth, but it had seemed like a better idea with the edge of teeth and hands.

'It seemed like a better idea with your hand around my throat and Nathaniel's mouth on my breast.'

'We can do that,' Nicky said.

'Totally,' Nathaniel said.

So we did.

65

Nathaniel requested an addition. He wanted my hands tied. I said, 'But with my hands tied and the gag it takes away my *no*, my safeword.'

'That would be the idea,' he said.

I debated, but it was something that Nathaniel had wanted for a long time, and with Nicky to partner him it seemed like a better idea. I totally and completely wouldn't have done it if it had been Nathaniel and Asher. He was a true sadist and a serious power tripper; I would never willingly put myself in a position with Asher to not be able to say *stop*. But Nicky, I trusted him more, so . . .

I sat on the bed between them, Nicky's hand squeezing the breath from my throat, controlling me with all that strength, while Nathaniel fitted the gag, forcing my mouth wide and wider like Nicky's kiss had done, so that the gag was like a continuation of the kiss. By the time Nathaniel had the gag fitted and tied behind my head, my body needed to breathe again and I was fighting the panic. I tapped out. Nicky released, and I found out that I could breathe both around the ball gag and through my nose.

Nathaniel came back around where he could see my face. 'Is it okay?'

I nodded.

He smiled and kissed my forehead. Then he picked up one of the straps that he and Nicky had threaded under the mattress earlier. It had a black nylon cuff on it that closed with Velcro on the end of it. The moment I'd seen the Velcro cuffs I'd known he brought them for me, not for him, because I liked the Velcro. I could, if I had to, get out of them, but up to that point they were secure and gave the illusion of me being trapped, but it was an illusion. Nathaniel liked leather cuffs, or handcuffs, because he liked more than just the illusion of being trapped.

To my questioning look he'd said, 'You like to be tied up when you're under stress, too.'

To that I hadn't known what to say, so I wisely let it go.

I lay down on the bed with Nathaniel on one side and Nicky on the other. Nathaniel fastened the first cuff securely around my wrist. My wrists were tiny enough that we actually had trouble finding handcuffs that fit me, but the Velcro went down nice and snug. My arms were out to the side, not directly overhead. I'd discovered that my shoulders didn't like being tied overhead for long, at all.

Nicky fastened the second cuff in place, though he had to take it down in size twice. He'd never tied me up before.

Nathaniel moved so he could look deeply into my eyes and said, 'Comfortable?'

I pulled on the cuffs, because I liked to struggle and often the fighting against the ropes, or whatever, was what caused real scrapes and bruising. I nodded.

He smiled, and it was a good, warm, happy smile.

Nicky was already settling down on the other side of me. Nathaniel mirrored him. My breasts already had red circles of Nathaniel's teeth in them, but as the two men grinned at each other and both moved their mouths down to my breasts, I was betting I was about to get fresh marks.

They started by sucking my nipples hard enough that I writhed and made small, happy protesting noises through the gag. Then they both wrapped their hand around the softness of my breasts, mounding them up so they could a better mouthful, and then as if they'd practiced it they put as much of my breast into their mouths as they could and bit down. I screamed through the gag, because it wasn't the gradual buildup that Nathaniel had done, but a zero to all-out. If I could have safe-worded, I would have, but then Nicky growled with my breast still deep in his mouth so that the sound vibrated around my breast. I looked down to find that his eyes had slid to lion amber, and there was that thrill of fear in me. I trusted him implicitly, but . . . but . . . that was the game.

Nathaniel more purred than growled, but the sound vibrated against my breast as well. His eyes were still lavender and human, but the look in them was not my submissive boy. A mix of personalities in the dungeon can change things, and I realized that something about Nicky brought out a more dominant side of Nathaniel.

They growled with my breasts in their mouths, teeth eased a bit, and then they both bit down so hard and sudden that I screamed, and even through the gag it held pain.

They both stopped and drew back. Nicky traced the edge of his bite marks where they went below the earlier ones that Nathaniel had made. 'I got a little blood on this side. Mmmm . . .' It wasn't much blood, just tiny red droplets filling in the indentations of his teeth, but he leaned over and licked the wound, and even that hurt.

I made protesting noises.

'No fair,' Nathaniel said. 'I didn't get to taste any blood. I was good.'

'I'll share, or you can make your own.'

Nathaniel looked up at me with a positively evil smile, and then slipped his mouth back over my breast. I was already making protest noises when he bit me. Hard enough that I screamed for real even through the gag.

He drew back to survey his handiwork. 'Now I have blood,' he said, happily. He leaned down and started licking the tiny red droplets on his side. Nicky bent to the wound he'd made and they both lapped and sucked at the blood. It had hurt for them to make the tiny wounds, but the sensation of them licking the wounds wasn't pain; it switched over to a painful pleasure, so that I made small noises through the gag that were halfway between protest and yummy noises.

Nathaniel looked up and asked, 'Was that too hard a bite?'

I nodded, yes, it was too hard.

'Now you've spoiled it,' Nicky said. 'If you hadn't asked we could have done it again.'

'We have to untie her sometime and I don't want her really mad at us.'

'Good point.'

Nathaniel moved lower on the bed.

'What are you planning to do?' Nicky asked.

'We're going to run out of time and I want Anita to enjoy the first time we use the gag on her, so I was thinking oral sex and then intercourse.'

'Sounds good, expect I want to do breath play while you eat her out.'

'She can't tap out now. It's a lot more dangerous this way,' Nathaniel said.

Nicky moved up the bed so he was looking directly into my face. 'Do you trust me to do this?'

I studied his face. His eye was human blue again. He seemed calm, steady. I did trust him. I finally nodded.

He rewarded me with a wonderful smile. 'You get started. I'll wait until she's close.'

'Hand me a pillow,' Nathaniel said.

Nicky handed him one and Nathaniel used it to prop me up just enough so that it was easier on the neck, and then he settled between my legs. I gazed down my body to see him give that evil smile again, before he began to lick delicately between my legs. He licked around the edges of me and then did a quick lick right down the middle that made me squirm, and then he settled down to business and licked and rolled that one sweet spot, burying his face deep against me, so he could trace and lick around every edge and crease of me. The warmth began to build inside me. My breathing sped up.

Nicky spoke low to me. 'He really is good at eating pussy.' He caressed my neck, gently, and then he settled his big hand around me, firm and tight, and as the warm pleasure began to build between my legs from Nathaniel's mouth, Nicky squeezed. He squeezed harder and more sudden so that I went from breathing to not, like a switch clicked over.

He stared down into my face while he choked me and Nathaniel ate me out. 'I love how dark your face is getting,' Nicky whispered.

The pleasured weight between my legs built, but I couldn't breathe and my body had trouble concentrating on both. Some people say that suffocation while you orgasm is a high, but to me it was already a distraction so that where I would have tipped over the edge, I stayed on the verge while my body fought not to panic. Nicky eased his grip, studying my face. I took a gasping breath, mostly through my nose.

'It's actually keeping you from orgasming, isn't it?' he asked.

I nodded.

'I want you to orgasm, so we can fuck you and you can feed on me, but I also want to choke you again.'

Nathaniel licked me deep and quick and that building weight of warm spilled over to pleasure. I screamed my orgasm through the gag, grinding myself against Nathaniel's mouth, riding the orgasm as he kept sucking me, bringing me in waves so that I wasn't sure it was just one, or a dozen. When he'd reduced me to an eye-fluttering, boneless, happy, floating afterglow, Nicky whispered against my cheek, 'Are you ready?'

I tried to think, *Ready for what?* Then I felt his hand at my throat, and even that couldn't make me control my fluttering eyelids enough to see his face. He wrapped that big hand around me and then squeezed. The choking was somehow intermingled with the orgasm's twitching pleasurable afterglow, so that my body didn't fight for air, there was no panic to think through, it was all one flowing piece of sensation.

I felt Nathaniel move the pillow and then felt him hard and ready as he pushed against my opening and then slid inside. The feel of him inside me after the oral sex, with Nicky still choking me, was amazing, but it was like my body couldn't concentrate on both at the same time.

Nicky let go of my throat, and I breathed in deep, almost like a sigh. Nathaniel found his rhythm and began to slide gently in and out of me. He had his eyes closed, head slightly to the side the way he did sometimes when he was trying to last and having to fight his body to do it. He found that spot just inside the opening and caressed himself over it again and again and again, until he brought me screaming, writhing, and spasming underneath him. He made a sound that was almost a cry of his own, his body shuddered, and then with one last thrust I felt him go inside me. It made me cry out again.

He pulled himself out of me and that made us both writhe again. He rolled over to one side of me and gasped, 'Oh, my God.'

Nicky said, 'My turn,' and then he moved between my legs, and even with Nathaniel having done the prep work he still had to push his way inside. 'She always stays so tight.'

'Not always,' Nathaniel said, 'but most of the time.'

Nicky shoved his way inside, and then he leaned over me so that I was staring directly into his face. 'I know you like rough sex. I pounded into you in the shower earlier, but I like knowing that I'm about to pound the fuck out of you and you can't say no, and you can't tell me be gentle. I know you wouldn't tell me that anyway, but I really like that you can't tell me to stop.' And then he did what he said, and started to pound himself in and out of me so that the sound of our flesh hitting together sounded almost like he was spanking me, but faster and harder than any hand. He used the strength of himself, the length, the width, all of himself, grabbing my hips, and holding my ass up at an angle so he could be up on his knees while he pounded himself into me as hard and fast as he could. I was almost, almost there, when he said, 'Can you please choke her one last time while I fuck her. I don't trust me doing it with the gag and the ropes.'

Nathaniel crawled up beside my shoulders and looked down at me. 'Yes?'

I nodded.

He put his much smaller hand around the front of my throat and squeezed. Nicky went back to pounding himself in and out of me so hard and fast that I couldn't keep track. 'Tighter,' he said. 'Make her face change colors.'

Nathaniel squeezed tighter, and that otherworldly strength was there. His hand was smaller, but he squeezed and I felt the blood rushing into my face.

'Hold her up,' Nicky said, and he lost his rhythm for a moment.

Nathaniel used his other hand in my hair to raise my face up so Nicky could watch. That seemed to satisfy him, because he found his rhythm again, hard and fast and deep, and he changed just enough angle so it was deeper, and it threw me over the edge into orgasm while Nathaniel's hands were still on me. I couldn't cry out my orgasm, but my body spasmed for me, and Nicky cried out, as he went inside me.

Nathaniel let go of me and eased me back against the pillows.

Nicky was above me, staring into my face, with his body still buried as deeply as it could go inside me. My eyes were fluttering back and forth so I couldn't focus as much as I wanted, but there was an eager, dark happiness to Nicky's face. I think he was watching the color change in my face.

'I love that you trust me this much,' he whispered.

The gag kept me from saying it back to him, but I did trust him that much, I really did.

66

Real food was had. We left Nathaniel back under the covers to sleep. Edward and I decided to divide and conquer. He would go talk to the local PD and see what they'd learned from the crime scenes and freshly discovered bodies. I'd go to the hospital and question Little Henry and see Micah. Nicky came with me, but Claudia kept Lisandro with her, so that when dark fell he could help manage the Harlequin vampires. They had a poor opinion of shapeshifters in general and had a hard time understanding that the people in charge of our bodyguards were all wereanimals, when vampires were so obviously superior. Yeah, they were beginning to get on everyone's nerves. She gave me Domino back as a partner with Nicky and me.

'Claudia, I'm not sure any of the weretigers can. They're great in practice and as regular bodyguards, but none of them have seen combat or the kind of slaughter we walked into last night.'

'I need Lisandro to help me with the Harlequin, and that's that, Anita. You don't want Dev, and Pride and Nicky don't work well together. Emmanuel is good, but he's not seen the hard stuff either. Domino wasn't trained to be some white knight super-warrior like the gold tigers; he was trained as a mob bodyguard and enforcer who can be pretty brutal.'

'But it's not the same kind of brutal as what we faced last night and today.'

'Look, I don't have time or energy to debate this; Domino is your guy for now.' She stood there hands on hips, all six foot six of her, in the conference room where we'd eaten. Her long black hair was in a tight ponytail; no makeup distracted from the high cheekbones and strong features of her face. She was what the Mexicans would call *guapa*, handsome rather than pretty; there was just too much of her, from the broad, muscled shoulders to the long, muscular legs and all the parts in between to be pretty, or even beautiful, though she was that.

'How much trouble are you having integrating the Harlequin with our guards?' I asked.

'Look, I want to keep all the guards I can around Jean-Claude. The Harlequin are fearsomely good when they aren't being whiny bitches. Jean-Claude coming here on the spur of the moment is a security nightmare, and now you tell me the rogue master vampire is a necromancer that can raise zombies and inhabit their bodies in daylight. This just gets better and fucking better,' she said.

I wasn't sure I'd ever heard Claudia curse before, which meant she was even more upset than she was letting me see.

'I'm all better; Jean-Claude can fly home.'

She gave me a look of such scorn that I had to fight not to squirm. 'He'll never leave now, not until you're out of danger.'

'Danger is sort of my job description,' I said.

'And don't think that doesn't piss me off, too.'

'Okay,' I said, 'is this just about security issues, or are you pissed about something else?'

'I don't know what you're talking about; just go and catch this bastard, so we can all go home.'

'That's the plan,' I said. I left the conference room with Nicky in tow. We were going to pick up Domino from his room at the end of the hallway.

'What's got her panties in a twist?' I asked.

'I don't know, but she's been on edge for about two weeks,' Nicky said.

'This much on edge?' I asked, looking up at him.

He shook his head. 'No, not this bad.'

'Good, because I was about to feel stupid for not noticing that one of our head guards was having some kind of personal issue.'

'Claudia won't let it interfere with the job, whatever it is,' he said.

I nodded, and knew he meant it, but I also knew that even with the best of intentions personal stuff bled onto everything sometimes. But since she didn't want to talk about it, I would let it go; unless it interfered with her job it really wasn't any of my business.

Nicky knocked on the room door at the end of the hallway, just by the door marked *EXIT*. The door opened and it was Domino. He looked slender beside Nicky and Dev. Domino was five foot ten but he was more slender in his build, which made him look taller than he was, because when you looked at him your eye didn't stop at the shoulders or the chest like it did on the other two weretigers. His two most striking features were his hair and his eyes. The hair was mounded on top in a soft mass of black and white curls; he'd recently started shaving the bottom layer of hair close to his head, so that it was almost a skater cut. The multicolored curls were natural, though he got a lot of club kids and Goths asking him where he'd gotten the great dye job. His hair showed his mixed tiger heritage, half white clan and half black. He was one of only a handful of black weretigers that had lived through the near-extermination of that clan. He'd been found in an orphanage by the white tiger clan; no one knew who his parents had been, only what they had been. He had two tiger forms, one white, one black, and he could also do tigerman form in both. His mixed heritage had made the white tiger clan treat him as not good enough to mate with, for fear of bearing an impure child. The clans mated with each other to keep the genetics healthier, but most babies looked like one side or the other and went to be raised with the clan that they most resembled. Domino was one of only two that I'd met who couldn't hide his mixed heritage.

His eyes were pure black tiger, like orange flame. They were startling enough that people thought they were contacts, like they thought the hair was dyed. In his black tiger form, those orange tiger eyes were Halloween beautiful. In white tiger form, they marked him as impure, because in every form his tiger eyes stayed the same, like all the clan tigers they were born with the eyes. Though there were clan tigers that had human eyes, they were considered weak by the other tigers and usually only had the form of a giant tiger as their beast.

His smile filled those jack-o'-lantern-colored eyes with such happiness. It made me feel guilty that I hadn't gone out of my way to greet him when he got to town and that I hadn't wanted him to bodyguard me today.

'Hey, Domino,' I said, and went to him.

He wrapped me in his arms, and I hugged him around the waist. He didn't have all his weapons on yet, which made it easier to hug, but meant it would take him longer to get ready to go; like so much about dating my bodyguards, it was a mixed blessing.

I went up on tiptoe still wrapped in the hug, so that he didn't have to bend very far for us to kiss hello. His lips were soft and the kiss softer. It might have grown into something more, but my phone rang and the ring tone was the *Hawaii Five-O* theme, which was what I used for most police that I worked with occasionally.

Domino knew the ring tone and let me go without a question. He moved back into the room to get his weapons. We followed and shut the door behind us as I answered the phone. It was Hatfield.

'Blake, everyone here is congratulating us on killing the rogue vampire, but before I celebrate I wanted to ask you and Forrester. Is it dead?'

I liked Hatfield a lot in that moment. 'No, I'm like ninety-five percent sure it's not.'

'I thought you'd say that.' She didn't sound happy about being right, but it was honest emotion.

Domino had his gear laid out on the neatly made bed as if he planned to pack it all neatly away. He was casual about a lot of stuff, but not about his job. He'd been trained as a mob bodyguard and enforcer, because the master of the city of Vegas was a mob boss who dated back to the days of Bugsy Siegel. Domino had been playing catch-up in some areas of the guards' training, because we had more ex-military and ex-police and mercenaries, running our crew, but for sheer brutality he'd probably seen his share. I'd met Max, the Master of Vegas. His first job in the mob had been as a leg-breaker himself, which meant in his day he hadn't been squeamish about getting his own hands dirty, and expected the same willingness from his people. Domino slipped his vest on and began tightening the straps.

'I wish I believed the big bad vampire died in the fire and explosion, but this thing can jump bodies. To truly kill it we have to keep it in one place long enough to die.'

'How do we do that?' Hatfield asked.

'If we can find the original body and destroy it, then chances are that'll do the job.'

Domino started putting his weapons in place. He got to carry more weapons when he came out with me as a sort of junior marshal, because he didn't have to hide that he was armed. Hiding weapons in everyday clothes could be a challenge.

'How do we find the body?' Hatfield asked.

'I'm going to question Little Henry at the hospital and Deputy Gutterman about the sheriff's attack and see if I can get a clue to a location.'

'Can't you just ask the vampires in custody tonight?'

'Yeah, but once night falls this rogue is going to be even stronger and harder to find and kill than he was earlier today, so I'd really like to find the original body and take care of things before the sun goes down.'

Nicky picked up a pocket-sized .308 pistol from the bed. He made some soft remark, but I knew that it was some remark on size and implying penis size comparison in some way. It was a guy thing. I knew that Domino had nothing to be ashamed of in that area. He got his Beretta .45 out of the holster at his side and made some soft remark back, probably belittling Nicky's size since he carried a nine-millimeter as his main gun.

Hatfield had been quiet while I watched the men. She finally said, 'Okay, agreed. What can I do to help?'

'Ted is on his way to you guys to see what we learned from all the new crime scenes we found.'

'I'll call him and be waiting. What do I tell the brass who want to declare the danger over?'

'Tell them to wait until after tonight. From the time the sun goes down until it rises again will be the test. If nothing happens, then maybe we got him, but I think it will be worse tonight.'

'Why?' she asked.

'What do serial killers do when they're cornered?' I asked.

'Suicide, or kill more people faster, usually.'

'Yeah,' I said.

'Oh,' she said. 'Damn, that is not a good thought.'

'If you want unicorns and rainbows, you're in the wrong line of work,' I said.

She gave a small, not entirely happy laugh. 'Well, that's the God's honest truth.'

'Yep,' I said.

Domino had his weapons in place. He slipped his lined leather jacket over it all. It didn't close enough to hide the vest, or his own nine-millimeter Glock in a MOLLE-rigged strap on the front of the vest, but as long as he was with me he could flaunt the guns and still not be charged with brandishing a weapon in public. What constituted brandishing differed depending on which police officer charged you with it and basically meant that they thought you were scaring the civilians by carrying openly. They bitched at civilians if they carried concealed, and they bitched if they carried openly; sometimes I thought the gun laws were designed to be confusing. But my badge, my warrant of execution, and the way the law was currently written covered them, and suddenly they didn't have to play by civilian rules.

'I'll call Forrester,' Hatfield said.

'We're headed to the hospital,' I said.

'Give my best to Sheriff Callahan and your fiancé.'

'Will do, and thanks.'

'Callahan is a good man and a better sheriff. He was one of those old-fashioned ones who would go out and visit with the people in his township. You know, he has to be voted in for sheriff every time.'

'No, I didn't know that, actually.'

'He really cares about his people, and he makes sure they know it. He's been sheriff up there at least ten years now.'

It sounded like Micah and the Coalition. 'I didn't know that either,' I said.

Nicky held the door; Domino went first, doing the bodyguard look-see, and then nodded. I went through, Nicky closed the door behind us, and we headed for the elevators.

'We're about to get in the elevator, so I may lose you,' I said.

'Bye then, and I hope we find the body before sundown,' she said.

'Me, too,' I said.

We hung up. The elevator doors opened. We got in and went out to hunt vampires. Sometimes you do it with a gun, sometimes by talking to the people they leave behind. We call them survivors, but once the vampires get you, the person you were dies, like any traumatized part of you never leaves that room, that car, that moment, and you walk forward a ghost of your former self. You rebuild yourself over the years, but the person you were isn't the person you become. The great bad thing happens, and you become a ghost in your own life, and then you become flesh and blood and remake your life, but the ghosts of what happened don't go away completely. They wait for you in low moments, and then they wail at you, shaking their chains in your face and trying to strangle you with them.

I'd see Micah first and try to help him untangle the chains of guilt and love he felt for his father. Then I'd talk to Henry. He was a combat vet, special forces; he knew trauma before the vampires took him, but this trauma had killed his father. Did anything that came before prepare him for that? Somehow I doubted that even special forces training could really prepare you for losing someone like this, and the survivor guilt, which had probably been part of the ghost he brought back from combat, had gained a brand-new shiny link to its rattling chain.

Real ghosts are so much easier to deal with than the kind we carry around in our heads. Most people haunt themselves more effectively than any spirit.

67

Micah's mom was in the hallway being comforted by Gonzales. She was crying, and for a second I feared the worst. My stomach tightened with dread, but I squared my shoulders and kept walking forward; no retreat, no surrender.

Domino spoke low beside me. 'Who is that?'

I answered, sort of under my breath, 'Micah's mom.'

'Really?' he said.

I glanced up at him but couldn't read his expression with his eyes hidden behind sunglasses. He didn't exactly look happy, though; I hadn't thought about the whole mixed-race thing being an issue for anyone. If anyone was going to have an issue it would be the clan weretigers, but Domino with his own mixed heritage hadn't been my pick for being bothered by it.

Bea's face brightened when she saw me, even through the tears, and I knew just by the relief that it wasn't her 'husband' dead, but something she thought I could help with. I had had people want me to raise their deceased loved ones before, but I thought Beatrice was saner than that.

She hugged me way tighter than I liked and didn't hesitate with having to work around all the weapons. She'd been a cop's wife for a long time; it probably wasn't the first time that she'd had to work around guns for a hug.

I did the only thing I could; I hugged her back, which made her hug me tighter. Talk about being punished for competency, but I ended up more holding her than hugging her. I realized that her legs were weak. I braced and held her up. The moment she felt my strength her legs collapsed. She had me by at least fifty pounds, probably closer to seventy, but lucky for both of us I didn't have a problem supporting her. It was just sort of unexpected.

Nicky asked, 'You need help?'

'Not yet.'

She hadn't exactly fainted, because she was still holding on, it was more like she was sinking in some emotional water I couldn't see and she'd decided to hold on to me. To her I said, 'Beatrice, Bea, can you hear me?'

Gonzales was there, sort of hovering. 'Bea, you okay?'

She started to sag more, and I said, 'Nicky, help me get her to a chair.' I could support her weight, but a body isn't balanced like a barbell. Bodies are much harder to lift, especially if you don't want to accidentally hurt the person, or they're wearing a dress, like Bea, and you don't want to flash the room, which I didn't.

A chair just suddenly appeared behind her with a uniformed officer holding it. Nicky and Gonzales both tried to help me ease her into it, so that it was too much help and we all got in each other's way. She looked pale, her eyes not focusing.

I touched her face. She was clammy to the touch. 'Bea, can you hear me?'

She blinked at me, gave a small nod, and said, 'Yes.' Her voice was hoarse.

'When did you eat last?'

She couldn't remember.

'How much water have you had?'

She hadn't had any today. Someone went to fetch her water, and another officer went for a candy machine. I knelt on one knee on the floor in front of her and let her hold my hand. I'd have said I was holding hers, but she seemed to need the touch.

We got some water into her, Gonzales holding the cup between sips. A candy bar put some color back into her cheeks. 'I'm sorry,' she said, in a small, hoarse voice.

'You have to take care of yourself better than this, Bea,' I said.

'I just want to spend as much time with them as I can.'

'Them?' I asked.

'Rush and Micah.'

Rush I understood. 'Micah will be back.'

'But the two of them together, I won't get to see that much longer,' and she began to cry.

I patted her hand, and glared up at Gonzales. He gave me a what-did-I-do? look. When Bea seemed well enough to sit safely without falling over, I left the officer with the water by her side and walked Gonzales a little way from her. Nicky and Domino trailed after us.

'How long have you been here with her?' I asked.

'Only a couple of hours,' he said. 'I didn't know she hadn't eaten or drunk something.'

'Has Micah had anything?'

'I don't know, he's in with Rush.'

'Shit,' I said.

I turned to the cops in the hallway. 'Guys, really appreciate you being here like this.'

They all made noncommittal gestures of support.

'But can you guys keep checking and making sure the family keeps hydrated and a little food in them?'

They looked at one another. It turned out that most of them had only just cycled back through to hospital duty, so they hadn't known. 'Sorry, Marshal, we'll look after Mrs Callahan better from now on.'

I didn't correct him that it was Mrs Morgan, but part of me wondered if the kids had hyphenated names. Probably not, or the secret would have been out years ago, but all the same they were a unit, a couple that happened to be three instead of two. I had a moment to wonder how Jean-Claude, Micah, Nathaniel, and I would handle a commitment ceremony. For that matter, would Jean-Claude want to involve Asher? Did I want Nicky involved? It all seemed too complicated now, which meant that something about the last few minutes had hit an issue for me. I didn't know exactly what issue had been hit, but it was something, because I was feeling less friendly about the whole idea of commitment anything.

I let the negative emotions sort of wash over me but didn't let them stick. I just let them go. I'd figure out what was bugging me later; right now I wanted to see Micah and make sure he was okay. All right, as okay as he could be under the circumstances. My head was already starting to ache from whatever emotional land mine the last few minutes had hit, but I'd learned that I didn't have to know exactly what was bothering me. I just had to acknowledge the problem, keep moving, and not act on the irrational impulses. Edward had saved me earlier when I would have taken out my issues on Nicky and Dev; now I had to save myself.

I took a few deep breaths, and it was a mistake, because I could smell the sweet-and-sour smell of something rotting, and I knew it was Micah's dad. The smell was almost too close to the smell of the corpses earlier. It was like some awful preview. And just like that, I wasn't okay.

'Bathroom, nearest,' I said.

Gonzales pointed down the hallway. 'Go right.'

I'd have liked to be cool, but I started running, not like running-for-my-life fast, but I really wanted to get to the bathroom before I threw up. Nicky and Domino jogged behind me, and I felt stupid having them trail me. In that moment I just wanted to be alone.

I found the bathroom, slammed into the door to push it open, and ran for a stall. I started throwing up before I got to my knees and had just enough awareness left to keep my hair back with one hand.

I felt someone behind me. 'It's me,' Nicky said. Though for once if the bad guys had wanted to get me, doing it while I was being violently ill was a good moment to choose. Nicky held my hair for me so I could use both hands to prop myself up. Meat does not throw up well. If I'd known it was going to be important, I'd have had the soup, or maybe just coffee, yeah, just coffee would have been great.

I knelt there, my forearms propped on the toilet, head hanging down, while Nicky held my hair in one hand and put the other on my forehead. His hand felt cool, and I knew it wasn't. He ran hotter than human-normal like most lycanthropes. The fact that his hand felt that cool meant that maybe I was sicker than I thought.

'Here are some paper towels; it might help,' Domino said.

I thought he meant *Clean up*, and was about to protest that I hadn't made a mess, but then Nicky's hand left my forehead and put something cold against the back of my neck. It was a shock to the system, but it felt good. Cool was better.

'Sorry,' I managed to say.

'For what?' Domino asked, but Nicky didn't ask. He knew, partly because he was my Bride, but partly because he understood how much I hated weakness of any kind.

I started fumbling at the toilet paper roll.

Nicky leaned over to help.

'I got it,' I said, and realized I'd snapped at him. 'I'm sorry.' I got some of the paper to finally come off the damn roll and wiped at my mouth.

'Do you want me to leave?'

'No.' I said it automatically and then a tiny part of me wondered if it was true. Hadn't I thought I'd like to be alone just seconds before I came in here?

Nicky let go of my hair and started to move out of the stall.

I reached back and grabbed his pants leg. 'Please,' I said, 'just give me a minute. I didn't mean to snap. I don't want you to go. Thank you for taking care of me.'

'You're saying all the right things, but I can feel what you're actually feeling, remember? You're irritated, angry even.'

'But not at you,' I said, with my hand still wrapped in the loose edge of his jeans. He had to get loose fit a lot, because the muscles of his thighs didn't fit in some of the tight jeans.

'Just because you're not angry at me doesn't mean you won't aim it at me.' There was a tone in his voice that I couldn't quite figure out, but it wasn't a good one.

'Please,' I said again, 'don't let your issues and mine do something bad. I just need to figure out what the hell is going on in my head.'

'Okay,' but he sounded cautious, as if he didn't trust . . . me. He was this big, physical guy, tougher and better than most of the guards, physically stronger than I would ever be, but in that moment I realized something I hadn't before. If I had been abusive to him, as my Bride he couldn't have done anything about it. Brides were pretty much helpless to say no to their masters. He even had to keep me happy, because if I was unhappy it made him unhappy. I wondered how close to the dynamics with his mother our relationship was, and then wished I hadn't thought of it. It was all too Freudian and weird. Why was I overthinking this? What the hell was wrong with me? And then I realized, this was what I used to do. I used to overthink relationships and poke them with a stick until they broke, and then I'd be able to say, *See, see, I knew it.* Fuck, what about this case, the last few minutes, had set me back to such old shitty habits?

I threw the toilet paper in the toilet and flushed away my lunch, and then I let go of Nicky's pants leg and held my hand up to him. I didn't need the help to stand, but it was a way of apologizing and letting him know how much I'd appreciated the help in these last few minutes, how much I appreciated him.

He looked down at me, his face arrogant, unreadable; the one blue eye staring down at me was harsh and unfriendly. I wasn't the only one who'd had old issues hit in the last few minutes.

There was a moment when I thought he wasn't going to relent, and that in a few thoughtless moments we'd ruined something between us. 'Just tell me to take your hand, help you up, and I have to do it.'

'I don't want you to do it because you have to, I want you to do it because you want to.'

A look came over his face; it was almost pained. 'Why do you keep giving me choices, Anita? You don't have to.'

'Maybe that's why,' I said. 'Because I don't have to.'

'That makes no sense,' he said, but he reached down and took my hand. He lifted me to my feet and backed out of the stall at the same time, so that we ended up out in the main part of the bathroom. He just kept staring down at me, as if he couldn't figure out what, or who, I was.

'I feel like I missed something,' Domino said. 'Did you guys just have a fight?'

'Almost,' I said.

'Are you all right?' Nicky asked.

'I feel fine now.'

'I've never seen you get sick like that,' Domino said.

I shrugged. Nicky and I were still holding hands as if we were both afraid to let go. 'I used to throw up at crime scenes pretty regularly.'

'You keep saying that, but we've never seen you do it before,' Nicky said.

'This wasn't a crime scene,' Domino said. 'What made you sick?'

'I smelled the decomp coming from his father's room and it was too close to last night.'

'The smell didn't bother you last night,' Nicky said.

'Trust me, it did,' I said.

Nicky gave a small smile and squeezed my hand. 'It bothered all of us, but not that much.'

'I have no idea why I got sick just now,' I said.

He drew me in so that our bodies touched. He was back to staring at my face, but it was a different look now, not arrogant or harsh, more like he was thinking about something really hard.

'What?' I asked.

He just shook his head. 'Maybe you need more sleep.'

'Always on a case,' I said.

Domino offered me a breath mint.

'You're carrying breath mints in with your ammo?' I said.

'We're lycanthropes, Anita; sometimes we eat stuff that a human isn't going to want to smell on our breath.'

I took the mint and spoke around it as I rolled it in my mouth. 'But you only eat stuff like that in animal form; once you change back to human it's a different mouth.'

'Is it?' he asked.

I frowned while I thought about it. 'Yeah, I think so.'

'Just think of it as a precaution,' Domino said.

I squeezed Nicky's hand, then let go so I could go to the sinks and wash my hands. I looked at him in the mirror as I asked, 'Do you have breath mints with you?'

'No, clan tigers are prissy bastards; lions aren't.'

'I suppose lions eat raw meat and then just suck the juices off each other, no mint needed,' Domino said.

'Yeah, we do.'

Domino rolled his eyes, as if the tougher-than-anyone-else talk was old hat from Nicky. 'I know, I know, only the werehyenas are a tougher society to survive in than the werelions. Weretigers are complete pansies compared to you guys.'

'Not in St Louis they're not,' Nicky said.

'What do you mean?' I asked, as I dried my hands.

'I don't know exactly how Narcissus got to be head of the werehyenas in our city, but he's seriously fucked with their societal norms.'

'How so?' I asked, and started for the door.

'Hyenas aren't tougher to fight than lions, but they are tougher on each other. They'll brutalize each other to a degree that we won't.'

'They brutalize each other,' I said, thinking of some of the 'play' rooms I'd seen at the club Narcissus in Chains. Lycanthropes could heal almost anything that wasn't done with silver, or fire, which meant that if you liked BDSM there were options that humans would never survive.

'I don't mean the bondage stuff. I mean they fight just to fight, and fights that break out at the spur of the moment can totally change their clan structure. Every other animal group has rituals for dominance fights. A fight that gets out of hand doesn't necessarily change anything, because if it's not formal, then the rest of the group can join in and take sides, or in some animal groups an informal fight doesn't count even if it results in a death.'

'Really,' I said.

Nicky opened the bathroom door and checked the hallway automatically before I followed him.

Domino answered. 'I don't know about every animal group, but if someone killed Queen Bibiana in Vegas outside of ritual combat, the challenger would die with her. Her guard, her son, or her husband would see to that.'

I thought about Bibiana, who was as delicate as I was, but all white and ladylike. She was horribly powerful metaphysically, but I hadn't thought about her having to defend herself in ritual combat. 'I can't quite picture her taking on all challengers in one-on-one combat,' I said.

'The White Tiger Clan allows the queen to pick a champion if she is a good enough leader that we don't want to lose her.'

Nicky went a half-step in front of me, and Domino a little behind. We didn't usually do the formal bodyguard stuff when I was carrying my badge. I might have said something, but I actually wanted to ask Domino another question.

'What if the queen wasn't a good leader and the clan didn't support her?'

'Then a vote can be called and if enough of the clan votes no, she has to fight her own battle.'

Nicky glanced back and said, 'Sounds like a way to assassinate a leader without actually doing the job yourself.'

'It's a way to spread the guilt around,' Domino agreed, as if there were nothing wrong with it.

'If you want the leader dead, you have to do it in a one-on-one fight. There are no substitute champions in our culture,' Nicky said.

'Of course, there aren't,' Domino said, 'because werelions are just that awesome.'

Nicky glanced back again, and it wasn't a friendly look. 'This is one of the main problems with the Coalition, Anita. We are different animals, different cultures, with very different rules. It's hard to bring us together when we can't even decide how to elect a leader.'

'Micah adapts to whatever animal group he's visiting,' Domino said.

'I've never gone out of town with Micah before,' Nicky said.

'I don't think he's gone up against any lions yet.'

The phrasing sounded odd to me. We walked around the corner and could see the police outside the room again, but I stopped walking. 'What do you mean, gone up against?'

Domino's face suddenly got as blank as he could make it. He was perfect bodyguard empty, with an edge of angry intimidation around the edges. His energy prickled down my skin, and the fact that he'd lost control of his beast that much meant my question had stressed him.

I turned completely around to face him. Nicky took up his best bodyguard position at my back, but standing so he could see both up and down the hallway; again it was more guarding than I liked them doing around the police work, but I let it go, because I had a bad feeling about why Domino was suddenly nervous.

'I asked you a question, Domino,' I said, voice sort of soft. It wasn't a good softness, though; it was a tone that said I was getting angry.

He looked behind me at the other man.

'Don't look at Nicky; look at me, and answer my question.'

'I'm not your Bride, Anita. I'm just one of your many tigers to call. I'm not even bound that tight to you, because you already had a white tiger when you found me, so you just bound my black half. I don't have to obey you.' He was going all distant and angry on me, which was something he'd done when I first met him, but he'd stopped doing it with me.

'What's to stop me from asking Nicky, then? He has to tell me.'

'He's never traveled with Micah.'

'He can't answer the question, can he?' I asked, staring at his sunglasses, as if I could see his eyes through them, but I'd found that even if I couldn't actually see someone's eyes, staring as if you can through dark glasses unnerves some people.

'No, he can't,' Domino said, and he was arrogant and angry, and his power pushed like heat against my skin.

'There's a reason that Micah never takes Nicky, or Dev, or anyone who couldn't keep a secret from me, isn't there?'

'Don't do this now, Anita, not with Micah's dad and family,' Domino said.

'Don't do what? Find out that you've all been keeping something from me, including Micah?'

Domino's hands started to flex over and over. It wasn't exactly making fists; it was more like a cat will knead with its claws. It's a sign of high anxiety among all the big-cat lycanthropes. Domino knew I understood what it was, and the fact that he was doing it anyway meant either that he was that desperate to calm himself down or that he couldn't help it, which meant he was fighting for control. That scared me, because Domino had excellent control of his beast; if he was that stressed, then the answer to my question was even worse than I'd thought.

'Jesus,' I said, 'Micah's fighting for dominance to bring the groups into the Coalition?'

Domino shook his head, his hands kneading the air, fingers tensed and arched as he fought the growing heat that seemed to shimmer around him. I turned my head to the side and could see the 'heat' rising off him. It was a bad sign.

'Anita, after what happened with Ares, if he loses it in front of the cops, they will shoot him,' Nicky said.

I tried to calm myself down, because I couldn't even think past the thought of how many times Micah went out of town to talk to different groups. No one could win that many fights in a month and have no injuries to show for it, and Micah wasn't big enough, or physical enough . . . He was a leader, but not that kind.

'Ease down, Domino,' I said. 'I don't want to lose you because of something stupid.'

He bit his lower lip and shook his head, as if I'd asked him another question.

'I'll let it go, because honestly your reaction just now is answer enough.'

He took a few deep, even breaths and I felt him shove the heat of his beast back in its metaphorical box. I was finally able to shield enough that I'd only felt it as heat and not as a tiger. My own cats hadn't even tried to surface. I was getting better at this. We all were. I just didn't know how much better Micah had gotten at parts of it, like lying to me.

Domino finally spoke in a low, careful voice as if he were fighting to control even that. 'I swear to you that Micah doesn't fight every time he leaves town. Diplomacy and . . . softer methods work most of the time.'

'What does *softer methods* mean?' I asked.

Domino's power spiked like a fever burning against my skin.

'Let it go for now, Anita,' Nicky said. He moved so he was blocking the police's view of Domino.

I counted slowly to ten, though without being able to do the deep breathing that should have gone with it, it wasn't nearly as calming. 'I won't ask you any more questions right now, Domino, I promise.'

I couldn't see around Nicky's body, but I could feel that another wereanimal was coming closer. Their energy breathed along my skin like a breath of hot air. This power stirred my beasts and I 'saw' in my mind's eye my hyena stand up and shake itself like the big dog she resembled. She started trotting down a long, sunlit hallway that was usually shadowed, but the hyena trotted in the light, and tall yellowed grass appeared for her to do a curious sideways lope of a run. She moved so awkwardly compared to the cats, or the wolf, but she was still coming, and if I didn't get control of her the hyena would try to burst out of my body and become real, but I was angry. Anger made everything harder to control. I was angry and afraid, because Micah was my size and no matter how tough you are, when fighters are equally trained, size matters. The thought of Micah going up against someone Nicky's or Dev's size made my skin run cold. The fear seemed to puzzle the hyena because she whimpered and sat down looking at me with those odd brown eyes, such a human color if the pupils hadn't been slitted like a cat's.

'Control yourself,' Nicky said, softly.

I closed my eyes and tried. I fought for calm, fought to find my still center, but Micah was my still center, and he'd been risking his life for years and I hadn't known. I felt stupid. Had I really thought that diplomacy alone had made all those animal groups across the country join our Coalition? Yeah, I had. I'd had faith in Micah's ability to persuade, to lead, to manipulate and bargain. I even knew that he had done all those things. I knew that he had slept with some of the female shapeshifters to seal the deal, or to gain allies who would help persuade the group leaders to our way. That was probably what Domino meant by softer means; Micah had told me about the sex, because he hadn't wanted me to find out from anyone else. But the few times he'd come home injured, or with injured guards, he'd told me it just got out of hand, but in the end they had persuaded them.

Had Micah ever come home without the group agreeing to join us, eventually? No, he hadn't.

I was calm again, but it was the calm of water. It's only still until the next breeze touches it. I opened my eyes.

Nicky looked down at me. 'You okay for this?'

I nodded.

He stepped to one side and I was looking at Socrates. His skin was the color of coffee with one cream in it, his tightly curled hair cut tight on the sides and long on top, a lot like Domino's hair, but Socrates' hair was thick enough that it stayed in the nearly square top-layer shape almost like a hedge trimmed into a desired shape. His eyes were brown, but not the brown of the animal sitting inside my head now. Socrates' eyes were perfectly human.

The hyena sniffed the air and made a laughing, cackling sound that raised the hair on my arms. I had a moment to wonder if I'd made the sound out loud with my human mouth and throat, but I didn't think so.

Socrates rubbed his arms underneath his suit jacket. It gave me a glimpse of the gun at his waist. He was an ex-cop who'd been cut up when he helped bust an inner-city gang that had werehyenas for their enforcers. He'd been a hero, they'd cleaned out the gang, but he'd lost his badge and the job he loved.

'When did you gain my beast?' he whispered.

'When a bullet went through Ares and into me,' I said.

'It should take until the next full moon for you to manifest your hyena. That's two more weeks, but I feel it, smell it on you.'

'I'm precocious,' I said.

'You're something, all right,' he said, rubbing his arms again.

'You go out of town with Micah sometimes, don't you?'

'Why ask it like that, Anita? You know I have.'

I looked at him, just looked at him.

He looked past me to Domino. The look was angry, and eloquent, and seemed to be saying, *How could you be this stupid?* with a slight eyebrow raise and a tiny tilt to his head.

Domino's power flared again. 'I said nothing.'

Socrates' look didn't believe him, and neither did the rest of Socrates.

'Did you really think I'd never figure it out?' I asked.

He looked at me then and said, 'I don't know what you think you've figured out, so I can't speak to it.'

'Don't you lie to me, Socrates, not anymore.'

Gonzales started walking this way. My watching him made Socrates glance back, too. We had the attention of all the cops. I was letting my emotions get in the way of business, oh, hell, in the way of common sense. Cops are a curious lot, especially about anyone they may have to trust their lives to, so us arguing among ourselves wasn't going to reassure any of them.

'Is there a problem, Anita?' he asked.

If I said no, he'd know it was a lie, but . . . 'No,' I said, and the *no* was very firm, very certain. I'd actually made a waitress cry once by saying no. Gonzales didn't cry – he was made of sterner stuff than that – but he understood that it was an absolutely unmovable negative. Sometimes I spoke too forcefully and made waitresses cry by accident, but sometimes it was exactly the amount of force needed to stop people from asking me anything.

Gonzales looked at me, then looked from one to the other of the men. 'Okay, how are you feeling? You looked a little green.'

'Let's just say I'm wishing I'd stuck to something more liquid for lunch.'

He gave a little chuckle, but his eyes stayed wary and he did another glance around at all the men. His gaze came back to me and he showed me those suspicious cop eyes that said clearly I was full of shit and he didn't believe me. Didn't believe what, you might ask? He was a ten-year-plus veteran police officer; he didn't believe a damn thing that anyone told him.

A man called out from down the hallway. 'I thought you were tough, Blake. I hear you just tossed your lunch for no reason whatsoever.' It was Travers come to give moral support to Sheriff Callahan, and to continue to be a pain in my ass.

'What's your problem, Travers?' I asked, and it was a little loud just like his comment had been, because we were at the ends of the hallway from each other.

'You, you and your . . . men are my problem.' He was walking toward us.

I moved around Gonzales and started moving to meet Travers.

'Anita,' Socrates said, 'don't . . .'

I turned, pointed a finger at him, and just said, 'Don't even.'

Nicky caught up with me. 'What are you going to do?'

I realized that Travers was looking for a fight and so was I. I stopped walking and said, 'Fuck.'

He smiled at me.

But Travers didn't have any voice of reason with him; he was just this big, angry guy waiting for someone to take the first swing so he could swing back. His body language screamed, *Give me an excuse*.

'What are you smiling at?' Travers asked.

I realized he was asking Nicky, who turned and looked at him. Travers wasn't a rookie, he should have understood what that look meant, but he bristled, hands going into fists. Nicky planted one foot so he'd be able to pivot into his swing. I took a step ahead of him.

'Anita,' Nicky said.

'It's okay, Nicky.'

'It's not okay, Nicky,' Travers said, doing a bad and unflattering imitation of me.

'Travers, we are not going to let you use us to pick your fight.'

'They'll fight back, Blake, they can't help it. You kick a dog, it'll bite you.'

'They aren't dogs, Travers, nothing that domesticated.'

'No, not domesticated, pussy-whipped.'

'What is with everyone here and that phrase?' I asked.

Travers was right in front of us now. His hands were still fists; his arms were actually vibrating with anger. He wanted, almost needed, to hit something. 'You always hide behind your girlfriend, Nicky?'

'No,' Nicky said, and his *no*, like mine, was very firm, very sure of itself, and left no room for anything but the negative. He started to move closer to Travers, but I stepped between them.

I let down some of my shields, not all, not even all the way down, but enough so that when I touched Travers's arm I could draw on his anger. Being able to feed on sex was Jean-Claude's power, but I could also feed on anger and that was my power, my special little talent slice. I'd practiced until I could take the edge off someone's anger, like skimming off the anger, rage-filled cream, leaving bland but healthier milk behind.

I didn't so much feed on his anger, because that could cause confusion and get noticed by the other police. I sort of licked away a little bit of his anger, like taking the cherry off a milkshake.

Travers frowned, and looked lost for a second, and then he jerked back, holding his arm as if it hurt where I'd touched him. 'What did you do to me?'

'Why were you angry at us?' I asked quietly.

He shook his head, rubbing his arm. 'Do me a favor, Blake; next time I'm about to die don't save me, and don't have any of your damn vampires save me either.'

'You'd rather have rotted to death in excruciating pain than had Truth suck the corruption out of you?'

He looked at me, and there was real pain in his eyes. He whispered, 'Yes.' Looking into his eyes from touching distance, I knew he meant it. Something about Truth feeding on him had disturbed him so badly that he had decided dying was preferable.

I don't know what my expression was, but Travers suddenly turned around and walked fast for the elevators. He was still holding his arm.

Gonzales said, 'What did you do to him just now?'

'Just calmed his anger a little, I swear.'

'Do we care what happens to Travers?' Nicky asked.

'Care in what way?' I asked.

'Care if he lives or dies?'

'Truth risked his own life to save Travers, so yeah, alive would be good.'

'Then put him on suicide watch,' Socrates said from behind us.

I turned and looked at him. 'Why?' I asked.

'After I found out that I had lycanthropy and they were giving me a commendation for bravery and taking my badge, I thought about eating my gun. I know that look in someone's eyes.'

I looked at Nicky. 'You know that look, too?' I asked.

'If I hadn't had my brother and sister to keep safe, I'd have done it when I was a kid.'

I knew what 'it' was: suicide. Nicky had just told me he'd thought seriously about suicide when he was a teenager, or hell, maybe younger. I didn't know how old he'd been when the abuse started.

I took his hand in mine and didn't care if the other cops saw. I'd already thrown up for no real reason; they'd take points off for that. If they wanted to take more points off for me holding my lover's hand, let them. In that moment it was more important to reassure Nicky than to be the toughest badge in the room.

Nicky looked down at our clasped hands and smiled. That one smile was worth the teasing I might get for the hand holding.

'Why would your vampire friend saving his life make Travers suicidal?' Gonzales asked.

'I don't know,' Socrates said, 'but something about it spooked him.'

The door to the room opened, and it was Micah. He didn't have dark circles under his eyes; it was more as if the lack of rest had worn away some of the skin underneath his eyes so that he looked hollow-eyed and beyond exhausted. I'd seen him go with less sleep for longer and look a lot better, but sometimes it's not the number of hours, but what those hours hold that wears you down.

I'd been so angry with him just minutes before, but seeing those beautiful green-and-yellow eyes so tired, so discouraged, I just wanted to make it better. I let go of Nicky's hand and went to Micah.

He looked almost surprised, and then as I wrapped my arms around him, held him close, he held me back and buried his face in my hair. His breath shuddered, and then I felt something hot and liquid trailing down my neck. Everything that comes from the body is hot for a second or two, and then it leaves the body, touches the air, and loses its heat. Nothing showed that he was crying; his shoulders did not shake, he was almost utterly still, and with his face buried in my curls no one else could see what I could feel, his tears falling hot along my skin, then growing cooler as they flowed down my neck.

I held him, let his tears paint their salty trail across my skin, and I couldn't be mad at him; the only thing I could do in that moment was hold him. It didn't seem like much, but sometimes when everything else goes to hell, arms to hold you tight is everything.

68

Gonzales drove Beatrice home with promises from the police left in the hallway that they'd call at the first sign of any change. She kissed Micah and me good-bye and left without apologizing for having fallen apart. I'd have felt compelled to apologize, but that was me. Socrates took Domino back to the hotel, where he could release his inner tiger in peace and without getting shot by the police. Socrates also wanted to be farther away from me and my newfound inner hyena. He actually said, 'You have a tendency to find your animal to call pretty quickly, and that's not what we are to each other.'

'That's not what I am to any of the hyenas,' I said.

'Then I'd stay clear of us for a while,' he said.

It was good advice.

I persuaded Micah to come to the cafeteria with us. Nicky came with us, of course, but so did Micah's remaining bodyguard, Bram. He was still six feet of tall, dark, handsome, overly stern muscle, though he was built lean and not bulked the way Nicky was. Bram and Ares had been like light and dark copies of each other in so many ways. It was the first time I'd seen Bram since I'd had to shoot his favorite coworker and good friend. I wasn't sure what to say to him or if I was supposed to say anything. When in doubt on personal stuff I did my usual: nothing. If Bram brought it up I'd deal, but if he didn't I'd let it go until I could decide if and how to handle it.

Nicky went in front of us, Bram trailed behind, and Micah and I walked in the middle holding hands. He knew to hold my left hand so my gun hand was free. It was routine for me most of the time, but especially so when on the job and armed to the teeth for vampire hunting. It was nice that Micah remembered even under such emotional duress without my having to remind him. I loved him a lot for many reasons, but one of the biggest was his calm acceptance of this part of my life. Of course, knowing his dad had been a police officer the entire time Micah was growing up helped explain why he was okay with it.

We chose a table that put us in a corner so we had two walls at our backs and a line of sight through damn near every part of the cafeteria. Bram and Nicky moved to a table beside ours, automatically, like bodyguards do when they're trying to give you some privacy and still keep you safe.

It was a little weird for Nicky to go back into bodyguard mode and act as if he and Bram were the same to Micah and me. Nicky lived with us, traveling back and forth from the Circus of the Damned to the house in Jefferson County. He was the person most likely to be by my side when I wasn't with Micah, Nathaniel, or Jean-Claude. It seemed like it should make a difference, but I did want alone time with Micah. We needed to have a serious talk, maybe several serious talks, but first he needed food and water, or maybe coffee.

We turned our chairs so that we could both have our backs to the wall and sit with our legs lightly touching. He kept hold of my hand and laid his forehead on my shoulder. Again, it would have been a bit more romantic without the body armor, but I was on the job and had an active warrant, plus last time I'd been in the hospital I'd needed the vest.

I stroked the braid of his hair. It was in a tight French braid, which I knew Nathaniel had done before he left for the hotel. Neither Micah nor I could French-braid worth a damn, let alone our own hair. It wasn't as fun to pet his hair in the braid, but I knew that it would stay out of his face and just be overall easier to deal with than almost any other hairdo.

He raised his face and I was suddenly looking into those amazing eyes of his from inches away. They were green and gold, but that didn't do them justice. There was a ring of green around the pupils and yellow outside that. The amount of each color varied as the pupil expanded or contracted, and in dim light the green could look almost gray, but right at that moment the green was the paleness of new spring leaves, and the yellow the gold of elm leaves in the fall, as if he held both the newness of the year and the end of it in his eyes. The color was more startling because his skin had those darker undertones; when he had his dark summer tan the eyes were even more amazing. He'd tanned as dark as Richard Zeeman, our Ulfric, Wolf King, but his family did have Native American in their background. I'd asked Micah if his family had Native American, or Hispanic blood, like me, in their background and he'd simply said no. It was interesting that it had never occurred to him to explain his own mixed heritage. Either he never thought about it like that, or he'd assumed it wouldn't matter to any of us.

'I don't know how to do this, Anita,' he said, at last.

'Do what?' I asked.

'Regain my dad after all these years and lose him at the same time.'

That was Micah, straight at it, no hesitation, no prevarication, just hit right between the eyes, and then I realized it wasn't him at all. He'd been keeping something really big from me for most of the three years we'd been together.

'What's wrong? I just watched some thought go across your face,' he said.

'Everything that's happened since we landed here, and you're asking what's wrong,' I said, and did my best to smile.

He smiled back. 'Okay, you have a point, so you're telling me I'm imagining you thought of something just now.'

I sighed. I realized that I'd decided not to confront him about the dominance fights out of town until we got through this visit and back home. I didn't want to hit him while he was down, and the pain in his eyes when he came out of his father's room, that was down. But I'd waited too long; I could lie, but seldom to Micah. The fact that he'd managed to keep such a big secret from me for so long made me wonder if there were other secrets. I hadn't liked thinking it, and I really hated the thought of this conversation now when he was so low.

'I love you,' I said.

'I love you, too, but that sounded like a preamble to something bad,' he said.

'You know me too well,' I said.

'We're engaged; shouldn't we know each other well?'

I smiled. 'Fair enough, and I admit I was all ready to have a serious talk about something totally unrelated to your family, or the case here, but then I saw you, and . . .'

'And I completely fell apart,' he finished for me.

'I didn't say that; I think you're doing pretty damn well under the circumstances.'

He smiled. 'What did you want to talk about?'

'It has the potential for being a really big fight, Micah. Let's not do this now.'

'Something that big and you can honestly wait to discuss it?' he asked.

I nodded. 'I'm a little surprised myself, but yeah, I can wait.'

He put his head to one side and looked at me. 'Will I think it's a good idea to wait?'

'Yeah, I think you will,' I said.

He narrowed his eyes at me. 'Would you understand if I said you're being way too reasonable, and it's actually making me nervous?'

I laughed. 'Yeah, actually I would.'

He smiled, and this time it was brighter, more his usual smile. 'Tell me, Anita, because now I'm convinced that it's something about what my dad told us about Van Cleef and the pseudomilitary stuff.'

'It may not be pseudo, but it's not about that.'

He gave me a look.

'Promise,' I said.

'You know you have to tell me now, because I'll be thinking of the worst things.'

It was my turn to put my head against his shoulder. 'I'm trying to be reasonable, Micah; let me do it. Let me be the grown-up for once.'

He touched my hair, lifted my face so we were looking at each other. 'Now you're scaring me.'

'Damn it, we are both relentless in our own way,' I said.

'Yes, we are; it's one of the things I loved about you from the beginning.'

I held his hands, looked him in the eyes. I was afraid of this talk, because if he could keep this from me, then he was capable of keeping other things, big things, things that could blow us up as a couple. I realized I was afraid to have the talk, and afraid not to, which made no sense at all.

'And I loved that you loved that about me, because I'd had so many men who had hated it.'

'Then whatever it is, we can get through it, Anita. We both value too much about each other to let anything spoil everything.'

Sitting there holding his hands, looking at him, I believed him, but . . . I'd always believed him and now I felt like he'd lied to me, but . . . Oh, fuck it.

'Okay, here goes. Are you really fighting the leaders of the other animal groups to force them to join our Coalition?'

'Sometimes.' He said it as if it were nothing, ordinary, like *Of course*.

I tried to take my hands back, but he held on. 'Why are you angry?'

'Why am I angry? For the love of God, Micah, you've been going out of town and having battles to the death and you didn't think I needed to know that?'

'Lower your voice,' he said.

I wanted to yell louder, but he was right; I'd just said he was committing murder according to human law. I lowered my voice and leaned in closer, but my voice was still angry, just softer, like angry whispering.

'How could you keep that from me?'

His face closed down, his own temper showing. He didn't get mad often, but when he did it could be as bad as mine. This was going to go so badly.

'I didn't keep anything from you. I just didn't tell you.'

'That's the same thing, it's just words to cover it up,' I said.

He let go of my hands and said, 'Do you tell me every time you risk your life as a U.S. Marshal?'

'No, but that's different.'

'How?' he asked.

I wanted to say, *It just is*, but that wasn't an answer. I opened my mouth to explain the difference and stopped. I frowned at him. 'I see it as different, very different.'

'Why is it any different? They're both our jobs, and both our jobs can be dangerous.'

'But I didn't know your job was dangerous,' I said.

He studied my face. 'What did you think we were doing to get all the other groups on board with the Coalition?'

'I thought you were persuading them. I thought you were using diplomacy, logic that it just made sense to join.'

'I do most of the time, but you've been around enough shapeshifters,

Anita. You know that some animal groups aren't about logic or being reasonable.'

'If I'd thought about it, I guess I would have assumed that some of the bodyguards did the one-on-one combat for you the way that most of the Clan tiger queens have a champion.'

'I'm not a weretiger, Anita. You brought all of them on board when you were able to call all of them to us.'

'Magic and sex won us the weretigers,' I said.

'Yes,' he said.

'What won us the rest?' I asked softly.

'You know that I sleep with some of the female dominants.'

I nodded. 'You share me with enough people, I can't bitch.'

He smiled. 'You mean you don't have room to bitch, but you still could,' he said.

I shrugged. 'It would be stupid and unfair if I complained.'

He smiled wider and touched my face, gently. 'A lot of women, and men, are really unfair to their other half, Anita. You have a reputation for being unreasonable and violent, but you're one of the most practical women I've ever been with.'

'And you're the most practical man I've ever been with,' I said.

'Most people wouldn't think that was very romantic,' he said.

I smiled. 'A little ruthless practicality is very important in our lives.'

'Yes,' he said, 'it is.'

'When you can pick a champion, do you?' I asked.

'I do.'

Then I realized that he was taking people who were my friends, or more, and I thought about them being in danger. Fuck.

'What now?' he asked.

This time I just answered the question. 'I just realized that means that anyone who travels out of town with you is maybe in as much danger as you are. I should have known that.'

'You mean I should have told you, or you should have known?'

'Both, maybe, I don't know, but, Micah, you're my size; most animal groups are led by the biggest, baddest motherfucker they've got. How have you been winning so many fights? I've seen you in practice and you're good, but you're like me; we just don't have the reach. Most taller people have longer arms and legs; they can just hit us before we can hit them, unless we're lucky, or they aren't good at fighting, but to fight your way to the top of a pack, or a pride, you have to be good.'

'Usually, I do something utterly ruthless and very abrupt before they're expecting it. Leopards are fast, faster than most lions, or tigers; I just have to make the first blow count.'

'You mean kill them with the first blow,' I said softly.

'Yes,' he said, and studied my face. 'Does that bother you?'

I thought about the fact that he had been killing people fairly casually for years and I hadn't known. I didn't like that part, but I knew without a doubt that if he hadn't killed them, they would have killed him. I wanted him alive and in my life more than I wanted some humane ideal of the world.

'No, I don't think it does. If anything bothers me it's the fact that we're heading into their territories and forcing ourselves on them.'

'It started with invitations from groups that wanted to hear about the Coalition. They wanted to join, and then we had a few groups that attacked the ones that had joined us, because one of the things they agree to do is not to make war. We're trying to make a no-war rule that sticks like the Vampire Council did with the vampires, but lycanthropes don't have centuries of obeying a central government. Some of them want to keep their independence or simply think that werelions are better than werewolves, so they don't want to be in a mixed animal group, which is the whole idea of the Coalition.'

'Lions are the most aggressive. I'm assuming that you were able to persuade a lot of the hyena groups through sex since they're matriarchal.'

He grinned. 'Most of them, but honestly some of the animal groups prefer their own animal, so sometimes the guards help. I don't always like sex as rough as the hyenas do, or the lions for that matter. Some of the guards are happy to help out.'

'I'll bet they are,' I said.

He smiled. 'And if the leader has a reputation for being a very good and very ruthless fighter, then sometimes I kill lesser dominants in the group for insulting me; by most group rules, being disrespectful to a visiting leader can either start a war or I'm within my rights to do it. Watching me use the claws like switchblades unnerves other shapeshifters, and knowing I'm willing to kill over something small makes them afraid of what I'll do in an official fight.'

'I know that a lot of alphas can partially change their hands to claws, but yours are more like switchblades, neat and clean, and you might miss it if you blink. You are the best I've ever seen at it.'

'Thank you, I do my best.'

'But you scare the leaders into negotiating instead of fighting,' I said.

'It doesn't scare them, Anita, or not like you mean. Our culture is different from straight human culture; we value aggression and ruthlessness to a degree that most humans don't. It's not just that I'm willing to kill to get them to do what I want, it's that if they join with us they now know that I'll do whatever it takes to protect them.'

'You said you do use champions when you can; who usually?' I asked.

'Bram and . . . Ares did it when they could.'

'You won't have Ares to help you fight now,' I said, and my chest felt tight. I wasn't sure if it was mourning Ares, or the thought that I'd also killed someone who was keeping Micah safe in more ways than I'd known. I felt stupid and slow and like they'd all been keeping secrets from me.

Micah took my hands again. 'Don't do that to yourself, Anita.'

'Do what?'

'Don't beat yourself up about Ares. You did what you had to do.'

I nodded. 'If I had to do it over again, the only difference would be I'd shoot him when he first asked me to, before he shifted forms. If I'd done that the other cops would be alive and unhurt.'

He squeezed my hands and pulled me toward him, as he leaned over in his chair. He kissed me, and tried for it to be more than just lips, but I pulled back. He frowned at me.

'What's wrong? I thought we weren't going to fight.'

'I had a breath mint, but I threw up in the bathroom here. I think before we tongue-kiss you might want me to brush my teeth.'

He laughed and pulled me into a hug. 'God, I love you so much.'

It made me laugh, too. 'I love you more,' I said.

He pulled back enough to see my face. 'They sell toothbrushes in the gift shop.'

'Are you saying you want to kiss me more?'

'I want to kiss you as thoroughly as possible before you have to go back to work.'

I grinned. 'Okay, but first you need to eat and get some water in you.'

He frowned. 'How did you know I hadn't eaten?'

'Because your mother hadn't, and I think you're both neglecting the basics?'

The smile faded around the edges. 'I don't know what she and Ty are going to do without Dad. I keep thinking what I'd do if something happened to Nathaniel.'

I hugged him to me, putting my face against the braid that our other boy had done for him, and I realized that I was mad at him for not sharing information, but I had some serious info I hadn't shared yet. 'You know how you said that if you could you'd marry us both?'

I felt him nod, still cuddled into the hug.

'Jean-Claude proposed.'

He drew back, so he could see my face. He looked startled. 'When?'

'At the hospital.'

'What did you say?' he asked.

'I said yes.'

His face went very still, very careful. 'That's wonderful.'

I frowned at him. 'I know there's a lot to figure out, but if anyone can do it we can.'

He nodded. 'Of course you can.'

I frowned harder. 'Micah, you do understand that he and I talked about a group ceremony, not just Jean-Claude and me.'

'He is our master, Anita; even if there weren't Nathaniel he would never let you marry someone else.'

'I don't know who I'll legally marry, only one's allowed, but he and I talked about a lot of things. Does everyone get a wedding ring? I asked if everybody gets an engagement ring.'

He looked at me with a strange, uncertain smile on his face. 'What did Jean-Claude say?'

'That he didn't know the answers to my very reasonable questions but that I didn't just tell him no was more than he'd hoped for and that we'd figure it out.'

'Really, he said that?'

'He said that if he'd dreamt I'd have said yes, he'd have conspired with the other men in my life and made it the most romantic night of my life, and swept me off my feet.'

His smile was happier then. 'I can hear him saying that.'

'I asked him who would be part of the group, and beyond you and Nathaniel we aren't sure of anyone else, but we're not sure they aren't either.'

'Who else?'

I sighed. 'I'm worried what Asher would do if he's not included.'

'I am not marrying Asher,' Micah said.

I laughed. 'I know, me either, but Jean-Claude may feel differently. I don't know yet. I haven't had a lot of time to think about it.'

Then I realized I might need to say something else. 'When I had to leave Nicky down in the basement and I didn't know what would happen to him, I told him I loved him.'

Micah nodded. 'Nathaniel and I wondered how long it would take you to figure that out.'

I frowned at him. 'Did everyone know before me?' I asked.

'Everyone but Nicky, and Cynric maybe.'

That made my shoulders slump a little. 'I'm not sure how Cynric will take the group marriage thing.'

'If he's included, he'll be fine.'

I stared at Micah. 'You are joking, right?'

'Why, because he's young?'

'No, I mean, yes, I mean . . . Do you really want to be married to Cynric?'

'The only two people I want to be married to are you and Nathaniel.'

'But you'll marry Jean-Claude; why?'

'Because he's our master and you're his human servant and he introduces me as Our Micah.'

'How do you feel about that, by the way?' I asked.

'I'm not a fan, but he has to do something for the other vampires to make them not feel like you're cuckolding him with the rest of us. Prestige is very important with the vampires and the lycanthropes. He has to come first for you, or it would damage his power structure, our power structure that we've all worked so hard to build.'

'Is that why you don't mind the other vampires assuming that you're Jean-Claude's lover?'

He nodded. 'I'm secure, and besides, I am in love with Nathaniel. It's not like I'm all freaked out about being with another man.'

I leaned back so that we didn't have our arms around each other.

Micah kept my left hand in his, but we sat and looked at each other. We were both being cautious suddenly.

'So, you, Nathaniel, Jean-Claude, and me, and . . . who else?'

'I don't know,' he said.

'Are you in love with anyone else?'

'No, are you?' he asked.

'Nicky, and I love Cynric, but I'm not *in* love with him. I love Asher, but I'm not in love with him, and since he may force me to kill him someday I'd rather not be.'

He squeezed my hand. 'I know we're bringing him home before he ruins everything with the local werehyenas there, but I agree that he may force us to kill him.'

I nodded and felt inexplicably sad. 'Shouldn't getting married be happy and not so complicated?'

He laughed. 'We're talking about at least four of us in a group marriage and maybe more, Anita; that's complicated.'

I rolled my eyes and sighed. 'Okay, okay, I didn't mean that part.'

He laughed again and then said, 'One other thought. If we are doing this, then you need to tell Richard, or Jean-Claude does, before he hears it from somewhere else.'

I hung my head. 'Damn it, he's an ex.'

'An ex who you still have sex with occasionally, and who Asher lets top him in the dungeon, and who Jean-Claude and you, and sometimes Asher, all have sex with.'

'He doesn't have sex with the men.'

'You mean he doesn't have genital contact with them.'

I looked at him. 'Wow, that is what I meant, but that just . . . that was blunt of you.'

He smiled. 'I think if we're going to do this for real, we'll need to be blunt.'

'I'd love to argue with you, but I think I'd just sound stupid, so I'll pass.'

'I'll be honest: I'd love to marry you legally and have Nathaniel be a part of the ceremony like husband one and husband two, but Jean-Claude has to be a part of it, and probably the legal part.'

'Why?' I asked.

'First, his ego won't let it be anyone else. He's reasonable, ruthlessly practically, but like all the old vampires he's also arrogant. He's the first vampire king of America, and you are his queen.'

'I'm your queen, too.'

'Yes, but the shapeshifters are used to taking second place to the vampires in the power structure. They'll think it's normal that the legal spouse is Jean-Claude. The vampires have made peace with the thought that Jean-Claude looks the other way because he gets to sleep with all of us, too. They're a lot happier now that Envy has become one of Jean-Claude's regular lovers.'

'I can't sleep with everybody every night, and he does really prefer women to men, unless it's Asher.'

'He'd totally do Richard if our Ulfric would be okay with it,' Micah said.

'Not happening,' I said.

'I know.'

'You said once that you thought you'd have to sleep with Jean-Claude to be my leopard king, and you were relieved to find out it wasn't true, but you would have done it.'

'I would have done anything to save my people from Chimera, and Jean-Claude is not a fate worse than death,' he said, and smiled.

'No, no, he's not,' I said, and smiled back.

'I think I can eat something now,' Micah said.

'Good, I'll try some soup.'

'The lycanthropy keeps any of us from catching viruses, so you can't be sick.'

I didn't want to tell him it was the smell of his father's sickness that had reminded me of the smell of rotting corpses, so I said, 'I think something at lunch didn't agree with me.'

He accepted that, and for all I knew it might be true. We got food, and I started to get coffee, but the smell made my stomach roll again. I got water and soup. I also texted Edward to see if how he was feeling, because if there had been something wrong with the food then he'd be hit worse, because he didn't have the lycanthropy helping him stay healthy.

Edward was fine. I ate half my soup and was so done. I'd told Micah that I wanted to question Little Henry. Micah rushed his food so he could go back up with me and back up to his dad. Though we did stop off at the gift shop and get me a little travel toothbrush set. I did a quick oral cleanup in the bathroom and when Micah kissed me good-bye it was as thorough a kiss as you would ever want to do in public view of a hallway full of cops.

They gave us both good-natured ribbing about it. 'Get a room, Blake.' 'Another Callahan ladies' man, it figures.' The cops couldn't seem to decide which of us was the coworker to be teased and which of us was the 'girl.'

He and Bram went back into his father's room. Nicky and I went in search of Henry Crawford's doctor. I wanted to know if they'd found any fang marks on him, or any injuries at all. He'd looked unharmed, but that didn't mean he hadn't been; not every kind of harm leaves marks.

69

Henry Crawford wasn't that hurt and normally wouldn't have been on the same floor as Rush Callahan, but putting him a room just down the hallway from Micah's dad meant that all the cops hanging out there could help watch Henry's room, since vampires did have a habit of coming back for humans they'd singled out. Wolves will take the weakest in a herd, the easiest to kill. Though wolves are one of the traditional and most common animals to call for a master vampire, vamps don't think like wolves. They think more like lions.

Lions don't pick the weakest, though they can, and they will take opportunistic kills if offered, or even chase other predators off their kills and eat it. They'll even eat carrion, but when they hunt they go at it like some people enter a bar on Saturday night. They walk into the room, survey the crowd, pick out one they like, and think, 'I'll have that one.' People then spend the night seducing that person to take home for sex.

Lions pick the biggest, toughest water buffalo, or the fastest, juiciest-looking antelope, or whatever strikes their fancy, and then they throw overwhelming force at it. They live as part of a pride of lions, and the bigger the pride, usually, the bigger prey they will bring down, and the more arrogantly they choose it. Lions are the guy, or girl, who believes he, or she, really is God's gift to the opposite sex, and of course, you'll be flattered if they want you, and you will eventually say yes. Most of these people never turn into stalkers, because they are beautiful, sexy, and most people can be seduced. But lions, real lions, don't want sex from their prey, that's what other lions are for; they want to eat you, and unless the water buffalo can fight its way free early in the chase or have enough of its herd to fight back force against force, the lions will bring it down and eat it. Buffalo is big prey, so they kill it first; smaller prey sometimes gets eaten before it's totally dead. Most humans aren't big enough prey for vampires to kill us first. They toy with us, some because they enjoy it, because they can, but others because they're still deciding – do they want sex from us, or servitude, or are we just food?

Henry was still alive. The question was, had they just been playing with him, had they meant to make him their slave, or had the vampire that bewitched him grown to desire him? Food, torment, slavery, or sex; those were the choices between humans and vampires. How could I say that, with Jean-Claude's proposal just a few hours old? In my experience with vampires the overwhelming truth was they saw us as prey. I actually think it was a way of distancing themselves emotionally so they could feed on us. It was the same principle I used at crime scenes to distance myself from the victims. The bodies became *it*s, things, so I didn't run screaming. Live victims are harder; they demand more, and vampires can't feed on the dead.

Some of the vampire community called me a living vampire, but if I was, I didn't have the attitude yet. I would not have picked Henry Crawford junior at six foot seven, or his father, who had not been a small man either, as my victims *du jour*. I'd seen the group that had been out there in the woods looking for the lost, and there had been so many other men in the group who would have been easier marks than the Crawfords. Why them? Why go for the water buffalo when there'd been so many antelopes to choose from?

Several of my inner beasts sort of 'looked' up at me, if something inside you could look 'up.' They didn't talk like people talk, but I understood them all the same. Sometimes you get tired of antelope, and if you're big enough to take the water buffalo, why not? Until they took the Crawfords the vampires had taken tourists, some families with younger kids, hikers, one runner doing his route through the mountains, elderly couples in isolated areas. They'd been victims of opportunity, like the Crawfords, but everyone else had been much easier marks. Maybe the vampires were learning how to hunt and just decided to take bigger prey?

Tests on the blood around the man's groin had come back human and female. I was betting it was from the female vampire in custody, but we wouldn't know until we got the DNA tests back from the saliva in the bites she'd given to Travers. Because the vampires had lawyered up, we couldn't take DNA samples without them being awake and having their lawyer present. Ares' body had been considered too hazardous to test because of the lycanthropy. They'd been keeping Little Henry knocked out most of the time, because he'd been pretty hysterical any time he started to come to. They couldn't keep him doped up forever, but they also couldn't figure out what was wrong with him mentally and emotionally. Yes, he'd been through serious trauma and his father's death, but it was almost as if he were having hallucinations when he was awake and horrible nightmares if he slept without the drugs. Henry was a very big, strong guy to have the nurses waking him from nightmares or trying to control him during waking hallucinations.

Dr Bill Aimes was tall, athletic in that I-hit-the-treadmill-and-light-weights kind of way, with short blond hair and steel-rimmed glasses. He was stumped at how to help Little Henry. 'Is there anything that a vampire could do to him that would cause waking hallucinations and night terrors?'

'Some vampires can cause terror in a person and feed off it, like a sort of metaphysical snack, but usually they have to be physically closer to do it. It's usually a touch-distance kind of thing.'

'Could they be causing the fear and visions so they could keep feeding off him from a distance?'

I thought about it. 'I'd normally say no, but this vampire has done so many things that I would have said were impossible that I wouldn't rule it out. I can tell you, though, that if he's got a connection to a vampire, I should be able to sense it.'

'How would you sense it?'

'It's hard to explain unless you have a background in psychic ability,' I said.

He smiled and shook his head. 'No, I'm strictly a touch-it-and-it's-real person. I don't even believe in God, because I can't put him in a test tube.'

'You're an atheist?' I asked.

He nodded.

'Then you can't use holy objects against vampires, or faith against the demonic.'

'I think holy objects glow because of the individual's faith in them, and I've never met a demon.'

The way he said it made me ask, 'Do you not believe in demons?'

'If I don't believe in God, it's very hard to believe in the rest.'

'Angels?' I asked.

'Sorry, but no.'

'I'm so sorry,' I said, before I could stop myself.

'Sorry about what?' he asked.

'Your world is very . . . narrow, Dr Aimes. I find that sad, and it also means if vampires attack us you have to hide behind all of us believers.'

He laughed. 'I will hide behind you proudly and keep not believing in all the glowy stuff.'

'All right, you can hide behind me, but in the meantime I'll see what I can sense from Henry Crawford.'

'I hope you can give us some clue, because it's almost as if he's continuing to be freshly traumatized in the dreams and hallucinations.'

'Aren't night terrors by definition traumatizing?' I asked.

He seemed to think about that and then nodded. 'I suppose so, but these seem different. I've worked with patients with post-traumatic stress disorder and helped them work through some truly terrible memories, and all I can tell you is that there is something different going on here and I have no idea what it is.'

'Vampire mind games can fuck with stuff,' I said.

He grinned suddenly and gave a small laugh. 'Well, I guess you would be the expert on vampires.'

I agreed with him, gathered up Nicky, and went to see Little Henry Crawford.

70

Little Henry looked smaller lying down than he had standing up, and hospital gowns make us all look somehow shrunken and weak, but none of it could hide that he was still six foot seven, with a spread of shoulders that was almost wide enough to touch the metal railings of the bed. Who would look at this guy and think, *Him, I'll have him, and I'll totally fuck – him – up!*

Everyone in the search group had been physically smaller, so why him and his dad? I asked Nicky, 'Why did they take him and his father? They're both ex-military, ex–special forces, in good shape, and they are both well over six feet tall. You saw the other search team members; would the Crawfords have been your choice of prey?'

'None of the vampires I saw were ex-military. They're undead, but that doesn't give them experience they didn't have in real life.'

'You're saying they couldn't judge who was dangerous and who wasn't?'

'Not like you and I can.'

'But the two men are still huge; that's not something you need training to see,' I said.

'True.'

'It's like a lion pride going after a giraffe when there are plenty of gazelles to choose from.'

'But if you have enough lions you can bring down a giraffe, and if you have too many lions you need something that big to feed the pride. You said it yourself, Anita. This was the largest group of flesh-eating zombies you've ever seen.'

'Yeah, but they didn't eat the men – the zombies, I mean. The lions caught the giraffe but then didn't eat it; why not?'

'They ate one of them,' he said.

'But even the one they killed, they didn't eat it, not the way they did the others. You saw them, Nicky. They eat all the flesh. They ate enough to disfigure Crawford senior and kill him, but they didn't eat enough of him for the lion pride to be full of giraffe. It's like they were thinking more like serial killers than zombies.'

'Some vampires are serial killers,' he said.

'True, but that doesn't feel like what's going on. I mean, technically most vampires are serial killers, but it's because they have to feed on people, not because they want to kill them. Same outcome, but very different motives.'

'But the person ends up just as dead either way,' Nicky said.

'But serial killers get off on the torture, or the method of killing. The bodies down in the basement were just dead.'

'Throats torn out on most of the bodies I saw,' Nicky said.

'I didn't get much of a chance to see, but the ones near us had intact throats.'

'Probably tore out other major arteries and veins,' he said.

'Probably.'

'From what you've told me, the zombies should have just eaten everything they could hold in their stomach and then left the bodies to be found, or rot, whatever.'

'That's typical,' I said.

'So what caused these zombies to just kill the people and store them?'

I looked at him. 'Say that again.'

'They stored them like groceries, or cords of wood for winter,' he said.

'I thought about the pictures in my history books of the concentration camps with the bodies stacked on top of each other in piles.'

'They weren't piled haphazardly, Anita. It was neat, orderly stacks. You don't body-dump that way, and you don't stack like that for disposal.'

I had a thought for how he knew that, but instead I asked, 'Why would you pile them up like that?'

'It was a food cache.'

'Zombies, even flesh eaters, don't do that, Nicky.'

'Do ghouls do that?'

'If it's an old pack that's been around for a few years undetected, they'll start removing the freshly buried bodies from underneath so that the grave looks undisturbed, and I've seen them keep bodies in a crypt for eating later, but it's rare. I mean, I only know of two cases where ghouls were that organized. They're usually more animalistic.'

'A lot of predators store food for later, Anita. They drag it up trees, bury it under leaves, hide it from other predators, but they plan on eating it later, if nothing else finds it and eats it first.'

I thought about it; he was right about animal predators. 'Okay, if we think of it as just another kind of predator, then why so many bodies?'

'The group must be larger than we know.'

I shook my head. 'There aren't that many people missing. Even if you add up the vampires and zombies that we've already destroyed, there aren't enough missing to need that kind of food. The bodies were the missing, Nicky, if we could have left anything unburned to identify them from.'

'How many zombies would need that kind of food?'

'Hell, I don't know. I've never heard of a group that big.'

'Ghouls then; how many would feed off that kind of stored food?'

I thought about it and tried to figure it out. 'The largest ghoul pack I've ever heard of was more than a hundred, and it was in Eastern Europe. I guess something that big would need that kind of food.'

'But ghouls will eat badly decayed bodies, right?'

'Yes.'

'Will zombies?'

'No, they like fresher meat than ghouls.'

'So, either these zombies are more like ghouls and would have eaten the bodies as they continued to decay, or what?' he asked.

'Or the vampire was planning on needing more food,' I said.

'There's only one reason to need more food, Anita.'

'He's planning to make more zombies,' I said.

'A lot more, but we destroyed his creepy grocery store, so if he still raises that many zombies, where does the food come from?' Nicky asked.

There was a voice from the bed, hoarse as if he hadn't been talking much lately. 'Us, us.'

We turned and found Little Henry looking at us with big brown eyes.

'Us, who?' I asked.

'People,' he said. His eyes went a little wider, lips parting as his breathing sped up.

'What people?' I asked.

Henry opened his mouth and screamed, 'God! God! God!' He sat up in bed, clawing at the tubes and wires.

My cross flared to white-hot fire. I got out my gun, because when the cross flared it meant a vampire was nearby and doing bad things. Nicky had his gun out, too, so we were armed as the nurse and doctor came through the door.

'What did you do?' Dr Aimes demanded as he shielded his eyes from my cross and ran for his patient.

'It's a vampire,' I said. I'd known vampires that could be invisible in plain sight even to me.

Dr Aimes and a small blond nurse were trying to hold Henry so he didn't yank any more tubes out of himself, but it's hard to hold down someone that big. I'd have had Nicky help, but we had other things to do.

'Search the corners of the room by walking along the wall,' I said.

'You think the vamp has been here all along?' he asked.

'I don't know, but my cross says it's here.'

Nicky and I walked the perimeter of the room, guns out and ready, shoulder scraping the wall so even if it tricked our eyes we'd run into it. Invisible doesn't make you less solid.

I was half-blinded by the glow of my own cross. I thought about going for my sunglasses, but I didn't want to let go of the gun with either hand. I caught movement out of the corner of my eye, but it was the nurse being tossed across the room. Henry was still screaming, wordless, ragged, and frantic. Cops and more nurses came in to try to help hold him down, but their holy objects flared to blue-white light, too. The cops pulled their guns.

It was Deputy Al who asked, 'Where's the vampire?'

I explained what we were doing, and we had almost too many people searching the room while the medics fought to hold down Henry and he threw them around like toys. We finished our perimeter walk of the room. Nicky had gotten to the bathroom before I had, and he and another uniformed officer had checked it and called it clear. My cross was still white and blue and glowing, but there was nothing here.

'It's not here, Anita,' Nicky called to me over the screaming.

'There's nothing here,' Al said.

I glanced up at the ceiling; vampires could do that, but not while invisible. It took too much concentration to levitate and use mind tricks to that degree. If there'd been more shadows in the room, maybe a vampire could have done both, but the lights were full on and it was bright as day.

'Then help hold down Henry,' I said.

Nicky put up his gun, because I'd said so, and went to help the doctor and battered nurses. When he moved to help, so did a couple of the other bigger officers, and as soon as they touched Little Henry their holy objects flared brighter, going from blue-white to a pure burning incandescent white. His screams intensified, and he almost threw all that muscle off him, but one of them was almost as big as Nicky; they had enough strength to pin him to the bed.

I saw Dr Aimes pick up a syringe through the glow of the holy objects.

I yelled, 'Aimes, don't do it!'

Dr Aimes turned and looked at me. His glasses were gone, lost in the struggle. His cheek was already swelling a little. 'We have to calm him down. He's going to hurt himself, or someone else.'

'I know where the vampire is,' I said.

'What are you talking about?' He turned toward the IV tube with the syringe.

The room was small enough that I was there in time to grab his arm. 'It's in Henry.'

'What are you talking about?'

'Look at the holy objects when they touch him.'

He blinked at the bed as if he hadn't noticed, and maybe he hadn't. It looked like he'd gotten a good hit to the face. That can ring your bells and disorient you for a while. He turned back to me, looking puzzled. 'I don't understand.'

'I think I do,' I said, 'but it's going to be unpleasant.'

'More unpleasant than this?' Aimes said.

'Maybe,' I said.

'Will it help my patient?'

'Yes,' I said.

'Then do it.'

He should have asked more questions, or maybe I should have waited for him to recover from the blow that he'd had to the side of his head, but I didn't. Because he might get all cautious and reconsider and I didn't want that.

Nicky called to me from the bed, where he was still helping hold down Little Henry. 'What are you going to do?' Nicky was having to work at holding just one arm and part of the upper body. He could bench-press small cars if they had a balance point. He shouldn't have been having to work that hard to hold a human down, not even a really strong one.

I didn't know how to explain it to a room full of people with no psychic or vampire experience, so I said, 'I'm going to find the vampire.'

'How?' Deputy Al asked.

'Little Henry's going to help me.'

'How?' Al asked again.

'Easier if I just show you,' I said, and I started stripping off my weapons. All the men by the bed should have done the same, but there hadn't been time; now there was. I'd take off anything that Henry could grab and use against us, and then I'd have the men do the same one by one, and when we were as safe as we could manage, I'd go exploring. I'd go exploring inside Little Henry Crawford's mind.

71

They wrestled Little Henry into handcuffs on the metal bed rails, but he continued to thrash and jerk so much that Nicky said, 'The railings aren't going to hold; hurry.'

There was no beast inside Little Henry for me to call to mine. He wasn't a vampire that I could call with my necromancy. I'd broken ties between both types of preternaturals and their vampire masters, but I'd never tried to break a human free. I wasn't exactly sure how to do it, but Nicky was right; whatever I was going to do I needed to hurry.

I started with touch, because all vampire powers are greater with skin on skin. The moment I touched him I felt the power of the vampire. My cross flared white, hot, incandescent white just like the police officers' crosses had. Henry screamed louder, his voice growing ragged with the abuse. I tried to trace the power backward, but it was like I got lost inside Henry, like the very warmth and humanness of him somehow confused my power.

'Shit,' I said.

'What's wrong?' Dr Aimes asked, hovering close.

'If he were a lycanthrope or a vampire I could do this, but human is harder.'

'Do what? What are you trying to do?'

'Break him free of the vampire that's possessed him.'

'That's not possible,' Deputy Al said.

'I've done it before,' I said.

'It's impossible; once a vampire has you, they have you,' Al said.

I shook my head. 'Not to me, it's not impossible to me.'

I thought about shoving the cross into his skin. It would chase the vampire back for a few moments, but it wouldn't free someone who was already this deeply entrenched.

I walked around the bed to Nicky. 'Help me get into the bed.'

Nicky didn't question it, just picked me up.

Dr Aimes said, 'What are you going to do, Marshal?'

'I need to see his eyes, and I'm too damn short.'

Nicky helped lift me over those long, muscled arms that were still straining against the cuffs and the narrow metal bars of the bed. Two officers were still holding down his legs, or he would have bucked me off the bed. I tried to stay high on my knees above his body, but he was thrashing too much; I knelt over his chest, using both hands to grab his head. He was still shrieking, the sound so loud with me above his face that it was almost painful. My cross flared so bright that I was nearly blinded by it. I needed to see his eyes, and I couldn't. Did I dare take off the cross? But the other holy objects were so bright I wasn't sure it would make that much difference.

The skin of his face was cool against my hands, and I could feel the vampire inside him. I decided to treat him as if he weren't human, as if I had every right to expect him to respond to my power. 'Henry Crawford, Henry, look at me!' I put energy and power into my words.

He stopped struggling and blinked up at me through the edge of the lighted cross. 'Henry, Henry, can you hear me?'

He blinked, staring up at me as if he didn't know what I was.

'Henry, can you hear me?'

'I hear you,' he whispered.

'I'm going to set you free.'

'You can't. He told me I'm his forever.'

'He lied,' I said. 'They all lie.'

'Who?' he asked.

'Vampires.'

The cross light faded a little so I could see how green and brown his eyes were. Most people with hazel eyes really have brown eyes with a hint of gray, or green, but Little Henry's eyes really were green and brown all mixed together. I watched the pain and confusion in those eyes, and then I saw it, like a reflection of something dark. I would never know if I'd truly 'seen' it, or if it was my mind translating the untranslatable. The next moment the vampire threw its power into Henry and tried for me, but vampire was something I could understand.

I'd fought two other necromancers that had come back from the dead; one had almost killed me, but that was before I accepted what I was, who I was, and what that meant.

The vampire filled Henry with terror, and he drew breath to scream again, but I sent love in the place of fear. I sent the soft warmth of welcome and friendship; I offered a hand in the darkness. I offered Henry Crawford hope and a way out. I shone a light into the darkness that the vampire offered, and Henry turned to it the way humans always do; we need hope almost more than anything else, for without it we are lost. I helped Henry find his way back from the hell that the vampire had trapped him in, and I saw what he'd done to him. This vampire fed on fear and he'd kept Henry in perpetual terror during the day so he could feed off Henry's fear.

'You evil bastard,' I whispered.

His voice came out of Henry's mouth, but it wasn't Henry's voice. 'I am not evil, Anita Blake; he is mine, my slave to do with as I wish.'

'No, I say you cannot have him.'

'It is too late, he is mine!'

'Bullshit!' I threw my power into Henry, threw my necromancy into him like a guided missile seeking its target. Henry was just the sky that I was flying through, searching for the vampire, and Henry wanted to help me, because I had offered him the first peace and hope that he had since the vampires took him. Henry helped me, by wanting me to win. He opened himself up and didn't fight me as I sent a psychic gift into him that had no business being in a human being. I tried to make it a gentle passing, but in honesty I wanted the vampire more.

'He is mine, Anita Blake, mine!'

'NO!' I saw the vampire's body wrapped in dark cloth in what looked like a cave, or bare stone at least. It turned its head, and it was emaciated, skeletal, but the eyes – the eyes were alive, burning with fire as dark as the night itself.

'Yes, necromancer, the Mother of All Things breathed her power into me when you drank her down. She tried to escape to my body, but you would not let her go; thus I have her power but am free of her control. She did not control all the vampires merely for her own enjoyment. Some of us she controlled so we did not destroy all that is.'

'You can't destroy all that is,' I said.

'I can destroy all humans, with my power and hers combined. I am free from this body and free to enter others. The Mother took me with her when she tried to possess you and Jean-Claude and your others, but now I do not need anyone's help to ride the bodies of others.'

'Who are you?'

'Do you not recognize the feel of me, Anita? You and your lovers have tasted my power before. You denied me deaths once, but you and the police fed me in the mountains, and again in the hospital; with every death, I fed and grew stronger.'

'You are not the Lover of Death, you can't be.'

'Why can I not?'

'Your power feels completely different.'

'I was reborn when you slew our Mother; she filled me with her darkness, and I felt you filled with it, too. We are all that is left of her, Anita Blake, you and I.'

I stared into Henry's eyes and saw a body so ravaged by time that if he hadn't opened his eyes and moved I'd have taken him for a corpse, a long-dead corpse. 'You were in the basement. You just entered one of the zombies so you could move better in daylight. How did you get your body out in time and not burn?'

'I am the creator of my line; you know that rotting vampires do not burn in the sun. The flesh eaters are swift and strong; I carried myself to safety and hid in the woods while you killed all my hard work.'

'Apparently, you got some of Marmee Noir's necromancy that I didn't, but I got something you didn't get.'

'Lies.'

'You can only take over zombies you raise from the dead. I'll admit it's impressive that they don't have to be in the grave first, just three days or so dead for the soul to move on and you can raise them. Bully for you.'

'My vampires are more powerful than your master's.'

'Because you inhabit them and share some of your own power with them somehow, but you only take over the newly made ones; why is that? You were trying to take over your older bloodline vamps not that long ago; something about the Mother's power keeps you out.'

'I have no limits, Anita; I will prove that to you tonight.'

'Not with Henry you won't.'

'And how will you stop me?' It was Henry's face, but the sneering arrogance wasn't; it was like a stranger using the other man's face.

'Like this.' I called the *ardeur*, and I prayed that I could use it like a gentle scalpel to cut away only what needed to be gone but save the rest. I wanted to free Henry, not enslave him to me. My cross flared bright and brighter as I leaned down and laid the gentlest of kisses on his mouth. I thrust my power through that kiss and into him. The Lover of Death fought back, and if it had been night maybe he could have kept Henry, but it was daylight and I was a creature of the day, I had slain the Father of the Day, and taken over his powers as the Queen of Tigers, and from the Mother of All Darkness I had inherited the ability to break the unbreakable bonds between animal to call and master vampire, between vampire and their blood-oathed Master of the City, and between human servant and vampire master. It had been her gift and she had tried to use it on me more than once, and any vampire power that was used on me had a percentage chance of becoming mine forever. I was the weapon that the vampires had created, the perfect nemesis that the Mother of All Darkness, the Living Night, had forged simply by hitting me often enough and hard enough with the fires of her insane power.

Every holy object in the room flared so that I was physically blind to everything but the white light, but the parts of my eyes that saw in dreams, they saw the vampire as the light chased down the tie that bound Henry to him and burned it up like a fuse. I tried to thrust that light into the vampire himself, but he turned those night-dark eyes to me and whispered inside my mind, 'You have taken my servant, but you cannot take me. And now that you know I am alive I must destroy you, Anita Blake.'

I thought at him and 'heard' the words in the air of his hiding place. 'Right back at you, Morte d'Amour.'

Then he was gone, the cave or whatever it had been lost to my inner sight. I came back to myself straddling Henry's chest, the holy objects fading back to simple metal, and me rising up from the kiss.

I stared into Henry's eyes from inches away; they were too wide, lips parted, pulse beating in his throat like a trapped thing. I had a moment for my bloodlust to see that pulse, like candy to be licked away at until the juicy center popped in my mouth, but I'd worked too hard to free him to hurt him now. I wasn't new at this game anymore; I didn't have to touch his neck. I moved off, so that I was sitting on as much of the bed as his broad shoulders left, but at least

I wasn't straddling him. It was hard to have serious conversations with a man while you were straddling any part of his body.

'You okay?' I asked, and my voice sounded a little breathless, as if it had been hard work or something.

He looked around the room as if afraid of what he'd see, and then he said, 'I think so.'

Dr Aimes came over to the side of the bed and started checking his vitals. I think it was more for something normal to do than because he felt he needed to get Henry's temperature and pulse rate.

Nicky helped me down off the bed and then started handing me my weapons back. Al came over to us. He looked pale. 'I didn't think any of that was possible.'

'Things are only impossible until you find someone who can do it,' I said, as I tucked the last gun back in place.

'I guess so. So he made Henry his human servant?'

'Yeah.'

'Is that like someone who they bite a couple of times or something?'

'No, the really powerful ones don't have to lay a fang on someone to make them a servant.'

'I thought they had to bite you first.'

'Nope,' I said.

His phone rang, and he checked the Caller ID. 'Sorry, got to take this, glad you were able to help Little Henry.' He left to take his phone call.

Dr Aimes came over to me. 'I don't understand everything that just happened, but he seems perfectly fine now, a little shaken, but fine.'

'If you don't believe in angels I can't explain it to you,' I said with a smile.

'Are you saying you're an angel, Marshal Blake?'

I laughed. 'An angel, no, I would never claim that.'

'You were covered in white light at the end, almost completely hidden by the white glow of the crosses, and when you kissed him I swear I saw the light travel from your mouth into him.'

'I prayed for guidance to be able to free him without him coming to any more harm.' Yes, that was an edited version of what I'd prayed for, but God is okay with not explaining everything to everybody; if he weren't, he'd have left more explicit instructions for the rest of us.

'For a moment I could have sworn I saw wings in the light,' Aimes said.

I smiled and looked at Nicky. 'You see wings?'

He shook his head.

I smiled at the doctor. 'If you saw wings, Dr Aimes, they weren't mine.'

'Whose were they, then?'

I smiled wider. 'I believe in angels, remember.'

He looked shaken. 'You'll drive a man to drink, or to church, saying things like that, Marshal.'

'It's not my job to drive you to church and not my intention to drive you to drink.'

Dr Aimes looked at me. He had a look I'd seen before, but it was usually the first time people see a ghost, or a vampire, and they get good and truly scared for the first time.

'What is your intention, Marshal Blake?'

'I want to question Henry and see if we can get a clue where the vampire's body is. If we can destroy the original body, we can end this.'

'I'll leave you to question Mr Crawford. I think I'll go get that drink.'

'On duty?' I said.

'If any good science-loving atheist wouldn't need a drink after what I just saw, he's a better disbeliever than I am.' With that, he left.

The other cops were almost evenly divided between being scared by what they'd seen and being so impressed that it was almost worse, because I wasn't sure what they'd expect me to be able to do next time. Aimes hadn't been the only one who saw the white-shadowed outline of wings. I told them it was an answer to prayer, not me personally. I finally told one overly solicitous uniform, 'Trust me, I'm no angel.'

Nicky started laughing and couldn't seem to stop.

'Yuk it up, lion boy.'

That made him laugh harder, until he had to lean against the wall with tears trailing down from his eye. At least his laughing stopped any more weird theological questions; they just couldn't seem to talk about angels with this big, muscled bad-ass guy laughing his ass off beside me.

72

My phone rang, and it was Ted Nugent's 'Bad to the Bone,' which was Edward's ring tone.

'Hey, Ted, what's up?'

'All the older crime scenes that we found today were in Callahan's district almost without exception.'

'Really?'

'Yes, I don't think the sheriff was targeted by accident. Gutterman says that Callahan senior visited the isolated houses regularly, had coffee with them, checked on his older couples, or people with disabilities, anyone he was concerned about.'

'I take it those were a lot of the people who got hit,' I said.

'Yes.'

I said, 'Hang on a minute, Ted.' I turned to the cops and nurses with Henry. 'I'm going to take this call. I'll be right back; I have a few questions for you, Mr Crawford.'

'Marshal Blake, you just saved my immortal soul; you can call me Little Henry.'

I smiled. 'I don't know about your soul, I think that was yours either way, but I can't call you Little Henry when you're over a foot taller than me.'

He smiled. 'Everyone calls me that, and I'm taller than all of them.'

I smiled and made a vague motion at him, trying for noncommittal. I went out into the hallway with Nicky trailing behind. We walked a little way away from all the other police to have more privacy. 'I'm back, Ted.'

'I take it you cured Little Henry.'

'Yeah, that's a whole 'nother story, but it sounds like they took

Callahan out before he could piece together that they were hitting his people. The vamp's original body has to be in the sheriff's territory, somewhere that the sheriff would have known about.'

'Gutterman says that Al knows the area just about as well as the sheriff,' Edward said.

'Al left to take a phone call, but I can ask him about old mines, caves, anything with a rock wall and a dirt floor.' I told Edward about the vision I'd had with Little Henry.

'I called Al and told him to start making a list of places, but I'll call him again and add your information so he can narrow it down.'

'I love that you already had Al making a list.'

'And you're going to stay and see if Henry has any other information that will help us narrow the list down even further, aren't you?'

'Yeah.'

'Hatfield and I are making teams to go search the area now. If you want to be in on it, don't take too long questioning your new conquest.'

'Oh, God, Ted, don't say it that way, I worked really hard to not make him another conquest.'

'Sorry, bad joke; question Henry fast and get over here. I'll quote one of your favorite movies, "We're burning daylight."'

I grinned. 'You're one of the few people who knew I had a thing for John Wayne movies until very recently.'

'That one shitty night in the hotel and a marathon on the Western channel makes it hard to forget,' he said.

'Hey, you liked them, too.'

'True.'

'And the next day when we said we hadn't gotten much sleep, the other cops thought we'd had marathon sex,' I said.

'They wouldn't believe the movie marathon,' he said.

'They never do.'

'We're going to be ready to start searching in about forty-five minutes. Will you be ready?'

'Do my best, though I'm down a guard.'

'What'd you do to this one?'

'Nothing,' I said, and let the offended tone sound.

'Sure,' he said.

'I'll explain when we're out searching for vampires.'

'I was going to divide you and me up on different teams so that we could trust that at least two of the groups know enough about vampires to look in every place a body could be.'

'That makes sense, but I'll miss having you at my back,' I said.

'Same here, but we really are burning daylight, and I don't mean to go all movie line on you, but I have a bad feeling about tonight.'

'How so?'

'The Lover of Death is spooked now. He has nothing to lose by throwing everything at us.'

'You worried about zombies?' I asked.

'Aren't you?'

I thought about all the bodies we'd found in the house, like a creepy grocery store. Nicky had said you'd need a hell of a lot of zombies to store food like that. 'Yeah, I'm worried about more zombies.'

'Then question Little Henry, and I'll have SWAT meet you at the hospital to drive out with you. Hatfield and I will take our teams and start searching our sections. SWAT will have the map with the locations marked. Let's find the bastard before nightfall.'

'Will do,' I said. We hung up, and I went back to see if Little Henry remembered anything about a room with stone walls and a dirt floor.

73

Little Henry was already up and yelling for fresh clothes when we went back into the room. The hospital gown, which would have wrapped around me three times and tied twice, didn't reach his knees, and gaped in the back badly. The view was a nice one, but I looked away, because he wasn't mine to gape at. I'd worked too hard to not *ardeur* his ass to look at it now. Either Henry didn't realize he was flashing us, or he didn't care.

'I need clothes!'

'Mr Crawford, you didn't have any when you came in,' the small blond nurse told him, finally raising her voice back, just this side of yelling at him. She'd been the one he tossed across the room, though he probably didn't remember it.

'I've got an extra T-shirt in my tac bag that will fit you,' Nicky said.

Henry turned, his long, long hair in a tangle around him. 'Thank you.'

'But your inseam isn't going to fit in my extra pair of pants.'

I turned to the nurse, who was glaring at him. 'Can you find some scrub pants that will fit him?'

'I can try,' she said, and stalked past him.

I touched her arm as she went past, and she turned the glare on me. 'Thank you.'

'For what?' she asked.

'Doing your job. Henry doesn't remember throwing you across the room.'

Her eyes softened a little.

Henry said, 'I did what?'

'You fought the nice doctors and nurses when you were under vampire influence,' I said.

He looked at the nurse, who was my size but not as muscular. 'I am so sorry, did I hurt you? And I'm sorry I yelled just now.'

She shook her head. 'Not really hurt, no, bruised. Apology accepted, and I'll see about getting you some pants; we can't have you leaving in just a shirt.' She laughed at some inside joke.

'They won't have shoes either,' I said.

'What size do you wear?' Nicky asked.

'Twelve.'

'You're in luck; I got an extra pair in the car.'

'I appreciate it.'

'Not a problem,' Nicky said.

'You know, not to put too fine a point on it, but you're a civilian and we'll be riding with SWAT on this one.'

'I know most of the cops in town, Marshal Blake. My dad and I were the ones who led them out on survival searches and helped them do wilderness training around here.'

I nodded. 'Okay, but when they arrive, if you're not ready to go, we can't wait.'

'I'll be ready, but you can't leave without me anyway.'

'SWAT is bringing a map of our search grid.'

'I saw the same image you saw, but I know the place where he's holed up.'

'You recognized it?'

'I told them about it.'

'Tell me and I'll tell the others.'

'You'll never find it without me.' His face grew very serious. 'They were right to kill us; we'd find them anywhere in the mountains here.'

I wanted to correct him on his pronoun choice, but I didn't think it had been accidental, and if it had been it was too big a Freudian slip for me to deal with, I'd leave it to the professionals when he started therapy for the fresh PTSD.

'If you get the shirt and boots, he can at least be that much dressed,' I said.

Nicky shook his head. 'I'm your only bodyguard right now, so you have to come with me, or we take him down to the car in the scrubs they're looking for.'

'If I said I'll be fine until you get back, you would say what?'

He just looked at me, that one blue eye giving me attitude, and since it was Nicky it was a lot of attitude. 'That if this were a scary movie, I'd leave, and you'd be gone or dead when I come back, so we stay together.'

'Because it would be the kiss of death in a horror flick?' I asked.

'Because I'm your bodyguard.' He said it flat with no return of the humor I'd been trying for.

Henry said, 'I heard you two talking about how the zombies needed so much food and where they're going to get more.'

I looked at him. 'Sorry, I didn't think until too late that you might hear us the way people do when they're coming out of anesthesia.'

'It's okay, it helped wake me up. He'll start with Boulder and the surrounding towns.'

'Start how?' I asked.

'He's just going to keep raising the dead until they consume the living.'

'He's going to raise an undead army?' I asked.

Henry shook his head, sending his long golden-brown hair swinging as much as the tangles would allow. 'Not an army, more like undead locusts. He just wants them to kill as many people as possible, and he'll feed off each death. He feeds on fear and death.'

'I knew he originally fed on death, but I didn't know he was one of the night hags.'

'You mean nightmares?'

'Not exactly; *night hags* is a nickname for vampires that can cause fear in people and then feed on it from a distance. They can cause and feed on nightmares. Maybe that's where the idea of a nightmare comes from, but it's a vampire trick.'

'He showed me what he meant to do to the city.'

'How?'

'He put it in my head. At first I just saw it in my dreams, but then I started seeing it when I was awake anytime that I wasn't bespelled by his puppet.'

'The female vampire,' I said.

He nodded and suddenly looked very unhappy. 'She mind-fucked me, and then she was beautiful and I couldn't help but want her. She mind-fucked me with his help, and then she fucked me for real, or made me fuck her.' He gave a bitter laugh.

'You had no choice, Henry; you were under their spell, literally.'

'Please call me Little Henry. Straight Henry was my dad.'

'Okay, Little Henry. Vampires can make humans do anything they want once they have your mind thoroughly rolled.'

'I remember pieces of what they did to me, and that was bad, but what they made me do was worse, and Pop, he . . .' He looked away, shoulders hunching as if the memory were a blow.

'Don't try to remember today,' Nicky said.

Henry looked at him. 'The real stuff is hazy, or missing, but the dreams are crystal clear. They were his wish, his goal. He wants to turn everyone into a walking corpse like him. He wants to fill the city streets with walking dead that are faster, smarter, than regular zombies. You know how they say some people just want to watch the world burn?'

'Yeah,' Nicky said.

'Yeah,' I said.

'Well, he wants to watch it die.'

74

The nurse, whose name was Brenda, found scrubs that fit and a hair-brush and a hair tie so that Little Henry could put all that hair back in a braid. She'd also brought him little slip-on booties. He stripped off the hospital gown so that he walked out with us in just the scrubs and boots. Nurse Brenda gazed on the tall muscled yummy of him without a shirt like she was viewing property with an eye to purchase. Little Henry didn't notice, but Nicky did. He and I exchanged looks, then smiled and looked away. It wasn't our job to match-make, and honestly right now Henry's mind wasn't thinking anything but revenge.

While we waited for SWAT I tried to call Edward, but wherever he was in the mountains there was no cell service. I walked a little distance from Henry so I could call Claudia then; our head of security needed to know that the Lover of Death wasn't dead and had a whole new level of power and crazy. Nicky stayed talking to Henry, so I didn't go too far; if I did Nicky would feel compelled to follow me.

Claudia answered on the second ring. 'You okay?'

Something in her voice made me say, 'Yeah, but your voice says that I shouldn't be.'

'Seamus is missing,' she said.

'Oh, motherfucker,' I said.

'What? That's your curse for special occasions. Do you know where Seamus is?'

'Maybe.' I told her that the vampire we were hunting was the Lover of Death.

'He's supposed to be dead,' she said.

'Vamps that jump bodies are hard to kill, and harder to make sure of the kill. Apparently, when I was taking care of business with the Mother of All Darkness, she tried to spill herself into him and use him as her escape. I was stronger than she'd planned and it didn't work, but it worked a little. He's gained power from what she did give him.'

'Just like you and Jean-Claude gained from it,' she said.

'Yeah, except that he seems to plan on using his new-found power level to raise as many flesh-eating zombies and rotting vampires as possible and turn them on the humans.'

'That's bad, but what does it have to do with Seamus?'

'The Lover of Death bit him, rolled his mind. I was able to use my connection to hyenas to help him fight it, and his ties to his vampire master probably helped him fight it better than Ares, but—'

She cut me off. 'But you thought Seamus was free of the mind control because the vamp that did it was dead.'

'I should have called you as soon as I suspected that the vamp wasn't dead, but I was trying to save one of our human victims and . . . Oh, hell, Claudia I didn't think about Seamus until you said it.'

'You think the Lover of Death has control of Seamus.'

'Yes, I do.'

'Well, fuck,' she said.

'Yeah,' I said.

'The Harlequin may not be as good as advertised, but they are good, some of them very good, and Seamus is one of their best fighters.'

'What's his weapons skill? I haven't trained with him much; our schedules don't seem to overlap.'

'Don't try hand-to-hand with him, he's wicked fast, Anita. Fredo nicknamed him Water because he's that smooth and fast. You shoot better than he does, but you and he both like knives. Seamus beat Fredo in knife practice, not just cut him like you've managed, but beat him.'

'Holy shit,' I said.

'Yeah, Fredo is the knife guy. I've never seen anyone beat him like that before.'

'If we have to shoot him, then his vampire master may die with him,' I said.

'I know that, but unless you shoot him, you're going to lose, and so is Nicky. If Nicky can land a blow, he's stronger, but he's not faster, and he's not better with the martial arts. We were thinking of letting Seamus help teach the mixed martial arts class.'

'He's that good,' I said.

'I'm afraid so.'

'Well, doesn't this just suck,' I said.

'Anita, I need you to tell Nicky that Seamus is the hand-to-hand fighter that I'd least want to face for real. Make sure he understands not to mess around; if he gets a chance he must kill him, because there won't be a second chance.'

'I'll tell him,' I said.

'Do I need to give you the safety talk, too?' she asked.

'You mean tell me not to try to trade punches with Seamus?'

'Yeah, something like that.'

I laughed, though it wasn't exactly a happy laugh. 'Trust me, Claudia, if I have to fight him without weapons it won't be because I didn't try to kill him first.'

'If you lose all your weapons you cannot fight him and live, Anita. You're good, but I'm not sure I could beat him, and I'm closer to his weight class.'

'SWAT is going with us.'

'Where are you?'

'Hospital parking lot, waiting for SWAT so we can roll out.'

'Lisandro and Dev are headed out the door now.'

'If Seamus is that good, he'll eat Dev for dinner.'

'Yeah, but if I were one of the fallen council members I'd want to kill the new vampire king of America. That means that I'm keeping good people here to keep Jean-Claude safe.'

'Agreed,' I said.

'Besides, you'll have a team of SWAT with you; they're pretty good for humans.'

'They're very good for anyone,' I said.

'Come on, Anita, they can't compete with our speed.'

'Yeah, but training counts, too.'

'You don't have to defend them to me, Anita. I respect SWAT and their abilities. I'm just saying they're human and Seamus isn't.'

'No arguments, and sorry if I was defensive.'

'It's okay. I'm going to talk to the Harlequin wereanimals and see if I can learn anything helpful about the Lover of Death.'

'If you get any info that will help, call me,' I said.

'You know I will,' she said.

'If SWAT gets here before Lisandro and Dev arrive, then we're gone. We need to use every bit of daylight we have.'

'Understood; I'll text Dev and make sure he and Lisandro understand.'

'You know my objections to endangering Lisandro, because he has a family. Why send him?'

'You know why, Anita.' She sounded softly chiding.

I sighed. 'Yeah, I have practiced with Lisandro and watched him against others. He's not the strongest of the guards, but he's wicked fast and he's got the best all-around speed, endurance, strength, and technique of anyone in the MMA classes, except maybe Pride.'

'Which is why one of them goes with you and one of them stays here, just in case.'

'It won't come to a one-on-one champion fight, Claudia.'

'Probably not, but if there comes a point where you can maneuver Seamus into fighting Lisandro and leaving the rest of you out of it, I'd do it.'

'You going to throw Pride to the hyenas, too?' I asked.

'No, we have a lot more guards here, Anita. We'll overwhelm him with skill and numbers.'

'But you'll still keep Pride with you, just in case,' I said.

'Yeah,' she said.

'Send someone extra to Micah, too,' I said.

'I will.'

'Keep them safe for me.'

'It's my job.'

'Speaking of jobs, SWAT just pulled in,' I said. I waved them over to let them know I needed to talk to them before we headed out. They spilled out of their black Tahoe looking all around six feet tall or over, broad of shoulder, trim of waist, like a sports team in body armor with weapons. Most SWAT and special teams were tall and athletic and had a certain *we are just that good* attitude. It wasn't bragging, it was just training combined with surety; most of them had spent their lives being the toughest and most competent person in the room.

'Kill this guy for us, Anita,' Claudia said.

'It's my job,' I said.

She gave a small chuckle. 'Yeah, I guess it is.'

I hung up and went to tell SWAT we knew exactly where the

vampire's lair was located. I also had to tell them that we had another shapeshifter that might have been mind-fucked like Ares. If this kept up, they were going to change the rules so I couldn't bring my furry friends along.

75

Two things kept us in the parking lot long enough for Lisandro and Dev to arrive and throw their gear in the back of our SUV: Little Henry's request to borrow a gun, and my explaining what had happened with Seamus. The gun would have normally been not only no, but hell no, but they all knew him. They knew his skills in the field and at the shooting range. He'd actually been in the military with Machet and Wilson, two of our SWAT guys. Machete and Willy, respectively – most SWAT units were big on nicknames. Some were name-based like these two, but others were just call signs, like Sergeant Brock was Badger, and Yancey, who had come to see me in the hospital, was Swan. He pulled off enough of his gear so I could glimpse the nearly black hair with its hint of curl, and the smiling brown eyes. He didn't look remotely swanlike.

'So you've had another shapeshifter deputy marshal go rogue?' he asked, studying my face as if he wanted me to say no.

'This master vampire's animal to call seems to be hyena. It gives him a step up on mind-fucking them.'

'Any of you other guys werehyena?' he asked.

Dev raised his hand, 'Tiger.'

Lisandro said, 'Rat.'

'Lion,' said Nicky.

Badger, whose skin was smooth and nearly as dark as the black gear he was wearing, said, 'So if you guys get bitten you're not going to try to kill us?'

'You're safe from us,' Dev said, smiling.

'Okay, Little Henry rides with us and draws us a detailed plan of the layout while we drive. We'll have an entrance plan by the time we get there.'

'Sergeant, not to put too fine a point on it, but the vampire rolled Little Henry, too. Being human doesn't keep you safe from a vampire.'

He touched the cross pinned to his vest. 'My faith will keep me safe.'

'Yeah, mine, too, but if a human servant or zombie that he controls rips it off you, we'll need a backup plan.'

'Vampires are your side of things, so you got to have a plan that will protect us from the vampire by the time we get there,' he said.

'I'll do my best.'

'That's all I ask.'

I looked at him a minute to see if he was kidding, then realized he wasn't. Here was a man who would expect your best, period. 'Then let's saddle up, we're burning daylight,' I said.

He and Yancey grinned at me and then each other. 'Another John Wayne fan— See, Badger, I told you I liked her.'

Badger nodded, still grinning. 'Let's mount up, we *are* burning daylight.'

Nicky drove, I rode shotgun, and Lisandro and Dev had the middle seat. We followed SWAT and Little Henry onto the main road, and away we went.

We were at the edge of town, about to head into the mountains, when a woman ran across the road in front of SWAT's Tahoe. Their brake lights flashed red, and Nicky had to slam on his brakes to keep from rear-ending them.

A zombie ran across the road in front of both cars, in the direction that the woman had run.

'Is that what I think it is?' Lisandro asked.

'It's not dark yet,' Nicky said.

Dev said, 'Here we go again.'

'Shit,' I said, and reached for my door handle.

76

The moment I opened the door I could hear the woman screaming. I'd have loved to have time to put together a plan, a formation, something, but we were out of time. We spilled out of the SUV and ran toward the screams. SWAT was out of their truck, too. I heard one of them yell something, but if we waited the woman was dead.

I had my handguns and my knives. The AR and shotgun were still in the truck. I was betting that SWAT was taking the time to gear up. They were probably right, but I'd seen the zombie move; it wasn't the shambling dead, it was fast, and when night fell it'd be faster.

We found them on the driveway between two small identical houses. Her legs were kicking uselessly at the ground, the zombie straddling her waist, holding one of her arms in its hands and eating the flesh off her forearm while she shrieked.

I drew the Browning, aimed at the zombie's head, and fired. The force of the bullet rocked its whole body, but it just turned and stared at us, mouth scarlet with fresh blood, the woman's arm still trapped between its rotting hands.

Someone exclaimed behind us, 'Sweet Jesus!'

The zombie kept chewing on the meat in its mouth, as if we weren't walking closer, guns out. It was like the ones in the mountain, in the hospital: no fear, no thought of saving itself. It wouldn't run, not while it had meat to eat. It had ripped the woman's arm to pink tendons and red muscle, blood pouring out of the wounds, drenching the zombie's chin and upper body.

I shot it between the eyes; the head rocked back, the round hole bled dark blood, and some of the back of the head was shaped wrong now, but it bent back toward the woman's arm. It was going to take another bite. I walked up almost point-blank and shot it in the mouth, twice, three times, until the mouth was shattered and most of the head was a red mess. It still tried to bend over the woman's arm and take another bite, except now it had no working mouth to bite with.

The woman was still screaming.

SWAT was with us now, and they had taken the time to get the big guns. 'Blow it to pieces, and start first aid on the woman,' I said.

'I give the orders here, Blake,' Badger said.

'Fine, you decide what we're going to do, Sergeant. We're going back to the car for the rest of our weapons, then we'll come back and help you with the woman and the zombie if it's still intact.'

I turned and went back for the car and the rest of the arsenal. Nicky followed without hesitation. Dev hesitated while we walked a step or two, but it was Lisandro who almost didn't come at all. We were almost to the car when he jogged up behind us.

'I can't believe you left that woman like that,' he said, as he came to the back of the SUV while we started getting out the long guns.

'SWAT knows basic first aid, and if we're lucky maybe we got the paramedic.' I slid the AR over me in the tactical sling and settled the shotgun into its sling and Velcro on the vest. I preferred the AR to the shotgun for the suburbs. I added extra ammo to match the guns, and I was ready.

We went back at a paced jog and heard more gunfire. Machete was firing into the zombie, keeping it off the woman. Badger was wrapping up the woman's arm. Yancey and Willy were watching the perimeter for more undead. They looked very organized and official.

'Nice of you to join the party, Blake,' Badger said.

The woman seemed to be unconscious. I didn't know if she'd fainted from fear or blood loss. 'If we'd waited to gear up, the zombie could have killed her before we got to her,' I said.

'You stay with the group unless ordered otherwise, Blake, is that clear?'

'I hear what you're saying,' I said.

Machete had finally reduced the zombie to something that could barely crawl; without fire it was the best we could do. I had grenades in some of the pockets of the tactical pants, but if I set a zombie on fire here it could run into a house and set it on fire before it burned enough to be immobile. Suburbs were hard, so many soft targets.

'We have to get her a hospital,' Badger said.

'Yeah, so much for hunting vampires,' I said.

Badger looked up and gave me a very unfriendly look. 'We can't leave her like this.'

'I know, and I'll bet almost anything that this isn't the only zombie attacking citizens right now.'

'I thought zombies couldn't come out during daylight,' Machete said, coming back with his rifle loose in one hand.

'They don't like daylight, but they can walk around in it, or most of them can. They'll be slower and a little more confused in daylight, so the flesh eaters will be faster and more deadly when we lose the sun.'

'It looked pretty damn fast,' Machete said.

'It was,' I said.

'The vampire did this, didn't he?' Yancey asked.

'Yeah, he did. We have to take her to the hospital. We'll have to protect the citizens of Boulder from the walking dead, so we won't get to the mountains before nightfall.'

'You're saying he did this as a diversion.'

'Yep.'

'How can he make them rise when he's miles away?' Willy asked.

'Good question, but I don't think he raised the zombies today fresh. I think he's just letting us see some of the ones he raised earlier. He's sacrificing them as a diversion from his real body. Destroying his original body is the only way to kill him and stop this from happening.'

'You ran after her first, Blake. You weren't willing to let her die so we could kill the vampire.'

I looked at Badger as he picked up the woman with her freshly bandaged arm and settled her like a child in his big arms. 'No, I couldn't just keep driving and let her die like this, and that is what he was counting on.'

'If you could have kept driving and let her die, then you wouldn't be human,' he said.

'By saving her and all the others who are being attacked right now, we're giving him time to have one of his servants move his body and missing the chance to kill him once and for all. It'll cost lives.'

Badger nodded. 'You're probably right, but I'm still glad we saved this woman.'

I sighed. 'So am I; damn it to hell, but so am I.'

77

When we got back to the trucks, Little Henry wasn't there. Badger said, 'I told him to stay here, damn it.'

'There he is,' Yancey said.

At the same time Nicky said, 'There,' and pointed.

I followed where he pointed, and it was Little Henry running toward us, using all that long leg to run as fast as he could, carrying someone over his shoulder like a sack of potatoes. There were two zombies chasing them.

'Go save his ass, then we got a hospital run to make,' Sergeant Badger said.

We had a second where SWAT looked at us and we looked at them. I said, 'We'll take the zombies, you secure the civilians.'

'Roger that,' Yancey said.

I wanted my shotgun when we got to the zombies, but once you had the AR on its tac swing for running, you had to hold it as you ran, or it tangled your legs. The shotgun in its cross-draw shoulder sleeve was fine for running; I'd just have to change guns when we got there. I started jogging toward the zombies and Little Henry. Dev, Lisandro, and Nicky did the same, all of us jogging with our ARs in our hands. The men fell in around me, jogging easily to keep up. SWAT was moving out to meet Little Henry and there was a moment when all eight of us were close. Then the zombies seemed to sense that their prey was getting away, because they suddenly picked up their own pace, and it was fast. Why was it that only the flesh-eating zombies ever moved like that? I started to run, using that otherworldly speed the way I had in the mountains, and my men paced me, easily. They could have outstripped my shorter stride, but they stayed with me, because I had a plan, I would tell them what to do; people with training like people with plans, and they'll stay with you as long as you keep having a plan and making decisions.

We left SWAT behind, because humans couldn't move like we could. We came even with Little Henry. He was running full out, long legs eating up the ground, the woman on his shoulder bouncing a little as he kept moving toward SWAT and we kept moving toward the zombies.

I let my AR slide to one side, keeping my left hand on it, and reached with my right hand to draw the shotgun out of its back sleeve. I had a few moments of running with a gun in each hand. Nicky was beside me with the same double-handed run. I stopped with a few yards between us and the running zombies. I let the AR fall from my left hand and put both hands on the shotgun, raised it to my shoulder, and snugged it into place as the zombies ate up the ground between us. Nicky mirrored me.

I called, 'Right.'

He answered, 'Left.'

I shot the knee of the zombie on the right. It stumbled, falling to the ground. The zombie on the left fell down as Nicky blew its leg out from under it, too. Lisandro and Dev moved up on both sides of us to flank the zombies. They got up off the ground on hands and the remaining leg, snarling, and launched themselves at us. Nicky and I shot them in the heads; at this distance most of the upper parts of the heads exploded. Their bodies recovered from the force of the shots and they got back up. Lisandro and Dev fired into their bodies. Again the zombies reacted to the physics, but they couldn't feel pain, or fear, and they were already dead, so they got back up. Nicky and I shot them again, took the rest of their heads. Lisandro and Dev concentrated on the other intact leg. They used their hands to start to crawl toward us. Nicky and I used the shotgun to blow a hand into red mist on each of them. Lisandro moved up and shot the arm that Nicky had taken the hand off in a series of rapid gunshots until the arm was destroyed. Dev did the same on the arm of my zombie. Nicky and I took the other hand on our zombies, and Lisandro and Dev took out the arms. The zombies lay on the ground with legs and arms ruined, no heads, their bodies destroyed, and the remains of the bodies started trying to wiggle forward.

Dev said, 'These things just never give up, do they?' He stared down at the zombies with a look that might have been fear, but he was trying to hide it, and he'd done his job perfectly.

'No, they don't,' I said.

'It's going to be a long night,' Lisandro said.

'Yeah,' I said, 'it is.'

78

We got the first woman to the emergency room and left the woman
that Henry had rescued there, too. She was shocky from the whole
nearly-being-eaten-by-zombies thing. There were other injuries from
zombie attack, including two police officers. There were zombie calls
from all over the city. So far it was just one or two zombies attacking,
but we still had an hour until full dark. I was betting that once night
fell we'd get more zombies in larger groups just like up in the mountains, except there we'd all been armed and trained. The normal citizen
wasn't going to fare very well against these things. Hell, a single officer
in a patrol car was going to have trouble if there was more than one
of them. You needed armed groups that knew how to shoot and work
together, and even then there might come a point where overwhelming
numbers, well, overwhelmed us. I stood there in the emergency room
letting the noise and the movements of it wash over me. Nicky stood
not far away. Lisandro and Dev were talking to the SWAT guys.
Who you going to call when it looks like you're really going to have
to survive the zombie apocalypse?

I knew exactly who to call. 'Ted, you know how you complained
that I had a zombie apocalypse and didn't invite you?'

'Yeah.'

'Consider yourself invited.'

He gave a small chuckle, the way some men will do when you say
something sexy.

'You're excited. After what we saw in the hospital and the basement
you're excited about this,' I said.

'Yeah, I am.'

'There's something wrong with you, you do know that, right?' I said, and laughed.

'Yeah, I do know. Give me your location.'

I had Dev bring it up on his phone's GPS and gave him the address. 'We'll have to keep moving around from one emergency to the next,' I said.

'Understood, we'll be there as soon as we can.'

'We?'

'SWAT, remember?'

'Yeah, me, too. And, Ted?'

'Yes, Anita.'

'Bring your flamethrower.'

He gave that excited sex chuckle again. 'For real, you're not just teasing this time?'

'Zombie reports from all over the area and it's still daylight. It's just going to get worse after dark.'

He gave that low, deep laugh again. 'You say the best things.'

'Conversations like this is one of the reasons people think we're doing each other.'

'Maybe,' he said.

'Someone on your end of the phone said something you didn't like about us, or me, and you're rubbing their face in it.'

'Would I do that?' The words were innocent; the tone was not. Someone must have done something that truly pissed him off for him to play into it like this, because he knew it hurt my reputation worse than his. People expect men to be sex-hungry bastards, it's the old boys-will-be-boys idea, but a woman who sleeps around is a whore. I hated the attitude, but I knew it was a reality in most people's minds. I didn't understand it; I mean, if you think sleeping around is bad, shouldn't it be equally slutty no matter if a man or a woman does it? Or equally okay?

'Get here as soon as you can, and let me know which of the guys with you pissed you off and I'll help you play with him, between killing zombies.'

'You sweet-talking thing, you,' he said.

That made me laugh. We hung up with both of us laughing. There were so many reasons that Edward and I were friends.

79

Yancey and Sergeant Badger came over to me. Nicky moved up to join us. 'If we destroyed the vampire's body, would this all end?' Badger asked.

'I believe so.'

'That's not very definite,' Yancey said, with a smile that couldn't take the worry from his eyes.

'This vampire is doing things that are not possible, so the best you're going to get from me is, I think that will work, but we thought another marshal in another city destroyed his body once before and you see how that turned out.'

'Why didn't it work?' Yancey asked.

'Because this vamp can jump bodies to other vampires he's made and zombies he's raised. I admit the zombie thing is a new vampire trick, even for me.'

'So he jumped to a different body; why will destroying this body work any better?' Badger asked.

'Because this is his original body. We destroy that and no more jumping around, or we hold him in the body he's currently using long enough to destroy it and him with it; that could work, too.'

'Hatfield's group is close to where Little Henry drew the map to, so they could detour and destroy the body.'

I thought about sending Hatfield toward not just the Lover of Death, but Seamus; it seemed like a good way to get her killed.

'That's not a good face. What's wrong?' Yancey asked.

'Little Henry still sulking because you sent his map via smart phone, and he's not included?'

'Yes,' Badger said.

'But that's not the look on your face; you don't care if Henry sulks about this. What were you really thinking?' Yancey said.

'What are you, an expert on my facial expressions?'

He just looked at me, crooking one dark eyebrow over those brown-black eyes.

'He's figuring you pretty fast,' Lisandro said.

I frowned at him.

He just smiled at me. 'It's just the truth.'

'Fine. I don't want to get Hatfield and the men with her killed.'

'You won't be doing anything to them,' Badger said. 'You will be here helping save lives, while she tries to do the one thing that could end all this before it gets out of hand.'

'Besides, Blake, you've got to stop believing that only you can save the world and give the rest of us a chance,' Yancey said.

'Hatfield is competent,' Badger said. 'Text her any information you think she needs to remember and let her do her job. Right now, I want you to tell us everything you know about flesh-eating zombies.'

'If you want to know about zombies in general I've got lots to share, but flesh-eating zombies, honestly they are so rare that there isn't a lot of information.'

'Tell us what you have, Blake. It's more than anyone else has,' Badger said.

I nodded. 'Okay, I can tell you this: When it gets full dark they will be faster, stronger, and even harder to kill.'

They exchanged a look between them. Badger sighed and rubbed his hand over his close-cropped hair. 'What can kill them?'

'Fire. Blow them up into small enough bits and you can burn the pieces at your leisure.'

'What about the bomb squad?' Nicky asked.

We all looked at him.

'If you know how to defuse a bomb, you know how to make one,' he said.

'That's a good idea,' Badger said.

'Not fair,' Yancey said. 'You look big enough to bench-press a truck and you're smart.'

Nicky grinned at him. 'I'm not just another pretty face.'

That made us all smile, and we were going to need all the smiles we could get tonight, or maybe that was my pessimistic side talking.

Wait, I didn't have an optimistic side, so it was just my naturally sunny disposition.

'Exterminators, too; they have to have one person at every company who's trained in extreme measures of pest control.'

'How extreme could it be?' Yancey asked.

'The last time I was up against a killer zombie, I had an exterminator team backing me up with a flamethrower, just in case, as I walked the cemetery looking for the original grave.'

'What would you have gained from finding the grave the zombie came out of?' Badger asked.

'A clue to who had raised it might have led us to where it was hiding during the day, or it might have told us why it had turned into a flesh eater. Most flesh-eating zombies are out for revenge of some kind; you give them their revenge and they often go back to being a normal shambling zombie.'

'Are these out for revenge?'

'Most violent zombies are murder victims. They rise out of the grave with revenge their prime motivator, and anything that gets between them and that revenge they will kill. Some of them resort to eating people who didn't harm them in life; again, no one knows why some killer zombies just strangle people to death, or beat them to death but never try to eat anyone.'

'Are these all murder victims?' Yancey asked.

I thought about that. 'Maybe; most of the ones we've been able to identify are all missing-person cases, so yeah, I guess they are, but the weird thing is they should all be trying to kill whoever killed them. Once they've killed their murderer they become harmless.'

'But they were killed by rotting vampires, right?' Nicky asked.

'Or other killer zombies, yeah,' I said.

'So what if you raise a zombie that was killed by another zombie? They can't kill their murderers, because they're already dead.'

'In a more normal zombie it could go one of two ways; either the death of their murderer would negate everything and they'd just not animate quite right, but they'd be peaceful, or they could be driven by revenge that they could never satisfy. Zombies that can't get revenge because their murderer has died sometimes do go on a killing spree until they get burned.'

'Are we saying that every zombie this rotting vampire raises is seeking revenge, but because he's dead to begin with they're slaughtering every-thing in their path?' Yancey asked, frowning as if he were trying to work it out in his head.

'I think you may have hit on it, but the difference is that these zombies seem to be under his control and murderous zombies are wild cards. They obey no one.'

'Would it be possible to raise a zombie as a sort of weapon?' Yancey asked.

Nicky and I said, 'Yes,' at the same time. We looked at each other. The night I met Nicky I'd saved myself – us – by turning the cemetery of zombies I'd raised against the bad guys. They'd made me raise the dead at gunpoint and threat of death to Micah, Nathaniel, and Jason and hadn't thought that giving me a cemetery of my own zombies tipped the odds in my favor.

I looked back at the other two men. 'It's pretty standard folklore that vaudun priests can raise a zombie and send it after their enemies.'

'Vaudun, you mean voodoo?' Badger asked.

'Same religion, different words. I usually say *vaudun*, because people are less likely to think all movie monsters. You say *voodoo* and people get very set ideas in their head. It's a perfectly fine religion and most believers are law-abiding citizens.'

'Does that mean that zombies see vampires, like the rotting vampires, as already dead?' Yancey asked.

I shrugged. 'I guess so, or they'd go after their murderers.'

'Or maybe they haven't found their murderers yet,' Nicky said.

'What do you mean?' I asked.

'If we gave them the two vampires you guys have in custody, and they were able to kill them, would the ones that those two killed go back to being ordinary zombies?'

'I don't know,' I said.

'You said that if a killer zombie can't find his murderer and have his revenge, he can start killing and eating anything that gets in his way, right?'

'Yeah.'

'Then shouldn't giving the vampires over to the zombies quiet some of them?'

'It might, but we'd be giving two legal citizens over to be torn limb from limb. Vampires are a lot harder to kill than humans usually, which means the vamps would stay alive a lot longer during the process.'

He nodded. 'Makes sense.'

'That would be a really bad way to die, Nicky.'

'Yeah.' He said it as if to say, *So what?*

'If we were just going to execute the vamps anyway, and it would save dozens of lives . . .' Yancey let his words trail off.

Badger looked at him. 'You could do that, give someone over to the thing we saw today?'

He shrugged. 'It's a thought; we're just brainstorming and gathering information, right?'

'They're rotting vampires,' Nicky said. 'If you can't teach them how to look human, the woman seemed to want to die.'

'They should have two forms; one should be totally human and as attractive as they were in life,' I said.

Dev and Lisandro came over to us. 'What has you guys all serious face?' Dev asked, smiling.

'We're debating on whether giving the two vampires in custody over to the zombies of their murder victims would make the zombies stop killing other people,' I said.

Dev's eyes widened and he went pale.

'Who came up with the idea?' Lisandro asked.

'I did,' Nicky said.

'You are a sick motherfucker,' Lisandro said.

'Yes, yes, I am,' Nicky said, totally unbothered by the comment.

Lisandro laughed, as if he couldn't quite believe it, but he did.

'You're not going to actually do it, are you?' Dev asked.

'They are citizens with rights, so no,' I said.

'Not if Anita thinks the vampires in custody committed some of the murders without being controlled by their master,' Nicky said.

'They'd still be legal citizens,' I said.

'But they'd be executed anyway; what does it matter whether you stake them during the day or feed them to the people they killed?'

'It does have an interesting sense of irony,' Yancey said.

'They're either people, with all that means, or they're not,' Dev said. 'You can't make them legal and fight for the law that gave them a second chance at life and then turn around and lie so that they lose that second chance.'

'That's directed at me, I take it,' I said.

'Yes, because it's your warrant and you are the expert on vampires. If you decide that they killed people without being forced to do it, then they're dead,' Dev said. He didn't sound happy, but he was right.

'And the marshal who holds the warrants has complete discretion on how the executions are to be carried out,' Nicky said.

'Is that true?' Yancey said.

I nodded. 'Yeah.'

'So you could do anything to them as long as they die eventually?' Yancey asked.

I nodded again. Olaf, alias Marshal Otto Jeffries, was known to torture his vamps before killing them; of course, torture was his hobby, but the badge and warrant gave him a legal outlet for his passion. It did make one wonder about the job, when a serial killer found it a good outlet.

'You look like you're remembering something bad,' he said.

I shook my head. 'I try to be humane when I kill, so let's table the idea until we get desperate.'

'We won't get that desperate,' Dev said, looking at me, very seriously.

'If he's as powerful a necromancer as I think he is, he could raise dozens of zombies.'

'What about the zombies in the morgue?' Nicky asked.

'What about them?' I asked.

'Were they all murder victims?'

'I don't know.'

'What would it mean if they weren't all murder victims?' Yancey asked.

'That every zombie this guy raises turns into a killer.'

'He's ordering them to kill,' Nicky said.

I nodded. 'Yeah, he has to be.'

'Well, this just gets better and better,' Yancey said.

'Don't most zombies need a ritual to raise them from the grave?' Badger asked.

'Yes,' I said.

'Does this necromancer need a ritual, and if he does, could we use that to find him?'

'I don't know for certain, but if he does, then yeah, potentially I could trace it back to him.'

'How would that work?'

'You know that old saying, about more than one way to skin a cat?'

'Yes.'

'There's more than one way to raise a zombie, and more than one way to catch a necromancer.'

'You have an idea,' Nicky said.

'Maybe.'

'Maybe is better than nothing, so let's hear it,' Badger said.

I told them my maybe.

'You're setting yourself up as bait; as your bodyguard I vote no,' Lisandro said.

'She's not bait,' Nicky said.

'She's going to do the metaphysical version of standing in the middle of a fight and yelling, *Come and get me!* That's bait,' Lisandro said.

'He's going to think she's bait, that's the point,' Nicky said.

'So she's bait.'

'It's not bait, it's a challenge. Anita is betting that she's the biggest, baddest necromancer,' Dev said. He was very serious as he studied my face.

'Don't mean to be a wet blanket,' Yancey said, 'but what if you're wrong? What if he's the biggest and baddest?'

'He won't be,' Nicky said.

I wasn't quite as confident as Nicky, but I was confident that if I raised my own mini-army of zombies, the Lover of Death wouldn't be able to resist coming around to check out the competition. It would distract him from the fact that Hatfield and her team of SWAT were hunting his original body. It might keep him from inhabiting it once darkness fell, and killing all of them. If she could destroy his original body, and I could trap him in whatever body he was inhabiting at the moment here in town and destroy that one, we could kill him, and we had to kill him, because we had to stop him, and dead is the stoppest stop of all.

80

The cemetery was one of the largest and oldest in the city. You could see the years marching across in the changes in the tombstones from ornate angels and beautiful sculptures to the nearly flat stone markers that were easier to mow around. It was like visible archaeology: centuries in a glance, and the change from looking up to heaven to staying low to the ground, and worrying more about ease of maintenance than about God and all his angels. The sunset was a spectacular spread of pink and purple and pale crimson all done in neon-glow colors, as if some disco queen's lipstick had been spread across the western sky and set on fire. I don't know if I'd ever seen the sky painted so bright with the dying of the light.

I took Nicky's hand as we watched the sunset. I wasn't sure this plan was going to work, and I'd decided that if the other cops wanted to give me grief about being up close and personal with my guys, so be it. We were about to enter a night that could be like the hospital, except with more zombies, and no hallway to contain them. If hundreds of killer zombies rose we were going to be either one of the safest spots in town, or one of the most dangerous. We wouldn't know which until it was too late to back out.

'The sunsets are always like that out here,' Yancey said.

It made me turn and look at him, Nicky's hand still in mine, so that my turning turned the big man with me. It was a couple thing, that turning with the hands joined so that you spent most of your time looking in the same direction.

'Really?' I said.

'You expect to get bored with another spectacular sunset, but you never do,' Badger said. They'd stayed with us in case our plan worked and the big bad showed up. Willy had found a vantage point and was waiting to do what snipers do best: shoot the bad guy on my signal. Machete was with him in case a zombie tried to sneak up and eat Willy while he was trying to shoot.

'How could you ever get bored of something that beautiful?' Dev asked.

'Most people stop seeing things they experience too often, even the amazing ones,' I said.

He shook his head. 'I don't understand that.'

'I like that you don't understand it.'

He smiled a little uncertainly. 'Do you stop appreciating the wonderful things in your life just because you see them every day?'

'No,' I said, and turned to Nicky, going up on tiptoe to kiss him gently. It earned me a surprised and very pleased look, which made me smile. He knew that I did not do public displays of affection when I was around the police often and especially not with my secondary lovers.

I walked over to Dev, put my hands on his arms, and looked up into that handsome face and those eyes with their ring of pale golden brown and blue around the outside. I went up on tiptoe and he leaned down so we could kiss.

I moved back from the kiss and stood flat-footed with my hands still on his arms. 'I don't grow tired of the wonderful things in my life, Dev. I value that you're afraid of the zombies and you're still going to stay here with us.'

'I'm your bodyguard, Anita; I would suck at my job if I left now.'

I smiled. 'I guess so.'

'I feel totally neglected,' Lisandro said. 'Aren't I wonderful, too?'

I laughed. 'I'm told your wife and kids think you're amazingly wonderful.'

He grinned at me. 'Yeah, they do.'

'I'm not married,' Yancey said. 'Do I get a kiss?'

'I know I started it, because of kissing more than one man at work, but don't let my PDA with my guys go to your head.'

'It didn't go to my head, I promise,' he said.

It took me a three-count to realize he'd made a double entendre. I laughed. 'I'd get mad, but that was clever.'

He grinned at me. 'Thank you, I'm pretty proud of that one myself.'

'You do throw the best parties.' It was Edward in his most cheerful Ted voice walking across the grass toward us. He had two SWAT officers with him, too. I knew that the other two were mirroring our sniper and spotter from a different vantage point. The local PD was allocating a lot of their best people to my very 'maybe' plan. I hoped we all lived.

Edward introduced the first one as Lindell, who was as tall as Dev, but so thin he probably had to fight for every ounce of muscle and every pound of weight. He was just built lean and willowy. Officer Shrewsbury was barely six feet, built solid, and moved in a tight coil of energy as if he were just waiting for someone to yell, *Go!* He was also a natural redhead, complete with the pale skin and freckles that usually went with it. Lindell's nickname was Paris. Shrewsbury's was Berry, as in Strawberry. No one offered to explain the tall, almost homely Lindell being named after the city of love, and I didn't ask. I'd learned that nicknames were personal, sometimes very personal, especially among the special teams.

Edward came up to me smiling broadly and radiating his alter ego, Ted.

'If you didn't bring your flamethrower, I'm going to be disappointed,' I said, smiling.

'It's in the car, Anita; you know I never tease unless I'm planning to come across.'

I smiled at him and gave a small eye flick behind him. He made the smallest eye-slide to the side Paris was standing on, which meant Paris was the guy who had been giving Edward enough grief about our supposed love affair that he'd begun to play with him.

'I know you're always good for anything you promise, Ted.' I put a smile to go with the teasing tone and looked up in time to see Dev puzzling down at me. I had totally forgotten about promising to help Ted tease someone, so had forgotten to mention it to my guys. Oh, well.

'Very important, everybody, when the sun goes down I will be having some vampires fly to meet us. They are my close friends and associates; do not shoot them thinking they're bad guys.'

'How do we tell one vampire from another?' Paris asked.

'Are you saying all vampires look alike?' I asked.

He frowned at me, then said, 'I'm saying that our main perp is a vampire, so how are we supposed to know the difference?'

'The three that are joining us will literally be flying in, as in coming from the sky on their own power. The bad vamp, as far as I know, can't fly.'

'I thought flying was just a story. You mean they can really do that?' he asked.

'A few master vamps can levitate; actual flight is a lot rarer, but these three can do it.'

'Who's coming to play with us?' Edward asked.

'Wicked Truth and one you haven't met yet, Jane.'

'A vampire named Jane?' Paris made it a question.

'Yep,' I said.

'I thought all vampires had cool names like Jean-Claude, or what was the other one you just said, Wicked True?'

'They're the Wicked Truth, think of it as a paired call sign,' I said.

'See, cool.'

I was beginning to think it wasn't personal with Paris; he just couldn't stop talking long enough to think things through. Maybe his nickname came from the fact that the mythological Paris had started the Trojan War.

Darkness came, and it wasn't the fading of the brilliant sunset that let me know, it was the feeling inside me as if a switch had been clicked over. It was as if I could breathe easier in the thin air, or as if I'd been holding some tension inside me all day that finally eased.

I felt Jean-Claude wake for the night. Knew when he opened his eyes and knew that he felt the cool night breeze against my face. I didn't envy Claudia explaining everything to him. I thought about Wicked and Truth and I could feel them, too. Feel them coming aware to the night and all the possibilities. Claudia would be telling them that they had been volunteered to stand at my back and be my metaphysical battery, and if Seamus showed up they, plus Lisandro, were probably the best chance we had at winning without just shooting him on sight. Since shooting him might kill Jane, too, and she'd done nothing, we'd try not to shoot him, but if we had to, we would.

Badger's radio crackled and he touched his mic on his vest. 'Roger that.' He turned to me. 'We're getting reports of packs of zombies.'

'How big?'

'Eyewitnesses are reporting anywhere from five to twenty, so probably somewhere in between.'

My phone rang and I knew the ring tone. I picked it up. 'Jean-Claude,' I said.

'*Ma petite*, what have you done?'

'My job.'

'I would stand by your side, you know that.'

'Claudia and I talked about it, but we learned from some of the older guards that if you are in person here, then the Lover of Death could make a direct challenge to you to try to take over as king of all the vampires here. It's too great a risk, and you know that.'

'I would be more power at your back.'

'Yes, but if I get hurt you have the ability to feed me energy and keep me alive. If we're both hurt, then we're screwed.'

He laughed, that wonderful touchable sound that seemed to glide down my skin as if he'd touched me with his hand. It made me shiver.

'*Ma petite*, you say the sweetest things.'

'You still know I'm right.'

'I would love to say I do not and fly to your side.'

'I love you,' I said.

'*Je t'aime, ma petite.*'

'Kiss Asher for me when he shows up tonight.'

'He will not be coming tonight. They have closed all the airports and roads into the city. The National Guard is being mobilized.'

'One little zombie apocalypse and they call out the big guns,' I said.

'You are the big gun, *ma petite*.'

'You can't see me smiling, but I am.'

'I can feel you smiling,' he said.

There was a prickly rush of cold that wasn't the night air. 'I sense vampire, gotta go. *Je t'aime, mon fiancé.*'

'That is the first time you have called me so; I love you, *ma petite*.'

I made the sign we'd agreed upon when I sensed vampire and hoped that the snipers remembered that just because I sensed vampire didn't mean it was bad guys. I reached out toward that sense of power and found Wicked Truth. I concentrated and could feel the air against their bodies as they literally flew toward me; they were just above us. If they hadn't been blood-oathed to Jean-Claude, and my lovers, I wouldn't have been able to pinpoint them so accurately, but they were mine. What was mine I could sense.

It made me try to sense Jane. She was blood-oathed to Jean-Claude, too, and I got a flash of vampire. I'd have known she was close and a vampire, but other than that I'd have been blind. So it wasn't just the connection to Jean-Claude. Was it being my lovers, or that I fed the *ardeur* on them, that made me be able to know so much about the Wicked Truth? Later, when we got through all this, I'd experiment and see what made the difference between the vampires I could track and the ones I couldn't.

The SWAT officers all tensed and at least touched their guns as the vampires landed. Edward took it in stride; he'd seen the show before. Truth touched ground a few seconds before Wicked, so that they were both crouched on the ground letting the momentum of landing sink into the earth itself, and then stood together, tall and handsome, their faces as close to identical as any brothers I'd ever seen. Only the hair was different, one slightly wavy and brown, the other straight, thick, and blond, plus one had slightly bluer eyes, the other a bit more gray, and choice of clothing. Wicked wore a pale designer trench coat that flared around an equally beautiful tailored suit, and Truth was back in his newly repaired knee-high leather boots; they looked like something that should have been worn to a Renaissance fair, but they were the real deal, not a modern imitation. We'd finally convinced him that modern jeans were a good thing, and a black pair was tucked into the boots. Under his black leather jacket I caught glimpses of one of his new black T-shirts, the one that read, *Don't Worry I'm Right Behind You, using you as a meat shield*, the second phrase in much smaller type. They walked toward me smiling. Wicked's smile seem to promise naughty mischief; Truth's was open and just happy to see me.

I met them partway, and normally I didn't greet them with a hug let alone more, but I was about to ask them to risk their lives, not as my bodyguards, but as my familiars, like a witch might use a cat. So I went to them and held a hand out to each of them. They exchanged a quick glance between them, all the surprise they showed, and then took my hands. I put an arm around each of their waists, sliding my arms under the trench coat and the leather jacket, sliding my hands over the texture difference between Truth's cotton T-shirt and Wicked's silk dress shirt, until I tucked myself in close between them. They gazed down at me with those mirror faces, the deep dimples in their chins like an extra grace to those handsome faces. Their arms slid around me, one across my shoulders, the other lower.

'I'm not complaining,' Wicked said, 'but why the effusive greeting for us?'

'I'm asking a lot of you tonight.'

'We're your bodyguards, Anita; if you need our lives, they are yours,' Truth said.

I hugged him a little tighter. 'I don't want your life, Truth.'

'Whatever you want, it is yours,' he said.

'Whatever our lady requires,' Wicked said.

'And that's why you got hugs,' I said.

Jane landed in a fall of black hooded cloak. It would match her outfit, so that she looked like a movie ninja until she pushed back the hood to reveal the very blond hair and the large blue eyes. I'd seen men react to the delicate beauty of her, until they got a taste of her coldness. She was about my size, delicate but curvy, because she'd been recruited from a time when to be too thin meant you were poor or ill. She was as silent and self-contained as any of the Harlequin vampires, as cool and controlled as Goran and his master were hotheaded and uncontrolled.

She stood and came toward us, moving in a glide that caused the black cloak to billow and wave around her almost as if it were alive on its own. I wasn't sure how she did it, but she wasn't the only one of the Harlequin who could make the cloaks distractingly dramatic. As Seamus was Water, because of his grace, she was Ice, because she let nothing ruffle her, and she was as inexorable as a glacier, and as patient. There was something a little scary about Jane. She'd never done anything to me, or said an unkind word, but she was unnerving somehow.

I untangled myself from Wicked Truth and turned to face her. Did I apologize for taking her animal to call into harm's way? 'I'm sorry that Seamus has been compromised.'

'He was doing his job,' she said.

Okay, so much for pleasantries. 'Can you sense Seamus?'

'Yes,' she said.

'Is he still bound to you?' I asked.

'Yes and no.'

'Explain.'

'The Lover of Death has not broken our tie completely. It is almost as if we are sharing Seamus, which is not possible.'

'If Seamus comes, we will give you a chance to win him back to you completely, but if he tries to fight us . . . we can't let that happen, Jane.'

'He is too dangerous, I understand,' she said.

'Do you understand the consequences?'

'If he dies, I may die. It is almost a certainty now that our Dark Mother is dead and no longer sharing her power with us. We, her guards, are much diminished.' Her voice never changed inflection. She might have been talking about what we'd do tomorrow if it didn't rain.

'I'm sorry for that, but I can't be sorry for why it happened.'

'Understood,' she said.

'Okay, then, I'll introduce everyone around.' I did, and Paris was the one who tried to flirt with Jane. She looked at him as if he were less than nothing, a pimple on the butt of the universe and she could have cared less. Wicked and Truth bothered the SWAT guys for the same reason that Dev, Nicky, and Lisandro did: SWAT wasn't used to meeting other men who made them for a moment think, *Would I win this fight?* They were friendly about it, but I knew that Wicked had picked up on it; I couldn't tell if Truth had, or if he cared. If we'd had more time Wicked would have played with them a little, gently, but he would have amused himself.

I was about to try to do something that most animators couldn't have attempted at all, and those who could would have needed a human sacrifice to even try, which was very illegal, but I'd had more than one zombie raising where the power wanted to spread outside the circle of power. The circle was to keep the zombie you raised inside just in case something went wrong, but it was also there to keep things out. There are things that will inhabit corpses, especially fresh ones, until the body starts to rot and then everything leaves it. I'd accidentally raised entire cemeteries before when people had died inside the circle of power. It had been enough energy that the circle had cracked and spread the power throughout the cemetery. One of the times that the energy had wanted to spread had been without a circle of protection and with a vampire at my back acting as my undead energy boost. I was going to try to replicate that, but this time I wasn't going to fight the power, I was going to indulge it. I was purposefully going to raise as many zombies as I could. I was chumming for the Lover of the

Death to come play with me. He thought that having some of the power of the Mother of All Darkness inside him made him a bad-ass necromancer; I was going to do everything I could to show him that I was better at it. I needed him to come close enough for me to raise a circle with him inside it, and then all I had to do was keep him trapped in the body he walked in with, and give the word to Hatfield to burn the one on her end. She still hadn't found the body, but she had found the old mine that he'd been hiding in. Little Henry had been right that it was a maze. I prayed she'd find the body before he showed up on this end, because if not we were fucked. To kill him, the body he was in and the body he'd started in both had to burn.

We were in the modern open area of the cemetery. It gave the snipers the best chance. It left us open for the same thing, but long gun wasn't Seamus's strong suit, and the Lover of Death wouldn't shoot us. If he killed us tonight it would be death by zombie, or rotting vampire, nothing as clean and neat as a bullet.

Nicky came to me and spoke low. 'Why are you delaying?'

He was right. 'I think I'm afraid.'

'That you can't do it?'

'No, that I can.'

'Why does that scare you?' he asked.

I took a deep breath and was honest with the gibbering voice in the back of my head. 'I've fought my necromancy for years to not do the very thing I'm about to do on purpose.'

'Create your own army of the undead?'

I nodded.

'What scares you about it the most?'

I looked up at him. 'That I'll enjoy it too much.'

'It's okay to enjoy what we're good at, Anita.'

'It's not okay to enjoy certain things, it's dangerous.'

'You mean how you're not supposed to enjoy killing people, or hurting them?'

I nodded. 'Yeah, like that.'

'Do you feel guilty about anyone you've killed?'

'No, not really.'

'Me either; now do this, Anita. Let your power out of its cage and see how far it runs.'

'What if it runs too far to put back in its cage?'

'If you're the one controlling the zombie army, I know it will be a good zombie army, because you are my moral compass and you always point true north, Anita. Don't let your doubts, or anyone else's issues, make you think otherwise.'

'Are you sure you're a sociopath?' I asked.

'Pretty sure, yeah; why?'

'Because somehow I didn't think sociopaths were good at being comforting.'

'We can be great at it, because we spend our lives play-acting, pretending so that we fit in and no one suspects that we have no idea why people are nice to each other.'

'You understand that was completely not comforting, right?'

'Yes, but I don't have to pretend with you; you already know that I'm a sociopath, and you love me anyway.'

Edward came up to us. 'Sorry to interrupt, but what's the holdup?'

'Me, worrying about things I shouldn't be,' I said.

'Want some help clearing your head?' he asked.

I shook my head. 'I'm good, Nicky helped.'

Nicky looked at Edward. 'She's having one of those what-if-killing-feels-really-good, doesn't-that-make-me-a-bad-person moments.'

Edward nodded as if that made perfect sense. 'Then it feels good. We can't really control what flips our switch; don't judge it, Anita, and just accept it.'

I wanted to argue, but it would have been beyond stupid to argue with the two sociopaths in my life. 'Why do I have moral quandary questions with the two of you?'

'Because you don't really have moral quandaries about violence, Anita, but you're afraid of being judged for enjoying it, so you only bring it to the two people in your life who won't judge you.'

I wanted to argue with Edward, but I couldn't. 'Well, fuck.'

'Pretty much; now go raise zombies like the kickass necromancer we all know you are.' He actually petted me on the head, which he knew I hated.

'Don't pet me,' I said.

'Sorry, but if you need to stroke off, I can help you; otherwise do your job so that the evil necromancer's undead army doesn't eat all the nice people in Boulder.'

'Does that make me the good necromancer, or just the other evil one?'

'It makes you our necromancer; now go play with the vampires and raise us some zombies.'

'Fine, you guys go stand somewhere else.' I went to get my vampires and embrace my inner necromancer. I hoped I was the good one.

81

Most animators need practice and training to raise the dead; I got training so I could stop doing it by accident. A beloved dog that crawled into bed with me when I was fourteen, roadkill that followed me like I was some nightmarish Pied Piper, and finally a college professor who had committed suicide and come to my dorm room so I could tell his wife he was sorry. I wondered if the lone shambling zombies that they'd occasionally find wandering around were accidents from untrained animators like I had been once. I'd learned to raise the dead with the traditional words, steel, ointment, and blood sacrifice, usually a chicken, but I didn't need them. The man who had trained me needed them, but in emergencies I'd learned that they were just window dressing for me.

Edward was in the shadows with his flamethrower propped up against a larger tombstone. He'd only get it out if I could trap the Lover of Death in the circle. If he used a zombie body then I'd have him, but if he chose to ride one of his rotting vampires, that was harder. It was a lot harder to make a circle of power that could hold a vampire in, or out. I believed I could do it, if I stopped being afraid of myself. I realized as I stood in the cool night sensing Truth and Wicked at my back that I was still afraid of who I was, what I was, and there was still a part of me that would have chosen a different talent. Necromancy had given me so much in my life that made me happy, and I'd still have been 'normal' if I could have magically made it so.

I thought about no Jean-Claude in my life, no Nathaniel, or Micah, because they'd come to me because I had animals to call through Jean-Claude's vampire marks. No one in my life who made me happy would have come into my life without my necromancy – not a single one. I thought about how happy I was, happier than I'd ever been, and I let go of the fear, the doubts, and decided to embrace all of me, truly, completely, and just trust.

I turned around and looked at the two vampires. I hugged them to me like I had when I first saw them tonight, but this time I let myself cuddle against their chests and raise my face up for a kiss. Wicked bent over me first and laid a gentle kiss upon my lips, and then Truth bent over me and started gentle, but the kiss grew and I moved my arm from around Wicked's waist so I could wrap myself around Truth and kiss him back, all eager lips, and tongue, and then I lost enough control that I forgot I was kissing a vampire and those dainty fangs are sharp. I tasted blood like sweet copper pennies. Truth made a small inarticulate sound and kissed me harder, lifting me off the ground with his arms around my upper body, so that my feet dangled inches above the ground. It could have turned to the *ardeur* and heat, but I chose that moment to call my necromancy, though *call* was not the right word, because that implies you have to coax it, call it like a reluctant dog. I just stopped holding it back, and it spilled up through my body into my mouth and the vampire that was kissing me. He cried out, his mouth coming away from mine, blood trickling down his lower lip. Wicked was at my back, hand curling in my hair, turning my head to kiss him, and the necromancy liked him, too. Animators can raise zombies; necromancers control all the undead. Wicked kissed me as his brother had, all mouth and tongue and teeth, and bled me a little bit more so that it was passion and blood and necromancy all intertwined. The men dropped to their knees and took me with them to the grave underneath us. The moment my body touched the ground, my necromancy flooded into the ground seeking the dead.

It hit the graves one after another like a stone tossed into water so that the power spilled out and out like rings in water, but it was earth underneath us that began to move like water. I heard startled cries and knew it was some of the police with us, but it was distant. The two vampires pressed to my body, and the bodies in the ground were all more real to me, because they were dead, and my power liked the dead.

Truth whispered against my face, 'Oh, my God.'

I said, 'Yes.' I got to my knees with Wicked wrapped around the back of me, his hands still caressing me; my hand was in Truth's, and with the vampires wrapped around me, the graves moved like water, spilling the zombies to the surface. They didn't have to climb their way out; my power brought them up whole and in one piece. But they didn't look like his zombies, they didn't look like corpses, they looked like people in their funeral finery.

It wasn't enough. I sent my power out and out seeking more, and found another graveyard, and I raised it, and even that wasn't enough. For the first time I didn't argue, or hold back, I just embraced how good it felt to find the dead and call them to me, because that was what I did. I raised them and then I told them to come to me, and I knew that the distant ones were making their slow, careful way to me.

I felt him almost on the other side of the city. My necromancy found him like iron seeking a magnet, but it was more than that; his power was seeking me, too. I realized in that moment that we both carried Her power inside us, and those pieces wanted to be whole again.

He came to me, not just because we carried pieces of the Mother of All Darkness, but because he was dead and all the dead are attracted to necromancers. He walked into our cemetery wearing the body of one of his own zombies, so that he was just one of many, though he looked rotted, and my zombies didn't, so that he stood out as he walked in with the first group of zombies I'd called to me.

'My power knows you,' he said.

'We carry the power of the Living Dark inside us,' I said.

'Yes,' he said.

Then two things happened at once. I drew a circle in my mind's eye in a large, sweeping arc, visualizing it glowing as it came up. The second thing was that Seamus leapt like a piece of the night itself toward me. Truth and Wicked moved in front of me, but Jane was there first. They fell to the ground in a whirl of black cloth and struggling bodies.

'You have put up a circle of power,' the Lover of Death said. 'How did you do that without blood to seal it?'

'I'm a modern necromancer; it's all about the shortcuts,' I said.

He didn't understand the comment, but it didn't matter, because Edward called out, 'Hatfield is a go.'

'Do it!'

I heard the little hiss, a hesitant click, and I threw myself backward to the ground, grabbing Truth and Wicked by their coats and taking them down with me, so that we were almost flat to the ground when the fire breathed over us orange and yellow and so hot that it made the night air shimmer in heat waves, and made the air above us so hot we were afraid to move.

The Lover of Death was engulfed in flames. Some of my zombies were caught in the edges of it, but the Lover of Death was lost in flame. He didn't scream at first, and then he did, wordless at first, and then, 'My body, you're destroying my body! No! NO! Half the Mother's power dies with me! Nooooo!' He charged toward us as he burned. Edward in the silver fire suit was between us and the burning zombie. I heard the *click* and *whirr* and *whoosh* again and fresh flame spilled onto him. He tried to run then for the edge of the circle, but when he got to that invisible line he could not cross it. He stood on the edge of it and screamed and burned and died.

Jane, Lisandro, Dev, and Nicky had pinned Seamus. Nicky's face was bloody. Dev's left arm hung useless, something very wrong at the shoulder. Jane and Lisandro seemed unharmed.

It took a long time for the flames to die, but when they did we decapitated the corpse and took out the heart, which was mostly blackened, fleshy charcoal. We put the main body in a body bag and separate bags for the head and heart. We'd turn them to ash and then dump them in three separate bodies of running water. Yeah, it was old-school, but we were destroying the last of a very old-school power. But first, there were zombies.

I dropped the circle of power so that I could feel all of them, and it wasn't just my zombies now, it was his, they were all mine. They waited passively for me to put them back. I turned to Truth and Wicked.

'I need fresh blood to put them back,' I said.

Truth dropped to his knees, my hand still in his. 'If it is my blood you need, my lady, it is yours.'

'I was thinking my blood,' I said.

He looked puzzled.

'Are you inviting us to take blood from you?' Wicked asked.

'Yes.'

'Come on, Truth, you take the right side, I'll take the left,' Wicked said.

'It's been a long time since we shared like that,' Truth said.

'Too long,' his brother said.

'Left and right of what?' I asked.

'Your lovely neck,' Wicked said, caressing his fingers down the side closest to him.

The thought of them both feeding at the same time tightened things low in my body and made other things wet. I promised myself we'd try this again, with more privacy and more sex, but tonight I just needed blood and power.

Truth faced front, and Wicked faced back; they kissed and licked my neck gently, teasingly, until I said, 'Do it, please.'

'We would like to do this in private some night,' Truth said.

'I'd already thought of that, so yes, but tonight, zombies,' I said.

They both nuzzled my neck and then wrapped their arms around me and each other. I felt them tense and fought not to tense myself, because that could make it hurt without more foreplay, or more sex. I let my breath out in a long shuddering sigh and they struck together as if they'd planned it. The pain was sharp and immediate, but the moment they started to suck, it switched over from pain to pleasure and my spine tried to bow, so that they had to hold me steady or I might have torn their fangs from my throat, spasming with small mini-orgasms. I thought about them doing this with sex added and my knees buckled. They held me in their arms and drank me down.

They had to hold me so I could stand while I whispered, 'With word, will, and blood, I bind you to your graves. Go back and walk no more.'

The zombies hesitated, and I saw that something that lurks at the edges of things pass through their eyes, and then it was gone like a shadow over the moon, and the zombies walked back to their graves and lay down on them. The graves rose back over them, semiliquid and rolling again to swallow them back. When the earth became solid again, you'd have never known the grave had been disturbed.

When every zombie I could see was tucked back in its grave, I stopped trying to be brave and let my legs collapse. Wicked and Truth lowered me to the ground and cradled me between them. I wasn't sure if it was the blood loss or that I'd finally found out the limits of my necromancy, but I was suddenly exhausted.

Sergeant Badger came and said, 'All the zombies have vanished, they're back in their graves. Good job, Blake.'

I nodded and managed to say, 'Thanks.'

Edward knelt by us, pulling the silver hood off the fire suit. He grinned at me. 'Whose the biggest, baddest motherfucking necromancer?'

I smiled at him, and said, 'This girl.'

'Damn straight,' he said.

82

Micah's dad's infection stopped trying to spread as soon as the Lover of Death died. The doctors couldn't explain it, but it was as if the body and the antibiotics could fight back now. His left arm may never be the same, but they think with surgery and intensive physical therapy he should be okay. There was a minor scandal about his happy three-some lifestyle coming to light, but the actual problem is that he doesn't live in his own township. They'll be working that out for a while, but watching Bea, Ty, and all the kids clustering around the bed crying happy tears, I knew they'd be all right. There are other jobs.

Nicky and Dev healed perfectly, which is one of the serious benefits to being a shapeshifter. Seamus seemed to have suffered no ill effects from being possessed, and he and Jane seem to be back to normal, but I remembered what she said about being diminished. Just as everyone close to us has gained power as Jean-Claude and I have gained power, so did the Harlequin from the Mother of All Darkness, so they're right, they have lost power. It explains why though they are amazingly good, they aren't the nearly indestructible super-ninja warriors that their reputation promised. It's like they lost their power source. Jean-Claude and I are the power source now, and the Harlequin just aren't as hooked up to us as they were to her.

We also discovered that a good portion of the Harlequin vampires are abusing their animals to call. We found a therapist who specializes in couples with abuse issues; she's one of the few willing to deal with preternatural clients, so we've started the Harlequin pairs in therapy. I'm not sure they all really understand the issues, or how hard real therapy is, but they're going and they're sitting through sessions. I'm taking that as a win.

Asher came into town the next night. He left his new werehyena lover, Kane, in their hotel room, so he could meet with all of us first. I'd honestly expected him to rub our faces in the fact that he'd found someone who wanted just him, so the fact that he didn't throw the man up in our faces means both that he thought about it ahead of time and that the man is important to him. He wants us to like Kane and him to like us. That gives us a bargaining position, so Asher has agreed to therapy, too. We told him that he'd been a month away from coming home when he did his best to nearly get himself killed by Dulcia and her werehyenas. We probably owe her a visit, or at least flowers and a bottle of some really good liquor. Jean-Claude suggested jewelry might be appropriate. Apparently, Asher had been a very bad boy in the last few days of his stay in her territory. Jewelry works for me, as a thank-you for not killing our stupid boy.

Micah's dad told Van Cleef and his people that my panwere powers weren't duplicable without my vampire marks and maybe my necromancy. I asked Edward for more info on Van Cleef, but he said no, unless he contacts me. I let it go, because no one keeps secrets like Edward. If he said no, he meant it.

Edward and Donna are trying to find a date that works for their wedding; as the best man I'm supposed to talk to their son, Peter, about the bachelor party. Peter is an eighteen-year-old boy; I think his ideas for the party and mine may not be the same, but if it's what Edward wants, I'm in. It looks like Nathaniel is going to be standing on Donna's side of the aisle, which still confuses me since she'd never met him before, but something about having one of my guys in the wedding seems to comfort her, so again, who am I to bitch? Besides, Nathaniel is excited about helping her plan the wedding. He's so much at better at this kind of thing than I am, though he'd probably be better at organizing the bachelor party, too.

We're still negotiating who is involved in our commitment ceremony. It seemed so simple and so right to say yes to Jean-Claude and yes to Micah and Nathaniel, but beyond that, who gets to put on a ring and say *I do*? Asher was totally crushed, and I think the only reason it didn't turn into one of his spectacular fights was that he'd missed us and knew that his homecoming was too fragile for him to throw fits. Micah and I are adamant that we are not committing to Asher. Nathaniel would, depending on how Asher does in therapy with his jealousy issues. Asher's new boyfriend, Kane, is totally against any kind of ceremony that ties Asher to us and not him. Dev surprised us all by proposing to Asher. He went down on his knees, took Asher's hand. It was sweet, and very Dev, and made Asher very happy, but . . . you knew there was a *but* somewhere in there, right? New boyfriend Kane was understandably upset that he'd just moved to a new city, given up his old animal group, and his job, and now his lover that he'd done all that for was going to marry someone else? I couldn't even blame him for it.

Other people who surprised us by being happy until they found out they weren't getting a ring: Cynric, Jade, Crispin, Envy, and Ethan. Nicky is okay either way; as he said, 'I know you're committed to me being in your life, Anita. I don't need a ring to make me feel loved.'

Maybe the reason the others want a ring is that I don't tell them I love them. If you don't feel loved, maybe the outward trappings like weddings and wedding rings become more important? I'd always thought that the wedding stuff was just an outward confirmation of inner truths, but maybe not. Perhaps for some people the wedding is the beginning of the commitment, the promise of more, and by not wanting to include everyone they feel like it's an ending, instead of a beginning. I don't know, but for now we've put the commitment ceremony idea on hold while we try to work through the emotional land mines that blew up in our faces.

Love is not a one-size-fits-all emotion; there are as many different kinds of love as there are people. We're trying to find a size that fits everyone in our life. Is there such a thing as an uber-ginormous-bigger-than-anything-else-in-the-world-large-size love? Sometimes you need to go big, or go home.

JOHNNY
SWANSON

JOHNNY SWANSON

by Eleanor Updale

David Fickling Books

OXFORD · NEW YORK

31 Beaumont Street
Oxford OX1 2NP, UK

JOHNNY SWANSON
A DAVID FICKLING BOOK 978 0 385 61642 3

Published in Great Britain by David Fickling Books,
a division of Random House Children's Books
A Random House Group Company

This edition published 2010

1 3 5 7 9 10 8 6 4 2

The Random House Group Limited supports the Forest Stewardship Council (FSC),
the leading international forest certification organization. All our titles that are
printed on Greenpeace-approved FSC-certified paper carry the FSC logo. Our paper
procurement policy can be found at www.rbooks.co.uk/environment.

Mixed Sources
Product group from well-managed
forests and other controlled sources
www.fsc.org   Cert no. TT-COC-2139
© 1996 Forest Stewardship Council

DAVID FICKLING BOOKS
31 Beaumont Street, Oxford, OX1 2NP

www.kidsatrandomhouse.co.uk
www.rbooks.co.uk

Addresses for companies within The Random House Group Limited can be found
at: www.randomhouse.co.uk/offices.htm

THE RANDOM HOUSE GROUP Limited Reg. No. 954009

A CIP catalogue record for this book is available from the British Library.

Set in 12/16 pt Goudy Old Style by Falcon oast Graphic Art Ltd.
Printed and bound in Great Britain by Clays Ltd, St Ives plc

Author's Note

Some things in this book really existed, even if they sound made up.

For example:

Bacille Calmette-Guérin (the BCG vaccine) was approved by the League of Nations in 1928. It was not widely used in Britain until well after the Second World War.

Craig-y-Nos Castle is still there, though it ceased to be a sanatorium in 1959, and is now a hotel.

Vivatone Radio Active Hair Restorer was on sale in the shops.

And 'Maud Dawson's Love Answers', 'For the Chicks', and the advertisement for Umckaloabo really did appear in *Reynolds's Illustrated News* in 1929.

But nevertheless, this is a work of fiction.

Chapter 1

ATHLETICS, AUTUMN 1929

The teacher was smiling, but he wasn't smiling at Johnny. He was looking over Johnny's head at the other boys, lined up behind him to take their turn at the High Jump. And it wasn't a nice smile. It couldn't be. The scar running from Mr Murray's eye to his chin pulled the skin of his lips to one side and gave him a permanent sneer, even when he was in a good mood. But now he really was sniggering – inviting the rest of the class to laugh at the smallest, thinnest boy as he struggled with the run-up and brought down the pole.

Johnny could feel his second-hand shorts flapping against his spindly legs. He knew he looked ridiculous, and that his only hope was to pretend that he thought it was funny too. Of course he would fail. He breathed in, clenched his fists and started his run.

Mr Murray called out to him, catching the moment to put Johnny off his stride. 'Right then, Squirt,' he shouted. 'Show us what you're made of!'

The boys gave a mock cheer. Johnny forced a smile and clattered into the bar.

After the fall he brushed the mud from his knees and swaggered to the back of the line, grinning, even though he wanted to cry. Mr Murray blew his whistle and put a stop to the laughter, swiping at Johnny's head as he passed. 'It's nothing to smirk about, Swanson. This country needs men, not insects like you. You wouldn't have got far in the war.'

The boys groaned. They were expecting another tale about Mr Murray's bravery in France, where his face had been torn apart at the Battle of the Somme in 1916 – two years before any of them were born. But the teacher blew his whistle again and turned to the next boy in line: the muscular captain of the football team. 'Now then, Taylor. Show Swanson how it's done.'

Everyone cheered as Albert Taylor cleared the bar with room to spare; and at the end of the afternoon Albert was the winner and the class hero. No one wanted to know Johnny, however much he tried to turn his humiliation into a joke.

Mr Murray put Taylor in charge of clearing the hurdles from the games field and set off for the warmth of the staff room.

Taylor delegated the job straight away. 'You need building up, Quacky,' he said, using the nickname he knew Johnny hated. 'The extra exercise might make you grow a bit.' He threw Johnny the key to the shed and turned to the others. 'Who's coming for a game of marbles?'

The rest of the boys were happy to leave Johnny to lug the equipment away while they ran off to celebrate Albert's triumph, and to laugh about Johnny's shame.

Johnny had almost finished tidying the hut when he was startled by a snuffling noise outside. Had the boys come back to taunt him? Were they waiting to jump on him as he left the shed? He couldn't make out any voices, but he thought he could hear sticks of wood bashing against each other. Maybe they were going to barricade the door so he couldn't get out. They all knew he'd just started a job after school. They'd love to get him into trouble by making him late for his paper round. He pushed hard at the door, hoping to knock away whatever barrier they had already built.

The door swung open easily. There was no one there – just a big wooden hoop rolling away across the field. Then he heard a whimper and looked round. A girl was lying on her back on the grass behind the door. She had half a dozen hoops around her neck, and more looped over each outstretched arm. Like a beetle flipped upside-down, she was wriggling but couldn't get up.

'You knocked me over,' she sniffled.

'I'm sorry,' said Johnny. 'I didn't know you were there.' Although the girl was wearing glasses, he could see that she was crying, and had been weeping even before the door hit her. He lifted the hoops off her and helped her to her feet.

'They made me carry everything,' she said, brushing the earth off her gymslip. 'It's just because I'm new.' Her voice had an unfamiliar sing-song lilt.

'I thought I hadn't seen you before,' said Johnny.

'I only started here on Monday. I'm in Mrs Palmer's class. They all hate me already. It's because of my accent.'

'Accent?' said Johnny, pretending he hadn't noticed it.

'I'm Welsh,' said the girl. 'And I've got a Welsh name: Olwen. For some reason, all the other girls seem to think that's funny. And they call me "The Owl" because of my glasses. My specs kept falling off when we were exercising with the hoops. They all laughed at me.'

'Everyone gets picked on for something,' said Johnny, acutely aware that Olwen was taller than him, even though she was in the year below. 'They get at me for being so small. That's how I ended up having to put away all our gear. I'll help you stack those hoops in the shed. My name's Johnny, by the way. Johnny Swanson.'

As Olwen passed him the hoops, she told him about her new home. 'We had to move here from Wales,' she said. 'My dad lost his job in Swansea, and we had no money at all. So he wrote to an old army friend from the war to see if he could help us out. Lucky for us, he said yes. I don't know what would have happened to us without him. Anyway, now we're living at Newgate Farm.'

'Where's that?'

'It's just outside town. Dad's supposed to be working there, but he and Mum are both ill. They were sick even before we moved, and the journey just seems to have done them in.'

'Have you got any brothers and sisters? Are they at this school too? If you've got a brother he should defend you against those horrible girls.'

'Just a sister. She's a baby. She's too young for school. And she's ill too, now. Mum was worried about her this morning. It's her breathing, see. Maybe the country air doesn't agree with her. I really should go home and see if she's any better. It's a long walk.'

Johnny remembered his job at the shop. 'I must be getting along too,' he said.

They ran to the school gate together. 'Don't worry about those other girls,' said Johnny, as they split up. 'They'll soon get used to you. But if you have any more trouble with them, just come and see me.' He wasn't really sure what he was offering to do on her behalf, but Olwen seemed pleased to have found a friend at last.

'Thank you, Johnny,' she said. 'I'll see you tomorrow then.'

'Yes. I'll look out for you in the playground before school.'

The boys were still playing marbles in the street. Albert Taylor made a kissing noise on the back of his hand and nudged one of the others. 'Little Quacky's got a pet owl,' he said in a voice just loud enough for Johnny and Olwen to hear.

Johnny made his way towards Hutchinson's General Store and Post Office, just down the road from school. Joseph 'Hutch' Hutchinson limped out. He wasn't an old man, not yet thirty-five, and he still had a full head of chestnut hair; but his injured leg slowed him down, and he was getting plump through lack of exercise. His brown overall strained over his belly as he busied himself rearranging a display of apples. Before Johnny even reached the shop, he could tell that Hutch was angry.

'You're late,' said Hutch. 'I had the papers ready ten minutes ago.'

'It was PE day. We were up at the sports field.'

'And I suppose you broke all the records?' Hutch scoffed, lifting the strap of a large canvas bag across Johnny's shoulders. He squeezed Johnny's skinny arm. 'There's nothing to you. If it wasn't for your hair, I wouldn't believe you were Harry Swanson's son at all. He was a fine strong man, your dad.'

'I know,' said Johnny. 'I've seen a picture of him in his uniform.'

'Yes, but that would have been taken after the army cut off his golden curls.' Hutch ran his fingers roughly through Johnny's springy hair. 'You're his boy, all right, even if you are a bit of a shrimp. Now be off with you. There's folk out there waiting for the racing results.'

Johnny preferred the evening paper round. Not many people took two papers a day, and the bag was lighter than in the morning, when he visited almost all the houses nearby. He ran from one to another, trying to get his job done as quickly as he could. At the last house, Miss Dangerfield's, he pushed the paper through the letter box, and in his haste he let it clang shut.

'Can't you do anything quietly?' Miss Dangerfield shouted.

Johnny stood on tiptoe and opened the letter box to apologize. A musty, 'old lady' smell wafted from inside. He could see Miss Dangerfield advancing along the hallway to pick up the paper: muttering, dressed all in black as ever, and leaning on her walking stick. As she approached the door, Johnny could see how her hair had thinned almost to baldness on the top of her head. She straightened up and caught him looking at her. She was furious.

'Get out of it,' she yelled. 'You've no business spying on me!'

'I'm sorry,' said Johnny, meekly.

Miss Dangerfield lifted her stick and shook it at the letter box.

Johnny pulled away, and let the flap snap shut

again. 'Sorry,' he cried once more. 'It's just that your letter box is so high up . . .'

But his voice was drowned out by her shouts. 'Blooming children. Nothing but a menace. And I suppose you'll leave the gate open as usual.'

He shut it carefully behind him, just as he always did, and ran down the hill.

Back at the shop, Hutch was closing up. 'I'm chucking out these old biscuits,' he mumbled, without looking up. 'They're stale.' He scooped a handful of soggy custard creams onto a piece of old newspaper. 'Interested?'

Johnny sensed from his awkward manner that Hutch felt bad about teasing him earlier. 'Yes please,' he said. 'I really am sorry I was late.'

Hutch waved Johnny off without another word.

Johnny took his time going home. He would have to go past Miss Dangerfield's, and he wanted to give her a chance to calm down. He stopped and sat on the low wall of the graveyard to eat the biscuits. He couldn't help reading the paper they'd been wrapped in. It was last Wednesday's *Stambleton Echo*; a boring page, full of advertisements. People were selling old gardening tools, baby clothes, prams and books. Then one advert caught his eye. It was set apart from the others, in a little frame, and said:

Johnny read and re-read the advertisement. The Secret of Instant Height. It was just what he needed. But where would he find two shillings and sixpence? He didn't even have enough money for the stamped addressed envelope. Still, he tore the advert out of the paper and put it in his pocket. By the time he got home he had made up his mind to do anything to get the money, and to send away to Box 23 for the answer to all his problems.

Chapter 2

THE PEACE MUG

Johnny's mother, Winnie, was already at home. The front door led straight into the kitchen – the only downstairs room – and as soon as Johnny opened it he could see that she was ironing. She was pressing sheets: crisp white sheets quite unlike the ones they had on their own beds.

'They're Dr Langford's,' Winnie explained apologetically. 'They weren't dry enough to iron while I was there cleaning. Mrs Langford let me bring them home to finish them off. I'd hoped to get them all done before you got here. Tea will be a bit late, I'm afraid.'

'I thought the Langfords sent all their stuff to the laundry,' said Johnny. 'I've seen the van outside their house.'

'If you ask me, they're having to cut down on that sort of thing since Dr Langford retired,' said Winnie. 'Mrs Langford asked me if I would do the bed-linen, and I couldn't really say no. We don't want them getting rid of me too. There's plenty of people looking for cleaning jobs these days. They wouldn't have any trouble finding a replacement.'

Johnny took one end of a sheet and helped his mother stretch it out, ready for folding. They had to kick the furniture to the edges of their tiny kitchen to make enough space to pull it tight. 'Are they paying you extra for this?' asked Johnny, walking forward to hand over his end and pick up the fold at the bottom.

'Well, I tried hinting,' said Winnie, 'but Mrs Langford didn't seem to want to get the point. I didn't want to embarrass her – or myself. It must be hard for her. She's used to better things. She's from a posh French family, you know.'

They passed the sheet to and fro between them, giggling as one or the other dropped a corner, or wrongly guessed which way to turn next. Johnny thought his mother worked quite hard enough cleaning the Langfords' house every day without doing their ironing, too. But he liked the smell of the clean linen hanging to air in front of the hearth. And it was good to have an excuse for the fire to be lit.

'How was your day?' asked Winnie, patting the neat rectangle of folded cloth. 'It must have been nice to be out of the classroom and up on the field for a change?'

Johnny didn't tell her about how he had been laughed at, nor about Olwen, Miss Dangerfield, or the biscuits; nor about the advertisement for the Secret of Instant Height – which was really all that was on his mind now. 'Yes,' he said. 'It was good to be outside. But it was a bit cold.'

'Well, come and sit in the warm,' said his mother, shifting the clothes horse to make room by the fire. She caught her arm on the hot face of the iron, and stifled a curse. 'Oh, how stupid of me to have left that there,' she snapped, licking at a red mark on her skin. 'Get me down the ointment. It's on the top shelf.'

Johnny climbed on the arm of a chair and reached up to where his mother had kept all the dangerous and delicate things since he was a toddler. There were a couple of dusty jars of pills; a fine china mug decorated with flags and the word PEACE, which had been given out at the end of the war; and a flat round tin with elaborate writing on the top: *Dr Sampson's Patent Ointment for Cuts, Burns and Stings. A Soothing Solution in All Situations*. The lid was going a bit rusty at the edges, but he managed to prise it off, revealing a block of pungent brown cream, with a trace of the last finger that had scooped out a little, months before. His mother dipped in again, and started rubbing the oily mixture onto her burn.

'You'd better put it back straight away,' she said, 'so that we know where it is next time. Make sure you put the lid on tight or it will dry up.'

So Johnny climbed on the chair again. And while he was up there, and Winnie had her back to him, sorting out the ironing things, he took a look inside the china mug. He'd always known that his mother kept money in it: special secret bits of change that she felt she could spare to save up for Christmas – and he'd always known that he mustn't touch it. But he could see that there were coins inside – most of them coppers, but some of them silver.

He knew he shouldn't even think of taking the money, but for the rest of the evening he planned what he would do when his mother was asleep. So in the middle of the night he crept downstairs in the chilly dark, and tipped the money out of the mug and onto the table. Although it was cold, his hands were slippery with sweat. He dropped a penny. The coin rolled and then spun on the stone floor. It seemed ages before it came to a stop. Johnny froze, certain that his mother must have heard it; worried that she might even be able to hear his breathing, which sounded appallingly loud to him. He had no idea how he would explain what he was doing if she came in, but he wanted the Secret of Instant Height so much that he had to take the risk. There was no sound from her room. He counted the money. It came to nine shillings and sevenpence. He only needed two-and-six, with a few pence more for the envelopes and stamps.

He gathered up three shillings, and carefully put the rest back in the mug. The level of money had obviously dropped. Never mind: tomorrow he would get some stones to put under the cash, so that the theft didn't show. But surely it wasn't theft? It was borrowing. He promised himself that he would replace the coins, little by little, with the money Hutch paid him for delivering the papers. He wouldn't spend it on sweets or comics. By Christmas there would be nine shillings and sevenpence in the mug again. His mother would never know that any had been missing. And in the meantime, Johnny would have the Secret of Instant Height. That was all he cared about now.

Chapter 3

SENDING OFF

The next morning, Johnny left the house earlier than usual to help his mother carry the basket of sheets back to the Langfords'. On the way Winnie stopped off to check on their neighbour, Mrs Slack. She was an elderly widow who looked pretty healthy to Johnny, but always complained that she was ill. Winnie had mentioned once that she had 'trouble with her nerves'.

'Shall I do this washing-up for you, Mrs Slack?' asked Winnie, rolling up her sleeves and putting the kettle on to boil.

Mrs Slack waved her arm weakly in the direction of the sink. 'I just couldn't face it last night,' she said. 'I don't know what's come over me. It's all I can do to raise a teacup to my lips. Heaven knows how the floor will ever get cleaned.'

Winnie took the hint and asked Johnny to find her a bucket; then, while Winnie mopped, Mrs Slack listed her symptoms. Johnny tried not to listen. There were a lot of references to 'down below'. Mrs Slack kept pointing at Johnny and then mouthing words silently. 'I'd see the doctor,' she said, at full volume, 'but I don't like to trouble him with my little problems.'

Johnny's mother knew that she meant she couldn't, or wouldn't, pay. 'Dr Langford's retired now,' she explained. Johnny could tell from her voice that she had said this many times. 'But I could have a quiet word with him if you would like me to. It would save you going to that new man across town.'

'No. No need to put yourself out,' said Mrs Slack, in a tone that even Johnny recognized as meaning the exact opposite.

'Well, we'll be off then,' said Winnie. And they left Mrs Slack tucking in to a boiled egg and moaning about how she would be on her own all day.

'Poor soul,' sighed Winnie as they started off up the hill, each of them holding one handle of the washing basket.

'Do you think she really is ill?' asked Johnny.

'Maybe. Maybe not. But she doesn't have much of a life, and someone's got to take care of her. If my mother was still alive, I wouldn't want her to be all alone like that. I'd hope someone would drop in and make sure she was all right. It's the least I can do.'

Dr Langford's house was up on the hill, directly opposite Miss Dangerfield's. The doctor was leaving as Winnie and Johnny arrived. He was much older than Johnny's mother, tall and spry, with wisps of grey hair at the back of a big bald patch. Johnny was fascinated by the way the structure of the doctor's skull showed through the thin skin on his head. There was a prominent vein to one side that looked like a river on an ancient parchment map. You could see it throbbing when he was excited. Sometimes it seemed almost ready to pop. Today, Dr Langford hadn't shaved properly, and there were clumps of stubble under his chin. His smart trousers were gathered into bicycle clips at his ankles.

'My goodness, Doctor,' said Johnny's mother. 'You're up early.'

'Yes, Winnie,' said Dr Langford. 'I had a call from the sanatorium at Emberley last night. I'm helping them with an emergency case. A little baby and her parents.'

'Oh dear, the poor people,' said Winnie.

'It's a shame,' said the doctor, 'but I have to admit

to a certain excitement. It's good to feel wanted even when you've retired.' He bent down and pinched Johnny's cheek in the way that adults think is playful, but actually hurts a lot. 'And where are you off to so early, my boy? Surely it isn't time for school yet?'

'He has his paper round,' said Johnny's mother. 'It gives him a bit of pocket money, you know.'

'Of course,' said Dr Langford. 'I've seen you pushing the newspaper through the letter box. I'm sorry ours is so high up. It must be quite hard to reach.' There was another painful pinch of the cheek. 'You must eat up all your food, son. You're a growing lad . . . or should be. How old are you now? Nine? Ten?'

'Eleven,' said Johnny, embarrassed, and all the more determined to get the Secret of Instant Height.

'Well, I must be off,' said the doctor, climbing onto his bike and adding, with a wink to Johnny, 'I'll give you a ride to the shop, if you like.'

He lifted Johnny up and helped him balance on the crossbar, then swung himself onto the saddle and started to pedal. The bike rocked unnervingly, and Johnny wished for a moment that he had turned down the offer. Winnie waved, but Johnny didn't dare take his hands off the handlebars to wave back. The bike looped in a circle, but then steadied and picked up speed as the doctor's bony knees pumped harder. Seconds later, they were zooming down the hill. Johnny loved the rush of the wind against his face, and whooped with delight as they sped past the church and pulled up, wobbling again, outside Hutchinson's General Store and Post Office. Dr Langford helped Johnny down and rode away.

Inside the shop, Hutch was standing behind the counter, sorting out the morning papers.

'Early today, I see,' he grunted, parking his pencil behind his ear. 'Makes up for last night, I suppose.'

Buoyed up by the joy of the bike ride, Johnny found the courage to ask a favour. He needed Hutch's help if he was to reply to the advert for the Secret of Instant Height. 'Hutch,' he said, 'I want to buy a postal order and some stamps. Would you mind opening the post office so I can get them now?'

'That would be most irregular,' said Hutch, severely. 'The post office mustn't open till nine o'clock.'

'But I'll be at school then,' said Johnny. He didn't mean to sound desperate, but it did the trick. For once Hutch contemplated bending the rules.

'What's so special about this postal order?' he asked. 'What's the rush?'

Johnny thought quickly, and his words tumbled out. 'It's for my mother,' he said, making up a story as he spoke. 'She needs to send it to my auntie, who's ill. It's to buy her a train ticket so she can visit us. Mum wants me to catch the first post. She told me to get an envelope too. And an extra envelope and stamp so Auntie Ada can write back.'

He realized that he was getting himself into trouble. In a few seconds he had invented a sick aunt and invited her to Stambleton. He could already see that this deception was going to be quite hard to manage, and he also thought that it didn't sound very believable. But Hutch seemed convinced.

'Well,' he said, fishing for the keys in his pocket, 'since it's a medical matter, I think I can bend the rules just this once.' Hutch took off his brown overall, rolled down his shirt sleeves, put on his black jacket and straightened his tie, as he always did when working in the 'post office' part of the shop. He unlocked the safe and got out a large book, a cash box, his official rubber stamps and a big ink pad. 'Very well, Johnny,' he said, peering through the grille that separated the post office from the rest of the shop. 'How much is this postal order for?'

*

And so Johnny left for his paper round with everything he needed to send off for the Secret of Instant Height. He stopped at the cemetery and laid it all out along the top of the wall. He took the newspaper cutting from his pocket and copied out the address of Box 23 onto one of the envelopes. Then he addressed the other to himself, stuck on a stamp and folded it so that it would fit inside the first. He wondered whether he should have written a letter to go with the postal order, but decided that the newspaper cutting would tell the people at Box 23 why he was contacting them, so he tucked that inside as well. He checked twice to make sure that everything was correct. Then he licked the glue on the outer envelope and stuck it down hard.

The church clock chimed the half-hour. He was running late. He decided to reverse the usual order of his deliveries, so that Miss Dangerfield would get her paper first. He didn't want to be in trouble with her again. There were too many other things to worry about. Suppose his mother discovered that the money was missing? Suppose Hutch found out that he didn't really have an aunt? He wanted to tell someone all about it: someone who wouldn't tell on him; who would sympathize, and reassure him that he had done

the right thing. He sensed that Olwen would understand. If he really hurried he might find her in the
playground before lessons began. He posted the letter
and started to run.

Chapter 4

THE MEDICAL

Johnny delivered all the papers before the school bell rang, but he couldn't find Olwen in the playground then, or at morning break, or at lunch time.

The last lesson of the day was Religious Knowledge. Johnny had been dreading it, because he hadn't learned Genesis, Chapter 46, verses 8 to 24: a long list of names which the teacher, old Mr Wilson, had set as a punishment for the whole class after a mass fit of the giggles the week before. Johnny had tried. He'd got as far as Reuben, Jacob's first born, and the sons of Reuben: Hanoch, and Phallu, and Hezron, and Carmi. But the sight of about thirty weird names looming ahead had driven him outside to kick an empty can around, and then he'd forgotten all about it. Now he was preparing himself for the thwack of a ruler against his leg, or a belt across his backside as a punishment.

Suddenly he believed in miracles. A big boy came into the classroom with a message for the teacher.

The lesson was cancelled. Everyone was to go to the school hall at once for a special assembly. There was a great scraping of chairs as the children jumped up, full of boisterous relief. It seemed that quite a few hadn't learned that fearsome list.

'No talking!' shouted Mr Wilson, who looked as surprised by the change of plan as the rest of them. 'Line up in alphabetical order and follow me.'

All the other classes were filing into the hall. The headmaster was on the edge of the stage, telling everyone to hurry up and to sit cross-legged on the floor so that the whole school could get in. It was only after Johnny had taken his place, crammed in between Albert Taylor and Ernest Roberts, that he noticed two people sitting on chairs behind the headmaster. It was the school nurse, and Dr Langford, with a stethoscope round his neck.

The headmaster called for silence and stillness. 'As you can see, we have a visitor. Many of you may already know Dr Langford.'

There was an outbreak of chatter as the children compared notes on visits to the doctor. Johnny started telling Ernest how he'd had a ride on Dr Langford's bike only that morning. The teachers, who were sitting on chairs all round the edge of the hall,

31

shushed everyone quiet. Mr Wilson leaned forward and slapped Johnny on the head to shut him up.

The headmaster continued, 'Dr Langford has informed me that the family of one of our pupils has become infected with a serious illness.'

There was another buzz of talking, quickly stopped by the staff.

'Silence,' barked the headmaster. 'This is a most important matter. We have no reason to suppose that any of you are ill, but it is necessary for you to be checked straight away. You must all strip down to your underwear and make your way to the stage. Fold your clothes neatly, and leave them to mark your place.'

Johnny was horrified. He hadn't expected to have to undress today. He was wearing his oldest pants and vest. They were full of holes, and badly needed a wash. He knew he'd be teased by the other boys, especially Albert Taylor who, because of the alphabet, was right next to him. He expected Ernest Roberts on his other side to have a go at him too. Ernest lived a few doors down from the Swansons. He had been Johnny's friend and playmate until that term, when Mrs Roberts had taken him to the optician and he'd been prescribed thick spectacles. The boys at school were no kinder to Ernest than the girls had been to

Olwen. Constant jokes about Ernest's glasses had made him crack. Now he did Albert Taylor's bidding in return for his protection. He'd become Taylor's shadow, doing his homework and doling out insults and menace on command. If that meant persecuting his old friend, Johnny, for being short and poor, it was a price Ernest felt he had to pay.

Shivering with fear rather than cold, Johnny slowly pulled off his jumper and shirt. He saw Mr Wilson advancing again, ready to strike. Johnny winced, but Wilson reached across him and wrenched at Albert Taylor's arm instead, revealing an inky trail that ran from his wrist to his elbow.

'What's this, boy?' shouted Mr Wilson. 'See me after school.' He gave Taylor's arm a quick twist as he flung it down again, and Albert huddled into himself, trying to hide the list of biblical names he'd written on his skin: Jamin, Ohad, Jachin, Zohar, Shaul, and many more. From the stage, the headmaster sent one of his nasty stares across to the group of boys around Taylor. It promised trouble in the future.

But the head had more pressing business. 'Right,' he said when everyone was undressed. 'Now come up, class by class, one by one, to see the doctor. Then go back to your places and get dressed again.'

Another murmur ran through the hall. 'Silence!' cried the headmaster. 'The doctor needs quiet. He has to listen to your chests.' Everyone except Taylor obeyed. He was whispering threats into Johnny's ear, blaming him for Mr Wilson's attack. 'If you weren't so small, he'd never have been able to see me,' he said, while Ernest Roberts surreptitiously ground his heel onto Johnny's foot as they stood in line. Johnny looked round the hall to see if Olwen was being taunted too. He spotted Mrs Palmer's class, but she wasn't among them.

Dr Langford came to the front of the stage and explained what he was going to do. 'Now, children, I am going to listen to your lungs, but you're also going to have a special test, which will show us very soon whether you have been infected. All I have to do is make a little scratch on your wrist . . .'

There was a mass cry of '*Urggh!*'

'. . . No, really, you will hardly notice it, and in two or three days I'll be able to tell whether any of you might need treatment. But don't worry. That's very unlikely indeed.'

The doctor briskly examined each child. Occasionally he asked the school nurse to make a note of something, or had a little chat with a child he knew well. When Johnny's turn came he smiled. 'Well, I never thought I'd be doing all this when I saw you this morning,' he said.

'What are you checking for?' asked Johnny.

'TB, I'm afraid,' said Dr Langford, scraping Johnny's wrist while he was distracted. He lifted Johnny's vest and listened to his stethoscope. 'But I'm sure you've got nothing to worry about, my boy. Your chest is nice and clear.' The school nurse put a tick against Johnny's name, and moved the line on.

When everyone had been dealt with, the headmaster had a quick conversation with the doctor while the last of the children got back into their clothes. Then he called for quiet again and addressed the school. 'I'm sure we're all very grateful to Dr Langford for giving up his time to come here today. Now, there's no more time for lessons, so we'll stay here in the hall until home-time. Mr Wilson, perhaps you would like to lead us in some prayers.'

Mr Wilson stepped forward and prayed for the safe recovery of sick people everywhere. As the bell went to mark the end of the day, everyone burst into the same question: who was the child whose family illness had caused all this fuss?

In the playground, Albert Taylor's sister rushed up,

flushed with pride at being able to tell her big brother the news. 'It's that new girl,' she said. 'The one I told you about. The Owl. Mrs Palmer says she's gone back to Wales. Good riddance to bad rubbish, that's what I say.'

'What's wrong with her?' asked Taylor.

'It's TB,' said Johnny, glad to have inside information, and hoping it would earn him some credit with Taylor. 'The doctor told me.'

'And what's that, then?'

'I don't know,' said Johnny. 'But Olwen told me her family were ill.'

Taylor sneered, 'Yes. You were talking to The Owl last night, weren't you, Quacky?' He pulled his sister away from Johnny. 'Better keep away from you. You might have it too. We all might catch it.'

'But the doctor says I'm all right,' said Johnny as the crowd of children ran off.

Mr Wilson approached. He was trying in vain to catch Albert Taylor before he dodged his punishment for trying to cheat in the scripture test. Johnny plucked up the courage to ask him what TB was.

Mr Wilson shook his head. 'It's a very grave disease. A very grave disease indeed. It attacks the lungs. It can be deadly. We've had it here once before – a bad outbreak during the war. Several families were affected. We lost some pupils. That's why they built the big sanatorium at Emberley. But there hasn't been a case in this school since. Let's hope this is just a false alarm.'

Johnny ran to pick up his bag of newspapers at the shop. He took a detour through the graveyard towards the end of his paper round. This time he looked at the dates on some of the gravestones. There were a lot from 1916. He noticed some family groups. Three of the Roberts family were buried in one plot, and there were four Dangerfields, all children, who had died within months of each other. Could they be relatives of Miss Dangerfield up on the hill?

A voice started shouting: 'Hey! You boy! You boy. Get out of there!'

Johnny spun round. Through the branches of a holly bush he could see a black hat on the other side of the graveyard wall. A netting veil covered the face of the short, dumpy woman who was wearing it, but he knew at once that it was Miss Dangerfield herself. She was angry. 'Get away from those graves,' she cried. 'What do you think you are doing!'

'I was only looking,' said Johnny. 'I was just wondering if they were your family – if it was TB.'

'That's none of your business,' snapped Miss Dangerfield, raising her walking stick.

'But I just wanted to ask—'

'How dare you? You nasty little squirt. They were worth a hundred of you. Be off with you.'

Johnny ran away to finish his deliveries, wanting to know more about the bodies under the slabs, but too frightened to ask again.

Chapter 5
LETTERS

Johnny asked his mother about Miss Dangerfield and the TB, but Winnie had not lived in Stambleton in 1916, and knew less about the epidemic than Johnny did. She reassured him about the disease. If Dr Langford said Johnny was healthy, she was sure he was right. But other children had been told more lurid stories, and for the next few days the talk in the playground was all about TB, with graphic descriptions of victims gasping for breath, coughing up blood, and wasting away or just dropping down dead. Everyone was watching their wrists for signs of a reaction to the test. Dr Langford had said he'd be looking for a red bump at the point where a tiny trace of bacteria had been introduced. In art class, Ernest Roberts dabbed on some paint to make it look as if his scratch had flared up into a livid inflammation, but in fact everyone was boringly clear.

Johnny was still worried about Olwen. But when he asked at school whether anyone had heard anything about her they just teased him, so he kept quiet. He wondered in secret what had happened to Olwen's family. This disease was so bad that she had been sent away, and yet everyone said there was no cause for concern. Johnny was confused. But he was excited as well, hoping every day that he would get a reply from Box 23 containing the Secret of Instant Height. He met the postman in the street, and asked if he had seen an envelope addressed to John Swanson Esq. No, said the postman, there hadn't been any letters for Johnny's house that week. Even Hutch was concerned. He could see that Johnny was unusually anxious.

'Have you heard from that aunt of yours yet?' he asked.

'No. Nothing,' said Johnny. 'I hope she's all right.'

'Is she your mother's sister?' Hutch paused for thought. 'I suppose she must be. I knew your father all his life, and he never had a sister. Does she live where your mother comes from? Nottingham, isn't it?'

'Yes,' said Johnny, feeling he should at least tell the truth about his mother's origins, even if everything else was a lie. He was saved from further questions when a customer came in, but he realized that he would have to sort out this Auntie Ada business pretty soon. Maybe he should say that she had died. But then Hutch might send condolences to his mother. And Hutch might mention Ada to her anyway, dead or alive. It would be only natural if Winnie went into the shop. Johnny would have to keep Hutch and his mother apart. He needed yet another plan.

That night, Johnny got home first. There were two letters on the doormat, one addressed to him in his own handwriting, the other an official-looking brown envelope, with his mother's full name, 'Mrs Winifred May Swanson', typed boldly across it. As Johnny picked them up, he heard his mother coming. He just had time to stuff his own envelope into his pocket before she reached the front door.

'What have you got there?' she asked.

'It's a letter. For you,' he said. 'It looks important.'

Johnny was desperate to get away to read his own letter, but he stayed and watched while Winnie opened hers. She was still wearing her hat and coat, standing by the dim oil lamp in the kitchen. If you'd been looking through the window, you might have thought she was Johnny's sister. Like him she was short and slight. From a distance it was hard to believe that she was thirty. But close up, her puffy hands, raw with housework, and the worry-lines on her brow told a different story. The wrinkles grew more pronounced than usual as she took a single typed sheet out of the envelope. Then she flopped down onto a chair.

'What is it, Mum?' asked Johnny, still grasping the letter in his pocket. 'Is it bad news?'

He could see that she was trying to compose herself, to reassure him that there was nothing to be concerned about. Then she looked him straight in the eye. 'Johnny,' she said, 'I think you're old enough to know. It's from the landlord. The rent's going up after Christmas. We're going to have to find an extra three shillings a week.'

'But that's more than I make from the paper round in a fortnight,' said Johnny.

'Oh darling, I wouldn't ask you to pay it. I'll just have to try to find an extra job.' She started mumbling to herself: 'But there's not much work around. Maybe I could take in some washing. But how would I pay for the soap, and the fuel to heat the water?'

Johnny couldn't help it. His eyes went to the Peace Mug on the high shelf.

'No,' said his mother. 'We're not touching the

Christmas money. I'd sooner go without breakfast than use that. Anyway, it would only last a few weeks. It's staying up there. I'm not even going to count it till December.'

Johnny was half relieved that his mother was unlikely to find out he had taken money from the mug, and half ashamed at what he had done. But at least he had his own letter, almost throbbing in his pocket, begging him to open it. At least Box 23 had replied. The money from the Peace Mug hadn't been wasted.

Winnie pulled herself up from the chair, took off her hat and started slowly unbuttoning her coat. Johnny knew he should find some words of comfort, or come up with an idea for raising money, but he couldn't wait to open his letter.

'I'm just going to the lav,' he said, striding out to the yard, where a tiny, damp shed housed the lavatory. It was getting dark, and he could only just make out the writing on the envelope. He tore it open. Inside was a piece of paper that looked as if it had been ripped from a notebook. It was folded into four, with *The Secret of Instant Height is . . .* written in heavy black ink on the outside. Now Johnny was scared. What would it be? Would he have to take medicine, or mix some chemicals? Where would he get them from? How would he pay for them? He couldn't bear to open the note. But he had to know the secret. He had to find out how to grow taller. Maybe then he would be able to do jobs that brought in more money. Then he could help his mother with the rent. The lavatory seat didn't have a cover, but he sat down without lowering his shorts and looked again. *The Secret of Instant Height is . . .* He unfolded the paper. There were just four words written inside: *Stand on a box.*

He couldn't believe it. That was all it said. He had been tricked. He could feel the blood pumping round his ears as he blushed with shame. Two shillings and sixpence had been wasted – plus the cost of the envelopes and the stamps. He had stolen his mother's money, and thrown it away just when she needed it most. And that wasn't all. At any time Hutch might ask Winnie about 'Auntie Ada', and Johnny would have a lot of explaining to do. Everything would come out. He would be shown up as a fool, a liar and a thief. And now there was another thing. He had wet himself.

Chapter 6

CLEARING UP

Johnny stood with a blanket round his middle while his mother filled a tin bath with warm water, to wash him, and then his clothes. Winnie was sympathetic. She thought Johnny's 'accident' must have been brought on by worry about the rent, and she blamed herself for telling him about it. He said nothing of how he had been tricked over the advertisement, and covered his embarrassment by babbling on with ideas for raising more cash.

'I could do more work at the shop,' he said. 'Hutch is always complaining that he's too busy. I'll ask him tomorrow.' As he spoke, Johnny thought of another advantage. He could keep his mother away from Hutch, so she wouldn't find out about 'Auntie Ada'. 'And if I'm working there,' he added, 'I can bring our groceries home with me. You won't have to go shopping at all. That will give you more time to take on extra work, if you can find it.'

Winnie was wringing out Johnny's sopping shorts.

'I don't know how we'll get these dry in time for school tomorrow,' she said. 'I think I'll have to light the fire again.'

So Johnny felt even more guilty, seeing money go up in smoke because of him.

He didn't sleep much that night. For the first time in years, he took his old toy rabbit to bed with him, clutching its floppy body for comfort as he worried about the rent, the Peace Mug money, and his new friend Olwen, somewhere in Wales, possibly facing death. Every time he felt close to sleep a new anxiety arrived and he was wide awake again, imagining homelessness, shame and disease. At one a.m. he was weeping, trying to think of ways to get back at the people at Box 23. Should he tell the *Stambleton Echo* about the Secret of Instant Height? Shouldn't they know that a scam was being run from their own paper? He might not be the only one who had been tricked into sending a postal order. The person who put in the advert might be making a fortune . . .

And that's when the idea came to him: so clear and exciting that he sat bolt upright in bed. *If they can do it, so can I*, he thought. *If I could fall for a trick like that, surely plenty of other people would too!*

He spent the rest of the night thinking out his plan. At first he was full of enthusiasm. He got out of bed and paced the room, muttering to his toy rabbit. He would have to find out how the advertising pages worked, but that wouldn't be difficult. After all, he had plenty of papers in his delivery bag every day. There must be something printed in them to tell you how to place an advert. He'd put one in as soon as possible, and sit back to wait for the replies.

The replies! How would he get them? He couldn't have them sent to his house, or Winnie would find out what he was doing. He knew she wouldn't approve. He'd need a box number, like the Instant Height people. But then he'd have to find a way to slip over to the newspaper offices to collect them. And he'd need to work out how to cash postal orders without arousing Hutch's suspicion.

By half past one it all seemed too complicated. Johnny got back into bed. How could he hope to organize such an intricate scheme when he already faced the problem of disposing of 'Auntie Ada' in a way that would stop Hutch mentioning her to his mother? Surely he should see to that first . . .

He nuzzled up to the rabbit's threadbare fur, breathing in its familiar dusty smell as he tried to work out what to do. Maybe he should just own up and tell Hutch that 'Auntie Ada' had never existed ... Or maybe ... Maybe ... He yawned, and felt himself drifting off to sleep at last, only to be jolted awake again by the sound of the town hall clock striking two, and the arrival of another idea.

Maybe 'Auntie Ada' should stay in his life. Perhaps she could be part of his advertising plan. Johnny would explain to Hutch that his mother couldn't do her own shopping any more because she was busy looking after her invalid sister. And he would account for the postal orders by saying that he was cashing them on behalf of his aunt.

It was brilliant. But Johnny knew it was wrong. At a quarter to three he resolved to abandon the whole thing, deciding it would be simpler to admit what he had already done, and to face his mother's anger and (worse) her disappointment. He wiped his tears on the rabbit's ears, envisaging the scene as he confessed to stealing the money. Then he imagined what would happen if the advertising scheme worked. He pictured himself cashing postal orders, replacing the money in the Peace Mug, and even contributing to the rent. That felt better. At three o'clock he changed his mind one last time. He would risk it after all.

He snuggled under the blanket and started thinking up adverts that might trick the readers of the *Stambleton Echo*. He wanted to find things people were embarrassed or ashamed about so that, like him, they wouldn't want to tell the world how they had been swindled.

His own experience that day gave him his first idea: *Stop your baby wetting the bed.*

He wouldn't be too greedy. Perhaps he'd only ask one shilling for the answer to that. And the answer would be: *Make him sleep in a chair.*

Johnny was desperate for morning to come. He couldn't wait to get started. His legs wriggled uncontrollably every time he thought about the money that stupid people would send him. Somehow, soon after half past three, he finally slipped off to sleep with a smile.

But success didn't seem quite so certain in the chilly morning mist when, almost too tired to walk, he set off for the shop with his damp shorts chafing against his skin.

Chapter 7

THE LANDLORD

Johnny was glad to see that Hutch was in a good mood, whistling as he unpacked a delivery and stacked cans of tinned peaches into a pyramid on the shelf behind the counter.

'Hutch?' said Johnny. 'Is there any chance you could find me some more work here? I could come on Saturdays if you like, and in the holidays, too.'

'So you've had the letter then,' said Hutch, without looking up.

'What letter?' asked Johnny, panicking for a moment at the thought that Hutch might somehow know he'd been fooled into buying the Secret of Instant Height.

'The rent letter. There were some folk in the pub last night complaining about it. It looks as if he's gunning for all of you.'

'Who? Who's gunning for us?'

'Young Mr Bennett, up at the big house on the hill. I never liked the boy. Though he's a man now, of course. Just back from Cambridge University, so they say. He's inherited everything from his father. The factory, the farm, the whole estate. He owns your house now.'

'And he's the one who's putting up the rent?'

'Yes. Yours and everyone else's. He owns an awful lot of property round here. His family always have. But you people on Dagmouth Lane will get the worst of it.'

'Why us?'

'Because his father – old Mr Bennett, God rest his soul – kept all your rents specially low. He built those little houses just before the war. He did it to make money of course. Dagmouth Lane was just a bit of old wasteland then, and he saw a chance to make a profit out of it – renting out homes to factory workers and getting back the wages he paid them. But when the war came, and so many husbands and fathers were killed, he had a change of heart. He made sure Dagmouth Lane went to people like your mother. People who were suffering.' Hutch took out his handkerchief and blew his nose. Johnny hadn't noticed that he'd got a cold. 'Poor Winnie was only a girl then. She and Harry had been married just a few months, and I doubt whether your dad even knew she was expecting you when he went off to fight. After he was killed, Winnie needed a roof over her head, but with you on the way she couldn't get enough work to pay much rent – so old Mr Bennett let her have the house you live in now. She still had to pay, but much less than that house could have fetched. He did the same for lots of other families. He was a good man.'

'I know,' said Johnny. 'Mum talked about him when he died. But she didn't expect the rent to go up.'

'Well, she knew the father, but she doesn't know the son. He was only a lad in the war. He didn't have to fight, and he's not interested in the sacrifice people like your father made. He can only see those houses as a drain on his income. And to be fair, some people could pay a bit more now. Look at Mrs Roberts – she's married again. Her Alf's got a good job.'

'But my mother hasn't. She has to look after me, and the house, and go out to work. She works all the time. She can't afford to pay more.'

'I understand, son,' said Hutch, more warmly than he had ever spoken to Johnny before. 'And now she's got that sister of hers to worry about too.' Johnny flinched at the reminder of Auntie Ada.

Hutch continued, 'I'll see what I can do for you. I won't be able to pay you much, mind. But it might be enough to help a bit. And I'll expect you to work hard.'

'Don't worry, I will.'

'You can stay on after your evening paper round every day and sweep up. And you can help me unpack some of the deliveries.' As he said that, Hutch's hand slipped, and the pyramid of tins fell to the floor. Johnny collected them up and started rebuilding the display.

'This can's got really badly bashed,' he said. 'And the label's ripped.'

'Put it to one side,' said Hutch. 'I'll have to sell it at a discount. No one's going to want to pay full price for that.'

Johnny put the dented can under the counter.

Albert Taylor and Ernest Roberts were waiting outside with their pocket money. Strictly speaking, Hutch didn't let customers in till nine o'clock, but everyone knew he could be persuaded to sell a newspaper or two earlier, and today was the day the comics arrived. Hutch let the boys in. They were polite to him, but when his back was turned they made coughing noises at Johnny.

'Heard from your girlfriend?' said Taylor. 'Is she dead yet?'

Johnny pretended not to notice, and raced out of the shop to deliver the morning papers.

At the end of the day, when Johnny had helped tidy up, Hutch reached under the counter and handed him the damaged tin of peaches. 'Take this home to your mum,' he said. 'Tell her it's not charity. It's your pay for the extra work you've done.' Then he looked sternly at Johnny. 'I won't always be so generous, mind.'

But Johnny saw it as the start of a new role for him. From now on he would take stuff home from the shop whenever he could. That way his mother wouldn't go in there and Hutch would never get the chance to ask her about Auntie Ada. It had been a good day. For on his paper round he had looked in all the newspapers to find out how to place adverts. He reckoned he could get his secret business up and running with just one more raid on the money in the Peace Mug. He would write out his first advertisement in bed that night.

Chapter 8

THE SANATORIUM

The next morning Dr Langford gave Johnny another exhilarating bike ride down the hill. Hutch was not there when they arrived at the shop. The doctor propped his bicycle against the wall and waited with Johnny.

'I might as well pick up my paper here,' he said. 'I'll be at the sanatorium all day, and there's no point in you taking it to my house if I'm not in.'

'Is that a flat tyre?' Johnny asked, pointing to the front wheel of the bike.

'Oh dear. It looks as if we went over something sharp,' said Dr Langford. 'Yes, here's the culprit.' He showed Johnny a tiny nail sticking into the rubber. 'Never mind, I'll have it fixed in no time.'

The doctor opened the saddlebag and handed Johnny a long tin with rounded ends. Johnny wriggled the lid off. Inside there were some metal levers, sand-paper, assorted patches, a tube marked RUBBER SOLUTION, a crayon, and a few bits and pieces Johnny couldn't identify at all.

The doctor turned the bike upside down and asked Johnny to pass him one of the levers. Soon he'd worked the inner tube of the tyre out from under the rubber tread. It hung like an empty sausage skin. Dr Langford unclipped the pump from the bicycle frame and inflated the tube. 'Come here, Johnny,' he said. 'Keep quiet and tell me if you hear a hiss. With a bit of luck we'll find the hole pretty quickly. If not, we'll have to dunk the tube in a puddle and look for some bubbles.'

Johnny put his head close to the doctor's and listened. 'There it is!' they cried together.

'Crayon!' said Dr Langford, as if he were talking to a nurse in an operating theatre. Johnny passed it to him, and Dr Langford marked the spot.

As the doctor got to work on the puncture, Johnny found the courage to talk to him more freely than he had before. It was easier when they weren't looking directly at each other. Johnny cleared his throat. 'Dr Langford?' he said. 'Can I ask you an embarrassing question?'

The doctor seemed uncomfortable, too. 'I'll be happy to talk to you, Johnny,' he replied, without looking up. 'But you will have to come and see me at my old surgery. I can open it up specially for you, if you've got something on your mind.'

'Oh no,' said Johnny. 'I didn't mean that sort of embarrassing. It's just that I'm ashamed that I don't know this already. You said you were going to the sanatorium. My teacher talked about it too. What exactly *is* a sanatorium?'

The doctor laughed, and asked Johnny to pass the sandpaper. 'Oh, is that all? What a relief. Well, if they taught Latin at that school of ours, you'd be able to work it out. It comes from the verb *sanare*, meaning "to cure", or "to heal", and the adjective *sanus*, *–a*, *–um*, meaning "healthy". It's a place of health: a kind of hospital. But a special one. It's just for people who've got tuberculosis. That's the disease I was checking you for at school the other day. We sometimes call it TB, or consumption.'

'Everyone's talking about it at school. They say it makes you cough up blood and shrivel away to skin and bone.'

'That's one way of putting it, yes,' said Dr Langford. 'It usually affects the lungs, but it can strike other organs, too. It can give you a very nasty condition called scrofula – horrible purple lumps on the neck.'

Johnny automatically put his hand to his own

throat and started feeling for bumps, rolling the sound of the word 'scrofula' round his mouth.

'Rubber solution!' said the doctor. 'It's the little yellow tube.' Johnny gave it to him, and he continued working on the bike with the dexterity of a surgeon, chatting on about diseases. 'In the olden days they thought scrofula could be cured by a touch of the King's hand. They called it the King's Evil. But it was really just another kind of tuberculosis.'

'And tuberculosis is TB?'

'Yes, but we doctors have yet another name for it. Here's a special word for you, Johnny. This one's from ancient Greek: *phthisis*. It's one of my favourites. Just eight letters, but quite a tongue-twister – and only one vowel, if you don't count the "i" twice.' He spelled it out for Johnny. 'Remember that word, son. Try it out on your teacher and see if he knows what it means. You might need it in a crossword puzzle one day.'

As the doctor stuck a patch over the repair, Johnny tried to fix the word in his memory, saying it again and again; flicking from the first 'f' sound of the 'ph' into the 'th' and then on to the hiss at the end. 'It sounds like a curse,' he said.

'Well, the disease certainly is,' said Dr Langford.

'I'm sorry to say that it's often fatal. Some people get better, but there's no absolute cure. We do our best for patients with fresh air, good food and exercise. And we keep them away from other people, so that they don't pass on their germs. Last time there was a TB outbreak in Stambleton we had a big collection to build our sanatorium a few miles out in the country, so there would be less risk in the town.'

'Was that when all the Dangerfields died?'

'How do you know about that?'

'I've seen the gravestones in the cemetery.'

The doctor shook his head. 'Poor Miss Dangerfield. First her beloved brother and his wife were taken by the disease, then their children died, one by one. She nursed them all, you know. I'll never forget the sight of her weeping over the tiny body of her last dead nephew. And after all that, she lost her fiancé in the war. She was already getting on a bit then. It was her last chance of happiness. She's the only Dangerfield left now. It's no wonder she looks so much older than she really is.' He changed the subject without a pause. 'Any chalk in that tin? We need it to stop the repair sticking to the inside of the tyre when the tube goes back in.'

Johnny passed the chalk. 'Why didn't Miss Dangerfield catch TB? Why haven't you?'

'Well, you know, Johnny, we doctors have a way of staying healthy. And it's like all diseases. Not everyone who comes into contact with a nasty bug gets sick. If they did, the human race would have been wiped out long ago. But some people – babies especially – can pick up tuberculosis very easily. And they can die from it. Anyone can. Mind you, some French doctors have come up with a vaccine . . .'

'A what?'

'Vaccine – that's another good word for you (double "c" – you don't get that very often). It's a special medicine to stop you getting a disease in the first place. It's a wonderful thing – made of living cells. But it's very hard to produce – they have to grow it in a special liquid made from potatoes.'

Johnny laughed. 'Potatoes?'

'Yes, I know it sounds comical, but it's actually a very tricky process.' The doctor picked up the lever again, and carefully manoeuvred the inner tube back inside the tyre. 'It's not something you can just boil up in your kitchen. You need controlled laboratory conditions. But if you get the process exactly right, the vaccine contains a tiny dose of the disease.'

'Isn't that what was in the test you gave us?' Johnny held out his wrist to show that he was in the clear.

'A vaccine's much more potent than that. It's strong enough to teach the blood to fight against invading germs, but it doesn't make people ill. Do you want some more strange words? This vaccine's called Bacille Calmette-Guérin. We make it easier for ourselves by calling it BCG. It's named after the Frenchmen who developed it – lucky devils.'

'Lucky?'

The doctor wiped his hands on his trousers. 'Oh Johnny,' he chuckled. 'There's nothing a medic wants more than his name attached to something: a piece of equipment, or a disease.' He screwed the nozzle of the bicycle pump back onto the valve. 'That way your memory lives on even after your death. I knew them both, you know – Calmette and Guérin – when they were starting out on their research, long before the war. In fact that's how I met my wife. She's a distant relative of Professor Calmette.'

'Mum told me she was French,' said Johnny, looking longingly at the pump. 'But she doesn't sound foreign, does she?'

Dr Langford turned round. 'Would you like to do this bit?' he asked, and Johnny gladly got to work re-inflating the tyre. The doctor set an empty apple box on its end and sat down. 'Well, she's been living here for more than forty years, remember. And her English was pretty good to start with.' He smiled, and his eyes grew moist as he thought back. 'It was the first thing I noticed at that dinner party in Lille all those years ago. She's very well educated. From a fine background. It was good of her to give it all up for a humble English doctor.' He cleared his throat and slapped his knees. 'Still, as it turned out, her family lost everything in the war, so it's probably just as well that she married me.' He reached over and felt the wheel. 'That's enough now. Leave it for a bit to make sure it doesn't go down again.'

'But the professor,' said Johnny; 'the one who made the vaccine – did he survive?'

'Oh yes. He's still around – though, like me, he's ageing now. I saw him quite recently. My wife and I went over to visit the laboratory where they produce the vaccine. France has gone overboard for it. They're giving it to babies – free.'

'Why don't we have it here?' asked Johnny, collecting up all the bits and pieces from the pavement, and putting them back in the tin.

Dr Langford sighed. 'It's complicated. There's a law

against bringing new medicines into this country unless they've been approved by the government.'

'So why don't they approve it?'

'All sorts of reasons. Some people are against vaccination on principle – they think it's wrong to interfere with Nature; and there are big-wigs here who aren't convinced that the BCG works. But the fact is, Johnny, we British have never liked being taught anything by the French. Our government is paying British scientists to search for a British treatment. They haven't come up with anything yet, and I don't think there's any need for them to try.'

'Couldn't you tell the government to let us have the French vaccine?'

'Oh, I'm a nobody as far as they're concerned.' Dr Langford dropped his voice. 'But, as it happens, I do have a little plan for something that might change their minds.' He looked around, cautiously. 'Now you mustn't tell anyone, Johnny, but when I last went to France I didn't come back empty-handed.'

Johnny was excited at being let into a secret. He pulled up a crate of his own and sat down close to the doctor. 'You brought the vaccine with you?' he whispered.

'Not exactly. I brought some of the culture – the

cells from which it's made – and I've passed it on to someone who has access to a laboratory. We're trying to keep it alive and grow it on to create a reliable supply. If we can, we're going to run a little trial – just enough to prove to the authorities that it works, and to persuade them to use it here.'

'But aren't you breaking the law? Suppose they find your lab. Won't you get into trouble?'

'Possibly, Johnny. But I'm an old man. I'm happy to take that risk, just in case I can save some lives with the vaccine.'

'And you could give it an English name. It could be called after you: "the Langford Treatment", or something like that.'

The doctor laughed. 'That does have an attractive ring to it. But I don't think it would be fair. I'm only copying what the French are doing. I think we'd still have to call it BCG.'

'Can I come and see it? Will you take me to the laboratory?'

'No, Johnny. I've already told you too much. And anyway, the lab is far, far away from here, out in the wilds. The project is entirely in the hands of my associate at the moment.'

'When will the vaccine be ready?'

'If all goes well, we may have a little before the end of the year, but it will be a long while before we can produce enough to get the government to change their policy. For the time being they'll just have to keep on building special hospitals, like our sanatorium.' Dr Langford rose and turned his bike the right way up, wheeling it backwards and forwards along the pavement to check that the repair was good.

Johnny was enjoying getting to know the doctor better. Now that they were at ease with each other, he plucked up the courage to ask a question he'd had in mind all along but had kept to himself, for fear of appearing love-struck, or nosy. 'Dr Langford,' he said, cautiously, 'do you know anything about Olwen? Is she all right?'

To Johnny's relief, the doctor answered without a trace of amusement or disdain. 'The little Welsh girl? When I examined her, she was perfectly well. But she's gone back to Wales to stay with relatives. She'll be safe there, and I've passed on the name of an excellent sanatorium nearby that will take her in if she does develop symptoms. I'm afraid her parents and her sister were too sick to travel with her. They're in the sanatorium here. I'm sorry to say that the baby is desperately ill.'

'Can't you give it some of your vaccine – as soon as it's ready – even just a little bit?'

'It's too late for that, Johnny. You have to take the vaccine before you get sick. But I wish I could give it to all the other babies in the country. I really do.'

Johnny heard a wheezing noise behind him. It was Hutch, hurrying towards the shop, panting, and carrying a cardboard box.

'Has he got phthisis?' Johnny whispered to the doctor anxiously.

Dr Langford laughed. 'No, he's just out of breath.' He steadied the bike against a lamppost and walked towards Hutch. 'Can I give you a hand with that, Mr Hutchinson?'

'Thank you, sir,' Hutch puffed, handing the box to the doctor as he fumbled in his pocket for the keys to the shop. 'It's the poppies for the Remembrance Day collection. There was a bit of a mix-up, and I had to go and collect them at the station. I got held up.' He tapped his bad leg. 'I'm not as fast on my feet as I'd like to be.'

Inside the shop, Hutch hurriedly sorted the newspapers. 'I'm sorry, Johnny,' he said. 'This is going to make you late for school. There's no way you'll finish the round before the bell goes. And people will be furious that their papers are late. Don't let them take it out on you. It's all my fault.'

'Don't worry about that,' said the doctor. 'No one will be angry with me if I'm delayed getting to the sanatorium. I'll take Johnny on his round on my bicycle.'

So Johnny hoisted himself onto the crossbar, and the two of them delivered all the papers in record time. The doctor told him more about the sanatorium, and passed on another new word – *haemoptysis* (or spitting up blood). Not many people were out at such an early hour, but those who were waved happily at the old man and the boy. All except Dr Langford's neighbour, Miss Dangerfield, who always had a sharp contempt for anything out of the ordinary. She was polishing the brass numbers on her garden gate as Johnny and the doctor reached the end of the paper round.

Dr Langford rang the bell on his bike and shouted, 'Good morning, dear lady. Behold! Your paper!' as Johnny thrust it into her arms.

That was bad enough for Miss Dangerfield. Anyone might have seen. But it got worse. Johnny and the doctor both stuck out their legs and cheered as the bike freewheeled down the hill back to the shop. Miss Dangerfield had one word for it: 'Really!'

Johnny got to school just in time, and in class his mind slipped from images of illness back to his money-making scheme. He thought ahead to what he would do after he had raised enough cash to pay the rent. He would keep going with the adverts until he could afford to buy himself a bicycle.

Chapter 9

THE ADVERTISER

While Winnie threw herself into looking for extra work, Johnny got down to business. That night, after his mother had gone to bed, he raided the Peace Mug again and wrote out his Stop Your Baby Wetting the Bed advert, following the pattern of the one for the Secret of Instant Height, which was painfully imprinted on his memory. After school the following day, he hurried through his evening paper round and ran to the headquarters of the *Stambleton Echo*, a tall building by the canal. He could hear printing machinery thumping away below him as he climbed the steps up to an entrance marked OFFICE.

Johnny pushed open the heavy double doors, panting for breath, just as the woman in charge of the advertising department was getting ready to leave for the day. He'd already worked out what to say. Auntie Ada was going to help him out again. He had taken great care to make his handwriting look as neat and grown up as possible.

'Excuse me,' he puffed, standing on tiptoe to see over the high counter that separated the staff from the visiting public. 'Excuse me, madam. I've been sent with a message. My aunt wants to put an advertisement in your paper.'

'Which paper?' said the woman, impatiently.

Johnny was mystified. 'The *Echo*,' he said.

'Which *Echo*? The Hampton, the Balgrave, the Stambleton . . .'

'Stambleton,' said Johnny. 'I didn't know you did the others too.'

'Those, and the *Dorford Chronicle*, the *Mardly Trumpet*, the *Nethercross Express*—' It sounded as if she was ready to go on for a long time.

Johnny interrupted, 'They're all written here?'

'They're all printed here. And your aunt can advertise in any or all of them.'

Johnny was ecstatic. He had no idea that his adverts might be seen by so many people. 'Oh, all of them. I'm sure she'd want that.'

He handed his advertisement to the woman. She put on her glasses and started counting the words. Johnny had already done that several times. He knew that *Stop Your Baby Wetting the Bed. Send a postal order for one shilling and a stamped addressed envelope to Box*

X added up to twenty-one words. It would cost him one shilling and sixpence. He had the money in his pocket. He was slightly worried that it might cost more if the box number was in double figures, like the horrible 'Box 23'.

'That will be sixteen shillings and ninepence,' the lady said, as if it weren't a small fortune.

'Oh, I thought it would be one and six,' said Johnny, sheepishly. 'Twenty-one words. It says so in the paper.'

'That's for one advert, for one week, in one paper – and without a box number,' said the lady.

'Oh, but Auntie says she must have a box,' Johnny gulped, on the verge of tears. 'She doesn't want strangers to know where she lives. She wants you to collect the replies.'

'I quite understand,' said the lady, lifting her glasses to peer down at Johnny. 'A woman can't be too careful these days. But a box is sixpence a week.'

'But I've only got one and six,' said Johnny, putting his coins on the counter. 'And I have to get the advert in. She told me to run here. I don't know what to do.' He could feel his eyes starting to sting.

For once, being small and pale worked wonders for Johnny. The woman smiled sympathetically, put her glasses back on and examined the advert again.

'Well, you could have twelve words in one newspaper for a shilling,' she said. 'Let's see if we can cut this down.'

She showed Johnny how 'stamped addressed envelope' could be abbreviated to 'SAE'. 'One shilling postal order' could be written as '1/– PO'. She assured him that everyone would know what that meant. Like the box number, and 'SAE', it would count as just one word.

They ended up with: *Stop Your Baby Wetting the Bed. Send 1/– PO & SAE to Box 5.*

'I shouldn't really be showing you that,' said the lady, who was getting ever more friendly. 'Strictly speaking, I ought to encourage you to write more, so that we can charge extra. The other week someone came in with a little advert like this, and I persuaded him to spell out everything in full and put in the whole address of the paper. It pumped the price right up. I think I even got him to pay for a border round it. But he wasn't a nice man. He was really rude. I don't see why I should have to put up with discourtesy.'

Johnny thought back to the Instant Height advert. He hoped the lady was talking about the person who had tricked him into parting with money for that. 'Well, my auntie will certainly be very grateful that you have been so helpful to me,' he said in his best voice. 'Now I really mustn't hold you up any longer. Goodbye, madam.'

'Goodbye,' said the lady, smiling at his politeness. 'Tell your aunt she can collect the replies on any weekday during office hours.'

'She'll probably send me,' said Johnny.

He was on his way through the door and the lady was putting on her coat when she added, 'Oh, how silly of me. I forgot to take your aunt's name and address.'

Johnny hoped his panic didn't show as he made up a fictitious address on the spot. Auntie Ada was becoming ever more real. And she had a surname now. It seemed to come to him from nowhere, but afterwards he thought it fitted her rather well. From now on she was Mrs Ada Fortune. She'd have to be married. 'Miss Fortune' just didn't sound right.

Chapter 10

IN BUSINESS

After a week, Johnny returned to the newspaper office. He was late again. There was no way he could deliver all the papers and get there much before five o'clock. As before, the lady was in a hurry to leave.

'I have quite a journey,' she said. 'I live in Mardly. The bus goes at twenty past.'

'I'm sorry,' said Johnny, concealing his delight that she was not a Stambleton resident. He'd been worrying for days that she would realize he'd given a false address. He turned on the charm again. 'Do forgive me for coming at this hour. My aunt has sent me to collect the replies to her advertisement. It's Box Five.'

The woman turned to a rack of pigeonholes and took out a large envelope. She peeped inside, then sealed the flap. 'Take care of it,' she said. 'There are a few letters in there. They might have money in them. Mind how you go.'

Johnny couldn't wait to get away and open the

package. 'I won't hold you up any longer, madam,' he said, nodding politely on his way out. He dashed down to the edge of the canal and hid there until the woman had locked the door and set off for her bus stop. Then he tore open the big envelope. There were four smaller packets inside. Each of them contained a postal order for one shilling and a stamped addressed envelope for Johnny's reply. Johnny remembered how he had felt, assembling his letter to the people offering the Secret of Instant Height. For a moment he pictured the senders of these letters, desperately hoping for the solution to their babies' bedwetting, not suspecting that they were being tricked. But then he gathered up the postal orders. Four shillings. It was enough to cover the cost of this first advert, and to fund another, with money to spare to go back in the Peace Mug. He put the image of the anxious parents to the back of his mind, tucked everything back in the big envelope, and stuffed it down his jumper.

Up in his bedroom that night he wrote *Make him sleep in a chair* on four pieces of paper, and put one in each of the stamped addressed envelopes. Next morning, he popped them in the post box outside Hutch's shop. All day he checked and rechecked that the postal orders were still in his pocket. After school, when the post office was open, he asked Hutch to cash them on behalf of Auntie Ada. The sound of the four shilling bits jangling together as he ran cheered his journey home through the rain.

Over the next couple of weeks Johnny had a run of successes with:

Free yourself from rats . . .
Free yourself from mice . . .
Free yourself from spiders . . .
Free yourself from noisy neighbours . . .

and

Free yourself from nosy neighbours . . .

All of which had the answer,

Move house.

Not only were there no complaints, but one woman even sent in for the solution to her spider problem when she had already been tricked over the mice. *Get into Films* did well. There seemed to be a lot of would-be starlets around. For a shilling Johnny told them to *Go to the cinema*.

It was all very time-consuming. But Johnny had more time on his own now. His mother had found an extra job behind the bar at a run-down pub on the other side of town, and Johnny spent most evenings alone at home, making up adverts and practising Auntie Ada's flowing handwriting.

There were disappointments. No one seemed to want to know how to scratch itches without leaving unsightly marks (*Wear gloves*), but there was a huge demand for a way to stop your husband disturbing you with his snoring (*Sleep in a different room*). That one brought the Peace Mug back to its original level. Hutch seemed to believe that all the postal orders belonged to Auntie Ada. Johnny had told him that she did needlework in her sickbed, and sold it by post.

Some of the people who answered Johnny's adverts didn't send postal orders, but paid with unused postage stamps. At first Johnny was annoyed by that because, despite his growing business, he hardly ever sent any letters of his own. Then he had the brainwave of using the stamps for a different kind of scam. He put in an advert saying:

I will pay your rent for a year.
Send 15/– PO to cover expenses.

Eight people fell for it. They each received their rent for a year. Unfortunately for them, the year was 1066, and all they got was 3d. in stamps, which Johnny reckoned would have been enough for a fairly handsome property in those far-off days. There was one angry letter of complaint, sent to the box number. At first Johnny was worried. What if the disappointed customer told the newspaper what was going on, and they tried to track down Ada Fortune? Then (since he had plenty of stamps) he hit on the idea of writing back, using some of the language he'd seen in the law reports in the papers. He added in one of the best words Dr Langford had taught him: *haemoptysis*. He thought it sounded important, and he guessed that anyone stupid enough to think that a stranger would pay their rent for a year wouldn't know that it meant 'spitting blood'. Johnny used some of his earnings to buy thick paper and envelopes, and in his ever-improving handwriting he concocted a polite but firm letter, from a false address in London, in which he said that his legal advisers, and those of the news-paper, were in agreement (having consulted authorities on the law of haemoptysis) that there had been no deception, since no year had been specifically mentioned in the advertisement. He generously offered not to charge for the administrative costs that had been incurred in responding to the unjustified complaint. Johnny hoped that the angry man wouldn't try to contact him again. He didn't.

But, lucrative though it was, Johnny knew he had been lucky to get away with the rent scam. He understood now that people were much more likely to complain if they had paid a lot of money; and fifteen shillings was too much to ask for anything. It was safer to lure twenty people into parting with a shilling than to trick one into paying a pound. So he got rid of the remaining stamps with a cheap – but successful – offer:

Official Portrait of the King. 1/–.

Johnny had meant to be a little more honest, and to say 'miniature portrait', but he wasn't sure how to spell 'miniature', and anyway, it was always good to save a word in an advert. There were no complaints, even though the suckers had at least ended up with a stamp (worth anything from one penny to sixpence) to put on their angry letters. No doubt they agreed with Johnny that they would have looked pretty daft if they'd admitted falling for that trick. But it was a good one. Johnny worked out that once his costs were covered, he was making a profit of anything from 100 to 1100 per cent, depending on the value of the stamps he sent to his patriotic customers. True, the actual amounts that reached the Peace Mug were very small, but he was beginning to dream of bigger projects, with mighty returns.

And there was one unexpected side effect of all the effort. Winnie ran into Johnny's form teacher, Mrs Stiles, in the street one Saturday morning.

'Oh, Mrs Swanson,' said Mrs Stiles. 'I'm so very pleased with Johnny this term. His work has improved immensely. It's very neat indeed.'

'I'm delighted to hear it.'

'Yes, and it's not just his presentation. His maths is coming along in leaps and bounds. He's especially good at money sums.'

Later that day, when Winnie told Johnny what his teacher had said, she thought he was blushing out of proud embarrassment. She knew nothing of the guilty secret that was burning his cheeks.

Chapter 11

UMCKALOABO

Just before half-term, Dr Langford came to school again, to check that everyone was still clear of TB. He got Johnny's class off Geography this time. He was becoming rather popular. Then, during the week of holiday, Hutch gave Johnny jobs in the shop every day. Johnny saw Hutch at work in the stockroom, behind the counter, and in the post office. They had time to chat, and got to know each other better.

The store was always busy, with customers wanting everything from groceries to knitting patterns. There was a wooden booth near the door with a bench and a telephone inside. People came from all over town to use it. Some stayed inside for ages, and it smelled strongly of stale cigarette smoke. Johnny tried not to listen to the muffled, one-sided conversations seeping out through the sliding door, but sometimes he just couldn't help it. So he knew all about the deputy headmaster's attempt to get another job, and the vicar's daughter's entanglement with someone called

Michael, who appeared to be married. One day he heard Mrs Slack on the phone to some distant relative, droning on about her health and how she couldn't cope at home. At first he was appalled to find the old lady virtually begging for money, but he felt better about her when she continued:

'I don't know what I'd do without Mrs Swanson. She comes in every day to see that I'm all right and never asks for a penny. She's a marvellous woman. Sometimes I think she's all that's keeping me alive.'

He never told his mother what he had heard. He thought she would be angry with him for listening in. In the weeks to come, he was to wish that he *had* said something. But by then it was too late.

When it was quiet in the shop, Johnny had the chance to study the newspapers, looking at the advertisements for ideas. He knew the best adverts were in the Sunday papers, but he could never get a good look at them on the day, because the shop was shut; he just saw the headlines as he posted each copy through a letter box. To read them properly he had to wait till Hutch threw his own copies away; so when Johnny fished *Reynolds's News* out of the bin on the Monday of half-term, it was covered in brown circles from the bottom of Hutch's teacup.

Johnny opened out the huge newspaper. It took up almost the whole counter. He had to move aside the charity collection tin and a jar of Liquorice Allsorts to make room for it. He turned the pages, leafing through news and fashion tips, the sheet music for a popular song, a short story, cartoons, theatre reviews, and display adverts for cars and London department stores. Among the small ads, one entry caught his eye immediately. It was headed: CHEST DISEASES, and it went on:

'Umckaloabo acts as regards Tuberculosis as a real specific'
(Dr Sechehaye in the 'Swiss Medical Review').
It appears to me to have a specific destructive influence on the Tubercule Bacilli in the same way the Quinine has upon Malaria.'
(Dr Grun in the King's Bench Division).

If you are suffering from a disease of the chest or lungs – spasmodic or cardiac asthma excluded – ask your doctor about Umckaloabo, or send a postcard for particulars of it to Chas. H. Stevens, 204–206 Worple Road, Wimbledon, London, S.W.20, who will post same to you Free of Charge.

Readers, especially TBs, will see in the above few lines more wonderful news than is to be found in many volumes on the same subject.

Johnny read the advert through several times, trying to get his tongue round the strange word 'Umckaloabo'. It sounded like something from Africa. With his practised eye, he couldn't help calculating the price of such a wordy advertisement in a high-circulation paper. With all the special layout to make it look like a news story, you wouldn't get much change from three pounds. Chas. H. Stevens of Wimbledon must have great faith in what he was selling, particularly as he wasn't asking his customers for any money up front.

Johnny's heart quickened. Maybe this advertisement was indeed the 'wonderful news' it claimed to be. Perhaps Mr Stevens really had found a cure for TB. If that was so, shouldn't Dr Langford be told? Perhaps he could use Umckaloabo to help Olwen's family. Johnny knew the Langfords didn't take *Reynolds's News*. They wouldn't have seen the advertisement themselves. He took out some scissors from the drawer under the counter and carefully cut it out.

*

After work, Johnny went straight up the hill to Dr Langford's house to tell him about Umckaloabo. Mrs Langford opened the door. She was tall and slim, like her husband, but while his limbs tended to flail around in an ungainly way, hers moved with an effortless grace, even though she sometimes put her hand to her back, as if it hurt to bend. Her steel-grey hair was twisted up at the back in a chignon. Johnny knew that was what it was called because he'd seen a diagram showing how to do it in the paper only that morning. Winnie had often admired Mrs Langford's clothes, saying how well-made they were, and how well co-ordinated. Johnny had no opinion on how Mrs Langford's skirt and blouse were constructed, but he could see that they matched. Both were a deep shade of blue.

'Hello Johnny,' said Mrs Langford. 'Are you looking for your mother? She went home hours ago.'

'No. I've brought something for Dr Langford,' said Johnny, pulling the crumpled cutting from his pocket. 'It's important. I think Dr Langford ought to know. Someone's found a cure for TB.'

'Well, if they really have, he'll be fascinated. Not to say amazed. Let me have a look at that. You'd better come in.' She took the cutting and showed Johnny into the drawing room. 'You sit by the fire and get warm. Now, where are my glasses?'

Johnny watched her search the room, which had more places to lose things than in his entire home.

She ran her hand along the bookshelves, shook out plump cushions, dug down the back of the soft sofa and shuffled though piles of newspapers and magazines. 'I don't know where they get to. I must have had them just before I came to answer the door. Now, let's see. What was I doing when you arrived?' She paused and thought back. 'That's it. I was sewing. I was sitting just where you are now.'

'Oh, I'm sorry,' said Johnny, jumping up. 'I didn't know this was your chair.'

'Don't be silly. You're my guest. You can sit where you like. Just forgive me a moment.' Johnny heard her knees click as she bent down and scrabbled on the floor behind his feet. She pulled out a work basket. An old sock dangled from under the lid. 'I remember now. I slid it there when the bell rang – just in case it was the vicar or someone like that. I wouldn't want him to catch me darning holes!'

Johnny held the basket while Mrs Langford, sighing, hauled herself back up again. Then she took it back, and lifted out her spectacles. 'If I had sixpence for every time I've lost these, I'd be a very rich woman,' she joked. 'I've seen people with their glasses on special strings round their necks. Rather an ageing effect, I've always thought. But perhaps the time has come for me.'

Johnny was already mentally composing a new advert: *Never Lose Your Glasses Again*. He was wondering whether to send people real string, or just the suggestion that they could tie up their glasses themselves. Maybe he could charge more if he used coloured ribbon . . .

Mrs Langford straightened out Johnny's cutting, and looked at it through her spectacles. 'Oh, Umckaloabo. I've heard of this. There was a big row about it a few years ago. This Charles Stevens was struck off because of it.'

'Struck off?'

Mrs Langford explained: 'Struck off the Medical Register. It means the authorities took away his right to practise medicine. He's not allowed to call himself a doctor any more. He was making wild claims about an unproven drug. He's what we call a quack.'

'A what?'

'A quack. A fake doctor.'

'They call me Quacky at school,' said Johnny. 'But it's nothing to do with doctors. It's because of my name: Swanson. It makes them think of ducks.'

'That's not very nice of them,' said Mrs Langford. 'But boys will be boys, I suppose. They called my husband Longfeet when he was at school, because he was so tall.'

'What's all this?' said Dr Langford, who had just entered the room. 'Oh, hello Johnny. I wasn't expecting to see you. Nothing wrong, I hope?'

'No,' said Johnny miserably, unable to disguise his disappointment at finding that the advertisement was a trick.

Mrs Langford passed the cutting to her husband. 'It's Umckaloabo again,' she said.

Dr Langford patted his pockets. 'Can I borrow your glasses a minute?' he asked. His wife passed them over, with a wink to Johnny. The doctor sighed. 'So he's still making money out of it. It's a disgrace, giving false hope to worried people and pocketing the proceeds. I thought we'd seen the back of this Stevens character.' Dr Langford was still reading the advertisement. 'He lives a long way away. Wimbledon.' He looked up at Johnny, grinning. 'You know what Wimbledon is famous for, don't you, son?'

Johnny shrugged. 'Don't ask me.'

'Tennis.' There was an awkward pause. The doctor seemed to be waiting for something. 'Do you see? Do you get it? Has the penny dropped?'

'I'm sorry?' said Johnny, embarrassed and confused.

'It's just that . . . well . . . you know . . . this Umckaloabo stuff. It's a Wimbledon racket.' The doctor paused again. Eventually Johnny got the joke, and mustered a half-hearted laugh.

Mrs Langford threw the cutting on the fire.

'I bet hundreds of people will answer that advertisement and pay good money for rubbish,' said Dr Langford. 'It's not right.'

'Why don't you put your vaccine in the paper then?' asked Johnny.

The room fell silent, and Mrs Langford gave her husband a stern look. The doctor, shamefaced, put a finger to his lips. 'I shouldn't have told you about that, Johnny. It's absolutely secret. I could get into a great deal of trouble if anyone finds out what I'm doing.'

'You mustn't mention it to anyone,' said Mrs Langford, trying to sound kind, but looking more agitated than Johnny had ever seen her. She turned to her husband, muttering something under her breath.

Johnny felt embarrassed, and cross with himself for getting the doctor into trouble with his wife. He interrupted. 'Don't worry. I won't tell anyone. But I still don't understand. Why is it all right for this man

Stevens to advertise something that doesn't work, and against the law for you to sell something that does?'

'Because real medicines have to be controlled, Johnny. Powerful drugs can do harm as well as good. You can bet your life that almost everything you see advertised in the paper is useless. You'd be astounded at what people will fall for in the small ads.'

Johnny didn't say that he knew only too well. He could feel himself blushing as his mind flashed back to that moment by the canal, when he had last thought of his customers as real people who were being tricked. Dr Langford had put that feeling into words: *It's a disgrace, giving false hope to worried people and pocketing the proceeds.*

Johnny wanted to get away from the awkward atmosphere. It wasn't just his hidden shame over the adverts. He didn't want to get trapped in between two quarrelling adults, and he felt guilty that he had made such nice old people angry with each other. 'I think I'd better go home now,' he said, as politely as he could. 'I'm sorry to have troubled you.'

'That's quite all right, Johnny,' said Dr Langford, showing him to the door. 'I know you were only trying to help.'

'I was thinking of Olwen,' said Johnny. 'I know it's too late for your vaccine to work on her, but it sounded as if this Umb . . . Umber . . . whatever it's called, might help. But if that's no good, what will happen to her?'

'I'm afraid I can't say. I don't even know exactly where she is. She's not my patient. She's probably not even ill at the moment. All I know is that she's with relatives in Wales.' The doctor lowered his voice. 'Now remember, son. Mum's the word. Don't tell anyone about the vaccine. Understand?'

The door closed behind him, and Johnny could hear raised voices. He crept round to the drawing-room window, hoping to be able to make out what the Langfords were saying, but he could only catch fragments of the argument.

Mrs Langford was furious: '. . . couldn't resist it . . . totally unnecessary risk.'

The doctor was trying to reassure her: 'He won't tell anyone . . . Who's going to listen to a boy? . . . doesn't know where the laboratory is.'

'I just wish you'd never got involved . . . not even going to make us any money . . . scrimping to make ends meet . . .'

Johnny heard a door slam and the voices disappeared.

He set off down the path, only to find Miss Dangerfield waiting at the gate. After seeing Mrs Langford in her trim clothes, Johnny noticed how Miss Dangerfield's shapeless old-fashioned layers of black swept along the muddy ground, and how short and stooped she was underneath her funereal fringes and flounces. Even so, her fierce nasal voice was chilling.

'I've been watching you,' she said. 'I saw you hovering by that window. Hoping to break in, I shouldn't wonder.'

'No, Miss Dangerfield. I wasn't. I was just listening—'

'Listening!' She grasped Johnny's shirt and pulled him towards her. 'Eavesdropping – that's what I call it.'

'No. Not that,' said Johnny, shaking. 'I'd just been inside, talking to Dr Langford.'

Miss Dangerfield was spitting with contempt. 'You? Inside? Don't be ridiculous. Why should Dr Langford want to talk to you? What were you talking about?'

Johnny had only just promised to keep quiet. He could see how concerned the Langfords were that no one should know they had brought the BCG to Britain. He said nothing. But he knew Miss Dangerfield would take his silence as a sign of guilt.

'I thought as much!' she said when Johnny failed to speak. 'You're a liar as well as a thief.' She pushed him away. He wanted to run, but his legs wouldn't move. She grabbed his hair and shook him till his eyes watered with pain. 'You get away from here, and don't come back!' she yelled, turning him round and poking her walking stick into the small of his back. 'I'm warning you.'

After what the doctor had told him about Miss Dangerfield's sad past, Johnny had begun to feel a bit sorry for her. But not now. Not after how she had just treated him. To Johnny she was a miserable old woman once again. Instead of walking away, as he knew he should, he did something he'd never done in the presence of an adult. He made a very rude sign and said an even ruder word. Then he ran.

Chapter 12

THE PRIVATE BOX

Every afternoon a man with a wide moustache came up to the post office counter to ask if he had any mail.

'Why does he do that?' asked Johnny. 'Why doesn't the postman take him his letters?'

'Oh, he's got what we call a private box,' said Hutch. 'He has all his letters addressed here, and he collects them himself.'

'Why would he want to do that?'

'Well. There could be all sorts of reasons. He might be travelling, and picking up letters from several post offices on his route. Or he might not like the folk he lives with to see what letters he's getting. Or perhaps he doesn't want the people who send the letters to know exactly where he lives.'

'But they could come here and ask you,' said Johnny.

Hutch stood tall and took a deep breath. 'They could, Johnny, but I'd never tell them,' he said in his official 'post office' voice. 'I'm a servant of the Crown, and a private box is called a private box for a reason. That man's identity and his address are a confidential matter. The very fact that he has a private box is private. I probably shouldn't even be talking to you about it now.'

Johnny could instantly see the advantages of a private box at the post office. He wanted one. If the replies to his adverts were delivered to the shop, he wouldn't have to walk to the newspaper offices so often. He was getting worried about the lady there. She seemed to like him, but that was becoming a problem. He always tried to collect Auntie Ada's letters just before closing time, but even then she wanted to chat. Once, she had suggested that they should walk to her bus stop together, and recently she'd raised her eyebrows at some of the adverts he took in. How long could he trust himself not to say something that would make her suspicious? What if she herself responded to one of the adverts? She had already seemed rather too interested in *The Answer to Smelly Feet* (*Wear a clothes peg on your nose*).

Since her company owned most of the newspapers for miles around, Johnny couldn't avoid the lady, even when he moved his business from one local paper to another. But if his post could be sent to Hutch's shop, he might be able to start advertising in different places – perhaps even the national papers, which had more readers. Now that he had more money, Johnny could send in his advertisements by mail, paying for them with postal orders and stamps he received from his customers. He might even be able to phone the advertising departments. His voice was still high. They would believe he was Ada Fortune.

'I think Auntie Ada should have a private box,' he said to Hutch casually. 'She must worry about the people who buy her needlework knowing our address. The last thing she needs in her state of health is surprise visitors. And if her letters were delivered here in the first place, I could cash her postal orders with you and take the money straight home. She wouldn't have to wait so long to get it. How much does a private box cost?'

'Not much,' said Hutch. 'But listen, the poor woman's an invalid, and I know your family's having a rough time at present. I won't make her pay. I'll cover the costs myself.'

Johnny tried to protest. But before he got the words out, he realized that he couldn't offer to pay the fee himself. He mustn't let on that he had a stash of money at home.

'No, I'll pay,' said Hutch, interrupting Johnny's garbled rejection of the offer, which he took as simple politeness. 'I insist. It will be a pleasure. But it must all be done properly. You take this form home and get your aunt to fill it in.'

So, that night, Johnny created Ada Fortune's first official document, beautifully signed. The next day, Hutch marked it with his rubber stamp and filed it away.

'Tell your auntie that her address is now PO Box Nine, Stambleton, Warwickshire. In future I'll keep her letters aside, and you can take them home with you.'

Even though the new address would add a few pence to the cost of each advertisement, Johnny knew the private box was going to make his life a lot easier, and he spent the rest of half-term dreaming up new projects. When he looked through the national papers he saw that most of the advertisements were about health and self-improvement. It was obviously a lucrative market, and although Dr Langford had struck a nerve with his criticism of quack medicine, Johnny could see that sending out remedies offered a solution to another problem. He needed to convince Hutch that Auntie Ada really *was* doing needlework in exchange for all those postal orders. It was time to be seen posting parcels on her behalf. But there was no need for Johnny to sew anything. Hutch would never know what was inside the packages, so Johnny could fill them with 'cures' for everything from sleeplessness to sore toes.

He had no trouble finding a list of illnesses: years of accompanying his mother on her visits to Mrs Slack had exposed him to the human version of a medical encyclopaedia; and the graveyard on his paper round had everything he needed to fulfil the orders. He pulled the juiciest leaves off the evergreens, and collected the most beautiful fallen autumn foliage from the ground. There were seed husks, conker shells, acorns, and twisted pieces of twig.

He was tugging the feathers off the corpse of a pigeon when he heard a rapping noise. It was Miss Dangerfield, bashing her walking stick on top of the wall.

'Hey! You boy! What do you think you are doing?'

Johnny had to think fast. 'Oh, hello, madam,' he said, playing for time. 'I'm . . . I'm . . . It's Nature Study. I have to collect some specimens for school.'

'Don't you "madam" me! And don't you "Nature Study" me! I know the school is on holiday. Nature Study indeed! You're up to no good. And where's my paper?' Johnny put his hand into his bag to get it for her. 'Not here, you fool! I don't want it here, do I? I want it at home. And you're late. Mr Hutchinson pays you to deliver the newspaper to my house. And you're late!'

Somewhere inside himself Johnny knew that it was pointless to argue, but after her unkindness the other day, and with the safety of the graveyard wall between them, he couldn't resist pointing out the flaw in what Miss Dangerfield was saying. 'But I'm on my way. And anyway, you're not there, are you? I mean, you're here. So you wouldn't know I was late, would you? If you were there, I mean. Which you're not.'

'Don't you answer me back, boy.'

'I wasn't answering back—'

'Yes you were, and you're doing it again now. I've got a good mind to report you. Now get off up the hill and deliver my paper.'

Johnny placed a few more leaves in the bag.

Miss Dangerfield banged her stick on the wall again. 'Do it now, I tell you! And if there's any dirt on that paper, I'm cancelling my order. I've got my eye on you, boy. Indeed I have.'

Johnny ran off up the hill and finished his deliveries. He'd enjoyed the brief moment of standing up for himself, but he was worried about Miss Dangerfield. Suppose she had gone straight from the graveyard to the post office? She might be telling on him now. He might lose his job just when the rent was about to go up. He needed his base at Hutch's, with its postal orders, stationery and stamps, to keep the money coming in. He had to get back, to talk his way out of trouble.

Hutch was sweeping up, looking stern. 'I've had a complaint.'

'I know. Miss Dangerfield told me she was going to talk to you.'

'Talk! She ranted. She raved. Lucky for you, she knocked over the display of sugar with that stick of hers, and she flounced off before I could make her any promises. But I'm warning you, Johnny. Stay on the right side of her. I won't be able to defend you for ever.'

'I'll try,' said Johnny, meaning it, because he knew his business interests could be smashed by one blow from Miss Dangerfield's cane.

He had no time to lose. He must make the most of the post office while he still had access to it. So he bought a notepad and some brown paper from Hutch and went home to compose a host of adverts to put in right away, and to wrap up his stock of 'cures' ready for a quick dispatch. He had no idea whether any of the leaves were poisonous, so he put a note in each parcel saying FOR EXTERNAL USE ONLY. He'd seen that written on the tin of Dr Sampson's Patent Ointment for Cuts, Burns and Stings.

According to the nature of the problem, he told his customers to slip the leaves, husks and feathers under their pillows, in their underwear, or down their socks. To his horror, his first victim wrote straight back to say that the 'cure' had worked. His heartburn had disappeared as soon as he had put dried potato peelings down his vest.

Chapter 13

RAKING IT IN

The TB scare had died down by the end of half-term. Normal lessons seemed even more tedious after the brief burst of excitement, but that wasn't the only reason Johnny was sad to go back. It meant a pay cut from Hutch, and reduced the time he could spend running his business. Even so, he got some profitable ideas at school.

On the first day back, they were studying light waves in Mr Marshall's Science class. The teacher pointed to Ernest Roberts, who was sitting next to Johnny.

'Roberts. Take off your glasses.'

'But I won't be able to see the blackboard then, sir.'

'That's the point, Roberts.'

Ernest took off his specs, and the teacher threw a square of cardboard in his direction. Without his glasses he couldn't catch it, and it dropped to the floor. Johnny picked it up.

'Well, Swanson. Tell us what that is.'

Johnny was bemused. 'It's just a piece of cardboard, sir.'

'Look carefully. Do you notice anything special about it?'

Johnny examined it closely. 'It's cut from a packet of hair restorer, sir.' He read out the label. '*Vivatone Radio Active Hair Restorer. Grey banished. No dyes. No stains.*'

Everybody laughed.

'The other side, Swanson. Look at the other side.'

'It's just plain, sir. But there is a little hole in the middle.'

'Exactly, Swanson. A hole. What we call a pinhole. And why do you think it's called that?'

'Because you made it with a pin?' shouted Albert Taylor.

'Well done, Taylor. I made it with a pin. Now, Roberts. Look through that pinhole and tell me what you can see.'

Ernest Roberts shut one eye and looked through the pinhole with the other.

'I can see you, sir. Perfectly clearly.' He read the heading off the blackboard: '*Optics*. It's magic, sir.'

'No, Roberts, it's not magic,' said Mr Marshall. 'It's science,' and he drew a diagram on the board to show

how the pinhole concentrated the light waves so that they hit Roberts's retina at just the right spot.

'Cheaper than a pair of glasses, eh, Roberts?' he said. 'Someone should put it on the market. Talk about money for old rope.'

Johnny was already devising a new advert in his head: *The Secret of Instant Sight.* There was plenty of old cardboard in the shop. He knew Hutch would let him have it for nothing.

And the remark about 'money for old rope' wasn't lost on Johnny either. He found some twine in the graveyard. He cut it up into short lengths and tied them into bracelets, to be worn on painful wrists and ankles. The potato-vest man bought one, and wrote again, convinced that his arthritic joints were much relieved.

Despite being back at school, Johnny couldn't stop himself. He saw financial opportunities everywhere. *Reynolds's News* had a popular feature:

MAUD DAWSON'S LOVE ANSWERS
Is your burden too hard to bear? Let me share it!

The answers to the questions seemed like downright twaddle to Johnny. He was sure he could do better than Maud Dawson, and charge people for his advice. He put an advert in the *Saturday Post* (calling himself Ada Ardour), offering advice on anything, in return for a shilling and a stamped addressed envelope. He was overwhelmed with requests for help. Some of the letters were several pages long, and went into embarrassing detail about love affairs. This was typical, if less explicit than most:

> *Dear Miss Ardour,*
>
> *I am engaged to be married next year. My fiancé says he loves me, but he is insisting that I must give up cycling when we are married, and he says we cannot have any pets, though I love dogs and cats. We argue about all these matters. Should I give in? I worry that if we continue in this way he may cease to consider me sweet natured, and that we may be getting into a habit of dispute which will continue after the wedding.*
>
> *Yours in desperation,*
> *Anxious of Ambleside*

Johnny had no doubt that Maud Dawson would advise 'Anxious of Ambleside' to be dutiful and to yield to her fiancé's demands. He took a different view, and wrote back:

Dear Anxious of Ambleside,

This man does not sound very kind. Leave him, keep your bike, and get a dog. This may cause you embarrassment now, but you will thank me in years to come.

Confidentially yours,
Ada Ardour

He was pleased with his reply, and let his mind play with the scene in Ambleside as 'Anxious' told her boyfriend to get lost. But then he had visions of the jilted lover tracking him down, and added at the bottom:

Of course, this is only advice, and your decision will be entirely your own. Ada Ardour takes no respon-sibility for the eventual outcome.

He liked the expression 'Confidentially yours', and it went on to become the regular heading on his 'agony' advertisements. And he added that extra sentence on the bottom of all his advice letters – just in case.

'Confidentially Yours' was entertaining (and educa-tional) for Johnny, but it was also tiring work, with each letter needing an individual reply. He dreamed up another scam where his customers would do most of the work. 'The Poetry Police' offered to send critical advice to aspiring poets at two shillings a time. Johnny read the poems, but he sent all the poets the same few words of encouragement: *A good effort. Do not be afraid to experiment.* And he kept the poems. One came in handy for English homework. Then he spotted a competition in the Sunday paper. Underneath 'Maud Dawson's Love Answers' was a column headed 'For the Chicks'. It was a sickly item, aimed at children, written by someone who called herself 'Aunty Betty'. She was offering prizes for 'Fairy Verse'. Johnny just happened to have a poem about fairies amongst his haul. He sent it in under his own name, and his mother was awash with pride when a letter arrived from the paper, enclosing a five-shilling postal order for Johnny. She was moved when he insisted on putting his winnings towards the rent money. She didn't know that he was hiding even more cash inside the floppy body of his old toy rabbit, which sat on top of the wardrobe in his bedroom. And she had no idea that he was buying food at the shop. Whenever Johnny came home with something for the larder, he always said that Hutch had sent it, because otherwise it would just have to be thrown away.

Every morning, Johnny set off with a stash of letters in his school satchel. Most were replies to his hapless customers, but there were always at least three new adverts, destined for papers all over the country. Soon he couldn't get to sleep at night until he had everything in order for the next day. He began to take a pride in his 'work'. Only once did he have a real attack of conscience. It came as the result of one of his least sophisticated efforts, based on the simple formula of the Secret of Instant Height. Anyone who sent Johnny a shilling to find out how to *Make Your Money Go Further* was told to *Roll it down a hill*. Twenty people fell for it, and so Johnny would have made a pound; but there was one postal order he felt he couldn't cash. It was from Mrs Langford. This wasn't the first time Johnny had been given the chance to trick someone he knew – Albert Taylor's mother had fallen for the snoring scam, and he'd been glad to take her money – but the doctor was so generous with his bike rides that Johnny felt it would be unforgivable to cheat his wife out of a shilling. He remembered Mrs Langford darning socks on the day he'd visited them, and her harsh words to her husband about how poor they were becoming. He put her postal order straight into the stamped addressed envelope and sent it back.

But the other nineteen applicants all got the silly answer. And none of them complained.

Chapter 14

REMEMBRANCE DAY

Not long after the half-term break there was another day off school. That year, 1929, 11th November fell on a Monday, and everything closed down for a big parade and religious service to honour those who had died in the Great War. But the papers still had to be delivered, so Johnny was up early as usual. When he got to the shop, Hutch was polishing his medals. He had three, hanging from multi-coloured ribbons, and a round silver badge with a crown and the King's initials intertwined. Around the edge, it said: For King and Empire. Services Rendered.

Johnny picked it up. 'Mr Murray's got one of these,' he said. 'He wears it all the time at school.'

'It's what you got if you were discharged from the army because you were wounded,' said Hutch. 'I must have been one of the first to have it. I got shot right at the beginning of the war.' He slapped his leg. 'I was one of the lucky ones. I only saw one battle, and I survived.'

'Mr Murray doesn't seem to think he was lucky.'

'Well, he wasn't really. He got hit in the face. It ruined his whole life. Turned him into such a bitter man. I'm OK. I'm still doing what I did before. Everything changed for him.'

'What? Do you mean he wasn't a teacher before the war?'

'Him? A teacher? Do you think he'd ever have wanted to be a teacher? He hates it. Surely you've noticed that?'

'I've noticed that he hates me,' said Johnny. 'He's so mean and cruel.'

'He doesn't really hate you, I'm sure,' said Hutch. 'But he's angry. He never wanted to fight. He didn't volunteer like me. He was called up towards the end of the war. He was a good-looking man – hoping to become an actor, you know. He can't do that with half his face shot away, and now he's stuck with a job he doesn't like and can't afford to give up.'

'But why take it out on me?'

'He probably doesn't mean to. You probably just make him feel guilty.'

'Guilty? Why?'

'Because your father died and he survived. It's hard for us veterans, you know. I don't think many of us are going to take pride in being able to march in the parade today. We'll be thinking of all the dead men who deserve to be there. And there'll be plenty of others angry that we're still around, when their loved-ones are gone. That Miss Dangerfield lost her sweetheart. Your own mother lost your dad. She'd be a saint if she wasn't jealous of the women who got their husbands back.'

'But she's proud of how Dad died. This morning she got out the little plaque with his name on, and the scroll the King sent when he was killed. She keeps them in a special box, you know, with the letter they sent about how his body couldn't be recovered. Mr Murray says that means he was blown to bits.'

Hutch winced. 'Who knows, Johnny? Who knows? It was chaos out there. Half the stories about what happened to people must be lies or guesswork. But whatever happened, your mother is right to hang on to her pride. The trouble is, it's all wearing off a bit now. During the war we were heroes. Now I'm just a man with a limp, and your Mr Murray is a bitter bully with an ugly face. We'll have our parade, but some people won't even bother to go. And next year there'll be even fewer who'll brave the cold. There's plenty of folk who think we should put it all behind us. Maybe they're right. The war's been over for more than ten years now, after all.'

Hutch was staring into space, and Johnny felt awkward seeing him so emotional, so he picked up the bag and set off on his paper round. The square was being prepared for the ceremony, and the band was rehearsing stirring marches and sad laments for the dead.

At ten o'clock, Johnny and Winnie took their place by the war memorial. Johnny quickly found his father's name, but this year he noticed two Hutchinsons and a Murray there too. He hadn't realized before that those two had lost brothers. Gradually other people joined the crowd – all of them well wrapped up in winter clothes, stamping on the stone cobbles to keep their feet warm. Towards half past ten, Dr Langford and his wife arrived. They both looked smart. She was wearing a stylish black coat with a wide fur collar, bought in the days when they still had plenty of money. Her hair was pulled back into a tight bun under her hat, showing off the fine features beneath her wrinkled skin. Even Johnny could tell that she was naturally elegant. Maybe it was that French blood the doctor had told him about.

Mrs Langford exchanged some pleasant words with Winnie as they waited for the parade to begin. Dr Langford quietly shook hands with several of his former patients. He pinched Johnny's cheek in his well-meaning, but painful, way.

The bandsmen were just lifting their instruments to start playing when a large black car swept into the square. Johnny was collecting cigarette cards with pictures of all the latest models, and he recognized it straight away as the most luxurious of the set: it was a Rolls-Royce Phantom II. A whisper ran through the crowd as people realized who had arrived. It was young Mr Frederick Bennett, the new landlord, making his first public appearance in Stambleton since his father's death. Seeing the parade about to start, he strode over to find a place at the front of the spectators, followed by a very thin woman whose long fur cloak flapped open to reveal a startlingly short dress. She squealed as her high-heeled shoes slithered on the uneven cobblestones. The couple wriggled in between the Langfords, right opposite the vicar, who was about to signal the start of the service. Frederick Bennett kept whispering to Mrs Langford during the hymns and between the prayers. No one else said anything, but it was as if a shout of disapproval rang around the square. At eleven o'clock Johnny could sense that his mother was having trouble holding back tears, and he took her hand for the two-minute silence. The atmosphere was ruined by several bouts of coughing from Mr Bennett's companion, whose automatic 'Pardon me' came out louder than even she could have expected.

After some marching by the old soldiers, and the laying of wreaths, the Mayor made a short speech. Then the crowd dissolved into little pockets of chatter. Johnny overheard more than one comment that Frederick Bennett wasn't a patch on his father; but he couldn't help being impressed by the car. He watched as Mr Bennett and his companion climbed back into the huge automobile. He saw them lighting cigarettes and giggling together before Bennett turned the wheel and the car screeched away towards his big house.

Dr Langford put his hand on Johnny's shoulder. 'There goes your new landlord, Johnny,' he said. 'What do you make of him?'

Johnny tried to be polite. 'He was a little rude,' he said. 'Do you think his wife is ill?'

'No. And I don't think she's his wife either, Johnny. Don't worry. That cough of hers probably has more to do with the cigarettes than any disease.'

'So she hasn't got phth . . . phthis . . . whatever it's called?'

'Phthisis . . . TB . . . No.' Dr Langford chuckled. 'She's not going to end up in the sanatorium.' And he winked, adding, 'I'm pleased to say.'

'Actually, I wanted to ask you something about the sanatorium,' said Johnny. 'I was wondering if I could visit Olwen's family there? I thought they might know how she's getting on in Wales. I've been worrying about her a bit. I could ask them for her address. I could write to her.'

'That's very sweet of you,' said the doctor, making Johnny blush. 'But I'd advise you to stay away. You'd probably be safe, but it's best not to take any risks. In any case, the sanatorium has very strict visiting rules. It's usually relatives only. This Olwen isn't a relation of yours, is she?'

'No. Just a friend. And I haven't known her very long. I've never even met her parents. They wouldn't know who I was.'

'Why don't you leave it to me, then? I still go to the sanatorium from time to time. If you want to send them something or write them a note, I'd be happy to take it with me next time I'm called in to help with a case. Just come to my house and drop it off.'

Johnny said thank you, and promised to take something round in the next few days. Then he rejoined Winnie, who was talking to Mrs Langford. Mr Bennett was the subject of their conversation, too.

'The family were my husband's patients,' said Mrs Langford. 'So of course we've known him most of his life. His father and my husband were very close, you know, particularly towards the end.'

Johnny hoped that Winnie would steel herself to ask for a pay rise. He thought that perhaps, since Mrs Langford had just been reminded of how his mother had been widowed so young, she might show some pity. Winnie had sensed the moment too. 'You've heard that Mr Bennett's putting our rent up, I suppose?' she began, nervously. 'We may have to move out of the house.'

'Yes, dear,' Mrs Langford cut in, patting Winnie's hand. 'Times are hard. Hard even for us, I'm afraid. We're all going to have to tighten our belts.'

Winnie understood the signal. There was no prospect of more money from the Langfords; so she tried asking for something else. 'I'm going to have to get extra work elsewhere,' she said. 'I wonder if you could possibly write a letter of recommendation – for me to show to people I ask for jobs?'

Mrs Langford seemed relieved that Winnie had taken the hint. 'Of course,' she said. 'I'll do it today. Maybe you would like to come round to collect it? In fact, come anyway – shall we say about four o'clock? I've just asked Mr Bennett and his young lady to supper, and you can help me prepare.' Johnny noted that there was no mention of any payment for the unexpected work. Without waiting for a reply, Mrs Langford turned to call her husband. 'Come along, Giles,' she said, not wanting to raise her voice on such a solemn occasion. 'We'd better be getting home.' There was no response, so she sent Johnny. 'Run along and ask my husband to come here, dear,' she said, and Johnny did as he was told,

The doctor was caught up with chit-chat, but he understood Johnny's sign language, and Johnny returned to tell Mrs Langford that her husband wouldn't be long.

Mrs Langford pulled Johnny to one side and whispered to him. 'About the other day,' she said. 'That advertisement and what my husband was talking about. You understand, don't you – whatever happens, whoever asks you, however much you feel like boasting' – she squeezed his arm so tightly that he couldn't doubt her seriousness – '*not a word.*'

'Of course.'

'I mean it, Johnny. I'm depending on you. Now get back to your mother. She needs you, today of all days.'

Johnny could see that his mother was exhausted, and sadder than he had ever known her. She walked towards the memorial, took off one glove, and stroked the letters that made up her dead husband's name. This wasn't the moment for Johnny to reveal that he could make their lives more comfortable. He would have to wait until he could explain what he had been doing in a way that wouldn't make Winnie angry. But he was happy, because in his heart he knew things were about to get better.

But then, suddenly, they got very much worse.

Chapter 15

MISSING

The very next evening Johnny got home from his paper round to find his mother on her hands and knees, sorting out the cupboard under the sink. It was always a bad sign. Whenever Winnie was worried or upset, she would take refuge in unnecessary cleaning.

'What's wrong, Mum?' he asked.

'Nothing,' she said unconvincingly. She turned and knocked over her bucket of soap suds. Johnny grabbed the mop and soaked up the water before any harm was done, but Winnie was already in tears.

Johnny pulled out a chair and sat her down at the table. 'I'll put the kettle on,' he said. 'Now, what is it?'

'Oh, I'm probably just being silly,' said Winnie, blowing her nose. 'It's the Langfords. They've disappeared. When I got to their house this morning the door was locked and the shutters were closed. I rang the bell. I knocked. There was nobody there.'

'Well, they haven't cancelled their newspapers. I delivered them as usual, morning and evening.'

'Did you notice anything?'

'No. I just put the papers through the letter box.' Johnny didn't mention that he liked to get up and down that hill as fast as possible since all the trouble with Miss Dangerfield. 'Maybe they've just gone to visit friends or something?'

'But I'm sure they would have told me. I was there yesterday afternoon, remember? They didn't say anything about going away. In fact Mrs Langford suggested I should leave my basket and my apron there, since I'd be back again so soon. That's one of the things I'm worried about. I need my basket. I need my apron. I need my money too. They should pay me on Friday. What if they're not back by then?'

'They probably will be. And anyway, we'll manage,' said Johnny, tempted to tell her about the secret hoard of cash upstairs. 'I bet you'll go round in the morning and everything will be just as it should be.'

'Well, let's hope so. I'm sorry, Johnny. It's just with the worry about the rent and everything . . .' She wiped her eyes on her sleeve. 'Oh my! Look at the time. I'd better get going or I'll be late for the pub. There's some cheese on the windowsill for your tea. Will you be all right?'

'Of course. I've got lots of homework to do,' said

Johnny, who wanted to get cracking on his latest brainwave (*Send 2/6 for the Secret of Living to the Year 2000. Full refund guaranteed in the event of failure.*)

'You're such a good boy – working so hard. Now don't be afraid to turn the light up. We're not so poor that we can't afford a drop of oil. I won't have you ruining your eyes in the dark.'

'Don't worry about me, Mum. I'll be fine. You run along, and I'll come with you in the morning to see what's going on at the doctor's. I bet everything will be back to normal.'

But the next morning the Langfords' house was still locked up. Before the evening paper round, Johnny wrote a note to Olwen's parents, wishing them well and asking how to contact her in Wales. He even enclosed a stamped addressed envelope for their reply. He chose a box of toffees for the doctor to take to the sanatorium with the note. Since it was early closing day Hutch was busy in the stockroom, so Johnny put the money for the sweets under the cash register and set off to deliver the papers.

Johnny knocked on the Langfords' door, hoping that the doctor would be back, so he could pass over the present for Olwen's parents. There was no answer, and the shutters were still closed. He posted the newspaper through the letter box. It was too high for him to look through, so he couldn't tell whether the previous day's papers had been picked up. Johnny wondered where the Langfords could have gone, but then another thought struck him. What if they were inside, locked in? Suppose they were sick, or even dead? He clambered onto a window ledge, and tried to climb the drainpipe to look in upstairs. The pipe wobbled and pulled away from the wall. As he struggled to keep his balance, he felt a sharp blow across his back. It was Miss Dangerfield's walking stick.

'Got you! You little burglar,' she said as he dropped to the ground.

Johnny tried to explain. 'I'm not breaking in, Miss Dangerfield. I'm not a thief. I'm worried about the Langfords. There's no sign of them. I thought they might be trapped inside.'

'Trapped inside? Don't give me that! You know they're not there. You wanted to get in and steal something while they're away.'

'Are they away?' said Johnny.

'That's no more any of my business than it's any of yours.'

'But it is my business in a way,' said Johnny. 'They haven't cancelled their papers.'

She prodded him with her stick. 'Now get up. And talking of papers, get on with delivering them. Have you got mine?'

Johnny opened his bag to get Miss Dangerfield's copy of the *Evening Echo*. She spotted the toffees nestling alongside. 'And how do you explain these?' she asked, grabbing the box. 'Where did you get them? Stolen from Mr Hutchinson's shop, I shouldn't wonder!'

'No. I paid for them. I was bringing them to Dr Langford.'

'What! You were giving the doctor a present? Credit me with some intelligence!'

'No, they're not for him. They're for a friend. Well, for her parents actually.'

'Oh really? And what's the name of these people?'

Johnny realized he'd never known Olwen's surname. 'I'm not sure—'

'Ha! You're not sure. You're giving a box of expensive sweets to people you don't know! You expect me to believe that?' She steered him towards the gate, bashing his legs with her cane. 'Come with me. I'm taking you back to the shop.'

'But—'

'Silence! You can explain yourself to Mr Hutchinson. He's got a telephone down there, hasn't he? I may even ask him to call the police.'

She marched Johnny down the hill, and battered on the door of the shop. Hutch unlocked it, and let her in. Miss Dangerfield slammed the box of toffees down on the counter.

'Proof!' she cried. 'I tried to tell you the other day. I said this boy was up to no good, and I was right. I caught him climbing into the doctor's house, and now this. He's been stealing from you as well.'

Hutch picked up the box and looked up to the shelf. There was indeed a gap in the display.

'But I paid for them, Hutch!' Johnny croaked through the tears he had been fighting all the way to the shop. 'I tried to tell her. I paid for them. They're mine.'

Miss Dangerfield looked at Hutch. 'Is that true? Did you sell them to him?'

Hutch fumbled with the box. 'To be honest, I don't remember doing that.'

'It's a police matter,' said Miss Dangerfield. 'The boy should be locked up.'

Johnny, still crying, was trying to explain. 'You were

in the stockroom,' he sniffed. 'I had to go on the paper round, so I took them—'

'What did I tell you!' cried Miss Dangerfield,

'I took them, but I put the money under the till. It's probably still there now.'

'A likely story!' scoffed Miss Dangerfield as Hutch ran his hand along the counter and found the two-shilling piece.

'Here it is!' he said with relief.

'Ha!' said Miss Dangerfield. 'A trick. The boy's even more devious than I thought.'

Hutch took control. He opened the shop door. 'Thank you, madam, I'm sure you were only trying to help, but I will deal with things from here. Leave the boy with me, and I will talk to him.'

'You should sack him. Don't forget, I saw him breaking into the Langfords'—'

'I will ask him about that, too,' said Hutch in a polite, but firm, tone. 'Goodnight, now, Miss Dangerfield. I really must close the shop.'

She left, mumbling complaints, and Hutch bolted the door. Johnny expected him to laugh about the old woman, but he was furious.

'After all I've done for you! After all that. She says she caught you red-handed. You were trying to break in.'

'I wasn't. I was trying to have a look to see if something had happened to the Langfords. Their house is all locked up.'

'So? Maybe they've gone away for a few days.'

'Why didn't they say they were going?'

'How should I know?

'Suppose they're locked in? Suppose they're sick or something?'

Hutch was getting exasperated. 'Don't be daft. He's a doctor. And they've got a telephone. What are the chances of them being stranded inside their own house? You're just letting your imagination run away with you. Miss Dangerfield was right about one thing. It's none of your business.' He took a deep breath. He looked stern. 'Now, I've promised her I'll deal with the matter.'

'No!' Johnny's nose began to run. 'No! Don't sack me, Hutch. Please.' He looked at Hutch with desperate pleading in his streaming eyes.

Hutch was calming down. 'I'm not going to sack you, but I'm taking you off that part of the paper round, and I'm knocking sixpence off your pay. I'll deliver Miss Dangerfield's papers myself until the Langfords get back and all this blows over. You keep away from there.'

'All right,' said Johnny.

Hutch handed him the box. 'You'd better take these. But remember, you're not going to have so much money in future. You certainly won't be able to spend it on fancy sweets.'

'They weren't for me,' said Johnny, and he explained about Olwen's family at the sanatorium, and how the sweets had been a present.

Hutch's mood softened. 'And you paid for them out of your own money?'

Johnny sniffed. 'Yes,' he said, letting Hutch believe he had been saving up his wages.

'Well, that's very good of you, Johnny,' said Hutch, handing over his handkerchief so that Johnny could dry his eyes. 'I'm impressed. I think Miss Dangerfield has misjudged you, and if there's one thing I can't stand it's people making false accusations. But you keep away from her – and from the Langfords' house until they get back. She might go straight to the police next time, and trouble with the police is the last thing your family needs at the moment.' Hutch put the toffees back on the shelf, and gave Johnny his two shillings. 'Charity begins at home, son,' he said. 'Give this to your mother, if you feel you can spare it. Now, get off home, and don't be late tomorrow.'

Johnny was almost exhausted with relief, but he ran home, hoping to catch Winnie before she left on her long walk to the pub. He met her as she was closing the front door, and he walked with her, trying to explain what had happened before she heard about it from Miss Dangerfield. Winnie understood how horrible it was for Johnny, being accused of something he hadn't done, and why he'd wanted to see in through the Langfords' upstairs windows, but she was angry with him for climbing and breaking the drainpipe.

'It was a stupid thing to do,' she said. 'Dangerous, too. That house looks good, but everything's starting to fall apart. If you wanted to look in upstairs, you should have gone up a tree or something.'

'I still could,' said Johnny, inspired by Winnie's throwaway remark.

'But you can't risk being seen by Mrs Dangerfield. She'd be back at the post office complaining about you all over again.'

'Not if you come with me. She wouldn't dare tell me off if you were there.' Johnny was getting excited about his plan. 'Come on. You want to know what's inside, too, don't you? Let's go together.'

'What, now? said Winnie, startled. 'But it's dark.

And it will still be dark before you go to school in the morning.'

'All right then – later tomorrow. When it's light. I'll get out of school at dinner time. Meet me at the Langfords' and I'll climb a tree in the garden and tell you what I see.'

'I'm not sure,' said Winnie. 'I'll sleep on it.'

She did, and in the end her concern over her basket, her apron, and whether she would ever get her wages over-rode her natural caution. Johnny climbed an old pear tree. He'd hardly had time to steady himself before he heard the sound of a sash window opening. But the noise was coming from over the road.

'You boy!' shouted Miss Dangerfield. 'You, boy, get away from there!'

'Oh no,' said Winnie, quivering with fear. 'You'd better come down, Johnny. She's seen you.'

'Just a minute, Mum,' said Johnny. 'I'm up here now. I might as well carry on. You pretend you're angry with me, and I'll stay up here till I've had a good look.'

So Winnie started shouting at Johnny while he clambered through the branches, looking into the Langfords' house. He tried to sound as if he was answering back rudely, but he was really giving Winnie a running commentary on what he could see. They made a good team, but all Johnny had to report on was a row of empty bedrooms and a tidy study.

'Well, that was a waste of time,' said Winnie as they strode back towards the gate. 'I feel terrible now. That was really wrong, looking in someone's windows. We'll just have to accept that the Langfords have taken off without paying me. Maybe they'll explain it all if they ever come back, but until then, Hutch wants you to stay away from here, and so do I. Promise me you will.'

'All right. I promise.'

'Good boy,' said Winnie, taking his hand. 'We'll just put all this behind us.'

Miss Dangerfield was still watching from an upstairs room, muttering to herself about 'that Swanson woman'. It seemed that she was just as bad as her nasty little son.

Chapter 16

THE CLONG

The weekend came and went, and the Langfords were still away. Nobody apart from Johnny and Winnie seemed bothered, so Johnny decided to use his new advertising skills to try to find them. He was already intrigued by the 'personal columns' in the newspapers, where people put in strange messages that meant nothing to anyone but themselves. He'd seen: *Masham. Contact Dawkins. Something to your advantage*, and, *Cad. I don't care. So there. Flopsy.* Now he composed one of his own: *Langford. Please contact Swanson. Worried.* At threepence a word, he had to drop something to get the cost down to a shilling. He decided to lose the 'please', but keep 'worried', which he had already substituted for 'urgent'. Even at a shilling it was expensive compared with his other adverts, because of course it wasn't going to bring in any money. He knew from his deliveries that the Langfords read the *Stambleton Echo* and the *London Times*. He put his advert in the London paper, since they could get that anywhere, and he was pretty sure they weren't in Stambleton.

A fortnight later, there was no response.

But the rest of Johnny's advertising business was booming. Letters were still coming in from the lovelorn and the poets, one of whom was now writing to 'PO Box 9' with a new creation, and two shillings, every few days. A new advertisement – *Make Your Shoes Last Twice as Long* – was a big hit in a Norfolk newspaper. There were no complaints about the answer: *Hop everywhere. Remember to change legs.*

The rabbit on top of the wardrobe was becoming quite heavy with money. One Tuesday in December, almost a month after the Langfords had disappeared, Johnny thought he would cheer up his mother on her night off from the pub by spending some of his cash on a cake for tea. He told Hutch that Auntie Ada was paying for it, but he planned to knock it about a bit on the way home, and pretend to Winnie that Hutch had sent it because it was damaged and would other-wise be thrown away.

Both Hutch and his mother had forbidden him to approach the doctor's house, and for weeks Johnny had gone home the long way round; but tonight it was raining and the wind was rising, and he couldn't resist taking his old route past the Langfords'. The days were so short now that it was dark whenever he wasn't at school, and he was sure that in the bad weather Miss Dangerfield wouldn't be outside to spot him, even if she still cared what he did.

Did he imagine the light? He walked up the hill into the December gale, with his head down most of the time to keep the sharp sleet out of his eyes. But he looked up now and then, trying to make out the shape of the Langfords' house against the moonless sky. He'd always thought that the house must have been built by someone who'd made up the plans as he went along. From one side it appeared to have four floors; from another, only two. Wings stuck out in all directions, each with its roof sloping at a different angle. By day it was easy to spot the house, but in the dark, with nobody home, nothing was clear.

But maybe the Langfords were back? Johnny was sure, even from halfway down the hill, that he saw a glow in one of the upstairs windows. He started running towards it, but it was gone. Then it was back again, lower down now, and moving. He caught a glimpse of a silhouette. Was it a person, or the shape of one of the branches between him and the house, bouncing in the strengthening wind? He ran to the front gate.

Usually it squeaked as it opened, but tonight the sound couldn't be heard above the din of the storm. There was a noise from the back of the house. Was it a car, or another blast of wind? The gale was so strong now that Johnny struggled simply to walk forward, clutching the cake inside his coat; trying to keep it dry.

He banged on the front door. There was no answer, and the shutters were still closed across the windows, but he had a feeling that something had changed – that someone had been there just before him. The drift of leaves that had collected on the front step over the past month had almost disappeared. Had it been blown away by the storm, or had somebody kicked it aside to open the door?

Johnny thumped again, rang the bell, and waited. But nobody came, so he set off for home, still protecting the cake, and bursting to tell his mother that someone might have been inside.

He arrived dripping wet and full of babble. Winnie stood silently by the table as he jabbered about what he thought he had seen. At first he didn't notice that she wasn't speaking – that she didn't seem to be taking in what he was saying about the Langfords and the light. Then he sensed that she was angry. Of course! She had told him not to go there. She must be cross. He stopped talking. She still just stood and stared down at the table.

It was laid for three. That was strange. They never had visitors. It was always just the two of them, if that. More often these days they each ate alone, because Winnie was out at work so much. Johnny looked around. There was no one else in the room.

'Is someone coming to supper?' he asked. Then he saw a chance to get back his mother's favour – he unbuttoned his coat and took out the cake. 'What a stroke of luck!' he said. 'Hutch gave me this as I was leaving the shop. He was throwing it out because – well, you can see. It's got a bit squashed. No one would want to buy that now, would they?' He knew he was talking too much – saying too many words too quickly to sound as casual and convincing as he wanted to. But at least the cake really was soggy and deformed after its journey home in the rain.

Winnie still said nothing.

Johnny felt he had to fill the gap. 'Who's coming, Mum? Who's the extra place for?'

'Can't you guess?' said Winnie, in a voice laced with a bitterness Johnny seldom heard.

Johnny was stumped. How could he know who she'd invited to share their meal?

Winnie's voice had a note of sarcasm now. 'It shouldn't be too difficult for you. After all, you know her better than I do.'

'Who? I don't know, Mum. Tell me. Don't make me guess. I can't think of anyone.' His mind raced through the women they knew, but none of them ever came inside the house, let alone to tea. Could it be someone important? One of his teachers perhaps? Please, no. Not that. Mrs Slack? Or worse, Miss Dangerfield? Was Winnie trying to make peace with her?

Winnie stood still, stern and smouldering. Then she snatched the cake from Johnny and slid it out of its wet paper bag straight onto the table. She picked up the bread knife and thrust it towards him so hard that for the first time in his life he thought she might really want to hurt him. 'You cut it,' she spat. 'Does she like cake? How much does she want? You decide. You're the one who knows all about her.'

With a blow of physical horror, Johnny realized why his mother was so angry. A few days before, in the shop, Hutch had named the sensation that Johnny was experiencing now. They had been quietly unloading a delivery when Hutch had stopped dead and clapped his hand to his mouth. Johnny had wondered if he was ill, but Hutch explained that he wasn't unwell, he had just had a terrible 'clong'. A 'clong', he said, was 'a rush of cold sick to the heart'. It was what happened when everything was going well, and you suddenly realized that you should be somewhere else, or had let somebody down, or were about to be found out. For Hutch, that day, the clong came when he recalled a promise to provide refreshments for the Mayor and Mayoress as they paid an official visit to the Chamber of Commerce. The event had already started, and Hutch had done absolutely nothing about it. It had slipped from his mind completely. Until the clong.

Now Johnny felt that same chilly, electric sickness. There was a metallic buzz in his joints, and his body seemed to be gearing up to run, though his feet were too heavy to move. He could feel his brain lurching to invent explanations, but failing to find even two coherent words. He wished he was still outside, with that wonderful expectation of how happy his mother would be to hear about the lights at the Langfords', and to see the wonderful cake. But there was no chance of happiness now. Because before his mother spoke again, Johnny knew what she was going to say:

'Go on, Johnny,' she shouted, with a catch of hysteria in her voice. 'Cut her a slice. Go on. Cut a nice slice of cake for your Auntie Ada!'

Chapter 17

THE ROW

'**H**ow could you?' cried Winnie. 'What were you thinking of? How could you make me look so . . .' She couldn't find a word for the humiliation she had felt when she'd run into Hutch in the street, and he had asked after her invalid sister. 'I didn't know what he was talking about.'

'He didn't tell me that he'd met you when I did the papers after school,' Johnny mumbled.

'Well, let's hope that means he doesn't know you're a liar. But he must have thought I was terribly rude.'

'What exactly did he say?'

'He said that Ada's needlework seemed to be selling very well. I just stood there, wondering who Ada was. Then he said how good I was to take my sister in when times are so hard. I thought he'd mistaken me for somebody else.'

Stupidly, Johnny seized on that as an opportunity to try to wriggle out of trouble. 'Maybe he had. Maybe there's someone else with a sister called Ada—'

'Someone else! Someone else who also has a son called Johnny who delivers Hutch's papers for him? Oh, and who also, I hear, sends letters for this Auntie Ada, and deals with all her money.'

Johnny stuttered out the beginning of a limp explanation: 'It's not . . . I haven't . . . It's just . . .'

His mother kept talking. 'I just stood there. What could I say? Thank goodness it was raining. In the end I rushed away, pretending I was cold. How could you, Johnny? How could you lie like that?' She didn't wait for an explanation, but carried on. 'Do you think for one minute that I would have stayed in this town if I'd had family somewhere else? Do you think I would have let old Mr Bennett put me in this cheap house if I'd had relatives to help me pay my own way properly? Oh, I wish I'd had a sister – or anyone to help me out when your dad was gone. Now everyone will think I was turned out by my own family. They'll think you're a . . .' She paused and wiped some spittle from her mouth. 'They'll think I had you without being married at all. They'll think that's why I'm on my own.'

'I'm sorry,' said Johnny weakly. 'I was trying to help.'

'Help? How does it help to invent an extra person?

What were you trying to do? Did you make up this story to get Hutch to give you all that food you've been bringing home from the shop?'

'No!' Johnny was outraged at the idea that he'd been begging for charity. 'Not that. Hutch hasn't . . .' He was about to tell her that he'd been buying the extra food. But then he realized that would mean revealing another lie – about the adverts and the money he'd been making. Instead, he tried to explain how the myth of Ada had come about. 'It just got out of hand. I needed a postal order—'

'A postal order? What would you need a postal order for?'

How could Johnny explain it all? How could he tell her about sending off for the Secret of Instant Height? About stealing from the Peace Mug? About telling Hutch that the money was for Auntie Ada's ticket to visit them? How could he account for all the other postal orders, or admit that, for more than three months, he had been placing trick advertisements in newspapers all over the country?

His mother kept on at him. 'What does a postal order have to do with this "Auntie Ada"?'

'It's just . . . It's just . . . It's just I said to Hutch that we needed to send her some money, so she could get a train and come to stay, because she was ill. And stamps for the letter. He wouldn't have opened the post office specially if it was just for me.'

'Opened up specially? What on earth did you need the post office for anyway? You're a child, Johnny! Children don't need postal orders and stamps. What were you up to?'

Johnny decided to tell part of the truth. 'I needed to place an advertisement,' he said.

'A what? You? *You* needed to place an advertisement?'

'A personal message. I've seen them in the papers. It's how people get in touch with each other when they don't have an address.'

'But why would you want to send a personal message?' She changed her voice to make 'personal message' sound la-di-dah.

'To find the Langfords,' said Johnny. 'I asked them to contact us. *Langford. Contact Swanson. Worried.* It cost me a shilling.'

'A shilling of your own money?'

Johnny, his heart pounding with guilt, stood still, staring at his feet, letting her believe it was.

'And you told Hutch it was for this auntie – this Ada?'

'Yes,' muttered Johnny, still not looking up.

Winnie thumped the table. 'Well you shouldn't have. You mustn't tell lies, Johnny. I've always told you that. It only leads to trouble.' She was still cross, but she was calming down. 'First thing tomorrow you're going to put this right. You're going to tell Hutch what you've done, and you're going to apologize. Do you understand?'

Johnny sniffed. 'Yes,' he said, though he had no idea how he would find the words to untangle everything. 'I was only trying to help. I thought if the Langfords came back you could get your wages and have your job with them again. I'm sorry.'

Winnie picked up the knife and fork she had set on the table for Ada. She turned to put them back in the drawer. 'Well, perhaps you thought you were doing your best,' she said. 'But it hasn't worked, has it?'

'What?'

'The advertisement. The Langfords haven't been in touch?'

'No.' Johnny slumped down into a chair.

Winnie took the seat on the other side of the table. Her voice was almost normal now. 'I've been trying to find the Langfords too, you know. When I ran into Hutch today I was on my way back from the sanatorium. I went there on the bus after you'd gone to school.'

'You didn't tell me you were going,' said Johnny, hoping to switch the blame and make Winnie feel guilty now.

'I wasn't sure I would go until the last minute,' she said. 'I thought they'd just turn me away and say I was being nosy if I asked if they knew where Dr Langford was. But then I had an idea. I had that letter of recommendation from Mrs Langford. I could pretend I was going to see if they had any cleaning jobs.'

Johnny stopped himself pointing out to Winnie that what she'd done was a kind of lying. 'Did they know where the Langfords have gone?' he asked.

'No. In fact they hadn't even noticed that Dr Langford was away. He doesn't have any work there just now. That case he was helping with . . . well, I'm afraid the little baby' – she paused, and tried to break the news kindly – 'passed away.'

Johnny felt another blow to his stomach. 'It was Olwen's baby sister, wasn't it?'

'Yes. I'm sorry, Johnny, but I think it must have been.'

'Does Olwen know? What about her mum and dad? They're in the sanatorium too, you know.'

'I wasn't going to ask about them, was I, Johnny? I don't even know them. Neither do you. I don't know why you're so obsessed with them. You only talked to that Olwen once, didn't you?'

'Yes, but I liked her. She was nice to me. We could have been friends. And it must be horrible for her, worrying about her family, all alone and far away.'

'At least she won't be ill, if they got her away in time. But listen, Johnny. I've got something else to tell you. It turned out that I didn't have a wasted journey.'

'What?'

'Well, as it happens, they *do* need cleaners. I'm going to start work at the sanatorium tomorrow.'

Johnny was horrified. 'What? You can't!'

Winnie began to sound enthusiastic. 'You should see it, Johnny. It's a really nice place – huge wards, and workshops, a library, a gymnasium, gardens. And it's good money. They have to pay well there. People are too frightened to go.'

'Of course they are! And they're right. It's dangerous. Dr Langford as good as told me that himself. He told me not to visit. You might get their disease. Phthisis. It's TB – consumption. You might die. Olwen's sister died!'

'I've got no choice, Johnny. The rent goes up in a couple of weeks.'

'But I can get us money,' said Johnny, desperate to tell her about the advert scam, but terrified of making her as angry as she had been before.

'You? How? Don't be silly. I'm the one who should be providing for you.'

'I won't let you go to the sanatorium,' Johnny insisted, throwing in his own bit of news. 'And anyway, what if the Langfords are back? You can work for them again. Remember? I told you. I saw lights up at the house tonight.'

Now Winnie was angry again, with a rage that had been buried by the fury over Auntie Ada. 'That's another thing!' she yelled. 'You shouldn't have gone there. You promised you wouldn't.' She was almost crying. 'Oh Johnny, what's happening to you? You've lied to Hutch. You've invented this silly aunt. You've disobeyed me. Don't we have enough troubles without all this?'

They were both weeping now, and both furious. Johnny picked up the cake and threw it against the wall. His mother jumped to her feet, knocking over her chair. She grabbed her coat from the hook on the back of the door.

'I'm going out,' she said. 'I'm going to look for those lights of yours.'

'I'll come too,' said Johnny, reaching for his jacket.

Winnie pushed him back. 'Oh no you won't. I want to be by myself. I may be a while. You get off to bed. I'll see you in the morning.'

She slammed the door behind her, and strode into the storm.

Chapter 18

WINNIE'S WALK

Winnie stomped up the hill. The wintry rain was even harder than before. In her rage, she'd forgotten her hat and gloves, and she was soaked and freezing before she reached the Langfords' house. Water was cascading from a gutter above the drainpipe that Johnny had pulled away from the wall nearly a month before. The windows were still tightly shuttered. Winnie rang the bell and thumped the door with her fists; then she went all round the house banging on windows, rattling the back door and peering though the misty glass of the conservatory. She shouted the Langfords' names, yelled hellos and, as she was overtaken by tears, gave out animal wails of anger. But there was no one there. She wandered aimlessly down the other side of the hill, away from home, towards the shops. She slipped on some mud and landed awkwardly, hurting her wrist as she tried to save herself. Back on her feet, she pushed wet strands of hair out of her eyes, smearing dirt across her face.

There was no one on the streets. They were all warm and snug in their homes – those who weren't in the pub of course. Winnie could hear the tinny plink of the piano before she turned the corner and saw the lights. She never went to that pub. She saw enough of the one she worked in, on the other side of town, and she couldn't afford to be a drinker anyway. But tonight she had a little money in her pocket – the change from her bus fare to the sanatorium. She was cold and unhappy. She pushed open the door. She recognized most of the faces, though she knew none of the people well. Everyone stopped speaking as Winnie walked to the bar, muddy and dripping. Mr Murray from the school was there. Winnie tried not to stare at his hideous wounded face, but she didn't want to seem repelled by it either.

He was equally thrown by her wild appearance. 'Good evening, Mrs Swanson,' he said, awkwardly.

Winnie couldn't reply. She was too shaken by the argument, and too embarrassed by the knowledge of what she must look like, to engage in conversation with one of Johnny's teachers.

The pub chatter gradually got going again, and the pianist restarted his tune. Everyone ignored Winnie as she huddled in a corner, sobbing, and struggling to make one little drink last for the rest of the evening.

Johnny went to bed in tears, and listened out for his mother's return. He wanted to tell her how sorry he was, and he decided that if she wasn't too angry when she got back, he would try again to stop her going to the sanatorium. If that meant coming clean about the adverts and the money in the rabbit, he would have to do it. He tried to stay awake, but somehow he missed the click of the front door and Winnie's soft steps on the stair. Very early next morning he was woken by his mother's voice outside his bedroom.

'Johnny, I've got to go,' she said. 'Don't be late for your paper round.'

It took him a moment to wake properly and get out of bed. By then she had left. He thought she must still be angry. He couldn't have known that she didn't want him to see her setting off for her new job looking pale and dishevelled, in a wet and muddy coat.

Chapter 19

NEWS

The rain had stopped, and Johnny made it to the shop in good time, prepared to be brave and to apologize to Hutch about Auntie Ada. But Hutch was cheery. He didn't mention his conversation with Winnie the previous day, and Johnny decided that it must have made much less of an impression on him than it had on her. He decided to leave his explanation until the evening, when the shop was shut and Hutch wasn't so busy. He got his deliveries done and went to school, where he spent the day mentally rehearsing his speech to Hutch, and thinking of ways to make peace with his mother. By the end of the last lesson, he felt ready to come clean.

As soon as he was outside the school gates, he knew that something strange was going on. There were groups of women gossiping in the street. No one was ever collected from school by their parents, but today Mrs Taylor was there, waiting for Albert and his little sister. She took them aside and started talking in a frenzied whisper. Albert looked alarmed, but excited. Johnny tried to listen in, but he couldn't make out any details before Mrs Taylor pulled her children further away. What had happened? Hutch would know. The shop was a great place for news, and as it was early closing day, he would have time to talk. Johnny ran all the way there.

A car was parked outside. Johnny had never seen it before. He peered through its windows. The back seat was covered with clothes, messy papers, maps and empty cigarette packets. Hutch came out. He put his hand on Johnny's shoulder.

'I was only looking,' said Johnny.

'That's all right, son,' said Hutch, in a tone that was meant to reassure him, but was so kind that it gave Johnny a jolt of panic. Hutch steered him towards the shop. 'Come inside,' he said. 'I've got something to tell you.'

A man in a brown suit and a soft hat was leaning half in and half out of the wooden telephone booth, just inside the door. He was lighting a cigarette. Johnny noticed it was the same brand as the ones in the car.

'May I have another word with you, Mr Hutchinson?' the man called as they went past.

'I'll be back with you in a moment, sir. This is my delivery boy. We just need to sort a few things out.'

Johnny didn't understand. The bag of newspapers was always ready for him, behind the counter. Why was Hutch taking him through to the stockroom?

'Sit down,' said Hutch, pointing to a tea chest. 'Johnny, lad, I've got some bad news.'

'Mum?' cried Johnny, terrified that something had happened to her at the sanatorium.

'No, Johnny. I'm sure your mother is all right. It's Dr Langford, Johnny. I'm very sorry to be the one to tell you this, but I'm afraid Dr Langford has died.'

'Where? How do you know?'

'He was found up at his house a couple of hours ago. Miss Dangerfield called the police when she noticed a window had been broken. She thought there might have been a burglary. But when the constable got in to have a look, he discovered the doctor's body.'

Johnny buzzed with shock, excitement and indignation. 'So Dr Langford was in there, dead, all this time, while everyone thought he was away? I told you. I said—'

'Well, no, Johnny. That's what I thought at first too. But that gentleman out there is a newspaper

153

reporter, and he's told me the police are sure that Dr Langford died last night.'

Johnny thought back to the lights he had seen; then his mind started running on. 'What did he die of? Where's Mrs Langford? Was she there too?'

Hutch silenced him. 'Calm down, Johnny. I don't know many details yet, but I think it's right for me to tell you this. According to that reporter, the police think that Dr Langford was murdered.'

'Murdered? How? Why?'

'I don't know. The detectives are still up at the house. But I thought that since you knew Dr Langford well, you should hear the news from me.' Johnny was staring ahead. Hutch wasn't sure whether he had taken everything in. 'Would you like me to come home with you to tell your mother?'

'She won't be there. She's working at the sanatorium at Emberley today, and she's going to go straight on to her job at the pub tonight.'

'She'll probably hear about it there, poor woman. I'm so sorry. I know the doctor was very kind to you both.'

Johnny was stunned. He could hear his blood pumping round his ears, and his arms and legs were tingling. He remembered that he was supposed to be doing his paper round. 'I'd better go,' he said, jumping up and strapping on the bag. 'People will be waiting for their newspapers.'

'Only go if you're sure you're all right,' said Hutch. 'But Johnny, I think it will be best if I do the round in the morning. There's nothing in tonight's paper, but this business is bound to be all over tomorrow's. I wouldn't want you to have to handle the . . . the details . . . if you see what I mean.'

Johnny left with the newspapers, and Hutch went to talk to the reporter again. The news was already sweeping the town, and as Johnny passed from house to house, more people spoke to him than usual. Some even came to the door to take the paper from him rather than waiting for it to drop through the letter box. They were all disappointed that the discovery of Dr Langford's body had come too late to get into print, but they gave Johnny titbits of gossip, and he passed on the rumours as he went. By the end of his round he knew a little more: there were four police cars and an undertaker's van up at the house; the body still hadn't been removed; and the neighbours were being questioned.

Even though it meant breaking his promise again, Johnny couldn't resist climbing the hill to see what was going on; but a constable was holding back a growing crowd, and it was too dark to see the Langfords' house at all. So, since he'd finished his deliveries, he turned back towards the shop. He was overtaken by a bicycle racing downhill at speed. For a moment he thought it was Dr Langford, and he recalled those thrilling early morning lifts, perched on the crossbar. But it wasn't Dr Langford. It was a policeman. That was when it hit him. The charge of shock and excitement that had carried him through the past half-hour drained away. It was replaced by a sad emptiness he had never known before. He would never see Dr Langford again. There had been a murder. Here. In Stambleton. And the victim was someone he knew.

Chapter 20

QUESTIONING

When Johnny got to the bottom of the hill, the policeman's bicycle was outside the shop. Hutch opened the door and let Johnny in. The reporter was leaning on the counter. The constable was standing stiffly, with his helmet under his arm.

Hutch spoke first. 'Johnny, the officer wants to have a word with you. Strictly speaking, your mother should be here, but I've explained that she's at the sanatorium. They've sent a fast car for her, but I don't think she'll arrive for a while. Would you like me to stay with you while the policeman asks you some questions?'

'Yes,' said Johnny, taking off his bag. He turned to the officer. 'Do you know who killed the doctor? Is Mrs Langford all right?'

'I'm the one asking the questions, son,' said the policeman. He coughed, and gestured towards the reporter. 'Would you mind waiting elsewhere, sir?' he said, and the reporter grumpily went out to sit in his car.

Hutch bolted the door behind him. Then he brought out the high stool from behind the post office grille, and helped Johnny up to sit on it. The policeman put his helmet on the counter and took out his notebook.

'Now then, Johnny,' said the policeman, 'I'm told you knew Dr Langford well?'

'All my life,' said Johnny. 'And my mother is their cleaner.'

'Yes, your mother. We'll get to that.'

Johnny wondered what he meant.

'When were you last at Dr Langford's house?'

Johnny could feel himself blushing with guilt. 'Last night,' he said, looking at his shoes. Hutch let out a sigh. Johnny hoped he wouldn't tell the policeman that he'd forbidden him to go there.

'Were you there with your mother?' asked the officer.

'No. I was on my own. I was on my way home from the shop.'

'What time was this?

'About half past five. I thought I saw a light inside.'

'A light? Where?'

'Upstairs at first, just for a moment. And then downstairs, I think. I went to look, but there was nobody there.'

'You're sure of that? You didn't see or hear anything else?'

'It was raining, and windy. I might have heard a car.'

'You might have heard a car. A big car? A small car?'

'I don't know,' said Johnny. 'It was just a noise really. I'm not even sure it was a car.'

'And where was your mother while you were at the Langfords' house?'

'At home. She was already there when I got back.'

'And you both stayed at home for the rest of the evening?'

'Yes. Well, I did. She went out.'

'Where did she go?'

'I don't know.'

The policeman looked up from his notebook. 'You don't know? She didn't tell you? She doesn't tell you where she is when she goes out?'

'Yes, she does usually. But last night was different. I don't think she knew where she was going. She was angry. We'd had a row.'

'A row. What about?'

Johnny didn't know what to say. He couldn't explain all about Auntie Ada, especially with Hutch sitting there listening. But he knew he should tell the

159

truth, even if it wasn't the whole truth. 'It was about money. And I was cross because she was going to work at the sanatorium.'

'And why were you cross about that?'

'Because she might catch a disease there. But she said she had to go, because we need the money now that she's not getting paid by the Langfords.'

The officer licked his pencil and started writing again. 'So the Langfords had sacked her?'

'Oh no. But they went away. They've been gone for about a month. But they didn't say they were going, and Mum hadn't been paid when they left.'

'And she was angry about that?'

'Well, a bit. But not just angry. Worried. We both were. And she needed her basket and her apron. She'd left them at the Langfords' house, you see.'

'An apron, you say. What was it like?'

'Pink. And embroidered with flowers. She made it herself.'

The policeman paused to make some more notes, then he asked, 'And what time did your mother go out last night?'

'I don't know. It might have been about seven o'clock, I suppose.'

'And she was angry when she left?'

'Yes. Very angry.'

'And what time did she come back?'

'I've no idea. I tried to stay awake, but I'd fallen asleep.'

'So it was late?'

'It must have been. I was lying there for ages, till long after the wind died down. I know I'd heard the clock strike ten.'

'And this morning? Did she tell you where she'd been?'

'No. I didn't see her. She had to leave early for her new job.'

They were distracted by the bell of a police car speeding along the High Street.

'That will be them bringing your mother here now,' said Hutch. 'We'll soon get all this cleared up.'

But the car sped past the shop and onwards up the hill. The reporter started the engine of his own car and followed it.

Johnny turned to the policeman. 'Was my mum in that car?'

'Probably,' said the policeman. 'I think the detectives up at the doctor's house want to speak to her.' He turned to Hutch. 'This is a serious business, Mr

Hutchinson. The investigation may take some time. We'll have to make arrangements for this young chap to be cared for.'

Johnny was horrified at the thought of being taken away, but Hutch told the officer that wouldn't be necessary.

'The lad has an aunt at home,' he said. 'I'm sure she'll keep an eye on him.'

Johnny knew he should speak now. He should tell Hutch that he'd never had an auntie. But then he would have to explain about the postal orders and the adverts, and he couldn't do that in front of a policeman. And if the officer knew there was no one at home, Johnny might be sent away to be looked after by strangers until Winnie got back. His mouth was dry, his chest was heaving with every breath. He jumped down from the stool and raced for the door. 'I want to see my mother,' he cried, tugging on the handle. It was no use: the door was locked. 'Can't I go where she is?'

'No,' said the policeman firmly. 'That's out of the question.'

Hutch could see that Johnny was getting distressed. He put his arm round him and moved him back into the middle of the shop. 'I'll give you the makings of supper for you and your Auntie Ada,' he said. 'It's best that you wait at home for your mother to come back. Have you finished with Johnny, Officer?'

'For now, yes,' said the policeman. 'But think hard, Johnny, and see if you can remember anything else about last night. If you do, tell Mr Hutchinson here, and he can phone us at the police station or up at the Langfords' house. And don't talk to anyone else, Johnny – especially that reporter I saw here before. Make sure any information comes straight to us.'

Hutch saw the policeman out, then did as he had promised, gathering together the ingredients to make supper for two. Johnny started the speech he had memorized at school, relieved at last to have the chance to explain what he had done: how there was no Auntie Ada, and how he would be alone at home without his mother. 'Hutch,' he began, 'Hutch, there's something I've got to tell you—'

A car zipped to a halt outside. It was the reporter, back again from the crime scene. He battered on the door, asking to be let in to use the phone. Johnny's confession would have to wait.

Hutch and Johnny listened in as the reporter rang his news desk. He was twitching with excitement, holding the receiver between his shoulder and ear as he tried to light a cigarette while jabbering to his editor. Clearly some of the policemen had broken their own rule about not talking to the press. 'It's better than I thought,' the reporter panted down the phone. 'There may be two victims. They've got a suspect who had a motive for killing both the Langfords. They're ransacking the house, and they're going to search the garden in the morning. The suspect's denying everything, and refusing to say where the second body's hidden, but they're going to question her all night . . . What? Yes, that's right: *her*. The suspect is a woman.'

At that moment Johnny realized why the policeman had been asking him so many questions. His mother was in very deep trouble indeed.

Chapter 21

THE SUSPECT

It was clear the reporter had no idea that Johnny was the suspect's son. Before Hutch could steer Johnny out of earshot, the man rattled out his story for the next morning's paper to the person on the other end of the phone.

'OK. If you're ready, I'll start dictating,' he said. 'It'll need a good headline: BARMAID QUIZZED IN BLOODY DOUBLE MURDER, or something like that.' He took a drag of his cigarette and began, occasionally consulting scribbled notes, but obviously composing his article as he went along:

'*Mystery surrounds the discovery, in Stambleton yesterday, of the corpse of retired doctor Giles Langford. At first light today police begin the grim search of the Langfords' garden for the remains of his wife, Marie, feared to be the second victim of a savage double killing.*'

He paused to let the typist catch up.

'*Dr Langford was found in a pool of blood yesterday afternoon, after a neighbour observed a broken window on the first floor of his house. She suspected a burglary, but when police arrived at the scene they found that the hole in the window was too small and too high to climb through, and that there was no sign of forced entry elsewhere. They believe that the Langfords may have let their killer into the house. Both front and back doors were locked from the outside, suggesting that the murderer might be someone, such as a domestic servant, who had access to a key. A barmaid, who was once the Langfords' cleaner, was being questioned by police last night.'*

Johnny lurched towards the phone box, trying to interrupt the man; to say that Winnie wasn't really a barmaid and had never been given keys to the Langfords'. If she had, she would have gone inside weeks ago to see if everything was all right. But Hutch grabbed hold of Johnny, stopped him speaking and pulled him into the stockroom as the reporter flipped to another page of his notebook and continued:

'Giles Langford (seventy-two) was well respected in the area for his work during the tuberculosis outbreak in 1916. Trained at St Bartholomew's Hospital in London, and Lille University in France, he . . .'

Hutch closed the door. 'You mustn't talk to that man,' he whispered. 'Remember what the officer said.' He handed Johnny the bag of food. 'Now, you get home to your auntie. I'll stay here to close up.'

'Hutch . . .' said Johnny, thinking that he really should say that there was no aunt, and that he would be going back to an empty house. 'Hutch . . .'

But Hutch shooed him out of the back door. 'Go now, Johnny, before he gets off the phone. You don't want him asking you any questions.'

So Johnny ran home, and sat at the table with food enough for two but absolutely no appetite at all. There was nothing unusual about him being alone – these days Winnie was often out working in the evenings – but Johnny felt her absence more than ever. His mind raced over what he had heard. He tried desperately to persuade himself that the evidence didn't point towards his mother, but he could see that it might. And yet never, not even for a second, did he believe that Winnie was guilty of the crime. When he closed his eyes, he imagined Dr Langford on the floor surrounded by blood. He was worried about Mrs Langford too. Was she lying somewhere in the garden? Poor Mrs Langford. Had she already been there when he went up to the house in the storm? Had he walked past her body? Had he seen the murderer silhouetted against the light?

He went upstairs to his room. He needed something to do, to take his mind off the horrors up on the hill and the image of his mother in a cell. Usually, he'd have had a clutch of replies to PO Box 9 to deal with, but Hutch hadn't given him any that night. He understood now why Winnie fell to cleaning and sorting when she was worried. He tidied up his few possessions and made his bed. He unpacked his satchel. He'd already done his homework (during a History lesson) to give himself time to write out some new adverts at home. On any other night, that would have filled the hours till bed time. But he couldn't do it now. He couldn't think up silly jokes to trick people out of money. Because it was all his fault. Johnny could see that. If he hadn't invented Auntie Ada; if he hadn't done the adverts; if he hadn't lied, Winnie would never have stormed off that night, and none of this would be happening.

He opened the door to his mother's bedroom. These days he hardly ever went in there, but he remembered how he used to climb into bed with her when he was little, and how she would cuddle away his nightmares and kiss away his fears. The room was perfectly tidy. There was nothing to do in there. Winnie's nightdress was hanging on the bedstead. It still smelled of her. He spread it out on the bed and lay down alongside it. Then the tears came. He cried till he ached.

And suddenly it was morning. Johnny was still wearing yesterday's clothes, the pattern of Winnie's bedspread was imprinted on his cheek, and it was time to get up.

Chapter 22

GUILTY

He went to the shop even though Hutch had told him not to, but Hutch wouldn't let him deliver the papers. While Hutch was out doing the round, Johnny read the copies kept on the counter for sale. Most of them had brief versions of the story that added nothing to what he already knew. Several ended with a phrase he had seen in papers before. He'd always thought it rather comical, but today it had an ominous ring. A *woman is helping the police with their enquiries*. That was his mother they were talking about.

He desperately wanted to see her: to tell her that he knew she was innocent, and to find out whether she needed anything. It wasn't far to the police station. He was sure he could get there and back before Hutch had finished the paper round. He felt bad about leaving the shop unlocked, but he thought Hutch would understand.

*

Johnny had never been in the police station before. From time to time he'd seen people going in or out, but the doors always swung shut behind them. He'd imagined the scene beyond those doors: rows of cells, with frantic prisoners shaking at the iron bars, and fierce guards snarling, truncheons at the ready, making sure that no one escaped. So it was a bit of a disappointment to discover that the inside of the police station looked rather like the office at the Stambleton Echo. There was no sign of any criminals at all.

Johnny found himself in a small room with a dark wooden counter. There was no one behind the desk, just a silver bell and a sign saying: RING FOR ATTENTION. Johnny rang the bell. Nothing happened. He didn't know what to do. He didn't want to get into trouble for ringing it twice, but what if no one had heard it? He decided to wait, and sat down on a hard wooden bench, reading a poster about the penalties for riding a bicycle without lights.

He was just about to reach for the bell again when the door behind the counter opened, and a large policeman came through, backwards, pushing the door with his bottom. He was holding a teapot and a mug, and had a thick slice of bread and jam gripped

171

between his teeth. As he swung round, he noticed Johnny. He let the bread drop onto the counter and put down the pot.

'I didn't know you were there,' he said, gruffly. 'You should have rung the bell.'

Johnny was about to say that he had rung, but then he thought it might sound like answering back, and he could sense that the policeman wouldn't like that.

'What do you want?' asked the policeman, angrily picking up the bread, which had fallen jam-side down.

'I'd like to see my mother, please.'

'And who might she be?'

'Winifred Swanson,' said Johnny. 'She's helping the police with their enquiries.'

At the sound of Winnie's name, the policeman drew himself upright and adopted a more formal tone. 'Mrs Swanson is here, yes. But I'm afraid you can't see her. We don't let children in to see the prisoners. This isn't a playground. Only adult relatives or legal representatives.'

'But she hasn't got any adult relatives.'

'Don't be silly, boy. Everyone's got adult relatives.'

'But . . .' Once again Johnny got the silent message that arguing would only make things worse. He tried asking a question instead. 'When will she be coming home?'

'Not for some time, I should think, son. Though it's not my place to say. Your mother is in a great deal of trouble. Murder is a capital offence.'

A capital offence. Johnny knew what that meant, but hearing the policeman say the words made him admit to himself, for the first time, that there was a chance that Winnie would be put to death. A capital offence meant the gallows. Murderers were hanged. In all the agony of last night, Johnny had never imagined that he might lose his mother for ever. He was suddenly drenched in sweat. There was a rush of sickly acid from his stomach to his throat. Surely, now that the police had talked to Winnie all night – now that they could see how quiet and gentle she was, and she'd had a chance to explain everything – surely they couldn't believe that she was guilty? And yet this policeman seemed to think it was possible. It was all a dreadful mistake. Johnny tried to say so, but the officer silenced him.

'Now be on your way. I'm a busy man.'

'Please would you tell her that I came? Tell her Johnny was here?'

'Do I look as if I have time to pass on messages?'

Johnny stopped himself saying yes. 'But if she asks . . .'

He had gone too far. The policeman had had enough, and wanted to get back to his breakfast.

'Look, son. I've got work to do. And you should be getting off to school, shouldn't you?'

'But . . .' It was no good. 'Please give her my love,' Johnny called as he went back through the swing doors. He ran to the shop in tears, imagining his mother alone in a cell, facing the death penalty.

Hutch returned looking ashen, and mumbling swear words under his breath. 'You're going to have to be careful, Johnny,' he said. 'There are people out there who have decided your mother is guilty before she's even been charged. I don't dare repeat some of the things I've heard this morning.'

'She didn't do it, Hutch.'

'I know, son. I'm sure she can't have done. But the police seem to think they have enough evidence against her. They're not looking for anyone else. If we knew as much as the police, perhaps we could prove that they should.'

'How can we find out?'

'Well, if your mother could afford a fancy lawyer,

174

he'd check everything. But I know there's no money for that. It looks as if it's down to you and me, son.'

Someone was tapping on the shop door.

Hutch shouted, 'We're not open till nine o'clock,' without looking up. The knocking continued. It was the reporter again, signalling with fancy hand gestures that he wanted to use the phone.

'I'd better let him in,' said Hutch. 'And anyway, he might have some new information. You go and sit in the stockroom. I don't want him to know you're here.'

Hutch tried to get on the right side of the reporter as soon as he opened the door. 'Sorry, I didn't realize it was you,' he said. 'You're up early.'

'I've got to move fast on this one,' said the reporter. 'I want to get everything I can into the early edition. If they charge her, we won't be able to print much until she comes up in court.'

'And how long will that be?'

'Well, there'll have to be a remand hearing very soon if they want to keep her in custody, but the magistrates can put big restrictions on how much of that we can report. The police will make their case for holding her in jail, but we can't put all the evidence in the paper in case it influences a future jury.'

'And have the police got a good case?' asked Hutch.

175

'Seems like it to me. She was seen there on the night of the murder, and her apron was found at the scene, soaked in the doctor's blood. It certainly sounds as if she's the criminal type. I've been talking to that Miss Dangerfield. She's told me all about her.'

Johnny was tempted to burst out of his hiding place and punch the man, or at least to tell him what a nasty, cruel woman Miss Dangerfield was. But he stayed where he was, listening, as the reporter continued:

'And this Swanson woman had a motive. The police know why she went to the Langfords' house. They owed her money.'

Johnny had another clong. He felt shaky, and his mouth was dry. He realized why the police thought his mother had a motive for murdering the Langfords. He had told them. He had explained to the constable the night before that Winnie hadn't been paid, and he had said that she was angry, though he hadn't dared say why. He'd even described Winnie's apron: the pink one with the dainty daises. So Johnny was as much to blame as Miss Dangerfield. He had given the police a reason to believe that his own mother was a killer.

The reporter went to the phone. He closed the

door on the little kiosk, but Hutch and Johnny could still make out what he was saying to his editor. He was relishing the story. It involved High Society now: for the suspect had revealed that the Langfords had entertained young Mr Bennett and his fiancée to supper on Remembrance Day – the last day that anyone had seen them alive. Now the detectives were planning to drive over to the Bennett mansion to talk to the most powerful man in town.

'I'd better hurry,' the reporter yelled down the phone. 'I want to get there before the police do.'

It gave Johnny an idea. This was his chance to get close to the men in charge of the investigation – to find out what they knew, and to persuade them that Winnie couldn't possibly be guilty.

Chapter 23

HIGH-CLASS INFORMATION

Without a word to Hutch, Johnny ran out of the shop before the reporter had even put down the receiver. He dived into the back of the reporter's car, cramming himself down onto the floor and pulling some of the rubbish from the seat on top of himself in the hope of being camouflaged. A minute later the reporter jumped into the front, lit up a cigarette, and accelerated away. With his ear pressed against the floor of the car, Johnny heard the rumble of the main road, dull thumps as they turned onto a country lane, splashes as the wheels rocked through puddles, and then the crunch of gravel as the car drew up outside Mr Bennett's grand house.

The reporter got out, leaving his door open. Through a gap under the seat, Johnny saw him walk across to talk to a man who was washing Mr Bennett's car.

The reporter stroked the bonnet. 'Quite a beast. A Phantom Two, isn't it?'

'Watch it,' snapped the man, wiping the part the reporter had touched. 'I've just polished that bit.'

'Sorry. Takes a bit of looking after, I should think?'

'The engine's fine, but it's like any other car: if you drive through the countryside, you have to clean off the mud. Mr Bennett wants it spick and span for this afternoon.'

'Where's he off to?'

The handyman stopped rubbing the car and looked quizzically at the reporter. 'Who wants to know?'

The reporter drew closer to the man, and offered him a cigarette. Johnny couldn't hear everything now, but from the tone of the mumbled words he guessed that the reporter was trying to get information about Mr Bennett, and to talk his way into the house. Johnny was scared that it wouldn't work. If the reporter was sent away, his own journey would be wasted. So he wriggled over to the other side of the car and opened the door as quietly as he could. Then he slithered out and crawled into some shrubs by the front door. The winter leaves were sparse. If the reporter turned round he would be certain to spot Johnny curled up there, trying to hide. But Johnny was saved when a police car rolled in and pulled up right by the flowerbed.

A man got out and planted his huge foot within inches of Johnny's head. He was wearing ordinary shoes, not the boots that uniformed policemen had. His brown raincoat almost brushed against Johnny's face. Johnny was frightened, but he was glad he'd come. These were real plain-clothes detectives: the top men. Fortunately the man by the flowerbed didn't detect Johnny. He strode straight over to the Rolls-Royce, and after some stern words the reporter got back in his car and drove away. Another policeman rang the doorbell and spoke to the butler, who let the visitors in and closed the door. Johnny crept round the outside of the house, trying to get out of sight of the handyman, who was polishing the car again. He was hoping to find another way into the house.

The back door was open, and there was no one around. Johnny could hear the butler in the distance, talking to the policemen.

'If you would be so good as to wait in here, gentlemen, I will tell Mr Bennett that you wish to see him.'

Johnny made his way in the direction of the voices. He followed a dark corridor leading from the servants' area to the front of the house, and stopped where the drab linoleum met the polished marble of the circular entrance hall: a vast open space, with doors all round the edge, lit by a dome of glass. He saw the butler emerge from a room on one side of the ring and walk across to another, directly opposite. Johnny guessed that the policemen were in the first room and Mr Bennett in the second. There was an ornate coat-rack on the wall to his left, not far from the door to the policemen's room. He recognized the overcoat Bennett had worn on Remembrance Day, and his girlfriend's long fur cloak. He heard voices: Mr Bennett and the butler were about to come out and cross the hall. If Johnny stayed where he was, they were bound to see him. If he went back down the corridor, he might not be able to hear what they were saying. On impulse, he ran round the edge of the room and slid behind the fur cloak. It almost covered him, but didn't quite reach the floor. He reached up, grabbed the hook, bent his knees and pulled his feet out of view just in time. It was just as well. The policemen heard Bennett coming and strode into the hall to meet him. Johnny had to stay very still. His arm ached with the strain of supporting his weight, and he wedged his feet against the wall to get steady. With his other hand, he felt a slit in the side of the cloak, where the lady would have put her arms through. He slowly pulled it up to his face. The fur tickled his nose, but he could see now. The butler looked annoyed. No doubt he thought the policemen should have stayed where he had put them, but Johnny was glad they hadn't. In the echoing rotunda he could hear every word.

'That will be all, Maxwell,' said Bennett, and the butler nodded an automatic 'Very good, sir.' He strode off, almost brushing against the fur cloak on his way to the servants' corridor.

Frederick Bennett had not been up long, and was still in his dressing gown. He'd been toying with his breakfast when Maxwell had announced that the police wanted to see him, and he'd come to meet them with the newspaper in one hand and a piece of toast in the other.

'A bad business,' he said, using the toast to point to the story about the murder. 'Langford was our family physician, you know. Perhaps that's why you've come?'

'Indeed, sir,' said the older of the two detectives, who introduced himself as Inspector Griffin. 'We were wondering if you might be able to throw some light on the Langfords' whereabouts for the past month. We gather that you and your fiancée dined with them on November the eleventh.'

'Absolutely,' said Mr Bennett, 'though Miss Carmichael and I are not engaged to be married, Inspector. We never were, and I'm pleased to say that we never will be. Miss Carmichael has returned to her job at the Gaiety Theatre in London.'

The inspector gave Bennett an understanding smile. The tale of a rich young man temporarily infatuated with a show girl was a familiar one. He returned to the point. 'It seems that you may have been the last people to see the Langfords before they disappeared.'

'Disappeared?' Bennett sprayed crumbs from his mouth as he finished the last of his toast. 'They didn't disappear, Inspector. Whatever gave you that idea? No. They went to France. They may have left a bit abruptly, but they told me they were going.' The junior detective got out a notebook and started writing as Bennett continued. 'They talked about it over supper that night. I remember clearly. Mrs Langford received a telephone call while we were there. One of her relatives – a cousin, I think – was seriously ill. They were going over to visit her – to see if they could help. I imagine it's quite useful to have a retired doctor in the family at a time like that.'

'I dare say,' said the inspector. 'So you are sure they both went?'

'Yes, but Mrs Langford wrote to tell me that her husband was on his way back. The letter came only the other day. I may still have it. Would you like me to try to find it?'

'That would be very good of you, sir,' said the inspector. Johnny could tell he was trying not to show too much enthusiasm about a possible lead.

'Come this way, then, gentlemen,' said Bennett, leading them into a third room, right next to the coat-stand. When they were all inside, Johnny let his feet drop to the floor and shook out his aching arm. Then he edged along to look round the door-frame. It was Mr Bennett's study. He was facing the window, rummaging through large piles of papers on the desk. The two detectives stood on either side of him. To Johnny's relief, all three had their backs to him.

'It should be here somewhere,' said Bennett, 'unless I threw it out straight away. To be honest, I only glanced at it when it arrived. It didn't seem very important at the time.'

'I quite understand, sir,' said Inspector Griffin, 'but do please have a look if you don't mind.'

'I've had a tremendous amount of correspondence since my father died: letters of condolence, family business, and so on. Things still aren't straight after more than a year. There are rather a lot of bills, I'm afraid – what with the state of the stock market, and death duties, of course. You know how it is.'

The inspector grunted sympathetically as Bennett leafed through his paperwork.

'Ah! We're in luck,' said Bennett, holding up a sheet of paper. 'There's no address, I'm afraid. Just a date – Friday the thirtieth of November nineteen twenty-nine.' He lifted a silver-framed calendar from his desk. 'So, let's see, that's two weeks ago tomorrow.'

'Exactly so,' said Inspector Griffin. 'It should give us an idea of the whereabouts of Dr and Mrs Langford on that day at the very least. Would you be so good as to read us the rest of the letter?'

Bennett continued: '*Dear Frederick, Do forgive me for taking so long to write, but as you know we left for France in rather a hurry. Giles and I both want to tell you formally how grateful we are for your generous donation towards the work of the sanatorium at Emberley.*'

Bennett cleared his throat with mock modesty. 'I was very impressed with what Dr Langford and his colleagues were doing there. TB is such a wretched disease. One has to give what one can.' The policemen nodded. Bennett continued reading. He was walking around the room now, and every now and then Johnny had to dart back to avoid being seen.

'*It was quite unexpected, and I assure you that my only motive in inviting you to supper was to enjoy the pleasure of your company, and that of your charming friend—* Well, not quite so charming, as it's turned out. But never mind . . . *My cousin's health* – Ah, I was right: it was a cousin – *My cousin's health is improving somewhat, and my husband feels that he should be able to return to England in ten days or so.*'

The younger policeman, more smartly dressed than Griffin but rather quiet, Johnny thought, for a detective, spoke for the first time. 'It all fits. He was killed on Tuesday. That's ten days exactly after the letter was written.'

Inspector Griffin still had his back to the door, but Johnny could tell from an angry flick of his wrist that he disapproved of the interruption. The polite wave that followed indicated that Mr Bennett should continue reading:

'*I, however, will stay in France to help with her convalescence. We will leave Avignon* – Ah, Avignon. That was it. That's where they went – *leave Avignon next week for a country hotel where I intend to stay until after Christmas. Once again, thank you for your generosity. Your friend, Marie Langford.*'

He folded the letter and offered it to Inspector Griffin. 'You may keep this if it is of any interest to you.'

The inspector took it with a grateful bow. He looked over the letter. 'So we can assume that Mrs Langford is abroad.'

'Yes. That's a relief, anyway,' said Bennett. 'It means you can be pretty sure she's safe.'

Johnny was thrilled to hear it. At least that was one worry off his mind.

Inspector Griffin nodded. 'As you probably read in the paper, we have been looking for another body, just in case, sir. I think we can stop that search now. But we need to inform the poor lady that her husband is dead.'

'How will you find her?' said Bennett. 'She must have left Avignon already. All we know from the letter is that she's at a country hotel somewhere in France. That's not much to go on.'

The second detective spoke again. 'No. And we don't even know where she was staying in Avignon. If we did, we could ask the people there where she and her aunt moved to.'

Griffin interrupted him. 'Do you still have the envelope, by any chance, sir? Perhaps an address was written on it. It's the continental way. Even a post-mark might help.'

'I'm afraid not, Inspector. I put envelopes on the fire as soon as I open them. Otherwise I would be drowning in paper here.'

'I quite understand. But what a shame. I fear it may take some time to locate Mrs Langford.'

'I only hope she doesn't read the English news-papers, wherever she is. It would be awful for her to hear about her husband's death from the press.'

'Indeed, sir. But we will do our best to find her, and to break the news as gently as we can. I don't think we need detain you any longer.'

Mr Bennett started ushering them towards the door. Johnny slid back under the fur coat just in time. As Bennett opened the front door he said, casually, 'It says in the paper that you have a suspect. May I ask who it is?'

'Well, strictly speaking, I shouldn't tell you, sir. But I'm sure we'll be charging her today. It's the Langfords' cleaning woman, sir. A Mrs Swanson. Do you know her?'

'Not to speak to. But she's one of my tenants. She lives in one of the houses on Dagmouth Lane. I'm planning a lot of improvements on that part of the estate.'

Johnny would have liked to add that any building works were an excuse to drive up the rent, but he held his tongue as Bennett stopped on the doorstep and continued: 'Funnily enough, now I think about it, I remember Marie Langford mentioning Mrs Swanson over supper that day. She said the woman was looking for extra work. She asked me if there were any jobs here. Apparently Winnie Swanson is a bit hard up.'

'That's what we've heard too, sir,' said Griffin, holding out his hand to say goodbye. 'It seems that money may be at the heart of all this.'

'The things people will do for cash,' said Bennett, shaking his head. 'It beggars belief.'

Johnny wanted to talk to the detectives, to convince them that his mother was innocent. It was why he had come. But now he could only do it if he revealed that he had been hiding and listening in to everything they'd said. For a split second the brave part of him – the part that would do anything for his mother – urged him to show himself; but in an instant his fear of getting into trouble triumphed. He even persuaded himself that being caught would make things worse for Winnie. He stayed hidden under the cloak.

He heard the door close, and the police car pull away. He regretted his decision straight away. The chance to meet the inspector had gone, but he was still at risk of being caught. He was trapped for as long as Mr Bennett stayed in the hall. Johnny sensed that Bennett was walking towards him. He peeped through the slit again, only to see Bennett staring straight back, his eyes filled with contempt. Johnny held his breath; then Bennett broke the tension, turning to shout down the corridor to the butler.

'Maxwell! Some fresh coffee in the morning room!' Johnny relaxed as Bennett started walking away to restart his breakfast, but then he stopped, and yelled again: 'And Maxwell, get rid of that fur coat. Miss Carmichael won't be coming back.'

A distant shout of 'Very good, sir' came from the kitchen. Johnny panicked. He couldn't leave his hiding place while Bennett was in the hall, but there was no way he could risk staying there till Maxwell re-entered and tore the cloak from its peg. He watched Bennett walk slowly back to the breakfast room, but a heartbeat later he heard Maxwell coming up the passage. The butler turned towards the coat-stand and looked the fur up and down. But his hands were full. He sniffed. No doubt he'd deal with the coat after he'd put down his tray.

As soon as Maxwell was in attendance on his master, Johnny ran for the back door. He didn't want to risk meeting the handyman, or walking on the noisy gravel at the front of the house, so he crossed the grounds till he found a wall. It was a long walk back to the post office, but he was elated to have got away, and glad to be carrying Hutch the good news that Mrs Langford was safe.

Chapter 24

THE HEARING

Winnie was due to appear in court on the next Wednesday afternoon. Wednesday was early closing day in Stambleton. All the shops shut at noon, including Hutchinson's General Store and Post Office, and Hutch told Johnny that he would go to the court to see what happened. Johnny, he said, wouldn't be allowed in, and must go to school as normal.

Of course, nothing was 'normal' at school now. Johnny had never been paid so much attention; but it wasn't the kind of attention he enjoyed. The other pupils stared at him and whispered about him, but no one came near. Some had been told by their parents not to have anything to do with him. The teachers were stiff and formal, and didn't know what to say. Only Mr Murray made any reference to Winnie's arrest. Johnny's class were in the gym, using the wall-bars and climbing ropes. Mr Murray curled a rope into the shape of a noose, and lolled his head to one side with his tongue hanging out. Everybody laughed.

On the day of the hearing, Johnny was stuck in a classroom, trying to imagine what was going on. Hutch had explained that this wasn't the big trial: it was to decide whether the police had enough evidence against Winnie to justify keeping her in prison, so that the case could go on to a more important court. Johnny knew what that meant, though Hutch didn't spell it out: a court that could impose the death penalty.

Hutch got to the court as early as he could, determined to find a seat in the public gallery. There was quite a crowd. With all the shops closed, lots of other people were free too, and everyone wanted to hear why the police were so sure that Winnie had killed Dr Langford. If they had gone to see a monster, they were disappointed. Winnie looked tiny, standing alone in the shabby shift dress she'd had on when she was arrested. She stayed still, with her head down and her hands clasped in front of her, throughout the proceedings. Her mousy hair flopped forward, hiding her face. Hutch had hoped to catch her eye – to give her a reassuring nod, at least – but she didn't look at the public gallery once. Her voice was so weak when she confirmed her name that the magistrate had to ask her to speak up.

The policeman who had discovered the body described the scene. Then a doctor testified that the victim had definitely not died of natural causes, but from a blow that had opened a blood vessel in his head. It was possible that he had been punched, and had fallen against the mantelpiece. In his opinion, the state of the corpse suggested that the murder was committed some time between five and eight o'clock on the night of Tuesday 10th December.

Then Miss Dangerfield was called to the stand. There was a titter as she confirmed her full name: Letitia Euphemia Gladys Dangerfield. Dressed in black, as ever, she looked stern and trustworthy as she swore to tell the truth. The prosecuting lawyer asked her why she had called the police on 11th December.

'Because I had noticed a broken window at the Langfords' house.'

'And at what time did you notice it?'

'At about ten in the morning. I called the police immediately, but it took them rather a long time to come.'

'That's as may be, Miss Dangerfield. One can perhaps forgive the police for not expecting a broken window to be important.'

'But I told them I thought there might have been a burglary.'

'And what made you think that?'

'Because the night before I had seen someone behaving strangely in the garden.'

'And do you see that person here today, Miss Dangerfield?'

'I do, sir.'

'Would you be so good as to point them out to us?'

Winnie, pale and weak, flinched as Miss Dangerfield lifted her walking stick and waved it at the dock. 'That's her,' she bellowed. 'Mrs Winifred Swanson.'

'Thank you, Miss Dangerfield. Now tell us, at what time did you see her?'

'It must have been between seven o'clock and seven twenty. I had finished my supper, and I had not yet turned on my radio-gramophone.' She said the word 'radio-gramophone' with great relish, glad to boast to the court that she owned one. 'I can be sure of the time. That night I listened in to a talk by Professor W. W. Watts on "The Origins of Life". I have consulted the *Radio Times*. It began at seven twenty-five.'

'And why do you say that the accused, Mrs Swanson, was behaving strangely?'

'Because she was. It was pouring with rain, and she

was running around with no hat on, shouting abuse and wailing.'

'And what, exactly, was she saying?'

'I couldn't hear. The rain and the wind were too loud.'

'But you said it was abuse.'

'I could tell by the tone. And anyway, I know the kind of woman she is.'

'Yes. I'll come back to that. But first, could you tell us, had you seen Mrs Swanson near the Langfords' house before?'

'Many times. She was their cleaner. She came every day.'

'And was it customary for her to behave in this manner?'

'No, sir. But there had been some strange episodes lately.'

'What do you mean by that?'

'Ever since the Langfords went away, I'd seen the accused and her son loitering around the house. On one occasion her son was trying to break in. On another he was climbing a tree in the garden. His mother was with him. I got the impression that they intended to burgle the property while it was empty.'

'Did you inform the police?'

'No, sir. Of course, now I wish I had.'

'And on the night when Dr Langford died – did you actually see the accused enter the house?'

'No, sir. It was dark and stormy. I did not have as good a view as usual.'

'But in your opinion, could she have gone inside?'

'Yes, sir.'

'And did you see her leave?'

'No. Obviously it was still dark, and the weather was bad, and as I said, from seven twenty-five onwards I was sitting down, listening to my radio-gramophone. I would not have been able to hear her. My radio-gramophone is a Lissenola New Era. That model is equipped with an extremely powerful loudspeaker.'

The lawyer stifled a smile. 'So I believe, madam. Now, you said the house was empty. But as we know now, Dr Langford was at home. How long had the Langfords been away?'

'I'm not sure, sir. They didn't tell me they were going.' She sounded rather put out about that. 'I know they were still there on November the eleventh, because I saw Mr Bennett visit them in his big car.'

'And when did Dr Langford return to the house?'

'I don't know.'

'You saw nothing to suggest he was back?'

'No, sir – and I keep a good eye out.'

There were some more giggles from the public gallery. The lawyer hushed them with another question.

'I'm sure you do, madam. Now, tell me this. During your observation of the house over the years, have you formed an opinion of the accused and her relationship with the Langfords?'

'I dare say Mrs Langford treated her kindly. But I thought the accused got on rather better with Dr Langford. Lately I'd sometimes see them meeting and talking together, very early in the morning, outside the house. Dr Langford even gave that son of hers rides on his bicycle.'

'Are you implying that the relationship between Mrs Swanson and her employer might have been too close?'

'You might infer that, sir, if you choose to.'

Winnie wasn't too sure what all this 'imply' and 'infer' stuff meant, but she could tell what Miss Dangerfield was suggesting, and she cried out, 'No. That's not true.' But it was too late. Miss Dangerfield had managed to introduce an extra element into the case against her.

The lawyer followed it up. 'Miss Dangerfield, in your long observation of the accused, have you noticed anything else about her character?'

'Well, I know she works in a pub. Some way from our part of town.'

'In a rough area?'

'Indeed. And I know she can't control her son. That time he was up a tree in the Langfords' garden, she was there, shouting at him, but she didn't seem able to make him come down.'

'Could you hear what she was saying to him?'

'No, I can't quite recall. I believe my radio-gramophone may have been on at the time. But whatever she was saying, it wasn't having any effect.'

Hutch sat in the public gallery, trying to be hopeful. Despite all the bad things Miss Dangerfield had said, as far as he could tell all she'd really proved was that Winnie was outside the doctor's house on the fateful night. And how much notice would the court take of a sour spinster's picture of Winnie's character? If Miss Dangerfield was the only witness the police had against her, perhaps things weren't as bad as they'd seemed.

But she wasn't the only witness. Hamish Alexander Murray was called to the stand. It was the PE master from school, wearing a suit rather than his usual sports kit. The lawyer asked him to state his name, and then confirmed that he was a teacher, and that his facial injuries had been sustained in the war. Hutch could see why he was doing that – to make Murray sound like a hero so that his evidence would be more convincing.

'Mr Murray,' said the lawyer, 'on the night of December the tenth – that is, the night before Dr Langford's body was discovered – where were you?'

'I was in the Black Horse public house, sir.'

'And in the course of the evening, did you see the accused?'

'Yes, sir.'

'Now let us be clear. She was not serving behind the bar?'

'No, sir. She doesn't work there. I believe Mrs Swanson works in an altogether different class of establishment. She came into the Black Horse for a drink.'

'And what time was that?'

'About seven thirty. Maybe seven forty-five.'

'And you are sure this was on December the tenth?'

'Yes, sir. It was the night of the storm. She was soaking wet when she arrived, rather bedraggled, and behaving strangely, I remember.'

'And she was alone?'

'Yes, sir. I noticed that. I'm sure everybody did. Not many respectable women go into pubs by themselves.'

'Indeed,' said the lawyer, hoping the magistrate would draw the obvious conclusion about Winnie's character. 'And how would you describe her demeanour?'

'She looked distressed. Wild, I'd say. Her hair was all over the place, and she was covered in mud. She wouldn't meet my eyes when I tried to say hello. I would say she was in a real state.'

'A state? A state of shock?'

'More agitation . . . as if something had just happened to her, or as if she had just done something exciting. Desperate, if you get my meaning. More like an animal than a human being.'

The public gallery took in a collective gulp of breath. The lawyer raised one eyebrow just a little, and carried on. 'Did she speak to anyone else?'

'Just to order a drink.'

'An alcoholic drink?'

'I believe so. Then she sat alone in the corner. She was trembling. I was surprised. You'd think she'd be at home, looking after her son. After all, there's no man in the house.'

*

Hutch left the court. Even though it was early closing day, the evening papers had to be sorted and delivered. It was just as well that he had to go. He was seething at the picture of Winnie that was being painted, layer by layer; and he knew he should get away before he said something and landed himself in trouble. He wished he'd got to know Winnie better over the years; but she hadn't lived in Stambleton before her marriage, and after Harry Swanson's death Hutch had been afraid of being too forward – of seeming too interested in a young war widow, new to town. Yet Hutch knew enough about Winnie and about her son to find it impossible to believe in her guilt. He could think of nothing he could do to help her, but he was determined to shield Johnny from the worst of the evidence, and from the public reaction to her plight.

Even so, when he got back to the shop and found Johnny outside waiting eagerly for news, he had to be honest. 'You'll have to be strong, son,' he said. 'It isn't over yet. I don't think your mother will be home for Christmas.'

Chapter 25

ALONE

Hutch was right. The court decided that Winnie should face a full trial at the end of January. Johnny knew that would bring more torture at school. He'd already been given a new nickname: 'Swingson', which constantly reminded him that his mother might hang. He couldn't face new taunts, so he composed a letter from Auntie Ada, saying that 'under the circumstances' it might be appropriate for him to start the Christmas holidays a little early. The headmaster agreed, with relief.

So Johnny had some free time; but he wasn't allowed to visit his mother, and anyway the prison was two bus rides away. Hutch said he would go next Tuesday, when he'd be closing at lunch time, because it would be Christmas Eve. He told Johnny to make Winnie a card, wishing her well. Hutch would take her a present: something nice to eat, from the shop. But there was the best part of a week to wait until then, and no more school for Johnny.

When Winnie was arrested, he had worried constantly that someone would find out he was living on his own; but far from being troubled by busybodies, Johnny was frozen out by the people of Stambleton. No one visited. Nobody came to their door when he delivered their newspapers. People crossed the street rather than stop and talk to him. He couldn't tell whether it was embarrassment or contempt that made them do it. He could feel himself being stared at, but no one came near enough to insult him or sympathize. He didn't want to talk to them either. He stopped playing in the street. Alone in the house, he'd lost the urge to keep busy by tidying up, and even before the hearing he had found himself writing out adverts again. He'd felt guilty at first, after his realization on that terrible night that they had been the cause of the trouble, but he just couldn't stop himself; and he wanted to keep Auntie Ada alive so that he wouldn't be taken away to a children's home.

But Johnny had plenty of time to think, and his determination to persuade the world that his mother couldn't be a killer was gradually matched by an obsession that the real murderer must still be on the loose. Johnny realized that he knew something the police did not: Dr Langford had been working on the

BCG vaccine – or at least someone at a laboratory 'out in the wilds' had been doing it on his behalf. Suppose that was the reason he had been killed? Johnny remembered how determined the Langfords had been to keep it a secret – how worried they were that someone might find out. What if somebody had? Johnny agonized about his promise not to say anything. Mrs Langford had been unambiguous: *Whatever happens, whoever asks you, however much you feel like boasting – not a word.* Did that mean he shouldn't tell the police? Dr Langford was dead. He couldn't suffer any more. But what about Mrs Langford? She might get into trouble if Johnny spoke out. But maybe she was in danger anyway. Suppose the killer found her in France, or was waiting for her to come home, so that he could strike again? Johnny decided that he would have to break his silence. After all, the police were used to keeping secrets themselves. Then he remembered how much the reporter had found out about his mother from officers who couldn't resist passing details on. Was it worth the risk? In the end he decided that if it might save his mother, it was. On his first day off school he steeled himself to go back to the police station.

*

This time the desk sergeant recognized him straight away. He was just as hostile as before.

'What do you want? Your mother's not here any more. She's in the big prison now.'

'I know. I want to talk to you. I want to help you find the real killer.'

'We already have the real killer, son.'

'No you don't. My mother could never hurt anyone. Someone else did it.'

'And you know who, do you?' The swing doors opened, and a man came in from the street. The policeman broke off from talking to Johnny. 'I'll be with you in a moment, sir. This won't take long.' He turned back to Johnny. 'Well? Do you have a name to give me?'

'Not a name, exactly,' said Johnny. 'It's a bit more complicated than that.'

The newcomer was leaning against the counter and looking down at Johnny with a patronizing smile. Johnny felt he couldn't go into details of Dr Langford's secret in front of a complete stranger.

'It's private, too,' said Johnny, hoping the policeman would take him somewhere they could speak without being overheard.

The policeman laughed. 'If it's so private, you'd

better keep it to yourself, son. I've got better things to do with my time. Now this gentleman would probably appreciate a little privacy. You'd better be on your way.'

'But it's important.'

'I said get out of it.'

Johnny stood for a moment, stuttering, but the policeman just pointed to the door. 'Now, sir, what can I do for you?' he asked the man.

'I want to report a lost dog.'

The policeman started making a note. Without even looking up, he bellowed at Johnny again. 'Go!'

Johnny knew there was no point in staying. He ran away, not letting the tears of fear, anger and dismay break through until the door swung shut behind him.

That afternoon he hit on a different tactic. He would write down his ideas about an alternative killer in a note to Inspector Griffin. He thought at first that he would do it in Auntie Ada's name, but then he envisaged the scene when the inspector came round and found out that she didn't really exist. So he wrote everything out as neatly as he could, and signed it himself. He slipped it into his bag when he went on the evening paper round, and as soon as the last newspaper had been put through the last letter box, he made his way to the police station again. He was barely through the door before the desk sergeant was shouting at him.

'Wasting police time is a crime, you know.'

'I just want to drop off a letter for Inspector Griffin.'

'A letter about what, exactly?'

'It's about the murder. To help him find the person who did it.'

'And why should he listen to you? He already has the murderer in custody, as you know only too well.'

'But she didn't do it!'

'So who did?'

'I don't know exactly. But all my ideas are in this letter.' Johnny put it down on the counter.

'And why should Inspector Griffin take any notice of that? Why should he believe a small boy trying to save his mother, and ignore witnesses who've given sworn evidence against her in court?'

'Because I know something they don't know.'

'And it's all in here?' said the sergeant, picking up the envelope.

'Yes. Please take it.'

'Oh, I'll take it, son. I'll take it and I'll file it in the appropriate place.'

'Thank you,' said Johnny. But his momentary relief turned to anguish again as the sergeant tore the envelope in two and dropped it behind him.

'Now I'm warning you, boy,' he said. 'I've had enough of your time-wasting. Keep away from here.' The sergeant lifted a flap in the counter and walked through to the 'public' side of the room. Through the gap, Johnny could see the torn letter in the waste-paper basket. The policeman grabbed his arm and manhandled him through the door. 'I don't want to see you here again,' he hissed as Johnny tumbled down the steps. 'I've a good mind to come round to your house to tell that aunt of yours that if she can't control you, we'll put you with someone who can.'

As he helped Hutch close up the shop Johnny worried that the police were ransacking his home and discovering that there was no Auntie Ada.

Hutch noticed his agitation. 'Are you all right, son?' he asked. 'You don't seem yourself today.'

Johnny wanted to tell him everything, but he didn't think he should betray the Langfords' secret to anyone except the police, and he feared that if he told Hutch that he'd lied about his auntie he might lose the only person he had on his side.

'No. Well. I'm just worried about . . . Well, you know,' he said.

'I understand,' said Hutch, awkwardly restraining himself from giving Johnny a hug. He took a jar of strawberry jam from a shelf. 'Here. Take this home to your auntie. She must be worried too, poor thing.'

Johnny took the jar and ran home. The door was still locked, and there was no sign that anyone had been inside. He got a pillow and some of his mother's clothes, and pulled round the big armchair so that it had its back to the door. He pulled the curtains almost shut, leaving just enough of a gap to satisfy anyone who was determined to look inside. Everything was arranged so that they would think they saw an old woman asleep by the fireplace. He hoped they'd be too polite to try to wake her up.

Chapter 26

THE FARMER

Even with the pretend Auntie Ada in place, Johnny was lonely – perhaps even more lonely than before. Sitting by himself, eating jam straight from the jar with a spoon, he desperately wanted to talk to someone, to tell them what was happening to his mother, and how no one except Hutch believed that she was innocent.

He decided to try again to find Olwen. Although he had met her only once, she'd been on his mind ever since. She'd been kind when everyone else was bullying him, and she hadn't heard any of the nasty rumours about Winnie. He felt that she would understand. He wanted to write to her, but all he knew was that she was with relatives somewhere in Wales. He remembered that she had lived on a farm outside Stambleton, so next morning he set off to walk there, hoping the farmer would know her new address. It was a harder, colder walk than he had expected, and even when he reached a sign saying NEWGATE FARM (which was nailed to a very old-looking gate), a long track wound its way towards the farmhouse. Johnny was trudging round a corner when a battered van came the other way. He jumped aside, expecting it to pass, but the driver, a weather-beaten man wearing an ill-fitting suit, stopped and spoke to him.

'Where are you going?'

'To the farmhouse. I want to talk to the farmer,' Johnny said.

'I'm the farmer. What can I do for you? There's no work here – if you're looking for work, that is. You seem a bit young for that.'

'No, I don't want a job. I'm looking for information. I'm trying to find someone who used to live here.'

'Well, there's no one at home. And I'm on my way to a funeral. That's why I'm all dressed up like this,' the farmer said, running his finger inside the stiff collar of his shirt. 'I can't stop for long, but you can get in if you want, and we can talk in the warm.'

Johnny climbed in and sat beside the farmer. He'd hardly ever been in a car before, let alone a big van like this. It was a real treat. 'Thank you,' he said. 'It's nice to get out of the wind. Do you mind if I ask you questions?'

'Not at all,' said the farmer. 'But you'll have to

speak up. I need to leave the engine running, otherwise it could conk out and I might never get it started again. Now, who are you trying to find?'

'It's a girl called Olwen. She came to my school in September. But she had to leave again. I think her baby sister died.'

The farmer gripped the steering wheel. 'I wish I could help you. I've been trying to find her myself, poor love. It's her father's funeral I'm off to now. He's being buried near that big sanatorium up at Emberley. Her mother's only been gone a couple of weeks. Olwen's all alone now – though she probably doesn't know it. Her folks packed her off to try to keep her safe, and now it's too late to ask them where she is.'

'Olwen told me you knew her dad in the army.'

'He saved my life – dragged me from a shell-hole at the battle of Ypres. He carried me on his back all the way to the dressing station. We lost touch after the war, but I couldn't refuse him when he wrote saying he was in trouble. I'd promised I'd do anything for him. He was desperate. I thought I could give him a roof over his head and a job.'

Johnny had read stories like that in the *Boy's Own Paper*. It was thrilling to hear that such heroism and gratitude happened in real life. He'd often wished that someone would appear on his doorstep with a tale about his own father's war exploits, but this was the next best thing. He was proud on Olwen's behalf, and glad that the farmer had done the decent thing.

'It was kind of you to help them,' said Johnny. 'I know Olwen was grateful. It was one of the first things she told me when I met her. Hasn't she written to you since she went away?'

'Not a word. I think that's odd, don't you? You'd think her people would be in touch. I wish I'd taken more notice when they sent her away, but it was all such a rush, and it wasn't my business, was it?'

The farmer sounded as if he wanted Johnny's forgiveness. Johnny tried to make him feel better. 'Oh, I'm sure you did everything you could. They were lucky you helped them in the first place.'

'To be honest, there have been moments when I've regretted it. People don't trust my milk since they brought the TB here. And burials don't come cheap, even without fancy carriages and flowers.'

'So there won't be anyone else at the funeral?'

'Probably not, unless the hospital's found somebody. But it's not fitting for anyone to be buried without a friend at the graveside, so I'm going: as a last thank-you for what he did for me, and on behalf of the relatives, you might say. It doesn't seem right for young Olwen to miss her chance to say goodbye, but what can I do?'

'Dr Langford said she'd gone back to relatives in Wales.'

'Ah, but Wales is a big place. I know they were from Swansea, but who's to say where their relations live? I couldn't even track down their old home. I must have had their address once, when her dad first wrote to me, but I'm darned if I can find the letter anywhere. If I'd known all this was going to happen, I'd have taken more care. I never expected them all to drop dead before I had the chance to ask where Olwen was.'

'Do you think I could come to the funeral too?' asked Johnny. He remembered a phrase he'd heard his mother use. 'I'd like to pay my respects.'

'Well, that's fine talk from one so young. You're not really dressed for it, but I don't see why not. There won't be anyone there to take offence.'

Johnny looked down at his tatty clothes. In his mother's absence he hadn't paid any attention to washing or ironing, and he knew he must be even more grubby than usual after his long walk. 'I really would like to come, if you don't mind, sir.'

'It will be a pleasure to take you. And good company for me,' said the farmer, releasing the brake.

The van rolled forward, let out a couple of loud bangs, and moved off, bumping so much on the uneven road that Johnny's bottom kept bouncing off the seat. They both started to laugh. That didn't seem right on the way to a funeral, so they decided to sing hymns instead. After 'All People That on Earth Do Dwell', 'He Who Would Valiant Be', 'Praise My Soul the King of Heaven' and 'The Lord's My Shepherd' they arrived at the graveyard at Emberley.

A young vicar was waiting for them. He supervised the burial with minimal ceremony. The gravediggers started filling in the hole, and Johnny and the farmer returned to the van. Johnny was trying not to cry. He was sad about Olwen's father, even though he had never met him, and about Olwen's sister and mother in two fresh graves nearby; but really he was thinking about his own mother, and how she might be buried soon unless he could do something to save her. He wanted to tell the farmer about it. But he couldn't find the words.

In the end, it was the farmer who brought the subject up as they drove back towards Stambleton. He wasn't meaning to, but he recalled that Johnny had mentioned Dr Langford.

'So you knew the old doctor?' he said. 'I couldn't believe it when I heard he'd been murdered.'

'Oh yes, said Johnny. 'I've known him all my life. He was a really nice man.'

'A terrible business. Dr Langford was a real gentleman. And so good with children. He took good care of a fair few at that sanatorium. They were his two specialities, see: children and TB. You should have seen him when we had the epidemic in 1916. I don't think they'd ever have built that sanatorium without Dr Langford raising money and making speeches everywhere. It was thanks to him that Olwen's family were taken in there as charity cases. We've been robbed of a good man. I can't imagine why anyone would want to kill him. That evil barmaid had better swing for it.'

Johnny didn't know what to say. Should he risk letting on who he was? Should he try to explain that Winnie wasn't guilty? Best to say nothing, he thought. He'd be out of the van in a few minutes. He might never see the farmer again. He stayed quiet. But the farmer filled the silence: 'Do you know her? You're from Stambleton. She has a kiddie about your age. You must have seen him at school. You must have come across his mother?'

Johnny started to stutter a reply. He could hardly get any words out. He didn't want to sound as if he was disowning Winnie, but he didn't know how to explain why he hadn't mentioned her before. He wanted to tell the farmer all about her, and how she couldn't possibly have committed the crime. All he managed to do was make himself sound shifty.

The farmer was suddenly suspicious. 'Hang on a minute,' he said, glancing across at his small passenger, 'why aren't you at school today?'

'I don't go any more,' said Johnny. 'I can't because—'

'What's your name?' said the farmer, driving faster and faster as it dawned on him who his passenger might be.

'Johnny . . .'

'Johnny what?'

'Johnny Swans—'

'You're that boy, aren't you?' gasped the farmer, slamming on the brakes so hard that Johnny was thrown forward against the dashboard. 'You're that woman's brat. Get out. Get out! You've got a nerve. I can't believe you tricked your way into my van.'

'But you asked me in. I was only—'

'I should have known. A boy of your age wanting

to go to a funeral? You're sick. Go on. Get out. Now!'

Johnny fumbled with the door handle. At last he was able to climb down onto the road. They were still a couple of miles from Stambleton. The farmer tried to move off, but the engine had stopped, and he had to get out and crank it with a handle. He stood in front of the bonnet, cursing.

'She didn't do it,' Johnny shouted, with tears in his eyes. 'She's innocent.'

The farmer didn't look up. Swearing under his breath, he kept cranking the engine until it spluttered and started running again. Then he pulled out the heavy iron handle and waved it at Johnny. 'Get out of my sight!' he yelled; and, terrified that the man was going to beat him or fling the handle at his head, Johnny turned and started running towards town. A few seconds later the van swept past.

Johnny was shocked by the speed with which the kind man had turned on him. His words had revealed more about local gossip than Johnny had dared to imagine. People really hated Winnie. And there was no hope now of finding Olwen, the one person who might not know what had happened; who might listen to Johnny's version of the story, take pity on him and understand his grief.

Chapter 27

OUTCASTS

At least Johnny had Hutch. He went straight to the shop. It was quiet. A few people came in to buy stamps or cash their pensions at the post office. Some had Christmas parcels to send. One or two used the phone booth just inside the door. But several people cancelled their papers, and even more followed Miss Dangerfield's example and decided to shop elsewhere for their food.

'It's because of me, isn't it?' said Johnny as he and Hutch tidied the stockroom to make space for goods that wouldn't sell. 'It's my fault.'

'No, it's because of me,' Hutch said. 'Because I'm standing by you. And it's the fault of no one except the small-minded people of Stambleton. I'll take over the paper deliveries for a while. I don't want you to have to face abuse every day. You can do extra jobs for me here instead.' He brought down some cardboard and paint from a high shelf. 'And you can start right now. I want you to make some notices. We're going to have to have our post-Christmas sale a little early. This year, it's a pre-Christmas sale. If cut prices don't lure people back in here, nothing will.'

Hutch had a large stock of aluminium teapots filled with Christmas biscuits. He'd ordered them as a seasonal novelty before his customers had deserted him. Other shops were selling them for five shillings. Hutch was marking them down to 3/6. Cheese, ham and bacon were all reduced to a shilling per pound. But the real crowd-puller was to be Keiller's Assorted Chocolates at only tenpence for a half-pound box, with boxes twice the size going for only sixpence more.

So Johnny set to work. Hutch gave him a list of discounts, and Johnny translated them into posters, using bright colours, with lots of red, to make them look Christmassy. He got a ladder and climbed into the window to put up the posters and to build towers of chocolate boxes to attract passers-by. He painted CHRISTMAS SALE in huge letters at the top of the display, and set about arranging tins of crab meat in the shape of a crab, and iced cakes in the shape of a snowflake. Johnny was concentrating hard, determined to produce a show that would bring back the customers Hutch had lost because of him. He didn't notice the growing crowd that was watching him work until they started a rumbling chant. Maybe it was the sign saying KEILLER'S CHOCOLATES that set them off. Soon they were all shouting: 'Killer's son! Killer's son! Killer's son! Killer's son!' Johnny looked up. It was already dark outside, but in the light from the window he could see a few faces he recognized. Some of them were people he knew from his paper round: folk who only a few weeks ago had given him a cheery wave every morning. Albert Taylor and Ernest Roberts were both there on their way home from school, and in the thick of it all was an elderly woman. She looked strong and feisty – you might even say 'in robust health'. It was Mrs Slack, who had apparently recovered from her ailments now that Winnie was no longer available to care for her.

As the abuse grew louder, Johnny went to the front of the window and put his face close to the glass so that she could hear him. 'Mrs Slack,' he cried. 'Please! You know my mother is a good woman. Please tell everyone. Please tell them everything she has done for you!'

'Done for me!' shrieked Mrs Slack. 'Done for me! I'm lucky she hasn't done for me! Every day she came round my house – looking for things to steal, I shouldn't wonder. Or trying to poison me. Strange that I've been better since she's gone, isn't it? String her up, that's what I say!' And she joined in the chant, which was growing louder and more vicious: 'Killer's son! Killer's son!'

A brick flew in, showering Johnny with glass. Hutch rushed to the window, drawing jeers from the crowd, to pull Johnny back into the shop. His weak leg trailed behind him, bringing down the ladder, and with it the paint pot. Red liquid spilled everywhere, and the crowd screamed, 'Blood! Blood! Killer's son! Killer's son!'

The mob was frightening, but its members were not brave. The sound of a police whistle quickly dispersed them; but not before some had reached through the broken glass for chocolate boxes and teapots.

When the crowd had gone, Johnny started shivering uncontrollably. 'It's shock,' said Hutch. 'Come and sit down.' He took Johnny into the stockroom, sat him on a crate and wrapped a sack around his shoulders. 'You'd better keep warm,' he said. 'They say sugar's good for shock, you know. I'll see what I can find.' He was back in no time with a chocolate bar and a fizzy drink. 'Perhaps you'd better go home.'

'No, Hutch,' said Johnny. 'I'll be all right in a minute. Let me stay here. I'd rather be with you.'

Hutch was touched to have Johnny's confidence. 'You sit here for a while then,' he said tenderly, 'and I'll start straightening out the shop. You can join me when you're feeling better.'

So Hutch and Johnny spent the rest of the day clearing the mess and boarding up the window.

'Shouldn't the police arrest those people?' said Johnny. 'We know most of them. We could tell the police their names.'

'No point,' said Hutch. 'I don't think that would win us many friends, do you?'

'But what about the stuff they stole? Aren't you going to report them for that?'

'Who?'

'Well, Albert Taylor for one. And Ernest Roberts. I saw them there.'

'You saw them?'

'Yes, I did. And I don't see why they should get away with it. They've been horrible to me for ages. We should tell the police.'

'You saw them steal the chocolates?'

'Well, no. Not exactly. I didn't see them actually do it. But I know it was them. I just know it.'

'Oh, Johnny,' sighed Hutch. 'Listen to yourself. Can't you hear who you sound like?'

'Who?'

'Like someone who saw your mother at the Langfords' house? Like someone who saw her sitting in a pub? Do you actually know that Taylor and Roberts plundered the window display?'

Johnny was ashamed of himself. 'No,' he whispered.

'Then I think it's best if we say no more about it, don't you?'

'All right. But you'd better close down the shop, Hutch,' said Johnny. 'It isn't safe for you here.'

Hutch disagreed. 'We'll see off those bullies,' he said. 'And we'll beat them by carrying on. I won't close. In fact, I can't close. I have to stay open, because of the post office. It's my duty. It's as simple as that.'

When Johnny arrived home that night, he found a pudding basin on the doorstep. He recognized it as the one Winnie had used to make Mrs Slack a treacle sponge on a cold day at the beginning of December. It was half full of a golden liquid. Johnny didn't stop to investigate what that might be. He could guess. He tipped it away, and dashed the basin against the wall.

Alone inside, he barricaded the door in case anyone tried to break in. He tore up some old newspapers to try to get a fire going in the grate. There was something in one of them about the effort the police were making to find Marie Langford in France, so they could tell her about her husband's tragic death. They didn't seem to be having any luck with their search. Johnny wondered whether they were trying hard enough. Perhaps, if he could find her first, before the police had a chance to poison her mind against Winnie, Johnny might persuade Mrs Langford to help clear his mother's name. At the very least she could tell everyone how honest and reliable Winnie had been in the past. She might even be able to suggest another suspect for the murder. If only he could make contact with Marie Langford, wherever in France she might be.

Someone rapped on the door. Johnny jumped up and turned down the lamp, so that whoever was outside would think the house was empty. But the knocking came again. Then a half-familiar voice. Johnny worked out who it was just before the man said his name. It was the reporter.

Johnny went over to the door. 'Go away,' he

shouted. 'I'm not allowed to talk to you. The police said so.'

'And why should you do what the police say?' asked the man. 'They've put your mother in prison. They don't believe she's innocent. Why should you listen to them?'

'I don't want to get her into any more trouble,' said Johnny.

The reporter pushed open the letter box. Johnny could see his lips moving. 'Pardon me for saying this, Johnny, but when you're on trial for murder, you can't really get into any more trouble. What are they going to do? Hang her twice?' His lips and teeth settled into a sneer.

Johnny felt sick at the thought that his mother might die. 'Go away,' he said, trying to push down the flap of the letter box. 'Leave me alone.'

The reporter pushed back. His voice softened. 'All I want to do is talk to you about your mother. I'm not going to write anything about her in the paper. I'm not allowed to until the trial. But when it's over, everyone is going to want to know about her – what she was really like. Only you can tell me that, Johnny. If you don't tell me the nice things about her, I won't be able to write them down. I'll have to rely on people like Miss Dangerfield. Do you want me to go and talk to her again?'

'No, I don't. And stop talking as if Mum is going to be found guilty. She didn't do it. I know she didn't. Why aren't you and the police trying to find out who did?'

Now the reporter's eyes filled the slot in the door. 'That's a good point, Johnny,' he said. 'Do you have any ideas about who might have done it? I'd love to hear them. Let me in, and we can talk in the warm.'

'It's not very warm in here,' said Johnny.

'Well, maybe I could give you the price of the coal you'll burn while you're talking to me. Perhaps a little more than that. And remember, I can't help your mother if I don't know enough about her to make her case. Let me in, Johnny. Please.'

Johnny was on the point of giving way when he heard footsteps coming down the lane. There were at least two men, and they were getting closer. He could hear their voices. They sounded drunk, but he couldn't make out what they were saying. Then he heard the reporter again. He was shouting now.

'Get out of it!' he yelled.

Johnny peered through the letter box. He could see the reporter grappling with the men. He held one of them by the hair while he punched the other, bringing up his knee to hit him in the groin. Then, while that man rolled on the floor in agony, he jabbed his fingers into the other's eyes and wrenched his arm behind his back. Johnny winced with pain just watching.

The reporter kicked the man on the ground. 'I said clear off. Keep away or I'll get you again. And I'll tell the police too. Do you hear?'

The men swore at him, but they slunk away, back up the narrow alley. The reporter knocked on the door again, and this time Johnny let him in. His lips were swollen and his knuckles were bleeding.

'Why were those men after you?' asked Johnny.

'They weren't after me, son. They were after you. But you won't be troubled by them again. Not if they think I'm protecting you. If there's one thing the war did for the likes of me, it taught us how to fight. Those youngsters didn't have a chance. But you'd better be careful. Watch where you go. Especially after dark.'

The reporter blotted the blood with his handkerchief. Johnny dragged over the armchair, casually dismantling the pretend Auntie Ada. He climbed up to get the ointment down from beside the Peace Mug on the high shelf. 'Thank you,' he said, with his back to the reporter. He felt he owed the man a smear of antiseptic, even if he wasn't supposed to talk to him.

The reporter took the opportunity to get a conversation going. 'Are you getting enough to eat?' he asked, looking around the bare room for signs of food.

Johnny opened a cupboard and showed off the things Hutch had given him since Winnie's arrest. Everything was in tins: ham, peas, some sweet evaporated milk. 'I've got a bit of cheese, too,' said Johnny. He reached across to the windowsill and took down a little parcel wrapped in greaseproof paper. 'Do you want some? I'm afraid I haven't got any bread.'

'That's very kind of you, Johnny,' said the reporter. He put his hand in his coat pocket. 'I've got a couple of apples here. Why don't we share them?'

So Johnny got a knife and two plates from the side of the sink. At first he was going to give the reporter his mother's plate – the chipped one with blue roses round the edge – but then he thought he'd keep that one for himself. He didn't want a stranger to have it. The reporter had Johnny's: plain white, with a red rim.

The apples and cheese went well together, and the reporter started asking casual questions about Winnie while he crunched his way through the fruit. At first Johnny kept his answers short and factual. Then he found himself talking more and more about his mother: how she had been left completely alone when his father was killed, because neither she nor Harry had had any family left by 1918. He described how she looked after the neighbours, how hard she worked, and how worried she was about the rent going up. The reporter listened, and sympathized, and gave Johnny a handful of coins when he left.

'Be careful, Johnny,' he said. 'Lock the door behind me when I go. And if you think of anything else you want to tell me, just get in touch.' He wrote his office telephone number on a piece of paper and handed it over.

As he bolted the door, Johnny felt glad to have met someone who really cared about him. He thought he might ask Hutch if he could use the phone tomorrow. Maybe he could persuade the reporter to help him track down Marie Langford in the hope that she might prove that Winnie wasn't a killer. Perhaps it would be all right to break his promise and tell the reporter about the BCG so that he could help to find the real murderer.

But then Johnny noticed that something was

missing from the mantelpiece. The reporter had taken the photograph of his father. It was the only picture of Harry Swanson that Johnny had ever seen. As far as he knew it was the only image of him anywhere. And that man had taken it. Taken it without asking. Johnny decided to have nothing more to do with him. He would search for Mrs Langford by himself.

Chapter 28

TAKING CHARGE

Johnny realized that his best bet for finding Marie Langford was to use the two tools he knew so well: the post and the newspapers. He put a new personal message in the *London Times*, quoting Auntie Ada's box number, and he helped Hutch sort letters that came into the post office, looking out for anything addressed to the doctor's house. He reckoned that since Mrs Langford was abroad, and didn't know that her husband was dead, she was bound to write him a letter sometime – especially with Christmas coming. The police had the same idea, and an officer came in every day to check for letters from France, but nothing turned up. The policeman wasn't at all interested in doing anything about the broken shop window. He seemed to think that bad feeling against Hutch and Johnny was only natural.

Hutch tried asking the policeman about the investigation. 'Is there anything new? Have you found out any more about the murder?'

The officer's response was steely: 'We've got all the evidence we need. And even if there was a development, why should I tell you, in view of your relationship with the accused?'

Over the weekend, Johnny filled the long evening hours devising new money-making schemes. The rent rise was now only days away, and the savings inside his rabbit wouldn't last long. He couldn't afford to be high-minded about advertising. He roughed out a couple of offers: *Give Your Home a Country Feel*. People who sent him sixpence would be told: *Walk around in muddy boots*.

He even thought of putting a little free sample of dirt into the envelopes. Perhaps he'd add a few seeds, too. He could easily get some from the plants in the graveyard. Maybe he could say they were magic seeds. He got that idea from the posters outside the Playhouse. They were doing *Jack and the Beanstalk* as the Christmas pantomime.

Johnny's most frequent correspondent, the aspiring poet, had sent ten poems at once, asking what the Poetry Police thought of them. Johnny spent two whole evenings writing his replies, glad of the one-pound postal order that had arrived with them, and determined to give value for money so that the man would write again. He put the poems in a stack by the fire, ready to use them as fuel; but then he had another idea. He cut them up into strips, each containing one line of verse, and shuffled them up. A quick advert in the *Stambleton Echo* offered:

The Poetry Kit:
I send the verbiage, you make the verse.
3d. per line.

He ran to the advertising office first thing the next day, and managed to get the advertisement into that evening's edition. The lady behind the counter thought it was one of his auntie's better ideas. The kit would, she said, make an excellent Christmas present. She was right. The response was immediate and enthusiastic.

By Christmas Eve Johnny was confident that he would be able to pay the rent for the whole of January, right up to the date of his mother's trial. He was glad about that, but he was tormented by the thought of how Hutch would react if he found out how he had got hold of so much money.

'I see your auntie is still sewing,' said Hutch when Johnny presented a pile of postal orders for cashing before the post office closed down for Christmas. 'That's good.'

Johnny was on the point of telling him the truth about Ada when a customer came in. Trade was so slow that Hutch could not afford to ignore her, even for a second, and Johnny didn't want to risk reminding her of 'the Bloody Barmaid of Stambleton', so he dived into the stockroom. Yet another chance to own up had come and gone.

Chapter 29

THE PRISON VISIT

In the stockroom, Johnny re-read the letter he had written for Hutch to take to his mother. In it, he apologized for making her so angry on the night they'd last been together, and insisted that the whole terrible mess was his fault. He swore he would do everything he could to get Winnie out of prison. Somehow it didn't seem right to sign off without wishing her a happy Christmas, even though he knew there was no chance of that for either of them. It was nearly noon. Before long, Hutch would be setting off for the prison. Johnny imagined his mother alone in her cell, wondering whether anyone was doing anything to get her released.

In fact, Winnie was worrying about Johnny. She had no idea what had happened to him after her arrest, and no one would tell her. A lawyer, appointed by the court, had been to see her, but had offered little hope. It was clear that he, like the police, saw her conviction as inevitable. Winnie wondered whether she would ever see Johnny again. She was devastated that their last words to each other had been so harsh, and felt that she had let her son down, even though she was innocent of any crime. She was lonely in her cell, but terrified whenever she was let out to exercise with the other prisoners – even though they kept their distance, assuming that she was capable of killing. Winnie had hardly eaten for nearly a fortnight, and was even skinnier than before. There was no mirror, but she knew that now, more than ever, she matched the description Mr Murray had given the court of the dazed and desperate creature he had seen in the pub on that awful night. Her hair was lank and greasy, and she badly needed a proper wash.

When the prison guard took her into the visiting room, Winnie was surprised to see Hutch, large and embarrassed in his best suit, sitting at a tiny table with his bad leg stretched out to one side; but she was thrilled that at last she would have news of her son.

'How's Johnny?' she blurted out, before correcting herself and adding, politely, 'It's so kind of you to come, Mr Hutchinson.'

'Oh, it's a pleasure,' said Hutch, automatically.

'Well, not a pleasure, of course, but you know what I mean.' There was an awkward pause before he continued. 'I brought you some food from the shop: a little pork pie and some chocolates. But they were confiscated on the way in.'

'What a shame. But thank you, anyway. Let's hope the warders enjoy them.'

Hutch was impressed that she had enough spirit to muster a little joke. He took Johnny's letter from his pocket. 'They did let me bring this in. They read it first, of course. They said he's got lovely handwriting.'

'Yes, he has, hasn't he?' said Winnie. 'I'm so proud of him.' She held the envelope against her cheek and cried.

Johnny sat alone in the kitchen, wondering how Hutch was getting on, and wishing he could have gone to the jail. As it got dark outside, he could hear carol singers in the street. He didn't light the lamp. He wanted them to think the house was empty. He couldn't face Christmas cheer, or the prospect of another visit from the thugs the reporter had seen off the week before. But he opened the door when he heard Hutch coming. He recognized his rhythmical limp in the lane. Johnny hoped that Hutch had stopped off at the shop on his way back. He was hungry, and it would be nice to have something special for Christmas. But Hutch arrived empty-handed, looking grave.

'Oh, my boy. What are you doing alone here in the dark?'

'Nothing. I was just thinking about Mum. How is she?'

Hutch sighed. 'As well as can be expected, I suppose. She's worried about you though.'

'She doesn't need to be, Hutch. I hope you told her that. I can look after myself.'

'I told her you were in fine form. But she told me something too – something I should probably have guessed for myself.' Hutch paused, and looked away. Johnny wondered for a moment if he was about to hear a horrible revelation about the court case. But it was a different thing entirely. Hutch took a breath and announced: 'Johnny, I know about your Auntie Ada. Your mother has told me all.'

Johnny was caught between relief that the pretence was over and fear that he was in deep trouble. He couldn't bear the idea of losing Hutch as well as everyone else. 'I'm sorry,' he said. 'I wanted to tell you, but I didn't know how.'

Hutch felt sympathy for the boy, but also outrage at how he had behaved. He tried to stay calm. 'I have to say, Johnny, that I'm shocked. Shocked and disappointed that you have lied to me for so long. In any other situation, I might look for a way to punish you, and I won't put up with being deceived again.' Johnny bowed his head, and Hutch continued in a more friendly tone. 'But what matters now is that you shouldn't be here on your own – especially at Christmas. I'd never have let you come back here every night if I'd known. I've agreed with your mother that you will come and live with me until this business is over.'

'Until after the trial you mean,' said Johnny. 'They'll let her out then, won't they?'

'Yes,' said Hutch, trying to sound convinced. 'It will all be finished then. Now, you run along and get some things together.'

Johnny was back in a trice with a few underclothes tied up in a shirt. Hutch was touched to see that he clung to a toy rabbit as if he would never allow himself to be parted from it. 'If there's anything valuable in the house, you'd better bring that, too,' he said. 'Just in case anyone breaks in while you're away.'

Johnny put down his things and climbed up to get

the Peace Mug. He went up to Winnie's room, lifted a loose floorboard, and took out the box in which his mother kept his father's medals and important family papers. There was nothing else he wanted to take. Except his father's photograph, of course. But that had already gone.

Chapter 30

AT HOME WITH HUTCH

Johnny had never been in the flat above the shop. Compared with his own home it was luxurious, with electric light, lino on the floor, and an indoor bathroom with hot and cold water on tap. At Hutch's suggestion, Johnny had a bath as soon as he arrived, using expensive soap he had stacked in displays but never seen out of its box. Hutch went downstairs to the shop and got Johnny a toothbrush and some of the newest tooth cleaner, which came as a paste in a tube, and bubbled into a sweet minty foam in his mouth.

Afterwards, Johnny found his way to the kitchen. Hutch was mashing potatoes. The room was quite bare, with lots of empty shelves. 'I use the shop as my larder,' Hutch explained. 'I only bring things up here when I need them.' Like the bathroom, the kitchen was full of steam. Hutch had speared two holes in the top of a tin of stewed steak and was heating it up in a pan of boiling water on a trim little gas stove. He had pudding ready alongside: a can of pineapple chunks and a tin of condensed milk. Johnny had seen it advertised in the paper. *Doctors tell other doctors what wonderful results they have had with Nestles Milk,* said the advertisement. He'd thought of stealing that line for one of his own enterprises. But he supposed there wouldn't be any more of them now.

Johnny watched, hungry and amazed, as Hutch stirred large knobs of butter into the potatoes. He kept Hutch talking about the visit to his mother; but he knew the question that was bound to come, and eventually Hutch found the words:

'Now then, Johnny,' he said gravely. 'If there never was an Auntie Ada, where did all those postal orders come from?'

Haltingly at first, but then with relief, excitement and even a hint of pride, Johnny told Hutch everything, from the Secret of Instant Height through to the Poetry Police and Confidentially Yours.

Hutch tried to be kind, well aware of the torment Johnny was enduring, but he couldn't disguise his disapproval of what the boy had done.

'This can't go on. Good heavens, Johnny! Can't you see why it's wrong? Can't you imagine how those people you tricked are feeling?'

'I don't need to imagine. I know. They did it to me first, remember?'

'But that doesn't mean you can do it to other people! It doesn't excuse making total strangers send you money for nothing!'

'They always got something. Even if it wasn't exactly what they were expecting.'

'And what's all this about you selling stamps?'

'I haven't been selling them.'

'You said they were portraits of the King. People paid for them. That's selling stamps.'

'Oh.'

'And selling unused stamps is against the law. If you're not a properly qualified postmaster, that is. I should know. I can show you a copy of the regulations if you want.'

'I didn't realize—'

'And it's worse than that. Presumably, to make any money, you must have been selling stamps at more than their face value?'

'How do you mean?'

'Well, when you sent someone one of these "official portraits", how much did you charge?'

'A shilling.'

'And you sent them one-shilling stamps?'

'Of course not. Penny stamps; threepenny stamps; sixpenny stamps. It depended on what I had at the time.'

'So you were making a profit.'

'That was the point.'

Hutch thumped the table. 'But that makes it even worse. It's a crime, Johnny. You have committed a crime! Here we are with your mother unjustly imprisoned and you really *are* a criminal. I should turn you in, Johnny. I might even lose my job if I don't.'

Johnny was blinking hard, trying not to cry. 'I'm sorry,' he said weakly. 'I was only trying to help.'

Hutch was still angry. 'Well, you haven't helped, have you?'

'I've got enough money to pay the rent.'

Hutch couldn't stop himself. His next words spilled out before he could think. 'But your mother might die!'

The silence that followed wrenched at them both. Eventually Hutch had to break it. He could see that Johnny was on the verge of tears. Hutch was calmer, but still stern. 'Well, Johnny, it's all got to stop now, hasn't it? I'm not going to tell the police: for your mother's sake, if nothing else. But if any more letters come to that private box, we'll just return them unopened to the main sorting office.'

'No, you can't do that!' cried Johnny, thinking of the advert in the personal column of *The Times*. He explained how he was looking for Mrs Langford in the hope that she would be able to help prove Winnie's innocence. 'You see, Hutch, it's not just that Mrs Langford can tell everyone what a good woman my mother is. She can give new evidence.'

'Like what, exactly?'

'For a start, she knows my mother didn't have any keys to her house. The police don't believe Mum, but they'd believe Mrs Langford.' Johnny wondered whether he should break his promise and tell Hutch about the BCG. He started cautiously: 'And there's another thing. *Someone* killed Dr Langford, and if it wasn't Mum, it must have been somebody with a reason. Mrs Langford might know who it was, and why.'

Johnny was surprised by Hutch's response. 'Your mother was talking about that too,' he said. 'She's been running over in her mind everything she knows about the Langfords, looking for a motive for the murder. And she thinks it might have been something to do with the doctor's work. I thought he'd retired completely, but apparently he was still keeping his hand in. He'd hinted to your mother that he was involved with some sort of new medicine. Something to do with TB.'

'Phthisis,' said Johnny.

Hutch jolted with shock. 'I beg your pardon?' he said, thinking Johnny had used a dirty word.

'Phthisis. It's another word for TB.' Johnny felt his way cautiously, wondering how much Winnie knew, and what she had told Hutch. 'Dr Langford told me about it. He was hoping they'd find a cure.'

'Well, your mother thinks he might have done that, or that he knew a way to stop people getting it in the first place. He told her about some vaccine they've developed in France. It's called BBC or something.'

Johnny realized that Dr Langford had been incapable of keeping his mouth shut. It bolstered his theory that the killer was a medical rival or a blackmailer who had found out what the doctor was doing. He felt relief wash over him. He wasn't really breaking a confidence by talking about the BCG. The doctor had told Winnie; and now she'd told Hutch. Surely it didn't count as a secret any more?

'Mum's right,' he said. 'Has she told the police?'

'She's tried to. But they won't take any notice. They don't want to hear about anything that spoils their case against her. And anyway, she doesn't know for certain that it's true.'

'But it is. Dr Langford told me himself. He was involved with someone who's making the vaccine.'

'Who? Where?'

'All I know is that they're working in a laboratory "in the wilds" – somewhere they won't be found. I heard Dr Langford say that.'

Hutch was despondent. 'So it could be anyone, anywhere. What good is that?'

'If we could find Mrs Langford in France, we could ask her where the laboratory is. And we could warn her. She might be in danger too.'

'But how can we track her down when the police can't?'

'Do you think they're really trying? I went to the police station to tell them all this, and they wouldn't even listen. If they've decided Mum did the murder, why would they want to look for someone else? Why should they spend a fortune trying to find Mrs Langford abroad?'

Hutch shook his head. 'It looks as if it's all down to us now, Johnny.'

'I've tried to trace her. I've done that advert.'

'But if Mrs Langford's in France, she's hardly likely to see it, is she?' said Hutch. 'I think we need to do another advertisement, Johnny – something bigger that stands a better chance of being noticed. We can ask anyone who knows Mrs Langford's whereabouts to get in touch.' He paused for thought. 'And we need to put it in all the major national and regional papers so that whoever was working with Dr Langford might see it.'

'But that will cost a fortune.'

'Don't worry, son, I'll pay. But I think we'd better keep our identities secret, don't you, just in case the murderer gets the idea we're on his trail?'

'You mean . . . ?'

'Yes,' Hutch sighed. 'Auntie Ada can have one more outing. And we'll use her private box as the address for the reply.'

Chapter 31

LOOKING FOR MRS LANGFORD

Hutch made up a bed in the spare room at the back of the flat. Johnny lay down surrounded by boxes of official Post Office forms which Hutch felt were too important to be kept in the stockroom downstairs alongside the custard powder and fish paste. He clutched his old rabbit, just as he had at the beginning of this business, on the night when he'd wet himself after the revelation that the Secret of Instant Height was a trick. He was exhausted, but unable to get to sleep in the unfamiliar surroundings; and he was excited by the idea of having Hutch to help him search for Mrs Langford and the real murderer. He wondered who it was. It had to be someone who knew about the BCG. Another doctor perhaps? Maybe someone from France? It could even be the man with that useless drug from Africa. After all, he'd be out of business if someone found a way to stop people getting TB. Johnny tried to remember the name at the top of the advert Mrs Langford had thrown onto the fire after Dr Langford's joke about the Wimbledon racket. Umba . . . Umca . . . Umcka . . . Umckaloabo. He drifted off at last to the exotic rhythm of the word. He had completely forgotten that tomorrow would be Christmas Day.

Hutch hadn't, and Johnny woke to find presents at the end of his bed. He knew where they had come from. He recognized the chocolates, jellies and candied fruit he had unpacked when they'd been delivered to the shop weeks before, and which had so spectacularly failed to sell since his mother's arrest. Of course he knew that Hutch must have crept downstairs to fetch them in the middle of the night, but somehow he almost believed in Santa Claus for the first time in years. The Christmas lunch he and Hutch enjoyed together was the most lavish meal he had ever eaten, but he couldn't really enjoy it because the person he loved most in the world wasn't there.

After the meal, he and Hutch sat down together and composed their advertisement. After a lot of deliberation they came up with:

Langford
Anyone knowing the whereabouts of
Mrs Marie Langford,

widow of the late Dr Giles Langford,
believed to be staying with relatives in France,
is kindly invited to contact
PO Box 9, Stambleton, Warwickshire.
This is a matter of the utmost importance.

They got it into the first post after Christmas, and it was in papers across the country before New Year.

Over the next week, a number of letters arrived addressed to PO Box 9, but they all turned out to be replies to Johnny's last spurt of adverts before he had confessed all to Hutch. With Hutch watching over his shoulder, Johnny sent all the money straight back.

Then a letter came that didn't contain a postal order. It was just a small sheet of paper saying:

I do not know where Marie Langford is, but if you value your safety, you will stop asking questions.

It was unsigned.

Hutch looked at the postmark. 'It was posted in Brecon,' he said.

'Should we go to the police now?' asked Johnny.

'I'm not sure,' said Hutch. 'Maybe we should try to find out more first.'

'Where is Brecon, anyway?'

'It's near Swansea, I think. In Wales.'

'I know someone who comes from Swansea,' said Johnny, excitedly. 'Olwen. That girl from school I told you about. If we could find her, maybe she could help.'

'Don't be silly. That way we end up searching for two people, not just one. And anyway, what use can a child be?'

Johnny had to admit that Hutch was right. 'I know,' he said, calming down. 'I didn't really mean it. We'll have to do something else.'

Hutch was thinking. 'We could put in another advertisement – in the paper that covers the Brecon area. How about: *Langford. Any news? PO Box 9, Stambleton.*'

'No,' said Johnny. 'Don't mention Stambleton. That's put the wind up someone already. Let's get a box number at the paper this time, and ask them to send any replies on to us.'

Hutch found out the phone number of the local paper, and called to ask about their advertising rates. He was allocated Box 102. He sold himself a postal order to cover the fee, and asked Johnny to write the message out neatly, and to put everything into an envelope.

Johnny went upstairs and did as he was told. But sitting there with pen and paper, he couldn't resist working out the wording for another advert that had come into his mind in an idle moment. He thought quite a few people might fall for it, and though he knew Hutch wouldn't approve, he felt uncomfortable without any cash coming in. After all, he couldn't live off Hutch's kindness for ever, especially with business so bad, and he wanted to keep paying the rent on the house in Dagmouth Lane, ready for his mother's return.

He still had some postal orders he'd received just before Christmas, from people who had been so desperate about the behaviour of their pets that they had written in to find out how to *Solve the Problem of a Barking Dog*. They had each paid a shilling, only to be told to *Swap it for a cat*.

Johnny wasn't particularly proud of that one. But as so often, a simple idea had turned out to be very lucrative. He knew Hutch would never cash the postal orders now, and he thought he should probably return them to his 'customers', but he had lost their addresses when he had sent back their stamped addressed envelopes. So he thought it wouldn't do any harm to use them to pay his next advertising fee. There was enough for a few more words than usual. He wrote out the advert:

Change Your Appearance Permanently.
Unhappy with the way you look?
Transform yourself Instantly and For Ever.
Send 1/– to Box 102.

With only a moment's hesitation, he popped it in the envelope alongside Hutch's personal ad about Mrs Langford. He sealed the letter and took it downstairs just in time to catch the postman, who was collecting the outgoing mail.

The response to both advertisements was quick and surprising. A week later, Hutch answered the phone in the kiosk by the shop door. People who had no phone at home occasionally arranged to take calls there, but at that moment (as was so often the case since Hutch had taken Johnny in) there were no customers in the shop.

'Hello,' said Hutch.

There was a pause while the person at the other end spoke.

Hutch replied in his 'post office' voice. 'I'm sorry, that's quite impossible. The identity of a box holder is a confidential matter . . .'

Johnny was weighing flour from a huge sack into three-pound bags, and it took a little while for him to notice that Hutch's tone had changed, and that he was leaning out of the phone booth, clicking his fingers to attract Johnny's attention.

'. . . but as it happens,' Hutch was saying, 'the lady is in the shop at the moment. I'll put her on.' He called across to Johnny, hoping he'd take the hint that the person on the phone was calling in response to the advertisement about Mrs Langford. 'Ada!' he shouted. 'Ada. You have a telephone call.'

Hutch handed Johnny the phone, but stayed close, listening in.

'Hello?' said Johnny, hoping that his voice sounded more like a woman's than a boy's. 'Can I help you?'

'You can help yourself, darling,' said a man's voice at the other end. 'You must be mad if you thought I wouldn't spot that new advert in the local paper. *Langford. Any news?* Well there's no news, and there won't be any. I told you before. Keep your nose out if you want to stay safe. Do you hear? And remember. I know where you are.'

The line went dead. Johnny was scared. It was true. The caller knew where Ada lived, even if he was unaware that she didn't exist. And if he came to Stambleton, he wouldn't have any trouble finding the post office. He might use force to get Hutch to say who Ada really was. Things could turn nasty. But the man on the phone had given Johnny and Hutch some important information, too. He was the author of the threatening letter; he was involved in the Langford case; and, most importantly of all, he had a Welsh accent.

Almost as soon as he had posted the Change Your Appearance Permanently advert, Johnny had regretted it. He had made a solemn promise to Hutch to stop the advertising scams, and he had broken his word the first time he was tempted. He prayed that no one would reply, and dreaded the arrival of a package from the Welsh newspaper, even though it might contain information about Marie Langford. He could picture Hutch's rage if he found that the contents of Box 102 was a haul of postal orders and stamped addressed envelopes. So he was relieved that Hutch was out on the paper round when a fat letter arrived from Wales.

Johnny took the packet upstairs to open it, sensing that Change Your Appearance Permanently had been one of his greatest successes. He was right, but the old feeling of excitement was mixed with a sense of shame as he split the seal. No one had answered the personal ad, but there were thirteen replies to the other one. Despite his promise to Hutch, Johnny knew he would secretly write out the answer thirteen times and stash the postal orders inside his rabbit. He shuffled through the stamped addressed envelopes. Most of them were cheap little things, the kind Hutch sold for 4d. a dozen. One was thicker, with scalloped edges to the flap. Another was pink and scented. Halfway through the pile, he found a buff-coloured envelope that looked as if it had come from an office. It was made out to an address in Wales, and the distinctive, curly handwriting seemed familiar. The address read:

Mrs J. W. Morgan
Craig-y-Nos Castle
Near Brecon
Wales

He couldn't remember where he had seen the writing before. He was pretty sure that it was different from the earlier, menacing, note from Brecon, but he thought he'd better make sure. He'd put that one aside in his mother's box, safe with the medals and birth certificates in case he ever needed to show it to the police. He compared the two. He was right. There was no similarity at all. And yet he was sure he had seen the writing on the new envelope recently. Was it an old customer? One of his lonely hearts, perhaps? If it was someone unlucky in love, they might well want to change their appearance. But how could he ever check? He had burned all their desperate letters, to keep himself warm when he had been alone at home.

He went to put the threatening letter back in the box. And that was when he saw it. There, alongside the telegram announcing his father's death, was the testimonial that Mrs Langford had written for his mother on Remembrance Day. The envelope said simply:

To whom it may concern

The similarity to the writing on the new envelope was unmistakable. The 'w' of 'whom' began with a swirl on top of the first downstroke, almost like a child's drawing of a snail's shell. 'Wales' in the new address began in the same way, and so did the 'w' in J. W. Morgan. The 'con' in 'concern' matched the end of 'Brecon'. Johnny unfolded the letter of recommendation. The 'w's in the heading 'Mrs Winifred May Swanson' both had snail-shell swirls. There was also a flourish on the last leg of the 'm's, just like the 'm' in Morgan on today's envelope. Johnny knew what that meant: Marie Langford and J. W. Morgan were the same person; Marie Langford was not in France – she was living in a castle in Wales; and for some reason she wanted to transform herself instantly, and for ever.

Chapter 32

THE DARK ROCK

Johnny put the stack of new letters under his mattress and ran down to show Hutch the new envelope from Brecon.

'Hutch! Hutch! We've got a reply,' he shouted as he bounded into the shop.

Hutch had only just returned from delivering the papers, and he was preoccupied with opening up for the day.

'Look, Hutch! Look! It's in Mrs Langford's handwriting.' Johnny thrust the envelope in front of Hutch, who took it and examined it carefully.

'And what does she say?' he asked.

Johnny was silent.

'We said, *Langford. Any News?* What's the reply?' Hutch looked inside the envelope. It was empty. He was puzzled for a moment, and then furious. And Johnny knew at once that he should have covered his tracks more carefully.

'Johnny,' said Hutch, sternly. 'Johnny, tell me, and

tell me honestly. Why has this woman sent us an envelope addressed to herself?'

It was a sorry scene, which might have had terrible consequences for Johnny had it not been pensions day, with a stream of customers coming in to use the post office. In whispered conversations between transactions, Johnny admitted that he had run one final scam in the Welsh paper, and Hutch left him in no doubt that he was even angrier than before. But his rage was tempered by the need to be polite to the customers, and the dawning realization that at last they had a lead on Mrs Langford's whereabouts. Hutch was intrigued by the address:

'Craig-y-Nos Castle. It sounds like an imposing place.'

'How can we find out more about it?' said Johnny. 'Shall I go to the library?'

'No. I doubt you'd find much about Wales in there.' Hutch pushed back his shoulders and straightened his tie. 'I think this is a sufficiently important matter for me to use my Post Office contacts.'

So Hutch put in a long-distance call to his opposite number in Brecon, more than 150 miles away. Johnny listened in to them sharing Post Office chit-chat (both of them had received a circular from Head Office saying that they must empty the coin boxes on their telephones at least once a month; both of them thought that an unnecessary imposition). Then Hutch asked his question. His bad leg was twitching. Johnny could tell that he didn't like lying.

'I've got a letter. It's somehow ended up here, and I'm thinking that it might be important. It has that sort of "urgent" look you get a feel for, if you see what I mean. But the handwriting is very bad. Let me tell you what I think it says.' He read out the Craig-y-Nos address, spelling it out with all the hyphens, and pretending to have trouble reading it, though it was, in fact, perfectly legible – if a little unusual.

Johnny could hear the voice of the man at the other end, but he couldn't work out what he was saying in the long pauses between Hutch's questions. Eventually Hutch ended the call. 'Right you are, then. Many thanks. I'll forward it on.'

Johnny couldn't wait to hear what Hutch had found out.

'Well,' said Hutch, as he put down the receiver. 'That was very interesting indeed. This Craig-y-Nos place. The name means Dark Rock, or Rock of the Night.'

'Never mind that,' said Johnny, impatiently. 'Where is it? What's it like?'

'It really is a castle, apparently – but a modern one.

And it used to belong to a famous opera singer: Adelina Patti. She spent a fortune on it. It's got its own theatre, massive grounds, even its own station. Oh, she was a big star before the war.' Hutch seemed to have become infected with the Welsh postmaster's long-windedness.

Johnny interrupted again. 'What would Mrs Langford be doing staying with an opera singer?'

'Ah, but that's the thing, see. Madame Patti's long dead. And Craig-y-Nos Castle isn't a private residence any more. It's been turned into a hospital.'

Johnny gasped, and Hutch delivered his next fact with a flourish of triumph. 'And guess what kind of hospital it is?'

Johnny was bursting with anticipation, desperate for Hutch to get on with it.

Hutch puffed out his chest, and announced: 'Craig-y-Nos Castle, Johnny, is now a sanatorium.'

'That's it!' yelled Johnny. 'Mum was right. That's what this whole business is all about. Everything's linked to phthisis.'

'It seems so, Johnny. But please call it TB like everyone else.'

'Shall we tell the police?' said Johnny. 'Surely they'll listen to us now?'

'Yes, I'll phone them straight away.'

Hutch went back into the booth. Johnny hovered outside trying to listen in, but Hutch dropped his voice very low when he heard the bell on the shop door announce the arrival of a customer. Johnny served her. She was curt with him, like most people nowadays, and made it clear that she had only come in because she had unexpectedly run out of matches, and it wasn't worth her while to walk to another shop to buy some more. She left just as Hutch slammed down the phone. Johnny opened the door to the kiosk, hoping for good news. Instead he found Hutch punching the wall with rage. He had never heard him curse before.

'It's no good,' said Hutch. 'Johnny, there's nothing we can do to get through to those people. They've made their decision. As far as they're concerned, your mother's guilty, and anything you or I say is just made up to try to get her off. He wouldn't even give me time to tell him that we'd found Mrs Langford.'

'So what can we do now?' said Johnny. 'Do you think we should go to Craig-y-Nos ourselves and find out what's going on?'

'I'd like to, Johnny. Believe me, I would. But I can't leave the shop.'

'Surely it wouldn't matter if you closed – just for a day or so?'

'The shop would be all right,' said Hutch. 'To be honest, it's costing me money to open since all this fuss. It's the post office I'm worried about. I have a legal duty to run it. People need the service. I can't just shut it down.'

'But what would happen if you were ill?'

'I'd have to contact Head Office, and they would send a substitute postmaster. But they wouldn't like it. And if they found out afterwards that I hadn't been ill at all, I'd probably lose my job. I'd never be able to be a public servant again.'

'But they needn't find out.'

'Not if we fail, Johnny. But what if we succeed? If we can solve the murder, your mother will be let out, and there will be lots of publicity. Questions will be asked. My lie would be exposed.'

Johnny was fired up by the thought that they might succeed, and that with Mrs Langford's help Winnie might be freed. But he could see Hutch's point.

'I'll go by myself,' he said.

'Are you serious?' said Hutch.

'Of course I am. My mother and Mrs Langford are

both in danger. It looks as if I'm the only one who can help them. I really have to go.'

Hutch was thoughtful. 'I'm not sure I should let you. I promised your mother I would keep you safe.'

'Hutch, I'm sorry,' said Johnny defiantly. 'I know I should do what you say, but if you don't let me, I'll just go anyway. There's no way you can stop me. I've got enough money to buy a ticket. If you help me, I might at least get on the right train.'

Hutch gave in eventually, and looked up the route and train times in a large book he kept under the counter in the post office. He worked out that if Johnny started early enough, it was just about possible to get to Craig-y-Nos and back in one day. He made Johnny a packed lunch for the journey, and wrote a list of the stations where he would have to change trains.

'If you have any problems, ask a lady,' he said, 'or the guard or the ticket collector. Don't stick your head out of the window – you might get it knocked off. And don't use the lavatory while the train is in a station – it's not allowed.' He asked for the list back and scribbled something new on the bottom. 'It's the phone number here, in case you hit trouble.

You'll have to ask the operator to put you through.'

'I know how to work the phone,' said Johnny wearily. 'I sometimes went to the telephone box by the Town Hall to send in adverts. It meant I could use papers all over the country.'

'But how did you pay them?'

'Oh, I sent postal orders. Sometimes I could put two or three adverts on one bill. The *Yorkshire Post* even gave Auntie Ada an account.'

Hutch shook his head. 'So much knowledge for one so young,' he said.

Johnny didn't dare tell him that he'd never been on a train in his life.

Chapter 33

JOHNNY'S JOURNEY

Johnny loved the railway. He often watched from the footbridge over Stambleton station as snorting steam engines powered through on their way from places like Birmingham, Rugby and Crewe to all parts of the country. Even the little local trains that puffed to a stop at Stambleton were exciting.

On board for the first time, Johnny rocked with the rhythm as the wheels bumped over the joints in the track. He stared out at the unfamiliar perspective on the town he knew so well, and then, only minutes later, on a rural landscape he had never seen before. He adored the smell of the sooty steam that blew in through the little sliding window at the top of the compartment. It mingled with the aroma of cigarettes and pipe-smoke clinging to the itchy upholstery, which left patterns on the backs of his legs. Hutch had put some comics in his bag, but Johnny didn't want to read. There was too much to see. And anyway, he was worried in case he missed the two connections he would have to make before arriving at Penwyllt, where a station had been built at Adelina Patti's own expense especially to serve Craig-y-Nos. Johnny thought how much Dr Langford would have loved those place names, heavy with consonants and mystery.

His last change involved a cold wait for the local service to Penwyllt. There was a refreshment room at the other end of the platform. Johnny wondered whether they would let him sit inside to keep warm. He had a shilling in his pocket, but Hutch had given it to him for use in emergencies only, and he didn't want to be forced to spend some of it on a cup of tea. He decided to go in, sit down, and see if he got thrown out. It would be worth the embarrassment to have the chance to get the feeling back in his feet and fingers again. But as he pushed open the door, letting out a blast of steamy brightness, he caught sight of a group of women surrounded by baskets and parcels, chatting and laughing together. They were wearing uniforms with broad aprons and large white hats. Johnny guessed they must be nurses from the Craig-y-Nos sanatorium, returning after a day out at the shops.

Johnny had brought the 'J. W. Morgan' envelope with him so that if he were stopped by anyone at the sanatorium he could say that he had come to visit her, and at the very least buy himself some time. But what if the nurses talked to him now? What if they asked him who he was and where he was going? What if they made a fuss of him so that he didn't get a chance to look round the sanatorium secretly, to try to find out what was going on there? Or, worse still, what if they didn't believe him, and sent him back to Stambleton when he was so close to Craig-y-Nos. He decided to stay out of the nurses' way for as long as he could. Reluctantly he gently let the door close again, and walked up and down the platform, trying to keep warm.

A porter cleared his throat and spat onto the rails. *Haemoptysis*, thought Johnny, remembering Dr Langford again. In the cold, his excitement was waning, and the sight of the nurses and the porter's sputum had reminded him why the sanatorium existed. It wasn't just Mrs Langford's prison. Craig-y-Nos Castle must be full of people with a deadly disease. For the first time on this adventure Johnny was frightened. Until now he hadn't let himself admit that if he went to Craig-y-Nos he might catch TB. He might die. It was stupid to put himself in contact with all those germs.

Now he wanted to go home. After all the bravado and exhilaration that had buoyed him up through the journey so far, Johnny was at last struck by the madness of this whole adventure. He was only a boy. He was in unfamiliar territory, and he didn't really know what he was looking for. He might meet a murderer: that Welshman on the phone had already threatened him. Why had he ever come up with the idea of trying to investigate Craig-y-Nos on his own? Hutch should never have allowed him to set off in the first place. You could tell that he wasn't used to looking after children. His mother would never have let him go.

His mother. That was why he was doing it. Johnny might be afraid; he might long to go back to Stambleton; but he knew that if he did, someone else could die. Winnie was in real danger. He was facing a risk – but her fate looked certain. Johnny imagined what would happen if he failed to find Mrs Langford. Although he was staring at columns of figures on the railway timetable, all he could see was the hangman putting a noose round his mother's neck. He couldn't get the image out of his mind. He knew he had to carry on.

When the little train came in, Johnny watched to see which carriage the nurses chose and then got into the other one. He was all alone. As the train rattled along, the scenery grew ever greener and more dramatic, with waterfalls gushing down rocky hills. Occasionally Johnny caught a glimpse of a mighty building nestling halfway up the valley. Part of it was made of sparkling glass, the rest of solid brown-grey stone. It had two towers: one tall and pointed with big white clock-faces on every side, and a stout square one with battlements on top, like a castle in a history book. Although it was early afternoon, the winter light was already fading, and the building looked sinister in the gloom. It must be Craig-y-Nos.

Chapter 34

AT CRAIG-Y-NOS

Penwyllt station was high on a windswept hill. There was no sign of the castle now, nor of any people apart from the station master and the group of nurses who had just got off the train. A cart was waiting to take them to Craig-y-Nos. Johnny buttoned up his coat, pulled down the big woolly hat that Hutch had insisted on lending him to keep warm, and followed the cart down the hill. The road twisted in huge loops, and Johnny managed to keep up by running in a straight line, taking short cuts through the bushes, ducking down so that he wouldn't be seen. He stayed outside the gates of the castle, watching as the cart turned into a courtyard and drew to a halt alongside a fountain in the shape of a golden bird. The driver helped the nurses climb down, and they ran inside, too busy with their bags and their gossip to notice a little boy in the shadows.

Close up, the castle looked friendlier than it had from a distance. As well as the two big towers there were smaller turrets, sloping roofs, and all sorts of out-buildings joined together with walls and arches. The windows were wide, not at all like the arrow-slits Johnny had expected (and even hoped for). They made the place look more like a country house than a fortress. Through the glass, Johnny could see that the rooms had electric lights, and warm fires in the grates. He walked round the outside and looked out across the valley. At the back of the castle the ground fell away steeply, and Johnny could hear rushing water down below. There must be a river at the bottom. It was almost dark now. Nurses were wheeling beds and chairs inside from the gardens. Even in early January they believed in exposing their patients to fresh air whenever they could. The beds seemed rather short. The chairs were small. All at once Johnny realized that Craig-y-Nos was a children's hospital. He was going to find it easier to blend in than he had expected.

Nevertheless, he was careful. He crouched in a corner of the courtyard, waiting for the nurses' chatter to die away before risking going inside. He saw a child shuffling along in the shadow of the wall. Like him, she was trying not to be seen, but his eyes were drawn towards her at once because of her shoes. They were far too big for her and the laces were undone, so she couldn't help making a clattering, dragging noise as she crossed the stone path to a back door. She wore a heavy coat over her pyjamas. That was the wrong size too. Its sleeves hung down past her hands, and the pockets were bulging. Johnny guessed that she'd been up to no good – that she'd borrowed someone else's clothes to sneak outside from one of the wards, and wouldn't want to be caught as she found her way back in. He followed several paces behind her, hoping that she would lead the way through parts of the building where no one would spot him either.

He tracked her from one corridor to another, past dormitories and treatment rooms, a laboratory, workshops and a kitchen. Through half-open doors he caught glimpses of nurses busying about their work, and he knew that sooner or later he was bound to be discovered, but he wanted to see as much of the hospital as he could before then, if only so that he could plan his route to make a quick getaway if he had to.

A sudden cry and a crash behind him made him instinctively spin round. Someone had dropped some plates. There was uproar in the kitchen, but the corridor was empty. He was safe. He hadn't been seen.

He turned back again. The girl had been startled by the smash as well, and she too had looked in the direction of the noise. Now she was staring at Johnny through her round glasses.

'Who are you?' she asked.

Johnny reached into his pocket for the J. W. Morgan envelope, ready with his explanation.

The girl interrupted: 'I've seen you before somewhere . . .'

As she spoke, Johnny recognized her too. 'Olwen?' he asked. 'What are you doing here? I'm Johnny. Johnny Swanson. You came to my school in Stambleton. I tried to find you . . .'

Olwen's words came out in a rush of excited surprise. 'You were nice to me there. You were the only one. Have you seen my family? Are they here too? I've been so worried. They don't tell us anything in this place, you know. We might as well be in prison. We're not allowed letters or anything like that. I've been hoping for so long that Mam and Dad would come to get me. Oh, what a relief that you're here now. There's nothing wrong with me, you know. My uncle should never have put me in here.'

Johnny was panicking. It was clear that Olwen didn't know that her parents and sister were dead;

even if she'd imagined the worst, she was frantically clinging to the idea that all was well. He knew he would have to tell her what had happened, but he couldn't find a way to begin. He tried first to explain that he hadn't come to Craig-y-Nos for her.

'I didn't even know you were here,' he said. 'I'm looking for someone else. But, Olwen, I have got some news.'

'About my family? You know how they are?'

'Yes,' he said, realizing instantly that he had accidentally given her hope.

'Are they coming for me? Have they sent you with a message?'

He stuttered something unintelligible, and was saved by the sound of footsteps. Olwen grabbed his arm and tugged him down some stone stairs. 'In here,' she whispered urgently, opening the door to a dark windowless room that smelled of antiseptic and damp. It was full of boxes, like Hutch's stockroom. Dismantled beds and bits and pieces of medical equipment were propped against the walls.

'No one will find us,' she said. 'They're all too scared to come in. Even some of the nurses think there's a ghost down here.' Olwen was giggling. 'They say it's where Madame Patti was laid to rest after she died.' She put on a dramatic voice: 'They embalmed the body on this very table.'

There was just enough light for Johnny to see Olwen hoisting herself up onto a marble slab in the middle of the room. She sat there with her feet swinging in mid air. 'Close the door,' she said. Johnny did, and they were suddenly in total darkness. One of Olwen's shoes fell off. Johnny gasped in fright.

Olwen laughed. 'Don't be silly. There's nothing to be scared of. I don't believe in ghosts – and even if they do exist, I think I'd like to meet one. I'd ask what it's like being dead. Wouldn't you?'

Johnny was glad Olwen couldn't see his face in the darkness. He hated hearing her talk so casually about death when he had such bad news for her.

She was badgering him for information. 'Come on, then. Tell me what's going on. But be quick, mind. I've got to get back to the ward before the nurses notice I'm missing.'

'Were you running away?'

'No, though I'd love to if I had anywhere to go. It was my turn to go down to the bins to see if there was any left-over food. I've got some stale cake here, and a bit of cheese rind if you want it.'

Johnny could hear her digging into her coat

pocket. 'Stop it, Olwen,' he said. 'Be quiet for a minute. This is no time for messing about with cake. I've got something serious to say.'

Olwen's tone changed. 'Is it the baby? They took her to the sanatorium, you know. Mam promised they would make her better.'

Johnny took a deep breath. Even in the darkness he could tell that Olwen had guessed part of the truth and didn't dare ask the question that was really on her mind. He forced himself to answer.

'I'm sorry, Olwen. Your sister died. I know that the doctors did everything in their power, but she was desperately ill. They couldn't save her.'

He waited for Olwen to ask more. He wanted her to prompt him to talk about her parents, but there was silence. 'I'm sorry. I'm really sorry,' he said. He was trying to speak normally, but his voice came out in breathy croaks. Olwen still didn't say anything, and Johnny knew he had to carry on. He swallowed hard. 'It's not just the baby,' he said. 'It's your mother and father.'

'Have they come to collect me? If the baby's dead, they don't need to spend all their time looking after her any more, do they? They can take me home now, can't they?'

'No, Olwen. They can't come.'

'Are they ill too? Is Dad still bad?'

'No, it's not that . . .' Johnny could tell he was making a mess of it, taking far too long to break the news, and dangling another moment of false hope. In the end he had to accept that there was no easy way to say it. 'Oh, Olwen, I'm so sorry. They died too.'

If he'd expected anything, he'd been prepared for tears; but Olwen was suddenly angry. 'No they're not. Don't lie. They're not,' she shouted. 'Someone would have told me.'

Johnny fumbled in the darkness for her hand. 'Please, Olwen, believe me. It *is* true. I've seen their graves. They both had TB, and they both died in the sanatorium at Emberley. I'm sure someone would have told you if they could, but I don't think anyone knew where to find you.'

'But you did.'

'No I didn't, Olwen. I tried to tell you before. I came here for another reason. Something really important.' He knew at once that it was the wrong thing to say.

Olwen snatched her hand away. 'Really important? How? My family are dead. What could be more important than that?' She was sniffing now. She must be crying.

'Important to me, I meant. And to my mother.' It seemed wrong to be changing the subject, but he wanted to explain. His words started tumbling out. 'There's someone here who might be able to save my mother's life. It's Mrs Langford. The old doctor's wife from Stambleton. Do you know her? Is she here? She might be calling herself Mrs Morgan.'

He could tell that Olwen wasn't really listening. She was sobbing quite loudly now. He wanted to comfort her, but didn't know how. He fumbled in the dark, trying to put his arm round her, but they both pulled away, startled at the sound of brisk footsteps on the stairs.

'We've been here too long! They're looking for me,' Olwen gasped through her tears as she slipped down from the table.

'Please, don't say that I'm here,' Johnny whispered back, fearing Olwen might tell on him in revenge for his bad news. He stumbled into a pile of boxes and curled up behind them, hoping that nothing would show if someone came looking.

The door swung open and the light from the stairway flung a huge silhouette of a nurse across the back wall. The points of her starched headdress looked like horns on an angry bull in the contorted image.

A fierce voice boomed out. 'Here you are! I might have known. You come out from there, young lady! This time you've gone too far!' Johnny heard Olwen sobbing as the furious nurse dragged her from under the table. 'I've had enough of you and your disobedience. Now stand up and stop that stupid crying!'

Through a gap in the boxes Johnny saw the nurse shaking Olwen, tearing off her overcoat and rummaging through its pockets.

'What's this? Cake! Cheese! Have you been thieving again?'

'No, not stealing. It doesn't belong to anyone. It's rubbish.'

'As if you don't get enough for nothing! You'd better watch your step, my girl, or you'll get thrown out. And then where will you be? That uncle of yours doesn't want you back, you know. If you ask me he's dumped you here, living off charity. Can't say that I blame him. Nobody would want you, you nasty, deceitful little madam!'

Johnny wished he could defend Olwen. He wanted to jump out and tell the nurse about Olwen's parents, and how she'd only just found out that she was all alone in the world. But he had to stay quiet. The nurse wasn't looking for him, and with luck she wouldn't spot his hiding place. But it hurt to hear Olwen under attack.

'I said stop that stupid grizzling!' The arm of the giant shadow rose and swung. There was the unmistakable sound of flesh striking flesh. 'Now, what have you got to say for yourself?'

Olwen sobbed and started to speak. 'It's my mam and dad. And my sister—' she began, but the nurse was in no mood to listen.

'I don't want excuses. You've been here long enough to get over homesickness. Stop that snivelling and tell me where you got this food.'

Olwen was shaking with tears as the nurse slapped at the thin fabric of her pyjamas.

'You've been rooting through the dustbins, haven't you? You're just a greedy, stinking animal. No better than a pig.'

Olwen's next breath, caught up in tears and snot, came out as a noisy snort.

The nurse held the coat in the air. 'And what about this? It looks like Dr Howell's. Did you take it from the staff cloakroom? You know you're not allowed to go in there.'

Olwen sniffed. The nurse picked one shoe up off the floor and wrenched the other from Olwen's foot.

'You're coming with me to take these things back straight away. And since you like delving in dirt so much, you can spend the rest of the day scrubbing the outside toilets. You can start with the boys'. You'll miss all the fun and games tonight, you nasty, scheming, ungrateful child!'

Olwen tried to speak, then bowed her head and left the room. The nurse followed her and slammed the door behind them, shutting Johnny in the dark again.

Chapter 35

THE THEATRE

Johnny was furious with himself for saying nothing while Olwen was being attacked by the nurse. He made a silent promise that he would try to sort out Olwen's predicament as soon as he'd completed his own mission. Then he waited until there was no sound from the other side of the door, and crept out into the corridor to search for Mrs Langford.

He could hear the angry nurse again, shouting somewhere in the distance. There were other noises too. He knew that only luck had stopped him being discovered already. After seeing how the nurse had treated Olwen, he doubted whether anyone would give him a chance to explain why he was there. Every time he turned a corner he dreaded walking into a potential captor. Each creak and footfall was amplified in the part of his mind where terror lived.

Then, all at once, he found himself in a corridor with a dead end. He could hear footsteps: brisk, feminine footsteps, closing in behind him. Someone was coming, and there was no way out. Panicking, he rehearsed his cover story: how he was there to find a Mrs J. W. Morgan – how he had brought her an important message that he had promised to deliver in private and in person. As the clicking of high-heeled shoes grew nearer, he flattened his body against the wall.

Except it wasn't a wall. He was leaning on a pair of double doors that slowly began to give way under the pressure of his back. The footsteps were getting nearer, so he allowed himself to slip through into the dark unknown on the other side.

His eyes started adjusting. He could tell that this was a huge space, like the assembly hall at school. Then the doors opened again, swiftly and deliberately this time, and he squashed himself behind one of them as somebody came in. With the clunk of a heavy switch, there was a blast of light that blinded him for an instant. He blinked, then sneaked a look round the side of the door, trying to keep himself out of sight. With the lights on, the hall was transformed into a glorious theatre. Its blue walls and ivory ceiling were heavy with golden images of angels and harps. The flat curtain across the wide stage was decorated with a gigantic painting of a warrior queen in a chariot pulled through the clouds by two white horses. At first Johnny was stunned; then he remembered what Hutch had told him: a famous opera singer had built a theatre as part of this grand house before it became a sanatorium.

A woman was shuffling between rows and rows of chairs, setting down a sheet of paper on each seat. Johnny recognized her straight away. He had known that upswept hair, the long graceful neck and those elegant movements all his life. It was Marie Langford. He couldn't believe his luck and ran towards her. 'Mrs Langford!' he cried. 'I've found you.'

She looked at him with horror and disbelief. 'Johnny?' she gasped. 'What on earth are you doing here?'

'I had to find you, Mrs Langford. You must help me. Mrs Langford, it's awful. They think my mother killed your husband. She's in prison, Mrs Langford. She might die!' He hugged her tightly, burying his face in the rough tweed of her suit.

She pulled his arms away and sat down on one of the chairs. 'Be quiet, Johnny,' she said, looking anxiously around to make sure that no one else was in earshot. 'And don't call me Mrs Langford. No one here calls me that. If you let them know who I really am, we could both be in a lot of trouble.'

'So you are J. W. Morgan, then?'

'What? How do you know that?'

Johnny took the crumpled envelope out of his pocket and handed it to her. 'Change Your Appearance Permanently,' he said. 'You answered that advert. Mrs Langford, I know you want a disguise.'

Mrs Langford sat in silence, turning over the envelope while Johnny burbled on. 'I knew it was you. And I've worked it all out. Someone is holding you prisoner here, aren't they, Mrs Langford? That's why you need the disguise, isn't it? You want to escape.'

Mrs Langford was still for a few more seconds, then nodded, gazing down at the letter. 'Tell me more, Johnny,' she said quietly. 'Tell me everything you know.'

'Well, I know that my mother didn't kill Dr Langford for a start—' He stopped suddenly, remembering Olwen's reaction to unexpected news. 'Oh, Mrs Langford. I'm sorry. Forgive me. Did you know? Your husband is dead.'

She didn't raise her head, but nodded, and whispered, 'Yes, Johnny. I know.'

'He was murdered, Mrs Langford. While you were in France—'

'In France?' She paused and mumbled, 'Oh yes . . .'

Johnny was getting excited and talking more quickly. 'And the police think my mother did it. But she didn't, and you can tell them she didn't. The police won't take any notice of me. But they'll listen to you. You know she'd never do a thing like that, don't you?'

Mrs Langford said nothing.

'Help me, Mrs Langford. Tell the police it was nothing to do with my mother. You must know it wasn't. And you must have some idea who it was. I've worked that out too. It must have been somebody who knew about the BCG. Was it the Umckaloabo man? Was it somebody here? There was a Welshman who warned me to stop looking for you. Is it him, Mrs Langford? Did he kill your husband? Is that why he's hiding you here? To keep you quiet?'

Mrs Langford pulled Johnny close to her and whispered urgently, 'Johnny, you're the one who had better keep quiet, or you are going to make things very difficult for both of us.' She split her pile of papers in two and handed him half. 'Come on. Help me put these out on the seats, and I'll try to explain.'

291

Johnny took a look at the heading on the top sheet. It read:

THE STAFF OF CRAIG-Y-NOS PRESENT
CINDERELLA

He understood now why the nurse had told Olwen she'd be missing 'fun and games'. 'A pantomime? Is there going to be a pantomime?' he asked.

'Yes, Johnny. Tonight everyone at Craig-y-Nos will be in this hall. It's a special treat. Now, come on. I haven't got long to finish getting things ready.'

They walked between the rows putting out the programmes, and Mrs Langford began. 'As you know, my husband was doing some important work to do with TB. One of his old students, Dr Howell, was producing the BCG vaccine for him – here, in the laboratory.'

Dr Howell. Johnny had heard that name just a few minutes earlier. Olwen had been wearing his coat and shoes.

Mr Langford continued: 'My husband got him some of the original culture, and told him how to do it.'

Johnny's mind ran on. 'And then Dr Howell got jealous, and killed your husband so he could pretend the vaccine was all his own work.'

'Oh Johnny, what a clever boy you are,' said Mrs Langford. 'But it was worse than that. You see, Dr Howell wanted to sell the vaccine.'

'Like the Umckaloabo man? The man who put that advert in the paper!'

'Yes, Johnny. Just like him. But of course Dr Howell couldn't advertise BCG openly because it was against the law for him to have it. So he planned to frighten people into thinking their children might die if they weren't immunized, and then to charge them a fortune to buy the BCG secretly. He was going to target rich people. He knew they'd pay him a lot of money if he promised not to tell anyone that they'd used an illegal vaccine.'

'So it was a kind of blackmail too?' said Johnny. 'Dr Langford wouldn't have liked that.'

'No indeed,' said Mrs Langford. 'My husband wanted the vaccine given free to all children, just as it is in France. He was terribly shocked when he found out about Dr Howell's plans. He protested, and he paid with his life.'

Johnny interrupted her. 'So Dr Howell was waiting

for your husband when he got back from France. Waiting to kill him, so he couldn't spoil his plans. I guessed ages ago that it must be something like that,' he said, triumphantly. 'I tried to tell the police, but they just wouldn't listen. But surely you could have told them?'

'No, Johnny. I haven't been at liberty for a moment since my husband died. This man, this Dr Howell . . . he watches over me all the time. I have to stay in his cottage overnight, and in the daytime I work here as a secretary. He got me the job so he could guard me round the clock. He's told them I'm his aunt—'

'Mrs J. W. Morgan!' said Johnny, understanding instantly how a fictitious aunt could be useful. 'I see it all now.'

'Exactly,' said Mrs Langford. 'So that's it. I'm trapped.'

Johnny jumped in, thrilled that his theory was proving to be correct, and Mrs Langford nodded in agreement as he babbled through the story. 'He knew where to find you in France, he brought you here so you couldn't tell anyone about him, and he's been keeping you prisoner ever since. Which is why you wanted the disguise. You wanted to get away . . .'

'Yes. About that, Johnny. I don't really understand. How are you connected to that advertisement?'

Before Johnny could reply, a man in a white coat strode in through the double doors. He shuffled from foot to foot anxiously, nibbling at his fingernails.

'Get a move on,' he said roughly. 'We haven't got much time.' Johnny listened hard. Was this the same man who had threatened him on the phone at the post office? He wasn't sure. The accent was the same, but no doubt lots of people in Wales spoke like that. The man continued, getting more agitated: 'One of the nurses held me up. Some nonsense about a girl stealing my coat. I could have done without that, today of all days. Anyway, it's up to you to make sure this panto starts on time. Are you absolutely sure that everyone is coming?'

'Yes, of course, Dr Howell,' said Mrs Langford, and Johnny froze beside her. Now that he'd heard the name, he was certain that he was in the presence of a murderer.

Mrs Langford kept her composure. She took the remaining programmes out of Johnny's arms. 'Thank you for your help, son,' she said, as if he were one of the patients and had simply been lending her a hand. 'I'll finish off here. You run along, now.' She bent down and added in a whisper, 'Come and find me in the office after the show has started.'

Johnny turned to leave. 'Of course, Mrs Morgan,' he said at the top of his voice, trying to give Dr Howell the impression that he was just another inmate. He was grateful to Mrs Langford for giving him a chance to get away from the menacing man; and he was determined to make good use of the time before he saw her again. He set off to find the outside toilets, and Olwen, who would by now be scrubbing them out as her punishment.

Chapter 36

IN THE TOILETS

It wasn't hard to find the boys' toilets. Johnny needed only to follow his nose. This might be a hospital, but boys in a hurry could lower the tone of a lavatory anywhere. The smell was familiar from school, and the chilly brick block was very similar to the grim outdoor shack in the playground back in Stambleton. At least here there were electric lights, though all they did was show up the chipped surface of the long porcelain trough that served as a urinal, the rude words and pictures scraped into the peeling paint of the cubicle doors, and the muddy footmarks swirling in the stinking liquid on the grey stone floor. There were even footprints on the ceiling. Johnny worked out how they'd got there. A thick pipe crossed the room high up above the doorway. If you swung on it and kicked really hard, you could hit the roof. He was tempted to have a go, but this was not the time.

Olwen, still in her pyjamas, was in the far corner,

297

on her knees with a bucket, sniffing in time to the rhythm of her scrubbing brush. She didn't respond to Johnny at first.

'Olwen?' he said. 'It's me. Johnny. Olwen! I need your help.'

Gradually her scrubbing slowed and she looked up, pushing a stray strand of hair out of her eyes with the back of her wrist. 'Why should I want to help you? Why should I want to help anyone? All my people are dead, and no one here cares. They don't even want to know anything about it.'

'I care, Olwen,' said Johnny. 'I really do. And there's someone else too. She's bound to want to help you. I tried to tell you before. It's Mrs Langford, the doctor's wife from Stambleton. Or widow, I should say.'

'I don't know what you're talking about.'

'Do you remember the doctor who came to take your sister off to the sanatorium?'

'Of course I do. He's the one who sent me back to Wales. He said it was for my own good. But my uncle didn't want a child in the house, and he was scared that I was bringing germs with me. So as soon as I caught a cold, he put me in here and then he moved away. Do I remember that doctor? If it wasn't for him

I'd never have been dumped here. I wish he was dead.'

'He *is* dead, Olwen,' said Johnny. 'I've been trying to tell you about it ever since I got here. Dr Langford was murdered.'

'Serves him right.'

'Olwen! How can you say that? He was a nice man. He was good to me, and I know he must have thought he was doing the best for you.' Johnny told Olwen about the murder. 'Anyway,' he said, drawing his explanation to a close, 'Dr Langford's wife is here. She's calling herself Mrs Morgan, and she's the person I've been looking for.'

'So?' Olwen was still dazed by her own news.

'Mrs Langford's in trouble, Olwen. We have to help her. There's a man called Dr Howell. He's the real murderer, and he's holding her prisoner.'

'Dr Howell?' Olwen was shocked. 'But he's really kind. He didn't make a fuss at all when the nurse told him I'd taken his coat. I think she was really disappointed. She says she's going to report me to Professor Campbell instead.'

'Who?'

'Professor Campbell. He's in charge of the whole hospital. The nurse said she'll recommend a very severe punishment.'

'I'm sorry about that, Olwen, but if you ask me, Dr Howell's only pretending to be pleasant. Mrs Langford seemed really scared of him. Your problem with Professor Campbell isn't nearly as serious as what he might do to her.'

'But what's that got to do with me? Or you, for that matter?'

'I told you. Everyone thinks my mother killed Dr Langford. She's in prison, and only Mrs Langford can put her in the clear. If she doesn't, do you know what will happen to my mother?'

'Just think yourself lucky you've got a mother,' snarled Olwen. '*I* haven't. Not any more!' She started crying, and Johnny knelt down on the wet floor to try to comfort her.

'I know,' he said, 'and I'm truly sorry. But if I don't do something to stop it, my mother will be found guilty. Do you know what that means? It means that they'll hang her. They'll make her stand with a noose round her neck and then they'll open a trapdoor so that she falls through and is strangled by the rope. Her body will be left swinging there, dead, and afterwards she'll be buried in an unmarked grave. And then I won't have a mother either. Is that what you want? I'm sorry you've lost your family, but why should I lose my mother too? You must be able to imagine how that will make me feel.'

Olwen's voice softened. 'I dare say I can.'

'Then help me.'

'How? What on earth can I do? I'm stuck here scrubbing the floor.'

'We've got to call the police. And we must go to that man – that Professor Campbell you talked about. We can tell him the truth about Dr Howell. But the police first. We need a telephone. Do you know if they have one here?'

'There must be one in the office, I suppose. I don't know. I've never been in there.'

'But you know where the office is, don't you?'

'Of course I do.'

'Well, show me, please. I've got to meet Mrs Langford there after the pantomime's started. If I get there first I can use the phone before she comes. And while I'm doing that, you can find Professor Campbell and tell him that Mrs Langford – Mrs Morgan – is in danger. Say that he's got to protect her from Dr Howell.'

Olwen tried to protest: 'He won't take any notice of me. If that nurse has already told him about the coat, he'll think I'm just trying to get out of trouble.'

Johnny was desperate. 'But he might believe you. Olwen, you're my only hope. There may not be time for me to phone the police *and* find Professor Campbell. I don't even know what he looks like. Please. Do this for me, and when we've dealt with Dr Howell – or even if it all goes wrong and I get caught – I'll tell the professor everything that's happened to you. I promise. I'll make sure he does something about it. Now come on. I've got to make that phone call.'

'All right,' Olwen sighed. 'I'll show you the way to the office. Then I'll try to find Professor Campbell. But we haven't got long for that, either. He's in the pantomime, you know. He's one of the Ugly Sisters. He's probably getting into his costume now.' She dropped her scrubbing brush into the bucket and Johnny helped her to her feet. 'Follow me,' she said. 'It's dark enough for us to take a short cut across the courtyard. But keep your head down. We don't want anyone to see that we're there.'

Chapter 37

THE OFFICE

Johnny and Olwen cut across the yard. Olwen pulled him into the bushes beneath the office window. 'Lift me up,' she said. 'I'll look in and see if there's anybody there.'

'Climb on my back,' said Johnny, crouching down in the mud; and Olwen stepped on him and pulled her chin up to the level of the windowsill.

'The lights are off,' she whispered. 'There's nobody inside. But there is a telephone. I can see it on the desk by the typewriter.'

'Right. Tell me which door it is and I'll go in,' said Johnny.

'What if it's locked?' said Olwen. 'And what if someone sees you in the corridor?'

'I could go in through the window. Can you get it open if I raise you a bit higher?'

Olwen pushed at the window, and it started to lift up.

'Swap over,' said Johnny. 'I'll stand on you and climb in.'

Neither of them was very big, but somehow they managed to launch Johnny over the sill. He dropped down onto the floor inside the room. As soon as he landed he knew it would be hard to climb back out. But he'd deal with that later. The important thing now was to phone the police. He picked up the receiver and dialled the operator. It seemed to take ages for the mechanism to click and whir its way to a connection, but at least that gave him time for a brainwave. He breathed deeply, and when a response came from the other end he spoke calmly, in his most adult high-pitched voice:

'Hello. My name is Mrs Ada Fortune. I'm calling on behalf of Professor Campbell at the Craig-y-Nos sanatorium. We need the police here on a matter of the greatest urgency and importance.'

The operator wanted more details.

'I'm afraid I am not at liberty to go into the particulars. Suffice it to say that this is a matter of life and death. Hurry, please.'

Johnny slammed down the receiver, hoping that would help convince the operator that something serious had happened, and rushed to the door. Olwen was right. It was locked. He dragged the chair from the desk to the window, but it swivelled beneath him when he tried to jump up, and without Olwen to give him a push he couldn't manoeuvre his body over the sill. He looked around for something higher and more stable to climb on. There was only the desk; but it was at least three times the size of his kitchen table at home and, with rows of drawers on both sides, far too heavy for Johnny to pull across the room.

He was stuck there. He turned on the desk lamp and looked around, hopelessly searching for another way out. It was a drab, functional place. There was a bookcase full of files, an etching of the King on the wall, and a notice board covered with lists of staff and their rotas. Johnny saw that Dr Howell was on duty that night. Alongside was a newspaper cutting about a huge donation raised for the hospital in a local collection at Christmas. Johnny's eye was naturally pulled to the small ads at the side of the page. A sheepdog needed a new home. Someone else was selling an unused wedding dress. And then he saw it: his own advert, *Change Your Appearance Permanently*. That must be where Mrs Langford had seen it. It explained why she hadn't answered the personal message in the same edition appealing for news of her whereabouts. That must have been printed on a different page.

There was nothing Johnny could do except wait for

Mrs Langford to come. He pulled the chair back to the desk and sat down, wondering whether to phone Hutch, if only to let him know that he was safe (so far), but that would mean talking to the operator again, and he didn't want her to get suspicious. The desk was littered with piles of paper. There were brown envelopes, just like the one Mrs Langford had sent to Johnny, and leaflets everywhere, some in English, some in French. All of them seemed to be about TB. Many were annotated in Mrs Langford's snail-shell handwriting. It reassured him that he was in the right place. This definitely was her office. What a relief! With luck, it wouldn't be long before the police arrived and she could tell them the truth about the murder. Dr Howell would be arrested, and Mrs Langford and his mother would both be safe. Johnny leaned over to read the sheet of paper that was sticking out of the typewriter. It was headed *The War Against Tuberculosis*. On the next line it said:

Future Mothers! Young Housewives! Did you know that Tuberculosis kills 25 per cent of infants born to parents with the disease, or growing up in infected surroundings?

Johnny turned the wheel at the side of the machine so that more of the writing would show.

It also kills, sooner or later, many children born of healthy parents, and brought up in healthy households.

But did you know that there is something you can do to protect your children?

You can VACCINATE them.

He recognized the style. He had read claims like that about everything from tonic wine to disinfectant. He guessed that Mrs Langford was typing an advertisement. Dr Howell must be making her do it as part of his plan to sell the BCG vaccine. Johnny wanted to read more.

Then he heard a voice outside. It was Mrs Langford. She had come, as she had promised, to meet him there. He'd just have to explain that he'd climbed through the window because the door was locked. She would understand. But as she turned the key he heard someone else; and he recognized that voice too. Dr Howell was with her. There was no way he would forgive Johnny for breaking in. There was only one place to hide. Johnny turned off the lamp and slid down from the chair. As Mrs Langford switched on the main light, he crawled into the arched footwell under her desk. It smelled of furniture polish, perfume and shoes.

'What's that window doing open?' said Mrs Langford, striding across the room. 'I could have sworn I closed it earlier.'

Dr Howell laughed. 'Maybe Professor Campbell's been in. You know what a demon he is for the healing power of fresh air.'

Johnny was surprised at how friendly they sounded. Mrs Langford chatted happily as she shut the window, 'Well, I'm not ill,' she said, 'and I don't like a draught.'

'I see you've got the leaflets done,' said Dr Howell.

Mrs Langford sat at the typewriter. Johnny had to squash himself even deeper into the tight space to make sure she couldn't feel him with her feet. He hoped she'd have the presence of mind to say nothing if she realized he was there. He listened hard. He couldn't see anything now. Mrs Langford's legs blocked off what little light had come through the arch, and the footwell had no opening on the side facing the door. But at least that meant no one could see Johnny.

'Here you are,' said Mrs Langford. 'I've just finished

the last translation.' The typewriter gave a mechanical ripping noise as she pulled out the page. 'You see. There's nothing to worry about. Everything's ready to go.'

'Just as well,' said Dr Howell, sounding anxious. 'Time's running out. Are you certain that absolutely everyone will be in the theatre?'

'Of course. That's the whole point, isn't it? It took me ages to talk Professor Campbell into including the entire staff. Mind you, I convinced *myself* in the end. It's silly to have a beautiful theatre and not to make use of it. And it's true: nothing will make the children laugh louder than the sight of all the doctors and nurses dressed up in silly costumes. Old Campbell thinks you've made a real sacrifice, offering to be the only doctor on call. You've done yourself some good there.'

Johnny was confused. Why was Mrs Langford being so nice to Dr Howell? Why did she seem so relaxed, and he so nervous? It sounded as if they were planning to do something while the pantomime was on; but what?

The corridor outside started to fill with childish chatter and the rattle of beds being wheeled into the theatre. Johnny could hear Dr Howell pacing the room and muttering.

'I wish they'd hurry up,' said the doctor. 'We need everyone out of the way.'

'Calm down,' said Mrs Langford. 'And for goodness' sake stop biting your nails. Now listen. Don't be alarmed, but there's something else we've got to deal with first.'

'What?' said Howell, clearly annoyed. 'There's little enough time as it is.'

'Remember that boy you saw me with in the theatre?'

'The one who was helping you with the programmes? Not really. I wasn't taking much notice.'

'Well, he's coming here in a minute.'

'What! Why?'

Johnny couldn't understand. Why was Mrs Langford talking about him?

'He's not one of the patients. He's from Stambleton—'

'What! Have you lost your senses?' Dr Howell thumped his fist on the desk somewhere near Johnny's head.

'I said calm down. We can deal with him. He's come here looking for me.'

'But how did he find you?'

'Never mind that. He doesn't know anything, I'm

pretty sure of that. He's got it into his head that you are holding me here against my will.' She giggled. 'He wants to rescue me!'

'Why on earth . . . ?'

'He's the son of that cleaner. The one they've arrested. He wants me to go to the police, to prove that she didn't do it.'

Under the desk, Johnny was beginning to panic. Why was Mrs Langford telling Dr Howell so much? How could she be so stupid? Even though he couldn't see Howell, Johnny could tell that he was jumpy. Maybe he'd strike out if things didn't go his way. Couldn't Mrs Langford imagine what he might do to them both; especially with everyone else out of the way?

Dr Howell's next words started the awful explanation forming in his mind. 'So he doesn't know the truth?'

'Absolutely not, it seems. It's rather sweet really, little Johnny coming all this way to ask me, of all people, to help his mother. He has no idea how important it is for us that the police think she did it.'

'But where is he?' asked Dr Howell. 'What have you done with the boy?'

'Nothing, yet,' said Mrs Langford, 'but I've asked

him to meet me here once the pantomime has started. He should come any time now.'

'Have you gone mad? We don't want anyone around—'

'He won't be here for long. Or he needn't be, if you've got the courage to do something about him.' Her next words terrified Johnny. 'A little injection perhaps? It would only take a jiffy.'

Chapter 38

DEATHWATCH

Dr Howell sounded shocked. 'Now look – I can't just—'

Mrs Langford's voice grew cold and stern. 'But you have to. There's no alternative. We can't risk him surviving. He's determined to save his mother. He might start asking questions.'

Johnny was frozen with fright. All he could see was Mrs Langford's legs, casually crossed at the ankles, with one foot twirling in circles as she calmly plotted his death.

'But we can't. It's not that simple. For one thing, we'll have to deal with the body.' Howell sounded horrified.

'And can you think of a better place in the world to do that? We've got sheets and blankets, wheelchairs, trolleys, miles of parkland and a rushing river. Even a drip like you could make someone disappear here!'

Howell lurched round the desk and grabbed Mrs Langford, pulling her up out of her chair. Johnny could tell by the way her feet twisted and rose onto tiptoe that Howell was using all his might against her; but her voice stayed strong as she took control, saying icily, 'The boy might walk in at any moment. Is this what you want him to see? It's no more than he'd expect, you know. He thinks you're out to hurt me. He'd run straight off to get help.'

Howell slackened his grip, and Mrs Langford's feet steadied again.

'Look, we haven't got much time,' she said. 'Have you got a key to the dispensary?'

'Of course.'

Mrs Langford walked over to the door and listened. 'It's all quiet out there. Everyone's in the theatre now.' She spoke with great authority. 'Go quickly and get something that will do the trick straight away. I'll keep him here if he arrives before you get back. Don't worry. He trusts me. He thinks he's protecting me. He has no idea that he's the one who's in danger.'

But of course Johnny now knew only too well, and under the table he was quaking.

Dr Howell opened the door to leave, and the sound of the pantomime overture burst into the room, followed by joyous laughter as the Ugly Sisters took to the stage. For a moment, Johnny contemplated the idea of coming out from his hiding place while Mrs Langford was alone. He might be able to reason with her, or to overpower her and run away. But he couldn't be sure. She might grab him and hold him till Dr Howell got back with whatever he was collecting from the dispensary. He couldn't take the risk. Shivering and sweating with fear, he curled up even tighter as Mrs Langford returned to her chair and stretched out her legs. The toe of her shoe was a hair's-breadth from his face. He dared not breathe too deeply in case she felt the warm damp air against her skin.

Then the door handle rattled, and she was on her feet again as a burst of hisses from the theatre accompanied Dr Howell's return.

'OK,' he said. 'But this boy of yours had better come soon. We haven't got long, remember.'

Johnny heard clinking glass, and things being put down on the desk, just above his head. He pictured jars of poison and hypodermic needles waiting for his arrival in the room.

Mrs Langford was calmly planning out how the ambush would work. 'You stand behind the door,' she said to Howell, 'then I'll coax him over here. You can grab him from behind. It will all be over in an instant.'

Dr Howell and Mrs Langford stopped talking. They

waited for Johnny with only the faint sounds of *Oohs* and *Aahs* from the pantomime to break their silence. All Johnny could do was try to stay still, and hope that somehow something would happen to make him safe.

Eventually Dr Howell spoke. 'I thought you said the boy was on his way,' he snapped, from his position beside the door.

'He'll come,' said Mrs Langford. 'He's probably just making sure the coast is clear.'

Under the table, Johnny's terror was mixed with curiosity. He still wanted to know what it was that Mrs Langford and Dr Howell had originally been planning to do while the pantomime was on. It was obvious that Mrs Langford had organized the play simply to make sure that the two of them could be alone together. They kept saying that there wasn't much time, and that they had to get Johnny out of the way first. But before what? What were they talking about?

After a few minutes, as a song struck up in the theatre, Dr Howell started pacing again. 'Come on! Come on, boy!' he muttered impatiently. He started rearranging the paraphernalia of death on the desk. Every shuffle and clink made Johnny's heart thump harder. Then Dr Howell rushed back over to the door. 'He's here!' he cried.

'Oh my goodness!' said Mrs Langford, flustered for the first time that night.

Under the desk Johnny wondered what they meant. Suppose it was Olwen, come to report back to Johnny and Mrs Langford on her mission to Professor Campbell? There was no way Johnny could warn her – nothing he could do to stop her entering the room. *Please, Olwen*, he prayed. *Please don't come in!* He heard the squeak of the handle, and a chorus of 'Look behind you!' from the children at the pantomime as the door opened. He felt sick, expecting a scream as Dr Howell grabbed Olwen and administered the poison.

Instead, a man spoke. *The police! Of course! It's the police. They've come!* thought Johnny as a wave of relief swept over him. But no. It didn't sound like a policeman.

'Hello, you two.'

Johnny knew that voice. He'd heard it on Remembrance Day and again the day after Dr Langford's body was discovered.

'That was a hell of a drive! Got anything to drink?'

It was the voice of Johnny's landlord, Frederick Bennett. But what on earth was Mr Bennett doing at Craig-y-Nos?

Chapter 39

A MATTER OF PRINCIPLE

Back in Stambleton, Hutch had closed up the shop for the night. He was on his way upstairs to the flat when the doorbell rang. Hutch limped back down and pulled on the string of the brown roller-blind that covered the glass in the front door. It snapped up to reveal a policeman. Hutch's thoughts went straight to Johnny. He unlocked the door and let the officer in. He was relieved that the policeman hadn't brought bad news – or at least not bad news of that type.

The officer took off his helmet and addressed Hutch in a portentous tone. 'Mr Hutchinson, I regret to say that I have been sent to investigate a very serious matter.'

'I'll be delighted to assist you, Officer, if I can. I have been trying to help for some time, but have received only rebuffs.'

'This is not about the murder, sir. We have received a complaint.'

'A complaint? About me?'

'Not about you, sir. About one of your customers.'

'Which one? Who? What have they done?'

'I can tell you, sir, that this is an allegation of fraud. Of obtaining money by deception. But I'm afraid I cannot tell you the name of the culprit.'

'I quite understand if it is a matter of confidentiality. But how can I help?'

'It's not a question of propriety, sir. I'm not telling you the name because I do not know it myself. That is why I have come to you.'

'I don't understand. I have hundreds of customers,' said Hutch, adding, under his breath, *Or I did have until recently*. 'I'm afraid I know little of what they do outside this shop. I certainly am not aware of anyone trying to defraud me.'

'As far as I know, you have not been defrauded, sir. But I think you will sympathize with the victim if I tell you the nature of the evidence. The complainant asserts that he has twice sent money to someone using a private postal box at this post office – and both times he has been the victim of a trick.' The policeman consulted his notebook. 'The complainant paid sixpence to find out how to save money on tea. Fair enough, you might think. In this day and age we're all looking for ways to make economies, and the gentleman was hoping to be put in touch with a supplier charging reasonable prices. All he got was advice that he should "stop using sugar and milk". He might have overlooked that, had he not received another note, in the same handwriting, when he paid a shilling for an appliance to take the backache out of cutting his toenails. That note said, "Get someone else to do it for you." '

Of course, Hutch knew immediately what the policeman was talking about, but he wasn't going to let on. He waited for the officer to say more.

'Now, I have been given the number of this private box,' said the policeman. 'It is the link between the two advertisements, and I am asking you to tell me the identity of the person who has rented it. Then I will be able to proceed with my enquiries.'

Hutch paused. He was in no doubt what his reply should be, and it would be the same whether the matter involved Johnny or not. 'I'm sorry. I can't help you,' he said.

'But surely you know who holds this box? No doubt they come in here to collect their mail?'

'I dare say they do. And I dare say I know the name. But I have to tell you that his, or her, identity is a matter between that person and the Post Office.'

'But this is a serious allegation.'

'That's as may be. And if it is serious enough, no doubt you can persuade a judge to issue you with a warrant permitting you to acquire the information you seek. But until then, I'm afraid my duty is to protect it.'

The policeman was beginning to get cross. 'But, Mr Hutchinson, you are already co-operating with us over Dr Langford's mail. You've let me and my colleagues examine that every morning.'

'May I remind you, Officer, that Dr Langford was murdered? Now, that *is* a serious matter. And of course, Dr Langford is dead. His relationship with the Post Office is now profoundly altered.'

'But be reasonable, man. The chances are that we'll get to the bottom of this fiddle, if fiddle it be, in the end anyway. We'll just find out sooner if we don't have to go through the rigmarole of getting the courts involved. Come on, Mr Hutchinson. It's PO Box number nine. Now, you know whose box it is, don't you?'

Hutch tried not to let his face show a thing.

The policeman tried again. 'Is it somebody local, or someone passing through?'

Again, Hutch stood silent.

'Am I going to have to take this higher?'

'It seems so. Officer, if you had paid for me to protect your privacy, I expect you would want me to keep my word?'

The policeman was exasperated now. He turned to go. 'I will be consulting my superiors. I'd rather you didn't leave the premises, Mr Hutchinson. I may be back before too long.'

'Certainly, Officer,' said Hutch. 'I was not planning to go out, anyway, and that is why I will be here. I think that if you ask your superiors you will find that you have no more right to restrict my movements than you have to demand the information you desire. We will talk again when you have satisfied yourself as to the legal position.'

The policeman left, muttering under his breath. He was fed up with Hutch and his pomposity. What right had he to be so proud, when he'd taken in that kid – the son of a killer?

Chapter 40

CONSPIRATORS

'What do you mean, a complication?' shouted Mr Bennett.

Mrs Langford tried to explain. 'There's a boy,' she said calmly. 'He's come here from Stambleton. He's Winnie Swanson's son. He's been looking for me.'

'What! How on earth did he find you?'

'I don't know. But he's coming to this room at any moment, and we're ready for him.'

Johnny could imagine her motioning towards the deadly drug waiting on the desk.

'Look, I don't need to be part of anything like that,' said Bennett. 'You deal with the boy. Give me the next batch of vaccine and you can have your share of the money for the last lot. Get a move on. I don't want to hang around.'

'Here's the box,' said Howell.

There were two thuds on the desk. Bennett had thrown down a couple of packets of money. 'There you are. Not a bad piece of work, eh? The whole batch gone. You were right, Marie. We can hook in customers every way. We can play on them as rebels who want something illegal; or as social climbers after something no one else has got; or as anxious parents worried that their babies might get sick. I tell you, by the time I've finished with them, they're scared *not* to buy it. I could do with those leaflets you promised me, though. I need to make the medical details more convincing. Some people prefer things in black and white.'

'Here they are,' said Mrs Langford. 'It's word-for-word what they say in France. She declaimed the first sentence grandly: '*Faites préserver vos enfants contre la tuberculose par le vaccin BCG* . . . Save your children from TB with the BCG vaccine. I've copied out the whole thing – except for this bit here of course.'

Bennett read out a sentence in a schoolboy French accent. '*Délivré gratuitement par l'institut Pasteur sur demande du médecin ou de la sage-femme.*'

Mrs Langford translated it for him: 'Delivered for free by the Pasteur Institute at the request of a doctor or midwife.'

Bennett laughed, but Howell was serious.

'It should be free,' he said. 'I never wanted to charge for it.' Bennett groaned as Howell continued, 'This doesn't feel right. I only helped Dr Langford because he wanted to save lives, and now we're exploiting people.'

Johnny was beginning to work out what was going on. Perhaps he'd been wrong about Howell. Maybe he had never meant to get involved. It was *Bennett* who was at the heart of the sales scheme, and Bennett was so clever that he was even giving Howell and Mrs Langford some of the takings so they would share his guilt.

But Johnny shuddered when Mrs Langford's voice broke in, with a sarcastic ring. 'Forgive me, Doctor, but I don't see you turning down your share of the proceeds. And why are you so high-minded about human life all of a sudden?' Johnny heard her pick up a glass jar from the desk. 'Look at this, Bennett,' she hissed. 'When you came in, our saintly friend, the doctor, was preparing to kill somebody!'

'I told you. I don't want to know about that,' said Bennett. 'I'm off.'

Johnny heard Howell step aside, blocking Bennett's path to the door.

'Don't go yet,' said Howell. 'I want to know what to do about the boy.'

'I've told you what to do,' said Mrs Langford. 'We haven't any choice.'

'But won't someone come looking for him?' said Howell. 'Maybe he told someone he was coming here.'

'Will you stop worrying!' said Mrs Langford. 'He's alone, I'm sure of it. And better still, he's told me that the police won't listen to him. Even the boy himself is convinced that I was in France at the time of the murder. That letter you made me write seems to have done a good job, Bennett.'

Johnny was trembling in his hiding place, sure now that he and his mother were both doomed. He was still trying to make sense of what Mrs Langford was saying.

Dr Howell was bemused too. 'What letter?' he said. 'What have you two been up to behind my back?'

'Don't be so dramatic,' sneered Bennett. 'We haven't been keeping anything from you. We had to do something to fill in a few gaps. It was our own fault. We didn't think things through properly at the beginning, when you made the Langfords come here in such a rush . . .'

'I had to,' said Howell. 'The culture wasn't growing properly. I needed Dr Langford's help, or we'd never have got the vaccine going.' He sounded close to tears. 'But neither of us wanted to sell it. It was just you two!'

'But you're in on it now, Howell,' said Bennett. 'You've already supplied the stuff, and now you've given me more.' He tapped his parcel. 'How will you explain this to the police?'

'They're not going to worry about that when I tell them how Dr Langford died!'

'You—'

Johnny heard the sound of a punch, a groan and a scuffle as the two men fought.

'Let me go!' screamed Howell, whose arm had been bent behind his back by Bennett.

Mrs Langford leaped up from her chair. 'You're not going to tell anyone anything, Howell!' she cried. There was a demonic chuckle behind the menace in her voice as she asked Bennett, 'What do you say, Frederick? Shall we do away with him, too?'

Howell was struggling against Bennett's grip. 'No! Don't! I'm not going to talk. Anyway, what could I say? I wasn't even there, was I?' His voice became muffled. Bennett had a hand over his mouth now. Johnny could hear Howell trying to shout. He was kicking too, trying to break away. Great blows from his feet thundered against the desk, and into Johnny's backbone.

Johnny could see Mrs Langford's feet pacing round

the desk. She tormented Howell as he squirmed against Bennett's grip. 'You know, you'll be much more useful to us dead than you've ever been alive,' she said. 'It's true, there'll be no more vaccine, but we'll be able to split the money we've already got two ways instead of three.'

Bennett picked up her drift. 'You're right, Marie. And if we're ever caught, we could say it was Howell's idea to sell the vaccine, and not yours at all.'

Johnny was stunned. So Mrs Langford was the mastermind. He had been completely taken in by her pretence of friendliness. He didn't want to believe it, but somehow it made sense. He knew that the Langfords had been hard up. Mrs Langford had even sent off for *Make Your Money Go Further*. And then Johnny felt a new twist of panic. To his undercurrent of terror was added a sickening wallop of guilt and regret. He was having another clong. He remembered showing Mrs Langford the Umckaloabo advert. He recalled asking why Dr Langford couldn't sell the BCG vaccine in the same way, and how the doctor had criticized Chas. H. Stevens, of Worple Road, Wimbledon, for making money by playing on the anxieties of the unwell. Had Johnny unwittingly given Mrs Langford the idea which had led to her husband's death and Winnie's arrest? Could she have thought up the whole scheme, and chosen Bennett to be her salesman? After all, as she herself had told Johnny when they'd talked in the theatre, the best customers were rich people: people who would keep quiet because they had a lot to lose if they were discovered. Bennett moved in those circles, and Mrs Langford had known him since he was a child. And Johnny knew that Bennett needed cash, too. He'd said as much when he'd joked with Inspector Griffin about the pile of bills on his desk. Johnny thought back to Remembrance Day, and Bennett's earnest conversation with Mrs Langford at the service. Then there'd been the sudden news that Bennett was invited to the Langfords' for supper. If the plot had been hatched that day, it would explain how unprepared they were when Howell had phoned during the meal to say that he needed Dr Langford's help.

Mrs Langford carried on taunting Dr Howell, whose shouts were still muffled by Bennett's grip. 'I really can't think of any reason to keep you alive, you know,' she said, with an air of exaggerated calm. 'It must be worrying for you. What a pity you can't move your arms. You could nibble those nails of yours even shorter. Maybe even make them bleed.'

'Come on then, woman, let's get it over with,' said Bennett, as Howell squealed and grunted. 'I can't hold him for ever.'

Johnny pictured Mrs Langford advancing on Howell with the loaded syringe.

Suddenly Bennett swore. Howell had bitten his hand and twisted out of his grip. Johnny heard more bumps and thrashing as the two men jostled with each other, lashing out and cursing. Howell threw Mrs Langford across the room, and Johnny stifled a gasp as one of her high-heeled shoes rolled under the desk, only inches away from him. He heard her pulling herself up again, panting. Then she let out a bizarre shriek and Dr Howell gave a desperate cry of resistance that was strangled into an agonized gargle, a wheeze and a cough. His rigid body thumped against the desk and onto the floor next to Johnny. Everything was still.

In the theatre, twelve chimes rang out as Cinderella ran away from the ball.

Chapter 41

COVER-UP

Johnny could sense frozen panic in the room.

Bennett spoke first. 'It's all right. It's all right,' he repeated as if trying to reassure himself. Then his tone shifted from distraction to resolution. 'I'm going,' he said.

'Take me with you,' said Mrs Langford, with a breathy coolness. 'Let's leave now, while there's no one around.'

'No. Someone would come looking for you. I couldn't risk having you in the car. The panto's nearly over. We wouldn't have time to get far before the body was discovered. We might even meet the police coming the other way.'

'Then stay. Stay and help me talk my way out of this. I can say that Howell attacked me, and you fought him off. We could make it look like self-defence.'

'No, I'm getting out of it. No one knows I've been here. There's no reason for me to be mixed up in this at all.'

Mrs Langford barred the door. Her tone had turned from pleading to menace. 'Unless I say something. After all, Howell's not around now to keep an eye on me. There's nothing to stop me telling everyone that you killed my husband.'

'Is that a threat?' Bennett sounded panicky.

Mrs Langford kept her spiteful calm. 'Take it how you like. I'm simply being practical. We're in this together, that's all. Keep your head, and we can come up with a story that puts us both in the clear.'

'How are you going to explain the poison? Isn't it a bit fishy that it just happened to be to hand?'

'I'll say Howell brought it with him. To kill me. To shut me up because I knew he killed Giles.'

There was a pause. When Bennett spoke, it sounded as if he was happy to go along with the plan. 'You should look a bit more roughed up,' he said. 'You'll have to play the victim a bit. A sweet little lady in the power of a homicidal brute.'

'Don't worry. Being a quiet, kind old woman is my speciality.'

Exactly, thought Johnny. *I was certainly taken in.*

Bennett and Mrs Langford stood in silence. Johnny was terrified that they would hear him breathing, and felt a rush of relief when the band in the theatre started playing 'Happy Days Are Here Again' and all the children in the audience joined in, filling the room with song.

'Maybe we should raise the alarm,' said Bennett. 'That's what you'd do, isn't it? If you'd really been attacked?'

'Yes, I'll call the police,' said Mrs Langford, limping round the desk to reach the phone.

Johnny's heart sank. If she got through to the operator, Mrs Langford might find out that the police were already on their way. She might panic. She might run. She might dive under the desk to find her shoe. She might see him. There might be some poison left in the jar, and Johnny knew now that she was not afraid to use it.

Mrs Langford lifted the receiver and dialled the operator. A second later she had dropped the phone. It swung to and fro across the mouth of the footwell. Johnny could hear the woman through the earpiece, shouting out, 'Hello . . . Hello . . . Hello?'

They were the same words used by one of two policemen who had just entered the room.

Johnny was flooded with joy. His earlier call to the operator hadn't been ignored.

Mrs Langford kept her creepy calm. 'Oh, Sergeant . . . and Constable . . . Thank goodness you are here,' she said, trying to conceal her bewilderment at their arrival.

Bennett took charge. 'This poor lady has been the victim of a savage assault,' he said. 'She was lucky I arrived.'

Then the door opened again and Johnny heard Olwen's voice: 'Johnny, are you in here? Mrs Langford? I've brought Professor Campbell.'

'What the devil . . . ?' said the policeman as everyone else in the room gasped in unison.

Johnny was feeling exactly as he had back in Mr Bennett's grand house, hidden under the big fur cloak. He could stay hidden and wait for a chance to run away, or he could show himself and intervene in the action. At Bennett's, fear had got the better of him. Now he took courage. He uncurled himself and shuffled out from under the desk. Everyone was paralysed – looking the other way, towards the door. And Johnny found himself just as aghast as they were. For there, holding Olwen's hand, was a six-foot-tall man with grotesquely rouged cheeks, wearing a multi-layered crinoline dress, hooped earrings and a fluffy blonde wig.

The senior policeman, with a deep Welsh voice, spoke for everyone. 'Will somebody please tell me what on earth is going on?'

Chapter 42

ARRESTS

'**I** can explain!' said Johnny, and everybody turned to face him.

'Johnny!' gasped Mrs Langford. 'Where did you come from?'

'I've been under the desk,' said Johnny. 'I heard everything. Officer, you must arrest that woman, and Mr Bennett, too. They haven't been telling you the truth.'

'But Johnny,' said Olwen, 'you told me Mrs Langford was in danger. It looks as if you were right.'

'No. I was wrong,' he gabbled. 'She killed Dr Howell. And Mr Bennett here, he killed Dr Langford.'

Bennett made a move for the door, but Professor Campbell opened his giant pantomime fan and blocked his path. 'This is preposterous,' said Bennett. 'I don't have to stay here and listen to the incoherent ramblings of a deranged child!'

'I think you'd better stop where you are, sir,' said

the sergeant, calmly. 'I'm sure we can get this cleared up.' He turned to Mrs Langford. 'Madam, perhaps you can enlighten us?'

Mrs Langford took a handkerchief from her sleeve and dabbed her eyes. 'It's as I said just now. Dr Howell attacked me, and Mr Bennett came to my rescue.'

'No!' cried Johnny. 'It wasn't like that. She killed Dr Howell, and she was going to kill me!' He pointed at Bennett. 'And he killed Dr Langford.'

'No he didn't,' came a voice. 'That's not quite right.' Everybody froze as Dr Howell's body began to stir. He sat up and spoke. 'It's all right. I haven't come back from the dead. I was only pretending. It seemed safer than letting myself be knocked about by those two thugs.' Howell pulled himself to his feet and seized the jar of liquid from the desk, hurling its contents into Mrs Langford's eyes. 'Did you really think I would murder a child? Did you really believe this was poison? You sick, depraved woman. Officer, she's your murderess!'

'But you're not dead,' said the sergeant in confusion. 'There is no victim.'

'Yes there is,' said Howell. 'Not me, Officer, but Dr Giles Langford, this woman's husband. She killed him. She's admitted it to me a hundred times, threatening to do the same to me unless I went along with her plans. And this man' – he pointed at Bennett – 'this man has forced me to hide her from the law.'

Johnny was stunned. Mrs Langford, a murderess? 'But she's an old lady,' he cried. 'Old ladies don't kill people! She loved her husband. He loved her. She can't have killed him.'

The sergeant interrupted. 'And where is the body – this Dr Langford?' he asked.

'Buried. In Stambleton, before Christmas,' said Howell.

'And my mother is in prison, charged with the murder,' said Johnny. 'And she didn't do it!'

'I don't understand,' said Professor Campbell. 'What has all this got to do with Craig-y-Nos?'

Dr Howell tried to explain. 'It all started when I took on some . . . some unconventional work for Dr Langford . . .' As the constable struggled to take notes, Howell told the story of how Langford had hoped to develop the BCG to do good, and how, in a panic on Remembrance Day, he himself had asked Langford to come to Wales to help him. 'I wasn't expecting Mrs Langford to come too,' he explained. 'I didn't know that she and Bennett had a very different plan for the vaccine.'

Mrs Langford interrupted. 'I had to come. I knew that if my husband was near a sanatorium he wouldn't be able to stop himself wandering around, chatting to people and hinting at what he was doing. I had to make sure he stayed in Howell's cottage. I knew he couldn't keep a secret. He'd even told that boy!'

Professor Campbell was struggling to keep up. 'You mean to say you've been cultivating a vaccine here? In our laboratory?'

'That's right,' said Howell. 'But at first my involvement was purely scientific. I was never happy about the idea of selling it.'

'So why didn't you tell someone what Bennett and Mrs Langford were planning?' asked the professor.

'I was scared,' said Howell, hanging his head. 'I'm ashamed to admit it, sir, but I was frightened. At first it was bad enough that I might ruin my career, but by the time I found out they wanted to sell the vaccine I knew that Mrs Langford had already killed once, and that Bennett had looked on while she did it. And I was right to be careful. Look what they tried to do to me when I finally crossed them!'

The sergeant, overwhelmed by the welter of information, opened his mouth to ask a question, but Johnny got in first.

'But why was Dr Langford murdered?' he said. 'You said he knew nothing of what his wife was up to.'

'Nothing until that final night,' said Howell, 'when I thought he was safely back in Stambleton. We'd finished here. The first batch of vaccine was a success, and I was sure I could carry on without Dr Langford's help. When Bennett came to collect him and his wife from my cottage to drive them home, I thought he was acting as a generous friend, not as a conspirator. They all left in good spirits.'

The policeman tried to intervene again, but Mrs Langford turned on Bennett. 'And you couldn't resist it, could you, you fool? Everything would have been all right. We were safely home. Giles would never have suspected a thing. But you had to boast about the money. You had to go and break his heart.'

'But you're the one who broke his head!'

The two policemen held Bennett and Mrs Langford back as they flew at each other.

'You know how angry he was,' Mrs Langford yelled at Bennett. 'You saw the fury in his eyes when you told him what we'd planned.'

Bennett sneered, 'Don't try to make it sound as if you were defending yourself.' He turned to the sergeant. 'She was frantic. First she flung an ashtray at him, and when that missed and went through the window, she bashed his head against the mantelpiece.'

'Don't you understand?' said Mrs Langford. 'He had to die. I couldn't live with him knowing that I was selling his dream.'

Howell spoke up. 'Listen to her. She's speaking as if she were doing her victim a favour – killing him to protect him from the knowledge of how she was funding their old age. Don't you see? She's lost her mind. She'd rather her husband died than that he knew she'd let him down. She killed the person she loved most in the world to shield herself from his disapproval.'

All eyes were on Mrs Langford. She was shaking and staring ahead blankly, as if re-playing the murder scene in her mind. 'There was so much blood,' she said, rubbing her hands on her skirt.

Bennett shouted at her again. 'But you didn't do anything to save him, did you? You were more interested in saving yourself. What's it going to sound like in court when I tell them you were on your knees mopping the floor before your husband was even dead?'

'My mother's apron!' said Johnny as the constable closed his notebook, defeated by the rush of revelations. 'You used my mother's apron, didn't you? That's why the police suspected her in the first place.'

Mrs Langford snapped into defiance. 'What about you, Bennett? You can't pin it all on me. You made me write that letter, remember? And you showed it to the police, to make out that I was in France. How are you going to explain that? Or why you drove me back down here and forced Howell to give me shelter? I'm not a fool. I know you didn't do that for my sake. You wanted me here to make sure Howell kept producing the vaccine. And you hid me from the police because I might have told them you were involved – not just in selling illegal medicine, but in the murder, too. Well, you can't get out of it now. I'm going to tell them everything. You're up to your neck in all this, and if I swing for it, so will you.'

'My crimes are going to look pretty pathetic alongside yours,' sniffed Bennett. 'You've killed your husband, you tried to kill Howell, and you wanted to kill the boy . . .'

Johnny joined in: 'And you would have killed my mother! She still might be hanged because of your lies. Oh, Mrs Langford! Mum and I thought you were our friend. We've never done anything to harm you. I even wanted to rescue you when I thought you were imprisoned here by Dr Howell. But you're the jailer. You knew they'd arrested my mother. You knew she was innocent and you did nothing to help her.'

The sergeant unfastened the handcuffs from his belt and nodded to his constable to do the same.

'I'm not sure I'm following all this, Officer,' said Professor Campbell, flapping his fan. 'It seems I have been sorely deceived by Dr Howell and Mrs Morgan – or should I call her Mrs Langford? I thought they were among the most diligent members of my staff! No doubt there are some arrests to be made here.'

Howell sat down on the edge of the desk, put his hands, with their well-bitten fingernails, over his face, and cried. 'I'm sorry,' he sobbed. 'I don't know how I got caught up in all this.' Johnny wondered how he could ever have believed that Howell was the murderer, and that Mrs Langford had been scared of him.

The sergeant at last got a chance to speak. 'I think I had better call Stambleton and see what they want me to do with the prisoners.'

Johnny picked up the dangling receiver. He heard a high-pitched 'Hello?' The operator was still on the line. She had been listening in to everything. Her garbled version of events would be all round the district by morning.

Chapter 43

ANOTHER PLACE, ANOTHER FIGHT

Far away from the mayhem at Craig-y-Nos, Hutch was sitting in an armchair reading (or rather dozing with a book on his lap and his glasses sliding down his nose) when he heard the doorbell. It was ringing hard and repeatedly. It must be the policeman, back with his warrant. Hutch had been in the chair for so long that his bad leg was stiff, and it took him a while to get down the stairs and into the shop. He turned on the light, hoping it would signal that he was on his way, but the bell kept going, nagging him to answer the door.

Hutch opened up. It wasn't the policeman. It was the reporter, as impatient as ever. 'I thought you were out,' he said.

'I was asleep,' Hutch said crossly. 'I'd nodded off. I'm allowed to do that in my own home, aren't I?'

'What about the boy? Couldn't he answer the door?'

Hutch said nothing.

The reporter continued: 'The boy. Johnny Swanson. He is here, isn't he? Very brave of you to take him in. And just as well, as it's turned out. I've had a look at his house. Every window smashed now. And rude words on the door.'

Hutch was still not fully awake, but he was uneasy. The boy. He hadn't heard anything from Johnny. Did that mean he was all right, or in trouble? Could the phone have been ringing while he was sleeping upstairs? All the fuss about the policeman's attack on Post Office protocol had distracted Hutch from thinking about Johnny. And now he realized that he had no idea exactly where the child was. It was nearly ten o'clock. There was only one more train due in to Stambleton. He hoped Johnny would be on it.

The reporter asked again, interrupting Hutch's thoughts, 'Mr Hutchinson? The boy, Mr Hutchinson? Is he well?'

'Well? Yes . . . he's well. Just not here tonight. I'm all alone. Is that all you wanted to know?' Hutch tried to usher the reporter back towards the door.

'Oh no,' said the reporter. 'I didn't come about Johnny at all. Like you, I don't like being up so late, especially for work, but they've sent me to check on

345

a story. Trouble is, this one involves the paper itself, and we never like that sort of news to go public. The police have been round at the office, asking about bogus adverts that we've printed in our paper, tricking people into parting with money. Apparently it involves a post office box here. Have the police been to see you too?'

'Yes, they have. But I couldn't help them. I can't go giving out people's personal details just because some policeman decides he wants them. I told him to go off and get a warrant.'

'And did he?'

'I don't know. He hasn't come back yet.'

'Well, we'd better wait for him together. Then maybe we can clear all this up tonight.'

Hutch didn't want to take the reporter up to his flat. He hated the idea of the man mooching about among his things and looking for signs of Johnny. So he gave him the chair he kept for old ladies to sit on while they were doing their shopping, and dragged out the high stool from behind the post office counter for himself. He perched on it uncomfortably, but he preferred to be higher up than his unexpected guest. Their conversation was fitful. Both of them were getting more and more annoyed.

The reporter turned to the subject of the trial. 'So whatever happens, you will accept the verdict?' he asked.

'I don't think I'll face a problem there. Mrs Swanson will be found not guilty, I'm sure.'

'And that's the reason you've taken her son under your roof?'

'That, and the fact that the poor boy has no one else in the world.'

'You don't see it as a conflict with your responsibilities as a postmaster?'

Hutch corrected him: 'Sub-postmaster.'

'Oh, *sub*-postmaster. Of course. No doubt standards are somewhat lower for a *sub*-postmaster.'

Had he been less tired, Hutch would not have risen to the bait. But he was worried about Johnny, and about the possible return of the policeman, and the one thing he could not stand was cynicism about his duties as an employee of the Post Office.

'Standards are the same for everyone involved in public life,' he said.

'Public life! That's raising your status rather high, isn't it, Mr Hutchinson? Selling stamps, fruitcakes and carrots counts as "public life" now, does it? I'll try to remember that I'm in the presence of an eminent

347

public official when I next pop in for some toilet paper!'

Before he had finished the last word, Hutch was off his stool and had the reporter by the lapels. They were both ex-army men. They both knew how to fight. The reporter had the advantage of height; Hutch had bulk, and familiarity with the terrain. He knew just when he could reach out and grab a jug or a wooden butter-pat to use as a weapon. The two of them wrestled and rolled, bringing jars of sweets down from the shelves. Soon the floor was covered in bulls'-eyes, pear drops and cough-candy twists. The reporter lurched towards Hutch and slipped on some humbugs. He grasped for something to steady him, but only found one of the bags of flour Johnny had filled the day before. The packet exploded under the force of his grasp, showering both men with white powder. The reporter picked up the high stool and swung it round, hoping to knock Hutch off balance. Hutch caught the other end of it, and tried to change its trajectory. The reporter pushed back, and the two of them lurched and skidded towards the front of the shop. Then, at the last minute, the reporter let go of his end, and Hutch was pulled by his own weight right through the front door, splintering the wood and breaking the glass.

It was not his lucky night. He landed right on top of the policeman, who had come to report that an angry judge, called away from a delightful dinner party, had refused to issue a warrant for the information about PO Box 9.

The equally angry constable took great pleasure in escorting the sub-postmaster and the reporter to the police station.

Chapter 44

TRANSPORT

In Wales, the sergeant was on the phone, making arrangements for a special van to take his prisoners to Stambleton.

'What about me?' asked Johnny, rummaging in his pocket. 'I've got a return ticket, but it's getting late. I might not be able to catch a train tonight.'

Professor Campbell broke in while the sergeant continued his phone call in the background. 'I'm sure I could make arrangements for you to stay here.'

'Thank you,' said Johnny, trying not to sound as unenthusiastic as he felt. 'And, Professor, if you don't mind, there's something I want to talk to you about.' He was remembering his promise. 'It's Olwen, sir.' Johnny told Professor Campbell how Olwen had been orphaned, and how badly the nurse had treated her.

Olwen gave way to tears again. The professor enfolded her into a hug. Her slight body sank into the soft folds of his Ugly Sister dress.

'Don't cry, my dear, we will sort this out too,' the professor said, kindly.

'Is Olwen very ill?' asked Johnny. 'Does she really need to stay here?'

'No, the symptoms she came in with have cleared up. It wasn't TB after all. In fact, she shows all the signs of immunity. I've thought for some time that she could be discharged. We've been having trouble contacting her relatives.'

'My uncle's dumped me,' sniffed Olwen. 'And now I'll be here for ever.'

'Can't she come home with me?' asked Johnny.

'Does she have relatives in Stambleton who could look after her?'

'Well, no,' said Johnny. 'Not family exactly. But there's a farmer who knew her parents. I don't know his name. Or better still, the postmaster. He looks after me. He's called Mr Hutchinson . . .'

'I can't let Olwen go to just anyone. We must get permission from her legal guardian. She will have to stay here for now. But we will look into the matter. Perhaps you could ask this Mr Hutchinson to get in touch with me?'

'I should phone him anyway,' said Johnny. 'He must be wondering what's happened to me. I need to tell him I won't be coming home tonight. He might be worried.'

The sergeant finished his conversation and put down the receiver. 'No need for that,' he said. 'We're going to take you. Inspector Griffin's given us permission to commandeer Mr Bennett's car. He wants it back in Stambleton so they can search it for evidence. I'll be driving you myself.'

Johnny could hear angry shouts from Bennett in the police van as the sergeant opened the door of his precious limousine.

'Why don't you go in the back, son,' said the policeman. 'It's a long way, and you'll be able to lie down and get some sleep. Look. There's a blanket here.' Johnny slid across the shiny leather seat. The sergeant shook out the soft woollen travelling rug and tucked it around Johnny's legs.

'I'm not tired,' said Johnny. His excitement at being in a car at all was immense, but to be in this car, a Rolls-Royce Phantom II, made his blood fizz. On his only other rides he'd been hidden on the floor of the reporter's battered Morris Oxford, and bounced around in the farmer's ageing van. He didn't want to miss a moment of this journey.

Settling into the driver's seat, the sergeant fumbled

around until the headlights came on and the engine purred into life; then he pulled out of the courtyard, followed by the police van. Olwen stood on the steps of the building waving, and the professor flapped his fan in a final farewell.

Chapter 45

COMING HOME

Hours later, Hutch and the reporter were still sitting on an uncomfortable bench in a corridor at Stambleton police station. Hutch was worrying about Johnny. What if he got back to discover the door bashed down and the shop ransacked? He wanted to tell a policeman about Johnny, but he didn't want the reporter to hear, even though they had long since patched up their quarrel. In any case, the desk sergeant was busy with something else. The phone was ringing well after midnight. A couple of drunks were taken out of the cells and allowed to go home. Plain-clothes detectives arrived, including Inspector Griffin. Hutch recognized him from Winnie's court hearing. He knew Griffin was a very important police-man. He hoped he hadn't been called in to deal with the fight in the shop. A criminal conviction could mean the end of Hutch's Post Office career.

At one a.m. there was a shout of 'They're here!' and all the staff who were on duty gathered by the door.

'They made good time,' said a constable.

'Well they had a fast car,' said another. 'Kindly supplied by one of the prisoners.' Everybody laughed.

The reporter sensed that he might be missing a story, and tried to join the crowd of policemen. He was manhandled back to his place. A few minutes later, a strange procession of tired, deflated people passed by the bench he shared with Hutch. First came Mrs Langford, handcuffed to a stocky policeman wearing an unfamiliar uniform. She was stooping, and looked ten years older than she had before her husband was killed. Behind her was a young man in a white lab coat with his hands chained together. Even so, he managed to raise them to his mouth to nibble his nails. He was followed by another officer, manacled to a well-dressed man who was trying to shield his face with his hat. The reporter had to be forced back to his seat again when he saw that it was Frederick Bennett. At the end of the line – the only one who was smiling – was Johnny Swanson. The grumpy desk officer had shown no reservations about letting him into the building this time.

Johnny ran over to Hutch, babbling on about Mrs Langford being the murderer, and how his mother would have to be freed.

'Thank you so much for coming, Hutch. I'm sorry they've kept you up so late. It was a long drive.' Johnny couldn't disguise how much he had enjoyed his trip in Mr Bennett's grand car, even if the policeman who'd driven it had sometimes shown a dizzying unfamiliarity with the controls.

Hutch was embarrassed. He came clean. 'The fact is, Johnny old chap, I didn't know you were on your way. I got here under my own steam, you might say.'

Johnny didn't understand. But he did notice that Hutch and the reporter were both covered in a dusting of flour, with patches of unidentified foodstuffs sprayed across their dishevelled clothes.

Hutch began an explanation. 'This gentleman and I had a bit of a . . .'

'A bit of an altercation, you might say,' said the reporter.

'About what?' asked Johnny.

Neither of them wanted to admit that it had been, at least in part, about Johnny and his mother.

'Good question,' said the reporter. 'I really can't remember.'

Inspector Griffin approached them. 'Mr Hutchinson, I believe,' he said, holding out his hand.

'I must apologize for my behaviour,' said Hutch,

assuming that Griffin had come to question him about the fight at the shop.

'Never mind that,' said Griffin. 'It was your own property you damaged, and if this gentleman is prepared to let the matter drop, I think we can forget the whole episode. The person I'm most eager to talk to is this young chap.' He tousled Johnny's bouncy curls. 'Mr Hutchinson, would you care to sit in? I understand that you've been looking after Johnny while his mother's been . . . away.'

'Of course,' said Hutch, and he accompanied Johnny into the interview room, where the three of them sat down at a small bare table. Inspector Griffin took notes as Johnny explained what had happened in Wales, summed up the vaccine plot, and described how Dr Langford had died.

Inspector Griffin scratched his head. 'Thank you, Johnny,' he said. 'I think I understand. You've been very helpful.'

'It's really Mum I wanted to help,' said Johnny. 'She can come home now, can't she?'

'Yes, indeed. There'll be some formalities, but we'll get her back to you as soon as we can.'

'What will happen to Mrs Langford and the others?' asked Johnny. 'Will they all be hanged?'

'I can't say. Dr Howell should get away with a prison stretch. It sounds as if he's guilty of contravening the Therapeutic Medicines Act, and of obstructing the police; but things look bad for Mrs Langford, despite her age – and Bennett certainly seems to be implicated in covering up the murder, even if he didn't strike the fatal blow. Don't worry, Johnny. You're safe. We'll be keeping them under lock and key until we can confirm what you've told us.'

'It's all true, I promise.'

'Yes, Johnny,' the inspector said kindly, 'I believe you, but there's no way a court would accept your word as evidence on its own. With a bit of luck the three of them will speak out against each other, but the trouble is, a jury might think they're each trying to save their own skin. We really need someone else, too. If only there were another, adult, witness to all this.'

'I was thinking on the way home,' said Johnny. 'There is somebody else – someone who might have heard Bennett and Mrs Langford plan the BCG scam, at least, and may even know the truth about the murder.'

'Really? Who?'

'Mr Bennett's girlfriend,' said Johnny. 'She was

there on Remembrance Day. She went to supper at the Langfords' that night. I've been wondering what happened to her.'

'Bennett said they had parted,' the inspector said.

'I know,' said Johnny. 'I was there when he told you.'

Inspector Griffin raised an eyebrow.

'I didn't mean to listen in, but I was hiding. I'd gone to see Mr Bennett myself, but you asked him everything I wanted to know,' Johnny confessed.

'I'm glad to hear that you approve of my methods,' laughed Griffin. 'I recall him saying that the young lady was now performing at the Gaiety Theatre in London. I will make contact with her in the morning.'

'But the thing is,' Johnny continued excitedly, 'what if she's not there?'

'Why shouldn't she be?'

'Because her cloak was still in Mr Bennett's house the morning after Dr Langford's body was found. I know. I was hiding behind it.'

Hutch let out an exasperated sigh, and Griffin shook his head. 'It sounded to me as if she went away after a disagreement,' he said. 'Maybe she flounced off without it.'

'But suppose . . .' said Johnny. Then he saw the

look on Hutch's face, and was reminded of all his warnings about jumping to conclusions.

The policeman wanted to hear more. 'What are you suggesting?' he asked.

'Only that there might, possibly, be something suspicious about her disappearance, too,' said Johnny, stopping himself from making wild allegations.

Inspector Griffin was lost in thought for a moment. 'Have you mentioned this to anyone else?' he asked.

'No. Just you,' said Johnny. 'And Hutch knows now, of course.'

Hutch put his finger to his lips. 'I won't tell a soul,' he said.

Inspector Griffin's tone was serious. 'I'd appreciate your silence, sir. We will follow up this lead first thing in the morning. This could be an even more convoluted case than I thought.'

Hutch stretched out his bad leg and stifled a yawn. 'Is that all for tonight, Inspector? I'm sure you'll agree that Johnny should really be in bed.'

'Yes. We can talk again tomorrow.' Griffin closed his notebook. 'But before you go,' he said casually, 'tell me, Johnny, how did you know that Howell, Bennett and Mrs Langford were going to meet at Craig-y-Nos last night?'

'I didn't,' said Johnny. 'I'd never even heard of Craig-y-Nos until Mrs Langford replied to one of my advertisements.'

Hutch put his head in his hands.

The inspector was bemused. 'Your what, Johnny?'

'Well, you see, I put in this advert' – he knew it off by heart – '*Change Your Appearance Permanently. Unhappy with the way you look? Transform yourself Instantly and For Ever.*'

Hutch could see Inspector Griffin registering that Johnny was probably the culprit in the case of PO Box 9.

Griffin was silent for a moment and then spoke sternly. 'You may not be aware, Johnny, that while you've been in Wales this force has been dealing with an allegation of fraud in relation to advertisements very like the one you've described.'

Johnny had another clong. With a few unguarded words he had landed himself in trouble. He felt sick with shame. He had already faced Hutch's wrath over his adverts. Now the police knew. He had heard of guilty children being tried in the juvenile courts and sent away to special schools. Would that happen to him, just when his mother was coming home? Had he messed things up yet again? Would Winnie's freedom be laced with new worry and grief?

The inspector could see that Johnny was panicking. He was stern but understanding. 'Johnny, I know you've been through a lot in the last few weeks. We may be able to resolve the matter of the advertisements if I give you the name and address of the person who has complained, and you send him back his money.'

Johnny sighed with relief. 'Thank you, sir,' he said gravely. 'I promise I'll do it tomorrow.'

'In that case,' said Inspector Griffin, 'I think it is time you went home.' He stood up and took a step towards the door. Then he stopped abruptly and turned to Johnny, thinking out loud. 'So Mrs Langford wanted a disguise . . .' he mumbled. 'She must have been planning to get away – to hide and leave Bennett and Howell to face the music. Perhaps she was even planning to pin Langford's murder on them.'

'And?' said Hutch, not really following the policeman's train of thought.

'Well, it just might help me when I'm talking to the others. If I can show that Mrs Langford was preparing to double-cross them even before their plot was discovered, it might break down any last vestige of loyalty between them.'

Johnny interrupted. 'There wasn't much sign of loyalty when they were arguing in Wales. If you ask me, it's more likely that she was going to kill the others so they couldn't tell on her, and then change her appearance so she would never be found.'

Inspector Griffin nodded. 'Either way, sending off for that disguise shows how devious she's been. If she tries to defend herself against the murder charge by saying it was self-defence or a single moment of madness, we'll be able to demonstrate how she kept on plotting to save herself.'

'I'd never have thought she could be like that,' said Johnny.

'You'd be surprised,' said Inspector Griffin, 'how people behave after they've killed. I've seen quite a few murderers in my time. Many torture themselves with guilt; but some plot a killing in cold blood, and then seem perfectly normal – even congenial – once they've got rid of the person they despised. Others, who've surprised themselves by killing, entirely lose their grip on what's right and wrong.'

'Is that what's happened to Mrs Langford?' asked Johnny.

'I'd say so. She killed a decent, loving man. No one else matches up to her estimation of him, and no crime she might commit in future can seem as bad to her as what she's already done. So why shouldn't she kill again? That's why she thought nothing of threatening you and Howell. She might eventually have moved on to another stage, enjoying killing and taking a pride in avoiding capture. Some killers even manage to convince themselves that they're not guilty, when all the evidence points the other way.'

'And some suspects really are innocent, despite appearances,' said Hutch severely.

Inspector Griffin knew he was thinking of Winnie. He gave an embarrassed cough. It was the nearest he came to an apology. 'Anyway, Johnny,' he said, trying to lighten the mood, 'that advert of yours may have done the trick in solving this crime. I think we'll be able to turn a blind eye to how it got in the paper – just as long as there are no more.'

'Oh, I promise,' said Johnny, meaning it. 'I'll never, ever do it again.'

Hutch interrupted. 'There's something I would like to ask Johnny, if I may,' he said to the detective.

'Go ahead,' said Inspector Griffin, hoping for another revelation that might advance the case.

'Well, Johnny,' said Hutch, 'I was just wondering . . .'

'Yes?' said Johnny. 'You know you can ask me anything, Hutch.'

'I was wondering. How *do* you transform yourself instantly and for ever? What's the answer to that one?'

Johnny was abashed. He looked at his feet and muttered, 'Cut your head off.'

Hutch shrugged his shoulders. 'Not one of your best, son,' he sighed. 'Maybe it is time to call it a day.'

Chapter 46

RELEASE

The next day, the phone in the wooden booth at Hutch's shop kept ringing. There were calls from newspapers, well-wishers, and Inspector Griffin, who was over at the prison organizing all the paperwork so that Winnie could come home. Johnny told Hutch about his meeting with Olwen, and persuaded him to phone Professor Campbell at Craig-y-Nos to find out how she was. It was hard to get through. The Welsh sanatorium was also besieged by the press, but eventually Hutch had some news for Johnny.

'Well, he wouldn't tell me much over the phone,' he said. 'Quite right, of course, I could be anybody. But it seems that Olwen's going to stay at Craig-y-Nos until her next of kin are found. But the professor promised to pass on a letter, if you want to write to her.'

'Of course I do,' said Johnny.

'If you're quick, we can get something in the post tonight. Then, I hope, we'll be able to go and pick up your mother as soon as I've closed the shop. Inspector Griffin has offered to take us to the prison in his car.'

Johnny and Hutch waited in the police car while Inspector Griffin went into the jail to complete the last of the formalities. He seemed to be gone for ages, though it was really only a quarter of an hour; and Johnny started to worry that something had gone wrong. To avoid crowds gathering outside the prison, Griffin had told the press that Winnie wouldn't be released until the next day.

In the chill of the evening the deserted street was made even gloomier by the shadow of the high prison wall. There was a small door cut into one side of the massive prison gate. Eventually, it opened, throwing a rectangle of light across the street, and Inspector Griffin stepped out. At first Johnny feared he was alone, but then the detective turned and helped a tiny figure through behind him. Winnie was weak, and bewildered by her sudden freedom, but she spread her arms wide as she saw Johnny leap from the car and run towards her.

'Mummy!' Johnny cried, calling her by the name he hadn't let himself use since he was ten. He wanted to tell her everything, but all he could say was: 'Oh, Mummy! Mummy! You're back! You're back!'

Winnie's voice cracked as she hugged him and whispered, 'Yes, darling. And I know I'm free because of you. Oh, Johnny. I couldn't be more proud of you.'

By now they were both in tears, and inside the car Hutch was reaching for his handkerchief.

Winnie's neighbours had been busy all day. Anxious to pretend to themselves that they had never despised or disparaged her, they had mended the windows of her house and cleaned off all the slogans from the walls. The farmer from Newgate had driven to town with some eggs and milk. He left them on the kitchen table with a note humbly apologizing for being so cruel to Johnny, and he laid a fire in the grate. Even Mrs Slack brought something. It was a pan of hot soup. Johnny wouldn't eat it. He was scared it might contain an extra, yellow, liquid ingredient; but he told Winnie he just wasn't hungry. He didn't want her to know all the horrible details of his time alone at home.

'At least with Bennett in jail, the rent won't be going up,' said Johnny, as he sliced the pie Hutch had brought for their supper. 'And you don't need to go out to work for a while, Mum. I managed to save up some cash while you were away.'

Hutch and Winnie, sitting in front of the fire, exchanged a glance that told Johnny she knew about the advertisements. He was relieved not to have to explain it all himself. He started to say sorry.

'We'll talk about that some other time,' said his mother, pouring him another cup of tea.

Johnny and Winnie both slept late the next day. After breakfast they had a visitor. It was the new doctor, who had taken on Dr Langford's patients when he retired. He gave Winnie a thorough check, and examined Johnny to make sure he had not picked up any nasty germs at Craig-y-Nos.

'Everything's fine, Mrs Swanson,' he reassured Winnie, as he put away his stethoscope. 'Keep him off school for a week or two, just to make sure he's not brewing anything. After that I'll do regular tests, but I don't think you have anything to worry about with this splendid young lad.'

The doctor had a copy of the morning paper in his bag. The reporter who had christened Winnie 'the Bloody Barmaid' had written an article based on all the nice things he had learned about her during his conversation with Johnny over the apples and cheese.

THE ANGEL OF STAMBLETON
By Our Special Correspondent

Winifred Swanson, the war widow freed from prison (see page 1), was today hailed by friends and neighbours as a credit to the community, caught in a web of intrigue woven by the real killers of Dr Giles Langford. 'Winnie was always there with a smile and a kind word,'said Mrs Edna Slack (57). She visited me every day Nothing was too much trouble for her. I was lost without her when she was taken away.' Millicent Roberts (34) spoke of Mrs Swanson's devotion to her son, Johnny. 'She worked all hours to keep a roof over that boy's head,' said Mrs Roberts.

WAR HERO

Young Johnny never knew his father, Private Harry Swanson (pictured, right), who was killed in France within days of the end of the war, just a month after his 20th birthday.

BOY DETECTIVE

It was Johnny (11) who rescued his mother from the gallows. Police in charge of the case refused to speak publicly at this stage, but it is believed that they feel great admiration for Johnny's initiative and tenacity in proving his mother's innocence and providing evidence which led to the arrest of three new suspects. Johnny, a pupil at

Continued on page 5

That afternoon, Johnny went round to the shop, where Hutch had begun repairing the damage from the fight. He went upstairs to collect his rabbit, the Peace Mug and Winnie's special box of medals and documents. He remembered the twelve remaining 'transformation' letters under the mattress. Without regret, he put the postal orders into their stamped addressed envelopes, ready to return them to the poor fools who so badly wanted to change their looks.

When he got downstairs, Hutch was taking delivery of the evening papers. He cut the string on the bundle and opened out the top copy.

'Hey, Johnny, take a look at this,' he shouted.

There was a picture of Frederick Bennett on the front page. The headline was in bigger type than usual. Johnny could read it from the other side of the shop: LOCAL SQUIRE ON MURDER CHARGE.

'But that's not right,' said Johnny. 'I told them. Mrs Langford was the killer, not Bennett.'

'It's a different murder,' said Hutch, reading out the strap-line on the lead story. '*Actress's body found in wood*. You were right, Johnny. Bennett got his girl-friend out of the way.'

'What else does it say?'

371

'Not much. Remember what that reporter said when your mother was arrested? Once they've charged someone, the papers aren't allowed to print everything they know.'

The bell jangled as the battered shop door opened. 'I'm glad you were paying attention,' said a familiar voice. It was the reporter. 'You're right. There's a lot of detail that will have to wait for the trial.'

'Like what?' asked Johnny.

'Like the fact that the link to Bennett was confirmed by the blanket the body was wrapped in. It matches one that's still in the back of his car.'

Johnny remembered slumbering under that blanket on the journey back from Wales. He shuddered.

The reporter continued. 'The body was found in a wood more than twenty miles away. It chills me to think of it, but I may have seen the mud from that journey being washed off Bennett's car.'

Johnny recalled the scene outside Bennett's house too, but he said nothing.

'Apparently the body was in such a state that they had to identify it from the necklace in one of her publicity photos.'

Hutch flinched. 'That's enough,' he said, reminding the man that a child was present.

The reporter cast his eye around the shop and changed the subject. 'I see you're getting straight again,' he said.

Hutch nodded. 'I suppose you want to use the phone.'

'No, I haven't come here to work,' said the reporter. He took out his wallet and put two £5 notes on the table. 'I came to contribute towards the repairs, and to give Johnny this.' He handed over a small parcel, wrapped in brown paper and tied with string. 'Open it carefully,' he said. 'It's made of glass.'

Johnny tore off the wrapping. It was the photograph of his father, in a beautiful new tortoiseshell frame. Hutch came over to have a look. 'He was a grand man, your dad,' he said, holding the picture up alongside Johnny's face. 'I can see the likeness. He would have been proud of you.'

'I should never have taken it,' said the reporter, ashamed. 'I'm sorry. Forgive me.'

'Mum will be pleased to have it back,' said Johnny, curtly. He couldn't really find it in himself to forgive the theft.

'Since I'm here, Johnny,' said the reporter, taking out his notebook, 'I wonder if there's anything you'd like to tell me about Mr Bennett? A contact of mine in the police tells me you've been very helpful, giving them leads.'

'I've nothing to say,' said Johnny. 'I'm not supposed to talk to anyone until after all the trials are over.'

'He's right,' said Hutch, holding the door open. 'I think it would be best if you kept your distance for the time being, don't you?'

'My source had some nice things to say about you, too, Mr Hutchinson.'

'Oh, really?' said Hutch, surprised.

'He didn't go into details, but I gather we have you to thank for that complaint about the advertisements being withdrawn. Reading between the lines, I'd say someone had a word with the man behind PO Box Nine.'

'I couldn't possibly comment,' said Hutch.

'Of course not. I understand. You have a duty of confidentiality as a postmaster.'

'Sub-postmaster,' said Hutch.

'Let's not split hairs. If the adverts are going to stop, I thank you.'

Johnny said nothing as the reporter slapped him on the arm in a friendly gesture of farewell. 'So what's next for you, son?' he asked.

'I'll be going back to school soon.'

'And then what? When you leave school? Has this business given you a taste for detective work? Are you going to join the police? Or go into journalism perhaps?'

'I don't know,' said Johnny. 'I haven't really thought about it. Maybe I'll open a shop.'

As the reporter took his leave, Hutch started marking up the papers for the evening delivery round, feeling a glow of almost paternal pride.

Chapter 47

A NEW WORLD

A fortnight later, the new doctor visited again.

'I think it's time to send you back to school, old chap,' he said breezily. 'You'll be glad to see all your friends again.'

Johnny tried to look pleased, but he was dreading returning to the playground bullies.

On his first day he deliberately took longer than usual over his paper round, and arrived at school just as the bell was ringing. Mr Murray was standing by the gate, waiting to catch latecomers.

'Another lucky escape, eh, Swanson?' he snarled as Johnny ran to his classroom.

Mrs Stiles called the register: 'Morrison, Noble, Parker, Roberts, Swanson . . .'

She shushed the titter that ran round the room at the sound of Johnny's name. 'That's enough. Welcome back, Johnny,' she said, dipping her pen in the inkwell. 'It's good to be able to tick you off again. Taylor, Tompkins, Venables . . .'

At break time, Johnny dawdled into the yard with his head down and waited for the first taunts. To his amazement, he was quickly surrounded by children asking questions about the murder. He had never been so popular.

Albert Taylor broke through the crush and strode towards him. Johnny tried not to flinch, but he expected Taylor to lash out, verbally at least. Taylor reached for his pocket. What would it be? A knuckle-duster? A catapult? A knife?

It was a bar of chocolate. Albert broke off a square and offered it to Johnny. 'Here, Detecko. Take it.'

Detecko. A new nickname – short for detective – a name that played on Johnny's strengths at last. Taylor didn't need to spell it out to the others. From now on, anyone caught calling Johnny 'Quacky' or 'Swingson' would be for it. It was time to let Johnny join in their games.

In the weeks ahead, one of those games got quite nasty, and Johnny was far from proud of his part in it, even though it was exhilarating to be admired by Taylor's gang. The ill-will against Winnie had found a new home. It was redirected towards Miss Dangerfield. The old lady had never been liked, but now she was not even feared. Johnny did nothing to stop the boys who had once taunted him throwing bricks through her windows and painting LIAR across her front door. Her walking stick was found floating in the duckpond.

'Poor woman,' said Winnie, as she and Johnny sat over their tea one night. 'I know what it's like to have the whole town turn against you. I wouldn't wish it on anyone.'

Johnny pretended his mouth was too full to reply.

In the Easter holidays, a FOR SALE sign went up outside Miss Dangerfield's house just as a SOLD notice was taken down by the new owner of the Langfords' across the road. The young doctor had moved in. It was the last straw for Miss Dangerfield. He was unmarried, had a motorbike, and left his bathroom window open. She let the vicar know exactly what she thought of her new neighbour:

'If I stand on the stool in my bedroom, I can see him with his shirt off when he's shaving,' she said. 'It's too bad.'

On the day the removal vans came, Johnny climbed the tree in the doctor's garden to watch – just to make sure that Miss Dangerfield was really going. She was belligerent to the last, haranguing the moving men as they manhandled her furniture across her front garden.

'Mind that radio-gramophone!' she squealed. 'It's a Lissenola New Era.'

But she had lost her power. The men shrugged, and bumped the wooden cabinet against the gate.

Johnny ran down the hill to the shop to collect the papers for his evening delivery round. He was surprised to find his mother sweeping the floor.

'Hutch has offered me a job,' she said. 'He says I can help out here.'

Hutch looped the bag of papers over Johnny's shoulder and steered him out onto the pavement. 'I hope you don't mind, son,' he said. 'You can still do bits and pieces for me too, but I knew your mother needed the work. That doctor asked her if she wanted her old job back at the Langfords' place. I think we should keep her away from there, don't you?'

So through the summer, Winnie spent her days at the shop, and sometimes Hutch came round for supper at Johnny's house. Then, while Johnny did his homework, Winnie and Hutch would go out for walks, or to the pub, where Winnie was now a celebrity, not an outcast. School was better too. Even Mr Murray, seeing that Johnny was growing taller and stronger, included him in teams, and started picking on someone in the year below.

Every now and then Johnny got a new idea for an advert, but he managed to stick to his promise never to place one again. The poet still wrote regularly. For a while Johnny just sent his postal orders straight back, but the man pleaded with him for guidance on his writing, and so Hutch told Johnny that he could reply, so long as he never charged for his advice.

'Think of him as a pen-pal,' said Winnie. And that's what Johnny did.

Olwen wrote to Johnny too. She was still at Craig-y-Nos: stuck there, miserable, living on charity until her uncle was found.

'Can't we do something for her?' asked Johnny over supper one night.

'I've been looking into it,' said Hutch. 'I've had quite a correspondence with that Professor Campbell of yours. I didn't want to talk about it in case it all came to nothing, but I think I can tell you now.'

'What does he say?' Johnny asked.

Hutch took Winnie's hand. Johnny blushed at his tenderness and tried not to look. 'Well,' said Hutch, 'it may be possible for me to give Olwen a new home.'

'That's wonderful. Will she come back to Stambleton to live with you?'

Winnie answered. 'With us, Johnny. With all three of us.'

'You mean . . . ?' said Johnny, guessing the answer but still wanting to ask. 'You mean you are going to get married?' Halfway through the question his voice cracked and swooped into a different register.

'Well, that's the end of Auntie Ada,' laughed Hutch. 'She won't be making any more telephone calls!'

'Do you know, I'm rather sorry to see the back of her,' said Winnie. 'She may have caused a lot of trouble, but in a way she brought us together.'

'Yes,' said Hutch. 'We're going to be a real family, Johnny. You, Winnie and Olwen will come and live with me over the shop.'

Johnny thought for a moment, imagining his new life. 'Does that mean I'll be Johnny Hutchinson?'

Winnie glanced across at the picture in its tortoise-shell frame, and Hutch answered for her. 'No, Johnny. I couldn't do that to your dad. He might never have known you, but he would have been proud of you – of all your funny schemes and scrapes, and of the hard work and bravery that saved your mother's life. I couldn't take away his name from the last, and best, thing he left behind.' He patted Johnny's golden curls. 'Dear boy. I swear that in the years ahead I will love and care for you as if you were my own child. But I promise you, because I think it is the right and proper thing, that whatever happens, you will always be Johnny Swanson.'

A note about money

In 1929 British money worked in a different way:

The smallest coin was a farthing.

Two of those made a halfpenny (pronounced haypny).

Two of those made a penny.

There was a small silver coin worth three pennies, called a threepenny bit.

The sixpence was a slightly bigger silver coin.

Two sixpences made one shilling (worth twelve pennies, or 5p in modern money).

The two-shilling coin was called a florin.

A large coin, called a half-crown, was worth two shillings and sixpence.

A crown was worth five shillings.

After that there were bank notes, worth ten shillings (50p in modern money), one pound, five pounds, ten pounds, and so on.

One pound was worth twenty shillings, or two hundred and forty pennies.

Sums of money were written like this:

One penny	1d.
Sixpence	6d.
One shilling	1s. or 1/-
One shilling and fourpence	1/4
Two pounds, nine shillings and elevenpence	£2 9s. 11d. or 49/11

A daily paper cost 1d. A weekly comic cost 2d. (less than one penny in our 'new' money.)

In an age when very few people had bank accounts or chequebooks, sending even small sums of money through the post was impractical and insecure, not least because the coins were so heavy. For this reason, postal orders were popular. You paid the money in at your local post office, and received an official coupon which the recipient could cash in at their post office, or use again to send to someone else.

Without postal orders, Johnny Swanson would never have been able to run his business.